$\mathcal{K}$ylar had never started a~~~~~~~~~~~~~~~~

Approaching the Lae'~~~~~~~~~~~~~~~~
the stealth he'd used to ap~~~~~~~~~~~~~~~
simply walked past the s~~~~~~~~~~~~~~~
blazoned with a golden sun: the pure light of reason beating back the darkness of superstition. Kylar grinned. The
Lae'knaught were going to love the Night Angel.

Without provoking anyone, Cenaria had been invaded
from the east by the Lae'knaught, from the north by Khalidor, and now from the south by Ceura. It was about time
some of those hungry swords met each other.

Kylar ran, pulling his illusions around him, becoming the
Night Angel. As if through smoke, there were glimpses of
gleaming iridescent black metal skin, the crescents of exaggerated muscles, a face like Judgment, with brows pronounced and frowning, and glossy black eyes without pupils
that leaked blue flames. He ran past a knot of gaunt Cenarian recruits, wide-eyed, their weapons in hand but forgotten.
There were no crimes in their eyes. These men had joined
because they had no other way to feed themselves.

The next group had participated in a hundred burnings and
worse. A smoking black blade slid from Kylar's left hand.

"I judge you!" the Night Angel shouted. "I find you
wanting!"

Praise for *The Way of Shadows*

"What a terrific story! I was mesmerized from start to finish.
Unforgettable characters, a plot that kept me guessing, non-
stop action and the kind of in-depth storytelling that makes
me admire a writer's work." —Terry Brooks

"Kylar is a wonderful character—sympathetic and despicable,
cowardly and courageous, honorable and unscrupulous . . . a
breathtaking debut!"
—Dave Duncan, author of *The Alchemist's Code*

BOOKS BY BRENT WEEKS

The Night Angel Trilogy

The Way of Shadows

Shadow's Edge

Beyond the Shadows

Beyond the Shadows

BRENT WEEKS

orbit

www.orbitbooks.net

New York   London

Copyright © 2008 by Brent Weeks
Excerpt from *Orcs* copyright © 2004 by Stan Nicholls
All rights reserved. Except as permitted under the U.S. Copyright Act of 1976, no part of this publication may be reproduced, distributed, or transmitted in any form or by any means, or stored in a data base or retrieval system, without the prior written permission of the publisher.

Orbit
Hachette Book Group
237 Park Avenue
New York, NY 10017
Visit our Web site at www.orbitbooks.net

Orbit is an imprint of Hachette Book Group, Inc.
The Orbit name and logo is a trademark of Little, Brown Book Group Ltd.

Printed in the United States of America

First edition: December 2008

10 9 8 7 6 5 4

For Kristi,
for all the usual reasons,
&
For my dad,
for your excellence and your integrity,
and for raising kids who whisper, "Peep!"

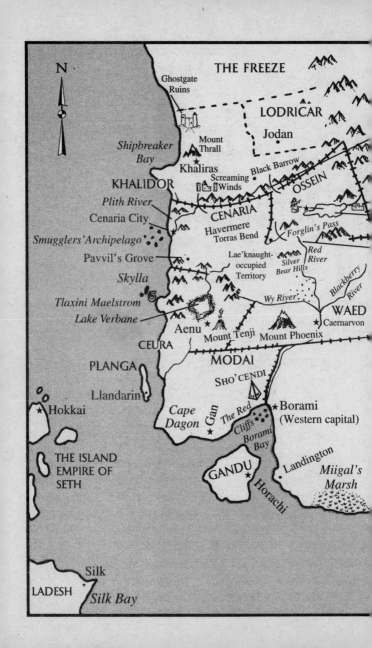

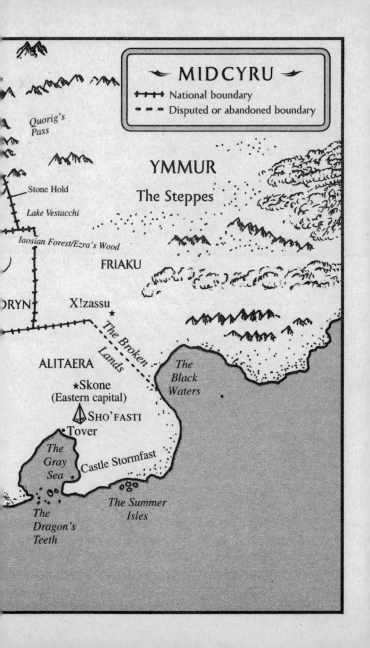

Beyond
the
Shadows

1

Logan Gyre was sitting in the mud and blood of the battlefield of Pavvil's Grove when Terah Graesin came to him. It was barely an hour since they'd routed the Khalidorans, when the monstrous ferali forged to devour Cenaria's army had turned instead on its Khalidoran masters. Logan had issued the orders that seemed most pressing, then dismissed everyone to join the revelries that were sweeping the Cenarian camp.

Terah Graesin came to him alone. He was sitting on a low rock, heedless of the mud. His fine clothes were so spattered with blood and worse they were a total loss anyway. Terah's dress, by contrast, was clean except for the lower fringe. She wore high shoes, but even those couldn't keep her entirely free of the thick mud. She stopped before him. He didn't stand.

She pretended not to notice. He pretended not to notice that her bodyguards—unbloodied from battle—were hidden in the trees less than a hundred paces away. Terah

Graesin could have only one reason to come to him: she was wondering if she was still the queen.

If Logan hadn't been so bone-weary, he would have been amused. Terah had come to him alone as a show of vulnerability or fearlessness. "You were a hero today," Terah said. "You stopped the Godking's beast. They're saying you killed him."

Logan shook his head. He'd stabbed the ferali, and then the Godking had left it, but other men had given it more grievous wounds than he had. Something else had stopped the Godking, not Logan.

"You commanded it to destroy our enemies, and it did. You saved Cenaria."

Logan shrugged. It already seemed long ago.

"I guess the question is," Terah Graesin said, "did you save Cenaria for yourself, or for all of us?"

Logan spat at her feet. "Don't give me that horse-shit, Terah. You think you're going to manipulate me? You've got nothing to offer, nothing to threaten. You've got a question for me? Have a little respect and just fucking ask."

Terah's back stiffened, her chin lifted, and one hand twitched, but then she stopped.

It was the hand twitch that captured Logan's attention. If she had raised her hand, was that the sign for her men to attack? Logan looked past her into the woods at the edge of the field, but the first thing he saw wasn't her men. He saw his own. Agon's Dogs—including two of the astoundingly talented archers Agon had armed with Ymmuri bows and made wytch hunters—had stealthily circled behind Terah's bodyguards. Both wytch hunters had arrows nocked, but not drawn. Both men had obviously taken care to stand where Logan could see them clearly, because none of the other Dogs were clearly visible.

One archer was alternately looking at Logan and at a target in the woods. Logan followed his eyes and saw Terah's hidden archer, aiming at Logan, waiting for Terah's signal. The other wytch hunter was staring at Terah Graesin's back. They were waiting for Logan's signal. Logan should have known his streetwise followers wouldn't leave him alone when Terah Graesin was near.

He looked at Terah. She was slim, pretty, with imperious green eyes that reminded Logan of his mother's. Terah thought Logan didn't know about her men in the woods. She thought Logan didn't know that she had the stronger hand. "You swore fealty to me this morning under less than ideal circumstances," Terah said. "Do you intend to keep your troth, or do you intend to make yourself king?"

She couldn't ask the question straight, could she? It just wasn't in her, not even when she thought she had total control over Logan. She would not make a good queen.

Logan thought he'd already made his decision, but he hesitated. He remembered how it felt to be powerless in the Hole, how it felt to be powerless when Jenine, his just-wed wife, had been murdered. He remembered how disconcertingly wonderful it felt to tell Kylar to kill Gorkhy and see it done. He wondered if he would feel the same pleasure at seeing Terah Graesin die. With one nod toward those wytch hunters, he would find out. He would never feel powerless again.

His father had told him, "An oath is the measure of the man who gives it." Logan had seen what happened when he did what he knew was right, no matter how foolish it looked at the time. That was what rallied the Holers around him. That was what had saved his life when he was feverish and barely conscious. That was what had made Lilly—the woman the Khalidorans crafted into the fe-rali—turn on the Khalidorans. Ultimately, Logan's doing what was right had saved all of Cenaria. But his father Regnus Drake had lived by his oaths, through a miserable marriage and miserable service to a petty, wicked king. He gritted his teeth all day and slept well every night. Logan didn't know if he was as much of a man as his father. He couldn't do it.

So he hesitated. If she raised her hand to order her men to attack, she would be breaking the covenant between lord and vassal. If she broke it, he would be free.

"Our soldiers proclaimed me king." Logan. said in a neutral tone. *Lose your temper, Terah. Order the attack. Order your own death.*

Terah's eyes lit, but her voice was steady and her hand didn't move. "Men say many things in the heat of battle. I am prepared to forgive this indiscretion."

Is this what Kylar saved me for?

No. But this is the man I am. I am my father's son.

Logan stood slowly so as not to alarm either side's archers, then, slowly, he knelt and touched Terah Graesin's feet in submission.

Late that night, a band of Khalidorans attacked the Cenarian camp, killing dozens of drunken revelers before fleeing into the darkness. In the morning, Terah Graesin sent Logan Gyre and a thousand of his men to hunt them down.

2

The sentry was a seasoned sa'ceurai, a sword lord who'd killed sixteen men and bound their forelocks into his fiery red hair. His eyes probed the darkness restlessly where the forest and the oak grove met, and when he turned, he shielded his eyes from his comrades' low fires to protect his night vision. Despite the cool wind that swept the camp and set the great oaks groaning, he wore no helmet that would muffle his hearing. But he had no chance of stopping the wetboy.

Former wetboy, Kylar thought, balancing one-handed on a broad oak limb. If he were still a killer for hire, he'd murder the sentry and be done with it. Kylar was something different now, the Night Angel—immortal, invisible, and nearly invincible—and he only served death to those who deserved it.

These swordsmen from the land whose very name meant "the sword," Ceura, were the best soldiers Kylar had ever seen. They had set up camp with efficiency that spoke of years of campaigning. They cleared brush that might conceal the approach of enemies, banked their small fires to reduce their visibility, and arranged their tents to protect their horses and their leaders. Each fire warmed ten men, each of whom clearly knew his responsibilities. They moved like ants in the forest, and once they finished their duties, each man would only wander as far as an adjacent fire. They gambled, but they didn't drink, and they kept their voices low. The only snag in all the Ceurans' efficiency seemed to come from their armor. With Ceuran bamboo-and-lacquer armor, a man could dress himself. But donning the Khalidoran armor they had stolen a week ago at Pavvil's Grove required assistance. Scale mail mixed with chain and even plate, and the Ceurans couldn't decide if they needed to sleep armored or if men should be assigned to each other as squires.

When each squad was allowed to decide for itself how to fix the problem and didn't waste time asking up the chain of command, Kylar knew his friend Logan Gyre was doomed. War Leader Lantano Garuwashi paired the Ceuran love of order with individual responsibility. It was emblematic of why Garuwashi had never lost a battle. It was why he had to die.

So Kylar moved through the trees like the breath of a vengeful god, only rustling the branches in time with the evening wind. The oaks grew in straight, widely spaced rows broken where younger trees had muscled between their elders' shoulders and grown ancient themselves. Kylar climbed out as far on a limb as he could and spied Lantano Garuwashi through the swaying branches, dimly illuminated in the light of his fire, touching the sword in his lap with the delight of recent acquisition. If Kylar could get to the next oak, he could climb down mere paces from his deader.

Can I still call my target a "deader," even though I'm not a wetboy anymore? Thinking of Garuwashi as a "target" was impossible. Kylar could still hear his master Durzo Blint's voice, *"Assassins,"* he sneered, "have targets, because assassins sometimes miss."

Kylar gauged the distance to the next limb that could bear his weight. Eight paces. It was no great leap. The daunting part was landing on a tree limb and arresting his momentum silently with only one arm. If Kylar didn't leap, he'd have to sneak between two fires where men were still passing intermittently, and the ground was strewn with dead leaves. He'd jump, he decided, when the next good breeze came.

"There's an odd light in your eyes," Lantano Garuwashi said. He was big for a Ceuran, tall and lean and as heavily muscled as a tiger. Stripes of his own hair, burning the same color as the flickering fire, were visible through the sixty locks of all colors he'd claimed from opponents he'd killed.

"I've always loved fire. I want to remember it as I die."

Kylar shifted to get a look at the speaker. It was Feir Cousat, a blond mountain of a man as wide as he was tall. Kylar had met him once. Feir was not only a capable hand with a sword, he was a mage. Kylar was lucky the man's back was to him.

A week ago, after the Khalidoran Godking Garoth Ursuul killed him, Kylar had made a bargain with the yellow-eyed being called the Wolf. In his weird lair in the lands between life and death, the Wolf promised to restore Kylar's right arm and bring him back to life quickly if Kylar stole Lantano Garuwashi's sword. What had seemed simple—who can stop an invisible man from stealing?—was getting more complicated by the second. Who can stop an invisible man? A mage who can see invisible men.

"So you really believe the Dark Hunter lives in those woods?" Garuwashi asked.

"Draw the blade a little, War Leader," Feir said. Garuwashi bared the sword a hand's breadth. Light poured from a blade that looked like a crystal filled with fire. "The blade burns to warn of danger or magic. The Dark Hunter is both."

So am I, Kylar thought.

"It's close?" Garuwashi asked. He rose to a crouch like a tiger ready to pounce.

"I told you luring the Cenarian army here might be our deaths, not theirs," Feir said. He stared back into the fire.

For the past week, since the battle of Pavvil's Grove, Garuwashi had led Logan and his men east. Because the Ceurans had disguised themselves in dead Khalidorans' armor, Logan thought he was chasing the remnants of the defeated Khalidoran army. Kylar still had no idea why Lantano Garuwashi had led Logan here.

But then, he had no idea why the black metal ball called a ka'kari had chosen to serve him, or why it brought him back from death, or why he saw the taint on men's souls that demanded death, or, for that matter, why the sun rose, or how it hung in the sky without falling.

"You said we were safe as long as we didn't go into the Hunter's wood," Garuwashi said.

"I said 'probably' safe," Feir said. "The Hunter senses and hates magic. That sword definitely counts."

Garuwashi waved a hand, dismissing the danger. "We didn't go into the Hunter's wood—and if the Cenarians want to fight us, they must," Garuwashi said.

As Kylar finally understood the plan, he could hardly breathe. The woods north, south, and west of the grove were thick and overgrown. The only way for Logan to use his numerical superiority would be to come through the east, where the giant sequoys of the Dark Hunter's Wood gave an army plenty of space to maneuver. But it was said a creature from ages past killed anything that entered that wood. Learned men scoffed at such superstition, but Kylar had met the peasants of Torras Bend. If they were superstitious, they were a people with only one superstition. Logan would march right into the trap.

The wind kicked up again, setting the branches groaning. Kylar snarled silently, and leapt. With his Talent he made the distance easily. But he'd jumped too hard, too far, and he slipped off the far side of the branch. Little black talons jabbed through his clothing along the sides of his knees, along his left forearm, and even from his ribs. For a moment, the talons were liquid metal, not so much tearing his clothes as absorbing them at each tiny point, and then they solidified and Kylar jerked to a stop.

After he pulled himself back onto the branch, the claws melted back into his skin. Kylar was left trembling, and not just because of how close he'd come to falling. *What am I becoming?* With every death reaped and every death suffered, he was growing stronger. It scared the hell out of him. *What does it cost? There's got to be a price.*

Gritting his teeth, Kylar climbed headfirst down the

tree, letting the claws rise and sink from his skin, stabbing little holes in his clothes and in the tree bark. When he reached the ground, the black ka'kari bled from every pore to cover him like a second skin. It masked his face and body and clothes and sword, and began devouring light. Invisible, Kylar advanced.

"I dreamed of living in a small town like that Torras Bend," Feir said, his back as broad as an ox before Kylar. "Build a smithy on the river, design a water wheel to drive the bellows until my sons are old enough to help. A prophet told me it could happen."

"Enough of your dreams," Garuwashi cut him off, standing. "My main army should be almost through the mountains. You and I are going."

Main army? The last piece clicked. This was why the sa'ceurai had dressed as Khalidorans. Garuwashi had drawn the best of Cenaria's army far to the east while his main army was massing in the west. With the Khalidorans defeated at Pavvil's Grove, Cenaria's peasant levies were probably already hurrying back to their farms. In days, a couple hundred Cenarian castle guards were going to face the entire Ceuran army.

"Going? Tonight?" Feir asked, surprised.

"Now." Garuwashi smirked right at Kylar. Kylar froze, but he saw no flash of recognition in those green eyes. Instead, he saw something worse.

There were eighty-two kills in Garuwashi's eyes. *Eighty-two!* And not one of them a murder. Killing Lantano Garuwashi wouldn't be justice; it would be murder. Kylar cursed aloud.

Lantano Garuwashi jumped to his feet, the scabbard flying from a sword that looked like a bar of flame, his body already in a fighting stance. The mountain that was Feir was only a little slower. He was on his feet, turning with naked steel in his hand faster than Kylar would have believed from a man so big. His eyes went wide as he saw Kylar.

Kylar screamed in frustration and let blue flame whoosh over the ka'kari-skin and the great frowning mask he wore. He heard a footstep as one of Garuwashi's bodyguards attacked from behind. Kylar's Talent surged and he back-flipped, planting his feet on the man's shoulders and pushing off. The sa'ceurai smashed into the ground and Kylar flipped through the air, blue flames whipping and crackling from his body.

Before he caught the branch, he dropped the flames and went invisible. He flipped from branch to branch one-handed, with no attempt at stealth. If he didn't do something— tonight—Logan and all his men would die.

"Was that the Hunter?" Garuwashi asked.

"Worse," Feir said, pale. "That was the Night Angel, perhaps the only man in the world you need fear."

Lantano Garuwashi's eyes lit with a fire that told Feir he heard the words "man you need fear" as "worthy adversary."

"Which way did he go?" Garuwashi asked.

3

As Elene rode up to the little inn in Torras Bend, utterly exhausted, a gorgeous young woman with long red hair in a ponytail and an earring sparkling in her left ear, was mounting a roan stallion. The stable hand ogled her as she rode north.

Elene was almost on top of the stable hand before the man turned. He blinked at her stupidly. "Hey, your friend just left," he said, pointing to the disappearing redhead.

"What are you talking about?" Elene was so tired she could hardly think. She'd walked for two days before one of the horses had found her. And she'd never found out what had happened to the other captives or the Khalidorans or the Ymmuri who'd saved her.

"You could still catch her," the stable hand said.

Elene had seen the young woman well enough to know that they'd never met. She shook her head. She had to pick up supplies in Torras Bend before she headed to Cenaria. Besides, it was almost dark, and after her days on the trail with her Khalidoran captors, Elene needed a night in bed and desperately needed a chance to wash up. "I don't think so," she said.

She went inside, rented a room from the distracted innkeeper's wife with some of the generous amount of silver she'd found in her horse's saddlebags, washed herself and her filthy clothing, and immediately fell asleep.

Before dawn, she pulled on her still-damp dress distastefully and went downstairs.

The innkeeper, a slight young man, was carrying in a crate full of washed flagons from outside and setting them upside-down to dry before he finally went to bed for the night. He nodded at Elene in a friendly manner, barely glancing up. "The wife will have breakfast ready in half an hour. And if—oh hell." He looked at her again, obviously seeing her for the first time. "Maira didn't tell me. . . ." He rubbed his hands on his apron in what was obviously a habitual gesture, because his hands weren't wet, and stalked over to a table piled high with knick-knacks, notes, and account books.

He pulled out a note, and handed it to her apologetically. "I didn't see you last night, or I'd have given it to you straight away." Elene's name and description were written on the outside of the note. She unfolded it and a smaller, crumpled note fell out. The smaller note was in Kylar's hand. It was dated the day he'd left her in Caernarvon. Her throat tightened.

"Elene," she read, "I'm sorry. I tried. I swear I tried. Some things are worth more than my happiness. Some things only I can do. Sell these to Master Bourary and move the family to a better part of town. I will always love you."

Kylar still loved her. He loved her. She'd always believed it, but it was different to see it in his own messy writing. The tears flowed freely. She didn't even care about the disconcerted innkeeper, opening and shutting his mouth, unsure what to do with a woman crying in his inn.

Elene had refused to change and it had cost her everything, but the God was giving her a second chance. She'd show Kylar just how strong, deep, and wide a woman's love could be. It wasn't going to be easy, but he was the man she loved. He was the one. She loved him, and it was as simple as that.

It was several minutes before she read the other note, this one written in an unfamiliar woman's hand.

"My name's Vi," the note said, "I'm the wetboy who killed Jarl and kidnapped Uly. Kylar left you to save Logan and kill the Godking. The man you love saved Cenaria. I hope you're proud of him. If you go to Cenaria, I've given Momma K access to my accounts for you. Take whatever you want. Otherwise, Uly will be at the Chantry, as will I, and I think Kylar will go there soon. There's . . . more, but I can't bear to write it. I had to do something terrible so we could win. No words can erase what I've done to you. I'm so terribly sorry. I wish that I could make it right, but I can't. When you come, you can exact whatever vengeance you wish, even to my life. -Vi Sovari"

The hairs on the back of Elene's neck were standing up. What kind of a person would claim to be such an enemy and such a friend? Where were Elene's wedding earrings? "There's more"? What did that mean? Vi had done something terrible?

The lead weight of intuition dropped into Elene's stomach. That woman outside yesterday had been wearing an earring. It probably wasn't—it surely wasn't—

"Oh my God," Elene said. She ran for her horse.

The dream was different every night. Logan stood on the platform, looking at pretty, petty Terah Graesin. She would walk over an army of corpses—or marry a man she despised—to seize her ambition. As it had that day, Logan's heart failed him. His father had married a woman who poisoned all his happiness. Logan could not.

As he had that day, Logan asked for her fealty, the round platform reminding him of the Hole where he'd rotted during the Khalidoran occupation. Terah refused. But instead of submitting himself so the armies wouldn't be split on the eve of battle, in this dream Logan said, "Then I sentence you to death for treason."

His sword sang. Terah stumbled back, too slowly. The blade cut halfway through her neck.

Logan caught her, and abruptly, it was another woman, another place. Jenine's slashed throat gushed blood over her white nightgown and his bare chest. The Khalidorans who'd broken into their wedding chamber laughed.

Logan thrashed and woke. He lay in darkness. It took him time to reorient himself. His Jenine was dead. Terah Graesin was queen. Logan had sworn fealty. Logan Gyre had given his troth, a word that meant not just his oath but his truth. So if his queen ordered him to stamp out the last few Khalidorans, he complied. He would always be glad to kill Khalidorans.

Sitting up in the dark of the camp tent, Logan saw the captain of his bodyguards, Kaldrosa Wyn. During the occupation, Momma K's brothels had become the safest places in the city for women. Momma K had accepted only the most beautiful and exotic. They had drawn the first Khalidoran blood of the war during a city-wide ambush that had come to be called the Nocta Hemata, the Night of Blood. Logan had honored them publicly and they had become his. Those who could fight had fought and died—and saved him. After the Battle of Pavvil's Grove, Logan had dismissed the rest of the Order of the Garter except for Kaldrosa Wyn. Her husband was one of the ten wytch hunters, and they'd go nowhere without each other, so she'd said she might as well serve.

Kaldrosa wore her garter on her left arm. Sewn from enchanted Khalidoran battle flags, it glimmered even in the darkness. She was, of course, pretty, with olive Sethi skin, a throaty laugh, and a hundred stories, some of which she claimed were even true. Her chain mail was ill-fitting, and she wore a tabard with his white gyrfalcon, its wingtips breaking a black circle. "It's time," she said.

General Agon Brant poked his head in the tent, then entered. He still needed two canes to walk. "The scouts have returned. Our elite Khalidorans think they're setting an ambush. If we come from the north, south, or west, we have to go through dense forest. The only way is through the Hunter's Wood. If it really exists, it'll wipe us out. If I were facing fourteen hundred men with only one hundred, I don't think I could do any better."

If the situation had arisen a month ago, Logan wouldn't have hesitated. He would lead his army through the open spaces of the Hunter's Wood, legends be damned. But at Pavvil's Grove they'd seen a legend walk—and devour thousands. The ferali had shaken Logan's conviction that he knew the difference between superstition and reality. "They're Khalidoran. Why didn't they head north for Quorig's Pass?"

Agon shrugged. It was a week-old problem. This platoon wasn't nearly as sloppy as the Khalidorans they knew. Even as they fled from Logan's army, they'd raided. Cenaria had lost a hundred men. The Khalidorans hadn't lost one. The best guess Agon could make was that they were an elite unit from some Khalidoran tribe the Cenarians hadn't encountered before. Logan felt like he was staring at a puzzle. If he didn't solve it, his people would die. "You still want to hit them from all sides?" Agon asked.

The problem stared at Logan, mocking him. The answer didn't come. "Yes."

"Are you still insisting on leading the cavalry through the Wood yourself?"

Logan nodded. If he was going to ask men to brave death from some monster, he would do it himself, too.

"That's very . . . brave," Agon said. He'd served nobles long enough to make a compliment speak volumes of insult.

"Enough," Logan said, accepting his helmet from Kaldrosa. "Let's go kill some Khalidorans."

4

Vürdmeister Neph Dada hacked a deep, rasping, unhealthy cough. He cleared his throat noisily and spat the results into his hand. Then he tilted his hand and watched the phlegm drip to the dirt before turning his eyes to the other Vürdmeisters around his low fire. Aside from the young Borsini, who blinked incessantly, they gave no sign that he disgusted them. A man didn't survive long enough to become a Vürdmeister on magical strength alone.

Glowing faintly, figures were laid out in military formations on the ground. "This is only an estimation of the armies' positions," Neph said. "Logan Gyre's forces are in red, roughly fourteen hundred men, west of the Dark Hunter's Wood, in Cenarian lands. Maybe two hundred Ceurans pretending to be Khalidoran are the blue, right at the edge of the Wood. Further south, in white, are five thousand of our beloved enemies the Lae'knaught. We Khalidorans haven't fought the Lae'knaught directly since you were all still at the tit, so let me remind you that though they hate all magic, *we* are what they were created

to destroy. Five thousand of them is more than enough
to complete the job the Cenarians began at the Battle of
Pavvil's Grove, so we must tread carefully."

In quick detail, Neph outlined what he knew of the
deployment of all the forces, inventing details where it
seemed appropriate, and always speaking over the Vürdmeisters' heads, as if expecting them to understand intricacies of generalship that they had never learned.
Whenever a Godking died, the massacres began. First
the heirs turned on each other. Then the survivors rallied
meisters and Vürdmeisters around them and began anew
until only one Ursuul remained. If no one established
dominance quickly, the bloodletting would spread to the
meisters. Neph didn't intend for that to happen.

So as soon as he was certain that Godking Garoth Ursuul was dead, Neph had found Tenser Ursuul, one of the
Godking's heirs, and convinced the boy to carry Khali.
Tenser thought carrying the goddess would mean power.
It would—for Neph. For Tenser, it meant catatonia and
insanity. Then Neph had sent a simple message to Vürdmeisters at every corner of the Khalidoran empire: "Help
me bring Khali home."

By answering a religious call, every Vürdmeister who
didn't want to throw away his life backing some vicious
Ursuul child had a legitimate escape. And if Neph tamed
these first Vürdmeisters who'd arrived from their post-
ings in nearby lands, when Vürdmeisters arrived from the
rest of the empire, they too would fall in line. If there
was one thing Godkings were good at, it was inculcating
submission.

"The Dark Hunter's Wood is between us," Neph mo-
tioned to encompass the Vürdmeisters, himself, and

Khali's bodyguard, a bare fifty men in all, "and all these armies. I personally have seen over a hundred men—meisters and not—ordered into the Wood. None has emerged. Ever. If this were merely a matter of Khali's security, I would not bring this to your attention." Neph coughed again, his lungs afire, but the coughing was calculated, too. Those who wouldn't bend the knee to a young man might be content to bide their time serving a failing old one. He spat. "The Ceurans have the sword of power, Curoch. Right there," Neph gestured to where his phlegm had fallen, at the very edge of the Dark Hunter's Wood.

"Has the sword taken the form of Ceur'caelestos, the Ceurans' Blade of Heaven?" Vürdmeister Borsini asked. He was the young blinking one with a grotesquely large nose and big ears to match. He was staring into the distance. Neph didn't like it. Had Borsini been eavesdropping when the scout reported?

Borsini's vir, the measure of the goddess's favor and his magical power, filled his arms like a hundred thorny black rose stems. Only Neph's vir filled more of his skin, undulating like living tattoos in Lodricari whorls, blackening him from forehead to fingernails. But despite his intelligence and power, Borsini was only in the eleventh shu'ra. Neph, Tarus, Orad, and Raalst were all twelfth shu'ra, the highest rank anyone aside from the Godking could attain.

"Curoch takes any shape it pleases," Neph said. "The point is, if Curoch goes into the Hunter's Wood, it will never come out. We have a slim chance to seize a prize we've sought for ages."

"But there are three armies here," Vürdmeister Tarus

pointed out. "All outnumber us, and each would happily kill us."

"Attempting to claim the sword will most likely end in death, but may I remind you," Neph said, "if we don't try, we will answer for it. Therefore, I will go. I am old. I have few years remaining to me, so my death will cost the empire less." Of course, if he had Curoch in hand, magnifying his magical power a hundredfold, everything would change, and all of them knew it.

Vürdmeister Tarus was the first to object. "Who's put you in charge—"

"Khali has," young Borsini interrupted before Neph could. *Dammit!* "Khali has sent me a vision," he said. "That's why I asked what the Ceurans call the sword. Khali told me that I am to fetch Ceur'caelestos. I am the youngest of us, the most dispensable, and the fastest. Vürdmeister Dada, she said she will speak to you this morning. You are to await her word by the prince's bedside. Alone."

The boy was a genius. Borsini wanted a chance at the sword, and he was buying off Neph in front of all of them. Neph would stay with Khali and the catatonic prince and when he emerged, it would be with "a word from the goddess." In truth, Neph hadn't wanted to go after the sword at all. But the only way he was certain the others would make him stay was if he'd tried to go. Borsini's eyes met Neph's. His look said, "If I get the sword, you serve me. Understood?"

"Blessed be her name," Neph said. The others echoed. They didn't fully understand what had just happened. They would, in time. Neph said, "You should take my horse; it's faster than yours." And he had woven a small cantrip into its mane. When the sun rose—at about the time a rider would get to the south side of the wood—the cantrip would begin pulsing with magic that would draw the Dark Hunter. Borsini wouldn't live to see noon.

"Thank you, but I'm an awkward hand at new horses. I'll take my own," Borsini said, his voice carefully neutral. His enormous ears wiggled, and he tugged at his enormous nose nervously. He suspected a trap and knew he'd avoided it, but he wanted Neph to think it was luck.

Neph blinked as if disappointed and then shrugged as if to cover and say it didn't matter.

It didn't. He'd tied that cantrip into the mane of every horse in the camp.

5

$\mathcal{K}$ylar had never started a war.

Approaching the Lae'knaught camp required none of the stealth he'd used to approach the Ceurans. Invisible, he simply walked past the sentries in their black tabards emblazoned with a golden sun: the pure light of reason beating back the darkness of superstition. Kylar grinned. The Lae'knaught were going to love the Night Angel.

The camp was huge. It held an entire legion, five thousand soldiers, including a thousand of the famed Lae'knaught Lancers. As a purely ideological society, the Lae'knaught claimed they held no land. In practice, they'd occupied eastern Cenaria for eighteen years. Kylar suspected this legion had been sent here as a show of force to deter Khalidor from trying to push further east. Maybe they just happened to be here.

In truth, he didn't care. The Lae'knaught were bullies. If there had been a shred of integrity in their claim of fighting black magic, they would have come to Cenaria's defense when Khalidor invaded. Instead, they'd bided their time, burning local "wytches" and recruiting among the Cenarian refugees. They'd probably been hoping to come to the rescue after Cenaria's power was obliterated and take even better lands for their pains.

Without provoking anyone, Cenaria had been invaded from the east by the Lae'knaught, from the north by Khalidor, and now from the south by Ceura. It was about time some of those hungry swords met each other.

A smoking black blade slid from Kylar's left hand. He made it glow, wreathed in blue flames, but kept himself invisible. Two soldiers chatting instead of walking their patrol routes froze at the sight. The first one was a relative innocent. In the other's eyes, Kylar could see that the man had accused a miller of witchcraft because he wanted the man's wife.

"Murderer," Kylar said. He slashed with the ka'kari-sword. The blade didn't so much cut as devour. There was barely any resistance as the blade passed through noseguard, nose, chin, tabard, gambeson, and stomach. The man looked down, then touched his split face, where blood gushed. He screamed and his entrails spurted out.

The other sentry bolted, shrieking.

Kylar ran, pulling his illusions around him. As if through smoke, there were glimpses of gleaming iridescent black metal skin, the crescents of exaggerated muscles, a face like Judgment, with brows pronounced and frowning, high angular cheekbones, a tiny mouth, and glossy black eyes without pupils that leaked blue flames. He ran past a knot of gaunt Cenarian recruits, wide-eyed at the sight of him, weapons in hand but forgotten. There were no crimes in their eyes. These men had joined because they had no other way to feed themselves.

The next group had participated in a hundred burnings, and worse. *"Raper!"* Kylar yelled. He slid the ka'kari-sword through the man's loins. It would be a bad death. Three more died before anyone attacked him. He danced past a spear and lopped off its head, then kept running for the command tents at the center of the camp.

A trumpet shrilled an alarm, finally. Kylar continued down the lines of tents, sometimes slipping back into invisibility, always reappearing before he killed. He cut loose some of the horses to create confusion, but not many. He wanted this army to be able to react quickly.

In minutes, the entire camp was in pandemonium. A team of horses dragging their hitching post bolted, the post whipping back and forth, tangling in tents and dragging them away. Men screamed, shouting obscenities, gibbering about a ghost, a demon, a phantasm. Some attacked each other in the darkness and confusion. A tent went up in flames. Whenever an officer emerged, shouting, trying to bring order, Kylar killed. Finally, he found what he was looking for.

An older man burst out of the largest tent in the camp. He threw a great helm on his head, the symbol of a Lae'knaught underlord, a general. "Form up! Hedgehog!" he shouted. "You fools, you're being beguiled! Hedgehog formation, damn you!"

Between their terror and his voice being muted by the great helm, few men listened at first, but a trumpeter blew the signal again and again. Kylar saw men starting to form loose circles of ten with their backs to each other, spears out.

"You're only fighting yourselves. It's a delusion. Remember your armor!" The underlord meant the armor of unbelief. The Lae'knaught thought superstitions only had power if you believed in them.

Kylar leapt high into the air, and let himself become visible as he dropped in front of the underlord. He landed on one knee, his left hand to the ground, holding the sword, his head bowed. Though the cacophony continued in the distance, the men nearby were stunned to silence. "Underlord," the Night Angel said. "For you I bear a message." He stood.

"It is nothing but an apparition," the underlord announced. "Gather! Eagle three!" The trumpeter blew the orders and soldiers began jogging to take up positions.

Over a hundred men crowded the clearing in front of the underlord's tent, forming a huge circle around him, spears pointing in. The Night Angel roared, blue flames leaping from his mouth and eyes. Flames trickled back down the sword. He whipped the sword in circles so fast it blurred into long ribbons of light. Then he slapped it back into its sheath with a pulse of light, leaving the soldiers blinking away after-images.

"You Lae'knaught fools," the Night Angel said. "This land is Khalidoran now. Flee or be slaughtered. Flee or face judgment." By claiming to be Khalidoran, Kylar hoped to draw any backlash onto the Ceurans-disguised-as-Khalidorans who were trying to kill Logan and all his men.

The underlord blinked. Then he shouted, "Delusions have no power over us! Remember your armor, men!"

Kylar let the flames dim, as if the Night Angel were unable to sustain itself without the Lae'knaught's belief. He faded until the only thing visible was his sword, moving in slow forms: Morning Shadows to Haden's Glory, Dripping Water to Kevan's Blunder.

"It cannot touch us," the underlord announced to the hundreds of soldiers now crowding the edges of the clearing. "The Light is ours! We do not fear the darkness."

"I judge you!" the Night Angel said. "I find you wanting!" He faded completely and saw relief in every eye around the circle, some men and women openly grinning and shaking their heads, amazed but victorious.

The underlord's aide-de-camp led his horse to him and handed him the reins and his lance. He mounted, looking like he knew he needed to start giving orders, reasserting control, getting the men to act so they wouldn't think, so they wouldn't panic. Kylar waited until he opened his mouth, then bellowed so loudly he drowned out the man's voice.

"Murderer!" Crescents of biceps and knotted shoulder muscles and glowing eyes were all that appeared, followed by a whoosh of flame as the spinning sword came alight. A soldier toppled to the ground. By the time his head rolled free of his body, the Night Angel was gone.

No one moved. It wasn't possible. An apparition was the product of mass hysteria. It had no body.

"Slaver!" This time, the sword appeared only as it jutted out of the soldier's back. The man was lifted on the sword and flung headlong into the side of the iron cauldron. He jerked, his flesh sizzling on the coals, but he didn't roll away.

"Torturer!" The legion's gentler's stomach opened.

"Unclean! Unclean!" The Night Angel screamed, its whole figure glowing, burning blue. It killed left and right.

"Kill it!" the underlord screamed.

Wreathed in blue flames that whipped and crackled in long streams behind him, Kylar was already flipping clear of the circle. Staying visible and burning, he ran straight north, as if heading back to the "Khalidoran" camp. Men dove out of his path. Then Kylar extinguished the flames, went invisible, and came back to see if his trap had worked.

"Form up!" the underlord shouted, his face purple with rage. "We march to the forest! It's time to kill some wytches, men! Let's go! Now!"

6

"Eunuchs to the left," Rugger said. The Khalidoran guard
said. He was so muscular he looked like a sack full of
nuts, but the most noticeable lump was the wen bulging grotesquely from his forehead. "Hey, Halfman! That
means you!"

Dorian shuffled into the line on the left, tearing his eyes
away from the guard. He knew the man: a bastard who'd
been whelped on some slave girl by one of Dorian's older
brothers. The aethelings, the throne-worthy sons, had tormented Rugger unrelentingly. Dorian's tutor, Neph Dada,
encouraged it. There was just one rule: they couldn't do
harm to any slave that would keep him from performing
his duties. Rugger's wen had been little Dorian's work.

"You staring at something?" Rugger demanded, poking Dorian with his spear.

Dorian looked resolutely at the floor and shook his
head. He'd altered his appearance as much as he dared before coming to the Citadel to ask for work, but he couldn't
take any illusion too far. He would be beaten regularly. A

guard or noble or aetheling would notice if a blow didn't hit the proper resistance or if Dorian didn't flinch appropriately. He'd experimented with altering the balance of his humors so that he might stop growing a man's hair, too, but the results had been horrifying. He touched his chest—now mercifully back to male proportions—just thinking about it.

Instead, he'd practiced until he could sweep his body with fire and air so as to be hairless. With the speed his beard came in, it would be a weave he would have to use twice a day. A slave's life included little privacy, so speed was essential. Mercifully, slaves were beneath notice—as long as they didn't draw attention to themselves by staring at guards as if they were freaks.

Slouch or die, Dorian. Rugger smacked him again, but Dorian didn't move, so Rugger moved down the line to harass others.

They were standing outside the Bridge Keep. Two hundred men and women were at the keep's west gate. Winter was coming, and even those who'd had good harvests had been beggared by the Godking's armies. For the smallfolk, it hardly mattered if the army passing through was enemy or friend. One looted, the other scavenged, but each took what it wanted and killed anyone who resisted. With the Godking emptying the Citadel to send armies both south into Cenaria and north into the Freeze, the coming winter would be brutal. All the people in the line were hoping to sell themselves into slavery before winter arrived and the lines quadrupled.

It was an icy clear autumn morning in the city of Khaliras, two hours before dawn. Dorian had forgotten the glory of the northern stars. In the city, few lamps burned—oil was too precious, so few terrestrial fires tried to compete with the ethereal flames burning like holes in the cloak of heaven.

Despite himself, Dorian couldn't help but feel a stirring of pride as he looked over the city that could have been his. Khaliras was laid out in an enormous ring around the chasm that surrounded Mount Thrall. Succeeding generations of Ursuul Godkings had walled in semicircles of the city to protect their slaves and artisans and merchants until all the semicircles of different stone had connected to shield the whole of the city.

There was only one hill, a narrow granite ridge up which the main road snaked in switchbacks designed to encumber siege weapons. At the top of the ridge the Gate Keep sat like a toad on a stump. And just on the other side of the rusty iron portcullis's teeth lay Dorian's first great challenge.

"You four, go," Rugger said.

Dorian was third of four eunuchs, and all shivered as they approached the precipice. Luxbridge was one of the wonders of the world, and in all his travels, Dorian had never seen magic to rival it. Without arches, without pillars, the bridge hung like a spider's anchor line for four hundred paces between the Gate Keep and the Citadel of Mount Thrall.

The last time he'd crossed Luxbridge, Dorian had only noticed the brilliance of the magic, sparkling, springy underfoot, coruscating in a thousand colors at every step. Now, he saw nothing but the building blocks to which the magic was anchored. Luxbridge's mundane materials were not stone, metal, or wood; it was paved with human skulls in a path wide enough for three horses to pass abreast. New heads had been added to whatever holes had formed over the years. Any Vürdmeister, as masters of the vir were called after they passed the tenth shu'ra, could dispel the entire bridge with a word. Dorian even knew the spell, for all the good it did him. What made his stomach knot was that the magic of Luxbridge had been crafted so that magi, who used the Talent rather than the foul vir that meisters and Vürdmeisters used, would automatically be dropped.

As perhaps the only person in Midcyru who had been trained as both meister and magus, Dorian thought he had a better chance of making the crossing than any other magus. He'd bought new shoes last night and fitted a lead plate inside each sole. He thought he'd eliminated all traces of southern magic that might cling to him. Unfortunately, there was only one way to find out.

Heart thudding, Dorian followed the eunuchs onto Luxbridge. At his first step, the bridge flared weirdly green and Dorian felt his feet tingling as vir reached up around his shoes. An instant later it stopped, and no one had seen it. Dorian had done it. Luxbridge felt that he was Talented, but Dorian's ancestors had been smart enough to know that not every Talented person was a mage. The rest of Dorian's steps, shuffling like the other nervous eunuchs', brought sparks out of the magic that made the embedded skulls seem to yawn and shift as they stared hatefully at those who passed overhead. But they didn't give way.

If Dorian felt some pride at the genius of Luxbridge, the sight of Mount Thrall brought only dread. He'd been born in the bowels of that damned rock, been starved in its dungeons, fought in its pits, and committed murder in its bedchambers and kitchens and halls.

Within that mountain, Dorian would find his *vürd,* his destiny, his doom, his completion. He would also find the woman who would become his wife. And, he feared, he would find out why he had cast aside his gift of prophecy. What was so terrible that he wanted to throw away his foreknowledge of it?

Mount Thrall was unnatural: an enormous four-sided black pyramid twice as tall as it was wide and extending deep below the earth. From Luxbridge, Dorian looked down and saw clouds obscuring whatever depths lay below. Thirty generations of slaves, both Khalidoran and captured in war, had been sent into those depths, mining until they gasped out their last breaths in the putrid fumes and added their own bones to the ore.

The pyramid of the mountain had been sheared straight down one edge and flattened, leaving a plateau in front of a great triangular dagger of mountain. The Citadel sat on that plateau. It was dwarfed by the mountain, but as one approached, it became clear that the Citadel was a city unto itself. It held barracks for ten thousand soldiers, great storerooms, vast cisterns, training places for men and horses and wolves, armories, a dozen smithies, kitchens, stables, barns, stockyards, lumberyards, and space for all the workers, tools, and raw materials needed for twenty thousand people to survive a year under siege. And even at that, the Citadel was dwarfed in comparison to the castle that was Mount Thrall, for the mountain was honeycombed with halls and great rooms and apartments and dungeons and passages long forgotten that bored into its very roots.

Neither the Citadel nor the mountain had been full in decades and with the armies sent north and south, the place was even quieter than usual. Khaliras was now home to only the smallfolk, a skeleton crew of an army, less than half of the kingdom's meisters, enough functionaries to keep the reduced business of the kingdom operating, the aethelings, and the Godking's wives and concubines and their keepers.

Head among those keepers was the Chief Eunuch, Yorbas Zurgah. Yorbas was an old, soft, perfectly hairless man, even shaving his head and plucking his eyebrows and eyelashes. He sat huddled in an ermine cloak to ward off the morning chill at the servants' gate. Before him was a desk with a parchment unrolled on it. His blue eyes studied Dorian dubiously.

"You're short," Chamberlain Zurgah said. He himself had a typical eunuch's height.

And you're fat. "Yes, my lord."

"'Sir' will suffice."

"Yes, sir."

Chamberlain Zurgah stroked his hairless chin with fingers like sausages encased in jeweled rings. "You have an odd look about you."

In his youth, Dorian had rarely seen Yorbas Zurgah. He didn't think the man would remember him, but anything that caused greater scrutiny was dangerous.

"Do you know the penalty for a man who attempts entry to the harem?" Zurgah asked.

Dorian shook his head and looked steadfastly at the ground. He clenched his jaw and, without raising his eyes, tucked his hair back behind his ears.

It was what he considered a stroke of genius; he'd

given himself silver streaks in his hair, paired with slightly pointed ears and several webbed toes. They were features that only one tribe in Khalidor possessed. The Feyuri claimed to be descended from the Fey folk and were equally despised for that and their pacifism. Dorian appeared to be half Feyuri, which was exotic enough and from a group despised enough that he hoped no one would stop to think how his Khalidoran half made him look a lot like Garoth Ursuul. It also explained why he was short. "It's the . . . other reason they call me Halfman, sir."

Yorbas Zurgah clicked his tongue. "I see. Then here are the terms of your indenture: you will serve whatever hours are asked of you. Your first tasks will include emptying and cleaning the concubines' chamber pots. Your food will be cold and never as much as you'd like. You are forbidden to speak with the concubines and if you have trouble with this, your tongue will be torn out. You understand?"

Dorian nodded.

"Then only one thing remains, Halfman."

"Sir?"

"We have to make sure you're a halfman after all. Remove your trousers."

7

Lantano Garuwashi sat in Kylar's path, his sword naked across his lap. Mountainous Feir Cousat stood beside him, meat-slab arms folded. They blocked a narrow game trail that led along the southern edge of the Hunter's Wood. Feir muttered a warning as Kylar approached.

Garuwashi's sword was unmistakable. The hilt was long enough for one or two hands; pure mistarille inscribed with gold runes in Old Ceuran. The slightly curving blade was inscribed with a dragon's head, facing the tip of the blade. As Kylar came closer, the dragon breathed fire. The flames traveled within the blade, and before them, Ceur'caelestos turned clear as glass. The flames rolled out farther as Kylar approached. Kylar brought the ka'kari to his eyes and saw Ceur'caelestos in the hues of magic.

That was when he knew the sword was the product of another age. The magics themselves had been crafted to be beautiful—and Kylar couldn't understand the least of them. He sensed playfulness, grandeur, hauteur, and love. Kylar realized he had a tendency for getting into things that were way over his head. Not least of which was trying to steal such a sword from Lantano Garuwashi.

"Drop the shadows, Kylar, or I'll help you drop them," Feir said.

Fifteen paces away from them, Kylar dropped the shadows. "So, mages can see me when I'm invisible. Dammit." He'd suspected as much.

Feir smiled joylessly. "Only one in ten men. Nine in ten women. I can only see you within thirty paces. Dorian could've seen you half a mile away, through trees. But I forget myself. Baronet Kylar Stern of Cenaria, also known as the Night Angel, war son of wetboy Durzo Blint, this is War Leader Lantano Garuwashi the Undefeated, the Chosen of Ceur'caelestos, of the Aenu Heights Lantanos."

Kylar clasped his left hand to his stump and bowed in the Ceuran style. "War Leader, the many tales of your deeds attest to your prowess."

Garuwashi rose and slid Ceur'caelestos into its sheath. He bowed and his mouth twitched. "Night Angel, likewise the few tales of yours."

The horizon was brightening, but it was still dark in the forest. It smelled like rain and coming winter. Kylar wondered if they would be the last smells he would experience. He smiled on the rising tide of despair. "We seem to have a problem," Kylar said. *Several, actually.*

"What's that?" Garuwashi asked.

I can't fight you invisible without killing Feir first, and even if I did, neither of you merits death. "You have a sword I need," Kylar said instead.

"Are you out of your—" Feir asked, but cut off at Garuwashi's raised hand.

"Forgive me, Night Angel," Garuwashi said, "but

you're not left-handed, and you move like the loss of your sword hand was recent. If you so desire death that you would challenge me, I will not deny you. But why would you?"

Because I made a deal with the Wolf. Mere hours afterward, Kylar had found Durzo's note that ended, "MAKE NO DEALS WITH THE WOLF." Maybe this was why. *I can't win.*

~Not unless I give you a hand,~ the ka'kari said in Kylar's mind. The black metal ball that lived within Kylar spoke rarely, and it wasn't always helpful when it did. *You're hilarious,* Kylar thought back at it.

Garuwashi's eyes flicked down to Kylar's wrist. Feir was agog.

Kylar glanced down and saw jet black metal writhing from his stump. It resolved itself slowly into a hand. He tried to make a fist, and it did. *Are you joking?*

~I'm not that cruel. By the way, Jorsin Alkestes didn't like the idea of his enemies coming back to life. If that sword kills you, you're really dead.~

Funny, the Wolf failed to mention that. Kylar wiggled the black fingers. He even had some sensation in them. At the same time, the hand was too light. It was hollow, the skin thinner than parchment. *Hey, while you're doing miracles . . .*

~No.~

You didn't even listen!

~Go ahead.~ It felt like the ka'kari was rolling its eyes. How did it do that? It didn't even have eyes.

Can you fix its weight?

~No.~

Why not?

The ka'kari sighed. ~*I stay one size. I'm already covering all your skin and making a hand for you. Invisibility, blue flames, and an extra hand not enough for you?*~

So making a dagger of you and throwing it would be a bad idea?

The ka'kari went silent in a huff, and Kylar grinned. Then he realized he was grinning at Lantano Garuwashi, who had sixty-three deaths tied to his hair, and eighty-two in his eyes.

"You need a minute?" Garuwashi asked, lifting an eyebrow.

"Uh, I'm ready now," Kylar said. He drew his sword.

"Kylar," Feir said. "What are you going to do with the sword?"

"I'm going to put it somewhere safe."

Feir's eyes widened. "You're taking it into the Wood?"

"I was thinking I'd throw it in."

"Good idea," Feir said.

"Perhaps a nice idea. But not a good one," Garuwashi said. He closed the distance between them in an instant. The swords rang together in the staccato melody that would climax in death. Kylar decided to feign a tendency to overextend on his ripostes. With a swordsman as talented as Lantano Garuwashi, he should only have to show the weakness twice and spring the trap the third time.

Except that the first time he overextended, Garuwashi's sword was into the gap, raking Kylar's ribs. He could have killed Kylar with that thrust, but he held back, wary of a trap.

Kylar staggered back, and Garuwashi let him regroup, his eyes showing disappointment. They'd barely crossed swords for five seconds. The man was too fast. Ridiculously fast. Kylar brought the ka'kari to his eyes and was even more stunned.

"You're not even Talented," Kylar said.

"Lantano Garuwashi needs no magic."

~*Kylar Stern surely does!*~

Kylar felt an old familiar shiver, an echo from his past. It was the fear of dying. With Alitaeran broadswords, Kylar could have crushed Garuwashi with the brute strength of his Talent. Against the elegant Ceuran sword, Kylar's Talent did almost nothing for him. "Let's get on with it," Kylar said.

They began again, Garuwashi feeling Kylar out, even giving ground, seeing what Kylar could do. But there was no holding back. Kylar had seen that. Soon Kylar would tire and try something desperate. Garuwashi would be waiting for it—how many desperate men had he seen in sixty-three duels? Surely every man who had survived the first clash of blades had the same sick feeling in his stomach that Kylar had now. There was no room for self-delusion once the blades began singing.

Something changed on Garuwashi's face. It wasn't enough to tell Kylar what he was going to do; but it was enough to tell him that Garuwashi thought he knew Kylar's strengths. Now he would end it.

There was a beat. Kylar waited for Garuwashi to advance, those damn long arms of his unbelievably quick, the stance fluid and sure.

"You feel it, don't you?" Garuwashi asked, withholding his attack. "The rhythm."

"Sometimes," Kylar grunted, his eyes not leaving

Garuwashi's center, where he would see any movement begin. "Once, I heard it as music in truth."

"Many died that day?" Garuwashi asked.

Kylar shrugged.

"Thirty highlanders, four wytches, and a Khalidoran prince," Feir said.

Lantano Garuwashi smiled, not surprised at Feir's knowledge. "Yet today you fight woodenly. You are stiff, slower than usual. Do you know why? That day you faced death no less than you do today."

Wrong, but I didn't know that then.

"Today," Garuwashi continued, "you are afraid. It narrows your vision, tenses your muscles, makes you slow. It will make you dead. Fight to win, Kylar Stern, not to not lose." It was disconcerting to hear good advice from the man who was about to kill him.

"Here," Garuwashi said. He lifted Ceur'caelestos and Kylar saw the edges go blunt. "I'll know when you're ready."

Feir leaned up against a tree and whistled quietly.

Garuwashi attacked again and within seconds, the dull sword scraped Kylar's ribs. A few more seconds passed in furious ringing and the dull blade grazed his forearm, then jabbed his shoulder. But even as the blows rained down on him, Kylar began to remember his master Durzo's merciless sparring. His fear receded. This was the same, except now Kylar had more endurance, more strength, more speed, and more experience than a year ago. And he'd beaten Durzo. Once. Kylar's vision cleared and his pulse slowed from its frenzied hammering.

"That's it!" Garuwashi said. Ceur'caelestos went sharp once more and they began.

Kylar was aware of Feir. The second-echelon Blade Master was seated cross-legged on the ground now, jaw slack. The man was muttering to himself, "Gabel's Game to Many Waters to Three Mountain Castles—good, good—to Heron's Hunt to—was that Praavel's Defense? Goramond's Dive to—what the hell? I've never—Yrmi's Bout, good gods, some variation on Two Tigers? Harani Bulls to . . ."

The fight accelerated, but Kylar felt a calm. He was, he realized, *smiling*. Madness! Yet it was so, and Garuwashi's thin lips were drawn up in a little smirk of their own. There was beauty here, something precious and rare. Every man wished he could fight. Few could, and only one in a hundred years fought this well. Kylar had never thought to see another master on a par with Durzo Blint, but Lantano Garuwashi might even be better than Durzo, a little faster, his reach a little longer.

Kylar dove behind a sapling a second before Garuwashi sheared it in two. As Garuwashi pushed aside the falling tree, Kylar thought. He only had one thing Lantano Garuwashi didn't. Well, aside from invisibility.

~Oh, don't use that! It wouldn't be fair*!~*

What Lantano Garuwashi didn't have was years of fighting against someone better than he was. Kylar was studying Garuwashi's style in a way Garuwashi had never needed study anyone's. It was straightforward. Garuwashi basically depended on his superior speed, strength, reach, technique, and flexibility to win. And—there!

Kylar went through half of Lord Umber's Glut and then modified it, twisting the last parry so Ceur'caelestos missed his cheek by a breath. His own sword gashed Garuwashi's shoulder—but Garuwashi's counter was already coming. Kylar threw up an arm and instinctively brought the ka'kari up along the ridge.

White light blazed and threw thousands of sparks, as if Kylar's arm were an enormous flint and Ceur'caelestos steel. Kylar's arm burned.

The warriors staggered back and Kylar knew that if Garuwashi had put any more force into that counter, it would have destroyed the ka'kari.

~Please . . . please don't ever do that again.~

"Who taught you that?" Garuwashi demanded, his face bright red.

"I . . ." Kylar stopped, confused. His left arm was throbbing, bleeding where Ceur'caelestos had scraped it.

"He means the combination, Kylar," Feir said, his eyes wide. "That move's called Garuwashi's Turn. No one else is fast enough to do it."

Kylar fell back into a ready stance, not in fear now, but futility. He'd thrown his best at Garuwashi and barely scratched him. "No one taught me," he said. "It just seemed right."

The anger dropped from Lantano Garuwashi's face in an instant. This was a man, Kylar saw, of sudden passions, unpredictable, intense, dangerous. Garuwashi drew a white handkerchief and reverently wiped Ceur'caelestos clean of Kylar's blood. He sheathed the Blade of Heaven.

"I will not kill you today, doen-Kylar, peace rest with your blade. In ten years, you will be full in your prime. Let us meet then in Aenu and fight before the royal court. Masters such as we deserve to fight with minstrels and maidens and lesser masters in attendance. Should you win, you may have all that is mine, including the holy blade. Should I win, at least you will have had ten years of life and glory, yes? It will be an event anticipated for a decade and retold for a thousand."

In ten years Kylar would indeed be in his prime, and what Garuwashi wasn't saying was that he would be past his own. Garuwashi would then be what, forty-five? Perhaps his speed and Kylar's would be equal then. He would still have his reach, and both would have a lot more experience, but that was the more precious coin to Kylar. Would the Wolf care if Kylar waited ten years? Hell, if Kylar didn't get himself killed, he wouldn't even see the Wolf for . . . well, probably ten years. Then again, if Kylar died on this sword, he wouldn't see the Wolf at all.

Grimacing, Kylar said, "You tell me, if I promised you that I was going to get something for you, would you want it now or in ten years?"

"If you try now, you'll die. In ten years, you'll have a chance."

A month ago, Kylar had one goal: to convince his girlfriend Elene that eighteen years as a virgin was quite enough. Then Jarl had been murdered while delivering the news that Logan Gyre was trapped in his own dungeon. Kylar's loyalties to the living and the dead had given him two new goals that had cost him the first. He'd abandoned Elene as he'd sworn he wouldn't in order to save Logan and avenge Jarl by killing the Godking. It had cost him an arm, a magical bond to the beautiful disaster named Vi Sovari, and an oath to steal Garuwashi's blade.

Now all Kylar wanted was to make sure his sacrifices hadn't been for nothing, and then to go make things right with Elene.

As if to punish him for his faithlessness, he now imagined her saying, "An oath you only keep when it's convenient isn't an oath at all."

"I can't put it off," Kylar said. "Sorry."

Garuwashi shrugged. "It is a matter of honor, yes? I understand. That is a—"

"Pit wyrm!" Feir shouted, leaping to his feet.

Kylar turned and all he could see was a hole tearing in space ten paces away, and through it, hell and rushing fire-cracked skin. In the forest, a big-nosed, big-eared Vürdmeister was laughing.

8

"$\mathcal{P}$iss. You're different, Halfman," Hopper said. He was a tall, lean, white-haired old eunuch who was training Dorian—*Halfman,* he reminded himself. Hopper handed him a pot.

"What do you mean?" Halfman asked.

"Two shits." Hopper handed Halfman two more chamber pots. Halfman emptied half of the piss into each, swished it around, and emptied the pots into an enormous clay jar set in a wicker frame. "A piss for every two shits. The rest of the pisses go last. They're easy. You get a puke or a slippery, you use two pisses on those. No one wants to smell that all day."

Halfman thought Hopper wasn't going to answer him, but after they finished emptying the pots into the enormous clay jars—six of them today, it meant one more trip for Halfman than usual—Hopper paused. "I dunno. Look at how you sit all straight."

Cursing inwardly, Halfman slouched. He'd been forgetting. Thirty-two years of sitting up straight like a king's son was dangerous. Of course, no one spent as much time with him as Hopper, but if the old eunuch had noticed, what would happen if Zurgah or an overseer or a meister or an aetheling did? His half-Feyuri appearance had already isolated him. He was regularly singled out for extra chores and beatings for imagined infractions. The nights he didn't go to bed aching were rare.

"Don't forget yourself. Puke—how the girls manage to nick wine is beyond me—if you do, well . . ." Hopper lifted his sandal-clad feet one at a time and wiggled his big toes. Those two toes were all he had left. He'd been caught teaching the bored women of the harem a dance, he said, and the only reason he'd been let off so easily was because Zurgah liked him, and the dance hadn't involved touching or speaking to the women. Other eunuchs, Hopper said, were killed for less. "Twenty-two years since my little dance. Twenty-two years I been with the chamber pots, and I'll stay with 'em till I die. Now help me with the empties. You remember the process?"

"One clean water rinses ten pisses or four shits."

"Bright one, you. Help me rinse the first forty, then you can take pots out."

They worked together in silence. Halfman had made no progress finding the woman who would be his wife. The Citadel held two separate harems, and several women were kept apart from either one. Halfman had been assigned to the common harem.

More than a hundred of Garoth Ursuul's wives and concubines lived here—wives were the women who had produced sons, concubines those who had produced either daughters or nothing, which were considered equivalent. Given that Garoth Ursuul had to be near sixty, all of the women were surprisingly young. No one ever said what happened to the old wives.

It was strange to be in his father's harem. He was seeing a different and oddly personal side of the man who had shaped him in a hundred ways. Like most Khalidorans, the Godking favored solid women with wide hips and full buttocks. There was a northern saying, *volaer ust vassuhr, vola uss vossahr.* Literally, "a man's horses and his brides should be big enough to ride." Most of the common women were Khalidoran, but the Godking's harems included all nationalities except the Feyuri. All were beautiful; all had large eyes and full lips; and he preferred taking them, Hopper said, as soon after their flowering as possible.

Life in the harem, though, bore little relation to the stories southrons told. If it was a life of luxury, it was also one of enforced boredom.

Each day, as he gathered the chamber pots from the concubines' rooms, Halfman stole glances at the women. The first thing he noticed was that they were always fully clothed. Not only was the Godking out of the city, but winter was coming. With no possibility of being asked to serve any time soon, some of the women didn't even bother brushing their hair or changing out of their bedclothes, though there seemed to be a form of social censure that kept anyone from slipping too far.

"They used to sit there all winter, half-naked and made up like fertility whores, huddled around the fires and shivering like puppies in the snow," Hopper said. "Now we give 'em a signal when His Holiness is on his way. Just wait'll you see it. You've never seen anyone move so fast. Or if one of them's called for by name, every last one of the others will descend on her. Khali's blood, you can't even see her for a good five minutes. Then when she comes out of that circle, you'd swear they traded her for the goddess herself. Much as they hate each other and scheme and gossip, when the Godking calls, they help each other. It's one thing to gossip and lie about a woman," Hopper lowered his voice, "but none of them wants to be the reason a girl gets sent to the aethelings."

Dorian's stomach turned. So they knew. Of course they knew. Dorian's seed class had been taught flaying on a disrespectful concubine. Dorian, as the first of the class, had been assigned her face. He remembered his pride as he had presented it to his tutor Neph Dada whole, even the eyelids and eyelashes intact. The ten-year-old Dorian had worn that face to dinner as a mask, making japes with his seed class while Neph smiled encouragement. God help him, he had done even worse things.

What was he doing here? This place was sick. How could a people tolerate this? How could they worship a goddess that delighted in suffering? Dorian sometimes believed that countries had the kind of leaders they deserved. What did that say about Khalidor—with its tribalism and endemic corruption held in check only by its deep fear of the men who styled themselves Godkings? What did it say about Dorian? This was his people, his country, his culture—and once, his birthright. He, Dorian Ursuul, had survived. He'd demolished his seed class one at a time, pitting brother against brother until only he survived. He'd accomplished his uurdthan, his Harrowing, and shown himself worthy to be called the Godking's son and heir. This, all of this, could have been his—and he didn't miss it for a second.

He loved many things about Khalidor: the music, the dances, the hospitality of its poor, its men who laughed or cried freely, and its women who would wail and keen over their dead where southrons stood silent like they didn't care. Dorian loved their zoomorphic art, the wild woad tattoos of the lowland tribes, the cool blue-eyed maidens with their milk-white skin and fierce tempers. He loved a hundred things about his people, but sometimes he wondered if the world wouldn't be a better place if the sea swept in and drowned them all.

As sacrifices for abundant livestock, how many of those blue-eyed girls had laid their mewling firstborn sons on Khali pyres? For abundant crops, how many of those expressive men had caged their aged fathers in wicker coffins and watched them drown slowly in bogs? They wept as they did murder—but they did it. For honor, when a man died, if his wife wasn't claimed by the clan chief, she was expected to throw herself on her husband's pyre. Dorian had seen a girl fourteen years old whose courage failed her. She'd been married less than a month to an old man she'd never met before her wedding. Her father beat her bloody and threw her on the pyre himself, cursing her for embarrassing him.

"Hey," Hopper said, "you're thinking. Don't. It's no good here. You work hard, you don't have to think. Got it?" Halfman nodded. "Then let's strap this on and you can work."

Together, they strapped the wicker basket to Halfman's back. There were thongs that wrapped around each shoulder and his hips to help him bear the great weight of the clay pot full of sewage. Hopper promised to have another pot ready by the time Halfman got back.

Halfman trudged through the cold basalt hallways. It was always dark in the slaves' passages, with only enough torches burning so the slaves could avoid colliding.

"I'm tired of banging toothless slaves," a voice said around the next intersection of hallways. "I hear the new girl's in the Tygre Tower. They say she's beautiful."

"Tavi! You can't call it that." Bertold Ursuul was Dorian's great-grandfather, and the man had gone mad, believing he could ascend to heaven if he built a tower high enough and decorated it solely with Harani swordtooth tygres. His madness embarrassed Garoth Ursuul, so he'd forbidden the tower to be called anything but Bertold's Tower.

Dorian stopped. There was a torch at the intersection and no way he could retreat without being noticed. The aethelings—for no one else spoke with such arrogance—were coming toward him. There was no escape.

Then he remembered. He was Halfman now, a eunuch slave. So he slouched and prayed that he was invisible.

"I talk how I please," Tavi said, coming into the intersection just as Halfman did. Halfman stopped, stepped aside, and averted his eyes. Tavi was a classic aetheling: good-looking if with a hawkish nose, well-groomed, well-dressed, an aura of command, and the stench of great power, despite being barely fifteen years old. Halfman couldn't help but size him up instantly—this one would be the first of his seed class. This would have been one Dorian would have tried to kill early. Too arrogant, though. Tavi was the kind who needed to brag. He would never make it through his uurdthan. "And I can fuck who I please, too," Tavi said, coming to a stop. He looked down each of the halls as if lost. His indecision froze Halfman

in place. He couldn't move without possibly moving into
the aethelings' path.

"Besides," Tavi said, "the harems are too closely
guarded. But the Tygre Tower's just got two dreads at the
bottom, and her deaf-mute eunuchs."

"He'll kill you," the other aetheling said. He didn't
look pleased to be having this conversation in front of
Halfman.

"Who's gonna tell him? The girl? So he'll kill her, too?
Fuck! Where are we? We've been walking this way for
ten minutes. All these halls look the same."

"I said we should have gone the other—" the other aetheling began.

"Shut up, Rivik. You," Tavi said, speaking to Halfman.
Halfman flinched as a slave would. "Khali, you stink!
Which way is it to the kitchens?"

Halfman reluctantly pointed back the way the aethelings had come.

Rivik laughed. Tavi cursed. "How far?" Tavi asked.

Halfman would have found some other way to answer,
but Dorian couldn't help himself. "About ten minutes."

Rivik laughed again, louder.

Tavi backhanded Dorian. "What's your name,
halfman?"

"Milord, this slave is called Halfman."

"Ooh hoo!" Rivik hooted. "We got a live one here!"

"Not for long," Tavi said.

"If you kill him, I'll tell," Rivik said.

"You'll tell?" The disdain and disbelief on Tavi's
face told Halfman that Rivik's days as a sidekick were
numbered.

"He made me laugh," Rivik said. "Come on. We're already late for lecture, you know how Draef will try to turn that on us."

"Fine, just a second." The vir rose to Tavi's skin and he began chanting.

"Tavi . . ."

"It won't kill him."

The magic was a slight concussion inches from Half-man's chest. It threw him back into the wall like a rag doll. The wicker splintered and the clay pot shattered, geysering human waste over Halfman and the wall behind him.

Rivik laughed louder. "We've gotta remember this next time we're bored. Khali's tits, it reeks! Imagine if we could break one of those pots in Draef's room."

The aethelings left Halfman gasping on the floor, wiping ooze from his face. It was five minutes before he stood up, but when he did, it was with alacrity. In the fear and in the miming of fear, he had almost missed it. The newest concubine could only be one woman. His future wife was at the top of Bertold's Tower, and she was in danger.

9

The pit wyrm tore through the hole in reality and went for Kylar. The great wyrm was tubular, at least ten feet in diameter, its skin cracked and blackened, fire showing through the gaps. When it lunged, its great bulk heaved forward and its entire eyeless front opened as it vomited its cone-like mouth. Kylar leapt as each concentric ring snapped out. Each ring was circled with teeth, and when the third ring caught a tree, teeth the size of Kylar's forearm whipped around into the wood. The pit wyrm sucked itself forward, its lamprey-like mouth inverting as the rings bit into the wood in turn, shearing a ten-foot section out of the tree trunk before Kylar landed.

Instantly, the pit wyrm lunged again. It had no visible means of propelling so great a mass. It didn't gather itself to strike like a serpent, but moved instead as if this were but one head or arm attached to a much larger creature crouched on the other side of that hole. Again, it went for Kylar.

He flipped through the air as the tree the pit wyrm had cut fell, crashing to the ground, throwing up dust in the misty morning light. Kylar grabbed a tree and spun, the ka'kari giving him claws enough to sink into the bark and throw him back over the pit wyrm's back. His sword flashed as he flew over the pit wyrm, but the blade bounced off the armored skin.

There was something white in the corner of Kylar's eye. He dropped to the forest floor and saw it: a tiny white homunculus with wings and the Vürdmeister's face, grinning at Kylar under an enormous nose. It clawed at Kylar's face.

Kylar blocked. The homunculus's talons sank smoothly into Kylar's sword.

The pit wyrm lunged again even as Feir hammered its side, his sword ringing in the mists but doing no damage, not even slowing the wyrm. The pit wyrm couldn't be distracted, wouldn't stop until it reached its target.

Its target wasn't Kylar. It was the homunculus.

Kylar dropped the sword and flipped once more. He landed on the side of a tree, thirty feet up, fingers and toes sinking into the wood. The pit wyrm slammed into Kylar's sword on the ground, the cone of teeth slapping around the homunculus, digging deep into the soil as each ring of teeth slapped forward, devouring the white creature and everything around it. The pit wyrm pulled back, shaking dirt and roots and dead leaves through the air. Satisfied, it began to slide back into whatever hell it had been called from.

Then it shivered.

Feir was still striking the creature. For some reason, he wasn't using magic. The mountainous mage struck again, a mighty hammer blow—with no effect.

By the time Kylar's eyes found the real reason the pit wyrm had shivered, Lantano Garuwashi was halfway through its body. He was hacking at it near the hole in reality. But he wasn't *hacking.* Wherever Garuwashi cut with Ceur'caelestos, the pit wyrm's flesh sprang apart, smoking. The look on the sa'ceurai's face told Kylar that the man was enrapt—he was the world's best swordsman, wielding the world's best sword, facing a monster out of legend. Lantano Garuwashi was living his purpose.

Garuwashi's sword moved with Garuwashi's speed. In two seconds, he had cut through the entire pit wyrm. The thirty-foot section of wyrm crashed to the forest floor, thrashed once, and then broke apart in quivering red and black clumps, dissolving in putrid green smoke until nothing was left. The stump writhed bloodlessly until Garuwashi slashed it with six slices in blinding succession and whatever was controlling it yanked it back into hell.

Kylar sprang off the tree and landed ten paces from Lantano Garuwashi. Having never fought a pit wyrm, the sa'ceurai couldn't have known that they didn't just appear; they had to be called. He let down his guard.

The big-nosed Vürdmeister acted before Kylar could, stepping out from behind a tree and unleashing a ball of green flame. Garuwashi brought Ceur'caelestos up, but he wasn't prepared for what happened when that sword came into contact with that magic.

When Ceur'caelestos met the vir, a dull thump shook the gold needles off the tamaracks. The morning mists blew outward in a visible globe, the moss shriveled and smoked on the trees, and the concussion blasted Feir and Garuwashi and the Vürdmeister from their feet.

Only Kylar was still standing, shielded from the magical explosion by the ka'kari covering his skin. The men fell in all directions, but Ceur'caelestos stayed in the center of its own storm. It spun once in the air and stuck in the forest floor.

Kylar swept Ceur'caelestos into his hand. The fallen Vürdmeister didn't try to stand. He gathered power, the vir on his arms wriggling in slow motion, their undulations becoming a movement that Kylar could strangely read—the magic would be a gout of flame three feet wide and fifteen feet long.

Before the Vürdmeister could release the flame, Kylar ran him through.

The Vürdmeister's cool blue eyes widened in pain, and then widened again in sheer terror as every inky rose-thorn tracing of vir in his entire body filled with white light. Light exploded from his skin. The Vürdmeister's body bucked and thrashed, then went limp. The vir was gone without a trace, leaving the dead man's skin the normal pasty hue of a northerner. Even the air felt clean.

In the distance, to the northeast, a Lae'knaught trumpet blasted the command to charge. It was far away—within the Dark Hunter's Wood.

"The bloody fools," Kylar murmured. He'd lured them in, but it was still hard to believe they'd fallen for it. He looked at Curoch. *The things I do for my king.*

~You're not really going to throw it away, are you?~

I gave my word.

~You have the Talent and the lifetimes it would take to become that sword's master.~

I can't exactly go out in public with a black metal hand, can I?

~Wear gloves.~

"We need to leave—right now," Feir Cousat said. "Using magic this close to the wood is like begging the

Dark Hunter to come. And there's some kind of magic beacon on the Vürdmeister's horse. I chased it away, but it's probably too late."

So that was why Feir hadn't used magic in fighting against the pit wyrm. Smart.

"You have taken my *ceuros*," Lantano Garuwashi said with a moral outrage that Kylar didn't understand. Then he remembered. A sa'ceurai's soul was his sword. They believed that literally. What sort of abomination would steal another man's soul?

"Did you not take it from someone else?" Kylar asked.

"The gods gave me the blade," Lantano Garuwashi said. He was quivering with rage and loathing, despair fighting to the fore in his eyes. "Your theft is not honorable."

"No," Kylar admitted. "Nor, I'm afraid, am I."

A plaintive howl unlike anything Kylar had ever heard ripped through the wood. It was high and mournful, inhuman.

"Too late," Feir said, his voice strangled. "The Hunter's coming."

The Wolf had told Kylar to stay back forty paces from the Hunter's Wood, so Kylar gave it fifty. He looked through the lesser trees of the natural forest to the preternatural height and bulk of the sequoys. He felt small, caught up in events vast beyond his comprehension. He heard the whistling of something speeding toward him. He hefted Curoch and threw it as far into the Wood as he could. It flew like an arrow. As it crossed into the air over the wood, it burned like a star falling to earth.

The entire forest began to glow golden.

The whistling stopped.

10

The three men stood side by side, staring into the wood. Feir thought that he was the only one who was properly terrified. Kylar had distracted the Hunter by throwing Curoch into the wood, but there was nothing to stop it from coming back.

Kylar calmly folded his legs and sat on the forest floor. The black skin retreated into the young man, leaving him in his underclothes. He studied the stump where his metallic right hand had been, barely noticing as the Wood's autumnal glow deepened to a bloody red and then began to lighten to green.

Lantano Garuwashi, now soulless, stared with disbelief. But he wasn't seeing anything except the disappearance of Ceur'caelestos. The man who would be king was suddenly *aceuran*—swordless, an outlaw, an exile, not even to be acknowledged. The cruel rain of implications was beating his future to dust.

In the last week, Feir had seen this man act publicly as if Ceur'caelestos had been destined for his hands. But in private moments, Feir had seen glimpses of the young hedge sa'ceurai with an iron sword, who knew that whatever excellence he attained, he would never be accepted among those born to greater blades. It was an enormous turnaround for a man who'd reconciled himself to hard realities—and now he was staring a new, much harder reality in the face.

Feir wondered how long it would be before Garuwashi decided to kill himself. Lantano Garuwashi wasn't a man who would easily give up his life. He believed in himself too much. But this disgrace would surely overwhelm that.

The thought left Feir oddly hollow. Why should he mourn Lantano Garuwashi's death? It would mean Cenaria would escape another brutal occupation and Feir would be released from his service to a hard and difficult man. But Feir didn't want Garuwashi to die. He respected him.

Magic flashed so intensely Feir's vision went white. It lasted only a fraction of a second. Kylar gasped.

Blinking away tears, Feir looked at him. Kylar appeared unchanged: still half-naked, still staring toward the wood. He stood slowly and stretched his arms.

"Much better," Kylar said, grinning.

He had both arms. He was whole. Kylar shook himself and his skin was cloaked in black again. He didn't cover his face with the grim mask of judgment; this time, he carried a slim black sword in his hand.

Lantano Garuwashi dropped to his knees and spoke to Feir, "'This path lies before you. Fight Khalidor and become a great king.' This you told me, and I heard only my heart's desire: that I would show those effete nobles in Aenu what their mocking was good for, that I would be Ceura's king. I did not fight Khalidor, and now my ceuros is lost. Thus has Lantano Garuwashi reaped death for faithlessness." He turned. "Night Angel, will you be my second?"

A brief look of confusion passed over Kylar, then his eyes showed recognition. After Garuwashi made a lateral cut through his own stomach with a short sword, his second would strike his head from his shoulders to finish the suicide. It was an honor, if a grisly one, and Feir couldn't help but feel slighted.

"Feir, nephilim, messenger from the gods whom I ignored, I would have you serve another way," Garuwashi said. "Please, carry my story to my warriors and to my family."

A chill went down Feir's spine. Not only would every sa'ceurai in the world know that Lantano Garuwashi had died here, but they would know Ceur'caelestos had been thrown into the Wood. No matter how Feir told the story, it would be retold until it fit Ceuran beliefs. The best swordsman, the best sword, and the deadliest place would be tied together forever in Ceuran myth. Every new sixteen-year-old sa'ceurai who thought he was invincible—in other words, most of them—would head for the Dark Hunter's Wood, determined to recover Ceur' caelestos and be Lantano Garuwashi reborn.

It would mean the death of generations.

Kylar's face changed. It started as black tears pouring from his eyes. Then his eyes themselves were covered in black oil. Then in a whoosh, the mask of judgment was back. Black eyes leaked incandescent blue flame. Studying Lantano Garuwashi, he cocked his head to the side.

Feir felt a chill at the sight of that visage. Any shred of childhood that had been left in the young man Feir had met six months ago was gone. Feir didn't know what had replaced it.

"No," the Night Angel pronounced. "There is no taint in you that demands death. Another ceuros will come to you, Lantano Garuwashi. In five years, I will meet you at dawn on Midsummer's Day in the High Hall of the Aenu. We shall show the world a duel such as it has never seen. This I swear."

The Night Angel slapped the thin blade to his back, where it dissolved into his skin. He bowed to Garuwashi and then to Feir, and then he disappeared.

"You don't understand," Garuwashi said, still on his knees, but the Night Angel was gone. Garuwashi turned wretched eyes to Feir. "Will you be my second?"

"No," Feir said.

"Very well, faithless servant. I don't need you."

Garuwashi drew his short sword, but for once in his life, Feir was quicker than the sa'ceurai. His sword smacked the blade from Garuwashi's hand and he scooped it up.

"Give me a few hours," Feir said. "The Hunter is distracted. With five thousand flies in its web, one more may go unnoticed."

"What are you going to do?" Garuwashi asked.

I'm going to save you. I'm going to save all your damned stiff-necked, infuriating, magnificent people. I'm probably going to get my damn fool self killed. "I'm going to get your sword back," Feir said, and then he walked into the Wood.

11

$\mathcal{A}$ high, tortured howl woke Vi Sovari from a dream of Kylar fighting gods and monsters. She sat up instantly, ignoring the aches from another night on rocky ground. The howl was miles away. She shouldn't have been able to hear it through the giant sequoys and the deadening morning mists, but it continued, filled with madness and rage, changing pitch as it flew with incredible speed from the Wood's center.

Only then did Vi become aware of Kylar through the ancient mistarille-and-gold earring. She'd bonded Kylar as he lay unconscious at the Godking's mercy. It had saved Cenaria and Kylar's life, and now Vi and Kylar could sense each other. Kylar was two miles distant, and Vi could feel that he held something of incredible power. She could feel him reaching a decision. The power departed from him, and he felt an odd sense of victory.

Suddenly, it was as if the sun were rising in the south. Vi stood on shaky knees. A hundred paces away, at the enormous sequoys of the Dark Hunter's Wood, the air itself turned a brilliant gold, radiating magic. Even to Vi, untrained as she was, it felt like the kiss of a midsummer's sunset on her skin.

Then the color deepened to reddish gold. Every dust mote floating in the air, every water droplet in the mists was a flaming autumnal glory.

When Vi was fifteen, her master, the wetboy Hu Gibbet, had taken her to a country estate for a job. The deader was some lord's bastard who'd made himself a successful spice merchant and decided not to repay his underworld Sa'kagé investors. The estate was covered with maples. That autumn morning Vi moved through a world of gold, carpeted with red-gold leaves, the very air awash in color. As she stood over the corpse, she had mentally retreated to a place where glorious crimson leaves weren't paired with pulsing arterial blood. Hu beat her for it, of course, and to those beatings Vi had mentally acquiesced. A distracted wetboy is a dead wetboy. A wetboy knows no beauty.

The howl ripped through the wood again, freezing her bones. Moving fast, terribly fast, it changed pitch higher and then lower and then higher, all in the space of two seconds, as if it were flying to and fro faster than anything could possibly move. Everywhere it went, it was followed by the faint, tinny sound of rending metal. Then came a man's scream. More followed.

There was a battle in the wood. No, a massacre.

All the while, the wood pulsed with magic. The flaming red was fading to yellow green and then to the deep green of vitality, the scent of new grass, fresh flowers.

"Kylar has given it new life," Vi said aloud. She didn't know how she knew, but she knew Kylar had put something into the Wood—and that something was rejuvenating the entire forest. Kylar himself felt invigorated, well in a way he hadn't felt in the week she'd shared the bond with him. Whole.

Vi felt something wrong behind her. Her hands flashed to the daggers at her belt. Then she was on her back. Even as air whooshed from her lungs, a crackling ball of blue energy hissed and spat through the air where she'd been standing a moment before.

The most Vi could do was gasp, trying to catch her wind. It was several blind seconds before she could sit up.

Before her, a man wrapped in dark brown leather put his foot on a corpse's face and wrenched a dagger from its eye. The corpse was wearing the robes of a Khalidoran Vürdmeister, and black, tattoo-like vir were still twitching under the surface of his skin. Vi's savior cleaned his dagger and turned. His feet made no sound. A multitude of cloaks, vests, pocketed shirts, and pouches of all sizes covered the man, all of them horsehide, all tanned the same deep brown and worn soft from long use. Twin forward-curving gurkas were tucked into the back of his belt, an unstrung scrimshawed short bow was slung over his back, and Vi could see numerous hilts protruding from his garments. He unlaced a brown mask that concealed all but his eyes and pulled it back around his shoulders. He had an affable face; wry, almond-shaped brown eyes; loose black hair; and broad, flat features with high cheekbones. He could only be a Ymmuri stalker.

Stalkers were reputed to be the greatest hunters of all the Ymmuri horse lords. They were said to be invisible in the forests or on the grassy steppes in the east where the Ymmuri lived. They never shot prey that wasn't running or on the wing. And they were all Talented. In other words, they were grassland wetboys. Unlike wetboys, they didn't kill for pay but for honor.

And fuck me if there isn't more truth to the stories about them than there is to the ones about us.

The stalker folded his hands behind his back and bowed. "I am Dehvirahaman ko Bruhmaeziwakazari," he said with an odd cadence that came from growing up speaking a tonal language. "You may . . . hearken? . . . call, yes, *call* me Dehvi." He smiled. "You are Vi, yes?"

Vi rose, swallowing. This man had snuck up on her—a wetboy—and thrown her to the ground easily, and now he stood smiling and friendly. It was as unnerving as having a blue ball of death pass inches from her face.

"Come," Dehvi said. "This place is safe no more. I will escort you."

"What are you talking about?" Vi asked.

"Magic . . . calls to? asks to? hearkens to? the demon of the Wood." Dehvi wrinkled his nose. Vi knew what he meant, but she wasn't sure what word he was looking for.

"Beckons!" he said, finding it. "That beckon means death."

"That call," Vi said, putting his words together slowly. Magic called the Hunter. The Vürdmeister had used magic, and Vi was Talented. The Hunter might be coming.

The stalker frowned. "These word give me difficulties. Too many meanings."

"Where are you taking me?" Vi asked. *And do I have any choice?* Her body relaxed to Alathea's Waking and her fingers dipped casually to check her daggers on their way to brush the dirt from her pants—except the daggers were gone.

The stalker regarded her coolly. Clearly she hadn't checked casually enough. "To Chantry."

He turned and knelt beside the corpse, muttering under his breath in a language Vi didn't recognize. He spat on the man three times, cursing him not with foul words as Vi cursed, but actually commending the man's soul to some Ymmuri hell.

"You wish to go?" Dehvi asked, offering her the daggers.

"Yes," Vi said, taking them gingerly. "Please."

"Then come. The demon hunts. Is best to leave."

12

When Dorian had first been studying to become a Hoth'salar, a Brother of Healing, he'd invented a little weave to mimic the symptoms of influenza by killing the life that inhabited the stomach, with devastating results that cleared up within a day or two. Several times, to Solon's and Feir's vast amusement, Dorian had used it for other than scholarly reasons. Now "influenza" swept through the eunuchs, and Halfman was pressed into double shifts and unfamiliar tasks. He'd even made himself sick first to eliminate suspicion.

Today, two of the most trusted eunuchs were sick. Halfman climbed the stairs to the Tygre Tower, an unheated basalt obscenity that looked on the verge of toppling in a high wind. He moved past thousands of the great marsupial cats. They looked like wolves with exaggerated maws, sword-like canines, and orange and black stripes. Everywhere one looked, the tygres looked back. There were tapestries, etchings, tiny statues, ancient mangy stuffed specimens, necklaces of teeth, paintings of tygres tearing apart children. The styles were a hodgepodge, unimportant. All that had mattered to Bertold Ursuul was that they featured sword-tooth tygres.

Dorian reached the top of the tower breathless, shivering from the cold, sorry that the food he'd carried had long lost its warmth, and apprehensive about who would be up here. If she were one of the Talented wives or concubines, she might smell the magic on him. The depth of the women's ensnarement was such that any who found a traitor would report him immediately.

Dorian knocked on the door. When it opened, his breath whooshed out.

She had long dark hair, large dark eyes, a slender but shapely figure under a shapeless dress. No cosmetics heightened her eyes and none rouged her lips. She wore no jewelry. She smiled and his heart stopped. He'd never met her, but he knew that smile. He had seen that dimple on the left side, a little deeper than the one on the right. She was the one.

"My lady," Dorian said.

She smiled. She was a small young woman with sad, kind eyes. So young!

"You can speak," she said, and her voice was light and pure and strong, the kind of voice that begged to sing. "They've only sent deaf-mutes before. What's your name?"

"It is death for me to speak, milady, and yet. . . . How afraid of them are you?" Halfman asked. Giving his real name was the ultimate commitment. He wanted to throw it down at her feet and abandon himself to her whim, but that was madness on a par with the madness he'd escaped by throwing away his gift of prophecy.

Jenine paused, biting her lip. Her lips were full, pink despite the coolness of this high tower. Dorian—for Half-man would never have dared—couldn't help but imagine kissing those soft, full lips. He blinked, forcing things carnal from his mind, impressed that this young woman was actually devoting thought to his question. In Khali-dor, fear was wisdom.

"I'm always afraid here," she said. "I don't believe I will betray you, but if they torture me?" She scowled. "That isn't much to give, is it? I will keep your confidence to the last extremity I can endure. It is a poor and lame vow, but I have been stripped of riches outside and in." She smiled then, the same beautiful, sad smile.

And he loved her. May the God who saved him have mercy, he couldn't believe it was happening so fast. He'd never believed in instant love. Such a thing could surely be only infatuation or lust, and he couldn't deny that he felt both. But at seeing her, he had an odd feeling of meet-ing an old friend. His Modaini friend Antoninus Wervel said such things happened when those who had known each other in past lives met. Dorian didn't believe that. Perhaps, instead, it was his visions. At Screaming Winds, he'd been in trances for weeks. Though his memory had been mostly scoured of those images, he knew he'd lived lifetimes with this woman in those visions. Perhaps that had primed him for love. For he believed that this was real love, that here was the woman to whom he would yield body and mind and soul and future and hopes, unflinch-ing. He would marry her, or no one. She would bear his son, or no one would.

It was either that—or the insanity Dorian had feared for so long had finally caught up with him.

"They call me Halfman," he said. "But I am Dorian Ursuul, first acknowledged son and heir to Garoth Ursuul, and long since stricken from the Citadel's records for my betrayal of the Godking and his ways."

"I don't understand," she said. Her forehead wrinkled. He'd seen that wrinkle, in his visions, when it had become a worry line, permanent on her brow. He had to stop himself from reaching a hand up to smooth it away. It would be too familiar. By the God, he thought he'd left all the confusions of being a prophet behind! "Why are you here?"

"For you, Jeni."

She stiffened. "You may call me Your Highness, or—as you have evidently come at great risk—you may call me Jenine."

"Yes, of course, Your Highness." Dorian's head swirled. Here he was, a prince himself, being granted permission to address a young girl by her full name. That grated. And it disappointed. Love at first sight was bad enough, but finding out that it wasn't mutual . . . well, he would have thought her a flighty girl if she'd thrown herself at him, wouldn't he?

"I think you'd better explain yourself," she said.

Stupid, Dorian. Stupid. She's far from home. She's seen her land laid waste by your people. She's isolated. She's scared—and you're not exactly at your best for romance, are you?

Ah hell, she thinks I'm a eunuch! There was a nice dilemma. How does one interject into a polite conversation, "By the way, in case you're ever interested, I do have a penis."?

"I know it seems implausible, Your Highness," he said. "But I've come to res . . . help you escape."

She put her hands on her hips—damn she was cute!—and said, "Oh, I see. You're a prince. I'm a princess trapped in a tall tower. You're here to rescue me. How droll. You can go tell Garoth I got teary-eyed and breathless—and then you can go to hell!"

Dorian rubbed his forehead. If only the snippets he remembered of his visions had given him good ways to deal with Jeni's—Jenine's—anger.

"All I need to know, Your Highness, is if you want to leave and risk death or if you'd rather stay in your comfortable tower until my father—who's old enough to be your grandfather—comes to take your dignity, your maidenhead, and your sanity. You're a little old for my father's preferences, but since you're a princess, I'm sure he'd give you a chance. If you produce a Talented son, you'll be allowed to live. You will watch him grow up only from a distance, so that your 'womanly weakness' doesn't cripple him. When he's thirteen years old, the two of you will be reunited and allowed to spend the next two months together. Then my father will surprise both of you by visiting personally and asking what you've taught his seed in the time he's given you. It doesn't matter. What matters is it will be the first time your son will have had a god's undivided attention. At the end of the interview, your son will be asked to kill you. It's a test few fail."

Her big eyes had gotten huge. "You didn't fail it, did you?"

"The north is a brutal mistress, Your Highness. No one leaves her without scars," Dorian said. "I've got a plan, but it won't be ready for five days, and everything depends on getting through the pass to Cenaria before the snow flies and the passes close. All I need to know is, if I risk my life to come again, will you leave with me?"

He could count the heartbeats while she thought. She surveyed her prison with clenched teeth. She pulled her high collar aside and Dorian saw a scar so wide he knew she must have been healed with magic almost immediately. A cut throat like that would have left her dead in a minute or two. "Back home in Cenaria, I was secretly in love. Logan was a good man, a true friend to my brother, intelligent, and half the women in the city were after him because he was so handsome—the other half were after him because he was heir to a duchy. Logan Gyre would have been a good match for me and for our families, but there was bad blood between our fathers, so I never dared hope my dream might come true. Then an assassin murdered my brother, and my father was left without an heir. He thought that if he made Logan his heir, it would forestall attempts on his own life. So Logan and I married. Two hours later, Khalidorans murdered my entire family to eliminate the heirs to the throne. But a wytch named Neph Dada thought I was too pretty to throw away, so he cut my throat in front of my husband and Healed me afterward. Logan they killed later, after subjecting him to gods know what tortures. These people have taken everything I love." She turned, and her eyes were molten steel. "I'll be ready."

Dorian picked up her bread knife. With his Talent, he elongated it and gave it two edges, while she watched. "There's an aetheling named Tavi," he said. "He's fearless while the Godking's still in Cenaria. He may come to . . . dishonor you. If he does . . . my advice is to only use this if you have the perfect opportunity. Otherwise, don't throw away your life."

The look in her eyes told him if Tavi came, Jenine would try to kill him. Failing that, she'd turn the knife on herself. And yet Dorian gave her the knife, knowing she deserved the choice.

"Now," he said, "perhaps we can speak of lighter things. Sorry that your food is cold. The hike up the damsel-in-distress's tower is a long one."

She smiled at that, a little, shy smile that reminded him of her age, and made him feel like a degenerate old predator. She fingered the dagger he'd shaped for her. "You really are a wytch, aren't you?"

"Not now. That magic is evil. I left it long ago and trained with the magi."

"Could you use your magic to bring me warm food?" Her eyes sparkled with mischief and as they laughed together, he fell in love with her all over again.

"If I could manage a disguise that convinced Yorbas Zurgah I'm a eunuch, I think I can warm your food. Here." And he warmed her gruel right then, hoping his I-do-have-a-penis was subtle enough.

She cocked an eyebrow at him. "Here I was thinking that if I'd been in an enchanted sleep and my prince needed to awaken me I'd have been out of luck."

"Uh, in the books I've read, he wakes her with a kiss," Dorian said.

"You've been reading the wrong books."

Dorian coughed and blushed, and Jenine giggled wickedly.

They spoke for hours. For the next four days, Dorian warmed the princess's meals, and the princess warmed to him. She was still devastated by the loss of her family and her kingdom and her husband, but his presence gave her hope. He saw the beautiful, sunny girl she had been emerge, and he saw evidence of the decisive, shrewd, charismatic woman she would become.

Dorian's respect and love and desire for her grew. They were the happiest days of his life.

13

Kylar's new right arm was still tingling. It looked just like the hand and forearm he'd lost a week ago except that it bore no scars and was the pallid shade of skin that had never seen the sun. The Wolf had thoughtfully given him a swordsman's calluses, but the rest of his skin was highly sensitive. The slightest breath of wind sent waves of sensation. The skin was hairless, but the nails were grown in and perfectly trimmed. The little finger that Kylar had broken as guild rat and that would never fully straighten before was now flawless.

The Wolf takes pride in his work. It's better than the hand I lost.

Kylar found his destrier waiting in the woods where he'd left it. Tribe carried him like he weighed nothing and it ate leagues for breakfast, but though he hated to admit it, the destrier intimidated him. Kylar was no horseman, and they both knew it. This morning, Tribe didn't give any trouble as Kylar approached him carefully, absorbing the ka'kari back into his skin before he came within sight.

As usual, Kylar had only worn underclothes beneath the ka'kari skin. The ka'kari could go over his clothes, but then the Night Angel looked lumpy—not exactly fear-inspiring. Tribe stared at him, making Kylar feel strangely self-conscious.

"Ah, son of a—" Kylar said. His underclothes had a huge hole right over the crotch. No wonder it was breezy. "Why do you do that?"

Tribe stared at him like he was crazy.

~Do what?~ the ka'kari asked.

"Eat my clothes!"

~I am the Devourer.~

"You could leave my clothes alone. And my swords."

~Some people like short swords.~

"People like swords with edges!"

~Good point.~

"Stop devouring my stuff. Understood?"

~No. Especially not when you ignore my puns.~

"It wasn't a request."

~I understand. I won't obey.~

Kylar was stricken silent. He grabbed worsted trousers, tunic, and his spare underclothes from the saddlebags and started to dress. He was stuck with this ka'kari for how long? Oh, right. Forever.

~You really don't understand this? You?~ the ka'kari asked. *~You, a man of flesh and blood and spirit, could not remain a mild-mannered herbalist for two months. But you expect me, a blend of metals and magic artificially infused with some small measure of intelligence and personality, to change my nature? As for the dull swords, I wasn't the one who sold Retribution, was I?~*

Kylar hadn't thought of that. Retribution's blade stayed

perfect, despite having been covered with the ka'kari for years. And he'd sold it for nothing.

No, he'd sold it to show Elene how much she meant to him. The thought of her made him ache all over again. Now he'd fulfilled his vow to the Wolf. Now, finally, he could find Elene and make things right.

Or at least more right. He reached up and touched the seamless earring in his left ear that chained him to Vi Sovari, who now was only miles away, heading east and north toward Forglin's Pass. Why was Vi going to the Chantry? Kylar pushed it out of his mind. That bitch was the last thing he wanted to think about.

Kylar suddenly grinned. "A small measure of intelligence and personality, huh?"

The ka'kari swore at him. Kylar laughed.

"Besides," Kylar said quietly, "I have changed."

"I believe you," a man said behind him.

In an instant, Kylar's sword was out. He spun, slashing. The man was tall like a hero of legend, his armor enameled white plate, with a polished mail coif that flowed around his shoulders in a cascade of steel. His helmet was tucked under his arm, and his face was gaunt, blue eyes bright. Kylar stopped the blade mere inches from Logan Gyre's neck.

Logan smiled. Kylar faltered. Abruptly, he sheathed his sword and dropped to a knee. "Your Majesty," he said.

"Stand up and hug me, you little puke."

Kylar hugged him and saw Logan's bodyguards, half a dozen of Agon's scruffy Dogs led by a beautiful woman with—of all things—a shiny garter on her arm. They were all staring at him suspiciously. Kylar upbraided himself for letting no less than eight people get so close before he noticed them. He was slipping. But then Kylar let his self-recriminations go as he felt his friend's embrace. Logan's months in the Hole had left too many sharp planes on his face and body for him to be handsome again yet, and feeling his slimness as he hugged Kylar was alarming, but there was an aura of rallying strength about him. Logan still had the same broad shoulders, the same noble carriage, and the same ridiculous height. "You're calling me little?" Kylar asked. "I probably outweigh you now. Smallest Ogre I've ever seen."

Logan laughed, releasing him. "You look good too. Except—" he turned Kylar's pale new arm over in his hand "—have you been sunning with one glove on?" He waved a hand absently. The bodyguards withdrew.

"I hacked the old arm off," Kylar said. "Had to get a new one."

Logan chuckled. "Another story you're not going to tell me?"

"You wouldn't believe me if I did," Kylar said.

"Try me."

"I just did."

"What is it with you and the lies?" Logan asked, incredulous, like Kylar was a kid with frosting and crumbs on his face claiming he'd never even seen a cake.

Kylar went cold. When he spoke again, his voice was as harsh and remote as Durzo Blint's. "You want to know why I lied to you for ten years."

"You were spying on me. I thought you were my friend."

"You pampered little fuck. When you were worrying about being embarrassed by the nude statue in the entry of your mansion, I was sleeping in sewers—literally—

because that's the only way a guild rat can stay warm enough on a freezing night to stay alive. When you were worrying about acne, I was worrying about the rapist who ran my guild and wanted to kill me. So yes, I apprenticed to a wetboy to get out. Yes, I lied to you. Yes, if you'd ever done anything wrong, I'd have told the Sa'kagé. I didn't like it, but I did it. But let me ask you this, you self-righteous bastard: when you were in the Hole and it was kill or be killed, what did you do? I lived in a Hole my whole fucking life. And you tell me who's more responsible for what Cenaria has become: my father, who was too weak to raise a child, or yours, who was too weak to become king?"

Logan's face drained. With his gauntness, it made his face look like a grey skull with burning eyes. His voice was flat. "To take the throne, my father would've had to murder the children of the woman he loved."

"And how many children died because he didn't? That's the burden of leadership, Logan: making the choice when none of the choices are good. When you nobles won't pay, others have to, people like me, kids with nothing."

Logan was silent for a long moment. "This isn't about my father, is it?"

"Where the fuck is your crown?!" Kylar demanded. Through the earring bond, Kylar could feel Vi's concern over the jumble of his emotions. She was feeling—dammit—Kylar tried to wall her out, push the feelings off to one side.

The big man looked haggard. "Did you ever meet Jenine Gunder?"

"When would I meet a princess?" It took Kylar a second to remember that Logan had been married to

Jenine—albeit only for a few hours. Khalidor's coup had come the very night of Logan's wedding. She'd bled to death in Logan's arms.

"You'd think I'd be over it," Logan said. "Honestly, I'd always assumed that a girl as beautiful and as happy as she was had to be stupid. What an asshole I was. Kylar, have you ever looked into a woman's eyes and found that she made you want to be strong, and good, and true? Protective, fierce, noble? Finding Jenine was finding something better than I ever dared to dream." Kylar didn't want to hear it. It reminded him of Elene. And if he thought about Elene, his anger would die. "I was supposed to go from that to Terah Graesin?" Logan asked. "I couldn't. Not for a crown. Not for anything."

"But I saw everyone on the battlefield, bowing to you."

"I'd given my troth . . ." Logan trailed off.

Kylar threw his hands up, despairing.

Logan's eyes filled with dim sorrow. "I did what I thought was right."

~Imagine a king who does that.~

Kylar looked at Logan as he hadn't looked at him even when he'd rescued him from the Hole. Then, he had only been able to see the physical wounds. Now he saw more. There was the gravitas of pain deep in Logan's eyes. "You'd do it again," Kylar said.

Logan forced a weak laugh. "Hey, I'm already having my doubts."

"No you're not."

The laughter died. "Yes, I am," Logan said quietly, his eyes never leaving Kylar's, his gaze never wavering. "But yes, I'd do it again. This is who I am." He had never been more royal.

Let me see him. Kylar put his hand on his friend's arm and saw Logan, through his own eyes, less handsome, but fierce, primal in the filth of the Hole, tearing raw flesh from a human leg with his teeth, weeping. There he was hating the Holers, sinking into the filth, becoming a Holer in his own eyes. There he was deciding over the hard knot of hunger that gnawed him day and night that he would share his next meal lest he abandon being human altogether. There he was, handing out food and hating those who accepted, but doing it. That small core of nobility became the most important possession Logan had, and he would pay any price for it.

That lesson was bound up with Serah Drake, who had been Logan's fiancée before King Gunder forced him to marry Princess Jenine. Logan had loved Serah once, but that love had withered over the years, finally propped up only by false kindness. He'd been planning to marry the wrong woman because he didn't want to hurt her feelings. Breaking his engagement had been the right thing to do, but it had seemed too cruel. But if they hadn't been engaged, Serah wouldn't have been at the castle the night of the coup. She'd still be alive. In the Hole, sharing food had been the right thing to do. It had seemed stupid, but in the end, the Holers helped Logan because he helped them first. Logan's failure and his success had driven home the same lesson: Do what you know is right, and you'll get the best consequences in the end.

It was, Kylar thought, why Logan might be great. You could count on him. He was loyal, he was honest, and he would fight to the death to do the right thing. Always.

"We've both come pretty far," Kylar said. "You think we can be friends?"

"No." Grimly, Logan shook his head. "Not friends. Best friends." Then he grinned, and the last year seemed to roll off Kylar's back. They were the kind of friends who would stand and be counted. For Kylar, who had always kept dirty secrets that threatened everything, the feeling was precious beyond words.

"What happens now?" Kylar asked.

"One more errand and then, well . . . I'm going to write a book."

Kylar tented his eyebrows. "No offense, Your Ogrishness, but what are you going to write a book about?"

"You know how I've always loved words. I'm going to write a book of words."

"I was under the impression that that's what most books are."

"Not composed of words. I'm going to write a book defining all the words in our language. I'm calling it a dictionary."

"You're writing in Jaeran?"

"Yes."

"Defining Jaeran words?"

"Right."

"So you'll have to already know Jaeran to read it?"

"You make it sound stupid," Logan said, scowling.

"Hmm." Kylar gave an I-wonder-why-that-is? shrug. The idea of Logan's commanding form sequestered in a candlelit study, squinting at manuscripts, was funny—except that Logan thought he was serious. Logan was scholarly, but he was no scholar. He was born to lead. This book idea was a pretense to shield him from seeing

Terah's mistakes and from his own impulses to do something about them.

Minutes ago, Kylar had thought he was done. He'd kept his oath to the Wolf. He thought that now he'd be free to go make things right with Elene. But now Terah Graesin was queen. She probably had a contract out on Logan already. The best way to cancel a contract was to cancel the contract-taker. And Terah Graesin deserved canceling. *One more kill, and I can change a country. With Logan as king, things can be different. There won't have to be guilds or guild rats anymore.* Elene was still safe in Waeddryn. He could do this in a week and be on his way.

"Look, we have to talk more, but first," Logan said, "I need to piss, and then I need to figure out what to do about the Khalidorans and this Lae'knaught army."

"What army?" Kylar asked.

"I just—what do you mean, what army? You have that look in your eye."

"Those Khalidorans aren't Khalidorans; the Lae' knaught've been wiped out, and we need to get to Cenaria before the Ceuran army does."

"The Ceuran—what? What?"

Kylar just laughed.

14

Dorian sat in the chute room, balancing the crap pot strapped to his back on the edge of one of the chutes. This was the last pot of the day, and Dorian was sore, exhausted, and grumpy—and he got to spend most of every day in the company of beautiful women. The chute room slave spent every day in this foul room, directing the slaves who brought in all of the Citadel's human waste and maintaining the sewage chutes, and he was the happiest slave Dorian had ever met. Dorian still gagged every time he opened the door. How the hell could Tobby be chipper?

Aching, Dorian stretched his back as he waited for Tobby to finish with the slave from the guards' quarters. Tobby pulled two levers, waited for a few moments, and then pulled a chain to the sound of distant clanking, then the man untied the top rope on his pack and Tobby tipped the pot over, sloshing the contents down the chute. A rope attached to the bottom kept the pot from following the sewage down the chute.

After he finished, Tobby walked over to Dorian. "This your last run?"

Dorian yawned and stretched. "Yes, I—" he lost his balance and the weight of the crap pot yanked him backward toward the open maw of a chute. He screamed—and jerked to a stop as Tobby threw himself against Dorian's knees.

For several moments, it was agony as the weight of the pot pulled against the sinews of his legs and stomach, trying to pull him into oblivion or rip him in half, but as the open-topped pot released its contents down the chute, the pain faded.

Once the pot was empty, Tobby was able to help Dorian out of the chute. "Trying to follow your predecessor, huh?" Tobby asked.

"What?"

Tobby chuckled. "Why'd you figure they needed another eunuch? Last harem carrier did what you just did . . . only I wasn't so fast that day."

"Shit," Dorian said.

Tobby laughed loudly like a braying donkey. Surely the man couldn't be amused by feces. Dorian began shaking from his brush with death. Good God, it hadn't even occurred to him to use his Talent.

"Funny thing is," Tobby said, "he didn't die from the ride. *They* killed him."

"What do you mean? Where does this chute go anyway?"

"Where does this shit go anyway?" Tobby echoed, then laughed again. "Down to the mines. Nearly drops on the heads a them sorry bastards. Soon as Arry fell in the chute, I routed him to one of the safe ones. Would have saved his life, if he had sense."

"Safe ones?" Dorian asked.

"You don't know shit, do you?" He punched Dorian in the arm. "Good one, eh? Eh?"

"Funny," Dorian said, forcing himself to smile ruefully.

"Didn't see that one coming, did ya?"

"Nope, didn't see that coming."

"I got a million of 'em," Tobby said.

"I bet." *If ever there was a man who deserved his slavery, I've met him.* "Why are some chutes safe?" Dorian asked.

"These chutes been here hunerds of years. First there was only one chute. At first it was a couple hunerd foot drop, from the bottom of the chute to the bottom of the chasm—well, after a couple hunerd years with twenty thousand folks shooting shit down it, there was no drop at all. Good ol' Batty Bertold got real nervous, thought an army or the pit slaves themselves might climb up the chute and attack the Citadel from within. So he built this. Now, when the shit gets within fifty feet of the bottom of the chute, we switch to a new chute. We let that first one sit until it's all soil. Then the pit slaves cart it up and the guards sell it for fertilizer. Course, I got to use all the chutes at least once a day so they don't rust up and so the pit slaves can't tell where the soil is firm under a few inches of crap and where the soup is deep enough to drown in. When Arry went down, I switched up the chutes so he'd have a chance."

"How fast can you do that?" Dorian asked.

Tobby tsked and pulled the third and the eighth lever and pulled the last chain. It took him about three seconds.

Dorian whistled, fixing the positions in his mind. "What happened to him?"

"He gave some shit to one of the meisters down there. Can't say I blame him, after what he'd been through."

"Sounds like he had a shitty day." Dorian felt dirty for the pun.

"Uh huh," Tobby said, not catching it. "Two meisters guard the pit slaves. It don't make 'em happy. They don't take no shit. They turned Arry inside out." He shook his head, somber. A moment later he grinned. "They don't take no shit, huh? Huh?" He punched Dorian's arm.

Dutifully, Dorian laughed. *I could take two meisters.*

When Dorian returned from emptying the crap pots, the concubines were keening. Dorian had never heard anything like it. He set the crap pot down and stared at Hopper.

"It's the Godking," the old man whispered, frozen by the sound from the next room. "We just got news. He's dead."

Dorian's heart stopped. *My father's dead.*

He wandered into the great room of the harem in a daze. Nearly two hundred women were gathered in the cold marble luxury of the place. They were tearing their clothes, ripping out their hair, beating their naked breasts, scratching bloody furrows in alabaster skin. Black tears rolled from kohled eyes. Some had flung themselves on the floor, weeping uncontrollably. Others had fainted.

In grief as in love and in drink, Dorian's people were extravagant, but these women's tears were not for show. They had all lived in awe and terror of the Godking, and few of them would have dared love him. None of his favorite concubines were here. No one would report who had wept and who had not. But His Holiness had been the center around which their lives revolved. Without that center, everything collapsed.

They would be compelled to throw themselves on Garoth's pyre to accompany him into the afterlife and be his slaves forever. And Garoth had always liked his women young.

Dorian saw one beautiful girl, Pricia. She was barely fourteen and just past her flowering, sitting alone, staring into space. She was still a virgin. Yorbas Zurgah had intended her as a present to the Godking when He arrived home.

"You have a chance," Dorian told her woodenly. "The next Godking might claim you."

"All my friends are going to die," Pricia said, not even looking at him.

Her answer shamed him. She hadn't been thinking of herself. This place was starting to make him think cynically, like the old Dorian.

The other implications of Garoth's death pounded Dorian a moment later. The Godking had left no clear heir, and whichever aetheling succeeded him would certainly kill off the others. If the concubines knew of Garoth's death, the aethelings would soon, if they didn't already.

Jenine!

Dorian burst into the eunuchs' room where he'd left Hopper.

"Get them all out of here," he ordered the old man. "Start with the virgins."

"What?"

"Hide them in my room. At least one of the aethelings will try to seize the Godking's harem as a declaration that he should be the next Godking. Or the guards may go crazy. You can't hide all of them, but at least the virgins will have a chance to be claimed by the next Godking. If they get raped, they'll die with the others."

Hopper nodded at once. "Done," he said.

Dorian ran up the Tygre Tower. The dreads guarding at the base of the tower were gone, and his heart dropped. He sprinted up the steps three at a time. He heard raised voices as he came up the last twenty steps. " . . . come, or I hurt you and then you come."

"All right," Jenine said, defeated.

The latch had been melted off the door. The fucker. It was Tavi, come to violate Jenine. Dorian kicked open the door just in time to see Jenine pull out the dagger he'd given her and bury it in a young man's chest. He screamed and his vir rose to the surface of his skin instantaneously. A white ball the size of a fist slammed into Jenine's chest and threw her across the chamber.

He turned at the sound of the door bursting open, but he didn't have time to move before Dorian's flame missiles hit him. Six burrowed through his chest and out his back before he fell facedown, dead. It wasn't Tavi. It was Rivik, Tavi's sidekick. Dorian went to Jenine.

She was whimpering, struggling to breathe, her chest concave with six broken ribs. Dorian put his hand on her chest, Seeing the damage. She relaxed as he washed away her pain. Bone after bone snapped into place seamlessly, and in moments, Dorian was done.

Jenine stared at him, wide-eyed. "You came."

"I'll always come for you."

She inhaled experimentally. "I feel . . . perfect."

Dorian smiled shyly and then started grabbing candelabra, tygre statuary, anything he could find made of gold.

"We can't carry all that," Jenine said.

Dorian dropped the unwieldy pile on the table. He winked at her and put his hands on each object in turn. One by one, they melted. The gold puddled onto the table, separating and connecting into lumps like quicksilver. The lumps began congealing, thinning, hardening, until each was flat disk bearing the likeness of Garoth Ursuul.

"What . . . how . . . ?" Jenine stuttered.

"The coins are only worth a fraction of what the art was, but they are a more *liquid* asset." He smiled as she giggled in wonder.

He allowed himself that smile, but things were not going according to plan. Dammit, everything was ready for tomorrow. The worst of it wasn't the wasted preparations, the lack of horses, the lack of warm clothing for the perilous crossing through Screaming Winds, the lack of dried food. It was that Dorian had used southern magic. Any meister who smelled him would sense it. Luxbridge might drop him into the chasm.

The chaos in the castle might not help them. More soldiers and meisters would surely be running about, and more aethelings definitely would. It meant that all Dorian's meticulous memorization of guards' watch routes and personal habits was for nothing.

Still, he was here, the armies of the Godking were not, nor were any of the Godking's older sons; Jenine was alive and safe, and the passes south were still open. In his wrath, he had vented far too much magic on Rivik, but he still had some left, enough to take care of a meister or even a Vürdmeister if caught unawares.

"What are you doing?" he asked as Jenine turned Rivik's body over. He didn't want her to have to look at that.

"I can't go like this. I'm taking his clothes," she said.

Together, they stripped Rivik. There was blood on the front of the tunic where Jenine had stabbed his chest, and six small burn holes on both front and back, but otherwise the tunic was fine. Rivik had been a slight youth, so the tunic was only a little big.

Jenine threw off her blouse and pulled on the dead youth's tunic, not asking Dorian to look away or turn his back. He stared at her slack-jawed, frozen, then looked away, embarrassed, then wondered why he was embarrassed and she was not, and looked again and looked away. He was twice her age! She was beautiful. She was brazen. She was being perfectly sensible; they didn't have time to be coy. Her head emerged from the tunic and she saw the look on his face. "Hand me the trousers, would you?" she asked nonchalantly.

The color in her cheeks told him it was a bluff, so he matched brazenness for brazenness and watched her as she pulled off her skirt. She snatched the trousers from his hands. "If you don't watch it, Halfman, you're going to be considerably more than half a—" she said with a significant glance at his trousers, but then her eyes went past Dorian to the body behind him. Her jest died and her high color drained away. "Let's get out of here," she said. "I hate this place. I hate this whole country."

She finished dressing in silence and pulled on the floppy hat Dorian had frequently worn to cover his own face as much as possible, piling her long hair on top of her head in a bundle. In the end, it was a poor disguise, not because of the clothes, but because Jenine didn't walk like a man, and couldn't learn in the few moments Dorian was willing to spare trying to teach her. But if she didn't look like a man, she didn't look like a princess either. They'd just have to hope everyone was distracted.

15

Feir had asked for two hours to get Lantano Garuwashi's sword out of Ezra's Wood. He had no idea how much of that time had passed. In fact, he couldn't remember how he'd come here. He looked up at the towering sequoys stretching to the sky.

Well, at least, he knew where here was. He was definitely in Ezra's Wood. He looked at his hands. Both of them were scraped and his knees hurt, as if he'd fallen. He touched his nose and could tell it had been broken and then set properly. There was still crusty, dried blood on his upper lip.

Dorian had told him stories about men who'd taken a blow to the head and forgot themselves, either forgetting everything before the blow, or more commonly completely losing the ability to remember anything at all after the blow. They could meet a person, the person would walk out of the room, and five minutes later return and be greeted as a stranger once more. For several moments Feir felt a panic rising inside him at the very thought, but aside from his nose, his head didn't feel as if he'd taken a blow. He could remember leaving Lantano Garuwashi, he could remember approaching the vast bubble of magics that surrounded Ezra's Wood, and he could remember the turmoil within those magics as—miles to the east— the Lae'knaught had entered the Wood and been trapped within it. Feir had used that turmoil as a distraction for his own attempt. But from that point, he could remember nothing.

He was facing the bubble now, as if he was leaving. He took a few more steps, disoriented and came around the trunk of another giant sequoy. Before him, not fifty paces away, just outside the magic, were Lantano Garuwashi and, oddly, Antoninus Wervel.

Maybe I have gone mad. Antoninus Wervel was a red mage, one of the most powerful and most intelligent men to walk the halls of Sho'cendi in decades. He was a fat Modaini man, and he'd been a casual friend for years. To see him sitting awkwardly cross-legged beside Lantano Garuwashi, who sat as gracefully as he did everything, was surreal.

Then the men saw Feir and both rose. Antoninus called something out, but though he was only forty paces away now, Feir couldn't hear him.

Feir walked straight to the wall of magic. Whatever clever magic he'd used to get into the Wood, it obviously hadn't been clever enough. He was alive only by the forbearance of whatever it was that lived here. So Feir walked straight through the magic. It slid around him, and for a moment, he could swear something in the Wood felt amused.

Then he was out.

"What are you doing here?" he asked Antoninus Wervel.

Antoninus laughed. "You escape the Wood, something no mage has done in seven centuries, and you ask what *I'm* doing?"

"Do you have my sword?" Garuwashi demanded.

Feir was carrying a pack strapped to his back that he hadn't been carrying when he entered the Wood. "Him first," he said.

Antoninus lifted his kohled eyebrows, but said, "I came with a delegation from Sho'cendi to recover Curoch. After the Battle of Pavvil's Grove, the delegation turned back. They were sure that if Curoch had been present in such a desperate battle with so many magi and meisters present, that someone would have tried to use it. No one did, so they decided to backtrack and follow other leads. The truth is, I don't think Lord Lucius trusts everyone in our delegation. He and I don't care for each other, but he knows where my loyalties lie, so he released me. So now it's your turn, Feir. Did you recover Ceur'caelestos?"

The Modaini was too damn smart. Feir could tell that the man had put together Feir, who'd held one nearly mythical sword, with the appearance of another nearly mythical sword and found no coincidence.

Feir opened the pack. There was a note inside with directions and instructions, written awkwardly, as if the hand writing it had been writing in an unfamiliar language. Feir read it quickly and remembered bits and pieces of what had happened in the Wood. Setting the note aside, he pulled a hilt out of his pack—a hilt only, with no sword. It was a perfect replica of the one on Ceur'caelestos, and it would fit Lantano Garuwashi's sheath perfectly. As long as the sa'ceurai didn't draw his sword, no one would ever know.

"What is this?" Lantano Garuwashi demanded.

"It's three months," Feir said.

"What?" Garuwashi asked.

"That's the time I need," Feir said. "I'm a Maker, Garuwashi, and I received instructions in the Wood—a prophecy left by Ezra himself, centuries ago. If you prefer death, I will be your second, but if you want to live, take this hilt. Antoninus and I will go to Black Barrow and do things no one has done since Ezra's time. I will make Ceur'caelestos for you by spring." Or at least a damn good fake. "You can be the king you've always wished to be."

Lantano Garuwashi stood for a long moment, eyes hot and then cold, trapped between his desires and his honor. He swallowed. "You swear you will bring me my ceuros?"

"I swear it."

Lantano Garuwashi took the hilt.

Logan and Kylar rode at the head of Logan's five hundred horse and nine hundred foot. Logan's bodyguards rode ten paces back, giving them privacy. The sharpened-tooth simpleton Gnasher rode in his usual spot beside Logan, but he didn't care what they might say; he just liked to be close. Kylar unrolled a worn letter.

"Whatcha got?" Logan asked.

Kylar gave him an inscrutable look, shrugged, and handed it to him. In small, tight handwriting, it said, "Hey, I thought it was my last one, too. He said I got one more for old time's sake. He might even have been telling the truth. Be careful who you love. Don't follow prophecies. Don't let them use you to bring the High King. Your secret is your most important possession. You're more important than I ever was, kid. Maybe for all those years I was just holding it for you. MAKE NO DEALS WITH THE WOLF."

"I assume this all means something to you," Logan said.

"Not all of it," Kylar said.

"Who's the Wolf?" Logan asked.

"Someone I made a deal with right before I found that letter."

"Ouch. And the High King?"

Kylar grimaced. "That was part I was hoping you could help me with."

Logan thought. "There was a High King who held Cenaria and several other countries maybe four hundred years ago, but Cenaria's been held by lots of different countries in the last thousand years. Sounds like an Ursuul thing. They're the only ones in Midcyru in a position to rule over other kings. I'd guess they're dredging up a prophecy to give themselves legitimacy. Is the secret what I think it is?" Logan asked.

"Here we are," Kylar said. They had circled Ezra's Wood, looking for signs of the Lae'knaught. Kylar said it was something Logan needed to see for himself.

Fifty paces away, Logan saw a wall of dead men. Hundreds of them pressed against an invisible barrier, trying to escape the forest. In places, bodies were piled twenty feet deep as men had clambered over the dead, hoping to reach the top of the invisible wall. There was no movement. No one was merely injured. Every body had been mangled, torn with sharp claws that must have had god-like strength. Helmets had been crushed flat. Heads were simply missing. Swords had been snapped like twigs. Even the horses were dead, heads torn off, sinews ripped through the skin, some muscles snapped instead of torn.

For as far as the eye could see into the sequoys, there was only devastation, and as far as the eye could see west and east, Lae'knaught were pressed against an invisible wall. They'd tested every place they could before dying, and found it everywhere impregnable. Gore still drained from the bodies, sliding against the wall like glass, but strangely, there was no smell. The magic sealed in even the air.

Logan heard vomiting from his bodyguards.

"The villagers of Torras Bend say someone tries to go into the Wood every generation. It happens so much that their term for suicide is 'walking into the Wood,'" Kylar said. Logan turned. Kylar's eyes were hollow, stricken. "I did this," Kylar said. "I lured them here so they'd fall into the Ceurans' trap instead of you. These souls are on my tab."

"Our scouts heard the fighting. That's why we held back. What you did here saved fourteen hundred lives—"

"At the cost of five thousand."

"—and maybe saved Cenaria." Logan stopped. It wasn't making a dent. "Captain," he said. "Bring the men forward in groups. I want everyone to see this. I don't want any Cenarian to ever make the mistake we almost did."

Kaldrosa Wyn saluted, obviously glad to be given a duty to take her away from the massacre.

Logan changed tack. "Kylar, I know you think you're

a bad man, but I've never seen anyone who will go to the lengths you will to do what you've decided is right. You are an amazingly moral man, and I trust you, and you're my best friend." Logan looked steadily at Kylar to let him read the truth.

Kylar gave a sarcastic, you-can't-be-serious grimace that slowly melted. The tension left his face as the truth sank in. Logan meant every word. Kylar blinked suddenly. Once, twice, and then looked away.

Oh, my friend, what have you gone through that being called moral nearly makes you weep? Or was it being called friend? Logan thought. He had been isolated for months in the Hole and found it hell. Kylar had been isolated for his entire life.

"But?" Kylar asked.

Logan heaved a deep sigh. "Not stupid either, are you?" Kylar flashed that old mischievous grin, and Logan loved him fiercely. "But you were a wetboy, Kylar, and now you're something even more dangerous. I can't claim that I don't know what you might do to Terah—"

"Do you really trust me?" Kylar interrupted.

Logan paused, maybe for too long. "Yes," he said finally.

"Then this conversation is finished."

16

"Dorian," Jenine said, "I think you should come look at this."

He stepped to the window and looked out over Khaliras. Marching into the city were twenty thousand soldiers, two thousand horse, and two hundred meisters. Dorian's little brother Paerik had returned from the Freeze. Serfs were piling out of the way of a group of horsemen who had advanced before the army. Dorian didn't have to see the banners to know it had to be Paerik himself.

Dorian and Jenine ran down the stairs two at a time, winding down and down to the base of the Tygre Tower. The grim cats favored him with their fanged smiles, mocking him. There was still time. If they could get to the front gate, they could cross Luxbridge a few minutes before Paerik arrived.

As always, the slaves' tunnels were dark. In the distance, figures clashed with sword and spell, but Dorian was able to take them around the worst of the fray. He could See his half-brothers from a great distance.

The path they were forced to take took them down a rough hewn stone tunnel past the Khalirium, where the goddess resided. The very stone down here stank of vir. Dorian rounded a corner a mere hundred paces from the castle's front gate and found himself staring at the back of an aetheling. Usually, he would have Seen the young man, but the proximity of the Khalirium confused him. He froze. Jenine yanked him back into the rough tunnel.

"Khali's not here!" the aetheling said.

Someone else cursed. "Moburu really took her to Cenaria? Damn him. He really does think he's the High King."

"So much for seizing Khali. What do we do now?" the first asked.

Khali was still in Cenaria? No wonder it didn't feel quite as oppressive down here as Dorian remembered.

"We gotta join Draef. If we help him stop Paerik at the bridge, he might let us live. Paerik or Tavi will kill us no matter what."

Dorian and Jenine scooted back into the tunnel as quickly and as quietly as they could, but it was almost fifty paces before it intersected with another hallway. No way they could run that far without the aethelings hearing or seeing them. As soon as they found a large cavity in the rough wall, Dorian pushed Jenine into it and then pressed himself as close as he could, but his thin sleeve caught on the stone and tore.

One of the aethelings stepped into the tunnel and raised his staff. A flame blazed up on it, illuminating the hall and his face. He was perhaps fourteen, as was the youth beside him. Both were short and slender and homely, bearing little of their father's robust good looks, and only a small portion of his power.

I can take them. Even with southern magic, Dorian was stronger than they were. But he didn't want it to come to that. *Come on, turn. Turn.*

If they turned, Dorian could take a shortcut and beat them to Luxbridge. With the advantage of surprise and with Khali hundreds of miles away, he could surely take this Draef and cross Luxbridge. Everything was so close he could taste it. Had not the God favored him already by holding off the snows?

Lord, please . . .

"I swear I heard something," one of the boys said.

"We don't have time for this, Vic," the other said.

But Vic strode forward, his staff held high. He came within ten paces and paused. Dorian readied himself.

Hold, a quiet voice said, cutting through the jumble of Dorian's thoughts. *Take the chutes.*

For a moment, Dorian believed it was the voice of the God. He could remember the exact positions the levers required. Dorian could easily overcome two meisters who weren't expecting him. From there, he and Jenine could climb out—there had to be a stair out for the meisters. Of course, he'd already thought about it for himself, but not for Jenine. The thought of riding a sewage chute down the-God-only-knew how many feet in the close darkness with the stench all around was horrible enough for him, and he'd been working human waste.

Jenine would think he was a coward, running away from fourteen-year-old boys. Maybe she wouldn't come with him at all. Maybe she would come, but despise him afterward. What kind of man makes the woman he loves crawl through shit?

Vic stepped closer. Five paces away now. Dorian was frozen, one eye exposed. Surely Vic would see them. He had to! And if Dorian didn't raise some defense, Vic would murder them where they stood. But if he did raise a defense, Vic would sense it. Either way was a decision.

It wasn't the voice of the God. It was the voice of fear. I can take them.

Dorian stepped out of the crevice and lashed out at Vic with fire missiles.

He recognized his mistake the moment the missiles diverted and flew down the tunnel toward Vic's brother. The boys were twins. Fraternal twins or Dorian would have recognized it at once. Twins could make a weave to protect each other at the expense of protecting themselves. That defense, if given fully, was far stronger than a meister could give himself.

The counterstrike came from Vic, much stronger than he should have been capable of. It was a hammerfist, a spinning blue cone that in his youthful enthusiasm Vic had actually embellished to look like a flaming fist. Rather than dodge it, Dorian had to stop it completely to make sure it didn't kill Jenine behind him. Another fist came a second later from Vic's twin, rattling stones down from the low ceiling of the tunnel. Dorian blocked it, too, suddenly aware of how much magic he'd used today. He was getting exhausted.

With fingers of magic, he reached beneath Vic's shield and twisted it onto himself. It surprised the boy so much that he abandoned his next attack. Down the hall, his twin did not. His next hammerfist was whipped in a tight circle by the shield that was now protecting Dorian, and arced into Vic instead. It crushed his body flat against the tunnel wall.

Dorian flung a single fire missile down the hall. With Vic dead, the twin was now unshielded, and the fire missile pierced his chest. He grunted and fell.

Picking up Vic's staff—the damn thing was an *amplifiae,* it was what had made the aetheling's blows more powerful than they ought to have been—Dorian pulled Jenine down the hall. They could still make it to the bridge. It was close now. The last hallway was clear, and though the mighty gate was closed, the sally port opened from the inside.

Almost there!

With a boom, the mighty double gates were flung open. The rancid stench of vir washed over Dorian and Jenine. Four young men stood before them, their skin awash with the knotted dark tattoo-like vir. They were ready; they'd sensed Dorian coming.

Dorian threw up a hurried shield, as thick as he could manage with the rest of his Talent, and turned to flee. The damned amplifiae didn't help at all; it was attuned to vir. In rapid succession, the shield absorbed a hammerfist, eight fire missiles, the staccato jabs of a needler, and the diffuse flame called a dragon tongue, meant to finish an opponent after his shields were down. But Dorian's shields weren't down, he could survive another wave so long as none of them dared a pit wyrm.

"Draef!" a young man called out triumphantly from behind Dorian. It was Tavi, with three of his own aethelings, blocking the hall's other exit. The first group stopped attacking Dorian instantly.

Dorian looked from one camp to the other, and they looked at him. He and Jenine were trapped between them. "Hold!" Dorian shouted. "I am Dorian Ursuul, the Son-That-Was. I know they expunged my name from the records, but I'm sure you've heard the rumors. I'm real, and you can't afford to attack me."

Tavi spat. "You're not even a meister."

"Why?" Draef asked at the same time.

"Even if I were only a magus, I won't go down easily. If either of you attack me, you'll leave yourselves open to be attacked by the other. But I am an Ursuul of the twelfth shu'ra." *Just a touch, just a touch.* He could manage that much and still not surrender to the vir.

Dorian reached down, and the vir rushed from the depths like a leviathan and rode the surface of his skin in great knots that obscured almost all of his skin. Quickly, he pushed it back.

The aethelings, all of them sixteen or seventeen years old at most, looked at him with awe. Several of the boys standing with Tavi looked on the verge of bolting.

"An illusion!" Tavi shouted, hysteria edging his voice.

"An illusion that smells?" Draef asked contemptuously. *Yes, Draef is the first of this seed class. Tavi's the pretender.* "What do you want?" Draef asked.

"Just to leave. I'll go, and then you can slaughter each other to your heart's content." As he addressed Draef, Dorian let his eyes go to the staff amplifiae he carried. He hadn't used the aetheling's hand speech in years, but with his body blocking Tavi's view, he moved his hands to signal over the amplifiae—*for you.*

Draef's eyes glittered. The amplifiae would be enough to turn the battle.

"Dorian," Jenine whispered. She was still slouched unassumingly by his side, trying to look like a body servant, and Dorian wasn't about to draw attention to her.

"Fair enough, get out," Draef said. His fingers signaled *when?*

Through clenched teeth, Jenine whispered, "Tavi's looking at me funny."

Dorian was trying to remember the finger speech vocabulary he hadn't used for so many years to answer Draef's question. There it was, he remembered. *When we get to the bridge.*

Draef looked satisfied, though tension still stood stark on every feature, and Dorian and Jenine started walking. Only now did Dorian risk a look back to Tavi. He was afraid that the young man's quick hatred might be roused even by meeting his eyes. Dorian had won, but with the overweening arrogance this aetheling possessed, it was best not to appear to take any joy in the victory.

The eight aethelings all had their eyes jumping from Dorian to their opponents on the opposite side of the hall. For them, any move Dorian made might be the distraction they or their enemy might take advantage of. And whether he made out of the hall alive or not, they would fight. Soon.

Out of the side of his mouth, Dorian said, "Remember to walk like a—" It was too late; Jenine had been drilled on proper comportment for far too long.

"She stays!" Tavi shouted suddenly and reached out with vir to grab Jenine.

The move set one of Draef's boys off. He threw up a crackling shield reflexively.

That unleashed a magical firestorm. Dorian threw a

shield around himself and Jenine. A fire missile made it through before the shield formed and scored his ribs. He hunched and almost lost the shield. Jenine grabbed him and held him upright.

The hall filled with magic, stroke and counterstroke, gouts of fire, lightning bolts that smote the rocks as shields diverted them, the rocks cascading from the ceiling turned into missiles themselves and hurled down the hall. Most of the attacks weren't directed at Dorian and Jenine, but they were in the line of fire.

Dorian's shield thinned, layer after layer snapping, melting, withering. The aethelings were all fresh. This battle would last long after Dorian's shields finally gave way. He was going to die, and worse, he was going to let Jenine die. He had failed her.

No, not while I have breath. God, forgive me for what I'm about to do. It was no true prayer to beg forgiveness while choosing to sin—but he meant it fervently all the same.

Dorian reached to the vir. It came, joyfully.

Someone was screaming, a terrible scream compounded a hundred times by the vir to shake every hall and tunnel of the Citadel. Dorian stood and flung his arms out. As they passed in front of him, he saw that his skin had totally disappeared beneath the all-absorbing, wriggling blackness. Nor did the vir stop at the bounds of his body. They lashed out from his arms—out farther and farther, like great wings—and came down on either side, barely registering the aethelings' last desperate attacks.

He felt the boys crunch beneath those mighty wings like beetles popping under his boot. Their shields broke like shells and the softness within was ground to gory smears on the rock.

The vir sang power and hatred and strength. *It is vile, and I love it.*

He stopped screaming, and it was long seconds before the sound stopped echoing back from the Citadel's halls. Dorian quieted the vir from his skin with effort. "Are you all right?"

Jenine's big, beautiful eyes were wider than he'd ever seen them. She tried to speak, couldn't, and nodded instead.

"I'm sorry," Dorian said. "It was that or die. We're almost there."

But as they stepped through the now-smoking gate, Dorian saw that he was wrong. Halfway across the glowing spans of Luxbridge was a man in a majestic white ermine cloak like Garoth Ursuul had worn. He wore the gold chains of a Godking around his neck and vir swam on his skin.

Dorian's brother Paerik Ursuul had come to claim his throne, and blocking the bridge with him stood six full Vürdmeisters.

17

On the third night, after they made it through Forglin's Pass and set up camp, Dehvi finally spoke to Vi. "Let us train together, wetboy."

"I'm not a wetboy," Vi said quickly.

"You were Hu Gibbet's apprentice."

Vi's mouth dried up. "Yes." The very name brought back ugly memories.

Dehvi drew a pair of sais. "The Night Angel did kill him."

"I know. I couldn't be happier." Vi wished she'd had the guts to do it herself.

The smile faded into puzzlement. "You seek no vengeance?"

"I've fucked men for smaller favors. I wanted to kill Hu since I was thirteen."

Dehvi scowled. "Too much talk." He bent over Vi's bedroll where she had put her sword. He poked the point of one sai at the juncture of blade and hilt and flicked her sword to her. She caught it and tested the edge. It was blunted with a thin shield of magic, but a strong blow would still cut. Dehvi checked all six points of his sais. Vi had never fought against sais. A sai looked like a short sword with a narrow blade, except that the hilts swept in a broad U for catching blades. Each tine was sharpened.

Holding the sais in one hand, Dehvi removed his horsehide cloak and draped it over a rock. Vi followed suit reluctantly. Then Dehvi turned, bowed, said something incomprehensible in Ymmuri, spun the sais in his hands, and took an impossibly low ready stance.

Vi's doubts about such a low stance were broken at the first clash. She lunged toward his face. He nearly leapt forward, catching her sword with one sai and then the other and twisting as he sprang like a snake. Vi's sword spun from her grasp and she found a sai touching her throat while the other jabbed the small of her back. Dehvi's face was impassive. He stepped back wordlessly and flicked her blade back to her.

She lasted fifteen seconds the second time, and didn't lose her blade, though Dehvi twisted it far out of the way and touched her ribs with the other sai. After a few minutes, she was beginning to understand. Then Dehvi changed stances. He sidestepped her first cut, not even using the sais, and swept her feet out from under her.

She pulled herself out of the mud and found him grinning. Hu Gibbet had leered at her sometimes, and mocked her often, but Dehvi's grin was innocent. It suggested that if she could see herself, she'd laugh too.

Suddenly, she was crying, hot tears spilling down her cheeks. Dehvi gave her the look she deserved: utter bewilderment. She laughed at the ridiculousness of it, rubbing her tears away. "Hu shit on everything, Dehvi. Every time he trained me, it was all mockery and bruises and humiliation. For fuck's sake, this is actually *fun*. And I'm learning so much more from you. You're better than he ever was. No wonder you kick ass."

"Asses I have kicked," Dehvi said. "Though finding them less sensitive than other places."

Vi laughed and blinked her eyes to keep that bizarre flood down.

"You did marry in Waeddryner way," Dehvi said. He tugged his own ear to indicate her earring. "But are not Waeddryner. Who is husband?"

Well, that helped with the crying. She cleared her throat. "Kylar Stern. Sort of."

Dehvi's eyebrows raised.

"It's, uh, complicated."

He shrugged and drew a sword. He touched the edge to make sure it was shielded, and they began sparring again. Vi sank into it, releasing her worries about the life she was fleeing from and the life she was fleeing to. Even as she lost, time and again feeling the dull poke of Dehvi's sword, for the first time she had the sense that fighting was something she was really good at. When she countered a move that had caught her before, Dehvi might barely nod, but it was as good as effusive praise.

Dehvi shifted fighting styles no less than six times, and Vi sensed that he knew quite a few more, but the last one felt familiar. Vi was sunk so deep into her own body that she barely noticed that she'd spoken until she saw Dehvi miss a step. Her riposte brushed his stomach. She'd said two words: "You're Durzo." Her eyes told her it was impossible. Her knowledge of illusory masks told her it was impossible. But she knew, and his reaction confirmed it. "What are you doing here?" she asked.

"It was the accent, wasn't it? Always takes me a while to get it back. You got some Ymmuri uncle or something?" Dehvi said, his voice abruptly Cenarian.

"You fight like Kylar. What are you doing here?"

"You bonded Kylar with the most powerful surviving set of compulsive wedding rings in the world. Was that your own idea?"

"The Godking put a compulsion on me. Sister Ariel said ringing was the way to break it."

"I thought Kylar was in love with that Elene girl. Why'd he marry you?"

Vi swallowed. "I sort of ringed him when he was unconscious."

Dehvi's expression went blank, and Vi had a sudden intuition that Durzo's blank look was as indicative of pending violence as Hu Gibbet's rages. Dehvi said softly, "I'm here to decide if I should kill you to free Kylar from the bond. You're not making much of a case for yourself."

She tossed her sword into the mud and shrugged. *Fuck it. Kill me.*

Dehvi-Durzo looked at her strangely, weighing her. "Have you ever felt that you were part of a grand design, Vi? That some benevolence was shaping your fate?"

"No," Vi said.

Dehvi laughed. "Me neither. Goodbye, Vi. Watch out for that husband of yours; he'll change you." Then he left.

* * *

Solonariwan Tofusin stood on deck as the Modaini merchant ship lumbered toward Hokkai Harbor. It had been twelve years since he'd been to the Sethi capital, the city he had once called home. The sight of the two great chain towers guarding the entrance to the harbor, shining white in the autumn sun, filled his heart to bursting.

As they passed between the towers, as always, his appreciation of the seemingly delicate towers became awe. Built during the height of the Sethi Empire, the chain towers stood on narrow peninsulas. The base of each tower abutted the ocean so the chain couldn't be attacked without taking the tower. The chains themselves lay under water except during maintenance and war. Then, the great teams of royal aurochs would winch the chains apart until they were at or barely below the water line at high tide and five to eight feet above it at low tide. During a battle, the aurochs would turn the chains. A single blade shaped like a shark tooth was attached to each link. Because of the half twist in the chain at each axle, a ship pressing against the mighty chains would find half the teeth chewing through his hull in each direction. It made the entire chain a saw that had destroyed more than one fleet, and deterred many more.

Above the sparkling blue waters—gods, Solon thought, the bay was a color to shame sapphires—Hokkai rose on its three hills. Above the ubiquitous docks already filling with wintering ships, the great city rose in thousands of whitewashed walls with red tile roofs. After the ugly hodgepodge of Cenarian architecture, it was a relief.

But the most beautiful sight of all, magnificent Whitecliff Castle reigning over the highest hill, filled Solon not only with awe but something akin to terror. *Kaede, my love, do you hate me still?*

After Khali and her Soulsworn had massacred everyone at Screaming Winds, Solon had had nothing to do. His friend Feir had left days before they knew of the danger. When the garrison commander ignored Dorian's warnings that Khali was coming, Dorian disappeared. Solon had been the only man to escape. He'd found himself suddenly without ties to anything. It had been Dorian's prophecy that had kept him from going home more than a decade ago. Solon had served Regnus Gyre as prophecy dictated—and failed. Regnus was dead. Solon had served for a decade, only to be dismissed the day before Regnus was murdered. Kaede was the Sethi empress now. She wasn't likely to be happy to see Solon, but if she killed him, so much the better.

He labored with the sailors. He could have paid for his passage, but no Sethi worth his salt would sit in a cabin while others were hoisting sails, not even on a wide-bellied Modaini merchant ship. The Sethi preferred small, light ships. It meant their merchants had to make twice as many trips, but they made them twice as fast. A Sethi ship also had to ride a storm rather than plow through it, but the Sethi accepted the ocean's whims and loved her and feared her equally.

As the ship came to rest in the bay, the Modaini merchant captain emerged from his cabin, his eyes and eyebrows freshly kohled. Solon always thought it gave the dark-haired Modaini a sinister aspect, but the captain was an affable man. He tossed Solon his pay and welcomed him to sail with him any time before going to speak with the harbormaster, who had rowed out to collect the harborage tax and inspect the cargo.

The harbormaster clambered up the webbing onto deck with the ease of a man who did it a dozen times a day. Like most Sethi, he wore no tunic until winter, and the sun had darkened his skin to a deep olive. He had a prominent nose, brown eyes, the figure-eight earring of Clan Hobashi, two silver rings on his right cheekbone, and two silver chains strung between the earring and cheek rings—an assistant to the harbormaster, then.

The man had barely spoken two words when he saw Solon and broke off in mid-sentence. Solon, still bare-chested as he had been for the whole trip, wasn't as tanned as most Sethi. But despite his light tan and the white hair growing in to replace the black, he was unmistakably Sethi—and he wore no clan rings. The harbormaster's long knife came out in a heartbeat. There were only two groups in Seth that wore no rings.

"What's your name, clanless?"

The Modaini captain looked aghast. He had never made a trip to Seth and didn't know their customs, which was why Solon had chosen his ship.

"Solon," Solon said, not giving his clan name, as an exile wouldn't.

The harbormaster grabbed Solon's chin and looked closely at his cheeks and ears, first on one side, and then, frustrated, on the other. His eyebrows tightened in confusion. Not only were there no scars where the clan rings had been torn out, but there were no scars from where the rings had been put in.

"Raesh kodir Sethi?" he demanded. *Are you not Sethi?*

"Sethi kodi," Solon acknowledged, his Old Sethi diction perfect.

The harbormaster released Solon's face as if burned. "What *was* your name?"

"Solonariwan Tofusin."

One of the Modaini sailors cursed. The harbormaster's tanned face turned green. He noticed that his long knife was still out and tucked it away as if it were scalding. "I think you'd better come with me . . . uh, your lordship."

"What's going on?" the captain asked.

Neither Solon nor the harbormaster answered. Solon clambered into the rowboat with the harbormaster. The sailor who'd cursed said, "The Tofusins reigned for five hundred years."

Not exactly. It was four hundred seventy-seven.

"Reigned? They don't anymore?" the captain asked, his voice strangled. Hopping into the rowboat, Solon couldn't help but smile.

"No, cap'n. The last one died ten years ago. If this one really is a Tofusin, there'll be all sorts of hell to pay."

That, on the other hand, is dead on.

18

$\mathcal{K}$hali's blood," Paerik swore, striding confidently across Luxbridge toward Dorian. "That was rather impressive. Who are you?" His eyes took in Jenine but dismissed her.

"It's all right," Dorian told Jenine, though it wasn't. He'd destroyed a few teenage boys who had underestimated him. Paerik Ursuul was a man in the prime of his powers. And he was fresh. And he had six battle-hardened Vürdmeisters backing him.

One of the Vürdmeisters whispered in Paerik's ear. Paerik straightened. "No, surely not. Dorian?" He stepped forward and Dorian stepped forward as well, not willing to let Paerik reach the end of Luxbridge unchallenged. Paerik smirked. Seeing that smirk, Dorian hated him, despised him, wanted to crush him.

"I am Dorian," Dorian said defiantly. Six Vürdmeisters and Paerik. Damn it, he only wanted to leave. The dark clouds overhead rushed past, coldly impartial.

"We thought you long dead, *brother*," Paerik said. "A mistake we shall soon remedy."

Dorian lashed out with vir and Talent both, splitting the weaves to sweep the Vürdmeisters off the bridge and at the same time yanking at the magical underpinnings to drop the bridge into the abyss.

They rebuffed the attacks with ease. Even with the amplifiae, Dorian was no match for seven Vürdmeisters together.

"Brother, brother," Paerik admonished. "This bridge will not drop a true-born Ursuul." He laughed and skulls embedded in Luxbridge seemed to laugh with him, their eyes glowing with magical fire. "Indeed, if any of Garoth's sons were in danger, it would be you, Dorian: the mage-trained."

"That's what I'm counting on," Dorian said. He stepped forward, out of the shoe he had cut free with his Talent, and put one bare foot on the bridge.

There was a flash as the last quarter of the bridge sensed a magus and unraveled.

Paerik screamed, falling with a shower of skulls that laughed no longer. He and the Vürdmeisters plummeted down and down. They flung vir at the distant walls, hoping to catch themselves, but the walls themselves were bespelled to deny magic purchase. The Vürdmeisters passed out of sight into the thick foul clouds of the abyss. Dorian could sense their magic for several more seconds, trying anything, everything, desperately. Then they winked out, all at the same time.

Before them, Luxbridge reformed itself. Dorian stepped back into his lead-lined shoe and tested it on the bridge. It flared green and began to turn transparent. He

had simply used too much Talent too recently for the thin
defense of the lead plating to be adequate, so he stretched
the vir forth once more and reached under the bridge to
steady it.

"We must go quickly," he told Jenine. "Stay close."

She nodded, biting her lip. By the God, she was beautiful. She was worth it.

Dorian stepped onto Luxbridge, and it held. It was even
more eerie, he thought, to walk across the span without the
skulls. Looking at the harmless skulls of the dead scared
him less than looking at clouds far beneath his feet.

In moments, they made the crossing. The guards standing at the Gate Keep gaped and dropped to their knees.
Dorian recognized Rugger.

"I'm sorry," he said. Rugger looked up, sure he
was about to die. Dorian Healed the man's wen with a
touch. Without the ugly protuberance, Rugger wasn't
half bad-looking. Rugger's hands went to his forehead,
disbelieving.

Hand in hand, Dorian and Jenine stepped through the
iron portcullis and looked over the city from their perch.

Paerik's army wound through the city and out onto
the plain. The front of it was just beginning the climb up
the ridge where Dorian and Jenine stood. The men and
women on the leading edge weren't soldiers; they were
meisters and Vürdmeisters, two hundred strong. And they
were already halfway to Dorian. They couldn't help but
have been aware of the magical firestorm he just been part
of. Every one of them had their eyes fixed on him.

"Are we going to die?" Jenine asked.

"No," Dorian said. "These people have lived under tyr-
anny so long, they have no idea what to do after you've

killed their leader. One more bluff, and we're on our way home." *What home is that, Dorian?*

"You really think you can bluff *that?*" Jenine asked, pointing to the entire army.

Dorian smiled, and he realized how long it had been since he'd thought about the future. He was no prophet now, but yes, he was sure. He was about to gamble it all for one last time. A few orders, a few curses, maybe a few deaths, and he and Jenine would be on their way to Cenaria. It would work. It could, anyway.

Something cold touched his cheek. Dorian blinked.

"What?" Jenine asked, seeing the hope die in his face. "What's wrong?" She followed his eyes up.

"It's snowing," he said softly. "The passes will be closed. We're trapped."

In the distance, barely audible beneath the hiss of falling snow, Dorian thought he heard Khali laughing.

Snow made the worst weather for invisibility. In Cenaria, snow usually melted as soon as it hit the ground, but tonight it was sticking long enough to show footprints. The sleet itself gave shape to Kylar's body as it ran down his limbs. Kylar had to move as slowly toward the Ceuran camp as if he were an assassin. At least he still remembered how to sneak. And at least the clouds blocked the moon. Still, it was cold. As usual, Kylar was only wearing underclothes beneath the ka'kari, and it wasn't enough.

He tugged at his earring, pushing down the distant awareness of Vi. Shivering, Kylar climbed a rocky knoll to get a better view. The Ceurans had four men camped on the windy hill, huddled around a banked fire, with oil-soaked torches nearby so they could give signals to the army below. Kylar sat five paces from a weary sentry. The man was a peasant foot soldier rather than a sa'ceurai. His armor was made of plates sewn onto fabric. Rather than being fastened with leather, which was durable but would harden and shrink if it got wet too often, Ceurans always fastened their armor with ruinously expensive Lodricari silk laces.

After the Battle of Pavvil's Grove, Garuwashi's plan had been to pull the Cenarian army east after his "Khalidoran" raiders while the main strength of his own army swept behind them and took the capital. It would have worked, but for something he never could have foreseen: walls.

Most of Cenaria's old walls had been cannibalized for their stones. By the time Kylar was a child, generations of Rabbits too poor to pay for masonry had finally left the Warrens without walls. The richer east side had seen a similar if slower erosion. But in the last few months while Kylar was gone, walls had appeared around the entire city. It was breathtaking. With Cenaria's endemic corruption, it would have taken five generations of kings and millions of crowns to equal what Garoth Ursuul's cruelty and magic had done in two months. Of course, he'd also had a ready supply of stone from all the houses Terah Graesin's followers had abandoned. And when those ran out, they simply demolished more homes and took what they needed.

Now, the Ceuran army was laid out in a crescent hugging the south and east of the city. On finding walls, Garuwashi's generals had prepared a siege until their leader could join them—which he had, by now. The west side of the city was an alternately boggy and rocky peninsula that held the Warrens. West of that was the ocean. North of the city were mountains and only one crossing of the Plith River. Garuwashi had contented himself with burning that bridge so he could concentrate his forces on the east side of the Plith and the two gates he would probably assault.

Garuwashi's army camped like the raiders Kylar had seen at the edge of Ezra's Wood. Tents made up a grid pattern, with small streets separating the tents and wider streets between platoons, commanders' tents at regular intervals, couriers' tents next to those, and latrines and fires laid out with precision.

What they didn't have were wagons. Whatever tunnels the Ceurans had taken were evidently not big enough, or too steep, or too claustrophobic for horses. Garuwashi had sacrificed everything for speed. The war leader himself had probably only caught up to his army in time to see the horror of the walls for himself. And now it was snowing.

This was not going to be a protracted siege. When Terah Graesin had left Cenaria, those who had followed her had put their possessions to the torch to keep them from falling into Khalidoran hands. How many granaries had gone up in those fires? Perhaps a better question was, how many bakeries and mills and warehouses were left? For their part, Lantano Garuwashi's men had the freedom of movement, but all the crops had been taken into the city long ago. Lantano's men could raid villages a few days out—but without horses, they couldn't bring the food back quickly, and they could only bring what they could carry. Even if they stole horses and built a few wagons, that would take time—and they had an entire army to feed.

Each side was going to be absolutely desperate within days.

Logan's force outside the walls wasn't likely to do much to sway the balance, not without communication with Terah Graesin. If they could tell the queen to hold on and not do anything stupid, Logan could use his cavalry to destroy any attempts Garuwashi made at foraging. In a standoff involving thirteen thousand foot soldiers, a few hundred horses could make all the difference. If Terah didn't do anything stupid.

Which meant someone needed to talk to her.

~Someone? Let me guess.~

Kylar had six hours until dawn. It was going to be a busy night. Before he left, just for fun, he tied the silk laces of the sentry's leggings together.

19

I'm sorry, Jenine," Dorian said. "I'm sorry we didn't leave earlier." With snow falling now, they would have had to leave a week ago to make it through the passes. A week ago, he hadn't even found Jenine yet. There was nothing he could have done differently. Still.

"You did everything you could. You were magnificent," Jenine said. The way she said it, with such bravery and unguarded admiration, told him she expected to die. Of course she did. Twenty thousand good reasons for that were marching through the city. She was so brave it made Dorian ache.

"I love you," he said. It just slipped out. He opened his mouth to apologize, but she put a finger on his lips.

"Thank you," she said. She reached up and kissed him gently.

It shouldn't have meant so much, those words, that kiss, coming from a girl who thought she was about to die, but they were liquid fire and hope and life to Dorian.

"We do have one chance," he said.

"We do?"

He shook himself and Halfman—at least the Feyuri ears and eyebrows and the less comfortable portions of his eunuch disguise—burst apart and disintegrated.

Rugger gasped. "Dorian?" he blurted out.

Dorian glared at him. Rugger dropped to his face. "Your Holiness," he said.

It was that simple. Garoth Ursuul had ruled absolutely, and if one disregarded the moral dimensions, he'd ruled efficiently and well. His death left a vacuum, and a people that expected to be ruled as they had been. They were a people accustomed to obeying orders instantly. Dorian and Jenine ran across Luxbridge and into the castle.

From somewhere deep in his mind, Dorian dredged up the correct sequences and shifted the halls so that the front gate led to the Lesser Hall, which then led to the Greater Hall, and finally to the throne room. The stones ground and shook, and obeyed him.

Before going to the throne room, Dorian ran to his old barracks. Hopper refused to open the door, so Dorian had to break it open. He quickly apologized to the terrified concubines, who all looked at him like they should know him, but didn't. Hopper recognized him faster and dropped to his face.

"Hopper, dammit, I don't have the time. Go to the Godking's chambers and get me the finest clothes you can as fast as you can. I need you girls to dress Jenine appropriately, and then I need two or three of you to be throne ornaments—but it's dangerous. Only volunteers, and only if you can be ready in five minutes."

"I don't want to leave you," Jenine said as he moved to go.

"If this is going to work, you must," Dorian said.

She started to protest, then nodded. He ran from the room.

He didn't go to the throne room. He went to his brothers' dormitories. They were littered with bodies. The aethelings had grasped what the Godking's death meant immediately. Several times in his search, Dorian saw younger children hiding beneath beds or in closets. He left them unharmed. All he was looking for were amplifiae, and in several of the rooms, he found many. The older aethelings had collected or created as many amplifiae as they could, knowing that one day they might be the difference between life and death. Dorian scooped as many as he could carry and ran to the throne room.

The throne room itself had been the site of one of the worst battles. Twenty dead aethelings and two Vürdmeisters sprawled in the shit and stench of death. Two young men were still alive, though too badly hurt to use the vir. Dorian stilled their hearts and took his throne amid the stench of burnt flesh and hair and the coppery smell of blood. All the amplifiae he had gathered were useless to him. He had some power left, but it would kill him to use what he would need to overmatch the number of Vürdmeisters marching toward the throne room right now.

Jenine and Hopper and two young concubines jogged into the hall, Hopper as awkward as his namesake.

"You look stunning," Dorian told Jenine. She was wearing green silks and emeralds. "Ladies," he told the concubines, "your bravery will not be forgotten."

"They're across the bridge," Hopper said. He produced some of Garoth's magnificent clothing, and the women stripped Dorian and dressed him as quickly as they could.

Dorian thought of the meisters hurrying here even now. Would they go slowly enough to try to read the residue of the battles they passed? What would they make of the gap in Luxbridge? He draped the heavy gold chains of office around his neck.

"You, there. And you, over there," he told the concubines. "Jenine, on the floor beside the throne. Sorry there's no chair. Hopper, over by the door in case I need you."

He sat then in the great onyx throne and as he put his hands on the sinuous arms of the chair, he felt connected to the whole Citadel, but most especially to its heart—its empty heart now, where Khali should have been. Dorian thanked the God that she wasn't there. He didn't know if he could survive that. He could feel the meisters approaching the great doors, so through the throne that made the Citadel like part of his body, he threw the doors open with a crash.

The meisters and Vürdmeisters hesitated. There were hundreds of them, and they took in the carnage of the dead aethelings and the easy majesty of the man on the throne at once. Most of them had obviously expected to see Paerik. Their jaws dropped. Others had known, had been able to read the vir to know he died—and, as usual, hadn't shared their knowledge with their fellows, hoping it would give them an edge.

"Enter," Dorian commanded, amplifying his voice enough that all could hear, but not booming as an amateur would. Vürdmeisters would not be cowed by a simple weave, and using it too forcefully would make them suspect him.

He let those who were able to read the battle read it. Then he waited. He let them look around the room, stare at the women, stare at the magic, even glance at Hopper. He let them look at him, let those who remembered him gasp and mutter about who he was. Dorian the heir, returned from the dead. Dorian, the rebel. Dorian, the defiant. Dorian, the erased. He waited, and it made him remember when his father had been grooming him to rule. They had walked one day together in a wheat field.

"How do you keep such ambitious people in your grip?" Dorian had asked.

Garoth Ursuul had said nothing. He simply pointed to a stalk of wheat that grew above its fellows and lopped its head off.

These men were the ones who had survived generations of that process. None of them spoke for ten seconds, twenty, a minute. Dorian waited until he was sure one young Vürdmeister was about to speak. Then with his vir, he flung a staff at the man.

Two hundred shields sprang up in the throne room. The amplifiae hit the young wytch's shield and fell to the ground. Dorian favored them with a condescending look and slowly the meisters lowered their shields. The young man who'd been about to speak scooted forward and picked up the staff, looking abashed. Then Dorian threw another amplifiae to the meister on his right. She caught it. Then he threw another and another until he'd dispensed all of the dozens he had, even his own.

There weren't enough for every meister, of course, but there were enough to make Dorian's point. A king didn't arm his enemies.

Dorian raised his vir to the surface of his skin, and

brought them not only into his arms, but up around his face. He allowed them to break through his scalp and form a living crown. There was pain there, pain as they broke his skin and as they broke through channels of power that he had blocked long ago. He was powerful again now. Powerful and dread.

"Some of you recognize me as Dorian, first seed, first aetheling, first survivor of training, first to accomplish his uurdthan, first son of Garoth Ursuul."

"But Dorian is dead," one of the younger meisters said, deep in the crowd.

"Yes, dead," Dorian said. "You have read the chronicles. Dorian is dead these twelve years. As now Paerik is dead. And Draef is dead. And Tavi. And Jurik. And Rivik. And Duron, and Hesdel, and Roqwin, and Porrik, and Gvessie, and Wheriss, and Julamon, and Vic. Dead, all of those who questioned my resolve. So now each of you has a choice. Will you question my resolve and try to take this throne, or will you gather my enemies and bring them to me?"

Dorian's face was perfectly impassive. It had to be. He had no Talent left, and no vir left if he wanted to live. The throne had some interesting powers, but not enough to destroy two hundred meisters.

He wondered suddenly if any of them realized how fragile he was. It wouldn't take an attack to destroy Dorian. It would only take a single sneer.

But these were men schooled not to sneer at authority, no matter how much they despised it. The moment stretched unbearably, and then one young man hit his knees before his Godking. Then another. Then it was a rush not to be the last.

This, at least, I owe you, father. You cruel, brutal, amazing man. They called you a god and you made them believe it.

The new Godking affected not to be surprised. He started issuing orders, and they obeyed, running to secure the safety of the concubines, running to capture the living aethelings, running to take care of the armies, to summon the leaders of the city and the highland and lowland chiefs, to gather the meisters who had gone into hiding during the fighting.

"What have I done?" Dorian asked Jenine quietly when it was done.

She didn't answer. There were still men and meisters in the throne room. It should have felt good to assume so much power, so much power to change everything he'd hated about his homeland. Instead, he felt trapped.

"Your Holiness," the young red-haired Vürdmeister who had been the closest to opposing him said. "If . . . if Dorian is dead, Your Holiness, what may we call you?"

Godking Dorian was impossible, of course. Not only because his father had wanted him dead. Dorian didn't want Solon or Feir or any magus to ever hear of this. Better they think him dead. *Looks like I had to go through the shit one way or the other, huh, God?* But the God didn't answer. The God was far away, and Dorian's challenges were here, immediate and deadly.

"I am . . . Godking Wanhope." Wanhope was an archaic word that meant despair. When he looked at Jenine, she looked frightened but resolute. He squeezed her hand. *She's worth it. We'll make it through this. Somehow.*

20

As Vi descended from the pass in the afternoon, the snows became sleet and finally rain. Forests yielded to farms, though she met no one on the road. Anyone with sense was inside. Vi rounded a corner and found herself staring at Sister Ariel, sitting on a mare with all the grace of a sack of potatoes. In contrast to how miserably drenched Vi was, the Bitch Wytch wasn't even wet. An inch above her skin and clothing, the rain sheared away, ran in rivulets over an invisible shell, and dropped to the ground. She smiled beatifically. "Hello, Vi. It's good to see you're alive. I received a very odd message this morning telling me to expect you."

"From Dehvi?" Vi asked.

"Who?"

"Dehvira-something Bruhmaezi-something," Vi said.

"Dehvirahaman ko Bruhmaeziwakazari?" Sister Ariel asked, getting both the cadence and the tone perfect. Bitch!

"That was it."

Sister Ariel smirked. "You are a very impressive young woman, Vi, but the Ghost of the Steppes—if not only a legend—is two hundred years dead. Someone was having fun with you."

"The what?" Vi asked.

"Why are you here, Vi?" Sister Ariel asked. "No lies. Please."

Instantly, Vi felt herself caught between rage and tears again, out of control. She'd never been like this before. Since murdering Jarl, she'd been a disaster. Ringing Kylar had only made it worse. Even the things that should have been good, like learning Hu was dead, and helping kill the man who claimed to be her father, Godking Garoth Ursuul, had instead only thrown her further off balance. "I'm here to become you, you bitch. To manipulate rather than be manipulated. To become the best." She tugged at her earring. "And to get this fucking thing off."

Sister Ariel's face stilled, her lips going white. "For your sake, I strongly suggest you come up with other reasons when the Gatekeeper interviews you. So how about you shut your mouth, and I'll pretend you're a normal young woman looking to join our sisterhood?"

It took a long time for Vi's rage to subside enough for her to nod.

They rode together through the rain and soon the city emerged from the low-lying cloud. "It's called Laketown," Sister Ariel said, "for the obvious reasons."

The city and the Chantry rested at the confluence of two rivers, which made a reservoir above Vestacchi Lake. All the buildings of the city and the Chantry rested on islands in the reservoir, the nearest of which was fifty paces from the shore. Arching bridges connected every island to its neighbors and several to the shore, but streets themselves were absent. Instead, low, flat punts navigated the waterways. Some of them were covered against the rain, others exposed. Regardless, the punts moved far faster than they should have.

Vi and Ariel entered the part of Laketown that had grown on the shores by the bridges, but all the merchants seemed to be huddled in their daub-and-wattle homes, with their chimneys or chimney holes smoking.

"By some ancient magic we still can't duplicate, the islands are actually floating," Sister Ariel said. "The entire dam can be opened and the islands flushed out into the lake in times of war. Of course, we haven't had to do that for centuries. And a good thing, too. I understand towing all the islands back up here is a lot of work."

"It's beautiful," Vi said, forgetting herself. "The water's so clean."

"This city was built at a time when magic was used to benefit farmers and fishermen. There were special streams in every city that would take the stains out of your clothing. There were plows that could be pulled by a single ox that would break six furrows in a single pass. There were free public baths with water as hot or cold as you wanted. Charms that kept meat from spoiling. People thought of magic as a tool, not only as a weapon. In Laketown, the slops and nightsoil are supposed to be thrown into these pipes that—see, no smell?—that take them directly to the dam. Of course, you can never get everyone to obey even a sensible law—like not throwing nightsoil in the water you drink—so the lake itself has spells that cleanse it."

Sister Ariel led them to a white punt on the far end of the dock. A boy dodged out into the rain to take their horses and Vi took her bags and stepped onto the punt. She took some comfort in Sister Ariel's obvious terror that the boat was going to capsize. As soon as they were settled on the low, wet seats, the punt began moving by itself.

Vi grabbed the side of the boat in a white-knuckled grip.

Sister Ariel smiled. "This magic, on the other hand," she said, "we can do. It's just too much trouble, these days." They skimmed quickly into the wide water streets and the little boat turned on its own.

"There are currents that shift on the turning of the glass. If you know what you're doing, you can get from one side of the city to the other going downstream all the way."

After a few minutes, they emerged into an enormous opening with no islands except the biggest one of them all. "Behold the White Lady. The Alabaster Seraph. The Chantry. The Seraph of Nerev. And for you now, Vi, home."

The Chantry had looked big before, but only now as they approached it did it become apparent how massive it was. The entire building was carved in the likeness of a winged, angelic woman. She was too solid to actually be alabaster, too perfectly white to be marble. The stone shone, even in the dim light of this dreary day. Vi imagined it would be blinding in the sunlight. As they came closer, Vi saw that what looked from a distance like erosion or pitting from age in the statue-building's surface were actually windows and decks for the myriad of rooms inside, each nearly invisible because the surrounding stone was the same dazzling white.

The Seraph's wings were half-unfurled, and she bore

a sword in her left hand, point down, and a cool look on her face. As the punt circled around the back of the island, Vi saw that the Seraph's right hand held a set of scales behind her back, with a feather on one side and a heart on the other.

Hundreds of docks crowded the back side of the island, and despite the rain, dozens of boats were loading and unloading all manner of supplies and people. Their white punt skimmed straight to the nearest set of docks, passing beneath an arch of living wisteria, impossibly still in bloom with a riot of purple flowers. The punt came to rest, and two sisters in black robes greeted them.

"Vi, go with them," Sister Ariel said. She paused, then added, "No threat they make is idle. It has been years since anyone died during initiation, but it is a possible. May whatever god you believe go with you. And if you believe in none, good luck."

The worst part wasn't that the last god Vi wanted with her now was Nysos, to whom she had offered her body and soul and the blood of so many innocents. The worst part was that Sister Ariel's good wishes sounded absolutely sincere.

21

The first step was breaking into the city. Kylar knew there had to be dozens of smugglers' routes, but that wasn't the kind of information smugglers handed out at Sa'kagé parties. He did know what he was looking for, though. It would be hidden within a few hundred paces of the walls, and it would emerge somewhere onto rock so as not to take hoofprints and wagon tracks, and it would be somewhere close to one of the main roads.

On the low hills surrounding the city, a month ago buildings had lined every road: taverns, farmhouses, hostelries, and any of the innumerable trade houses that catered to travelers who hadn't the coin for accommodations or services in the city. Now, there were no buildings.

The Ceurans had taken everything. They had dismantled every building and brought the materials into their camp. Kylar could only imagine the frenzy the Sa'kagé must have been in, trying to decide which tunnels to collapse and which to salvage, hoping to preserve their own way out of the city if all else failed.

He moved through the Ceuran camp slowly, dodging from shadow to shadow. He had eschewed invisibility for a hazy black, hoping it would be harder to see than the odd distortions of sleet hitting something that wasn't there.

His eyes should have given him a distinct advantage in searching for a smugglers' entrance. He finally found a large, low rock sitting feet from the main road with trees on either side of it. It was perfect. If the rock swung open, smugglers could pull their wagon onto the main road unseen and leave no tracks. Kylar brushed the sleet away from the rock and saw tell-tale scrapes from the iron-bound wagon wheels grinding against the rock. This was it.

Ten minutes later, he still hadn't made any progress. Every two minutes, he had to hide as a sentry made his rounds, and every five minutes a different sentry overlapped from the opposite side. Kylar couldn't blame the interruptions, though. He just couldn't find the catch that opened the door. Maybe it was the sleet, making his fingers clumsy with the cold. Or maybe he just wasn't as good as he thought.

Immortal, not invincible. Why'd Durzo have to be right all the time? Come to think of it, where the hell is Durzo?

The thought affected Kylar more profoundly than he expected. He'd lived for months thinking his master was dead. In all those months, Durzo hadn't bothered to come see Kylar. Kylar had thought himself his master's best friend. Even when Aristarchos ban Ebron had told him all of the heroes his master had been, Kylar had still thought that his relationship with Durzo was special. In a way, learning all the great men his master had been made

Kylar feel better about himself. But time had moved on, and apparently so too had Durzo. Whatever brief importance Kylar had had in that man's seven-century-long life, it was finished.

Kylar sat down on rock. The sleet soaked through to his underclothes in seconds. It made him feel even worse.

~Don't tell me you're going to cry.~

You mind?

~Wake me when the self-pity's done, would you?~

Damn you, you sound just like Durzo.

~So I stay with the man night and day for seven centuries and he rubs off on me. You only spent ten years with him, and look how much like him you are.~

That caught Kylar off guard. *I'm not like him.*

~No, you're just out here trying to save the world by yourself—again—by coincidence.~

He did this kind of thing a lot?

~Ever hear of the Miletian Regression? The Death of Six Kings? The Vendazian Uprising? The Escape of the Grasq Twins?~

Kylar hesitated. *Um, actually . . . no.*

The ka'kari sighed. Kylar wondered how it did that.

"I'm an idiot," Kylar said. He stood up. His butt was numb.

~An epiphany! Long overdue, too. But then, I've come to expect small things.~

Kylar walked to the wall. The last few hundred paces were empty of Ceuran soldiers—none of them were foolish enough to stray within bowshot. The only place the Ceurans had moved closer was along the shores of the Plith, where they were moving great quantities of rock to fill in part of the river. All along the shore and the approach to it, they'd built a corridor to protect the workers from arrows. The wytches had protected every approach to the city except the river. Kylar supposed that they'd figured a couple of meisters standing on either bank could keep any ships or swimmers from making it through the narrow passage. The Cenarians didn't have that luxury. This was where Garuwashi would attack. Once one bank was filled in enough, he could start sending skirmishers in.

If the sa'ceurai came and fought one-on-one with Cenarian soldiers, Kylar had no doubt who would have the larger pile of corpses at the end of the day.

Kylar walked to the wall. The great stones had been hardened with spells, and fitted more tightly to their neighbors than weight and mortar could accomplish. Kylar brought the ka'kari to his hands and feet.

~I should make you swim.~

Kylar smirked and felt the stone dimple under his fingers and toes. He began climbing.

Any hopes he had that Terah Graesin wasn't going to do something stupid died as he reached the top of the wall. With four hours until dawn, men were already preparing to attack the sa'ceurai. Most of the soldiers were still asleep, and the horses still in their stables, but a huge area had been cleared inside the south gate. Flags had been planted so that the regiments could find their positions first thing in the morning, and squires were scurrying around, making sure armor and weapons were in top condition. From the size of the area cleared, Kylar guessed that the queen was preparing an all-out attack at dawn, committing perhaps fifteen thousand men for the attack.

He squinted at the flags, doing the math. He wouldn't have said she had so many men.

The answer was in the flags nearest the gate. More than one flag bore a rabbit. The queen had conscripted Rabbits—and put totally untrained peasants at the spearhead of the attack on the most highly trained sa'ceurai in the world? Genius. It was one thing to throw your peasants against the other side's peasants when you had space to try to bring in cavalry from the side or something, but when the Cenarians came pouring out the gate, Garuwashi's sa'ceurai would meet them immediately. The battle would be confined to one front—the peasants would find themselves all alone, getting slaughtered, unable to move forward because of the sa'ceurai, unable to move back because the rest of the army was trying to get out of the south gate.

It would probably only be minutes before they panicked, and then it was only a matter of how many people would be slaughtered before Luc Graesin called off the attack and tried to shut the gates before the sa'ceurai got into the city.

Kylar dropped into the great yard and stole a leather gambeson from a pile, along with trousers and a tunic. A minute later, he stepped out from behind a smithy as a boy hurried past pushing a cart filled with cheap swords and pole arms.

"So the Rabbits get to lead the attack? Hit 'em at dawn?" Kylar said, waving at the battle flags. "How'd that happen?"

The kid lit up. "We volunteered."

"I know a man who volunteered to snort guri pepper sauce. It didn't make it a good idea."

"What are you saying?" the kid asked, offended.

"Why's the queen letting them go first?"

"It's not the queen. It's her brother Luc. He's Lord General now."

"And?"

The kid scowled. "He said the uh, the casualties would be highest among the first ones out. You know, till we took out their archers. The Rabbits ain't scared of nothing."

So the new Lord General manages to cull his bravest citizens and ensure a crushing defeat, all at once. Brilliant.

"You mind? I got work to do," the kid said.

Kylar stole a horse. He didn't have the time to walk to the castle. As he mounted, a groom came toward him. "Hey, who are you? That horse belongs to—"

Kylar brought the mask of judgment to his face in a rush and whipped his head toward the man, snarling, blue flame leaping up in his eyes and mouth.

The groom leapt backward and tripped into a horse trough with a yell.

Kylar rode as fast as he could. He left the horse and the stolen clothes before he got to East Kingsbridge and went invisible. He ran the rest of the way, leaving guards with their heads swiveling, trying to find where the patter of running feet had come from. Rather than run through the twisting, illogical halls of the castle, he climbed the wall. In minutes, he dropped onto the queen's balcony, which was still missing part of the railing where Kylar had freed Mags Drake's corpse. He looked inside.

The queen wasn't alone.

22

"Before I sent you after Sister Jessie, you said you'd been studying something for two years," Istariel Wyant, the Speaker of the Chantry, said. They were sitting in her office, high in the Seraph, sharing ootai and strategy. "What was it?"

"The *ka'karifer*," Ariel said.

"The what? My Hyrillic isn't what it used to be."

A doubtful look crossed Ariel's face. "Your Hyrillic was never what it used to be. If I recall correctly, your marks in all your language classes—"

"The question, Ariel," Istariel snapped, with more vigor than she intended. Only perhaps a dozen Sisters in the Chantry would recall how poorly she had performed in a few of her classes, and none of them would dare correct the Speaker. None except Ariel, who was not correcting her because she thought being Istariel's sister gave her license: Ariel would correct anyone.

"The bearers of the stones of stones," Ariel said. "Colloquially that would have meant stones of greatest power.

The original bearers were Jorsin's Champions of Light: Trace Arvagulania—fascinating, I think you would have liked her. She was one of the foremost minds of the age in an age famous for great minds. Probably not matched even to the present day, though I know Rosserti argues that Milovian Period is as important, I personally find his contentions regarding the Alitaeran succession to be weak: I think there were complete breaks with Miletian traditions during the Interregnum. But I'm getting side-tracked. Trace, this brilliant but horribly ugly woman—in some accounts the ugliest woman of the age, though I think those legends are as greatly exaggerated as most of the others— was given a stone that conferred all beauty upon her. The poets couldn't even agree what she looked like. I believe, in keeping with Hrambower's paper *Sententia*—damn all Lodricari scholars and their clotted syntax but there you have it—that the confusion was because the ka'kari's power was not that it shifted Trace's appearance, but that it directly affected viewers' perceptions of her, in each case making her what would be most attractive to them. Imagine the fortune Ezra could have made in cosmetics!" She waited for Istariel to laugh. She didn't.

"Fascinating," Istariel said, her tone flat.

"Of course that ka'kari disappeared and has never resurfaced. I imagine it would have, if it were anything but a legend. There is much stronger evidence in support of the red ka'kari's existence. Originally, it was given to Corvaer Blackwell—ironically enough, Lord Blackwell would henceforth be known as Corvaer the Red—and after he died during the Battle of Jaeran Flats, it was taken by a man named Malak Mok'mazi, Malak Firehands in our tongue, though obviously that translation doesn't preserve the alliteration. Accounts from both sides claimed that he fought from *within* the conflagration that swept the plain and broke the Gurvani army. Again, after his death—apparently fire isn't much good against poison—" Ariel barked a laugh, which Istariel didn't share. "Uh hmm, well, it seems to have reappeared in various hands throughout history. Some of those had credible witnesses. Herddios, whom we trust for all sorts of other stories that have checked out, claims to have personally—"

"Did you learn anything *new?*" Istariel said, doing to her best to feign interest. Limited interest.

Ariel licked her lips, her eyes flicking up to the ceiling as she thought. "I concluded that a review of all the currently available literature on the subject still left the most pertinent questions open. And most of the less pertinent ones as well."

"So it took you two years to figure out that you weren't going to figure anything out." It was a graceless way to put it, but then, with Ariel, it paid to be blunt.

Ariel grimaced. "That's why I was willing to go see about Jessie al'Gwaydin."

And not because your Speaker asked you to. For a moment, Istariel was jealous of her oblivious older sister. Ariel was a rock and the waves of politics passed her with sound and fury and she didn't even notice. She was a bore, but a useful one. Whenever Istariel had needed an expert opinion on the magical sides of dilemmas, Ariel could be loosed on the problem like a hound to scent. And she wouldn't share her findings with anyone except the books she wrote and Istariel. All in all, Ariel was worth far more than the trouble she caused. But did she have to be so boring?

If Ariel had turned her brilliant mind to politics. . . . Well, Istariel had thought of that before, in her more paranoid moments. If Ariel had the inclination for such things, Ariel would be the Speaker and Istariel would probably be some farmer's brood mare. The key to handling Ariel was understanding that she was a believer; not a believer in some god, but a believer in the Chantry. There was something endearingly naive in women who believed all that "Seraph's handmaiden" tripe. It made them far easier to handle than the magae who believed only in themselves. Point in a direction, say "good of the Chantry," and Ariel would do anything.

"Ariel, I've got a problem I need your help with. I know you've never accepted a tyro—"

"I'll do it."

"—but I want you to think about the good of the—What?"

"You want me to teach Viridiana Sovari so she's protected until she can destroy Eris Buel and the Chattel. I'll do it."

Istariel's heart jumped into her throat. So nakedly laid out, it was a plot whose discovery would bring down a Speaker. "Never say that!" she hissed. "Not ever. Not even here."

Ariel cocked an eyebrow at her.

Istariel smoothed her dress. "She's being initiated this evening?"

"As we speak. Apparently there are some difficulties. It's been hours."

Istariel frowned. "How Talented is this girl? Is she Eris Buel's equal?"

"No," Ariel said. "Not even close."

Istariel cursed.

"You misunderstand. She surpasses Eris Buel in every way. Vi Sovari is more Talented than I am."

Istariel's eyes widened. Like most Sisters, she was loath to admit when others were stronger. She would have thought Ariel, being so accustomed to being stronger than everyone, would chafe at the idea at least a little.

"Ulyssandra will be more Talented still, given five years," Ariel said.

"That's great news. But I don't have five years. I don't have one. I need you to turn this Vi Sovari into something special by spring. The Chattel are arriving then as a show of strength to make their demands heard." *And maybe to bring down a speaker.*

"You will make concessions," Ariel said, not quite a question.

"They wish us to start a men's school. Did I say wish? They demand. They demand recognition of their new 'order' and the attendant seats on the council, which would make them by far the most powerful order in the Chantry. By themselves they would have a majority in any vote that came to the floor. They demand a repeal of the marriage bans so they may marry magi. They demand a repeal of the Alitaeran Accords. The nations of Midcyru will have reason to fear that we wish to return to the Alkestian magocracy. These Chattel will unite the nations against us. We're a bastion of light in a dark world, Ariel. Concessions I can countenance. Destruction I cannot."

"What is it you want me to teach Vi?" Ariel asked. That was it; Istariel had her.

Istariel paused, stuck between discretion and wanting to make sure her dense sister did what needed to be done.

"Like we do with every Sister, help Vi figure out what her
strengths are, and train them."

Ariel's eyes widened and narrowed in a heartbeat. The
girl was nearly a battle maja, and they both knew it. In
fact, Ariel's response was so swift, Istariel thought she
might have suspected the order. Or maybe Ariel was just
that smart.

Well, there it was, as much discretion and direction as
Istariel could afford to give and still hope to retain her
seat if any word of this came out. Istariel would have to
keep her distance from Ariel and Vi, of course. Even Ariel
would understand that . . . if she noticed. Now, to smooth
things, to maintain the illusion.

"You are to be commended for bringing such great Talents into our fold, Sister Ariel. I don't believe two recruits
with such potential have been brought to the Chantry for
perhaps fifty years." She smiled. It was fifty years since
she and Ariel had arrived.

"Longer, surely."

"You deserve to be rewarded," Istariel said, her smile
freezing. "Is there anything I can get for your studies?"
Ariel, of course, would say service was enough.

"Absolutely," Ariel said.

By the time she left, Ariel had muscled Istariel into
consenting to every item. Ariel hadn't even had the grace
to offer something she didn't really want so Istariel could
say no and claim some small victory for her pride.

Istariel sat back and looked at her hair in her mirror,
wanting it to be perfect for her meeting with the Alitaeran
emissary. At least her blonde hair was still beautiful. She
had the other Sisters swearing it was magic that she could

have a mane so glossy and thick and perfect. It wasn't, but it always pleased her to hear the allegation.

Her mind cast back to Ariel's statement that she should be fascinated by ugly Trace Arvag-whatever-her-name-was. Istariel frowned, the face in the mirror showing any number of unattractive lines on a dignified but quite plain face. If Ariel had a sense of humor, Istariel would suspect she were the butt of a very subtle joke.

She snorted. Ariel, a sense of humor. Now there was a joke.

23

$\mathcal{K}$ylar peered through the glass inset in the balcony door. In the darkness of the queen's bedchamber, a couple was writhing on the queen's bed. From their frenetic pace, they were either very close to completion or very energetic. From habit, Kylar looked at the hinges of the balcony door, then realized they could squeal like a herd of pigs and never be noticed. He looked back through the window, suddenly shy. Still going.

A gentleman would wait. A wetboy would use the distraction. Kylar slipped inside.

The young man grunted and froze. Hands smacked loudly as the woman grabbed his buttocks and urged him to keep going. He thrust twice more, then wilted.

"Fuck!" Terah Graesin said, pushing him off her. "I thought I was going to make it this time."

"Sorry, Sis," Luc Graesin said.

Kylar felt suddenly lightheaded. The ka'kari whistled softly. ~*I haven't seen royal incest for a couple centuries, and that was in Ymmur, where it's expected.*~

Luc snuggled into Terah's side and laid his head on her chest. Considering that he was substantially taller and bigger than his sister, it was oddly submissive. Kylar was struck by the difference in their ages. Luc was perhaps seventeen and looked younger; Terah was twenty-five and looked older. How long had this been going on?

Durzo had taught Kylar that when something surprised you on a job, only one question mattered: does this change what I have to do? The answer now was no, unless Luc stayed all night. Kylar put aside all the speculations about what this meant and refocused. There was nothing to do but wait, so Kylar moved behind a pillar in a quiet corner of the room.

Luc propped himself up on an elbow. "Sis, I wanted to talk to you about tomorrow morning. This morning, whatever."

"You're going to lead your first battle," Terah said, pushing a lock of hair back behind his ear. "You're going to be safe. I've given the Guard commands to keep you back from—"

"That's just it, Ter." Luc got out of bed and began dressing. "I didn't fight at Pavvil's Grove. I didn't go on any raids. I didn't fight highlanders at Screaming Winds—"

"Do not bring up Logan Gyre."

"I'm the Lord Commander of the Royal Armies of Cenaria, and my experience of battle is limited to the fist-fight I had with the pig keeper's boy. I was ten. He was eight. I lost and you had him thrashed."

"Generals fight with their brains. Your scouts were instrumental to our victory at Pavvil's Grove," Terah said.

"How do you do that?" Luc asked, pausing in the act of lacing his tunic. "You fit two lies in one sentence. It wasn't our victory. It was Logan's. Why we rule now rather than having our heads on pikes, I don't know. And I completely botched handling the scouts. Men wondered if I was trying to screw up. I was so bad they thought I was a traitor."

"Who said that?" Terah asked, her eyes alight.

"It doesn't matter."

"What do you want, Luc? I've given you everything."

Luc threw his hands up. "That's what I'm trying to say! You've given me everything that a man might earn after a lifetime of—"

"What do you want?" she interrupted.

"I think we should stop."

"Stop?"

"You and me, Ter. Us. This." He wouldn't meet her gaze.

"Do you still love me?"

"Sis . . ."

"It's a simple question."

"Insanely," Luc said. "But if people find out, they'll install Logan in a second."

"Logan won't threaten us forever."

"Sis, he's a good man. A hero. You're not going to kill him."

She smiled dangerously. "Don't tell me how to rule, Luc."

"Terah," he said.

"You listen to me. You'll bitch and moan and fret, like always. And I'll take care of it, like always. I take the risks, you take the rewards. So why don't you and your conscience go fuck all the maids, while *I* get called a slut."

"You expect me to believe you didn't sleep with all those lords?" Luc asked.

She slapped him. "You bastard. They never laid a hand on me."

"So much can be accomplished without hands."

She slapped him again.

"Don't, don't do that again," Luc said.

She slapped him again. He did nothing.

"I let them call me a slut," Terah said. "I let you fuck other women. I wake up two hours before dawn on the nights you visit so a maid can change my sheets so that when my laundress—who's a Sa'kagé spy—washes them there's no evidence of us. Why? Because I love you. So I think I deserve a little gratitude."

Luc held her stare for a few moments, then deflated. "I'm sorry, Ter. I'm just scared."

"Go get some sleep. And come to me after your victory." Her smile held a promise.

Luc's eyes lit with boyish mischief. "How about I come to you now?"

"No," she said. "Good night, Luc."

"Please?"

"Good night, Luc."

After Luc left and the queen had been asleep for half an hour, Kylar drew his bollock dagger. It was pitted and blunted from the corrosive powers of the Devourer.

~Sorry.~

He reached out to prod Terah. Stopped. There were things more menacing than a pitted dagger.

Kylar studied Terah Graesin as he'd learned to study his deaders. She was a woman whose bearing and reputation were a greater part of her appeal than nature's gifts.

In this unguarded, unrouged moment, she looked more like a skinny farm girl than a queen: her lips thin, cracked, colorless. Her eyebrows tiny lines. Her eyelashes short. Her nose slightly hooked. Her milky skin marred by several pimples. Her face obscured by strands of loose hair.

In that moment, he couldn't help but respect Terah Graesin. She'd been born into one of the great families of Cenaria, but her spirit was indomitable. She had risen past men who despised her for her youth, her sex, her reputation. Terah Graesin hadn't become queen by accident. But here, Terah Graesin was just a woman alone, about to be woken by a nightmare.

Sometimes, Kylar couldn't help but pity the bastards. Durzo had taught Kylar that the best wetboy understood his deader better than the deader understood himself. Kylar believed it, but every time he did something calculated to inspire terror, he wondered if he was trading away his humanity. It was one thing to terrify goons. Was it different to terrify a young woman in the intimacy of her bedchamber?

But Terah Graesin wasn't merely a woman. She was a queen. Her idiocy would kill thousands—and she planned to kill Logan, the rightful king. *Act now. Doubt later.*

Kylar went to the other side of Terah's bed and pulled back the covers to give himself space to sit. With the patience of a wetboy, he eased his weight onto the mattress by degrees. Finally, he sat, legs folded, hands draped on his knees, back straight, the face of judgment angry.

The young queen was sleeping on her side, with her hands tucked under her pillow, so it was easy to grab the thick down blanket and pull it down. Caught between the necessity for patience—any rapid change would wake her—and the coldness of the room which would have Terah reaching for blankets even in sleep, Kylar pulled back the sheet to uncover her nakedness.

Kylar didn't look. If anything, he was disgusted. He wanted her off-balance, vulnerable. She stirred. He schooled himself to stillness, sitting upright once more, and began to glow a cool blue, gradually brightening.

This was the shaky part: a deader's startle response was involuntary. Scaring a screamer and telling them not to scream was futile. He could wake her with a hand across her mouth, but that wouldn't give the flavor of terror he was looking for.

Terah Graesin woke slowly, as he hoped. Squinted, then opened her eyes slowly. Blinked, once, twice as if against the dawn light that usually came in her windows. Focused closer, closer. Then, all in a rush, the Night Angel came into focus, eyes burning with blue flame, puffs of fire escaping his lips with every breath, body alternately invisible, wispy as black smoke, and gleaming hard iridescent black metal muscle. Her breath caught, and a squeak came out. Not loud, thank the God.

Her legs spasmed and kicked and she grabbed for the covers. Flailing, she scooted toward the edge of the bed. Kylar sat motionless as a god and reached out only with his Talent. He was still clumsy with this, but he made a lucky grab and caught Terah's throat with his first try. The hand of Talent pinned her to the bed.

Drawing up a rigid hand in a striking position called a knife hand, Kylar made it literal by forming the ka'kari into a leaf-shaped blade over his hand. He whispered, "A scream would be a mistake, Terah. Understood?" He used her name to make it more familiar, more creepy when she remembered it.

Eyes wide, she nodded.

"Cover yourself, whore. You reek of your brother's seed," he said. He released her throat and drew the ka'kari back from his hand. With jerky motions, she pulled up the sheets and held them in white-knuckled fists, drawing her knees up, trembling.

The Night Angel said. "While you rule my city, I demand you rule well."

"Who are you?" she asked, voice tight, still off balance.

"You will call off this attack. Garuwashi has no food. He can not hold this siege."

"You're here to help me save Cenaria?" she asked, incredulous.

"I will save Cenaria, with you or from you. Give me two days. Garuwashi doesn't know how bad it is in the city. He will negotiate."

Terah Graesin was already recovering. "He's refused me. He swore never to negotiate with a woman." That was news to Kylar. Why wouldn't Garuwashi negotiate?

"Not with you then," Kylar said. "With Gyre."

Her eyes lit with fury. "Gyre? You're Logan's creature? You were the one who saved us in the garden during the coup! All you cared about was him. You saved him, didn't you? You saved him and now you want him to get the glory. After all I've done to get here, you expect me to let Logan win? I'd rather die!" She stood haughtily and grabbed her robe from a chair. "Now I suggest—"

Kylar was on her. Before she could even think to scream, he slammed her onto the bed, straddled her, punched her solar plexus to knock the wind from her and clamped a hand over her face. He grabbed a hairpin from her bedside table and drove it through the meat of her arm. He let her gasp in a breath and then filled her mouth with the ka'kari to keep her from screaming.

Unable to expel her scream from her mouth, air gushed from her nose and blew snot all over his hand. He ground the hairpin back and forth, then grabbed another.

She bucked and kicked and tried to scream through her nose, so he blocked her nose with the ka'kari too.

Her eyes bulged and the veins on her neck stood out as she struggled in vain to breathe. She tried to flail, but Kylar had her arms pinned with his knees. He brought the hairpin into her view and touched the point to her forehead.

Though her throat was still working convulsively, Terah Graesin stilled. Kylar traced the point of the hairpin down her forehead, between her eyes, then across the delicate skin of one eyelid.

For a moment, he couldn't help but wonder what Elene would think if she saw him here, doing this. The queen's terror sickened him, and yet he held the cruel smile on his face. He lifted the hairpin away from her eye so she could see Judgment. "You'd rather die?" the Night Angel asked. "Really?"

24

The sight of the Alabaster Seraph growing larger as the punt approached did nothing to calm Elene. If Elene had read Vi's letter correctly—it seemed like so long ago now—Vi had ringed Kylar without his permission, with the very wedding earrings Kylar had intended for Elene and himself. Elene had never been so furious for so long.

She knew it was destructive. She knew it would eat her alive. Only weeks ago, she'd killed a man, and she hadn't felt the wash of hatred she felt now.

Elene knew she was being disobedient, holding onto her resentment, her righteous wrath. But it made her feel powerful to hate the woman who'd done her wrong. Vi deserved hatred.

The punt docked in a small slip magically shielded from the rain and the boatman pointed her to a line. Elene joined two dozen other people, mostly women, who had come to petition the Chantry. An hour later, when she gave her name and asked to see Vi, the Sister found a note about her and sent a tyro running.

Several minutes later, an older maja with the loose skin and ill-fitting clothes of a woman who's lost too much weight too fast came out. "Hello, Elene. My name is Sister Ariel. Come with me."

"Where are you taking me?"

"To see Uly and Vi. That's what you want, isn't it?" Sister Ariel turned and walked away without waiting for a response.

Many steps later, they stopped at a hospital floor with hundreds of beds, lining the circumference of the Seraph. Most of the beds were empty, but Sisters with green sashes moved among those that were occupied, sometimes touching the walls, which immediately turned transparent, letting in the diffuse morning sun.

"Is Uly ill?" Elene asked.

Sister Ariel said nothing. She led Elene past dozens of beds. Some of the girls on them had arms or legs wrapped in gauze, and here and there, ancient-looking magae slept, but most of the injured had no obvious wounds. Magical wounds, Elene supposed, didn't always leave evidence on the body.

Finally, they stopped at a bed, but the woman on it wasn't Uly, it was Vi. It took Elene's breath away. She had thought from the glimpse of the redhead on the trail that she'd never seen Vi before, but she had. Vi had been at the fateful last party at the Jadwin estate. That night, Vi had come as a blonde, wearing a dress that was a scandal in red. Elene remembered the swirl of emotions she'd felt that night clearly: shock that someone would wear such revealing attire, judgment, fascination. Elene—and every other man and woman—hadn't been able to take her eyes off the woman. Immediately after those first emotions, without ever losing her outrage, she'd felt jealousy, longing, the sick-stomach sensation of not measuring up to such beauty, wishing that she could attract such stares, and knowing she never would—and would never wear such clothes even if she could—but wishing all the same that she might, just for a few moments. Vi was that woman, and if anything, with her glossy flaming red hair rather than what must have been a blonde wig, Vi was even more striking.

Then, as Elene stepped closer to the bed, she saw Vi's other ear. She wore a single earring, mistarille and gold, sparkling in the morning light coming through the walls. It was half of the exact pair of beautiful wedding earrings Elene had pointed out to Kylar. The wash of emotions Elene had already been feeling suddenly had a boulder dropped in it. This was her competition? This . . . creature had ringed Kylar? No wonder he'd chosen her. What man wouldn't?

Unnoticed, Sister Ariel had come to stand beside Elene, and now she spoke, her voice barely a whisper. "When she's asleep, I see what a beautiful woman Viridiana would have been."

Elene shot a look at the Sister. *Like she could be* more *beautiful?*

"She is brittle and sick and hard and abused. Her character is as base as her body is beautiful. You'll see, when she wakes. She is a walking tragedy. The trade she was taught would wreck anyone with a soul. You know that from Kylar's experience. But Vi didn't just learn a sick trade, she learned under Hu Gibbet—all too often literally under him, from the time she was a child. Whenever I—old and fat as I am—see her asleep, I still get jealous. I still forget that Vi's beauty has been no friend to her."

Sister Ariel paused, as if captured by a thought. "In fact, the only friend she ever had—male or female—was Jarl, and the Godking compelled her to kill him."

Elene didn't want to hear it. "What's wrong with her? I mean, why is she here?"

Sister Ariel sighed. "Our initiation doesn't only require aptitude, it requires focus. Vi has aptitude to an almost appalling degree. She is as Talented as she is beautiful. I was and am worried that learning that may spoil her. Learning our art properly takes patience and humility, and women with enormous Talent tend to lack both. So I pushed her into the initiation immediately. With what she's done and been through in the last weeks, she had no focus at all, almost no will even to live. It was nearly a death sentence." She shrugged. "Elene, I know Vi has done you great wrong. These marriage rings are ancient. I'm studying the rings now to see if it's even possible to break the bond. I don't have high hopes. And I know—she confessed—that she ringed Kylar when he was unconscious. The other Sisters don't know that. It is considered one of the greatest crimes among us. Even if she did do it to save a country, and to save Kylar himself, Vi surely deserves whatever vengeance you would give her. If you choose, you should be able to wake her. If you wish to stay here at the Chantry, rooms will be provided for you. If you wish to speak with Uly, she should be finishing her morning classes in two hours. I will be in my room if you need me. Ask any tyro—any of the young women dressed in white—and they will take you wherever you wish to go."

With that, Sister Ariel left Elene alone with Vi.

Elene looked around as the Sister disappeared. There was suddenly no one else in sight. She touched the knife at her belt. She could kill Vi and simply leave. She'd killed now. She knew how.

She squeezed her eyes tight shut. *God, I can't do this.*

After a long moment, she breathed, unclenched her jaw, willed herself to relax, opened her eyes.

Vi lay as before, beautiful, peaceful, graceful. But instead of imagining her again at the Jadwin estate, attracting lust and jealousy like a lodestone, Elene imagined her as a child. Vi had been a beautiful child in the Warrens as Elene had been a beautiful child in the Warrens. Neither had emerged unscathed. Elene looked at Vi and chose to fix that child-Vi in her mind's eye, the beautiful, carefree little girl with flame-red hair before the Warrens had sullied her.

She's never had a friend. Elene didn't know if it was her own thought or the One God's voice, but she knew instantly what He was calling her to do.

Elene breathed deeply, frozen to the spot. *It's too hard, God. There's no way. Not after what she's done. I want to hate her. I want to be strong. I want to make her pay.* She spoke, and raged, and complained about the justice of making Vi suffer, and through it all, the God said nothing. Yet through it, she felt His presence. And when she was finished, He was still there, and Elene knew her choice was simple: obey or disobey.

She breathed deeply one more time, then sat in the chair beside Vi's bed and waited for her to wake.

From the stairs, staring through a crack in the door, Sister Ariel breathed for the first time in what seemed like many minutes. She released her Talent and eased the door shut. Another gamble, another win. She hoped her luck didn't run out any time soon.

25

After a two-hour wait with the nervous master of the docks, the Mikaidon came to collect Solon. The Mikaidon was the keeper of civil order in Hokkai, an office that not only put him in charge of law enforcement but also gave him considerable political clout, as he was the only person who could investigate and search noble persons and properties. Solon recognized him. "Oshobi," he said. "You've risen in the world."

Oshobi Takeda grunted. "So it is you." He wore the regalia of his office like a man who used it as armor, not ornamentation. Oshobi was perhaps thirty, muscular, and imposing. He wore his plumed helm open, of course, showing the electrum rings of Clan Takeda framing his right eye, with six steel chains connecting behind his head to his left ear. The fishes on his helm were gilded, as was his galerus, the leather and plate armor covering his left arm. His trident was as tall as he was. The type of net that dangled over his back, draping cloak-like from spikes on his shoulders, was usually edged with lead weights to help it spread out when thrown. Oshobi's net was weighted with small daggers. It could be used not only as a net, but as a shield or even a flail by a skilled warrior. Given the numerous scars and rippling muscles on Oshobi's bare chest, Solon guessed that a skilled warrior was exactly what Oshobi Takeda had become. He had grown into his name. Oshobi meant the great cat, or tiger, but Solon remembered the older boys calling him Oshibi: little pussy. Solon couldn't imagine anyone calling him that anymore.

"I request the honor of an audience with Empress Wariyamo," Solon said. It was a calculated statement, not asserting his own status, and recognizing hers.

"You're under arrest," Oshobi told him. In a blink, he lifted the net from the spikes on his shoulders. He looked like he wanted an excuse to use it.

The man was a cretin. Solon was a mage and Oshobi should remember it. Of course, Solon didn't look like one. After his decade serving Duke Regnus Gyre, he looked as hard and scarred as a warrior himself, albeit one with unnaturally white hair growing in. "On what charge? I do have certain rights, Mikaidon. If not as a prince," he brushed his unpierced cheek, "then certainly as a nobleman." His heart fell. So Kaede was furious. Should he be surprised?

"Your brother gave up all the Tofusins' rights. You can walk, or I can drag you."

What did my brother do? Solon had been at various schools learning magic for his brother's entire reign and Dorian's prophecies had sent Solon to Cenaria at the time of Sijuron Tofusin's death. They hadn't been close; Sij was a decade older than he was, but Solon's memories of him were pleasant. Apparently, Oshobi's weren't.

Solon said, "That's a tough one, Oshibi."

Oshobi flicked the butt of his trident at Solon's head. Solon caught the haft squarely in his hand and looked at the Mikaidon contemptuously.

"I'll walk," Solon said. His heart was turning to lead. During Sijuron's reign, Solon had been crisscrossing Midcyru with Dorian and Feir, searching for Curoch, so he hadn't been surprised that he hadn't heard much from home. And then, when he'd concealed his own identity and headed to Cenaria to serve one of Dorian's prophecies, he hadn't told anyone back home where he was going. But now, the silence seemed ominous. And in the years since, he hadn't been able to dispel his ignorance. From the necessity of keeping his identity secret, Solon had avoided all Sethi he saw, and those who saw him spotted the lack of clan rings and avoided him as an exile. But even the usual news one might hear from foreigners had mostly been lacking, as though the Sethi people hadn't wanted to share anything with outsiders.

But as they made their way to the castle, Solon soaked in the scents and sights of his old home and some of his tension eased. This land was balm to him. He'd forgotten how much he'd missed the red hills of Agrigolay. As the Mikaidon's stout, four-wheeled chariot rolled up the cobblestone road to the imperial palace, Solon's eyes were drawn to the west. As in most cities, the approach to the palace was jammed with buildings, homes, and shops as densely as possible. But in Seth, only the eastern side of the Imperial Way had buildings. The west side was centuries-old vineyards, rolling over the hills in perfect rows as far as the eye could see. The grapes hung heavy on the vine, and there were men checking their ripeness. The harvest would be any day.

Most kingdoms required their lords to offer a certain number of men for war every summer. In Seth, the levies were needed in fall, for the grapes. Already, Solon saw, enormous broad baskets had been stacked at the ends of the rows. There was no need for walls to protect the vineyards. The wines of Seth were its pride and its life's blood. No Sethi citizen would harm the vines, nor suffer a stranger to do so, and the theft of cuttings from these vines had precipitated war between Seth and Ladesh. The loss of half a dozen ships had been counted a small price when they successfully sank the Ladeshian merchantman that was carrying the cuttings back to Ladesh to begin rival vineyards, along with its escort. Ladesh had its silk monopoly, but anyone who wanted great wine bought it from Seth.

To Solon, like most Sethi, the vineyards were rich not only with beauty but also with meaning. The cycle of planting and grafting and pruning and nurturing and waiting—all resonated with meaning for every citizen.

They came over the last rise and Solon saw White-cliff Castle for the first time in twelve years. It was white marble, a testament to the vast wealth the empire had enjoyed at its height: no white marble was quarried on the islands, and shipping it across an ocean was so expensive that every time Solon saw the castle he was awed and almost ashamed of his ancestors' wastefulness. Outbuildings, smithies, barracks, servants' housing, barns, kennels, granaries, and storehouses ringed the hill cheek by jowl within the granite walls, but the crown of the hill was all castle. Steps broad enough for horses led up the first tier into the outer hall. The outer hall had a roof but no walls, leaving it oddly open to the elements. Enormous grooved marble pillars held a majestic roof of marble, onyx, and stained glass.

At the base of the steps, Oshobi drew his team to a halt. "Are you going to make this easy or hard?" he asked.

"I'm here to solve problems, not cause them," Solon said.

"Too late for that," Oshobi said. "There's a room for you on the first floor."

Solon nodded. A visiting noble would be put on the second floor, and he should have rated the third floor, but it was better than the dungeon, and it would give Kaede time to decide what to do about him.

They climbed the steps together, drawing only a few looks. Oshobi was obviously a familiar sight, and Solon's clothing was Cenarian, not Sethi, so from a distance, he supposed the lack of rings wasn't remarkable. Besides, it was almost harvest time, and everyone had too many things to do.

Sky watchers had aided the construction of the outer hall, so the stained glass panels provided art appropriate to the season. Currently, the sun lit the whole outer hall purple with scenes of harvest and grape crushing, women dancing in vats with their skirts held up higher above their ankles than absolutely necessary and men clapping and cheering them on. Elsewhere there were scenes of war, of sailing, of fishing, of grand balls, of festivals to Nysos. Some of the panels were brighter than others, reminding Solon of when he was a boy and a rare hailstorm had broken dozens of the panels. He remembered his father cursing their ancestors. Who would use glass for a ceiling? Of course there was no choice but to replace the broken panes, though the price was ruinous. One couldn't let one's entryway fall into a shambles.

Oshobi and Solon walked through the great black oak doors into the inner entry. Here, white staircases framed each side of the room, a great imperial purple carpet led further into the palace, and gold and marble statuary lined the hall. As they headed past the stairs to a side door, however, one of the smallest, oldest men Solon had ever seen came to Oshobi. The man stopped before he said anything, however, and gaped at Solon. He was the old Wariyamo chamberlain, a slave who had chosen to stay with the family permanently rather than take his freedom on the seventh year, and he obviously recognized Solon. After a moment, he recovered and whispered to Oshobi, who promptly reversed direction and gestured for Solon to follow him into the great hall.

They walked through the great hall, past decorative geometric patterns and starbursts—all designed with swords and spears. It was another wasteful display meant to send a message to visiting emissaries: we have so many armaments, we decorate with them. It was, Solon thought, a more reasonable waste than the stained glass. The great hall was empty except for the guards at the far door, and both of them were too young to recognize Solon. They opened the doors to the inner court promptly, so Oshobi wouldn't even have to slow. Oshobi led Solon past the great throne from which Solon's father and brother had ruled, and headed into the inner court.

The doors opened at the base of stairs, braced by lions.

They ascended twenty-one steps, and Solon felt his throat tightening. Then he saw her.

Kaede Wariyamo had black hair and perfect olive skin. Her eyes were deep brown, nose stately, mouth wide and full, neck slender. In keeping with the impending harvest, her hair was bound in a single tail and her nagika was simple cotton. A nagika was a dress that looped over one shoulder, the cloth gathered to the opposite hip and falling long to the floor, fully covering the ankles, leaving one breast bare. It wasn't, as Solon had explained to Midcyri on numerous occasions, that Sethi men didn't find breasts pleasing or innately feminine. They simply weren't erotic in the same way. In Seth, a man would comment on a woman's breasts as a Midcyran commented on a woman's eyes. But after ten years in Midcyru, Solon's pulse quickened to see the woman he loved and who'd once loved him so exposed. Kaede was twenty-eight years old now, and most of the innocent girl he had known had receded from her face. The intelligence had come more to the fore, and a steel that had once been buried deep now lay close to the surface. The holes of the clan piercings on her right cheek had long closed, but the dimples remained, showing the world she had not been born an empress.

Solon thought she was more beautiful than ever. He remembered the day he had left to train with the magi. He had kissed that slender neck, caressed those breasts. He could still remember the smell of her hair. It had been in this very room, where they'd thought no one would find them. He had wondered often when she would have made him stop, or if. But they'd never found out. Her mother, Daune Wariyamo, had found them and berated them both, calling him such foul names that had he been a little older he would have thrown her from the palace. Nor had she spared her daughter the vitriol. Solon had failed Kaede there. He had allowed his own shame to keep him from protecting Kaede, who was even younger and more vulnerable. It was only the first of his regrets with her.

"Oh, Kaede," he said, "your beauty would shame the very stars. Why did you never write?"

The sudden softness in her eyes steeled. She slapped him, hard.

"Guards! Take this bastard to the dungeon."

26

Men were gathering in the great yard before the city's south gate when Kylar arrived. The queen's messengers canceling the attack wouldn't arrive for a few more minutes. Kylar was almost certain that they would. However, Durzo had taught him that when you deal with human beings, never count on logic or consistency. Either way, Kylar's work wasn't finished.

The sa'ceurai were still sleeping. Kylar didn't make the mistake of thinking that this meant the morning's attack would take them off guard. They simply could sleep in and still slaughter Cenarians without missing breakfast.

The sleet had stopped, so Kylar was able to make good time to Lantano Garuwashi's tent. The war leader was asleep on a simple mat on one side of the room.

Kylar stopped at a table full of maps. He'd never seen such detailed maps. There were maps of the city with three different colors of blocks put on different objectives. Kylar wasn't even sure what the colors signified. There were maps of the city's surroundings, with elevation marked, the conditions of roads labeled, and a remarkably accurate chart of the Smugglers' Archipelago. Blocks with regimental flags stuck in them represented the various forces arrayed within and without the city, even the new Rabbit regiments, which meant they already had spies in the city who were managing to pass messages out. There were broader national maps, with both knowns and unknowns marked. They didn't know who held Screaming Winds in the north. They weren't sure of the Lae'knaught's strength in the southeast. But on the last map were blocks representing Cenaria's death.

Blocks on that national map represented Logan's force, guessed to be slightly larger than it was, and behind them, Ceuran reinforcements.

I'm not a general, I'm only a killer. And a fool. Kylar had glanced at what was in front of his eyes and thought he had a more accurate view of the situation than the city's generals. Lantano Garuwashi had rushed to the city without horses or baggage, but that didn't mean he hadn't told them to follow.

He had. They were just a few days out, behind Logan's army, and Logan had never seen them. In the meantime, Garuwashi had already dispatched a contingent of sa'ceurai to skirt Logan's force and go back to guard the supply train.

Among the papers were plans to hire pirates to cut off smugglers' routes into the city and others to encourage insurrection in the Warrens. They were already in negotiations with the Sa'kagé, which the generals knew had smuggling routes into the city. Currently, the Sa'kagé wasn't offering good terms, but the generals were confident that the Sa'kagé's offers would get sweeter as soon as the supply train arrived and the hungry Cenarians watched them feast.

Kylar felt sicker the more he read. Of course the Sa'kagé would treat with the Ceurans. It was one thing to refuse to collaborate with Khalidorans who wanted to wipe out all of Cenaria, quite another to betray a disliked queen to a reasonable man who wouldn't interfere with the Sa'kagé's business. As soon as that supply train arrived, Momma K would see the end. She would try to minimize the bloodshed, but which was better: For thousands to starve in the Warrens, or for a hundred noble heads to roll? The smuggling tunnels would soon fill with sa'ceurai.

"Night Angel," Lantano Garuwashi said in greeting, rising from his mat.

Checking, Kylar was sure he was still invisible. He looked at the papers in his hand, apparently hanging in midair. He dropped the invisibility. "Good morning, warleader."

Lantano Garuwashi was one of the rare men who looked more daunting half-naked than he did in full armor. There was no fat on his body, and where most quick swordsmen were built with lean muscles like Kylar, Garuwashi had the upper body of a blacksmith, each muscle sharply defined—and big. He had a smattering of scars on arms and chest and stomach, but not one of them was deep enough to have cut muscle and thereby impede his motion. They were the wounds of a man whose mistakes had been infrequent and small.

He shook his head as if to shake off sleep, but Kylar thought it was more calculated to rattle the bound ends of those sixty-odd locks in his own hair like a bowl full of marbles. Lantano Garuwashi grinned joylessly at Kylar. "I've been expecting you," he said.

Kylar couldn't believe it, but how else would he sleep so lightly that he woke at the sound of papers being turned fifty feet away? "If you expected me, there'd be fifty sa'ceurai ringing this tent."

"I knew you were coming as soon as my sentry reported that someone tied his leggings together."

Kylar's jaw dropped. "He reported himself?"

Garuwashi smiled, self-satisfied. Kylar wanted to think of him as smug, but it was an infectious kind of smile. "I punished him lightly and rewarded him well—as he expected."

"Son of a—" Every time Kylar took something for granted, he got hit in the face with it.

~Is there a lesson here?~

Kylar ignored the ka'kari. "So, if you expected me. . . . All this is guttershite." He dropped the papers on the table. "There's no supply train."

Garuwashi's grin faded. "It's coming," he said. "If you don't believe me, wait two days. You tell me, do you think all those reports could have been written between the time you were playing with my sentry and now? That would be a massive effort, wouldn't it? And it would be stupid of me to throw it away by telling you I expected you."

Kylar blinked. "So what's the game?"

Garuwashi began pulling on his clothes. "Oh, are we being honest with each other?"

"Might be quicker than lying."

Garuwashi hesitated. "Fair enough. I'm preparing to be a king, Night Angel."

"A High King?" Kylar asked.

Garuwashi looked puzzled. "You say this like it means something to you."

Kylar cursed his ineptitude. "A rumor I heard."

"Why would I wish to be a high king? Cenaria and Ceura are neither large nor distant from each other. Naming under-kings would simply give me rivals." He waved it away and tied the thin silk robe around his waist. "In a year, I will be king of Ceura. I have a reputation now and most of it serves my purposes. But in our capital Aenu, the effete nobles call me a barbarian. 'Skilled at war, yes, but can a butcher be king?' This is how they attack a man who is too excellent. So I have a small interest in capturing this city without killing. We both know that I can take Cenaria. I let you read long enough to see that, yes?"

"So what do you want?" Kylar asked.

"Surrender. Unconditionally. I will give you my word to be merciful. We will leave in the spring to claim my throne, and once I take it, I will grant this realm once more to your queen."

Kylar couldn't stop a twitch of annoyance.

Garuwashi caught it. "You prefer Duke Gyre be made king? Done. I will even restore half of the royal treasury. Beyond this, my men will spend the winter wiping out the Sa'kagé. Tell me, is not that alone worth the price of feeding and housing us? Is it not worth more than half the treasury?"

~Especially considering that the treasury's empty?~

Then Kylar realized Lantano Garuwashi knew that the Khalidorans had taken everything. Garuwashi was merely offering the queen a victory for her pride: You want half the treasury? Here's half of nothing! And letting his Ceurans talk of Garuwashi remitting half of the Cenarian treasury would help his reputation for magnanimity, no matter how little half was.

"You would have Cenaria trust you? You're saying this to a people who recently suffered under the most brutal tyrant imaginable?"

"It is a difficulty." Garuwashi shrugged. "We can do this however you please. But if my men must pay for this city with their blood, they will take blood in return. Take those papers to the queen. Take a few days to see if I'm bluffing. And by the way, this attack this morning, it's not a good idea. Send these rabbits after sword lords, and this siege will end today."

Kylar waved it off. "It's canceled already. Stupid idea."

"So, you do have the power to change things. I'd wondered."

It was a throwaway comment, but it struck Kylar. *How did I get here?* He was blithely negotiating for tens of thousands of lives and the fate of a country.

How would Logan take it? Kylar could obey the letter of his oath and everyone except Terah would win. He wouldn't kill Terah: Lantano Garuwashi would do it for him.

Garuwashi was an honorable man, but that wasn't the same as a good man. The Ceuran culture didn't require him to be apologetic about craving power. He would be true to his oaths. He would be merciful—by his own definition of mercy, and Kylar had no chance to get to know him well enough to know what that was. The Ceuran nobles called him a barbarian? What if they were right?

But Cenaria had more than lives at stake. Kylar hadn't stayed in the city long after killing Godking Ursuul, but everyone had been brimming with stories and pride about the Nocta Hemata.

Cenaria had been burnt to the ground, and something good was trying to grow in the ashes. Was Cenaria a land where the small became great despite overwhelming odds—as they had in the Nocta Hemata and the Battle of Pavvil's Grove? Or were they Midcyru's whipping boy— doomed to be overrun by their neighbors, fending off aggression only through the threat of such deep corruption that no one would want to rule them?

There were great souls in Cenaria. Momma K and Logan and Count Drake and Durzo were giants. Could they not be heroes as they might be in another country? Couldn't a Scarred Wrable have been a lauded soldier instead of a hired killer? Kylar thought so, but two things stood in the way: this man's invasion and Terah Graesin.

"I'm afraid I can't let you do this," Kylar said.

Fully dressed now, Lantano Garuwashi tucked his thumbs into his sash, which would normally hold his swords. It must have been habit, a not-so-subtle hint to whoever challenged him of Garuwashi's prowess. He removed his thumbs nonchalantly. "Are you going to kill me?" he asked. "I should find it difficult to fight an invisible man, but I thought we'd covered this ground already."

Kylar ignored him. He was looking past the Ceuran to the man's bed mat. There, for all the world looking like Ceur'caelestos, was a sword in its scabbard. A sword that Lantano Garuwashi hadn't tucked into his sash. A sword that Kylar had thrown into Ezra's Wood.

"Nice sword," Kylar said.

Lantano Garuwashi flushed. Though he smiled to cover it immediately, with his fair skin it couldn't be hidden.

"Whatever will your men say when they find out it's a fake? You have a vested interest in not spilling blood? How about a vested interest in not drawing your sword?"

Given the circumstances, Kylar thought Lantano Garuwashi mastered his rage rather well. His eyes went dead and his muscles relaxed. It wasn't the relaxation of a sluggard, but a swordsman's relaxation. Kylar had heard that Garuwashi once ripped out an opponent's throat before the man could draw his sword. He hadn't believed that an un-Talented man could do such a thing. Now he reconsidered.

Lantano Garuwashi didn't attack, though. Instead, he merely picked up his false Ceur'caelestos and tucked it into his belt. He forced a marginally pleasant expression to his face. "I have a secret of yours, Night Angel. You have an entire identity built as Kylar Stern. You wouldn't wish to lose that, would you? All your friends, all your access to the kinds of things the Night Angel couldn't find out on his own."

"Remind me to thank Feir for that." Kylar paused. Did this Ceuran never run out of tricks? "It would hurt me in any number of ways to lose Kylar Stern. But Kylar Stern isn't all I have or all I am. I can change my name."

"Changing a name is no great thing," Garuwashi admitted. "In Ceura we know this. We sometimes do it to commemorate great events in our lives, but a face—" he cut off as Kylar rubbed a hand over his face and put on Durzo's visage. "—ah, that is something else entirely, isn't it?"

"Losing my identity will cost me years of effort," Kylar

said. "On the other hand, if you can't draw your sword, you can't lead your men at all, no matter how overwhelming your strength is. I know Ceura well enough to know that a king can't rule with an iron sword, and there's no such thing as an aceuran sa'ceurai."

Lantano Garuwashi raised an eyebrow. He glanced at the sheathed sword on his hip. "If you wish to reprise our duel in the wood, I will oblige. Feir Cousat went into the Wood that day after my sword. As none ever has before, he returned, on my word as a sa'ceurai. I still bear Ceur'caelestos. If you force me to draw it, I will sate its spirit with your blood."

It was a serious oath, but the words of his vow didn't mean what he wanted Kylar to infer. "You bear nothing but a scabbard and a hilt. Say that I lie, Garuwashi, and I'll stand before your tent and challenge you before your army. Your sa'ceurai will tear you apart with their bare hands when they find you've lost Ceur'caelestos."

The muscles on Garuwashi's jaw stood out. He said nothing for a long time. "Curse you," he said finally. The iron in him seemed to melt. "Curse you for taking my sword, and curse Feir for making me live. He did come out of the Wood. He said he'd been chosen to make another Ceur'caelestos for me. He knew the sa'ceurai would never understand, so he gave me this hilt and swore to return by spring. I believed him." Garuwashi breathed deeply. "And now you come again to destroy me. I don't know whether to hate you or admire you, Night Angel. I almost had you. I saw it in your face. Do you never run out of tricks?"

Kylar didn't let his guard down. "You don't even want

Cenaria, do you? You just thought it would be another quick victory that would make your legend grow."

"What is a warleader without war, Night Angel? I was invincible before I took Ceur'caelestos, and now you wish me to lose—against Cenaria? You don't know what it is to lead men."

"I know what it is to kill them. I know what it is to ask others to pay for my mistakes."

"Do you know what it is to refuse to be satisfied with the meager portion life hands you? I think you do. Can you imagine me squatting in a field next to my one servant with my trousers rolled up, picking rice? These hands were not made for a hoe. You took this name Kylar Stern. Why? Because you were born with an iron sword, too.

"My men need food, but they need victory more. With me or without me, they are here for the winter," Lantano Garuwashi said. "The tunnels we widened to get through the mountains are rivers and ice now. If you expose me, the sa'ceurai will kill me, but then what? They will vent their fury on your people. For everyone's sake, Night Angel, let that go. Go instead and tell this queen to surrender. I give you my word that if she does this, not a single Cenarian will die. We will take nothing more than food and a place to winter. She will be granted her throne once more when we leave in the spring."

And you won't ask for anything else once you have Cenaria and Ceur'caelestos both, right?

Kylar shook his head. "You'll surrender."

"I can't," Garuwashi said through gritted teeth. "In

surrender, even Cenarians lay down their swords at the victor's feet."

Kylar hadn't thought of that. It wasn't the thought of surrender that was impossible for Lantano Garuwashi, it was the physical act.

"Maybe," Kylar said, "maybe there's a third way."

27

When Dorian's half-brother Paerik had brought his army to Khaliras to seize the throne, he had abandoned a vital post. The general who had served under him, General Talwin Naga, stood in front of the throne, explaining how the wild men would invade in the spring.

"Sixty thousand of them?" Dorian asked. "How could they raise so many?"

"Raise may be exactly the word, Your Holiness," the tiny Lodricari man who had accompanied General Naga said.

"Who are you?" Dorian asked.

"This is Ashaiah Vul," the general said. "He was your father's *Raptus Morgi*, Keeper of the Dead. I think you need to hear what he can tell you."

"I've never heard of such an office," Dorian said. And "raptus" didn't primarily mean keeper, either. It meant taker, stealer. Dorian's stomach turned.

"By your father's order and his father's before him, it was a quiet office, Your Holiness," Ashaiah Vul said.

He was utterly bald, with a knobby skull and a pinched face with nearsighted eyes, though he looked barely forty years old. "I was known only as the Keeper. Your father's Hands discouraged questions."

The Hands. There was another problem. Whoever led the informers, torturers, spies, and guards who served as the Godking's thousand hands had yet to show himself. Regardless, Dorian doubted Ashaiah Vul would dare lie about them.

"Go on," Dorian said.

"I think you may want to come with me, Your Holiness. I suggest you leave your guard here."

Is this the first attempt on my life? If so, it was rather clumsy. That made it all the more impossible to refuse. When the attempts on Dorian's life began, he had to defeat them ruthlessly. Then they would end. "Very well." Dorian signaled the guards to stay and dismissed the general.

In the hall, they immediately ran into Jenine. "My lord, I'm so glad to see you," she said, giving him a version of a Khalidoran bow mixed with a Cenarian curtsey, chin up, eyes closing demurely only for a moment, right hand sweeping into the Khalidoran courtiers' flourish while the left hand flared her skirt as she curtsied. She made the mixed curtsey look graceful, too. Obviously she'd practiced it. It occurred to him then that there was no Khalidoran form of a woman's salute to an equal male. Khalidoran women who were equals would nod to each other, but were always inferior to men in the same social rank, and invisible to men of lower rank. And all women prostrated themselves before a Godking. This was

Jenine's offering of a middle ground. He smiled, pleased with her solution.

Dorian nodded more deeply than any Godking before him would have. "My lady, the pleasure is mine. How may I serve you?"

"I was hoping to spend the day with you. I don't want to be in your way. I just want to learn."

Dorian glanced at Ashaiah Vul. The man, of course, had his eyes averted. He wouldn't dare to disapprove of a Godking's decisions, or to even look at a Godking's woman. "I'm afraid I'm going to go see something remarkably unpleasant. You don't want to see it. I don't want to see it. You should probably wait in the throne room. I'll be back shortly." Dorian turned.

"I do want to see it," Jenine interjected. Ashaiah Vul gasped at her audacity, then studied the floor once more as both of them looked at him, his face going red.

"A thousand pardons, my lord, I spoke hastily. Forgive my rudeness," Jenine said. She chewed her lip. "I—My father never looked at things he didn't want to see, and it got him and my whole family killed, our country laid waste. Dealing with things we don't like is part of ruling. My father refused to do it because he was weak and venal. How else am I to learn if not from you?"

"What I'm going to see is beyond anything your father had to deal with, real or imagined," Dorian said.

"Even so." Jenine was unmoved, and Dorian couldn't help but smile. He loved her strength, even as it surprised him.

"Very well," he said. "Ashaiah, show us what you were going to show me alone. All of it."

Ashaiah Vul said nothing, pretended to have no

opinion—and maybe, in fact, had no opinion. A God-king's unwelcome order was like a day of unwelcome weather. You might not like it, but you didn't have any illusions that you could change it, either. So Ashaiah took them deep into the bowels of the Citadel, and then into the tunnels of the mountain itself. Dorian could smell vir on the man, though not much. He was at best a meister of the third shu'ra.

Finally, Ashaiah Vul stopped in front of a door that looked like any of the hundreds of others this deep in the Citadel. The dust in this hall was so thick it was more like soil, and it was plain that this room hadn't been visited any more recently than any of the others. He unlocked the door and opened it.

Dorian held his vir as he followed the Lodricari into the darkness. His first sensation was that this room was huge, cavernous. The air was musty, thick, fetid.

Ashaiah mumbled an incantation and Dorian snapped three shields into place around both himself and Jenine. A moment later, light coursed up the arch where Ashaiah held his hand against the wall. It spread from arch to arch, across a painted ceiling over a hundred feet above. In a few seconds, light bathed the chamber.

This had been a library once, a place of beauty and light. The walls and pillars were the color of ivory and lace. The mural was like something out of a forgotten legend, light coming out of darkness, creation. It gave a sense of divinity and purpose. Long cherry shelves had once held both scrolls and books and tables had been arranged with space for scholars to study.

Now, it held clean, white bones. The chamber was hundreds of paces long, and half as wide, and everywhere, the books and scrolls had been removed. In their place, on every shelf, on every table, were bones. Old, old bones. Some shelves held entire skeletons, labeled with tags tied to their wrists. Some held skeletons of human bones but arranged in inhuman shapes. But mostly, the shelves held matching bones, with boxes for the small ones. An entire shelf of femurs. Boxes of finger bones. Pelvises stacked. Spines whole and in boxes for each vertebra. And skulls in a large central area: mountains of skulls.

Dorian dropped the shields. This was no attack. At least not on his body. "What is this?"

Ashaiah glanced at Jenine, then, obviously deciding he must speak the truth, said, "Should the wild men invade, this is your salvation, Your Holiness. It is your corpusarium. When General Naga speaks of the clans raising an army, this is what he means. Two years ago, a barbarian chieftain found an ancient mass grave and discovered a secret we had long thought was ours alone."

"Raising the dead?"

"Sort of, Your Holiness."

"Sort of?"

"The souls of men are inviolate," Ashaiah Vul said.

"I always liked purple."

Ashaiah blinked, not daring to chuckle. Jenine was too busy staring around in wonder. He didn't think she even heard him. "We don't have the power to bind men's souls to their bodies. Your predecessors tried to make themselves immortal doing that, but it never worked well. This is different. We call it raising because we use the bones of the dead and unite them with a kind of spirit we call the Strangers. The result is the krul. They were originally

called the Fallen because whenever they fall in battle, they
can be raised again if a Vürdmeister is present."

"Take me one step at a time," Dorian ordered, his quea-
siness increasing.

"It starts in the pits. It always has. The Godkings have
always said that the ore beneath Khaliras was powerful,
and that that's why the slaves and criminals and captured
enemies are forced to work there. It's a lie. We don't need
their service; we don't need the ore. We need the prison-
ers' bones and their agony. Their bones give us a frame.
Their agony draws the Strangers."

"What are these Strangers?" Dorian asked.

"We don't know. Some of them have been here for
millennia, but despite the length of their experiences, we
are a puzzle to them. They don't have physical bodies—
though my master said that once they walked the earth,
took lovers, and had children who were the heroes of old,
the nephilim. The southrons claim the name was because
the Strangers were once children of their One God who
were thrown out of heaven." He smiled weakly, clearly
regretting saying anything about a southron religion.

"What happened?"

"We don't know. But the Strangers long to wear flesh
again. So we take the bones of our dead and sanctify them
for the Strangers' use. Incidentally, this is why Godkings
have themselves cremated; they wish to avoid our use of
their bones."

"And then?"

"Real bones are necessary but not sufficient to give the
fallen a sense of embodiment, and it is for embodiment
that they trade their service. We give them flesh. It doesn't
have to look human. Some Godkings believed that any

shape is possible, putting human bones into a horse's or a dog's shape. It makes binding the fallen more difficult as they wish to be men, not horses, but it makes a fine horse."

"And the musculature, the skin and so forth, does it need to be crafted as painstakingly as the skeletons?" Dorian asked. He'd trained as a Healer, and he couldn't imagine the intricate magic necessary to create a whole living body.

"Given the correct skeleton and enough clay and water, the Strangers help the magic form muscles and ligaments and skin. They're never as sturdy as man. Godking Roygaris was able to craft krul that lived for a decade or more, but he was a brilliant anatomist. He was able to make krul horses, and wolves, and tigers, and mammoths and other creatures we no longer have names for."

"They function like living beings?"

"They are living beings, Your Holiness. They breathe, they eat, they . . ."—he looked at Jenine again—"defecate. They just don't feel as men do. Pain that would incapacitate a man will do nothing to them. They won't complain about hunger. They will mention it if it's gone long enough that they are about to stop functioning."

"They speak?"

"Poorly. But they can see better in the dark than a man, though not as far. Eyes are difficult to make correctly. They make poor archers. They have emotions, but the palette is different from men's. Fear is incredibly rare. They know that as long as the line of Godkings survives, if their body is destroyed, they will most likely be put into another sooner or later."

"Are they obedient?"

"Perfectly, in most circumstances, but they have an incredible hatred toward the living. They won't help build anything, not even engines of war. They only destroy. Experiments have been tried where a krul was put in a room with a prisoner and told that if he killed the prisoner, he would be killed in turn. Every time, the krul killed the prisoner. It was tried with women, with old men, with children: it didn't matter, except they killed children more quickly. You couldn't ask them to take a city and not kill those who surrendered. They also hunger for human flesh. Eating it seems to make them stronger. We don't know why."

"My father gathered these bones, but never used them." That was odd. Dorian turned it over in his mind. Perhaps Garoth Ursuul was too decent.

"Your pardon, Your Holiness. Your esteemed father did use them, once. When Clan Hil rebelled. Afterward, he noted that the Hil fought to the last man when they knew they would be eaten and profaned. Your father said he wished to have men left alive to rule; the krul wished only for ashes. He held them off for a great emergency. The emergency never came, so there's quite a stockpile."

"How many do we have?"

"About eighty-five thousand. When we organize them, we have to preserve their hierarchy. Their number system is different than ours."

"What do you mean?"

"Even our words for numbers are predicated on multiples of ten: ten, a hundred, a thousand, ten thousand, a hundred thousand, a million. Their number system is based on thirteen—my master said that was where our superstitions about thirteen come from. They're rigidly bound to those numbers. A meister can lead twelve krul himself, but if he wishes to lead thirteen or more, he must master a thirteenth, which is different—a white krul called a daemon. The white krul are faster, over six feet tall, and take more magic to raise. Platoons are thirteen squads—a hundred sixty-nine krul. So after you raise thirteen squads, if you wish to add a single krul, you must raise a bone lord. Bone lords speak well, they're smarter, tough, and they can use magic."

"Vir?"

"No. It's either the Talent or very similar. Thirteen bone lords make a legion. If you don't lead it yourself, a legion needs a fiend. Thirteen fiends make an army, twenty-eight thousand five hundred sixty-one krul. Your Holiness has enough for three armies, if you can master two arcanghuls to lead the other two armies. All told, that gives you a force of more than eighty-five thousand."

"What would happen if I had thirteen arcanghuls? What is that? Close to four hundred thousand krul?"

"I don't know, Your Holiness." The man looked fearful, however, and Dorian thought he was lying.

"Has it ever been tried? I won't have you lie to me."

The man blinked furiously. "The only rumors I've heard about that are blasphemous, Your Holiness."

"As Godking, I pardon your blasphemy."

The man blinked again, but after a few moments seemed to master his fear. "My predecessor, Keeper Yrrgin, said that the first of your line, Godking Roygaris, tried. He needed hundreds of thousands of skeletons for the attempt, so he invaded what is now the Freeze. Keeper Yrrgin said it was once a great civilization, filled with mighty cities. Roygaris took it with little difficulty, for they thought him their ally. And then he put them in camps and killed them all—an entire civilization. Keeper Yrrgin said that above the thirteen arcanghuls, Godking Roygaris found a rank he called night lords. With one night lord, Roygaris conquered the rest of the Freeze, and his armies only grew. He couldn't be content. He thought he was closing in on the mysteries of the universe. He thought if he could master thirteen night lords, he would master God. I can't imagine that there were ever so many people in all the world, but my master told me that he succeeded in capturing and putting to death almost five million people, and that there, above the night lords, he found . . ." the man face was pasty and sweating, his voice low and hoarse. "There he found Khali. She destroyed him and became our goddess. She gave us the vir to bind us to her and to make us destroyers. This is why agony is worship to her, because like all the Strangers, she hates life."

"What happened, Ashaiah?"

The man's voice was a whisper, "Jorsin Alkestes."

Dorian's heart went cold. He'd heard this history, but only from the southern perspective. The Mad Emperor and the Mad Mage. The conqueror and his dog. Now, Ashaiah was saying that Jorsin and Ezra had stopped a goddess and her army of five million krul.

"Elsewhere our armies would suffer losses in the day and be remade in the night. That alone made us almost invincible. But Alkestes somehow warded all of the great city of Trayethell and leagues around it so that the krul couldn't be raised there."

"Black Barrow?" Dorian asked. The city was in southeast Khalidor, but it had never been inhabited. It was cursed. No one lived within leagues of the place. Indeed, all of eastern Khalidor was sparsely populated. "Who else knows about these bones and about the krul?"

"I have a number of deaf-mutes who assist me. We take all the castle's and the city's dead. I never allow anyone in the larger chambers. Paerik and Moburu were the only ae-thelings who knew. General Naga learned it from Paerik. No one else."

No one else.

"So Paerik wasn't a fool," Jenine said, speaking for the first time since they'd entered the vast room. "With twenty thousand men, he was facing sixty thousand. Paerik didn't come here for the throne—or at least not only for the throne—he came for the krul. What does it mean, my lord?"

Dorian felt sick. She seized on exactly the crux of it. "My father suffered a huge setback by being stalled in Ce-naria. It was a distraction, a mistake. He thought he could grab it and send home riches and food, but the supplies he hoped to send home were put to the torch instead by the fleeing Cenarians." Dorian rubbed his face. "So when the barbarians come down from the Freeze, Khaliras will be indefensible. Its citizens would want to cross Lux-bridge and live here in the Citadel. As they wait out the siege, they'll have to be fed—and we have no food. Our military's good at following orders, but no good at taking initiative. If I throw them into a battle facing three-to-one odds, they'll get massacred. There's no way to win."

Jenine said nothing for a moment, then glanced around at the stacks and stacks of bones. "You mean there's no way to win except . . ."

He looked at the bones of men and thought of all the

stories of krul he'd ever heard, and he thought of dipping so deeply into the vir, and he thought of men dying no matter what he did. "Yes," he said. "There's no way to win except to raise these monsters. It will be an orgy of death."

"Whose deaths? The invaders' or your innocent people's?"

"The invaders'," Dorian said. So long as he did everything right.

"Then let us raise monsters," Jenine said.

28

After dressing appropriately, Kylar walked to Logan's tent. Logan's bodyguards nodded and pulled back the flap for him. The sun was poised on the horizon, but the tent was still dark enough that lanterns were needed to illuminate the maps that the officers, Agon, and Logan were studying.

Kylar joined the group silently. The maps were accurate, aside from missing the supply train.

"They outnumber us six to one," Agon said, "but they don't have any cavalry. So we ride out, the wytch hunters pick off a few officers and we melt back into the hills. We start gathering food so we can make it through the winter, and send out more scouts so we find any supply train they might have coming. It's the only way. They didn't expect walls. They'll starve before we do."

"The supply train is right here," Kylar said, pointing on the map. "It's accompanied by a thousand horse."

There was silence at the table.

"We have lost a scout in that direction," an officer said.

"Are you certain?" Agon asked. "How big is it?"

Kylar dropped a sheaf of notes on the table.

There was silence as the men picked up the rice paper sheets and read. Only Logan didn't read as the officers shared the notes back and forth. He stared at Kylar quizzically, obviously wondering what he was trying to accomplish.

"How did you get these, Wolfhound?" an officer asked, using the nickname the soldiers had given Kylar.

"I fetched." Kylar gave him a toothy smile.

"Enough," Agon said, throwing his papers down on the table. "It's worse than we feared."

"Worse?" the officer said. "It's a disaster."

"General," Kylar said to Logan, "can I have a word with you? Alone?"

Logan nodded and other men filed from the tent, carrying the notes for further study. "What are you playing at, Kylar?"

"Just making you look good."

"An impending slaughter makes me look good?"

"A disaster diverted makes you look good."

"And you have a plan."

"Garuwashi wants food and a victory. I propose we give them to him."

"Why hadn't I thought of that?" Logan said, uncharacteristically sarcastic. He was really worried, then. Good.

"It doesn't have to be a victory over *us*," Kylar said. Then he explained.

When he finished, Logan didn't look surprised. He

looked profoundly sad. "That would make me look good, wouldn't it?"

"And save thousands of lives and the city," Kylar said.

"Kylar, it's time for us to finish that conversation."

"What conversation?"

"The one about king-making and queen unmaking."

"I don't have any more to say."

"Good, then you can listen," Logan said. He rubbed his unshaven face and his sleeve fell to show the edge of the dully glowing green tattoo etched in his forearm. "People commonly misquote the old Sacrinomicon and say that money is the root of all evil, which is moronic if you think about it. The real quote is that the love of money is the root of all sorts of evil. Not as pithy, but a lot truer. In the same way, what I am capable of doing in the pursuit of power and sex, the man I choose for Logan Gyre to be will not allow. My hunger for food couldn't make me a monster in my own eyes. Not even when I ate human flesh. I was driven to that by necessity, not perversion. I suppose the same could be said for you, for killing. I saw it on your face when you killed my gaoler Gorkhy. You do it, but you don't love it. If you loved it, you'd turn into Hu Gibbet."

"There is a foul pleasure in it," Kylar said quietly.

"There's pleasure in having a full belly too, but for some it's dangerous pleasure. When I ordered you to kill Gorkhy, you didn't feel that." Logan saw his tattoo was uncovered and covered it. "I did. I gave an order and he died. I killed with a word. And I loved it. And I wanted more."

"So now what? You going to become a hermit, move to a cottage in the woods?"

"I'm not that selfish." Logan scrubbed a hand through his hair. "If I asked you, would you kill Terah Graesin?"

"Absolutely."

Logan closed his eyes. He'd obviously expected it. "If I didn't ask you, would you do it anyway?"

"Yes."

"Have you been planning it?"

"Yes."

"Dammit, Kylar! Now I know."

"So why'd you ask?" Kylar asked.

"To remove the excuse. Can you rule justly after you take the throne unjustly?"

"Good question to ask the woman who stole yours."

"How, Kylar?"

"Schedule a meeting with her and drink a lot beforehand."

"Dammit, man, how were you going to kill her?"

"A botched abortion. I'd poison whatever abortifacient she uses. Many of those potions are dangerous. If it appeared she'd taken double what her apothecary recommended, it would look like a tragic and shameful accident for a single, wanton young queen. If the nobles tried to cover up the details, the rumors would swirl around what a whore Terah was, rather than speculations that she was assassinated. And it would make the virtuous new king look even better."

"Gods," Logan breathed. "How long did it take you to come up with that?"

Kylar shrugged. "Couple minutes."

There was pain in Logan's eyes, as if he had to struggle to speak. "It's brilliant, Kylar. It's brilliant—and I forbid it."

"You forbid it?"

"Yes."

"And how do you propose to forbid me anything?" Kylar asked.

Logan looked astonished.

"Despite all my efforts, you're not my king. You can't forbid me a damn thing."

Logan's face darkened and all his usual conviviality drained away. It made Kylar conscious of just how tall Logan was. His lean seven-foot height made him a looming, merciless skeleton. "Know this," Logan said. "If I'm crowned because of Terah Graesin's murder, I'll have you executed."

"You'd kill me for Terah Graesin?"

"I'd execute you for treason. An attack on Cenaria's sovereign is an attack on Cenaria."

"She shouldn't be queen."

"But she is."

"You had no right to swear fealty."

"I did what I had to do to save the people, Kylar. Now I must abide by my word. Politics is ethics writ large."

"Politics is the art of the possible, and you know it," Kylar said. "On the eve of battle, the tides changed so you couldn't be king, so you changed course. The tides are changing again."

Logan folded his arms. His voice was granite. "My word stands."

"Can you love an idea more than you love a man and not become a monster? How many friends will you sacrifice on the altar of Justice, Logan?"

"If you force my hand, at least one."

They were standing on a precipice. Socially, Logan had

always been Kylar's superior. Morally, Kylar had always felt inferior, too. But they'd never been placed in a direct hierarchical relation. Now Logan was giving an order. He would not be moved.

Kylar could only accept his order and accept all his orders henceforth, or reject it and them forever. There was part of him that yearned to obey. He was convinced that killing Terah was the right thing, but Logan's moral compass was a more accurate instrument than Kylar's. What was it about submission that was so hard? Kylar wasn't being asked for blind servility. He was being asked to obey a man he knew and loved and respected, who in turn respected him.

The wolfhound is pampered by the fire. The wolf is hunted in the cold.

"Do you know how much I love you, Logan?" Kylar asked. Logan opened his mouth, but before he could say a word, Kylar said, "This much." And left.

29

Kylar was back in the city on his way to the one safe house he was confident hadn't been discovered during the Godking's reign when the ka'kari spoke.

~Would you be excited about Logan being king if he told you politics is the art of the possible and asked you to murder his rivals?~

I'm already damned. My crimes might as well accomplish something.

~So you'll serve clean water out of a filthy cup? You must have better tricks than I do.~

The safe house was on the east side, far enough from the fashionable areas that it had been on the city's outskirts. Now the building was gone. The entrance itself, a flagstone set flush with the ground, was only paces from the Godking's new wall. The neighborhood, once unfashionable, was buzzing with activity. After the Godking's death, thousands of people had fled the Warrens, either hoping to reclaim their lives or hoping to claim someone else's better life. The fires that the displaced had started on their way out of the city had left great swathes of it bare and black. Too few buildings remained to shelter everyone, even without the thousands who had left the city with Terah Graesin. Now they all were back, and there were no building materials to be found. With an army besieging the city and cold rains starting, people were desperate.

Kylar sat with his back to the wall to listen to the tones of the city. There was no way he was going to get into the safe house before nightfall. Even invisible, he couldn't lift a flagstone in the middle of what was now a de facto street without dozens of people noticing. The safe house had another entrance, of course. Unfortunately, a new wall was sitting on it.

The gossip was angry. Terah Graesin had stopped the free flow of traffic across the Vanden Bridge this morning, and it had nearly caused a riot. Kylar listened to a proclamation that promised a return to the way things had been before the invasion. The squatters would be driven back into the Warrens, and those legitimate merchants and petty nobility who had been uprooted would be granted their old homes and lands as soon as they could prove their claims. The herald was greeted with hisses and jeers.

"And how in the nine hells am I supposed to prove that I owned a smithy, when the queen burned it and my deeds to the ground?" one man yelled. Kylar would have been more sympathetic if he didn't recognize the man as a beggar. Others, however, joined a chorus of agreement.

"I'm not going back!" a young man yelled. "I lived in the Warrens long enough."

"I killed six palies in the Nocta Hemata," another shouted. "I deserve better!"

Before the crowd's fury gained more momentum, the herald beat a hasty retreat.

Within an hour, scribes were openly hawking badly forged deeds. An hour after that, a Sa'kagé representative showed up. His deeds were not only higher quality and much more expensive, he said the Sa'kagé guaranteed that no duplicate deeds would be forged. He could only sell deeds for this neighborhood, and he had an allotment of what kind of shops could be represented. Thus, unless the owner still possessed the original deed, Sa'kagé deeds were as good as gold. Within minutes, the non-Sa'kagé scribes had been chased off or coerced to join.

Meanwhile, food prices were skyrocketing. Tough loaves of bread that wouldn't sell for six coppers in the morning were selling for ten after a full day hardening in the sun. As the sun set, people improvised wood frames with cloaks or blankets stretched over them to make lean-tos against the wall. Others wrapped themselves tight in their cloaks, tucked their purses inside their tunics, and slept where they lay, alone or in groups for warmth.

Not everyone slept, of course. Darkness brought out the guild rats looking for easy bags. One even bent over Kylar, who hadn't moved in so long she thought him asleep. Kylar waited until the urchin—he couldn't even tell for sure under the grime but he thought it was a girl—had a hand on his purse. Then he struck, spinning the child into his arms, with both hands twisted behind her back and Kylar's other hand locked around her throat.

"Please, sir, I was up for a piss, and now I can't find my da."

"Kids who have parents don't say 'piss' when they talk to adults. What guild are you?"

"Guild, sir?"

Kylar clouted her ear, but not as hard as Durzo would have.

"Black Dragon."

"Black Dragon?" Kylar laughed softly. "That was my old guild. How much are dues these days?"

"Two coppers."

"Two? We had to pay four." Kylar felt like an old fart, talking about how much harder things were when he was growing up. He let her go. "What's your name, kid?"

"Blue."

"Well, Blue, tell the tall kid not to try that fat man's purse. He's not asleep. If you all get out of here for an hour, I'll leave enough to pay your dues for a week. If you don't, I'll yell that I've caught a thief and tell everyone to watch out for guild rats, and you'll have to move on anyway—and you'll all be lucky to escape a beating."

He let her go, and while she was gathering her crew, he went invisible and lifted the flagstone. Hidden doors set into the ground were never as secure as those set into walls. No matter how expertly constructed, once you opened a door in the ground, you displaced the dirt on the door as well as the dirt that inevitably got packed into the seams. It would be the last time Kylar could use this safe house. A safe house you were afraid to use wasn't a safe house at all, but Kylar needed a noble's clothing, gold, and—thanks to the ka'kari—new weapons.

Instead of climbing down the ladder, he jumped, and quickly pulled the flagstone shut. He checked his traps—one on the ladder and two on the door. All were intact. Then he opened the wood door slowly. The hinges protested and he made a mental note to oil them.

The tiny safe house was pristine, if stale. Kylar checked the top of one of the small chests. Across the latch was balanced a piece of his own hair. The hair, of course, wasn't a foolproof indicator of tampering. Even in a sealed safe house, your own entry could disturb the air enough to displace a hair, but if the hair was in place, it was unlikely that anyone else had entered.

Kylar shook his head. He wasn't even planning to stay here more than a few minutes, but Durzo's habit of checking traps and examining every corner for threats had sunk deep.

And where was Durzo? What had he been doing? Had he simply moved on to another life? Was it so easy for him to leave everything behind? The idea soured Kylar's mood. Durzo was the central figure in Kylar's life, and he'd abandoned him. Durzo had given him the ka'kari, a treasure of untold worth, but he hadn't given Kylar his trust—or his time.

A dusty glass case sat next to the dusty desk. Kylar opened the case. Inside, labeled in Durzo's neat hand, were dozens of jars of herbs, potions, elixirs, and tinctures. Durzo had told Kylar that some wetboys mislabeled their herbs deliberately, so as to confuse or kill anyone who stole from them. Durzo said anyone who had the resources and guts to steal from him could identify an herb or hire someone to do it for him. Kylar suspected the real reason was that Durzo couldn't bear to mislabel anything.

That he wouldn't mislabel his supplies, however, didn't mean that Durzo did label all of them. Durzo believed that safe houses had a one-in-four chance of being discovered in any given year, so he spread the most valuable items of his collection out among them to minimize losses. Managing such an inventory was probably half the reason Kylar's master had been so paranoid. For in this now-worthless safe house, in an unmarked vial smaller than Kylar's thumb, was a substance that looked like liquid gold. It had cost Durzo half a year and as much as a manse on Sidlin Way. Its proper name was philodunamos. Durzo called it bottled fire.

Whereas almost every other tool of the trade was mundane, if rarely known, bottled fire was magic. The only people who could make it were the Harani aborigines, whose magic was tied to emotion and song. After being driven from their lowland homes two centuries ago, they hadn't had access to the materials they needed to make philodunamos. How Durzo had known what those were, how he had gathered them, and how he had coached a Harani mage into making such a lethal substance, Kylar had no idea.

Sitting at the desk, Kylar rooted around until he found the gold-plated tweezers, a wad of cotton, and a candle. Then he couldn't find a tinderbox. Since he could see in the dark, he never carried one anymore. Without a tinderbox, he couldn't light the candle, without the candle, he couldn't clean the tweezers, without clean tweezers, he couldn't pull off a wisp of cotton to dip into the bottled fire, without the cotton, he couldn't test an appropriately tiny measure of the bottled fire. He swore under his breath.

~*Why do you make things so hard? Use me. I'm sterile.*~

You telling me there's no little ka'kari gravel out there?

There was a pause, then, unimpressed, ~*And I thought Durzo's humor was lacking.*~

Nonetheless, in a moment, the ka'kari puddled in Kylar's palm and formed an instrument with a flexible bulb on one side that tapered down to almost a needle-point on the other. Kylar had never seen anything like it before. ~*Squeeze me and put me in the philodunamos.*~

"You're amazing," Kylar said.

~*I know.*~

"Humble, too."

Kylar opened the vial and sucked out a single drop. He dripped it on a rag, closed the vial, and pushed his seat back. The ka'kari dissolved back into his skin. Kylar put the vial of bottled fire on the other side of the room and closed the herb cases, only drawing out one vial of water. The gold drop of philodunamos dried in moments, becoming hard and flaky. Kylar dropped the rag on the ground and dripped some water on it. The water wicked outward until it touched the philodunamos.

There was a whoosh of flame as high as Kylar's knee. The fire consumed the rag instantly and still burned for another ten seconds, then guttered out.

"It's tricky," Durzo had said. "Water, wine, blood, sweat, most anything wet should trigger it. But it can get unstable. So by the Night Angels, don't even open it if it's muggy."

Kylar smiled as he tucked the vial away. Sweat. He'd pour the bottle on Terah Graesin's incestuous bed if only such a death were public enough. He collected his clothing and gold and turned to grab a sword from the weapons wall, then something stopped him.

"You bastard," he said.

Hanging on the wall, impossibly, as if Kylar hadn't sold it for a fortune in a city two weeks' ride away, was a big, beautiful sword with the word Mercy etched on the blade. There was no explanation, no message of any kind— except for the smirk implicit in resetting Kylar's traps and replacing his single strand of hair. Durzo had redeemed Kylar's birthright. For a second time, Durzo was giving him Retribution.

30

Kylar stood in a hazy corridor decorated with brightly colored animals, facing a door. There were no sharp edges to anything. It was as if he were looking at the world through sleep-blurry eyes. The door opened without his touch, and as soon as he saw her, his heart lurched. Vi was lying on a narrow bed, weeping. She was the only thing in the world utterly clear, sharp, and present.

She raised a hand in supplication, and he went to her. She seemed as unsurprised by his presence as he was. For a moment, he wondered at that. Where was he? How had he come?

The thoughts disappeared the moment he touched her hand. This was real. Her hand was small in his, delicate and finely shaped, the skin as callused as his own. Unlike Elene's, Vi's third finger was slightly longer than her forefinger. He'd never noticed that before.

It was the most natural thing to sit on the bed and pull her into his arms. She lay across his lap and clung to him, suddenly weeping harder and grasping him convulsively.

He held her tight, willing his strength into her. He could feel her need for it. She was confused, lost, scared of this new life, scared of being known, scared of never being known. He didn't have to read her face, he felt it within himself.

She turned tear-swollen eyes to his face and he looked into her deep, green eyes. He was a mirror to her and he reflected back truth against every fear.

The tears slowed and her grip relaxed. She closed her eyes as if the intimacy was too much. She put her head in his lap, sighing, her body finally relaxing. Her long, fiery red hair was unbound. Though it was messy and tangled and crimped from where she had worn it in a ponytail all day, he was amazed. It was glossy, silky, mesmerizing, a color that only one in a thousand women had. His eyes followed a strand of her hair past tear-wet eyelashes to a nose with faint freckles he'd never noticed before to her slender neck.

Vi wore an ill-fitting plain nightdress. It was too short for her and the knot had come loose, leaving it gaping open. Her nipple was dark pink, small on her full breast, lightly puckered in the room's coolness. The first time Kylar had seen Vi's breasts, she'd exposed herself to shock him. This time, he could feel that she was unaware of it.

The unexpected innocence of Vi's exposure roused something protective in him. He swallowed and moved the cloth to cover her. Despite that Vi could feel him as clearly as he could feel her, she didn't notice. Was she merely that exhausted, or was she so divorced from her body that she didn't attach any significance to her breast being covered? Kylar didn't know, but either way, the wave of compassion he felt overpowered his desire. He barely glanced at her shapely legs, naked to mid-thigh, as he covered them with a blanket.

She burrowed into him, so vulnerable and so damn gorgeous he couldn't think straight.

He ran his fingers through her hair to call back the more protective feelings. Instead, Vi melted instantly, yielded completely, a wave of tingles coursing from head to loins. His heart lurched. The only thing he'd ever felt close to this was when he'd kissed Elene for half an hour and then spooned behind her, tracing kisses across her ears and neck and skimming his fingertips across her breasts—and it was always then that she stopped him, afraid of losing control completely. Vi sailed right over that brink. She was his, utterly, completely.

He was drunk on her ecstasy. The bond between them burned like fire. He couldn't stop himself. He slowly combed his fingers through her hair, rubbed her scalp, combed his fingers through her hair again. She shifted her hips, making tiny sounds. She rolled over in his lap so he could reach the other side of her head. It put her facing his stomach, inches from the undeniable evidence of his own arousal.

He froze. She felt it and her eyes flew open. Her pupils were pools of desire. "Please, don't stop," she said. "I'll take care of you. Promise." She gave the bulge of his trousers a peck.

Her casualness threw Kylar. There was a disconnect here, in what was supposed to be a connection. It wasn't *let's share this,* it was *let's trade.* It wasn't love—it was commerce.

"I'm sorry," she said, picking up on his confusion. "I

was being selfish." She threw back the blanket and in the illogic of a dream, her ugly nightdress was simply gone. In its place, a fitted red nightgown clung to her curves. She stretched like a cat, displaying herself to marvelous advantage. "You first. It's all yours."

"It's all yours," not "I'm all yours." She was offering herself like a sweetmeat. It was nothing to her.

The door opened abruptly and Elene stood there. Her eyes took in Vi, half-naked, draped over Kylar, her hand on his crotch and Kylar stupidly enjoying it.

Kylar scrambled out of bed. "No!" he cried.

"What?" Vi asked. "What are you seeing?"

"Elene! Wait!"

Kylar woke and found himself alone in the safe house.

Dorian was in his chambers with Jenine, poring over maps of the Freeze and the Vürdmeisters' estimations of the clans' strength, when the Keeper of the Dead entered. Dorian and Jenine followed the man into one of the cheerier rooms where a body lay wrapped in sheets. Two huge highlanders in nondescript southron clothes but with the bearing of soldiers stood after making their obeisance.

Ashaiah Vul opened the cloth around the corpse's head. The stench was magnified tenfold. The bald head had been split in half, but not cracked. Nothing had been broken or torn. There was simply a slice missing from his crown to his neck.

In that instant, Dorian knew not only the victim, but also the killer. Only the black ka'kari could make such a cut. Kylar had done this. The rotting sack of meat was

Dorian's father Garoth. His knees felt suddenly weak. Jenine came to stand close beside him, but she didn't touch him, didn't take his hand. Any show of comforting him would make him look weak to his men.

"How did you do this?" Dorian asked.

"Your Holiness," the highlander who had a birthmark over the left half of his face said, "we thought you'd want His Holiness's body for the pyre. There was a demon in the castle. It did this. The lieutenant went with our ten best men to kill it. He ordered us to take the body, sire. They were supposed to meet us, but they never came."

"How was your journey? Really."

The man stared at the floor. "It was real hard, Holiness. We got jumped three times. Sa'kagé twice and once some damn traitors in Quorig's Pass who went bandit after we lost at Pavvil's Grove. They thought we were carrying treasure. Red's not breathing right since I pulled the arrows out." He nodded at the other highlander, who didn't have red hair. "We hoped the Vürdmeisters might take a look once you're finished with us, sire."

"They weren't bandits. They were rebels." Dorian stepped forward and put his hand on the highlander's head. Red tensed, uncertain. He had blood clots and infections all through his lungs. It was amazing he'd lived as long as he had. "This is beyond the Vürdmeisters," Dorian said. "What about you?"

"I'm fine, Your Holiness."

"What happened to your knee?"

The man blanched. "My horse got killed. Fell on it."

"Come here. Kneel." The men knelt and Dorian was infuriated at the waste of their bravery. If Dorian weren't such a skilled Healer, one would die and the other live a cripple, and for what? To deliver bones. These heroes had made great sacrifices for nothing. "You have served with great honor and courage," Dorian told them. "In the coming days I will reward you appropriately." He Healed them both, though it was oddly difficult to use his Talent.

There was a low spate of awed cursing from the men as the magic swept them clean. Red coughed once and then inhaled deeply. They looked at Dorian with awe and fear and confusion, as if they couldn't believe that saving their lives was worth the Godking's own effort.

Dorian dismissed them and turned back to his father. "You sick bastard, you don't deserve a pyre. I should—" Dorian broke off, frowning. "Keeper, the Godkings always leave orders that their bodies be burned so that they may not be used for krul, yes?"

"Yes, Your Holiness," Ashaiah said, but he looked gray.

"How many times have those orders been obeyed?"

"Twice," Ashaiah whispered.

"You have the bones of every Godking for the last seven centuries except two?" Dorian was incredulous.

"Sixteen of your blood were used to raise arcanghuls and subsequently destroyed. We have the rest. Do you wish me to prepare a substitute corpse for Garoth's pyre, Your Holiness?"

Garoth Ursuul deserved no less for all the evil he'd done, but refusing his father a decent burial would say more about Dorian than it would about the dead man. "My father was monster enough in life," Dorian said. "I'll not make him one in death."

Only after the little man left did Jenine come hold his hand.

31

$\mathcal{W}$e're not going back, are we?" Jenine asked, coming before the Godking's throne. Dorian waved the guards away. He stood and walked to her, taking her hands in his.

"The passes are snowed in," he said gently.

"I mean we're not ever going back, are we?"

She said we. It made him tingle, that unconscious admission of unity. Dorian waved a hand at the gold chains of office he wore. "They would kill me for my father's crimes."

"Will you let me go?"

"Let you?" That hurt. "You're not my prisoner, Jenine. You can go whenever you wish." *Jenine.* Not Jeni. That formality had stuck. Maybe she feared she had merely traded gaolers. "But I have to tell you, I've just received news that Cenaria is under siege. The last warriors to make it through Screaming Winds saw an army surrounding the city."

"Who?"

"Some Ceuran general named Garuwashi and thousands of sa'ceurai. It may be that come spring—"

"We've got to go help them!" Jenine said.

He paused, letting her think. Sometimes she did act sixteen. "I could order my army to attempt the pass," Dorian said. "If they were lucky and the weather cooperated and the rebel highland tribes didn't attack while my army was spread out, we might only lose a few thousand. By the time we got there, the siege would probably be finished. And if we arrived in time and seized the city ourselves, do you think Cenaria would welcome us? The Khalidoran *saviors?* They will not have forgotten what my men did a few months ago. And my soldiers who lose brothers and fathers and sons in the passage, or who lost friends in the Nocta Hemata, will want the spoils of war.

"If I forbade rapine and murder, they might obey me, but it would plant doubts about me. Two hundred of my Vürdmeisters—that's more than half—have disappeared. I don't yet control the Godking's Hands, who are the only people who will tell me where those Vürdmeisters have gone, or who is leading them. Garoth Ursuul had other aethelings I haven't accounted for. I may be facing civil war in the spring. So if it came to it, who do you think the Vürdmeisters will follow, Khali, who gives them their power, or the once-treasonous aetheling?" The line between her eyebrows was deep with anguish now, helplessness, but Dorian wasn't finished. "And if they do follow me, and we are successful, what will your people say? They've installed a new queen, Terah Graesin."

"Terah?" Jenine was incredulous.

"Will the people welcome back young Jenine with a Khalidoran army? Or will they say you're a puppet, so young that I'm manipulating you, perhaps without your knowing it? Will Queen Graesin surrender her power?"

Jenine looked ill. "I thought . . . I thought it was going to be easy after we won. I mean, we won, right?"

It was a good question. Perhaps it was the only question that mattered.

"We won," Dorian said after a long moment. "But the victory cost us. I can never go south again. All of my friends besides you are in the south. They'll see my reign as a betrayal." That made him think of Solon. Had Solon even made it out of Screaming Winds alive? The thought made him ache. "If you want to assert your right to Cenaria's throne, I can deliver it, but that would cost you too.

"The price will be that everyone sees that a Godking has given you the throne. Do you think you're ready to rule? Without help? At sixteen, do you know how to pick advisers, how to tell when the chancellor of your exchequer is embezzling, how to deal with generals who see you as a child? Do you have a plan to deal with the Sa'kagé? Do you know why the last two Ceuran wars ended and what obligations you have to your neighbors? A plan to deal with the Lae'knaught who occupy your eastern lands? If you don't have all those covered, you'll need help. If you accept help, you'll be seen to be accepting help. If you don't accept help, you'll make mistakes. If you trust the wrong people, you'll be betrayed. If you don't trust the right people, you'll have no one to protect you from your enemies. Assassination has as long of a history in your kingdom as slaughter does in mine. Do you have an idea of whom you will marry and when? Do you plan to concede rule to your new husband, share it, or keep it?"

"I have answers to some of those questions, and I know some people I can trust—"

"—I don't doubt it—"

"—but I hadn't considered all of those." She got very quiet. "I'm not ready."

"I do have . . . an alternative," Dorian said. His heart pounded. He wanted to use the vir. In his old life, before the One God found him, he'd learned a glamour to seduce women. Now he could use it, just a little, just to help Jenine get over her fear and disappointment and to see Dorian as a man. He wouldn't make her do anything she didn't want to do.

He quashed the impulse. *Not that way.* If Jenine didn't choose him freely, it was all for nothing.

"Stay," Dorian said. "Be my queen. I love you, Jenine. You are the reason I came to Khalidor. This throne means nothing to me without you. I do and will always love you. A queen is what you are, what you are meant to be, and there is work for you here. My fathers haven't had queens; they had chattels, harems, playthings. Khalidor's people are no worse than any other, but this culture is sick. I thought once that I could run away. I see now that that's not enough. I've found my life's work: changing reverence for power to reverence for life. You have no idea what your mere presence will do. Our marriage will redefine marriage for this entire country. That's no small feat, and it will bring no small amount of happiness to the women *and* the men here."

"You want me to marry you because I'll help you in your work?"

"Jenine," he said quietly. "Lovers always want to make a private world. Just you and me and nothing else matters. The truth is, everything else does matter. Your family, my family, the different ways we were raised, the obligations we have, the work we do—it all matters. A marriage can be a refuge, but I'd be a fool to ignore what and who I am now, and what and who you are. But the answer is no, I don't want to marry you because I want you to help me. I want *you*. You're worth more than all the rest of it combined. I'd rather serve in a hut with you than rule all the world without you."

She averted her eyes. "You honor me, my lord."

"I love you."

She met his eyes now, but uncertainty still painted her features. "You are a good man, Dorian Ursuul, and a great man. May I think about it for a few days?"

"Of course," he said. His heart died a little. "Let me think about it" isn't the answer a man wants to his proposal. Of course, most men managed a little romance before asking.

In one way, he was horribly disappointed in himself. In another, he was content. He wanted Jenine's mind to consent to this match, not just her heart. Romantic feelings would come and go. He didn't want her to choose in haste and regret at leisure.

She excused herself and the guards let in Dorian's next appointment. It was Hopper. The man limped in quickly and prostrated himself. Jenine hesitated halfway out the door. She had told Dorian that there was something about

Hopper that she wanted to share with him, but they hadn't gotten around to it.

"Your Holiness," Hopper said, "the women have been in an uproar. They begged me to ask if you'll be accepting any of them into your harem."

Jenine turned away, as if embarrassed to be eavesdropping, but she didn't hasten to leave, either.

"Of course not," Dorian said. "Not one of them."

32

Terah Graesin had moved the coronation up. No matter that an army was encamped around the city, and that with their scant supplies already dwindling it was wildly inappropriate to have a party, Terah had decided she couldn't wait two months. Her coronation would be in three days. So Momma K had to come to the castle to meet the new court bard. She knocked on his door.

He opened, squinting, and looked about as pleased as Momma K expected. She'd commissioned a piece from him on their last meeting—for the queen's birthday. She hadn't mentioned the coronation was the same day. In retaliation, he'd gotten himself hired as the court bard, meaning she was paying for a piece he'd have to compose anyway.

"Do you know who I am, Quoglee Mars?" Momma K asked. As she stepped past him into his small apartment, he sniffed to smell her perfume. Quoglee's sense of smell was as good as his eyesight was bad. Her spies said he'd even spent time with Alitaera's royal perfumer.

He hesitated. Then, "You are Madame Kirena, a woman of great power and wealth." Quoglee's voice was a tenor so clear it was a pleasure even to hear him speak.

It was a pity nothing else about the man was beautiful. Quoglee Mars resembled nothing so much as a squashed frog. He had a wide, fleshy mouth that turned down at the edges, no neck, a perpetual squint, and a small round gut like a ball. Rather than trousers, he wore baggy yellow tights on his skinny legs, and he had a tiny tricorn hat with a feather in it. He was one of the ugliest men Momma K had ever seen, save for a few lepers far gone in their disease. "I heard your new tale, "The Fall of the House of Gunder." It was fearless. Beautiful. You should write more," she said.

Quoglee bowed, accepting the praise as his due. "I usually prefer the honesty of instrumentals. The pipe and lyre never lie, nor by their tones do good men die."

"An odd sentiment from a minstrel who's been chased from half the capitals of Midcyru because he can't stop himself from telling the truth." Which was why she'd asked if he knew who she was. At least he was capable of discretion. She smiled.

"May I ask why you're here?" Quoglee asked, squinting at her.

Damn all artists. Their bribes had to come as introductions to the influential, in gifts of clothing or instruments, in arranging special concerts and making sure they were well received. Of course, a bard rarely minded when some beautiful young music aficionado offered to polish his flute, either. But it all had to be discreet. The only punishment they could think to face for Momma K's displeasure was indifference. Years ago, Momma K had sent

a gorgeous little flute case to a newly popular bard called
Rowan the Red. The girl had given him some grossly ig-
norant compliment which she wouldn't have if she were
the educated young noblewoman she was pretending to
be. Instead of taking her to his room and giving her better
things to do with her mouth, Rowan had quizzed her and
publicly made her look a fool. It didn't take him long to
guess who might have sent her. When Momma K's most
gifted wetboy Durzo Blint had arrived a few hours later,
the bard was already writing a song mocking her and
making wild allegations, some of them true. No one ever
heard that catchy tune, or any other tune from Rowan the
Red, but it had been a near thing, and since then, Momma
K avoided bards when she could.

But bards were too good a resource to abandon. They
plied Momma K with every tidbit they knew and lapped
up every morsel she dropped. Indeed, they often gave her
new information, for bards were always present at parties
even if her other spies were not. But Quoglee was different. Quoglee's stories were rare, and the nobles regarded
them as absolute truth; other bards often repeated them.
He was hard to interest, but once that interest was piqued,
he was a bulldog.

"Do you know who I am, Quoglee Mars?" she asked
again.

Again, he hesitated. "You're the owner of half the brothels in the city. You're a woman who crawled out of the
gutter to climb higher than anyone would have believed.
My guess is you're the Sa'kagé Mistress of Pleasures."

"One of my girls has a small Talent of foretelling,"
Momma K said. "She doesn't dream often, but when she
does, she's never been wrong. Two years ago she dreamed

of you, maestro, though she'd never seen or heard of you and indeed, you hadn't yet come to Cenaria. She described you perfectly. She said a song burst from your mouth like a river. The river was the purest, clearest water she'd ever seen. She said I tried to stop it, but the waters overwhelmed me and I drowned. The next night she dreamed the same dream, but this time I tried to strike you down before you could sing, but the song was unstoppable, and again I drowned. On the third night, I swam. I think the name of your river is Truth, Quoglee Mars, so I ask again: do you know who I am?"

"You're the Shinga of the Sa'kagé," he said quietly.

Though she'd been prepared for it, hearing the truth spoken aloud frightened her. But this was why she'd hired Quoglee Mars in the first place. She'd paid him for a flute piece, then had her informants drop hints to him of a much bigger story, the kind of tale Quoglee couldn't resist telling. But the man was incredibly bright, and that made him dangerous. "How'd you learn?" she asked.

"Everyone knew you were Jarl's right hand. When he disappeared, none of the Sa'kagé's work was interrupted. Agon's Dogs continued training, the Nocta Hemata happened, and there was no rush of thugs' bodies floating in the Plith. The Sa'kagé isn't an organization to put off a struggle for succession just because there's a war. You've been Shinga for more than a month, haven't you?"

Momma K let out a long, slow breath. "Fifteen years," she said. "Always behind puppet Shingas. Shingas don't tend to die of natural causes."

"So what are you buying? I'm guessing you want more than a flute piece."

"I want you to sing a song of Terah Graesin's secrets."

"Do you know what those are?" Quoglee asked.

"Yes."

"Are you going to tell me?"

"No."

"Why not?"

"Because I've made my living telling lies and you know it. Because the truth is damning enough. Because you're renowned for winkling out the truth on your own."

"So if you can't dam the river, you wish to channel it. How do you propose to buy me off?"

"You want more than coin?" she asked, knowing the answer.

"Oh yes."

"Then I'll give you what you wish," she said.

"I want your story. You will answer every question I ask, and if you lie in any particular, I will use your tale to cast you in a devastating light."

"Now you tempt me to take my chances with prophecy and signal the wetboy I have waiting behind that curtain to kill you. A whore's truth has too many sharp edges. I will tell my story and not spare myself, but I will not share the secrets of the men I could destroy with what I know. It would be my death, and some few of them deserve better. I will give you more of my story, and more about the Sa'kagé, than you could ever learn alone, but that is all. And you will not tell it for at least a year. I have work to do first."

Quoglee's skin had turned green, making the impression of a frog complete. "You don't really have a wetboy behind that curtain, do you?" he asked.

"Of course not." Quoglee was a coward? Odd. "Do we have a deal?

He inhaled deeply, as if trying to smell the wetboy, and slowly he regained his balance. "If you tell me why you're doing this. I don't believe it's because of some whore's dream."

She nodded. "If Logan Gyre were king, Jarl's dream of a new Cenaria might come to pass. Things wouldn't have to be how they were for my sister and me growing up, or how they are for the guild rats now."

"Sounds awfully . . . altruistic," Quoglee said.

Momma K didn't let his tone anger her. "I have a daughter."

"Now that I didn't know."

"I'm the richest, most powerful person in this country, maestro. But a Shinga's power dies with her, and my wealth will be taken by whoever finally murders me. Having a daughter has cost me the man I love and quite nearly my life. But as much as she endangers me, I endanger her much more. I need Logan Gyre to become king because that's the only way I can go legitimate, and going legitimate is the only way I can pass anything on to my daughter except death."

Quoglee's eyes were wide. "You don't just mean to be a merchant or even a merchant queen, do you? You mean to establish a new noble house. How would you buy such a thing?"

"That's a tale I'll tell after the coronation. Do we have a deal?"

"You want me to learn a queen's darkest secrets and make a song of it . . . in three days? That's ridiculous. Impossible. There isn't a bard in Midcyru who could do such a thing. But." He paused theatrically, and Momma K

had to restrain herself from rolling her eyes. "But I am no
mere bard. I am a genius. I'll do it."

"Sing fearlessly, maestro. I will make sure your song
isn't interrupted."

Quoglee blinked rapidly and he sniffed again. "That's
it. Head notes of bergamot and galbanum with a third I
can't recall. The heart notes are jasmine and daffodil over
base notes of vanilla, iris, amber, and forest. Nuec vin
Broemar, the royal Alitaeran perfumer himself showed
me that perfume. He said it was his queen's own perfume.
No one else ever . . ." he trailed off, his eyes widening.

Momma K smiled, glad the gesture hadn't been
wasted.

A small tongue wet his wide, fleshy lips. "May I just
say, Madame Kirena, you frighten and intrigue me in almost equal measures."

She chuckled. "I promise you, maestro, the feeling is
mutual."

Scarred Wrable was on time. He always was. This time
their meeting was in the castle's statue gardens. Scarred
Wrable wore the hundred-colored robe of a hecatonarch,
the long sleeves covering his ritually scarred arms and
hands, the chasuble covering the lattice of scars across
his chest and neck. He smirked at her. "Yes, my child? Do
you have sins to confess, or sins to contract?"

Terah Graesin favored him with a contemptuous stare.
"You blaspheme, coming as a priest."

"Out of a hundred gods, there's got to be one with a
sense of humor. What's the job, Your Highness? If people

see you talking to me too long, they might think you really are confessing. They might wonder why."

"I want you to kill Logan Gyre. Sooner is better." She itched her bandaged arm. It was healing from where that damned shadow had stabbed her, but slowly.

Scarred Wrable spat on the brushed white gravel, forgetting he was supposed to be a priest. "Yah, right."

"I'll pay you twice what I paid you to kill Durzo Blint."

"Funny how you didn't tell me I was killing Blint until afterward."

"It turned out all right, didn't it?"

"Only 'cause I caught him unawares," Wrable said.

"I thought you said you fought him man to man," she said coolly.

He flushed. "I, I did, but it was a near thing. And you didn't pay me half enough."

"Oh, so that's it. Bargaining. How tiresome. Name your price, assassin."

"I'm a wetboy, as you should damn well know. I killed Durzo Blint. As to bargaining," he shook his head. "This ain't bargaining."

"How much?" Dammit, she'd worn high, thick sleeves to conceal the bandage on her arm, but it hurt, and she didn't dare touch it—not in front of Wrable, who'd tell the Sa'kagé.

"It would be a hell of a job, wouldn't it? They say Duke Gyre killed an ogre fifty feet tall at Pavvil's Grove. They say he's served by a madman with filed teeth who's ripped men clean in half and a two-legged wolfhound and a thousand sword whores. I even heard tell of a demon that came looking to save Logan, back during the coup.

That's a fearful lot of fearful friends that man has, and a fearful lot of fearful enemies a wetboy would make by killing him."

"I'll give you ten times the usual, and I'll make you a baronet, with lands." It was a princely sum, and she could tell Scarred Wrable was stunned at the amount.

"Tempting. But no. The only wetboy who'd take this job would be Hu Gibbet."

"Then send him to me!" Terah snarled.

"Can't. He's feeding the fish for taking jobs Mother Sa'kagé didn't approve. And Mother Sa'kagé has told all her little chicks, no jobs on Gyre."

"What?" Terah asked. "Don't you know who I am?"

"I will tell the Nine you tried."

Fury washed Terah to her toes. "If the Sa'kagé stands against me, so help me, I will destroy you all."

"By the High King's beard, woman!" Scarred Wrable said. "We said no to one job. There's a big difference between turning down a job and being your enemy."

"You will do this, or I will stamp you out," Terah said.

"That is a damn fool thing to say to a wetboy. But then you're a damn fool woman all round, aren't ya? Do you have any idea what Logan is doing this morning? No? While you're here trying to murder your allies, Logan is saving his."

"What are you talking about?"

"The Nine says that you have a week to take back your threats against them, and to give you a hint of what kind of a war you'd be starting, they've arranged for a small diplomatic disaster this morning. They ask that you keep in mind that future disasters need neither be small—nor diplomatic."

Ice shot down Terah's spine. They'd arranged a disaster already? Before she'd even threatened them? "How did you know?" she asked.

"We know everything," Scarred Wrable said.

"Your Majesty!" a servant came running into the statue garden. "The ambassadors from the Chantry and the Lae'knaught were both brought to your breakfast, as ordered. The stewards tried to seat both of them in the place of honor. They're furious."

"I didn't invite—" Terah turned to snarl at Scarred Wrable, but the man was gone.

33

$\mathcal{S}$olon," Kaede asked, standing in the darkness outside his cell, "why does my mother hate you?"

Solon sat up, brushing filthy straw from his hair. "What has she done?" It was early morning and chilly, and Kaede wore a purple samite wrap over her shoulders. Solon was relieved he wouldn't have to spend the interview trying not to gape at her breast like a mainlander—relieved and disappointed.

"Do you know why or not?" Kaede demanded. The steel in her voice reminded him of his visions when Khali came to Screaming Winds, trying to tempt him to his death. He'd known those visions were false because Kaede wasn't furious with him. Being right had never felt worse.

Standing, Solon walked to the bars. "It will not be easy to tell or hear."

"Humor me."

Solon closed his eyes. "After I completed my training with the blue mages twelve years ago, I came home, you remember? I was nineteen. I asked my father for permission to seek your hand. He told me your family would never consent."

"My mother never stopped at anything to advance my family. That's why I never understood her hating you. She should have been pushing me to marry a prince."

Solon lowered his voice. "Your mother feared that you were my sister."

In rapid succession, emotions flitted over Kaede's face: bewilderment, incredulity, understanding, surprise, revulsion, incredulity again.

"Kaede, I don't wish to slander either of our parents. The liaison was brief—only as long as my mother's last ill-fated pregnancy. When she and the baby both died, my father took it to be the gods' judgment on him. By then your mother was pregnant. Years later when my father noticed my interest in you, he requested a green mage come to tell him whether you were his daughter. In return for determining your patrimony and keeping their silence, I was to take my schooling with the green mages. Neither they nor my father expected me to show any Talent. They merely hoped to have a Sethi prince as a friend. As it turned out, I wasn't that Talented at Healing." Though he had met Dorian there, which had changed his life, and not only in good ways. "Regardless, they told my father that you were definitely not my sister, but your mother never trusted magi. Her fears told her that you looked more like my father than yours."

Kaede's eyes were cool. "How do I know any of this is true?"

"I wouldn't lie about my father. He was a great man. It wounded me when he told me he'd been faithless to my mother. It wounded him, too. He was different after she died. Can you think of anything else that makes sense of your mother's actions? Why don't you ask her?"

"Why didn't you come back?"

Solon's face was haggard. "I was nineteen when I learned. You were barely sixteen. I tried to reassure your mother that the mages were telling the truth. She thought I was threatening her. You were young and I didn't want to poison you against her by telling you. I had an offer for more training at Sho'cendi, so I took it. I wrote to you every week, and when you never responded, I sent a friend to deliver a letter personally. He was thrown out of your family's estate and told you were betrothed and you never wanted to hear from me again."

"I was never betrothed," Kaede said.

"Which I didn't find out until later. I was going to come home then, but a prophet told me I had two paths before me: 'Storm-riving, storm-riding, by your word—or silence—a brother king lies dead,' if I came home, I would kill my brother; if, on the other hand, I went to Cenaria, I might save the south from Khalidor."

"So did you?" Kaede asked.

"What?"

"Did you save the world?" Her tone had an edge of deep anger.

"No," Solon said. He swallowed. "I hid that I was a mage from a man who was like a brother to me, a man who would have become king. When he found out, he dismissed me. The next day, he was killed by an assassin I could have stopped had I been there."

"So you come home like a whipped dog looking for scraps."

Solon gave Kaede a gentle look, seeing pain under her anger. "I came home to make things right. I have no idea what happened here. No Sethi on the mainland will talk about it."

"You took the wrong fork of the prophecy," Kaede said. "You should have killed him."

"What?"

She pulled the samite wrap tight and looked out Solon's window. "Your brother was a horror. He squandered all the goodwill the people felt for your family within a year. His invasion of Ladesh cost us three of our four fleets, and the Ladeshian counterstroke cost us the last of our colonies. He forced my brother Jarris to lead a hopeless attack, and when it failed, he threw him in the dungeon. Where he was strangled. Sijuron claimed Jarris hanged himself. He forced the great families to sponsor week-long parties that they had no way of paying for. He raised taxes on rich and poor alike but gave dispensations to his friends. He built a menagerie that housed over a thousand animals. While people begged at the gates, he ordered silk beds made for his lions, and soon began throwing those who displeased him to those beasts. He liked to train with the military, but would order men killed for not really trying when they sparred with him—or for daring to bruise the imperial flesh when they did try. He took to carrying knuckle bones which he made anyone he encountered roll—the sides ranged from winning a purse of gold to death.

"I came across him one day and he made me roll, though usually the high families were exempt. I won. He made me roll again. I won four more times, until he had no more money. He was furious, so he ordered his retainers to pay me. I realized that he was going to make me roll until I rolled my death. So I challenged him to one last roll: I said let three sides be death, and the other three be marriage. My audacity intrigued him. He said that if I was going to beggar him, I might as well be his wife." Her eyes were cold with hatred. "Sijuron was quite the wit. He only gave me two of the six sides.

"I won. He kept his word and threw a huge wedding party at my family's expense. After he fell asleep, I cut his throat. I walked back to the great hall in my bare feet and my shift, my arms covered in blood to the elbows. The party was still going. It was barely midnight and those parties always had a curious frenzy: everyone knew they might die at the king's least whim.

"Everything stopped when I walked in. I sat in the king's seat and told them what I'd done. They cheered, Solon. Someone pulled his body into the great hall and the gentle nobles of this empire ripped him apart with their bare hands. I've been undoing the damage he inflicted on this kingdom ever since. In nine years, I haven't been able to fix half of what he destroyed in three."

Solon was aghast. "And you never married."

"Never remarried."

"Oh."

"I've been too busy. Besides, they call me the Black Widow, those who hate me. I don't mind. It's good that they fear me. For all that I'm a hundred times the monarch your brother was, I made missteps early and alienated some who might have been friends. I have learned since, but some men will never forgive a slight. My hold on this throne is a daily struggle—one that you could easily upset."

"I have no desire for a crown. I will swear that in front of all the court."

"Then what is it you want, Solon?"

His eyes never wavered. "Just you," he said.

"There is no just me," she snapped. "I am queen, but look at my face and you will see the holes where my clan rings were. Your cheek has never been pierced. Do you think that doesn't matter? If I am queen, what would you be?"

"Is a queen not a woman?"

"Not first."

"Is there any room beneath that crown for love?"

He saw glacial sorrow beneath the regal calm, and then it was gone. "I loved you once, Solon. When you left again, I was devastated. People prayed for your return, hoping you could restrain your brother, or later, hoping you'd replace him. I prayed for your return too, for other reasons. But you never came. I prayed even on the night of my wedding that you would come set things right. I prayed as your brother pulled me to his bed that you would burst through the doors. You didn't." Her voice was low, but cold. "Besides," she said. "I married your brother."

"But you said you—" he stopped, cursing his tactless stupidity.

She closed her eyes. "Afterward," she said. "I meant to get him so drunk that he'd pass out, but for once he wasn't in the mood to drink, and I—I was too frightened. I waited until it was over and he was asleep. Even after what he'd just done, I was barely able to cut his throat. In his sleep, he looked so much like you."

"I'm so sorry," Solon said.

She slapped him. Hard. "Don't you dare pity me. Don't you dare."

"It's not pity. It's love, Kaede. I hurt you, and I allowed you to be hurt, and I'm sorry."

"In two days, I marry Oshobi Takeda."

"You don't love him."

"Don't be stupid." Of course she didn't.

"Kaede, give me a chance. I'll do anything."

"You can watch the festivities from your cell. Good-bye, Solon."

Terah sat impatiently on the black monstrosity of a throne Garoth Ursuul had built. It had taken her half the morning to soothe the Lae'knaught and Chantry ambassadors. Her attempts to figure out who'd arranged her diplomatic disaster had been futile. Fingers pointed this way and that, and there was no telling who was lying.

Finally, Luc came in, resplendent in his cloth-of-gold Lord General's cloak, calfskin boots, and trim white tunic and breeches. "The rumors are true," he said, kneeling on the top step in front of her throne. "Logan has arrived with fourteen hundred men."

"They didn't lose anyone breaking through the Ceuran army?" Terah asked. The first report merely said that Logan had made it to the gates. Her orders not to open the gates for him had been diverted or ignored. She'd hoped the Ceurans might kill him for her.

Luc looked confused. "They didn't break through. They signed a treaty." Seeing the look on his sister's face, Luc hurried on. "When I demanded to know by what right they'd negotiated a treaty, they said by yours. They were surprised I didn't know."

Terah sagged into the throne. This had the Sa'kagé's grubby fingerprints all over it. "What are the details of the treaty?"

"I didn't ask."

"Idiot!"

He swallowed. "There are Ceuran wagons full of rice and grain going to every corner of the city. They're giving the Ceurans' food to our people."

"They let the Ceuran army inside the walls?"

"Just Lantano Garuwashi and the wagons. But the gates are still open. People are going out to the Ceuran camp and celebrating with them."

In minutes, Terah was on a balcony, looking over the city. It was a crisp autumn day, the sun bright but barely warm. Vanden Bridge was aglitter with sunlight reflected off hundreds of men in armor. "Logan's parading through the Warrens?" Terah asked. Why would he do such a thing? Who would feel safe there?

"The Rabbits worship him," Luc said.

The procession filed back to the east side and turned toward the castle. The streets had been crowded when Terah's army had paraded, but as Logan came, the city seemed to have emptied itself. The cheering itself sounded different. It scared the hell out of her.

"Summon my advisers," she said. "I need to know everything about this treaty before Garuwashi reaches the castle. Is he my ally, my vassal, or my overlord? Gods forbid, is he my husband? Go, Luc, go!"

34

After applying the appropriate makeup, Kylar secured Retribution to his back, dressed in loose rags so stinking and filthy he was loath to wear them, and donned a satchel full of nobleman's clothes. He reset the door's traps with poisons that would sicken but not kill and then perched on the ladder. It was early morning now and the exit was blind. He'd been waiting a quarter of an hour, attuning himself to the sounds of the street.

He heard the loud clop of a horse's hoof strike his flagstone. That was it. He waited one more second as he drew the ka'kari over his clothing and went invisible. He threw open the flagstone as a wagon passed overhead, crawled out, spun on his stomach, dropped the hidden door closed, and flung dust over the clean flagstone. The wagon's back axle caught on Retribution. It spun Kylar back around and dragged him for several feet before he twisted free. The driver cursed and looked back, but saw nothing.

Kylar stood, invisible, and made his way into an alley. He dropped the shadows and examined his rags to see

what damage the ka'kari had inflicted on them this time.
It wasn't bad, except for a few new holes in the back
that might show Retribution. He twisted the satchel to
lie across his back, affected a limp, and headed for the
Heron's Rest. It was at the crossroads of Sidlin and Vanden, and thus one of the few inns in the city where he
could enter in rags and leave in silks without attracting
attention.

He hadn't gone two blocks when he saw the ambush.
Guild kids were hiding amid the ashes and rubble that
clotted the alley. Most of them held rocks, but he caught
glimpses of one or two clutching Khalidoran swords, rel-
ics, no doubt, of the Nocta Hemata. There was time to
turn aside, but Kylar didn't for one reason: he saw Blue.
He'd forgotten to hide the money he'd promised her. She
might have even lived up to her side of the bargain and
moved her crew, though he doubted it.

The biggest kid in the guild was the first to stand up. He
was short for sixteen, and gaunt like all of them, though
he didn't have the distended belly of malnourishment that
some of the littles had. He held a Khalidoran sword and
his eyes darted around to the other kids for support. "Give
us your coin and that bag and you can go," he said. He
licked his lips.

Kylar looked around the circle. Seventeen of them, all
scared witless, most of them littles. Blue was squinting at
him suspiciously. He grinned at her. "I forgot to give you
this," he said, fishing in a pocket for a gold coin. It was
far more than he'd promised, but these kids could use it.
He tossed it to her.

One of the bigs mistook the move and whipped his
rock at Kylar's head. Kylar dodged and the missile nearly

brained another big on the other side. That big flung his rock and in a moment, the circle exploded in flying rocks and slashing steel.

With a surge of Talent, Kylar leapt ten feet in the air, flipped, drew Retribution, coated it with the ka'kari. As he landed, he spun in a circle, Silver Bear Falls to Garran's Zephyr, hacking the blades from the hilts of three swords. From Retribution, the ka'kari released a pulse of magic that rushed over Kylar's skin.

What was that?

~Impressive. Look.~

The guild had frozen, and even those bigs who were suddenly holding broken swords were staring at Kylar, not their swords. He glanced at himself and saw that somehow he'd lost his tunic and his skin was shining as if lit from within, as if he were bursting with barely re-strained power. *I didn't tell you to do that.*

~You wanted to stop them without killing them, didn't you?~

"I told you it was him," Blue said.

Kylar had an awful feeling of déjà vu. They thought he was Durzo. Had the ka'kari put that face on him, too? He was standing as Durzo had stood over a decade ago when Azoth's guild had tried to mug him. But now he was standing on Durzo's side. It looked different from here.

"It's Kylar," Blue whispered.

"Kylar," two kids echoed. The awe in their voices made it clear that they thought they were mugging a legend. Around the circle, rocks rattled to the ground. The circle drew back, the guild caught between flight and curios-ity. Only now did the bigs turn wide eyes to their faintly smoking swords, a few absently rubbing limbs or ribs bruised from flying rocks.

"How do you know that name?" Kylar demanded, feeling a sudden shiver of fear.

"I heard Jarl talking at Momma K's once," Blue said. "He said you were his best friend, he said you used to be Black Dragons. And Momma K told us once that the best Black Dragon ever apprenticed with Durzo Blint. I put it together."

Kylar couldn't move. Durzo had said it long ago, the truth always comes out. If these kids knew that Kylar was a wetboy and Durzo's apprentice, there was no telling how long before an enemy knew it. It might have spilled already, or his enemies might never think to ask a bunch of guild rats. There was no way to know.

It wasn't Kylar's fault, but "Kylar" had to disappear. His time was finished. If he ever came back to Cenaria, it would have to be as a different man with a different name and different friends or none. Kylar would have to abandon everything, as Durzo had abandoned everything every ten or twenty years. It was the price of immortality.

"Please, sir," the scared big who'd first confronted him said, licking his lips again. "Apprentice Blue. She's the smartest. She deserves to get out."

"You think this is out?" Kylar snarled. "I'll be dead inside a week!" He pulled the ka'kari to his skin and sent a jolt of blue fire through it. The kids threw up their hands to shield their eyes, and when they looked again, Kylar was gone.

35

Followed by generals, bodyguards, Lord Agon, and a bluff Ceuran named Otaru Tomaki, Logan and Lantano Garuwashi strode into the throne room. Logan knelt before the throne, as did the other Cenarians; the Ceurans bowed low; Lantano Garuwashi inclined his head, rings clacking in his long red hair.

"Arise," Queen Graesin said. She was warmly regal in a soft red gown with emerald piping, and matching jewels at her ears and throat. She descended the seven steps to where Garuwashi and Logan stood. "Duke Gyre," she said, smiling, "you have served us excellently. We shall reward you as richly as you deserve." She turned to Lantano Garuwashi. "Your Highness, it is an honor. Be welcome in our court."

Logan barely kept from breathing a sigh of relief. So she had gotten his letters after all. There had been something odd in her replies, a lack of the expected sneer. Perhaps she had decided that with her rule secure, she should start acting more like a queen.

"Please, call me Garuwashi. I am no king, yet," Lantano Garuwashi said, with a little smirk and something more besides. The traditional Ceuran doubled silk half robes over loose trousers tended to hide a man's build, but Garuwashi could have dressed in a pile of old sheets and still oozed masculinity. His hair shone like red gold, pulled back in a pony tail and interwoven with dozens of other strands, like a tiger's stripes. His jaw was pronounced, his face lean and clean shaven, shoulders broad, waist small, sleeves cut shorter than usual either for freedom of movement or to show thickly muscled arms. Terah Graesin, Logan saw, appreciated them; Garuwashi returned her glances boldly.

"Nor am I a queen, yet," she said. "Though it would please me greatly if you would be my guest at my coronation."

"I would be honored. And perhaps by this time next year, you can be my guest at mine."

"May I show you around my castle?" Terah asked, extending her hand to Garuwashi and dismissing the rest of them.

From the looks in their eyes, Logan expected Lantano Garuwashi would be mounting the ramparts in no time.

36

*H*er name was Pricia. She was the fourteen-year-old concubine who had wept for her friends and not for herself when Garoth died. She'd hanged herself with a silk belt. She was naked, her clothing folded neatly in a pile to one side, all her beauty gone. Her face was discolored, eyes open and bulging, tongue protruding, shit running down her fair legs. Dorian touched her and found her body only slightly cooled. From his touch, her body swung slightly. It was obscene. Dorian rubbed his face.

He should have known. The concubines had probably learned that Garoth's body had been recovered even before Dorian had. For the Godking's bodyguards, the recovery meant a small reclamation of honor. To the concubines, it meant death.

The former Godking's wives would be expected to join him on his pyre. Only the virgins and the concubines the next Godking desired would be spared. Dorian had said he was claiming no one. The women thought they would all be burned.

"When did you figure it out, Hopper?"

"Your Holiness?" Hopper asked. "I'm not sure I understand the question."

"Try again."

Hopper cleared his throat, fearful. "I was with the rest of the concubines. Pricia came into this room to fetch something. I had no idea—"

"Try. Again," Dorian said coldly.

Hopper searched Dorian's face, his eyes wide, panicky. He must have seen something that satisfied him, because he said, "Ah." The mask of fear dissolved and he bowed. "I knew you were an Ursuul after I told you that you seemed different. An eccentric slave would continue as before. A pretender would redouble his efforts to appear servile."

"What is your position within the Godking's Hands?" Dorian asked.

"I am their chief," Hopper said, inclining his head.

So it was as Jenine had suspected. Who better to keep an eye on the Godking's people and secrets than a eunuch whose awkward gait made him seem a buffoon? Hopper was at the confluence of the Godking's eunuchs, concubines and wives, and servants. Through them, he had eyes on every important Vürdmeister, aetheling, and general in the realm. "How did you really lose your toes?" Dorian asked.

"When His Holiness your father offered me the position, he said that would be part of the price. I welcomed the chance to make such a sacrifice." He smiled ruefully. "Being gelded, on the other hand, wasn't so welcome."

"He offered? Did you have the option to refuse?"

"Yes. His Holiness was always fair with us."

It was a new side to Garoth Ursuul, a kinder side than Dorian had known. It was unsettling. "Why didn't you expose me?"

"Because I didn't have anyone to report to, and I didn't know what you were trying to accomplish. By the time I did, you had accomplished it. It was, if you will pardon my presumption, one of my few failures as Chief of the Hands."

No wonder he didn't know what I intended. I didn't intend it.

Hopper swallowed. "Your Holiness, I suspect some of the aethelings and Vürdmeisters know what I am. I guard against mundane spying, but I have not the means to stop their vir."

It was astonishing how Dorian had blundered into success. He'd kept Hopper in the throne room the day he had seized power. The Vürdmeisters had come into the room and had seen not only a fearless Dorian, but Hopper off to one side, tacitly endorsing him. How much weight had that carried?

Dorian suddenly felt sick to his stomach. He suspected it was a lot.

He looked again at Pricia's body dangling in the room. Death was so common here that life wasn't considered sacred. Or did the cause and effect run the other way?

"What is your name, Hopper? Your real name."

"I was ordered to forget—I'm sorry, sire, my name was Vondeas Hil."

"I thought Clan Hil was annihilated." Garoth had used the krul to wipe them out.

"The Godking saved me from . . ." he hesitated. "From

the fleshpots. He thought I had potential. I did my best to prove him right."

The fleshpots. So the krul and their feeding habits were no great secret.

"Vondeas Hil, I will remember your name and the sacrifices you have made. Will you serve me as the Chief of my Hands?"

Vondeas bowed low.

"I have questions for you. Where are my two hundred missing Vürdmeisters?"

"Vürdmeister Neph Dada sounded a religious summons when His Holiness your father died. He called all Vürdmeisters to help him bring Khali home. Currently, your Hands believe them to be in your eastern lands."

Eastern Khalidor was sparsely populated. There were no major cities there, and hadn't been since Jorsin Alkestes had turned Trayethell into Black Barrow. "They're at Black Barrow?" Dorian asked.

"In its vicinity, at least. We don't know the exact location. Spies who've attempted to infiltrate the camp haven't returned."

Well, that at least was one problem that could wait. Meisters and magi, Vürdmeisters and archmagi had been smashing themselves against Black Barrow for centuries. Neph Dada at the head of two hundred Vürdmeisters was a serious problem, but at least Dorian would have until spring to consolidate his forces—and Neph wouldn't bother putting together an army. All Dorian's former tutor cared about was magic. Still, it was a problem that bore looking into.

"Redouble your efforts. I want to know what they're trying, and what—if anything—they've accomplished."

"Yes, Your Holiness."

"How many aethelings are completing their uurdthans?"

"Seventeen that I know of."

"How many of those are in a position to form a credible threat to me in the next six months?" Dorian asked.

"You must understand, Your Holiness, your father kept secrets even from me, so anything I tell you is complete to the best of my knowledge, and I did know more than he knew I did, but I cannot have full confidence that I knew all of his aethelings. I know that Moburu Ander lives and is attempting to subvert the wild men. I have reports that he believes himself to be some kind of prophesied High King. Your father cared little about that. He cared more that there appeared to be some evidence of collusion between Neph Dada and Moburu, though he and I believed any association between the two to be tenuous at best."

"Yes, I can't imagine Neph letting anyone live after they'd served his purpose. Nor would one of my brothers."

"The only other aetheling I know about was one I was not supposed to know, and I never learned his name. He was part of a delegation of war magi that Sho'cendi sent to recover Curoch. The magi made it as far as Cenaria, and witnessed the Battle of Pavvil's Grove, then returned to Sho'cendi, satisfied that Curoch was not present."

Dorian scowled. He had been certain that some of his brothers must be attempting to infiltrate the school of fire as he had been sent to the school of healing, but learning that one had been successful left the sick taste of betrayal in his mouth. He knew most of the magi that might have been sent on such a mission. Had he been friends with one of his own traitorous brothers? He shook his head. That was a distraction. Moburu and Neph were the real problem, and surviving until he could consolidate his men against them.

"Very well, Hopper. Thank you."

Hopper bowed once more, and when he straightened, he wore the slightly befuddled expression of Hopper once more.

"Dorian? Dorian, I've been looking all over for you," Jenine said, coming into the room.

Dorian was shocked to realize that he was still standing in a room with a hanged child. For all the good things he'd gained from learning to focus, he didn't think being able to ignore the ruin of a young girl was among them. By the God, it was a travesty, and he'd sat here, blithely contemplating politics. What was he becoming? His stomach threatened to rebel.

Jenine wore a shy smile. From where she stood, she couldn't see Pricia's hanged body. She was dressed in a simple gown of green silk that was gathered under her breasts. "I've made my decision," she said, walking forward. "I will marry you, Dorian, and I will learn to love you as you love me."

"Jenine, you shouldn't—" But he was too late. Jenine saw the hanged naked body and the first expression on the face of the woman he loved upon their betrothal was horror.

"Oh gods!" Jenine said, putting a hand to her mouth.

"I killed her," Dorian said and threw up.

"What?" Jenine asked. She didn't come to him.

"She killed herself rather than be forced to burn on Garoth's pyre," Hopper said quietly.

Dorian was on his knees. He blinked his eyes and grabbed a rag off the floor to wipe the vomit from his mouth. It was only after he wiped his beard clean that he looked at the cloth in his hand. It was Pricia's underclothes. They still smelled of her perfume.

He vomited again and staggered to his feet. This time he wiped his mouth on his cloak and turned so he couldn't see Pricia's body. "Hopper," he said. "Please take care of her. And double the watches on the concubines. Jenine, I need you to help me make a hard decision. It may have . . . consequences for our engagement."

37

$\mathcal{V}$i poured cold water into the basin from a copper pitcher and splashed her face. On the narrow desk by the door, she saw a note addressed to "Viridiana." Vi didn't touch it. She'd get ready when she was good and ready. The room was terrible. More like a broom closet. The unfinished stone walls were barely far apart enough to fit the narrow bed with its thin straw mattress. At the foot of the bed was a chest for her belongings and the washbasin. The chest was empty. They'd even taken Vi's hair ties. Tyros possessed only what the Chantry gave them. In Vi's case, that meant one ill-fitting white tyro's dress. The infuriating thing was that she knew that they had a dress that fit perfectly, as if Master Piccun had a fit of genius as he worked with what should have been terminally uninspiring wool and had somehow conquered the cloth to make Vi look beautiful.

That, obviously, was not the intended effect. That dress had been spirited away, and this white sack put in its place. They hadn't bothered tailoring a shift for her. The one she'd woken in was obviously used, if—she hoped—clean, and the previous owner had been fatter than she was tall. The shift didn't even come down to Vi's knees.

Vi brushed her hair back irritably. They'd taken her damn hair ties. She wasn't going to her lectures. She wasn't leaving the room. They'd taken enough. She looked around the room for something she could use. Her eyes fell on the copper pitcher. "To hell with them," she said to activate her Talent as she ripped off the handle. In a minute, her hair was pulled back into a fiercely tight braid. "To hell with them," she said again, and squeezed the copper into a tight circle binding her hair.

She picked up the note and unfolded it. "Viridiana, after your classes this morning, please come to the private dining hall. Elene wishes to meet you. -Sister Ariel"

Vi couldn't breathe. Elene? Oh, fuck. She'd known Elene would show up eventually, but so soon?

The door burst open and a wild-eyed, frumpy teenager stared around the room suspiciously, her arms raised as if she were summoning vast powers. "What's going on here?" the girl demanded. "You were using magic! Twice! Don't deny it."

Vi laughed, first nervously, then openly, glad for the distraction. The girl was practically wheezing from running. Her cheeks were flushed, sweat beading on her pale forehead under dark hair. She was fat enough and short enough that Vi wondered if this lard barrel had been the prior owner of her shift. She was perhaps fifteen, her white cotton dress edged with blue, and a brooch of gold scales prominent on her chest. "You got me," Vi said.

"You admit it!"

Vi raised an eyebrow. "Of course. Now get out. And knock next time."

"It's forbidden!"

"Knocking's forbidden?" Vi asked.

"No."

"Then try it next time, Chunky."

"My name is Xandra, and I'm the Floor Monitor. You used magic, twice. That's two days in the scullery for your first offense. And you disrespected me. That's a week!"

"You little shit."

"Swearing! Another day! They told me you'd be trouble." Xandra was shaking. It made her fat jiggle.

"You've got to be fucking joking," Vi said.

"Disrespect, swearing again! That's it! You'll report to the Mistress Jonisseh for a switching immediately."

"You call that disrespect, you squealing sow?" Vi stepped forward. Xandra opened her mouth and raised her arms. Vi said, "Graakos."

The shield snapped in place instantly, and whatever Xandra threw at her grazed right off it. Vi grabbed the girl's arm, twisted and heaved her out of the room. Xandra slid a good ten paces across the hallway's polished floor. As Vi stepped into the hall, she saw at least thirty little girls staring at her, wide-eyed, most of them under twelve.

"Please knock next time," Vi said. She turned on her heel and slammed the door.

From the hall, she heard Xandra quaver, "Slamming a door, that's—"

Vi opened the door and stared daggers at the girl, who

was still lying in a heap against the far wall. The words dried up in Xandra's mouth. Vi slammed the door again, and sat on her bed, picked up the note, tried not to cry— and failed.

38

In all his life, Kylar had never seen the people of the Warrens so happy. Agon's Dogs had stayed with the wagons full of grain and rice to manage the distribution. All the Dogs were members of the Sa'kagé, and they had taken it into their minds to make sure that the food was fairly distributed. "We got our bit coming," Kylar heard a Dog tell a scowling Sa'kagé basher. "I've heard it from high up. Now make sure those guild rats share!"

The Rabbits joined long queues that moved slowly but steadily forward, and a hard-bitten old coot broke out a tin whistle, sat on his new sack of rice, and began to play. In moments, the Rabbits were dancing. A woman soon had several pots boiling and anyone who dropped a measure of their rice or grain into one pot immediately could take a full, seasoned measure from another. She served bread and rice and soon wine. Someone offered herbs, someone else butter, another meat. In no time, it was a feast.

In a break between songs, one of Agon's Dogs stood up and yelled. "Ya might recognize me. I'm Conner Hook, and I grew up in this neighborhood. I seen ya and I know ya and I'm tellin' ya now, by the High King's bollocks, if any of ya come tru' the line twice, I'm callin' out yer name, and we're gonna fookin' add yer ass to the meat pot, got it?"

A cheer went up—and the line thinned considerably. For the Rabbits, to whom corruption was the unquestioned norm, it was a gift as unexpected as the free food itself. Kylar listened, and heard many a toast to Logan Gyre and many variations of the tale of him slaying an ogre and teary, drunken renditions of his speech establishing the Order of the Garter, and the word "king" muttered a dozen times. He smiled darkly, then froze.

He glimpsed a lean woman with long blonde hair on the far side of the square. In contrast to the Rabbits, she was so clean she was radiant, and he caught a flash of white teeth as she smiled. His heart stopped. "Elene?" he whispered.

The woman disappeared around a corner. Kylar went after her, pushing and dodging his way through the jubilant, dancing crowd. When he got to the corner, she was already fifty paces down the twisting alley, turning onto yet another. He ran after her with the speed of his Talent.

"Elene!" He grabbed her shoulder and she jumped, startled.

"Hi . . . Kylar, right?" Daydra asked. She had been one of Momma K's girls. Playing the virgin was her specialty. From a distance, she looked like Elene.

Kylar's heart lurched, and he wasn't sure if it was more from disappointment or relief. He didn't want Elene here. He didn't want her in this pit of a city or anywhere nearby

when he murdered the queen, but at the same time, he
wanted to see her so badly it ached.

She smiled at him awkwardly. "Um, I don't work the
sheets anymore, Kylar."

He flushed. "No, I wasn't—I'm sorry. I . . ." He turned
and made his way to the castle.

39

Feir Cousat and Antoninus Wervel emerged from Quorig's Pass after noon. As they approached Black Barrow,
the evergreen forest that carpeted the foothills ended.
Feir hunkered down in his coat against the deep autumn
chill and climbed a low rise. The sight took his breath
away. No one had lived in Black Barrow for seven hundred years. The land should have been long overgrown
with grass, trees, undergrowth. It wasn't. The grass, at
the least, should have been an autumnal brown. It wasn't.
Seven centuries ago, the decisive battle of the War of
Shadow had been fought in the early summer, and the
grass at Feir's feet was still short and green. He saw the
raw depression where a farmer's stone fence had been
pulled from the earth, the stones taken into the city so that
they might not be used as missiles by the enemy's siege
engines. Nothing had grown in the bare depressions that
marked where this fence had stood—seemingly only days
before. Time had stopped here.

Lifting his eyes, Feir saw more: ruts from the passage

of wagons, grass beaten flat by marching feet, holes for the firepits and latrine pits of an abandoned military camp. But no tents or tools. Anything that could be looted had been taken long ago, but everything that remained stayed unchanged.

That didn't only apply to the land. Two hundred paces away, the bodies began. First, a few marking the edge of the battle, and then hundreds, and then thousands, until in the distance the ground lay under a black blanket of the dead. The epicenter of death was a perfectly round dome of black rock the size of a small mountain covering the city and the hill where the castle had once been. At the base of the dome, siege engines on broken wheels, half-consumed by fires, tottered but hadn't fallen despite the centuries.

The dome was surrounded by a larger circle of magic in the land itself, miles across, called the Dead Demesne. Outside the circle, time continued, wind blew, rain fell. Inside the Dead Demesne . . . they didn't.

Feir rolled his great shoulders, readying himself. He cupped his hands close to his face and conjured a fire with his Talent. Then he stepped across the boundary into the circle of death. Nothing happened. He let the fire die.

"That's odd," he said aloud. Antoninus grunted in assent. Feir squinted at the air.

The Dead Demesne—like Black Barrow itself—was Emperor Jorsin Alkestes' work. He had made it lethal to use the vir within the circle, but because vir had similarities to the Talent, there was always some dissonance in the circle when anyone tried using the Talent. Little things would be different, like mage fire being red instead of orange. But Alkestes' weave was gone.

Feir rubbed his scruffy beard. It was good for him. He wouldn't have to factor it into the work he'd come here to do. But someone had broken what Jorsin made. That was not good.

Examining the air over the circle in the same way he had examined the circle in Ezra's Wood, Feir studied the magic. He could feel an emptiness in the weaves—the great magics Jorsin had woven didn't break without leaving a trace. Unfortunately, he couldn't tell much except that that the weaves had been broken recently. But to break a spell Jorsin Alkestes had made using Curoch would have required someone incredibly powerful here wielding some artifact, or a couple of hundred magi or Vürdmeisters working together. Feir couldn't imagine anyone with a shred of sense or decency participating in such a scheme. So that meant Vürdmeisters.

Jorsin's other weaves, the ones sealing the ground and sealing the dead, were perfectly intact. Feir didn't think they would be so easily broken, either. He hoped not.

Feir scanned the distant trees, suddenly queasy that unfriendly eyes might be hiding within them. He walked across the plain quickly, the air curiously odorless even as he approached the first body.

The creature was the black of a bloated corpse and man-shaped but ill-proportioned. Its arms were too long, its face too long, lower jaw jutting forward, ragged hooks of teeth stabbing up into the air from its lower jaw, mismatched black and blue eyes staring. It was massively muscled. Its skin was hairy, bordering on fur, and it had neither clothes, nor weapon. It was a krul. The meisters could not make life, but they could mimic and mock it. There were, Dorian had once told Feir, dark mirrors of almost every natural creation.

Feir and Antoninus walked on. It was going to get worse. A lot worse.

Soon, dead krul lay everywhere. Thousands had been killed bloodlessly by Jorsin's magic, but thousands more bore the marks of their deaths. Ugly faces had been crushed by war hammers or flailing hooves. Chests were caved in from being trampled. Throats were cut, torsos disemboweled, eyes hung by optic nerves from broken sockets, and blood glistened freshly in the wounds, never drying, never congealing.

Paths had been cleared through the bodies, and they followed them mutely. It wasn't long before Feir saw a human arm amid the krul, then a leg that appeared to have be half eaten. The bodies were piled knee-deep on either side of them. Then they began passing krul who'd been killed by magic. There were great craters in the battlefield empty of all but pulverized scraps of meat. Others had been burned or cut in half or shocked. Some had torn their faces to ribbons with their own claws.

The krul began to vary, too. Pure white krul with spiraling rams' horns led every unit of twelve, and larger ones seven feet tall appeared more rarely still. They walked past an entire platoon of four-legged feline krul the size of horses, with jet-black skin, sparse hair like a rat's tail, and exaggerated maws like a wolf. Rarer still were those like bears, easily twelve feet tall and with thick fur the color of new blood. As they trekked through the vast battlefield, it seemed every natural animal had found a dark mockery here. Bats, ravens, eagles, fanged horses, horned horses, even dark, red-eyed elephants carrying archers lay in ig-nominious death.

"The monsters," Antoninus said quietly. "Was nothing holy to them?"

Feir followed Antoninus's gaze and saw the krul children. They were most beautiful of all the krul, with balanced features, big child's eyes, pale skin close to a human shade, and long claws for fingers. These still wore their human clothes. Even the looters hadn't touched them. Feir almost gagged. They moved on, ever closer to the great black dome.

After a while, Feir felt inured to the horror. There were a thousand thousand permutations of death, krul of every shape and size and sometimes men and often horses, but the magical fixedness of it, the lack of smell, the stillness of the air, lent it a certain unreality, as if the dead were figures carved of wax.

If Jorsin was to be believed, one million one hundred thirteen thousand eight hundred and seventy-nine krul lay dead here. Various magi scholars had guessed that between five hundred thousand and a million krul would face them. Against fifty thousand men. The rest of Jors-in's armies had been drawn away by his own treacherous generals.

Then Jorsin had done all this, with Curoch—the very blade Feir had gone into the Wood to retrieve. Of course, he had only retrieved instructions. Curoch was safe in Ezra's Wood forever, and thank the gods for that.

"Well, here we are," Antoninus said as they finally touched the dome of Black Barrow. "Now we can forge our counterfeit Ceur'caelestos and save Lantano Garu-washi and all his men. Indeed, maybe all the south."

Feir said, "All we have to do is find Ezra's secret entrance to Black Barrow, find Ezra's workshop and his gold tools, find seven broken mistarille swords, rediscover a forging technique every present-day Maker says is a myth, find one giant ruby, and avoid detection by a couple of hundred Vürdmeisters plotting gods know what."

"Oh," Antoninus said, waggling his great, single kohled eyebrow, "here I thought it was going to take all winter."

40

A knock sounded on Vi's door hours later. "It's Sister Ariel. May I come in?"

"I can't stop you. There's no lock on the door," Vi said.

Sister Ariel came in. She said nothing for a time, staring around the bare room with apparent nostalgia.

"What do you want?" Vi asked.

"A bit nervous about going to the lecture, huh? Or was it your meeting with Elene that's got you acting more like a tyrant than a tyro?" Sister Ariel said.

"I fucked up," Vi said, sulking, knowing it, hating it, and sulking anyway. "Now they hate me, like always."

"They're twelve years old. They don't dare hate you."

"Is that supposed to make me feel better?"

"I'm not terribly concerned about your feelings, Vi. However, given the difficulties of your case and that I discovered you, and most of all because I couldn't come up with an excuse quickly enough, I've been put in charge of your tutelage."

Vi groaned.

"My feelings exactly. First of all, this room is entirely inappropriate for you."

"I get a better room?"

"You get to share a room. You were given a single in deference to your age. That was a mistake. You're isolated enough as is. As of this afternoon, you'll have a roommate. In case you're curious, the room will be only slightly larger than this one." Vi pitched back onto the bed. "Now, since you are my responsibility, you'll go to lecture. Now. Elene will have to wait until later."

Vi didn't move.

"Do we need to repeat certain lessons we learned on the trail?" Ariel asked.

Vi stood quickly.

"And by the by, lest you being put under my care be seen as a reward, all the punishments that your unfortunate floor monitor imposed will be carried out, as well as a few of my own. Follow." Ariel left, and Vi had no choice but to follow her like a whipped dog.

The Chantry had been constructed with beauty and practicality as its first considerations. Cost had obviously been no object. Even here, in the tyros' area, the arched ceilings were ten feet high, incised with a different pattern in every quarter. The tyros occupied the lowest level of the Chantry, though storerooms, archives, and the like lay beneath the water line. Because it was housed entirely within the giant statue of the Seraph, the interior of the Chantry was arranged in circles: living quarters arrayed along the quadrasecting halls, and lecture halls around the outside to take advantage of the sunlight necessary for magic.

Though white marble predominated, the tyros' floor didn't feel austere. A castle with so much stone would be cold and dark, but here the floors were warmed to welcome bare feet, and the ceiling itself was luminous. The walls were filled with bright, cheery scenes to comfort girls away from home for the first time: rabbits, unicorns, cats, dogs, horses, and animals Vi had never seen played together. They were drawn fancifully, but exquisitely.

Vi touched a painted pink puppy curled in sleep next to an impossibly friendly lion. Its eyes opened and it licked toward her fingers, its pink tongue pressing against the wall as if it were just on the other side of a glass. Vi yelped and jumped backward, clawing at her belt for a dagger that wasn't there.

"His name's Paet," Sister Ariel said. "He was one of my favorites. He doesn't wake until noon."

"What?"

"It's a timepiece. Watch this," Sister Ariel said, stopping outside one of the classrooms.

Gently, the ceilings pulsed violet, red, yellow, green, and blue in succession as a bell tolled. Seconds later, several hundred girls between ten and fourteen poured into the halls in a flood of noise and motion. Vi saw more curious glances than frightened ones. Apparently the rumors hadn't spread to the entire school yet. She folded her arms and scowled.

"Class starts in five minutes. Can you read and write?"

"Of course," Vi said. Her worthless mother had done that much.

"Good. I'll collect you at noon. Oh, and Vi? If you have a question during class, raise your hand. Sister Gizadin is

a stickler. When called on, stand with your hands behind
your back. If you don't, they'll think you're being disrespectful. Oh, and no magic. And remember everything.
Lectures are arranged in triads to help with that."

"Triads?" Vi asked, but Sister Ariel was already gone.

Five minutes later, Vi was seated in a too-small chair
at a too-small desk in the front row of a lecture hall.
Three walls were unadorned white stone. The east wall,
however, was as transparent as glass. The late morning
sun poured down, bathing Lake Vestacchi and the snow-
capped mountains beyond in light. The lake was the
deepest blue Vi had ever seen, and dozens of fishing boats
dotted the surface.

Vi barely noticed when her whispering classmates
suddenly quieted. A squat Sister tut-tutted and the wall
shimmered, becoming opaque white like the others in
seconds. Without preliminaries, Sister Gizadin began:
"There are three reasons glamours should be used sparingly. Anyone?" Not a girl made a move. "First, glamours
are unpredictable. Second, glamours are unnatural. Third,
glamours are unappreciated.

"*Unpredictable.* First, a glamour may affect only men
or only women or only children. Second, a glamour may
affect some people much more strongly than others.
Third, a glamour will attract people according to their
own predispositions. It may impart, particularly in men,
an overwhelming sexual desire for the caster. Or it may
impart a slavish servitude, where the person finds in you
every good thing they could imagine. Or it may impart a
simple attractiveness and persuasiveness.

"*Unnatural.* First, a glamour can operate by exaggerating a quality you already have. That could be exaggerating

your inherent attractiveness, or it could exaggerate people's perception of your courage or honor or strength, or it could exaggerate a bond such as friendship that you share with the glamour's target. Second, a glamour may feign the attractive features of another person. Third and most powerfully, a glamour may tap the subject's mind for what he finds most attractive. One man might say the caster was blonde and blue-eyed whilst the man beside him would swear she was buxom and green-eyed. But this type of glamour is unusual and challenging to use. And obviously, if the two men talk after that maja leaves, they will notice the discrepancy.

"That leads us to the third reason glamours should be used sparingly: Glamours are unappreciated. First—" she stopped, irritated. "Viridiana, stop fidgeting. You have a question?"

"What if you can control all that?" Vi asked, standing up and putting her arms behind her back, feeling like a child. "It's not that hard."

All the girls in the class looked at Vi as if they couldn't believe she'd dared speak.

"Do you really wish me to believe that you have natural mastery of one of the more difficult relational spells?"

"I didn't say mastery," Vi said defensively. The truth was, she was still off-kilter, the thought of having to go talk to Elene hanging over her like a death sentence—which, she realized, it might actually be.

"Unless you've actually cast this spell, sit and be silent."

Vi paused, then scowled. "I have."

"Oh? Pray tell." Sister Gizadin gave a condescending smirk.

Fine, bitch. "I was fucking this guy and he was having trouble waking the snake," Vi said. Sister Gizadin's eyes went huge. "So I kicked in a sex glamour. That usually does it in about five seconds. I mean, it's embarrassing. If you use too much, they're done before they get naked. With this one, the glamour did nothing. In your terms, I guess I was exaggerating my natural attractiveness. So I played around with it until I felt something give. His eyes glazed over and he started talking about my boyish figure—while holding two hands full of tit."

Sister Gizadin's mouth was open, but no words came out.

"Anyway," Vi said, "it wasn't hard. I mean, I'm most experienced with glamours for sex, but I figured those out with a pointer or two from a courtesan, so with Sisters teaching me, how hard can the other glamours be?"

For a long time, no one said anything. Vi noticed belatedly that everyone was gaping at her. Sister Gizadin's mouth closed. She began to speak, and then stopped. Finally she looked past Vi to a buck-toothed twelve-year-old who raised her hand. "Yes, Hana?" Sister Gizadin asked.

Hana stood with her hands behind her back. "Please, Sister, what kind of mage is a courtesan?"

Vi laughed.

That snapped Sister Gizadin out of it. "Sit, both of you!"

They sat.

"*Unappreciated,*" Sister Gizadin said. "Even if people's perceptions of the caster are not altered, there is still a feeling of wrongness after a glamour. During the spell, they won't notice they're being manipulated, but afterward, especially if they were wildly manipulated, they'll realize that their reactions were out of proportion. The irresponsible use of glamours is one reason why magae have historically been distrusted. No one wants to be manipulated, and in essence, glamours are all about manipulation. That's all. Class dismissed."

It was as if Vi had never spoken. Sister Gizadin didn't answer Vi's question, or Hana's. Indeed, she didn't seem affected in the slightest, except, Vi realized later, that she'd forgotten to teach the last portion of her lecture in triads.

Momma K adjusted the topazes hanging in her long hair, examining herself critically in Master Piccun's mirror. She'd found a note on her bedside table when she woke. It was written in Durzo's cramped hand, "I live. I will come for you." That was all. Bothersome man. She'd gotten up and dyed her hair one last time: a natural gray. No, silver, she decided.

Then she'd come here. It hadn't been easy to order Master Piccun to make her blue dress for the coronation more muted and higher cut than any she'd ever worn, but at least his hands had strayed when he took her measurements—as they always did. When his hands stopped wandering, she would know she was old.

"You are extraordinary," he said. "I have this meeting with every one of my beautiful clients. Normal women make new compromises with age daily, so it's less of a shock to them. Beauties seem to run into it all at once, and it happens here. They ignore my advice and order the latest fashion one more time, and then they see themselves. Some accuse me of making them look bad on purpose.

Others stare at the old stranger in the mirror, shocked. Always there are tears."

"I'm not much for crying."

"You know when I'm only flattering, Gwinvere. The body is my canvas, and I tell you, your body is years from that day of tears. You have something ineffable. You walk through life like a dancer, all strength and beauty and grace. I have this client, stunning girl, a bit muscular to be fashionable—I told her to start sitting on her ass and eating chocolates—but saved from being boyish by these hips and tits that would make a goddess green. By Priapus, the girl can wear anything—and will. I'd make her clothes for free, just to see her wear them."

"Now you're going to make me jealous," Gwinvere said. He knew she was kidding, though a small part of her wasn't. Aemil Piccun was talking about Vi Sovari.

"What I mean to say is that if I put up portraits of her and you at her age, a man would be hard-pressed to choose between you, but in person, it's no contest. Her beauty is wasted on her. She is divorced from her flesh, joyless. You, on the other hand, have this ability to enjoy a man enjoying you on any of a dozen levels. If I could imbue a dress with what you have, I would not be a tailor, I would be a god. Of all my clients, you will always be my favorite, Gwinvere."

She smiled, oddly moved. With Master Piccun, you always expected lechery, but you never expected him to mean anything by it. Now, he meant every word he said. "Thank you, Aemil. You warm my heart."

He grinned. "I don't suppose I've warmed any other parts of you, hmm?"

She laughed. "I'm tempted, but there are so many

women who will be needing discounts on their dresses for the coronation. They'd be so disappointed if I exhausted you."

"It's cruel to ruin a man by showing him what an artist of the bedchamber can do, and then denying him your talents for fourteen years straight."

"Fourteen?" she asked.

"Fourteen long, long years."

"Mmm," she said, relaxing almost imperceptibly. "It has been a long time."

He stepped close.

Momma K slipped away, opened the door, and beckoned the lissome noblewoman waiting in the front room. "Careful, sweetie, I think he'll want to start with the discount."

The noblewoman gasped. Master Piccun coughed. "Cruel, Gwinvere. Cruel."

41

Jenine had been spending her days trying to decide if Garoth Ursuul's wives and concubines would die. Dorian waited for her in the black rock halls that she usually lightened with her presence. But today, and for the days since he'd laid the question before her, that sunny presence had been clouded.

"My love," he said gently, "we have to decide today."

"Part of me hates you for making me decide, but this is what it is to be a queen, isn't it? You are wise, milord. If you decided for me, I would doubt you either way."

He breathed. When she'd said "part of me hates you," his heart stopped beating. Every Godking for centuries had been cremated with his wives and concubines, save for a few concubines that the next Godking wished for himself. If Dorian kept his first promise to Jenine, every woman in the harems would be obliged to throw themselves—or be thrown—onto Garoth Ursuul's pyre, with only the dubious reward of getting to spend all eternity as his slaves. The alternative was to claim all of them, which the Khalidorans would see as selfish and dishonoring to the dead, but a Godking was not expected to be selfless.

There was a third alternative, of course. Dorian could outright ban the practice of throwing the living on funeral pyres. In a few years, he intended to do exactly that. But he was already being painted as a soft southerner. The Vürdmeisters were sharks, and mercy would hatch a dozen plots against his life. What would Solon have told him to do? Dorian pushed the question aside: Solon would have told him to get the hell out of Khalidor.

"In some ways," he said, "if we are to change what marriage is to mean in these lands, it makes sense to let them die. From there we have a blank slate."

"So we throw away eighty-six women's lives to prove that women have value?"

Dorian said nothing. He offered his hand and she took it. They began walking toward his apartments. "I don't know how to take the cruelty out of the choice."

"I don't know if it will work, milord." Jenine always called him milord. She couldn't call him Dorian, of course. "Your Majesty" was too distant. "Your Holiness" was out of the question, and she knew what *Wanhope* meant: she refused to call her bridegroom "Despair." "There's something wrong with these girls. Did you know they're taken from their families when they're nine years old? They're trained to be exactly and only what the Godking wants. The only currency they know is the Godking's favor. They're not allowed to learn to read. They never go anywhere. They never meet anyone but each other and the eunuchs. It twists them. Yet they're not innocents. They gossip and backstab as much as anyone. Perhaps more, because they've nothing useful to occupy them. All the same, they're not animals either, though they've been treated as such. And most of them are just girls. I can't ask them to all die for me. You must claim them, milord, but I ask this: that you give each the choice. These women have never chosen anything for themselves. Let them choose now."

"You . . . you think some of them will choose death?"

"I heard women describe nights with Garoth that left them literally with scars—and they were proud of them. They really believe that your father was a god. Some do want to serve him forever."

Dorian felt like a stranger in his own land. He said nothing as they walked past a knot of aethelings who'd stopped in the hall, prostrating themselves until he passed. At the door of his apartments, he stopped and said, "Jenine, I swear to you that those women will be my concubines in name only. They will not share my bed."

She put a finger on his lips. "Shh, my love. Don't swear about what you can't control." He had a sudden sense that he'd done this before. He'd dreamed it, just last night, and had forgotten the dream until this moment. But in the dream, there had been a smell, harsh stench of . . . what? "If nothing else, I can control myself, my queen."

She smiled a sad smile too wise for her years. "Thank you, but I won't hold you to it."

"I'll hold myself to it."

She squeezed his hand, and then the sharp tang of vir hit his nostrils. He turned to the prostrate aethelings too late. Two boys without a mustache between them were standing, twin balls of green fire streaking toward Dorian and Jenine. They were barely five paces away.

Dorian watched, expecting the green missiles to pierce

his flesh. He was reaching for the vir, but it was too late to pull a shield together—but then the vir was there, already forming, already acting to protect him, pushing hard from below, only asking his assent.

Yes.

The green missiles were within a hand's breadth when the vir leapt up. The green fires twisted away, looped behind him and Jenine as Dorian threw his arms around her, and sped back toward the youths. There was a sound like eggs breaking and then sizzling meat as the missiles took each aetheling in the forehead, cracking their heads and scorching their brains, smoke puffing from perfectly round holes before they dropped to the ground, dead.

Dorian's shields sprang up around him and Jenine only then, though he'd acted as fast as he could. There was no other sound in the hall.

The dead children gaped at him, brains smoking. The living ones didn't dare look up. Fury rushed through Dorian. They hadn't just tried to kill them; they'd tried to kill Jenine. He looked at the Vürdmeister who was in charge of these aethelings. The man was cowering, prostrate, at the back of the line. Dorian couldn't think. The vir lashed out from his hand, yanked the man to his feet by his throat. He gave a strangled yelp, waving his hands in denial, before a huge fist of Dorian's vir smashed his chest against the rock wall.

Blood exploded over the wall and the aethelings at the back of the line, but no one moved. With effort, Dorian dropped the shields, pushed the vir down. His head was throbbing.

The aethelings had moved against him. It was a stupid, childish attempt, and it had almost succeeded because he hadn't thought to guard himself against boys who were eight years old. There'd been no follow-up to take advantage of the distraction, so Dorian couldn't know if the children had been directed by a Vürdmeister, unless it was simply to test Dorian's strength or to see if the vir would save him. In some ways, it wasn't important.

What was important was that something had to be done about the aethelings. They were vipers. If eight- and nine-year-olds had already acted, there was no doubt that the older boys were plotting, and a wedding would give them all sorts of opportunities. Delay looked like weakness, and weakness put not only himself but also Jenine in peril. That, he wouldn't tolerate.

Jenine started crying, and Dorian banished the aethelings and comforted her, but his mind was far away, and every thought was bloody.

42

$\mathcal{K}$ylar was dressed in servant's garb, and there were many new servants in the castle as Terah's retinue meshed with the remnants of Garoth's which had meshed with the remnants of King Gunder IX's, so getting into the servants' entrance was no problem. Once inside, he headed to the scullery and grabbed a tray of freshly polished silver goblets, balanced it in one hand, and walked toward the Great Hall. In the bustle and hum of activity and shouted orders and snarls of men and women under pressure working together for the first time, no one paid any attention to him. He was invisible not because of the ka'kari, but because of the practiced anonymity Durzo had spent so many hours teaching him.

For the moment, all of the tables were stored in the servants' room adjacent to the Great Hall. After the coronation, the tables would be carried in fully set. The goblets went onto one of the high tables adjacent to the queen's table. Unfortunately, her table was still empty: it wouldn't be set until immediately before the banquet, and then only under the watchful eyes of the Queen's Guard would her cupbearer lay out the castle's finest goldware for the high table with his own hand.

These were not insurmountable difficulties. However, Terah Graesin didn't have a reputation as a drinker, so if Kylar used a poison mild enough that her cupbearer wouldn't be affected when he tested her wine, she might not drink a lethal dose. The same was true of her eating utensils. She was a dainty eater.

So after setting down the goblets, Kylar grabbed a pile of rags dirtied in polishing the tables and headed down a back hallway. He walked purposefully, though he had no idea where the castle's laundry was. He scanned the ceilings and walls for the spy holes and crawlspaces that honeycombed the castle. When he saw a crawlspace, he leapt, grabbed the edge with his fingertips, and pulled himself up.

Inches from his face, a decaying web of vir criss-crossed the opening. Kylar's fingers were almost touching it. Hanging on by one hand, Kylar rolled the ka'kari through the web. The web popped harmlessly like a soap bubble.

From the secret passages, it was only a matter of finding his way. Kylar crawled or walked as the passages required and kept the ka'kari over his eyes so he could see every magical trap. In an hour, he'd found the royal treasury. The opening here was covered by stout iron bars.

The ka'kari made short work of that.

You know, before you came along, assassinating a queen would have been hard.

~Is that a complaint?~

As the sheered bars came off in Kylar's hands, he

stopped. *I'm like a god.* The thought jolted him. For some reason, it was the look on Blue's face that did it. Perhaps children didn't bother to cover their awe, or perhaps it was that he had been a Blue himself not so long ago. But as he thought about the awe in the guild rats' faces, he remembered the other faces: Caernarvon's Shinga's, Hu Gibbet's, even the Godking's face had held a note of awe. For the guild rats, it was a dream, for the others, a nightmare. But the incredulity was the same. He was the impossible.

For some reason, it had never sunk in. He was still Kylar, maybe still Azoth underneath it all. But now. . . . This was so easy. Kylar had longed to be more than guild rat. He'd longed to be more than wetboy. Now, he was more than a man. The rules didn't apply to him. He was stronger than a man, faster, a hundred times more powerful. Immortal. Death was temporary. If the most basic mortal concern—dying—didn't apply to him, what else didn't?

It was an intoxicating thought, but a lonely one. If he was more than a man, what communion could he have with men? Or women? The thought brought Elene sharply to the fore. His chest felt hollow. He would give his other arm if he could be with her again, his head in her lap, her fingers running through his hair, accepting him.

Odd, that. He could think of Elene with love, but as soon as his thoughts wandered near the hazy line of appreciation and desire—there, there was Vi with her red hair nearly glowing, the curve of her neck begging to be nuzzled, her eyes a challenge, nubile figure tempting him. He could sense her, somewhere far to the east. She was sleeping. Sleeping? At almost dinner time? Life at the Chantry must not be so bad.

He imagined slipping into bed behind her. Her hair was unbound, spilling over her pillow like a copper waterfall. Her hair was glorious, like some god had captured the last rays of the dying sun and given them to her. Kylar leaned close and inhaled deeply. Vi sighed in her sleep. She burrowed into him, her body conforming to his. His breath caught.

For a moment, he swore he wasn't wearing any clothes. Then they were back. Vi let out a moue of disappointment. *What the hell am I doing?* Certain now that he was indeed clothed, Kylar relaxed fractionally. Vi's breathing was slow and even. Kylar brushed a lock of hair behind her ear to see her face. She looked somehow smaller, more fragile, but no less beautiful. Without the customary tension, her face looked younger. She looked her age. Unlike Terah Graesin, whom sleep paled, sleep lent Vi's features grace.

Terah Graesin. The castle. *Where the hell am I?*

Seeing gooseflesh rising on Vi's arm, Kylar pulled the blanket up over both of them. He ran a hand gently from her shoulder down her arm. His hand continued down her hip to her leg. She was wearing a loose short shift and he stopped when his hand touched her warm, smooth skin. Then his hand came back up her leg, under her shift. He was a man out of control, his pulse pounding in his ears, the room indistinct, thoughts indistinct, only his nerves alive.

Her leg was lean, tight even in sleep. He trailed his hand over her hip. His fingertips glided over the depression between hip and navel, and then over her dancer's stomach, the perfect blend of warmth and soft over hard. He traced her lowest ribs as she breathed, still evenly though perhaps not so deeply as before, glorying in her. Kylar wasn't tall or thickly built, but Vi's slender form against him made him feel strong and tender and manly.

He leaned close, breathing her in, and then he kissed her neck. Gooseflesh rose, and this time he knew it wasn't the cold. He kissed her again, tracing her hairline. His fingers brushed the underside of her breast. Her back arched, grinding her buttocks against his groin. He was naked once more and her shift had ridden up. She was hot against him. "Yes," her whole body whispered, "yes."

A key grated in a lock. The sound was out of place. Then the other key grated, popping open a second lock.

~Kylar!~

I'm back. Sorry, I was . . . elsewhere.

~I'm in your body, Kylar. Some things you can't hide from me. Tumescence is one of them.~

Tumescence? What? Oh, God. *I didn't want to know that.*

Below, through the screen, Kylar saw the door to the treasury open. An officious little man clucked as he gazed around the barren room. There were only three chests. He opened the smallest and Kylar caught a glimpse of the crown, but the man sighed. "Where the hell is that pillow?" he muttered. He went out, closed the door, and began locking the locks.

Kylar pulled back the screen and dropped into the room, landing silently almost on top of the chests. He pulled the stopper out of the vial, formed the ka'kari into its bulb shape and drew out a generous dose of philoduna-mos. He stopped the vial and tucked it back into a pouch and grabbed the crown. It was a simple, elegant piece with only a few emeralds and diamonds on it. From the paucity of precious stones and gold in the other chests, Kylar guessed the simplicity had not been a stylistic choice. He modified the ka'kari even as he pressed the bulb, giving it a narrow brush as its tip, rather than a needle. As quickly as he dared, he drew a narrow band around the inside of the crown, with a glob at the back. As soon as Terah Graesin began to sweat under the gold band on her forehead, the bottled fire would wreathe her head in flames, and the glob would cause a small explosion into the back of her head. He didn't want Terah Graesin to be publicly burned; he wanted her dead. If she lived, the people's pity might offset their negative feelings for a time. If she lived, she would accuse Logan of the deed and execute him.

The philodunamos went on evenly, and dried quickly. The first lines Kylar had painted took on a flat gold sheen close to the color of the crown itself, although Kylar could see some ridges in it. He hoped the damn stuff didn't flake off. Still, he didn't guess that anyone was going to be putting it on before the coronation. It should be fine.

He heard a key in the lock at the same time he noticed that the glob of paint at the back of the crown was still wet. Unthinking, Kylar blew on it. He cut his breath off instantly, but saw one hard edge crack open and turn red. It glowed like a coal for a moment, then dimmed, even as a key rattled in the second lock. Kylar set the crown down gingerly in the chest and widened the ka'kari into a fan. He fanned the crown furiously as the key clicked open the third lock. He drew the ka'kari over himself, disappeared, and tried not to breathe.

The officious little man held a purple velvet pillow with long gold tassels off the corners. He closed and locked the other two chests, then lifted the crown reverently with two

hands—keeping his fingers on the outside, thank God—
and placed it on the pillow.

He walked out of the room. Kylar jumped back up
to the open screen, pulled himself into the crawlspace,
and headed for a place to change into his nobleman's
clothing.

Terah Graesin·was dead. She just didn't know it yet.

43

$\mathcal{V}$i woke in the darkness in a cold sweat. Sister Ariel had muttered darkly about some ineptitude or other that kept Vi from getting a new room and roommate immediately, but after the dream Vi had just had, she was glad to be alone.

She got out of bed, and the moment her feet touched the warm floor, dim light bloomed in the ceiling. Vi barely noticed. She pulled on the frumpy tyro's dress and headed out the door. Her stomach felt tight and sore. As she stepped into the hall, light bloomed like a star against the wall. Then, as if an unseen hand were drawing in big, bold lines, the light became a star suspended in a spider web, which was draped between an elk's antlers. The beast regarded Vi tiredly but stood to accompany her, the star illuminating her section of the hall with warm light.

Vi forgot herself and touched the beast. The light remained, but all else faded. The web around the star was replaced by an old iron lantern. The elk disappeared and in quick strokes was replaced with a bearded, fatherly woodsman. He nodded to Vi and lifted the lamp high. She touched the figure and it faded to be replaced with a grinning dog, balancing the star on its nose. She began walking, and it walked beside her. It was amazing. This entire floor was made to be a safe place for children.

In sudden fury, she punched the wall. The dog faded and a jester replaced it. Vi choked back a sob and hurried to the stairs at the center of the building. When she arrived at Sister Ariel's room, the door swung open before Vi knocked. "Come in," Sister Ariel said. She handed Vi a steaming cup of ootai. Her eyes looked bleary.

Vi was speechless. She stepped inside and took the cup in her left hand.

"Sit," Sister Ariel said. Her room wasn't large, and most of it was covered in piles of books and scrolls, but there were two chairs.

Vi sat.

"Pay attention and hold still," Sister Ariel said. She took Vi's swollen right hand and tsked. "*Savaltus.*" Pain shot through Vi's hand, then passed and her bruises faded. "You have an unfortunate habit of hitting things that are harder than your fist. The next time your recalcitrance evinces itself in self-mutilation, I won't heal you."

Vi had no idea what the words meant, but she got the gist. "I want you to make it stop," Vi said.

"Excuse me?"

"You tricked me into ringing Kylar. I want this damn thing off."

Sister Ariel cocked her head to one side, doglike. Her eyes gleamed. "Had a lucid dream, did you?"

"Fuck! Stop using words I don't understand!"

Something smacked Vi's butt so hard she screamed.

"The tongue is a flame, child," Sister Ariel said, her eyes cold. "We who speak to use magic learn to control it, else it burns us. Do you know what I was doing while you were studying today?"

"I don't give a shit."

Sister Ariel shook her head. "I have no moral qualm with your cursing, you fecal-mouthed cretin. When a guttershite curses, the world can't even hear it, Vi. When a maja curses, the world trembles. So I've come up with some punishments. I expect that you will exhaust them before I exhaust your defiance. But we're committed now. Your defiance makes only the path longer. *Sa troca excepio dazii.*"

Though she'd briefly seen the aura of magic surround Sister Ariel, Vi felt nothing. "What have you done?" she asked, eyes narrowing.

"That, my dear, is half the fun. With each new punishment, you get to guess. Now, you came because you had a particularly vivid dream, did you not?"

Vi stared into the bottom of her cup. Why was she suddenly squeamish to talk about sex? "It was him. He came to my bed. It was real."

"And?"

Vi looked up. "What do you mean and?"

"You dreamed of bedding a man. So what? Are you afraid you'll get pregnant?"

Vi's eyes locked back on the ootai. "We didn't, um, actually . . . you know."

"Then why are you here?"

"Is it because of the earrings?"

"Your dream? Definitely. They allow husbands and wives who can't be together to still communicate. Or conjugate. Only a few even of the oldest rings could do that, by the way. As I recall, not a few Sisters wasted decades studying it to find a way to pass messages instantly over great distances. It never worked. I can't recall why. But after the Third Alitaeran Accord banning magae from marrying Talented men, no one's studied it."

"So what I dreamed, Kylar dreamed?" Vi paled.

Sister Ariel looked at her quizzically. "That's what I said, isn't it?" It made Vi feel stupid all over again. "So it frightened you?"

"Not exactly," Vi admitted.

"Sometimes talking with you is like trying to master the Vengarizian Weave."

"Ah fuck this," Vi said. Suddenly, her mouth seemed to be on fire. She jumped to her feet, but Sister Ariel spoke and something hit the backs of her knees and she fell into her chair. "What the fuck was—"

Her mouth filled with fire again, and seeing the not-quite-suppressed smirk on Sister Ariel's face, Vi understood. After another five seconds, the pain stopped, leaving Vi gaping with pain and outrage. She touched her tongue, expecting it to be burned, but it felt normal.

"My mother used soap," Sister Ariel said, "but I couldn't figure out a weave for that. Now, you woke me for a reason. After you tell me what it was, you can go back to bed."

After thirty seconds, Vi realized Sister Ariel was serious. "Have you ever even fu—had sex?" Vi asked.

Sister Ariel said, "Actually, I lost my maidenhead riding a horse."

"I had no idea you were so coordinated." Vi had tried that once. It hadn't ended well.

Sister Ariel burst out laughing. "I didn't know you had such a wit," Ariel said. "I like you more and more, Vi."

Oh, *from* riding a horse, not *while* riding a horse. Vi laughed. She couldn't help it. She'd sooner die than squander even such a small bit of Ariel's regard. It was also an artful dodge of Vi's question. Hell, it was no use. Vi was tired and her stomach still felt as if she needed to shit. "I've—I've bedded dozens of men," she said.

"Good job," Sister Ariel said. "The correction, I mean, not the promiscuity."

"I never felt anything, with any of them, not since I was a kid. But with Kylar . . ."

"I'm no authority, but I think it's supposed to be different with someone you love."

That word set Vi off. "Not 'I didn't feel anything *for* them'! I didn't *feel* them! I'm totally numb down there. But tonight—" her mouth snapped shut. Since she was a child, fucking had been something Vi observed, something men did to her. Gradually her powerlessness had become her power. Men were slaves to their meat. Vi's body was simply currency, with the advantage that she could spend it again and again.

When she'd first thought of fucking Kylar, it had only been to think that after what she'd done to him, she owed him. Tonight had been horribly different. Different even from her earlier dream of Kylar. She had wanted Kylar in more ways than she could have imagined. Her body ached for him. It was like something lying so deeply asleep in her that she'd thought it dead was waking. Fucking Kylar wouldn't be a casual gift of the use of her body. It would be surrender.

"You have to get this earring off," Vi said. She was

shaking, cold sweat beaded on her forehead. "Please, before I go see Elene. She's still here, isn't she?"

"I'm sorry, child. Yes, she's here. You'll speak with her tomorrow." Sister Ariel sighed. "Viridiana, I've read everything I could find on those rings. The bond is unbreakable. It seemed like a good idea when they made them, I suppose. First they were used to bond a magus and maja who knew what they were getting into. Then others began to use the rings in political marriages. Kings and queens alike began to demand that the ringsmiths exaggerate the compulsion properties toward one side or the other, like yours are exaggerated to give you control. I don't know if we can understand the depth of human misery those magi wrought. But seeing what they had done, the Vy'sana, the Makers, took an oath to make such rings no more. They gathered those they could find and destroyed them and every text on their making. That ring in your ear is at least four hundred years old. That it survived to the present age is nothing less than a miracle."

"A miracle? You call this a miracle?"

Sister Ariel spread her hands helplessly.

Her carriage was waiting for her, but when Momma K got in, she wasn't alone. The dark blob in the opposite seat resolved itself into Scarred Wrable as soon as she sat. "Good evening, Momma K," he said. "Headed to the coronation?"

"As a matter of fact, I am. You need a ride?"

"I don't think so. It seems I've fallen out of favor with the queen."

"It seems?"

"I wake up from a good long drunk and go to get some hair of the dog and I got five guys telling me stories about what I did to the queen. Somehow, it's the wrong day. I was drunk, but I shouldn't have slept for a day and a half!"

Durzo. Her stomach twisted.

Ben Wrable's face was as pale as his scars. "It's Durzo, isn't it?"

"Don't be ridiculous. Durzo's dead."

"I know. I killed him, remember?" Oh, yes. Wrable had killed Kylar when Kylar had been disguised as Durzo. "He swore he wouldn't haunt me, but now my best client wants me dead."

"You still killed him. That had to be upsetting."

"You're not playing with me, are you? You didn't send some other wetboy to talk with Queen Graesin?"

"I didn't send anyone. I didn't arrange for the ambassadors to be insulted. I haven't moved against Terah Graesin." Yet. "Get out of the city for a while, Ben. Durzo probably just wanted to make sure you didn't take any more jobs for the woman who ordered his death."

Ben Wrable nodded, unthinking, and that unthinking nod confirmed what Momma K had suspected: it was indeed Terah Graesin who'd ordered Durzo killed. The bitch. Well, she'd get hers. Soon.

44

The Great Hall was filled with the cream of the realm, though given the hardships of the last year, that cream was more like watered milk. Many of the lords and ladies of the realm wore garments they wouldn't have had their servants wear a year ago. The number of nobles was also considerably reduced. Some had been killed in the coup or at Pavvil's Grove. Others had sided early with the God-king and had since fled. The chamberlain had done his best to fill in the ranks and bedeck the Great Hall appropriately, but the pageantry seemed thin. For once, however, there was no criticism. It was too hard to critique the royal guards' threadbare uniforms hastily patched with the colors of House Graesin while wearing a stained dress and borrowed jewels.

Kylar stepped in through a servants' entrance. He had no wish to be announced; he just wanted to see the effects of his handiwork. There was, however, one problem with the servants' entrance: it was full of servants.

"Milord? Milord?" a cheerful man asked.

"Uh, that will be all," Kylar said. *If I use you to cover these clothes, are you going to eat a hole in the crotch?*

~Hard to say.~ The ka'kari seemed to smirk.

"Ah, milord? Is milord lost?" The cheerful servant didn't wait for an answer. "Milord may follow me." He turned and began walking, and Kylar had no choice but to follow. Some servants, he thought, were too smart for their own good.

The servant marched him to the main entrance and handed him off to the chamberlain, a humorless man who looked him up and down, cocking his head like a bird. "You're out of order, marquess, you were to enter after your lord."

Kylar swallowed. "I'm sorry, you've mistaken me. I'm Baronet Stern. You needn't announce—"

The chamberlain double-checked his list. "Duke Gyre informed me pointedly that I was to announce you." He promptly turned and struck the ground with his staff. "Marquess Kylar Drake, Lord of Havermere, Lockley, Vennas, and Procin."

Feeling like he wasn't in control of his own body, Kylar walked forward. Eyes turned toward him, and more than once he heard "Wolfhound." Logan hadn't only legitimized Kylar by giving him a real title, unlike the baronetcy of Lae'knaught-held lands, he'd promoted him to dizzy heights. A marquess was beneath only the dukes of Cenaria. Kylar's chest tightened. It was a real title, with real lands and real responsibilities. Worse, Logan must have worked with Count Drake to have Kylar formally adopted. Kylar's bogus pedigree had been wiped clean. Logan was putting his own integrity behind Kylar. It was his last attempt to save Kylar from himself.

Kylar took his place to Logan's left in the front row. Logan smiled, and the bastard was so charismatic Kylar felt himself smiling along with him, too astonished to be pissed off.

"Well well, my friend," Logan said. "I half expected you to be slinking around up in the rafters. So glad you decided to join us mortals on the ground."

"Uhm, rafters, right. So overdone." Kylar cleared his throat, flabbergasted. "You're causing quite the scandal."

Still facing the front, Logan said, "I won't give up my best friend without a fight."

Silence. "You honor me," Kylar said.

"Yes, I do." Logan smiled, clearly proud of himself, but charmingly so.

"Did Momma K . . . ?"

"I came up with this all by myself, thank you, though Count Drake augmented it."

"The adoption?"

"The adoption," Logan confirmed. "Six rows back. Left side."

Kylar looked, and the blood drained from his face. In a section of poorer barons, a middle-aged blond lord and lady in even more modest clothing than most stood under the Stern banner. Beside them was a young man, as dark as they were light: their son, Baronet Stern.

"That might have been . . . awkward," Kylar said.

"We all need friends, Kylar," Logan said. "Me most of all. I've lost almost everyone I can trust. I need you."

Kylar said nothing. He noticed Logan's clothing for the first time. The duke was wearing a somber tunic and trousers, finely cut, but unrelievedly black. They were mourning clothes. Logan was still mourning Jenine, his whole family, many of his retainers, and perhaps Serah Drake as well. That old sick feeling rose in Kylar's stomach once more. Logan and Count Drake both were gambling their honor, which to each of them was his most sacred possession, on Kylar. Terah Graesin's assassination now would be more than a tragic difference of opinion. To Logan, it would be betrayal.

There was nothing to do. Marquess Kylar Drake sat in the front row, with eyes constantly on him. Perhaps the Night Angel could invisibly drop from the rafters and scoop up the deadly crown, but Marquess Drake could only watch the consequences of his choices unfurl. Kylar stood as Terah Graesin was announced, as she strode regally to the front, as the patr and the priest lifted prayers and blessed her coronation. Finally, the two divines and Duke Wesseros together lifted the crown from its purple pillow.

Not yet. Dear God, not yet. Kylar hadn't even thought of what would happen to those crowning Terah if she was already sweating. Symbolizing all the gods and the land itself, the three men placed the crown on Queen Graesin's brow.

Nothing happened. She accepted a scepter from Duke Wesseros and a sword from Lord General Graesin, held each for a long moment, then handed each back. The men bowed low, then she bade them rise as she sat. The men retreated, and Kylar's heart edged back out of his throat. Trumpets pealed and Kylar jumped. Everyone stood and applause thundered through the Great Hall.

The queen smiled as everyone cheered. She stood and gestured generously with her hands. Doors banged open on every side and a procession of servants streamed in, bearing tables and food. Musicians and jugglers mingled with the crowds as the servants rearranged the room for a feast. Kylar barely saw it. His eyes were latched on Terah Graesin.

Logan clapped him on the shoulder. "Well, that's that, huh?" Kylar didn't turn. "Come, Marquess Drake, tonight you sit at the high table."

45

$\mathcal{K}$ylar allowed Logan to usher him to a seat between a nattering forty-year-old third cousin of the Gunders, who was hoping to press a claim to the Gunder duchy, and Momma K, who was seated at Logan's right. She smiled at Kylar's open wonder.

"Don't tell me he got you a title, too," Kylar said.

"You forget, Kylar, I've been to more court functions than you have—although I admit, not many in the last decade. To the abiding fury of every eligible woman in the room, Duke Gyre chose to escort me this evening."

"Really?" Kylar asked, incredulous. Belatedly, Kylar remembered that Gwinvere Kirena had been the courtesan of an age, though she'd retired by the time Kylar knew her. She had doubtless escorted many of the lords in this very room to similar functions. He knew there had been a convenient fiction early in her career that Gwinvere was a visiting Alitaeran countess, but after a time, even that had been unnecessary. A woman as beautiful, as charming, as graceful a dancer, as skilled a singer, as adept a conversationalist, and as discreet as Gwinvere Kirena was the exception to many rules.

Momma K raised an eyebrow.

"Uh, sorry, I didn't mean . . ."

Logan came to his rescue, he said, "I asked her before anyone else could. I find there are so few beautiful women in this realm intelligent enough to form complete sentences."

"Yawp," Momma K said, in a perfect coastal Ceuran drawl. "Where's thet spittoon?"

Kylar laughed out loud. The truth was more likely that wearing mourning clothes and showing up with an older woman were the best ways Logan could fend off unwanted advances. If Logan had shown up with a young woman as his escort—or none at all—the matchmakers would have started in on him, mourning clothes or no mourning clothes. Kylar was still chuckling when he saw Terah Graesin, a few places beyond Logan, and his laughter died.

"Kylar?" Momma K asked. "Is something wrong?"

He shook himself. "I keep waiting for her head to explode." To his right, the nattering grasper gasped. He ignored her. He couldn't take his eyes off the queen. She drank. She leaned close to Lantano Garuwashi on her right and shared private observations. She jested with a lord at one of the lower tables who'd spilled his wine over his wife. She chatted with her brother who sat at her left. All the while, her death was waiting.

Kylar had expected it to explode soon after the crown was placed on her head, while she was still standing alone before the lords. Now, if he'd put too much philodunamos under her crown, he might kill others, too. Luc Graesin, though a relative innocent, wouldn't be much of a loss. But Lantano Garuwashi? Killing the legendary Ceuran would be disastrous.

"What I don't understand," Logan was saying to Momma K, "is why, out of all people, you are pushing Jarl's proposals." The name made Kylar pay attention.

"If I said it was because Jarl gave me hope, would you believe me?" Momma K asked.

A troubled look crossed Logan's face, and Kylar saw the old naive Logan briefly at battle with the Logan who'd spent months in the Hole. "I'd believe that was part of it," he said.

She smiled. "The fact is, Jarl's plans are not just good for the Rabbits—they're good for everyone. Do you know how much the average Rabbit spends when he visits a whorehouse?" She laughed at the look that crossed Logan's face. "I was being rhetorical, Your Grace. Three silver pieces. One on drink, two for the girl. I make one silver in profit. The average merchant buys wine, a meal, sometimes tobacco, sometimes riot weed, then a girl. I keep more than a crown in profit. And when nobles visit? Desserts, dancers, bards, jugglers, aperitifs, fine wines, plus other services you'd probably prefer I not mention. I take seven crowns in profit. So, if you were a cutthroat merchant queen, which would you choose?"

Logan's cheeks were pink, but he nodded. "Point taken." Kylar could barely believe his eyes. Logan, talking calmly about the economics of prostitution?

"The problem with how the people have looked at the Rabbits is that they see them as grubby, uncultured, and dangerous. I see them as potential customers."

"But you're not hurting for money. You own, what? half

of the, uh, houses of pleasure in this city?" Logan said. Momma K gave a feline smirk, and at that expression, Kylar realized that she didn't own half the city's brothels. She owned them all. "And I've heard you don't pay taxes, ever. Even if we were able to figure out exactly which magistrates in this city take bribes and which don't—" as Logan said it, Kylar realized Logan was speaking with the one woman in the city who *could* tell him—"if we removed them, you would suddenly have a raft of expenses you never had before. I can't imagine you'd come out ahead. If you were the city's most astute merchant, would you choose taxes or no taxes?"

"In the past twenty years, I've had nobles seize entire brothels no less than fifteen times. Banks I had an interest in have been seized ten times. I've lost sixty bouncers to nobles who resented being thrown out. In a particularly bad year, a certain high noble took a taste to killing whores, and I lost forty-three girls. When someone finally killed him, his father retaliated by burning six of my brothels to the ground, one of them with all of my employees locked inside." The coldness in Momma K's eyes was frightening. "So, while we can debate how many months without taxes pays for a seized brothel, ledger sheets can't explain what it is to find your young protégé has been kidnapped. They can't tell you what it is to live wondering how long it will be before the twist tires of her, and whether he will then kill her or release her. Your Grace, I have learned to use this city's corruption, but I shall not weep to see it destroyed."

Momma K's face was turned toward Logan, so Kylar couldn't read it, but her voice carried the ring of truth, and he heard depths to the stories that Logan couldn't know.

Momma K had been Shinga during all those atrocities. With all the Sa'kagé's resources, she could have brought her own justice to every case through men like Durzo Blint. But with every prostitute's death or ill-treatment, she had to decide if justice was worth the possible retaliation. After that nobleman had burned her brothels, Momma K could have sent a wetboy after him—but she'd have risked splitting apart the city in civil war. No wonder she'd turned into such a hard woman.

"I had no idea such things took place," Logan said.

Beyond him, Queen Graesin put a hand on her crown and adjusted it on her forehead. A bolt of lightning arced through Kylar, but nothing happened. He willed his muscles to relax and stabbed the untouched filet on his plate.

"The question is, is it possible?" Logan was saying. "I mean, building a few bridges over the Plith isn't going to change things. We'd be fighting against established interests."

"We ended slavery, and we did it without a war. The time is ripe. People have seen so much tumult in the last year that one more upheaval—if it gives them hope—could change everything. The Nocta Hemata showed the city that the Rabbits can be brave. Pavvil's Grove showed that they're willing to bleed for this country. Things can be made new."

Yes, as soon as the queen's head explodes.

There was something about the way she said "we ended slavery." She didn't mean we as in we, Cenaria. If she had become Shinga around the time Count Drake left the Sa'kagé, that meant she'd either been part of abolition movement, or she had decided not to oppose it despite the enormous profits it made for the Sa'kagé. She had to be

part of the reason Count Drake's enemies hadn't killed
him. Kylar wondered at her, this woman who had taught
him to read, who had championed him to Durzo, who had
helped end slavery and gave the guild rats a safe place
to stay in the winter. At the same time, she had ordered
dozens or even hundreds of kills. She had bribed magistrates, established dens of gambling and prostitution and
riot weed, extorted honest shop keepers, sprung crooks
from gaol, crushed her competitors by every means, and
enriched herself every step of the way. She was a fear-
some woman indeed. Kylar was glad that she'd always
liked him.

But none of these ideas would leave the ground while
Terah Graesin reigned. Yesterday she had sealed the Warrens. Tomorrow she was going to build new bridges?

Logan and Momma K continued their discussion, but
Kylar stopped listening and merely watched. Logan asked
piercing questions about the city's trades and economics,
who moved what, where merchants bought which goods,
what the tariffs were with different countries, how merchants avoided the more egregious taxes. That moved into
history and seamlessly into what they thought of the current state of the country, from who had been hurt worst by
the wars to who had cooperated with Khalidor and how
much of that would be held against them, to which lands
no longer had lords and who was pressing claims to them.
As Kylar watched, he realized that this must be what it
was like for a neophyte soldier to watch him fight. Logan
and Momma wove names and histories and connections
among nobles licit and illicit and business dealings and
rumors through their speech like masters of the loom.
Though Logan was clearly less experienced and had ac-

cess to only the licit half of the city's information, he still surprised Momma K from time to time with his analyses. And even as they were obviously engrossed in their own conversation, Logan took time to exchange pleasantries with Lantano Garuwashi at his left, who seemed intent on the queen anyway, and to make eye contact with the nobles at the lower tables who sought his glance, and thank the servers and even applaud the beaming new court bard who was terrifically talented even if he did look like a frog.

Beyond Logan, Terah Graesin was focused on her triumph, and enjoying it, accepting congratulations, drinking— dammit, poison would have worked—and flirting openly with both Lantano Garuwashi and her brother. There Kylar saw a microcosm of two reigns. Logan intent on bettering a country, Terah intent on herself.

And as the evening progressed, he realized that someone had cleaned the crown before the queen donned it. It put a decision Kylar had thought he'd already made back in his lap.

It was good to be with his friends. Here, at the high table, Kylar was suddenly legitimate, and no longer alone. He could stay here with the people he admired and loved. Momma K and Count Drake and Logan could be his companions for the rest of his life. He could find Elene and bring her back and give her this life. A life beyond the shadows. Maybe he didn't have to be the wolf in the cold.

Gods! He was immortal! Would it be so bad to let himself have one lifetime of happiness? Drake and Momma K had ended slavery while a corrupt king reigned. Surely between Logan and Count Drake and Kylar and Momma

K they could mitigate whatever damage a foolish queen did.

From the middle of the table, Queen Graesin caught Kylar staring at her. She winked.

As the feast ended, Queen Graesin stood and headed for one of the adjoining rooms arm in arm with Lantano Garuwashi. Lantano Garuwashi was graceful and intimidating in his broad, loose pants that draped like a skirt, and a silk shirt with starched tabs over his wide shoulders, leaving his heavily muscled arms bare. The rest of the high table stood next and Kylar moved to follow her. Logan put a hand on his arm and pulled a fat ring engraved with horses off a finger. "This is a symbol of your new office, Marquess." From a pocket, he produced another, much smaller signet ring shaped with what looked like tiny dragon. Kylar recognized it. "This is the ring of House Drake. Take them. There's life beyond the shadows."

Kylar had given his life before. He'd died to save the woman he loved. He'd died to get money to get out of Cenaria. He'd died for refusing Terah Graesin's contract on Logan. He'd died opposing the Godking. It had never been fun, but he'd begun to trust that he would come back. Every other death had cost him only the pain of dying. This death would cost him his life. He would have to leave forever. Start over completely in a far land. It would be like every one of his friends had died at the same time.

"You'll make a great king," Kylar said.

"How many men are you willing to kill for that idea?"

"It's not an idea. It's a dream. Now if you'll excuse me, Your Grace, the longer people see you talking with me, the more I will sully your reputation." Kylar turned and followed Terah Graesin into the next room.

"Your Grace," Momma K said, returning from mingling. "I think we should stay. I hear the new bard has composed a wonderful new song."

46

Quoglee Mars hadn't eaten. He would eat later, if at all, with the servants. But tonight, it didn't bother him. He wandered the tables and played whatever asinine music the threadbare nobles requested. He accepted their applause and moved on, eager to please the next batch of up-jumped plebeians.

After dinner, the castle was opened up and the tables spirited away so the nobles could mingle and have a chance to pay their respects and exchange a few words with the new queen. Entertainments had been spread through numerous rooms with desserts and liqueurs. Quoglee waited until the party had been going for a while before he mounted the platform where the high table had been. The guards who wandered the party had all wandered out, and several of the kingdom's more important nobles were in the room—and, most important, Queen Graesin wasn't.

Leaning his head down as if oblivious to them all, he began playing as only Quoglee Mars could play. For years, he knew, students of music would test their hand against this. Could they manage this overture in the time their tutors told them Quoglee Mars had played it? And some of them doubtless would crash through it with Quoglee's speed, and afterward, their tutors would tell them the difference between hitting notes and milking them.

Quoglee played impetuosity and youth, fervor and passion, sudden flares of anger, tempestuous, never slowing. Around that driving center, he wrapped sweetness, and love, and sorrow, pride against love, scaling higher and higher, with tragedy following a step behind.

Then, before the resolution, he stopped abruptly.

There was a moment of silence. The cretins were all looking at him, silent, expectant, not knowing if they could clap yet. He dipped his head, not even this perturbing him.

The applause was thunderous, but Quoglee held up a hand quickly, silencing it. The room held perhaps two hundred nobles, at least a hundred hangers-on, and dozens of servants. Miraculously, there were still no guards, and what speaking Quoglee had to do, he had to do without interference. "Today," he said in his stage voice, which carried better than a shout, "I wish to play something new that I've written for you, and all I ask is that you allow me to finish. This song was commissioned by someone you know, but someone who is more special than you know. It was, in fact, commissioned by the Shinga of your Sa'kagé. I swear every word of this song is true. I call it the Song of Secrets, and your Shinga wishes me to dedicate it to Queen Graesin."

*   *   *

"That's plenty far, Sergeant Gamble," Scarred Wrable said, stepping out of the shadows in a doorway that connected one of the side rooms with the Great Hall. With a practiced hand, he slid an arm between the sergeant's rich cloak and his back and cut through leather to bring the point of a dagger to rest against the man's spine. "There's nothing in there that interests you."

"What are you bastards doing in the Great Hall?"

"No theft, nor murder, and that's all you need to know, Sergeant."

"It's Commander Gamble now."

"It'll be the late Commander Gamble if you move that hand another inch."

"Ah. Point taken."

"In case you're thinking of raising an alarm, you might want to take a careful look around the room and tell me what you see."

Commander Gamble looked. Eight royal guards were in the room. Six of them were conversing individually with young male noblemen that the commander didn't recognize. The two others were stationed on either side of Queen Graesin and not talking to anyone, as they were commanded not to while guarding the queen. However, another group of three nobles near them did seem especially vigilant now that Commander Gamble studied them. He cursed aloud. He'd had no idea the Sa'kagé even had so many wetboys. "Let me guess that if anyone raises the alarm, you have orders."

"If you cooperate, not only will you and all these men live, but no one will blame you afterward. You might even keep your job."

"Why should I believe you?" Commander Gamble asked.

"Because I don't need to lie. I've got two dozen friends and a knife in your back."

Two dozen? Commander Gamble chewed on that for a moment. "Well then," he said. "Why don't we get a drink? I've got a special bottle—down in the kitchens."

Food paused, poised inches from open mouths, forgotten. Servants froze in the act of collecting glasses. For a moment, no one even breathed.

In a city of fatal secrets, Quoglee Mars had told everyone that he knew the greatest secret of them all. If that was the prequel to his song, what would his song hold?

Quoglee presided over the silence like the maestro he was, a smug smirk tugging at his lips. He judged the silence as if it were music, each beat of rest landing in perfect order. Then, a moment before the revelation could spark a firestorm of comment, he lifted one finger.

From the crowd, a woman's voice broke in a single high, clear note she held for impossibly long, and then, never pausing for a breath, it devolved into a plaintive run and finally words, decrying loneliness. All eyes turned to a barrel-chested soprano in ivory that no one recognized. As she sang, she strode through the crowd until she joined Quoglee on his platform. His voice joined hers, crossing and interweaving melodies, even as the words clashed, lovers singing of love and love denied.

From the corners of the room, the instruments, light viol and muscular bass and harp, played against the voices, but by the magic of music, each stood clear. The repetition

of the vocal pleas against the instrumental injunctions allowed the ear to follow one and then the next and the next.
Had it been speech, it would have been unintelligible. But
in music, every line was pellucid, individuated, stark in
its call. A sister's passion, a brother's confusion, youth
in turmoil, society frowning condemnation, secrets born in
the bedchambers of an exalted house. A woman defiant,
passionate, letting nothing stand in her way.

Though he didn't name them, Quoglee had taken no
pains to conceal the objects of his song, but as always,
some nobles caught on earlier than others. Those who understood couldn't believe what they were hearing. They
searched the room for guards, sure that someone must stop
this beautiful outrage. But no guard was at his post. The
Sa'kagé had chosen this night to unveil its power. There
was no way this could be an accident. This room, which
held two hundred of the kingdom's elite, now swelling
ever more as the curious came to see what held everyone transfixed, was normally protected by at least a dozen
of the Queen's Guard. Quoglee sang treason, and no one
stopped him. The beauty of the music and the seduction of
a rumor held the nobles in a spell. It was Quoglee's mas-
terpiece. No one had ever heard such music. The strings
warred with each other, and the forbidden love warred
with itself, the music claiming this twisted love was love
indeed, even as the boy twisted against his conscience and
the woman demanded her rights as a beloved.

Then, as they sang, finally in harmony, having declared
an armistice, surrendering to a forbidden love which must
remain secret, a new voice joined the fray. A young soprano, lean, in a simple white dress joined Quoglee and
the mezzo soprano, singing notes of such purity they tore

the heart. In her innocence, she stumbled upon a secret that would wreck a royal house.

The brother never knew. The elder sister saw all she had, all she desired, threatened by her own sister, and in her conflicted heart, she hatched a desperate plan.

Unnoticed by the rapt nobles, a young man had entered the chamber only moments after the first notes sounded. Luc Graesin made no move to silence Quoglee Mars. From the back of the room, he only listened.

The voice of Natassa Graesin spiraled into the Hole, betrayed by her own blood, murdered. She wailed, her voice discordant, fading into oblivion, her life a sacrifice to a perversion. The music played the matching leitmotifs of fatal secrets and Cenaria once again.

"Nooo!" Luc Graesin screamed.

The musicians cut off the last, lingering notes in shock. Luc burst through the doors, fleeing. No one followed.

47

Seeing Count Drake, Kylar slipped through Queen Graesin's entourage, but for once the casual invisibility of or-
dinariness failed him. A woman's hand touched his elbow.
He turned and found himself staring into Terah Graesin's
eyes. Those deep green Graesin eyes were breathtaking,
especially as Kylar involuntarily stared deeper.

In another place, another time, born to different parents,
Terah Graesin's evils would have been meaningless, for
she was merely obliviously selfish. She had desires, and
others existed to fulfill them. Her betrayals were casual
because she barely gave them a thought. Had she been
born a miller's daughter, the damage she did would have
been confined to jilted lovers and cheated customers.

"I thought Logan and Rimbold had told me everything
about you, Kylar Drake, but they could have warned me
how handsome you are," Terah said, flashing white teeth
that somehow reminded Kylar of a shark.

For some reason, the comment flustered Kylar. He'd
always considered himself very average-looking, but

looking into her eyes, he knew—knew—that she meant what she said, even if she was saying it aloud to flatter him. He blinked and began blushing and whatever it was that made him see into Terah faltered and disappeared. She chuckled, and it was a low, acquisitive sound.

"And such beautiful eyes," she said. "You've got eyes that make a girl think you can see right through her."

"I can," he said.

"Is that why you're blushing?"

That, of course, made him blush harder. He glanced back to Terah's ladies-in-waiting. They had dropped back. Apparently they knew that when Terah approached a man she wished to do so alone, but they were laughing prettily, no doubt at his expense. He caught a glimpse of one of them who didn't seem to be enjoying the comments, but then he lost her.

"Tell me, marquess, what do you see when you look in my eyes?" Terah asked.

"It would be highly indiscreet for me to say, Your Highness," Kylar said.

For an instant, her eyes filled with hunger. "Marquess," she said gravely, "a man risks his tongue for speaking indiscreetly to a queen."

"Tongues should be used to commit indiscretions, not to discuss them."

Terah Graesin gasped. "Marquess! You'll have me blushing."

"I'd be content with having you."

Her eyes dilated, then she pretended to cool. "Marquess Drake, I consider it my duty to know the nobles who serve me. You will attend me in my chambers."

"Yes, Your Highness."

Her voice softened. "Wait ten minutes. The guards will allow you through the door. I expect your . . . discretion." He nodded, smirking, and she paused. "Have we met? There's something about you that seems so familiar."

"Actually, we did meet once." During the coup. "I'm sorry I didn't make more of an impression on you." Six inches into your heart would have been about right.

"Well, we'll remedy that."

"Indeed."

She slipped away and Kylar saw Lantano Garuwashi fifteen paces away, staring at him. Kylar's throat constricted, but though he didn't look pleased, Garuwashi made no move toward him. Kylar looked around the room blankly, forgetting why he'd come in here in the first place. A girl broke away from Terah Graesin's circle and whispered to the guards at one of the doors. She turned. His eyes took in the large eyes, perfectly coifed hair, clear skin, full lips, narrow waist, and lean, firm curves. It was Ilena Drake. She was one of the queen's handmaidens. Kylar had the sense of dislocation. He'd looked away from a little girl for a moment and found a woman in her place. Ilena Drake was stunning. As she pointed him out to the guards to tell them to let him through to see the queen, her eyes suddenly met his. Her face was a mask of disappointment and disgust.

She thought she was being used to help her big brother cheat on her friend, Elene. She thought he'd become a marquess and was so enrapt by the idea of bedding a queen that he'd left everything else behind. Worse than the anger was the monumental disappointment in her eyes. Until now, Kylar could do no wrong in Ilena's eyes. He had been the slam. Until now.

Queen Graesin, having made her excuses, left the room. Kylar turned away.

Rimbold Drake disengaged from a conversation and was limping toward Kylar, leaning on his cane. His eyes went from Kylar's face to his hands, and the rings that weren't there.

"She's beautiful," Kylar said.

"She looks like her mother Ulana did twenty years ago. Albeit with more fire," the Count said, proud despite his grief. Ulana Drake had been as much of a mother to Kylar as he had allowed. She had been a woman unfailingly graceful. She had seemed to grow only more beautiful as the years had passed. Kylar told the Drake as much.

The Count's jaw tightened, and he closed his eyes, mastering himself. A few moments later, he said, "It's enough to tempt a man to curse God." His eyes were stony.

Kylar opened his mouth to ask a question, then closed it. In the next room, through the crowd listening to the bard, he saw a gorgeous blond in a blue silk dress cut so low in back it barely covered her butt. Kylar's breath caught. For a mad moment, he thought it was Elene. Damn guilty conscience. Daydra and her perfect ass moved deeper into the crowd as if looking for someone. *And you told me you gave up working the sheets.*

Drake seemed to come back to himself. He cocked an eyebrow at Kylar. "Yes?"

Coming back to himself, Kylar realized another good reason to keep his mouth shut. "Nothing."

"Kylar, you're my son—or can be, if you say the word. I give you permission to be tactless."

Kylar wrestled with that. "I wondered if it's harder for you when this shit happens. Sorry. I mean, I think what happened with Serah and Mags and Ulana is awful and senseless, but I don't expect the world to make sense. I wondered if it was harder for you, since you think there's a God out there who could have stopped it but didn't."

Count Drake frowned, pensive. "Kylar, in the crucible of tragedy, explanations fail. When you stand before a tragedy and tell yourself that there is no sense to it, doesn't your heart break? I think that must be as hard for you as it is for me when I scream at God and demand to know why—and he says nothing. We will both survive this, Kylar. The difference is, on the other side I will have hope."

"A naive hope."

"Show me the happy man who dares not hope," Drake said.

"Show me the brave man who dares not face the truth."

"You think I'm a coward?"

Kylar was horrified, "I didn't mean—"

"I'm sorry," the Count said. "That wasn't fair. But come, if she's following the usual routine, Her Highness will be expecting you soon."

Kylar gulped. Drake knew? "Actually, I uh, did kind of want to ask. . . . How much do you know about my gifts?"

"Is this the place to speak about that?" Drake asked.

"It's the time," Kylar said. There were three men, six women, and two servants eyeing him. Of those, only one servant—certainly a spy, though whose was anyone's guess—was within earshot, and he couldn't remain within it for long without rousing suspicions. Kylar caught the man's eye and the force of his stare sent the servant scurrying for another plate of canapés. "I see guilt," he said quietly. "Not always, but sometimes. Sometimes I can even tell what a man did."

Count Drake blanched. "The Sa'kagé would kill for such a power." He raised a hand to forestall Kylar's protest. "But given that you're not interested in blackmail, to me it sounds like a terrible burden."

Kylar hadn't thought of it that way. "What I want to know is what it means. Why would I have such a power, or gift, or curse? Why would the God do such a thing?"

"Ah, I see. You're hoping I can give you some kind of justification for regicide."

Kylar glared bloody daggers at the spy returning with a full platter of hors d'oeuvres. The man abruptly changed course, nearly dropping the platter. "The existence of such an ability suggests something about my purpose, doesn't it?"

Drake looked pensive again. "That depends on what you see. Do you see crime, or sin, or simply feelings of guilt? If crime, do you see all crimes from murder to setting up a market stand without permission? If you're in another country where an action that's illegal here isn't illegal, will a man crossing the border look different? If you see sin, you'll have to figure out whose definitions of sin apply, because I guarantee that my God and the hundred gods don't agree, or even Astara with Ishara. If what you see is feelings of guilt, does the madman without a conscience appear cleaner than the girl who believes that her parents died in an accident because she lied about finishing her chores?"

"Shit," Kylar said. "How come everyone I know is smarter than me? Whatever it is, I see the unclean. I want to know if that implies that I have a duty to do something about what I see."

"Trying to derive ought from is, are you?" Drake asked, smirking.

"What?"

"She may deserve to die, Kylar, but you shouldn't kill her."

"Everyone will be better off if I do."

"Except you, and me, and my daughter, and Logan, and Momma K, and everyone who loves you."

"What do you mean?" Kylar was caught off guard.

"Logan will put you to death, and losing you will hurt us deeply."

Kylar snorted. Some loss. "Sir, thank you for everything you've done for me, and everything you tried to do. I'm sorry I cost you so much."

Count Drake bowed his head and closed his eyes, leaning heavily on his cane. "Kylar, I've lost my wife and two daughters this year. I don't know if I can bear to lose a son."

Kylar squeezed the man's shoulder, marveling how fragile it felt. He looked into the count's eyes. "Just so you know," Kylar said, "you pass."

"I what?"

Kylar gave the man who'd once single-handedly introduced and abolished slavery in Cenaria a lopsided grin. "Whatever I see—guilt or whatever—you don't have it. You're clean."

A look of stunned disbelief shot across Drake's face, followed by something akin to awe. He stood transfixed.

"May your God bless you, sir. You certainly deserve it."

48

Dorian and Jenine were sitting together in the garden. He had dismissed his retainers, and for a time, they had sat without speaking. "I'm sorry I killed that Vürdmeister," Dorian said.

Jenine looked up, surprised. "Why? Because it upset me, or because it was the wrong?"

After a moment, Dorian said, "I could have dealt with him in a manner less . . . brutal."

"He was responsible for those aethelings, wasn't he?"

"Yes," Dorian said.

Jenine plucked a red flower with six petals, each bearing a purple starburst. Khalidorans considered a blooming starflower an omen of great good luck, because they bloomed only once every seven years. Conversely, a dead starflower was the worst luck. In this garden, they bloomed constantly, but each bloom would die within hours of being plucked. The vir was not good at sustaining life.

After regarding the flower in her fingers for a long

minute, Jenine said quietly, "Milord, I'm sure you know
that my father was a fool. What most people don't know
is that my mother was brilliant. My father feared her, and
he tried to marginalize her so she wouldn't grow more
powerful than he was. She knew it, and she let him because she didn't care to turn her mind to politics. It was
too rough, too dirty, too *brutal* for her. My father made a
thousand mistakes in ruling, but my mother's might have
been bigger because she chose not to rule. I lost the man
I love, a man who would have been a great king, because
of that. So I'm not going to turn away because ruling is
messy. My people will deserve better of me. Nor will I
settle for the soft hypocrisy of criticizing you as you face
threats I can barely imagine."

"I don't want to rule simply because I enjoy power.
If it's for that, then it's for nothing. I want to undo everything that my father and his fathers have made of this
country. I don't know if I can do it. I don't know if it can
be done."

A quick scowl passed across her face, but she didn't
speak for a few seconds. Dorian waited. Finally, she said,
"Milord, I see you usually being so decisive, so strong,
and then the next moment, you're in here, apologizing to
me for something you had to do. Maybe you could have
done it differently, but so what? There was an immediate
threat and you dealt with it. I'm trying to tell you that
you don't need to be weak for me. I've seen enough weak
men in my life. I guess my question is—and it's probably
the same question your people have—are you going to be
king, or are you just trying to stay alive until you can run
away?"

Her words caught him. He hadn't once thought of

himself growing old as Godking. Had that been because he couldn't remember even a fragment of prophecy with himself as an old Godking, or because he'd been afraid to throw in his lot wholeheartedly with this land? He hadn't thought about how things would be even a year from now. In thinking for such a short term, he'd ignored problems. He hadn't done anything to seal the highland tribes to him. He hadn't moved against Neph. He hadn't moved against the aethelings. If Jenine saw his hesitation as weakness, how many others did, too?

"I am king," Dorian said. "And I will be until the end of my life, however long that may be."

"Then rule as you must to be king."

"Do you have any idea what that means? Here, with these people?" Dorian asked.

"No," she admitted. "But I trust you."

Dorian had thought of Jenine as naive. But he'd been wrong. Jenine was inexperienced. There was a difference. And she might well yet be horrified by what experience taught, but her eyes were open. Nor did she have an over-flow of sympathy for the people who had killed her husband and her entire family. But a monarch had to be hard, didn't he?

Nodding as Jenine rose to go make more preparations for their wedding, distracted by his own thoughts, Dorian reached out with his Talent to lay a small weave on the starflower to preserve it. It was a simple weave and could make even the most delicate flower last a month. But Dorian had forgotten how much vir had been used in growing the flower. Vir and Talent touched and warred and the flower turned black and limp in Jenine's hands.

Dorian cursed. "I'm sorry, milady. You've given me

much to consider. You are wise beyond your years. Thank you." He plucked another starflower and wrapped it in vir for Jenine. It would last a few days, but then he'd simply pick another.

The royal guards let Kylar pass without comment. Ilena Drake stood near the door, arms folded under her breasts. "I'm sorry," Kylar told her.

"How could you do this to Elene?" she asked.

He walked past her and strode through quiet corridors, up the stairs to the queen's apartments in a fog. The ka'kari flicked out of his hand into the form of a dagger, then sucked back in. Out, in, out, in. Was it always this simple for Vi? Some flirtation, a little innuendo, and your deader isolated herself, arranged your entry, and helped keep your presence secret? After the lengths to which Kylar had gone for some kills, walking in an unlocked door seemed like cheating. The guards hadn't even taken the dagger from his belt.

Leaning against the door frame, he breathed deeply. He'd seen so much death in this place. Terah Graesin's room was Garoth Ursuul's old room. There had been statues of dead girls in the room bare weeks ago. What had they done with those statues of flesh made stony? If he ever found Trudana Jadwin, he would make Hu Gibbet look kind.

Such bloody, bloody thoughts. Kylar knocked.

There was the scuffing of bare feet on marble, and then Terah Graesin opened the door. Kylar was surprised she was still fully clothed. She stepped close and kissed him softly, luxuriously, their only contact in their lips. She moved slowly backward, sucking on his lower lip. He followed, letting her take the lead. She closed the door and stepped into his embrace.

"We'll have to be quick," she said, in between kisses on his neck. "I can't miss my own party, but if your tongue is half as talented as you suggest, I guarantee to reciprocate very soon." She giggled wickedly.

What surprised Kylar was how easy it was. Terah was taller than Elene, and her lips not as full, but teasing her was the same. He traced fingertips down the backs of her arms, then, feigning growing passion, slid one hand to the back of her neck and the other to soft curve of her buttock. From the interplay of starched stiffness and yielding flesh, he could tell she'd removed her undergarments.

He lifted an eyebrow and she giggled again. "Like I said, quick and clean. Later we can do long and dirty."

You poor bitch, you don't even know what this is. What was he doing? Why didn't he end this sad farce? *Finish the job, Kylar.*

Kylar closed his eyes as Terah pushed him onto the bed, but as soon as he did, he imagined Vi standing beside the bed. She looked pissed. Kylar's eyes flew open as Terah crawled over him. She tugged her neckline down. "Kiss me," she said.

Vi seemed to be standing right there, her eyes flaming, daring Kylar to do it and feel her wrath. The image made no sense, but that didn't make it any less powerful.

Terah made a pouting sound and tugged her dress lower, brushing her bare breast against Kylar's face. His ear felt suddenly hot. Sickness and revulsion washed through him. His stomach cramped.

There was a wordless scream of animal rage from the

doorway. Kylar blinked his eyes furiously, trying to clear away the black spots swimming in front of them. Terah barely sat up before a body collided with her, knocking her off of Kylar.

Kylar fell off the bed and staggered to his feet. As his vision cleared, he saw Luc Graesin on top of his sister, pummeling her with his fists and screaming obscenities. Finally, his chest heaving, Luc pulled himself off of her. "You killed Natassa," he said, drawing a short dagger from his belt. "You killed our sister."

"No," Terah said. "I swear." Blood was pouring from a gash across her eyebrow and her lips were fat and bloodied from Luc's fist.

The last piece of darkness Kylar had seen in Terah's eyes fell into place. "She sent a messenger to the God-king," Kylar said, "telling him Natassa was traveling to Havermere, and she arranged for there to only be two guards with her."

Terah gaped, but Luc's eyes never left her face. The guilt written there was plain. "I did it for us. She was going to betray us! For the gods' sake, help me, Kylar," Terah begged.

It was a mistake. She could have faced Luc down. The last thing she should have done was remind him of the other man she'd been about to fuck. Luc screamed again and stabbed her in the stomach. She shrieked and Luc cowered back, then attacked again, gashing her arm as she lurched to her feet. He stabbed at her back as she ran to a wall, caught the ribbing of her dress and dropped the dagger.

Terah found a bellrope and yanked on it over and over.

Luc picked up the bloody dagger and walked toward her, his face a mask of grief and rage, weeping and cursing. He stood in front of his sister as she collapsed on the floor. Kylar wondered if Luc saw what he saw. Terah Graesin without power, without the hauteur, was a pitiful shadow. She hunched into the corner, blubbering. "Please, Luc, please. I love you. I'm sorry. I'm so sorry."

Perhaps Luc did see the same thing as Kylar, because he stopped, paralyzed. He still held the dagger, but Kylar knew that he wouldn't use it now.

Terah's wounds weren't fatal, Kylar was certain of that, especially not with a green maja in the castle. Terah would recover, and she would owe the Chantry an enormous debt. She would put her brother to death and she would capitalize on people's sympathy for her to move against her enemies real or imagined. Poor Luc Graesin. The weak bastard wasn't even eighteen yet.

Kylar slapped the young man, hard, and plucked the dagger from his hands. Luc fell. "Look at me," Kylar told him.

The Royal Guards were on their way. They might arrive any moment. Kylar could cut Terah's throat, knock Luc senseless, climb out the window, and rejoin the party. Luc would be beheaded for treason and murder and Logan would be made king. Doubtless, whoever had told Luc about Natassa's betrayal intended exactly that.

Luc met his eyes and Kylar weighed the young man's soul.

Kylar cursed loudly. "You're no killer, Luc Graesin. You marched right up here, didn't you? Walked past a dozen witnesses? I thought so."

"What are you doing?" Terah demanded. "Help me."

Kylar looked into Luc's eyes again and saw a young man bound in chains not of his own making. Luc was no saint, nor purely a victim, but he didn't deserve death.

"Tell me one thing," Kylar said. "If you could take the throne, would you?"

"Hell no," Luc said.

He was telling the truth. "Then I give you these, Luc: first, knowledge: you're no killer. These wounds won't kill your sister. Second, your life. Make something of it. Third, I spare you a sight that would never leave you."

"What?" Luc asked.

Kylar punched him in the forehead. Luc dropped like a stone. Kylar rubbed Luc's bloody hands against his own. He cut Luc's tunic in two places with the dagger and finally stabbed him in the meat of his shoulder, shallowly.

Terah was aghast. "What are you doing?"

Kylar drew the mask of judgment over his face. "I've come for you, Terah." He let the ka'kari sink back into his skin.

She screamed. He grabbed a fistful of hair and pulled her to her feet. He planted the dagger in her shoulder, and with his right hand free, pressed it against her wounded stomach to get it bloody. He wiped the blood on both sides of his face and pulled the dagger out of her shoulder. He stood behind her, using her body as a shield between him and the door. She was begging, screaming, cursing, weeping, but Kylar barely heard her. He sighed and when he inhaled, he smelled her hair. It smelled of youth and promise.

There was the sound of jingling armor and heavy foot-steps pounding up the hall. A dozen Royal Guards burst into the room, bristling with weaponry. Behind them

Logan Gyre and Duke Wesseros and their guards pushed into the room. In seconds, they'd formed a half circle around Kylar and the queen. Dozens of weapons were leveled at Kylar.

"Put it down!" a royal guard yelled. "Put it down now!"

"Help me. Please," Terah begged.

"By the gods, Kylar," Logan shouted. "Don't do this. Please!"

For the job, it was perfect. Now dozens of witnesses had seen Logan command Kylar to stop. There remained only one thing. Kylar painted a desperate expression on his face. "Luc tried to stop me, and he couldn't," Kylar raved. "And you can't either!"

Kylar slashed the dagger through Terah Graesin's throat, and all the world screamed.

49

"Mother," Kaede said, coming into the study, "how are the wedding preparations coming?"

Daune Wariyamo raised her eyes from the papers spread all over her desk. She loved lists. "Our responsibilities are well in hand. Everyone has been informed of their precedence and the expected protocols. I only worry about Oshobi's mother. I'd say she has the brain of a hummingbird, except hummingbirds can hover for a moment or two. I expect the Takedas' half of the ceremony to be an unmitigated disaster." She pulled off her pince nez. "I heard some lunatic arrived, claiming to be a Tofusin."

A Tofusin, she said. As if there were more than one.

"He's nothing. Some white-haired freak," Kaede said, waving it away. "Mother, I want your opinion. An insult's been done to our family honor that may be on some people's minds as we go into this wedding, so I think I have to deal with it now. One of the cousins cuckolded her husband. She swears it was long ago and brief, but its effects continue. What should I do?"

Daune Wariyamo scrunched her eyebrows, as if the answer were so obvious that Kaede was stupid for asking. "A slut can not be tolerated, Kaede. A whore dishonors us all."

"Very well. I'll see it taken care of."

"Who is it?"

"Mother," Kaede said quietly, "I'm going to ask you a question, and if you lie to me, the consequences will be harsher than you can believe."

"Kaede! Is this how you to speak to your mother—"

"None of that, mother. What—"

"Your tone is so disrespectful, I—"

"Silence!" Kaede shouted.

Daune Wariyamo was too stunned for the moment to begin the usual tactics.

"Did you or did you not intercept letters that Solon sent to me?" Kaede asked.

Daune Wariyamo blinked rapidly, then said, "Of course I did."

"For how long?" Kaede asked.

"I don't remember."

"How long?" Kaede asked, her voice dangerous.

The empress's mother said nothing for a long moment. Then she said, "Years. Letters came every month, sometimes more often."

"Every week?"

"I suppose."

"What did you do with them, mother?"

"That Solon was worse than his brother."

"Don't you ever speak to me of that monster. Where are the letters?"

"They were a tissue of lies. I burned them."

"When did he stop sending them?" Kaede asked.

Her mother's expression went blank for a moment, then she said, "I don't know, ten years ago?"

"He didn't stop, did he? Don't you dare lie to me, by the gods, don't you dare."

"It's only a few times a year now. For all I knew, it was some impostor, hoping to break your heart again, Kae. Don't let this stranger ruin everything. Even if it is Solon, you don't know him. If you postpone this wedding, it could mean the end of you. Harvest is the only time for a queen to marry, and if you delay, the seas will be impassable. The lords from the other isles won't be able to attend. You need this. We can't offend the Takedas again."

Clan Takeda had been a thorn in Kaede's side since she'd taken the throne. They had angled and manipulated for years for this wedding, and if as a younger woman she had sworn she would never marry Oshobi, now she knew there was no other way. "Mother, is there anything else you haven't told me? Anything you want to confess?"

"Of course not—"

Kaede held up a finger. "I want you to think very carefully. You're not as good a liar as you believe."

Her mother hesitated, but the look on her face was that of a woman aggrieved that she could be suspect. "There's nothing."

Kaede had been wrong. Her mother was an excellent liar. Kaede turned to a guard. "Summon my secretary and the chamberlain."

"Kae, what are you doing?" Daune asked.

The officials stepped into the room in moments. Kaede had had them waiting outside. "Mother, the woman you called a slut and a whore is you. You betrayed my father and dishonored us."

"No! I never—"

"Did you expect to get away with it? You fornicated with an emperor—a man surrounded by bodyguards and slaves at all hours, and you the lady of a high house, with bodyguards and slaves of your own. Did you think no one would notice?"

There was real fear in Daune Wariyamo's face for the first time Kaede had ever seen. "It didn't mean anything, Kae."

"Until you got pregnant and didn't know who the father was."

Daune Wariyamo stood transfixed, as if she couldn't believe all of her secrets had yielded their rotten fruit on the same day. Around the room, officials and guards stood with mouths agape, barely daring to breathe.

"I wondered for years, Mother, why a woman so ambitious wouldn't want me to have anything to do with Prince Solon. It's because you were afraid he was my brother. You were afraid that your whoring would lead me, innocently, to an incestuous bed. Apparently your sense of honor is only diseased rather than nonexistent."

Tears were rolling down Daune's cheeks. "Kaede, I was young. He said he loved me."

"Did you believe the green mages when they examined me? I had no idea why at the time, I was only nine years old—too young to be showing Talent yet. They found out that I was a Wariyamo, didn't they? Weren't you relieved?"

"For a while. When Solon came home, a full blue mage at nineteen, he asked to see me secretly. That's when I knew. He tried to be so subtle, swearing how he would never hurt you, but under it all, there were threats, Kaede. What would happen when he got tired of you? What if I ever vexed him? He could destroy me with a word. I would be his slave for the rest of my life. What if you opposed him? He could lie, say the mages proved you were illegitimate. He was a mage himself; everyone would believe it. We'd lose everything. Our only hope was to keep him away from us. It wasn't like I was hurting him. I even got him an offer for more schooling at Sho'cendi, which was a high honor."

Kaede's face relaxed despite her fury. The decision had been made. The truth was out. Now there was room for sorrow. "So you ruined my chances of happiness because you couldn't believe that the man I loved would keep his word?"

"I was protecting us. No one's as good as they pretend to be," Daune said.

"True in your case," Kaede said. She turned. "Secretary Tayabusa, please record that the queen mother is henceforth stripped of all privileges and titles. She is banished from all the isles and territories of Seth, and if found on them after tomorrow, the penalty will be death. At dawn, Chamberlain Inyouye, you will have her accompanied to the harbor. You will pay her passage to whatever port she chooses. You will give her ten thousand yass, and make sure that she leaves. She may be accompanied by one servant if one can be found who volunteers to accompany her."

Everyone was stunned.

"Mother," Kaede said, "if this were the first time you'd lied to me, I wouldn't do this. It is, however, the last time.

Guards, I wish two of you to stay with her at all times. I doubt she will attempt to harm herself, but she has shown herself to be an adulteress and a liar. I don't expect theft is below her."

"You can't do this," Daune said, breathing so rapidly Kaede expected her to pass out.

"I already have."

"I'm your mother!"

Kaede stepped forward and put her hands on each side of her mother's face. She kissed her forehead. She took hold of the six platinum chains strung between her mother's cheek and ear and tore them out. Daune screamed, her ear torn to ribbons, her cheek dribbling blood.

Kaede said, "No, you are Queen Mother no more. You are Daune Wariyamo no more. Henceforth, you are Daune Outcast. Guards?"

The captain of the guard and his second stepped forward and took the outcast by each arm to lead her from the room.

"Kae! Kaede, please!"

"Captain," Kaede said as the guards neared the door, almost dragging their prisoner. "About what happened here . . ."

The captain looked quickly at each of his men. "You can be assured of my men's complete discretion, Your Majesty."

Secretary Tayabusa cleared his throat. "And I have written down the names of everyone in this room. If anyone speaks of this, they will be discovered and punished accordingly." He leveled a heavy gaze at each of the various servants and functionaries in turn.

"On the contrary," Kaede said, "no one will be punished

for speaking of what happened here. My dead mother shamed my family, and I will not grant her the mercy of covering her deeds in silence. Most of all, my betrothed and his family deserve to know the truth before they wed their honor to mine."

If the Takedas went ahead with the marriage obviously knowing the truth, they would have a harder time destroying her than if she married and then they "found out" about her shameful secret. Other than that, there were few things the Takedas could do. A coup was doubtful, despite Oshobi's popularity among the city guard. The Takedas' postponing the marriage until spring was most likely, and that would give her time. Time might give her opportunities. Best for her personally and worst for Seth, the Takedas might cancel the wedding and withdraw to their home island. That would mean they would come back in the spring for war.

At sunrise, Vi swung her feet over the side of her bed in her little room. She'd barely slept after leaving Sister Ariel, and she'd had horrible dreams about Kylar and oceans of blood. Maybe it was an omen. She was supposed to meet Elene this morning, first thing. She touched the water basin. "Cold," she said. When ice crystals began to spider across the surface, she broke the ice and washed her face, gasping despite herself. In minutes she finished her ablutions and pulled the ill-fitting tyro's robe over her ill-fitting shift. Vi tied back her hair with the white ribbons Sister Ariel had given her.

She heard the familiar scuff of Sister Ariel's steps before the Sister knocked on her door and came in without waiting for permission.

"You're up," Sister Ariel said, surprised. "You're going to see her?"

"She's up in the pommel of the Seraph's sword?" Vi asked.

"Praying still, Uly says. Vi," Sister Ariel paused. "You're one of us now. The Seraph will pay your debts. If you need to, you can offer her whatever it takes."

"I don't think she's looking for a bribe," Vi said.

"Nor do I." Sister Ariel paused again. "I expected I'd have to force you to go to her, Vi. The girl you used to be would never have done this. Well done."

Perfect, now it was impossible to back down.

Vi found the central staircase and began climbing. She was only a few floors up when the stones pulsed gently as they did every dawn. She paused on a landing as nearly invisible trickles of dust joined together into rivulets. They rushed past her feet as a small hole opened in the wall. The single day's accumulation of dust slipped through and the hole closed. Everywhere in the Seraph, the scene was repeated. Powered by the first rays of sunlight, all natural dirt was whisked away. Outside, the Seraph would appear to be briefly surrounded by a corona as magic repulsed dirt, grime, rain, or snow. The debris would cascade into the lake and there be dispersed by magic that kept the waters around the Seraph even cleaner than the rest of Lake Vestacchi.

There were, of course, still plenty of chores for the tyros. The magic was disengaged in any room where it might interfere with a Sister's experiments or sensitive artifacts, and it disregarded scraps of parchment, clothes, or anything else someone might leave on the floor. But without the magic, the tyros could have worked constantly and never been able to keep the Chantry clean. It was simply too big.

Vi reached one of the upper floors where full Sisters had their apartments. There was some pecking order to who had what floor and which Sisters got the treasured southern exposures, but Vi had no idea how it worked. Mercifully, no one was in the hall. Vi followed the un-flickering lamps to the southwest corner. The Seraph held a sword in her left hand, its point at her feet, the hilt coming above her waist, held slightly to one side. The pommel of that giant sword was capped with a round jewel. The room was a globe from which Sisters could see sunrise and sunset. The walls were always transparent. It was a sanctuary for those who needed to meditate or, as in Elene's case, pray.

Taking a deep breath, Vi opened the door. Elene was seated, looking toward the eastern mountains. The view was breathtaking. Vi had never been so high in her life. The punts in the lake below looked the size of her thumb. The mountains glowed. The sun was a jagged half-circle barely peeking over them. But Vi's eyes sought out Elene's face. Her skin glowed in the gentle light, her eyes deep brown, her scars softened. She gestured for Vi to come stand with her, not glancing away from the horizon.

Tentatively, Vi stepped up beside her. Together, they watched the sun rise.

Not daring to turn and look Elene in the face, but not able to wait another moment, Vi said, "I'm sorry if I interrupted your prayers." She drew her knife and rested it across her palms. "I made you a promise. I've done you and Kylar a great wrong. If you wish . . . I deserve no less."

Elene took the knife. After a minute, she said, "His mercies are new every morning."

Vi blinked. She glanced over at Elene and saw a tear tracking down her cheek. "Uh, whose?"

"The One God's. If he forgives you, how dare I not?"

What?

Elene took Vi's right hand with her left. Then she stood, shoulder to shoulder with her, looking at the newborn sun. She held Vi's hand firmly, but with nothing vindictive or tense in her grip. There was an aura about her of tremendous peace, peace so thick it slowly calmed Vi's taut nerves.

After a few minutes, Elene turned to her. Vi was surprised to find herself brave enough to meet the woman's eyes.

"I believe the God has a purpose for me, Vi. I don't know what it is, but I know it isn't murdering you." Elene threw the knife aside. "We're in a big mess, but we're in it together. All right?"

50

$\mathcal{V}$ürdmeister Neph Dada sat beneath an oak at the mouth of Quorig's Pass, awaiting his spy. He hadn't brought any of the two hundred Vürdmeisters he'd gathered to the meeting. If his spy was caught, he didn't want her to be able to tell the Chantry anything useful. Of course, the catatonic Tenser Ursuul and Khali had traveled with him, and he kept them close—but hidden.

Eris Buel arrived at moonrise. She was not an attractive woman. Her eyes were close-set, her nose long, and her chin weak. She looked rather like a rat in makeup. Too much makeup at that. And she had moles. Everywhere. Garoth Ursuul had long let it be known that his female progeny were worthless to him except as killing practice for the aethelings. It was half true. Most of the girls served to weed out boys too weak to murder their own sisters, but Garoth sent wytchborn girls away at birth.

Few became as valuable as Eris Buel. Years ago, Garoth learned that Eris had roused the Speaker's suspicions. Rather than lose her, Garoth had shipped her off to Alitaera and arranged her marriage to a nobleman. Eris had then caught the crest of a rising tide of resentment among the Chattel, the former magae who'd left the Chantry to marry. She was now poised to head that movement back to the Chantry, demanding recognition. Eris might even overthrow the Speaker.

"Eris," Neph said, dipping his head.

"Vürdmeister." Eris liked to think too highly of herself, but she could obviously feel the nearness of Khali. That was enough to put anyone off-balance.

"I have a task for you," Neph said. "One of our spies tells me a woman named Viridiana Sovari has bonded a man with a set of compulsive earrings. Given the bond, we expect he will come to the Chantry soon."

"I know the girl. She's the talk of the Chantry," Eris said.

"She doesn't matter. Let me be blunt. This man, Kylar, may hold Curoch. We've hired an extremely skilled thief to take it from him. We have reasons to trust our thief, but Kylar is very resourceful. He may track our man down. So as soon as our man steals the sword, he'll signal you by raising two black flags on a fishing boat visible from your room in the Chantry. Check three times a day. When you see it, collect the sword and leave the city immediately. The thief is not to see your face or know anything about you, just as you know nothing about him. You'll pay him. He knows how much to expect." Neph handed her a purse full of Alitaeran gold. She looked startled at the weight.

Neph was lying to her, of course. He did believe that Kylar had briefly held Curoch, but he'd also seen how Ezra's Wood changed on the day that Vürdmeister Borsini had gone to his death, trying to take Curoch from Kylar. The Sword of Power was gone; once something went into the Wood, it stayed there.

What Neph's thief was trying to steal was a normal sword, with one difference: it had been reported to Neph that Kylar's sword had a black blade. Kylar was hiding his ka'kari—the black ka'kari, the Devourer of magic—on his sword. Neph was certain of it. If he was wrong, he would likely be dead by spring. He was running out of options. The things he'd thought would be easy had turned out to be viciously difficult.

With two hundred Vürdmeisters, Neph had attacked the weaves Jorsin Alkestes had laid on Black Barrow hundreds of years ago. Even together, they'd only broken the first spell: now it was possible to use the vir within the Dead Demesne, the unchanging circle of land around the dome of Black Barrow. Before, anyone using the vir there would die instantly. It was better progress than anyone before Neph had made, but in itself, it accomplished nothing. All the millions of krul around Black Barrow were still magically sealed. No one could raise them. No one could raise the Titan Neph had found beneath the mighty dome of Black Barrow itself. With Curoch, Jorsin Alkestes had been more powerful alone than Neph was with two hundred Vürdmeisters.

Neph's few successes seemed like nothing. He'd stirred up the wild men in the Freeze. He'd taught their shamans to raise krul, though he'd deliberately taught them imperfectly, in case he ever had to face them himself. He'd sown rumors about the weakness of the new Godking among the highland tribes.

It would be enough to distract the new Godking, but

not enough for Neph to take the chains of office for himself. The Ursuuls had long claimed that only an Ursuul could take the vir from a meister. That claim had meant the meisters and Vürdmeisters had never been a threat to a true Ursuul—any magical fight would end instantly. Neph had been certain it was a lie. He had staked everything on the belief that once he held Khali, it would be a simple matter to learn to remove the vir from whomever he wished. But so far, he hadn't even come close.

If Neph didn't figure something out soon, any of the aethelings could show up any day and remove the vir from Neph himself.

There were ways out, but none was likely. If Neph actually recovered Curoch, of course, he could shatter Jorsin's work and anyone who rose against him even without the krul or the Strangers or Khali. If he could steal the black ka'kari, he could make it devour Jorsin's magics, raise the krul, and the krul would crush anyone who rose against him. He could use the black ka'kari to walk into Ezra's Wood and steal Curoch and everything else there. His last hope was to raise Khali herself. It had been Khali's wish for as long as she had been worshiped. It was enshrined in every Khalidoran's prayer: *Khalivos ras en me.* Khali, make your home in me. If Neph could give Khali a body, she would give him everything. Neph was preparing the magic and trying to find a proper host for Khali in case he needed to do it, but it was a last resort. Khali would surely teach him how to deny the vir to the Godking if Neph gave her true embodiment. But if Khali had a body, if she could give him everything, could she not also take everything from him?

Neph turned pensive eyes toward Eris. He needed, as

always with these arrogant children, to seal the lie. "If it is Curoch, Eris, I'll give you whatever you ask. But there are two things you should know. You have not the power to wield it even for an instant. It will kill you if you try. Second, I will kill you if you try." His vir squirmed up and down his arms as he laid a tiny weave on her. "I know you can untie that weave, but one of my other spies at the Chantry will be checking on you. If you tamper with it, she has instructions to kill you. Don't worry, the weave is small enough to escape any but the closest magical examination."

Eris's face paled. It would, of course, be her death if any loyal Sister found that weave. But Neph had also revealed that he had another spy close enough to her that the spy could check on the weave regularly. "How likely is it that Kylar has Curoch?" she asked.

"Not likely. But the prize is worth the possibility of losing you."

A green hue entered her skin. "I want Alitaera," she said defiantly. "That's my price. If it's Curoch, you'll take all Midcyru. I want to be queen of Alitaera. I have debts to repay."

Neph pretended to think about it. "Done," he said.

51

Kylar opened his eyes in darkness. His whole body ached, but he knew where he was instantly. Nothing else had the sewage-and-rotten-eggs smell of the Maw. They'd put him in one of the nobles' cells. He wouldn't have been surprised to find himself in the Hole, or dead. He was glad they hadn't killed him. It would be better for Logan if there was a trial first.

"I must have been twice your age when I killed my first queen," a familiar voice said. "'Course, I didn't make such a damn mess of it."

"Durzo?" Kylar sat up, but the man squatting on his heels across from him was unfamiliar. The laugh wasn't.

"I'm going by Dehvi now." The voice took on a tonal accent, "Dehvirahaman ko Bruhmaeziwakazari I have the honor to be." Durzo's voice came back as he said, "They used to call me the Ghost of the Steppes, or A Breath in the Typhoon."

"Durzo? Is that an illusion?"

"Call it advanced body magic. It was one of the things

I was going to teach you if you hadn't developed your Talent so damn slow. We've only got a few minutes. All the guards down here are honest, if you can believe it. And your trial's going on as we speak."

"Already?"

"Your pal the king seems to have high esteem for your powers. Almost accurately high. They drugged you. You've been unconscious for a week."

"Logan's the king?"

"Without opposition. He and Duke Wesseros are presiding over the trial. It's too bad you're missing it. You'd be amazed at what Gwinvere can get witnesses to say."

"Momma K's on trial?" Kylar asked. He was still off-balance. He couldn't place things. It was unreal to be talking with Durzo.

"No, no, no. But what she's doing is making sure the witnesses bring up Terah's indiscretions as many times as possible. The honorable judges are trying to quell the rumors, but Momma K's already won. No one thinks you killed a saint. That helps Logan, but you still killed a queen in plain sight of eighteen people. Logan wants to give you a nobleman's death, but they've already heard testimony that you're not a Stern—the Sterns were pretty adamant about that, go figure—and some lady who sat next to you at the coronation says you turned down the Drake's adoption. He gave you the rings and you refused to put them on. So you're looking at the wheel. I did that once. It's a real shitty way to die, especially for someone who heals as fast as we do."

"You came back," Kylar said. "You gave me Retribution. Again."

Durzo shrugged, as if it were nothing. He reached for a

pouch, then stopped himself. "You put philodunamos on the crown?"

Kylar nodded.

"You wonder why it didn't work? Someone cleaned it off. The laundress swears she dumped some cleaning rags into the water and boom! There was a fire. No one believes her. She lost an arm and her job."

Kylar's stomach turned. He'd nearly killed an innocent. Again. What could a one-armed laundress do?

"So," Durzo said. "Time's wasting. You want to live or die?"

"I'll take any way out that doesn't make Logan look complicit or weak." At Durzo's grimace, he said, "And don't tell me you wouldn't give your life for a friend. I know better."

Durzo grimaced again and stood. "You're the damnedest kid I ever met. Good luck."

"Master, wait. Am I . . . am I doing the right thing?" Kylar asked.

Durzo stopped and when he turned, there was a smile on his face. It was a rare sight. "It's a gamble, kid. You always put your money on your friends. It's something I admire about you."

Then he was gone. Kylar shook his head. How had he got himself into this?

Six royal guards arrived soon thereafter. None of them looked happy, but while two of them had the cautious air of professionals, the other four seemed either nervous or angry or both. One of the angry ones pulled Kylar to his feet. Kylar was, he noticed now, manacled to the wall, and still wearing the clothing he'd worn the night of the coronation. They'd been nice clothes a week ago. His and Terah's dried blood made the front stiff and reeking.

"So you're the big wetboy," the gap-toothed guard sneered. "You don't look so tough when you don't have a helpless woman shielding you."

"Sorry I made you look bad," Kylar said.

Gap-tooth hit him in the stomach.

"Please don't hit me again," Kylar said.

"You didn't make us look bad, you murdering bastard."

The captain said, "Don't be an asshole, Lew. Of course he did."

"Upstairs they're making him sound like a god. Wetboy-this, wetboy-that. Look at 'im. He ain't nothing." Lew casually backhanded Kylar.

"Lew, I—" the captain cut off as Kylar disappeared.

One by one the guards realized Kylar had vanished. There was dead silence for a moment. Then it was broken by the clang of manacles hitting the stone floor.

"Where the hell—"

"Sir! He's gone!"

"Block the door! Block the—"

The cell door slammed closed with all the guards inside. The lock clicked.

Kylar reappeared outside. Grinning, he waved the captain's keys at them.

"That didn't just happen," one of them said. "Tell me that didn't just happen." Another cursed under his breath. The rest still looked like they couldn't believe it.

"Captain," Kylar said, "will you please ask Lew not to strike me?"

The captain wet his lips. "Lew?"

"Yes, sir. Right, sir." Lew met Kylar's gaze and quickly looked away.

Kylar opened the cell door and the men shuffled out sheepishly.

"Should I, uh?" Lew asked, holding up the broken manacles.

The captain swallowed. "Uh, if you don't mind, Master . . . um, Kagé?"

Kylar put his wrists together. They put the manacles on him and walked out of the dungeons. No one said a word. No one laid a hand on him, either.

52

The courtroom was a large, rectangular hall that could hold hundreds of people. It was overflowing, and the doors had been thrown open so more people could stand at the back and watch. At the raised table at one end of the room, Logan Gyre and Duke Wesseros sat side by side. There were supposed to be three judges, but Logan hadn't wanted to impose the duty on the last surviving duke, Luc Graesin.

Facing the table was a small desk and chair inside an iron cage. The captain led Kylar to the cage and removed his manacles. The crowd watched, silently but with great anticipation, as though the wetboy was a monster on display who might gnaw the bars. Kylar stepped into the cage silently, glancing briefly at the gallery. Logan wondered if he was looking for friends. He wondered how many Kylar found.

The front two rows were made up of nobles. Lantano Garuwashi, silent but obviously wondering what Kylar was trying to accomplish, sat near Count Drake, whose jaw was set and eyes were grieved. Logan wondered how much Count Drake had known about his ward. Drake had been a model of integrity for as long as Logan had known him, and a Gyre banner man besides. The Stern family was in the second row, looking furious. The testimony had already established that they'd never known or seen Kylar, but they still felt their honor impugned. Aside from the usual nobles, there was a vast array of Cenarian humanity. The cream of the Warrens was here, men and women in fine clothes yet without titles. Logan wondered if all of those were Sa'kagé. He wondered how many were glad Kylar was here, and how many were grieved, or terrified for themselves that he might speak. Then there were a smattering of those drawn simply by the spectacle: a few Ladeshians, some Alitaeran merchants, and even a Ymmuri.

To Logan's right hand sat the witnesses. There were eighteen guards, as well as the grasping woman who'd sat next to Kylar at the coronation. Kylar sat.

"State your name for this tribunal," Duke Wesseros said.

"Kylar Stern."

"Sit down, Baron Stern!" Duke Wesseros barked as the unhappy nobleman jumped to his feet. The nobleman scowled and sat. "This court has accepted testimony from nobles who said you saved them during the Khalidoran coup. They called you the Night Angel. We have heard, sometimes despite our best attempts, about how you saved King Gyre from the Hole. We have heard you called Kagé, the Shadow. We even heard one man who claimed your name was Azoth. But one certainty we've established is that you are not, nor ever were, a Stern. What is your real name?"

Kylar looked amused. "I am the Night Angel, but if you'd choke on that, you can call me Kagé."

Duke Wesseros looked over to Logan. Logan had asked him to lead the proceedings. Logan nodded. "Kagé," Duke Wesseros said, "you stand accused of high treason and murder. How do you answer these charges?"

"Of murder, guilty. Of treason, not guilty. Terah Graesin was not a lawful queen. By marriage and adoption, Logan Gyre has been king since the death of King Aleine Gunder IX."

The courtroom erupted in whispers until Duke Wesseros raised his hands. He had threatened to clear the courtroom several times during the last week of testimony, and the crowd quieted quickly. "It is not your place to lecture your betters on Cenarian law."

"Then you tell me, Your Grace, was or was not Duke Gyre formally made King Gunder's heir and was or was not he married to Jenine Gunder, and did or did not that confer on him the right of succession?"

Duke Wesseros purpled, but said nothing. If he agreed, he would concede that Terah should never have been made queen and that he should have never sworn fealty to her. If he explained his decision was based on practicalities, he would sound like a weasel or a coward.

"I wouldn't have killed Terah Graesin if my betters had followed the law rather than their cocks and their coin purses," Kylar said.

This time, the whispers were forestalled by Logan's raised hand. He wore a thin gold band around his brow, but otherwise little to denote his kingship. "There is some truth in what you say. On the eve of Pavvil's Grove, some of us made regrettable compromises. In the end, however, Cenaria's nobility delivered into Duchess Graesin's hands the scepter and the sword, and we placed the crown upon her brow. It is not the prerogative of a commoner to shed blood to correct what he sees as the nobility's errors. Therefore, Kagé, you stand convicted of murder and treason."

A hush fell.

"This tribunal has further questions, which we ask you to answer for both your own sake and Cenaria's. If you answer fully and forthrightly, you will be granted a merciful death. If not, you will be bound to the wheel." Logan held his face impassive, but his stomach turned. The wheel was a cruel death, as bad as Alitaeran cruxing or Modaini drawing and quartering. It was the established punishment for treason. Only treasonous nobles were beheaded, and it had been established that Kylar was no noble. A merciful death for testimony was the most Logan could do for his friend.

"I will answer all I can without compromising my honor," Kylar said.

"Are you a member of the Sa'kagé?" Logan asked.

"Yes."

"Are you an assassin?"

Kylar sneered. "Assassins have targets. Wetboys have deaders. I was a wetboy."

There was a sudden electricity in the room, like thunderheads were rolling by. The crowd had become an audience, and they were pleased with the show. They were getting a chance to peek behind the veil at the Sa'kagé, and they wouldn't miss it for the world.

"'Was'?" Duke Wesseros interjected.

"I split with the Sa'kagé during the coup. I don't kill for money now."

"So you claim no one ordered you to kill the queen?" Logan asked.

"The Night Angel is the spirit of retribution. No one orders me to do anything, Your Highness, not even you." A thrill ran through the crowd at the show of defiance.

"Strike him," Duke Wesseros said.

One of the guards stepped up to the cage but hesitated.

"Strike him!" Duke Wesseros demanded.

The man hit Kylar across the jaw, not hard. Logan could swear the man looked scared.

"Who hired you to kill Terah Graesin?" Logan asked.

"I planned and carried it out alone."

"Why?" Duke Wesseros asked. "A wetboy might have escaped."

"If I wanted to, I could escape right now," Kylar said.

There were titters in the courtroom.

"Well, I don't know if you're a wetboy, but you're certainly an accomplished liar," Duke Wesseros said.

Kylar glanced at the guards who'd accompanied him up from the Maw. The men looked positively ill. Logan felt a tingling on his right arm and for a moment, could swear he saw something moving from Kylar's fingers like the shadow of a shadow. He looked around, but no one else seemed to notice anything. Then Kylar's expression changed like he was deciding against an impulse. Logan had seen the expression enough to know it. "I am an accomplished liar," Kylar admitted. "I guess it doesn't matter. You've already established that I'm not a Stern, and that I killed the queen, so let's finish this."

"You deny the Sa'kagé had any part in the queen's death?" Duke Wesseros asked.

"Are you a moron or a stooge?" Kylar shot back. "I've given Cenaria a king who can neither be bribed or blackmailed. The Sa'kagé is furious with me. The question you're too afraid to ask is whether the king ordered me to kill Terah Graesin."

Duke Wesseros jumped to his feet. "How dare you impugn our king's honor! Strike him!" The court was in an uproar.

Logan stood. "No! Sit!" It took half a minute for everyone to obey, but finally they did. "It's a fair question. A fair question for us to drag into the light, because everyone's going to be asking it quietly in the days to come." Then Logan sat.

"Many of you were at Pavvil's Grove. You saw Logan kill the ferali," Kylar said. Logan almost goggled. He and Kylar both knew he hadn't killed the ferali. It had been Kylar's assassinating the Godking that had defeated the beast. "Many of you hailed Logan as your king, but he wouldn't accept the crown then, would he? Do you think he was afraid of Terah Graesin then? How many of her banner men do you think would have stood by her on that day if Logan had taken the crown? He held his honor that day as he has every day of his life. Do you think that if he had ordered me to murder her on the night of her coronation that he would have welcomed me to sit by him at the high table? Do you think he is such a fool that, knowing what I was going to do an hour later, he would remind everyone what good friends he was with a wetboy? I've been a Sa'kagé spy on Logan Gyre for ten years. In that time, Logan came to trust me as his best friend. So it turns out that the question isn't whether he had me assassinate Terah Graesin, because he didn't. The duke who was once betrothed to a mere count's daughter has always had too much honor for that. The real question is if our new king will pardon his friend for the murder that put him on the throne." Kylar turned and met Logan's eyes for the first time. "Well, Logan, how about it?"

Whatever else Kylar's time straddling Cenaria's worlds had done to him, Logan saw that his friend had learned the way of rumors among both the peasants and the nobility. He'd fingered exactly the questions people would ask. Indeed, he'd set up everything so the questions could have only one answer. Logan had wondered why Kylar had allowed himself to be caught. He had no illusions that it had been because Kylar couldn't escape. Now he saw all the connections that Kylar had known other people would make. The first question when someone was assassinated was always, who benefits? When Terah Graesin died, the answer was clearly Logan. That wasn't why Kylar had killed her, though. He'd killed her for all of Cenaria's people, because she would have been a disaster as a queen. So Kylar had needed to kill her in a way that freed Logan of suspicion.

In a way, Logan had forced Kylar's hand with the seating arrangements at the coronation. The Sterns had been there. If Kylar hadn't been placed so prominently, he might have escaped attention, but with too much scrutiny, Kylar's disguise would collapse. When it collapsed, everyone would have known that Logan's best friend was in the Sa'kagé—that would be damning enough. After all, how could Logan be a reformer when he came to the throne smeared with charges of corruption himself? This was Kylar's answer: to shine a glaring light on everything and force Logan to show decisively where his loyalties lay.

Kylar had no doubt what Logan would do, Logan saw that. It was the right thing to do. It was the only thing to do. But Logan had recently lost his father, his mother, his fiancée, and his wife. How was he supposed to condemn his best friend to death?

Logan remembered the sick pleasure he'd felt at ordering Gorkhy's death. It was the pleasure of power, and he'd felt it again when men had bowed before him. But suddenly, he hated his power. Kylar was giving his life so Logan could have power. He trusted Logan that much, and Logan knew he had it in him to be a monster. But there was nothing to do.

His face stony, Logan said, "A pardon is out of the question. You were our friend, but our justice will not be swayed. Whatever your intentions, even if it was to make us king, you have done murder in this realm. Justice demands your death. Justice will be satisfied. As king, I demand you answer one more question. If you answer, we will grant you a merciful death. If not, it will be the wheel. Kagé, what are the names and positions of everyone you know in the Sa'kagé?"

Kylar sighed and shook his head.

53

$\mathcal{K}$ylar sat in the darkness and stench of his cell deep into the night.

He threw the ka'kari into the corner of the room. It bounced eerily noiselessly. He extended a hand and willed it back. It flew through the air as if on invisible strings and slapped into his palm. He threw it again and this time willed it to mold itself into a spike. He sucked it back through the air and when it hit his palm it squished and went back into his body.

He could escape. After he died this time, everything would be different.

He heard the sound of someone speaking in a distant hallway. A door opened, and soon Kylar heard the sound of a big man's footsteps. The face that eventually appeared, however, wasn't the one he expected.

"Lantano Garuwashi," Kylar said, standing and bowing.

"Night Angel." Garuwashi bowed equally low. "May I come in?"

Kylar smirked at how the man was treating this like a social visit. "Please."

Garuwashi unlocked the door and came in.

"How'd you get here?" Kylar asked.

"I asked permission."

"Ah."

"You rob me, Night Angel."

"How so?" Kylar asked.

"Our duel. It was to have been the height of our glory. A duel for the ages."

Kylar didn't know why, but that Lantano Garuwashi was peeved not to get to fight him five years hence somehow warmed Kylar. Perhaps it was the only way Garuwashi had to say that he would have liked to be Kylar's friend. "The Night Angels keep their word," Kylar said. "A Night Angel will be there, I promise."

"He will be your equal?"

"He may even be yours," Kylar said, grinning.

Garuwashi cracked a smile. He sat on the stone shelf opposite Kylar and folded his legs beneath himself. Kylar sat similarly on his bunk. "I don't understand Cenarian honor," Lantano Garuwashi said. "King Gyre will rule whether you do this or not. Why will you die for a people unworthy of you?"

"I don't know. I only know it felt like the right thing to do."

"Do you have a lover? Does she approve of this?"

Kylar hadn't even thought of it. The look on his face must have betrayed him, because Garuwashi shook his head, chuckling.

"You tell me, Night Angel, would you give *her* life to accomplish this?"

Kylar was as shocked that Lantano Garuwashi was asking the question as he was by the question itself. "I wouldn't ask anyone to die for my ideals."

"Yet you ask Logan to kill for them."

Kylar had no answer.

"Since you've never sent men to their deaths, let me make the question easier. Would your lover give her life to change this land?"

"Yes, gladly."

"Then perhaps she will forgive you one day."

Well, I plan to come back to life before she finds out. Instead, Kylar said, "I wouldn't have expected a sa'ceurai to care what a woman thinks."

Garuwashi burst into laughter. "No sa'ceurai wishes to marry a shadow. A woman should be as fiery as her hair. Ceuran women whisper on the streets and shout in the home. Young sa'ceurai think that means only in the bedroom." Garuwashi grinned. "They learn." Kylar couldn't help but smile too.

After a few more minutes, Garuwashi stood. "I must go," he said. "I will expect your successor at Midsummer's in five years. May your sword-soul shine ever brighter, Night Angel."

Lantano Garuwashi left, and to his surprise, Kylar slept.

He woke at the sound of a lock pick's scraping. He was alert instantly and stood stealthily. The door opened moments later, telling him that whoever was breaking into his cell was a professional. The locks on the nobles' cells were tight.

The door cracked open and Scarred Wrable's face appeared. He grinned to see Kylar awake and in a ready position. "You're Blint's apprentice after all, arn'tcha? Morning, lad."

"What are you doing here?" Kylar asked.

"There are two contracts out on you. One from inside. To kill ya." He meant inside the Sa'kagé. "The other one's from some nobles."

Kylar's eyes never left Scarred Wrable, though the man didn't have a weapon drawn. "Terah Graesin's folk?"

"Actually, some shadow saved a buncha lords during the coup. They think they owe you. You want to guess which contract I took?"

"Depends on who in the Sa'kagé took out the other one," Kylar said.

Scarred Wrable spat. "The one from inside wasn't from one of my usual clients, and Momma K likes you. I don't plan on betting against her. I took the nobles' contract." He drew a knife and extended it hilt first.

Kylar waved it off. "Tell them thanks, but I'm not here 'cause I can't escape."

"I told them you'd say that. They said I'd get half for trying. I don't know what you're trying to accomplish, but you're crazy brave."

"More one than the other, I think."

Scarred Wrable laughed. "How 'bout this, then. I lied when I said there's two contracts. There's three. Third one's same as the second: to free you. You got more friends than a wetboy oughta. You wanna guess who took it out?"

"Pray tell."

The wetboy grinned. "The king his own self. Iff'n I was king, I'd just let ya go. Guess nobles don't think like the rest of us. You coming?"

Damn you, Logan. Damn you for flinching. Kylar swallowed. "Staying."

Scarred Wrable's eyebrows lifted. Then he shrugged. "You oughta be a noble your own self. You're a man in love with death, Night Angel. See you on the other side."

54

They marched Kylar out of the Maw before dawn. His escort was fifty men. They bound his wrists with manacles behind his back, tied his elbows with hemp, and hobbled his feet. He was surprised when, instead of heading through the castle, the guards led him out the great double doors, up the black carven tongue, and out the throat of the Maw onto the rocky west side of Vos Island.

There was a barge waiting for them, and as soon as they chained Kylar to a post in the middle of it, they cast off, the men alert for threats from him or from any who might rescue him.

They had barely passed under West Kingsbridge when Kylar saw new construction on the Plith. Deep pilings had been sunk into the river bed south of Vos Island to support a central platform, which rested on the surface of the river. The pilings extended high above the platform and three spokes radiated from the center, supporting temporary spans to Vos Island, the Warrens, and the east side. The three-way bridge was temporary now, and low to the water, but the size and placement of the pilings told Kylar of the project's ambition. It would be a symbol of Logan's reign, a bridge that bound the city's sides and its government together. As they came closer, Kylar saw that what he had thought was merely the thickness of the temporary bridge's surface was something else.

Every one of the temporary spans—west to the Warrens, north to the castle, and east—was filled with people. The sun was barely lighting the sky, and there were thousands gathered. Everyone in the city had come. Even Lantano Garuwashi's soldiers had come.

As the barge came within sight, a cry went up, and it wasn't kind. These people loved Logan, Kylar knew instantly, and any traitor must be vile. From the safety of the mob, any fear they might have had for the Sa'kagé's avatar had vanished. Indeed, that probably made him more hated still. His disavowals in the courtroom made no difference; only the verdict mattered. The barge came closer and the yells were deafening. Looking on faces filled with hatred, Kylar supposed he was lucky the city had been starving—there was no rotten produce for people to throw.

Something splashed in the water twenty feet short of the barge.

"Shields up!" an officer barked.

The men crouched and raised their shields over their heads. Chained to the post in the middle, Kylar couldn't move. Rocks rattled off the shields and splashed in the water, then Kylar watched one arc perfectly. He turned his head. The rock gouged a furrow in his scalp and he staggered against the post, blood spilling over his ear. Another rock glanced off his shoulder and a third hit him in the crotch. The crowd cheered as he slumped.

He stood again, though spots swam before his eyes, blinding him. As they got closer, the hail thickened. Most of the throws missed, but rocks hammered his sides, his legs. A stone a handspan across landed on his foot, shattering bones. He screamed.

It was bad timing. A rock that would have been too high caught him in the mouth, snapping teeth and driving others through his lip. Another cheer went up.

Finally, the barge bumped against the platform. "Enough!" a woman shouted. Kylar lifted his head and saw a young woman in full armor standing in the center of the platform with her hands raised, trying to still the crowd. Then a stone hit him in the eye.

"Enough!" the woman shouted, but Kylar lost her voice under the shrieking voice of pain. His face was hot, his chained hands couldn't reach up to protect himself or feel the damage. Soldiers were jostling him, half carrying, half dragging him forward.

Kylar opened his eyes but could only see from his right. His first sight was of his bare foot, bleeding, ruined. It made him light-headed. He looked up, blinking, but blinking sent forks of lightning through his left eye. Blood was filling his mouth from his smashed lips. He didn't know if he'd swallowed or spit out the teeth, but jagged edges were all that remained.

When Kylar could finally try to make out the details, he saw that the platform was filled with Logan's retinue, including at least a hundred of Logan's bodyguards. Numerous other soldiers were scattered throughout the crowd, including along all three bridges, keeping a lane clear. On the far side of the platform, facing the castle, was the wheel. To one side, Logan sat in a gilded chair.

They dragged Kylar before him and a herald read out the charges. Kylar paid no attention to them. He looked only at Logan. Logan's eyes trailed over Kylar's wounds and he swallowed, but he didn't avert his gaze. His eyes met Kylar's and Kylar saw suffering as great as his own, but no wavering.

The herald finished with the charges with a question. "Yes," Kylar said loudly. "I killed Terah Graesin, and I'd do it again."

Logan stood and the muttering that had begun ceased instantly. "Kagé, Shadowed One, whom I knew as Kylar Stern, I owe you my life. You are a hero and I call you my friend, but you have betrayed this country and murdered her queen. I will not be a king who gives different justice to his friends. Kylar, my friend, I sentence you to hang by the wheel until you are dead."

Kylar said nothing. He merely bowed his head to Logan. Logan sat and made no attempt to quiet the crowd that now buzzed with the confirmation of the rumors they'd heard.

The soldiers dragged Kylar to the wheel. It was slightly taller than a man and open, with only four spokes radiating from the axle, which would be behind Kylar's back so he could face the crowds. There were blocks for his feet which adjusted at the ankle so his feet wouldn't slip free, a thick leather belt for his waist, and two sharply-ridged bars for handholds. The rest of the wheel bristled with iron spikes: all pointed inward.

The royal guards who'd brought him from the Maw began strapping him in place.

"Are you really the Night Angel?" Kaldrosa asked quietly, fitting the leather belt around his waist.

"Yes," Kylar said.

Kaldrosa leaned close as she strapped his wrist to the wheel and whispered, "There are two hundred fifty women here who'd be dead if you hadn't saved us from Hu Gibbet. It'll kill us to betray Logan, but if you—"

"Do your duty," Kylar said. He squeezed his eyes tight shut.

"Thank you," Kaldrosa said.

Once he was strapped in, the guards adjusted the spikes. If Kylar held himself in place, none of them would touch his body. However, as the wheel turned, he would have to support his weight by his ankles and by his hands, gripping knife-edged bars that would cut his fingers and palms to mincemeat. Once he weakened, the spikes would stab his sides, his legs, and his arms, enough to spur him to redouble his efforts, but never so deeply that they would kill. He would eventually die of blood loss, or his heart would burst.

As they finished, he lifted his gaze once more and scanned the crowd. He saw Momma K, and Count Drake. He saw the Chantry's ambassador faintly glowing in his sight, obviously hoping that this "Night Angel" would do something magical for her to report, and the Lae'knaught ambassador, dispassionate, more studying Logan's reaction than Kylar's suffering. He saw the women of the Order, horrified, one crying silently. He saw faces he had known from the Warrens, tavern keepers and whores and thieves and an herbalist. He saw nobles Kylar Stern had rubbed shoulders with and been ignored by.

Then Logan gave a signal, and the wheel rattled backward and settled down, water lapping over Kylar's feet.

Oh, yes, now Kylar remembered, there were more than

two ways to die on the wheel. The wheel itself was per-
pendicular to the flow of the Plith; it used the river's current to turn it. When Kylar was turned upside down, his
head would dip into the water low enough to cover his
mouth. It would only be enough to drown him if he was
unconscious and close to death anyway, but the coughing
fit would make him stab himself in dozens of places.

Logan nodded. The wheel began to turn.

55

*T*hank you for receiving me," Momma K said. She came out onto the castle balcony where Logan stood, his dinner untouched. He didn't lift his eyes from the river. It had been twelve hours since the wheel began turning. Behind him, Gnasher ate noisily and, with a total lack of stealth, stole Logan's biscuits.

"How could I deny you? When the Shinga plays, kings dance," Logan said flatly. He didn't turn. A wetboy had delivered her letter—her admission that she was the Shinga—just this morning. But the shock of it was muted by Logan's grief.

Momma K came to stand beside him at the railing. From this distance, all they could see was that there were still a few dozen people on the platform, half of them guards, and that the wheel was still turning. The signal flag to let Logan know when Kylar died still hadn't been raised.

"This changes everything," Momma K said.

"What hand did you have in Terah Graesin death?" Logan asked.

"None," Momma K said, "though not for lack of trying. I put Quoglee Mars on the right track, hoping he would discover that Terah betrayed her little sister Natassa. I even arranged for him to sing the night of the coronation. I made sure that no guards would stop him once he began, and I arranged for Luc Graesin to be there to hear it. I hoped Luc would kill Terah. Once you were king, I planned to have this talk with you regardless, though I was planning on waiting a month."

"In which time . . ." Logan led.

"The Ceuran food supplies and our own would run out," Momma K said.

"And?"

"I would come to you with enough food to feed the city through the winter."

Logan stared at her, not asking how she'd get it. "In return for what?"

"The thing is, Your Majesty, with this—" she gestured to the wheel—"you've proven that you have integrity. Integrity is rare here, but it won't change this city alone. You need allies for that, and if you want allies in this city, you will be seeking allies who have objectionable histories."

"Like you?"

"And like Count Drake, whom you conveniently forget was also once in Sa'kagé leadership."

Logan blinked.

"The point is, if you try to hold to account every official in the city who's ever taken a bribe or violated a trust or broken a law, you will have no officials."

"What do you propose?" Logan asked.

"The question is what you propose. What will the reign of King Gyre the First mean?"

Logan looked at his friend dying on the wheel in the distance. "I mean to make this mean something. I mean to destroy you Sa'kagé."

"That's a means, not an end."

"I mean to make Cenaria a great center of trade and learning, a place our people are proud to claim. We will be able to defend ourselves. We will live in peace, not in fear and corruption. The Warrens may never equal the east side, but I mean to make it possible for a man to be born in the Warrens and die in an eastside palace."

"How about a woman?" she asked lightly.

"Of course," he said.

She wore a small smile. "Sounds good. I'll take it."

A flash of anger passed over his face. "You could already buy a palace."

"I want you to appoint me duchess and grant me the Graesin lands, Your Majesty."

"There's not enough rice in the world to buy that."

It was his anger speaking. His best friend was dying. Momma K ignored it. "The Sa'kagé is a parasite latched onto Cenaria's face. Fully uprooting them is impossible, but their power can be broken. It may take years, and it will cost much of your treasure and perhaps your popularity. Success is not certain. Are you a king who can stay a course through a river of blood?"

Logan watched the wheel turn for a full minute. Then he said quietly, "While there is breath in my body, I will fight to make Kylar's death mean something. What will you do if I give you what you ask?"

"I will give you my complete loyalty. I'll be your

spymaster. Last but certainly not least, I'll destroy the Sa'kagé."

"Why should I believe that you would so casually betray an organization that must include every friend you ever had?" Logan asked.

"Friends? The Sa'kagé relieves us of the burden of friendship. The truth is, in all my years I had only three friends in the Sa'kagé. One was a wetboy named Durzo; Kylar had to kill him because of something I did. One was Jarl, who died trying what I'm proposing. The last is dying for it as we speak. What I propose is a betrayal, that's true, but it's not a casual betrayal. If we do this, we'll need to keep my appointment secret for a time. Once the Sa'kagé learns of my new loyalties, they'll go underground, and I need to speak with as many of them as possible before that."

"Can they be broken?" Logan asked.

"Not with swords alone."

"What can go wrong?" Logan asked.

"You want the short version or the long one?"

"The long one."

So she told him. Then she told him the plans she had in place to counter every one of those possibilities. It took an hour. She spoke succinctly and asked him questions as well: was he willing to use wetboys to do work the guards could not? How much amnesty was he willing to extend? Would thieves walk free? Bashers? Extortionists? Rapists? Murderers? What would be the penalty for those who took bribes in the new Cenaria?

"Our first strike will have to be sharp. Seizure of funds, arrests, making legitimate employment available. Large carrots, large sticks. And most of our plans will probably only last until the first sword is drawn."

Logan said nothing for a long time. Then he said, "If we do this, I won't put you in charge of uprooting the Sa'kagé."

"What?"

"I won't put that much power in your hands. You could destroy anyone with a word, and I'd have no idea if you were telling the truth. Rimbold Drake will be in charge. You will work for him. Fair enough?"

Momma K's eyes were cold for a long moment. Then they cleared. "I can see that taking orders is going to take some getting used to. Yes, it's fair. Perhaps you are the king who can do this after all. Your Majesty, I swear my fealty to you." She knelt gracefully and touched his foot.

"Gwinvere Kirena, I hereby establish House Kirena, peers among the great houses of the realm. I grant to you and your house in perpetuity the lands stretching from the Smugglers' Archipelago in the west to the Wy River in the east, and from the boundaries of Havermere in the north to Ceuran border in the south. Rise, Duchess Kirena."

She stood. "Your Majesty, there is one more thing. Yesterday I received confirmation of an earlier report that I hadn't believed. In each case, my sources had nothing to gain by lying. Both have been trustworthy in the past. I don't know how this is possible, but I believe it is true. I didn't want to tell you before we concluded our own negotiations because I didn't want you to think I was trying to influence them."

"That's a lot of hedging. What is it?" Logan asked.

"Your wife didn't die in the coup, Your Majesty. Jenine's in Khalidor. She's alive."

*   *   *

Some time after dark, the wheel stopped turning. Kylar jerked his head up. He blinked through the river water coursing from his hair and looked around. Blinking still hurt, but he could make out shapes now with the eye that had been blinded in the morning.

A young man in armor stood before him. Obviously, he was one of Logan's bodyguards. "I was given a message, Sir Kagé," he said. "Aristarchos is healthy and safe at home now with his wife and children. The Society wishes to thank you and hopes that stopping the wheel for a few hours is a small repayment." He glanced up one of the bridges.

Through the darkness, Kylar saw a Ladeshian man he'd never met. The man raised his hand in greeting, though in the darkness, no one but Kylar could have seen him. Then the Ladeshian walked away. So Aristarchos ban Ebron had survived his addiction. Kylar hadn't known he had a family. He wondered what Aristarchos's wife thought when her beautiful husband came back with blackened and missing teeth, his looks and pride sacrificed to a cause she couldn't understand. The Society thanked Kylar?

"We can only stop the wheel until dawn, Sir Kagé. I'm sorry."

But Kylar barely heard him. He unclenched his bloody hands from the knife-edged grips and let the belt and the ankle straps hold his weight. His head sunk to his chest.

"Kylar?" Vi asked. They were in a little room with two beds, a basin, and a small chest at the foot of each bed. A small figure was asleep on one bed, and Vi was propped up on one hand in the other. She looked worse than Kylar had ever seen her. Her eyes were red and puffy, her face blotchy, nose runny, and handkerchiefs wadded in her hands. "Gods, what have they done to you?"

He looked at the sleeping figure on the other bed and shuffled over to her. "Uly," he said. "God, she's getting big. Uly?"

"She can't hear us," Vi said. "We're not really here. Come, sit down."

Kylar sat with difficulty. He smiled wanly. "Uly's your roommate?"

Vi nodded. "Thirteen years old and she's better than me at everything."

"Tell her I'm sorry. I abandoned her like everyone else. I made a lousy father."

"Quiet. Lie down."

"Get blood . . . sheets," he said, but he didn't resist. He put his head in her lap and closed his eyes.

"Kylar, I think I can help you," Vi said, brushing his hair back. "But I need you to tell me what happened. Who did this to you?"

Her fingers were warm and gentle. It was an effort to speak. "Doing," he said.

"Doing?"

"I'm being executed for murdering Queen Graesin. Logan's the king. I did that, Elene. That's worth my life, isn't it?"

"Elene's not here, Kylar. It's me, Vi."

Kylar winced as a muscle in his back spasmed. He drew quick little breaths.

Vi laid both of her hands on him and the cramps released. He heard her gasp and then warmth flooded through his body and a blessed absence of pain.

There was a long silence and Kylar began fading.

Finally, Vi said, "But you'll come back, right? After you die?"

"No one ever explained it. Live every life like it's your last, huh?" He chuckled. He couldn't help it. He felt warm all over. When he opened his eyes to look up at Vi, she wasn't smiling. Her face was rigid with concentration and pain.

"Sleep," she said. "I'll help you all I can."

56

Logan rose before dawn. He hadn't slept. Sensing his mood, his guards hadn't slept either, but if they felt as wretched as he did, they concealed it. "I'm going to see Kylar," he told Kaldrosa. She nodded, having expected it. One of the things Logan was learning to hate about being king was that he couldn't go anywhere without a retinue. Given that the last two Cenarian monarchs—or six, if he believed Duchess Kirena—had been assassinated, it was reasonable. Still, though Logan hated dragging along twelve people with him wherever he went, it wasn't their fault, and it was beneath him to make their lives more difficult. So he simply had to act with more consideration.

Hot water arrived for his bath so promptly that Logan knew Kaldrosa must have told the kitchens hours ago that the king would require his bath early. It was a simple act, but illustrative. Many nobles ignored their servants as they ignored the ground beneath their feet. Logan's father had pointed out that a noble interacted with his servants more than he did with even his own family. It paid to treat them well, but it was a still rare servant who so actively anticipated her master's needs.

Logan stripped and bathed himself. As he scrubbed, he thought of how his apartments, though high above the Hole he'd lived in, had seen as much misery. Logan had seen the statues—hidden in a storeroom in the castle's bowels—of the Godking's women. They had all been young Cenarian noblewomen. Logan had known each by face and name and title. Every one of those women who had been so cruelly used, broken, murdered, and put on display. One of his first acts as king had been to return those girls to their families for burial. For some, there was no family left to return them to, so Logan had seen to those burials himself. He wished he could kill the dead Godking with his own hands, and the wheel would be too good for Trudana Jadwin, who had signed each statue as if they were pieces of her art. The room got brighter as Logan stood, dripping, naked, oblivious to the towel one of his bodyguards offered.

Jenine was, most likely, one of those women now. Even if he could get her back, she might well be bereft of reason. Regardless, she wouldn't be the woman he had lost. He had to be prepared for that, had to be ready to love someone broken, wounded beyond healing. The fucking monsters. The room brightened with a white-green incandescence as Logan's rage crested. He closed his eyes and exhaled. He mastered his outrage, his fury at his own ignorance, his impatience, and his hatred. He cooled them and fit them to his purpose. What would it profit to yell and smash things in his own castle while Jenine languished in Khalidor?

Logan opened his eyes and became aware of Kaldrosa

and Pturin, his short Ymmuri guard, gawking. The white-green lines etched in his forearm dimmed. Logan took the towel.

"The, uh, long-sleeved tunic?" Kaldrosa asked.

"Always. Thank you."

The sun was rising as Logan and his retinue arrived at the platform where Kylar was dying. The slow grind of the gears and the hiss of the flowing waters of the Plith, and the shifting strains of Kylar's weight on the straps holding him were the only sounds. Blood dripped from his sides where blades pierced his arms, his armpits, his ribs, missed his waist because the belt held him in place, but stabbed again into the sides of his thighs and calves. Blood dribbled from fists clenched around spiked hand-holds. Blood flowed freely from his scalp and each of his temples, refusing to clot because every revolution dipped his head underwater. He was a man limned in blood. And still he breathed.

There was another man who had been regarding Kylar in the dawn light, too. It was Lantano Garuwashi. He didn't turn as Logan approached.

The wheel turned Kylar sideways. Lacking the strength anymore to hold his body in place, he slid onto the points on the down side. As he inhaled, that motion made the spikes tear the holes in his chest larger. Blood welled up on the opposite side, and as he turned upside down, he made a feeble effort to hold himself up, but slid down. His head jabbed against three spikes and dozens more stabbed into his shoulders and arms. He took a deeper breath before his head went under water.

Logan's stomach clenched. It was with difficulty that he didn't throw up. He'd come to take his friend's body away, not to watch him suffer, not to watch him die.

Kylar's strength must have given way only minutes ago. It was impossible for a man to bleed so freely for long without dying. So Logan stood with Lantano Garuwashi and looked at what he had done for a minute, five minutes. Five minutes stretched to an unbearable ten, and still Kylar showed no signs of weakening further. It was unbelievable, impossible.

"Look at his feet," Garuwashi whispered.

For a moment, Logan had no idea what Garuwashi was talking about. There was nothing remarkable about Kylar's feet. They, at least, were spared injury. Then Logan remembered. When Kylar had been strapped to the wheel, they'd dragged him because a stone had crushed one of his feet. Another had blinded one eye. Now both feet and both eyes were whole. Logan's fleeting disbelief became wonder and then horror.

The wheel was intended as an excruciating death for traitors. It usually took hours. Kylar, however, was healing at an incredible rate. The wheel would kill him eventually, but after a day, he seemed like a man who had been on the wheel less than an hour. Logan had never intended such cruelty. This made the Hole look humane.

"You did right," Kylar said, startling Logan. His eyes were open, clear. "Go, my king. I'll be hanging around." He attempted a grin.

Logan abruptly began weeping. "How do I end this?"

Agon Brant cleared his throat. "Your Majesty, in times past when men were put on the wheel before a religious festival and a ruler wished to avoid defiling the city by having a man die during the festival, they would break the condemned's arms or legs so they'd be impaled more deeply on the spikes and die faster." He cleared his throat once more, never looking at Kylar. "I must also inform Your Majesty that the Lae'knaught ambassador is on his way. He refused to be put off any longer."

Logan closed his eyes and breathed deeply, slowly. He wiped his eyes and blinked. Looking up the makeshift bridge to the castle, he saw the Lae'knaught ambassador approaching. "Very well," Logan said. "Let him approach. Set up my chair and desk here." He'd deliberately leaked to the ambassador that he would be here, assuming the man would follow. Logan had meant to meet with the man in front of the wheel as a reminder of how hard Logan could be. But in his wildest nightmares he hadn't thought Kylar would still be dying while they met.

The wheel turned and Logan stood, facing it, watching Kylar until Agon Brant, acting as his impromptu chamberlain, announced the ambassador. "Your Majesty, Tertulus Martus, Questor of the Twelfth Army of the Lae'knaught, attaché to Overlord Julus Rotans."

Logan turned and sat at the field desk. Tertulus Martus's eyes flicked past him to Kylar. Standing, Logan's body obscured the visage of death. Sitting, it framed him. The ambassador couldn't look at him without being aware of the man dying behind him on the wheel.

"Your Majesty," Tertulus said. "Thank you for welcoming me, and congratulations on your recent ascension to the throne and your most glorious victories. If half the tales are true, your name shall live forever." He went on for some time. The Lae'knaught's Twelfth Army was their diplomatic corps. There hadn't been twelve Lae'knaught armies since before the Alitaeran Accords. Today, there were perhaps three—and maybe only two, given the massacre of the five thousand in Ezra's Wood. But Tertulus Martus had set the rudder before he began speaking, and he didn't even have to think as he spoke. His body was similarly controlled, betraying nothing. He stood with his feet fairly close together, so as not to appear combative. His hands were kept loose, so as to neither point nor clench into fists. His gestures were small. Logan watched his eyes instead.

The man was weighing him. This ambassador wasn't here to offer any deals, though he would surely soon offer something small. His anxiety to see Logan as quickly as possible came only from pressure from his superiors. They wanted to know if Logan was a threat. They had recently lost five thousand men, and they needed to know if this new king of an insignificant, corrupt kingdom could be trusted to do as Cenarian kings had done for twenty years: nothing.

Still saying nothing, Logan rose in the middle of the diplomat's sentence. With perfect calm, he knocked over the field desk, sending blank parchment, inkpot, and quill flying with a crash. He stepped on the desk and ripped off a leg.

With two mighty slashes, he broke Kylar's legs at the shins.

Kylar screamed. Deprived of support, his body sagged against a dozen blades under his arms. Jagged bones stabbed through the skin of his legs, gleaming wetly in the rising sun. He screamed again as the wheel turned sideways and the sides of his legs were pierced much more deeply. His head dunked under water in the middle of a scream and he came up coughing and retching.

His arms slid onto the blades again as he came fully upright and his screams trailed off into whimpers. Logan looked at the depth of the cuts and looked Kylar in the eye. There was great suffering, but there was no fear.

With two more heavy blows, Logan broke Kylar's forearms.

Kylar screamed again. Without the rigidity of those bones, his body sank unnaturally far, gravity stretching his arms like clay, his body sinking too far at every turn. He coughed blood with every breath, and blood streamed from him in rivers.

Logan heard several of his attendants throwing up, but he never turned away.

After seven revolutions, Kylar stopped coughing. The flow of blood slowed, and the tension in the distorted muscles relaxed. Logan gestured to a pair of the King's Guard. The wheel stopped. They checked for a pulse. There was none. They began removing the body.

Logan turned to Tertulus Martus, who for all his diplomatic training still hadn't managed to close his gaping mouth or narrow his wide eyes.

"Five hundred and forty-three years ago," Logan said, "a man was captured by a Khalidoran Vürdmeister and tortured for three months. This man kept his sanity, and his courage, and at the end of those three months, he escaped. He founded an order devoted to resisting and destroying black magic—Khalidoran magic. In time, this mission expanded to encompass the destruction of all magic and all who wield it. However, his order, the Laetunariverissiknaught, the

Bringers of the Freedom of the Light, still harbor an especial hatred of those who wield the vir."

"Your Majesty displays a remarkable knowledge of—"

"Silence!" Logan roared, pointing the bloody table leg an inch from Tertulus's nose. The man stopped. "For the last eighteen years, you Lae'knaught have been squatting on Cenarian lands. This will end. Here are your choices. First, you can pack up and leave immediately. Second, you can fight us. You recently lost five thousand men, and I have a battle-seasoned army that's getting bored—and a Ceuran army to whom I've sworn a battle that will live in history. We will crush you. Or third, you can marshal your armies and march to Khalidor beside us. That way you can fight those you say you truly hate, and have a chance to defeat them. If you fight beside us, I will give you a fifteen-year grant to the lands you now occupy. But, and I can't stress this enough, after that time, you will leave Cenarian lands forever. Regardless of your choice, my armies will march in the spring. We will head east first. If you don't join with us, we will wipe you out, and we won't stop at our own borders. We will notify every kingdom on whose lands you might hide that we are coming. Perhaps one of them might join you to fight against us. But then again, they might choose to join us. It depends on how much goodwill you've built up with your neighbors."

Tertulus Martus laughed nervously. "Those terms are clearly not acceptable, but I'm sure our negotiators will be able to find something mutually—"

"If you don't choose to fight beside Cenaria, you will

be choosing to fight against Cenaria. I win wars in such a way that I don't have to fight them twice."

"You can't come after us, not with your full strength, not with Khalidor to your north."

"Khalidor has suffered a great defeat and there are defensible passes between our borders. Khalidor doesn't hold any of my land. You do. I have made an oath to Lantano Garuwashi that he will have a great battle come spring. Together he and I can wipe you out. Such a victory, I dare say, would endear him greatly to the Ceurans back home. What we cannot do without you is destroy Khalidor. No matter what, the sa'ceurai will go home next summer. I have one year to destroy one or both of the greatest threats to my realm, so I've no reason to hold anything back, do I?"

"You're mad," Tertulus said, throwing away a lifetime of diplomatic training.

"I'm desperate. There's a difference. I have no intention of giving you a good deal, ambassador. You're overextended, weakened, surrounded by enemies, and quite frankly, you piss me off. I don't intend to negotiate. We've written up a treaty in full, with details on how your forces will be integrated with ours for the length of the war with Khalidor and details of how we will be sure that you leave Cenaria after your fifteen-year grant has expired. I will give you only enough time to take this to your Overlord, give him three days to discuss it with his advisers, and get back here. Any modifications he proposes will be considered a rejection of the treaty. That's all there is to it. On the other hand, if you truly hate Khalidor, if you hate black magic and how it has enslaved an entire country and seeks to destroy Midcyru, this is the opportunity of

a lifetime. We could destroy Khalidor once and for all."
Logan gestured and a scroll in an ornate case was brought
forward. "Now I advise you to get your horse. Your answer is due three weeks from today. Delinquency will be
considered a declaration of war."

57

Elene looked at the woman on the bed in the Chantry's hospital floor. Vi's eyes were swollen, her light freckles almost green against her pale skin. Two days ago, Vi had fallen unconscious with a cry as they'd been walking together. Elene had been surprised how well they'd been getting along, then this had happened. "Have you figured anything out?"

"It's definitely the bond," Sister Ariel said. That was good and bad. The only other guess they'd had was that Vi's rapid progress with her Talent had been hiding some flaw, and all her power had rebounded on her. From her talks with Sister Ariel, Elene had learned that Vi was terrifically Talented, but completely uneven in what she learned. Her wetboy training had enabled her to use her Talent easily, but she'd missed certain basics—and the Sisters had no idea which ones, so it seemed Vi mastered some difficult things as easily as breathing, and some easy things she couldn't get at all. When she'd collapsed, everyone had been frightened.

Of course, if it was the bond, that meant something had gone really wrong with Kylar. Elene looked at Sister Ariel.

"We've had pigeons from Cenaria that a treason trial was being concluded," Sister Ariel said. "I deduce from Vi's state that the sentence is being carried out even now. The wheel, I would imagine." She looked up and down the corridor. "With Kylar's special . . . gifts, it's taking longer than it should. And Vi has been helping him heal by taking some of his suffering onto herself. It's only making the inevitable last longer, so it's a cruel kindness, but it is well meant."

Kylar was dying, right now? Elene should have felt it, she should have known as Vi did. In fact, she would have, if Vi hadn't stolen her ring. Jealousy flashed through her, and she suppressed it only with difficulty. Dammit, why couldn't you forgive someone once and be done with it? "Why would she help him like that?" Elene asked.

"One can only guess. But then I don't claim to know much about love."

The word was a blow. Vi loved Kylar? This much?

Vi sat bolt upright and shrieked. Her eyes met Elene's. She grabbed her own shins. "No, I can't—I can't do it. I'm not strong enough. It hurts too much." She fell back on the bed, babbling, then shrieked again, holding her arms. "No, Kylar, no!" Then she lost consciousness, and Elene knew Kylar was dead.

Sister Ariel stepped forward immediately and grabbed Vi's earring. She tried to pry it off, but it wouldn't budge. "Dammit. The bond's not broken. Not even by his . . ." she trailed off, realizing that this place was too public to admit Kylar's immortality. "I was hoping—well, not hoping that he would . . . you know what, but that if he did, that the bond would break." Sister Ariel grimaced and looked away. "It was my last hope for you. The bond really is forever. I'm sorry, Elene. I'm sorry."

The walk through the golden halls of death was familiar now. Kylar glided forward, not really touching the ground. It was as if the mind constructed movement as walking, having to impose some order on a realm that existed without human analogues.

The Antechamber of the Mystery was exactly as he remembered it. The Wolf sat on his throne, yellow eyes lambent, hostility etched into his burn-scarred face. Two doors sat opposite him: the plain wood door through which Kylar would walk back to life, and the gold door leaking warm light around its edges, barred to him forever. The ghostly presence of others filled the room. They moved unseen, staring, talking about him.

"Congratulations, Nameless," the Wolf said. "You've proved you can sacrifice yourself like you don't care if you die. Like you don't give a damn about the living. How like the young." The wolfish smile was cruel.

Kylar was too tired to play games. The Wolf didn't intimidate him anymore. "Why do you hate me?" he asked.

The Wolf cocked his head, taken off guard. "Because you're a waste, Nameless. People love you more than you have any right to, and you treat them like they're shit to be scraped off your boots."

It was so unfair after what Kylar had gone through that

he threw his hands up. "You know what, to hell with you. You can make your little cryptic comments and hate me if you want to, but at least call me by my fucking name."

"And what name is that?" the Wolf asked.

"Kylar. Kylar Stern."

"Kylar Stern? The stern, undying dier? That's not a name; it's a title. It's a judge."

"Azoth, then."

"You are many leagues from that shitless, witless rat, but even were you he, do you know what azoth is?"

"What do you mean?"

The Wolf laughed unkindly. "Azoth is an old word for quicksilver. Random, formless, unpredictable, literally mercurial. You, Nameless, can be anyone and thus are no one. You're smoke, a shadow that melts away in the light of day. Kagé they call you. A shadow of what you could be and a shadow of your master, who was a titan."

"My master was a coward! He never even told me who he was!" Kylar shouted. He blinked. The depth of his rage left him shaken. Where had that come from?

The Wolf was pensive. The ghosts in the room fell silent. Then, in a murmur unintelligible to Kylar's ears, one of them spoke to the Wolf. The Wolf folded his hands over his stomach. He nodded, acquiescing. "Prince Acaelus Thorne of Trayethell was a warrior and not much else. Neither introspective nor wise, he was one of the rare good men who love war. He didn't hate himself or life. He wasn't cruel. He simply gloried in a contest with the highest possible stakes. He was good at it, too, and he became one of Jorsin Alkestes' best friends.

"That nettled one of Jorsin's other best friends, an easily nettled archmagus named Ezra, who thought Acaelus a charismatic fool who happened to be good at swinging a sword. In return, Acaelus thought Ezra a coward who took Jorsin away from where he belonged in the front lines. When the Champions were chosen—the men and women who were Jorsin's final hope of victory—Ezra intended to bond the Devourer himself. It was by far the most powerful ka'kari and he had sweat and bled for it. The only man to whom he would willingly surrender it was Jorsin. But the Devourer didn't choose Ezra. Or Jorsin. It chose the sword-swinger.

"Perhaps you can appreciate why it seemed odd that an artifact which by its nature was concerned with concealment would go to a man completely lacking subtlety."

It did seem odd, though the choice had obviously proved wise.

"The Devourer didn't choose your master simply because he was an obscure choice. It chose Acaelus because it understood his heart. Acaelus loved the clash of arms, but most men who love battle love it because it proves their mastery over others. If the Devourer had given itself to a man who loved power as Ezra did, it would have spawned a tyrant of terrible proportions. Think of a God-king made truly a god and you have a bit of it. What your master loved, at his core, was the brotherhood of war. He thirsted for the camaraderie of men risking all to come through for each other.

"The Devourer is nothing if not talented at setting up tensions. For your master to take the black ka'kari, he had to leave that brotherhood. He had to give up what he loved most and become known as a traitor. That tension forced Acaelus to become a deeper, wiser, and sadder man. Then of course, there was the Devourer's greater tension and

greater power. Your master was a man of war, but the
vagaries of war are such that even the mighty might be
clipped by a stray arrow or a falling horse or the mistake
of a friend. So your master lived with the tension of his
calling pulling against his fear for any he loved.

"Acaelus sought to live in peace. He had a few lifetimes as a farmer, a hunter, an apothecary, a perfumer,
a blacksmith—can you imagine? Yet though they were
full lives—sometimes married, even with children—they
were not fulfilled lives, for a man who denies what is essential to his being is a man who drills holes in the cup of
his own happiness. How could he help but resent those he
loved as they kept him from his calling? Here was a man
who could lead armies, who could defeat invasions almost single-handedly. This man was compelled to farm?
By his own love? Time and again, he returned to the
battlefield because the evil was too great to be ignored.
And sometimes he was victorious and there was no price
to pay. And sometimes his wife died, but it was worse
when his children died; his marriages never survived his
children's deaths. He was a man who never learned to forgive himself."

Kylar was missing some essential piece that the Wolf
thought he understood, but the man kept speaking, and
Kylar was so hungry to hear more about his master that
he didn't dare interrupt.

"So in the end, he sought to defeat the power of the
ka'kari by defeating love," the Wolf said. "He thought
that if he refused to love, death could take nothing from
him. He deafened himself to love's voice with killing and
whoring and drinking. He became a wetboy because wetboys cannot love. He was ultimately successful, and the

ka'kari abandoned him because he finally knew love's antithesis."

"Hatred?"

"Indifference. When Vonda's life was threatened, Durzo was relieved. The path he took was a reasonable one—he kept the ka'kari out of young Garoth Ursuul's hands—but the truth was that he didn't really care if Vonda died. That was what broke the ka'kari's bond."

"But he came back. Even after I bonded the ka'kari."

"Because he loved you, Kylar. He chose to die for you, to give up everything he still had—his sword, his ka'kari, his power, his life—for you. There is no greater love. Such a death was rewarded with new life."

"By who? You?" Kylar asked. The Wolf said nothing. "The ka'kari? The God?"

"Perhaps it is just the way greatest magic works: justice and mercy entwined. It's a mystery, Kylar. A mystery on a par with the question of why is there life at all? If you wish to answer the mystery by positing a God, you can, or you can say that it just is—and either way, be glad for it, for it is a gift. Or a most fortunate accident."

Kylar felt suddenly small in the workings of a universe vast beyond comprehension, vast and yet perhaps not ambivalent even to Durzo's suffering. One last life—a sheer gift. The ka'kari was even more strange and marvelous than he'd imagined.

"I thought . . ." Kylar shook his head. "I thought it was just amazing magic."

The Wolf laughed, and even the ghosts in the room seemed startled. "It is amazing magic, it just isn't *just* amazing magic. The most potent magics are tied to human truths: beauty and passion and yearning and fortitude and valor and empathy. It is from these that the ka'kari draw their strength as much as it is from the magic they are imbued with."

"And the darker truths?" Kylar asked.

"All human truths. Vengeance and hatred and glorying in destruction and ambition and greed and all the rest have power. The trick to being truly powerful is that your character be in line with the magic you attempt. Meisters make terrible healers. By the same token, most green mages have too much empathy to make war. The more fully human you are, the greater the diversity of your talents. The more deeply you feel, the more potent your gifts. That, Kylar, is why you called the ka'kari. You ached for love. Not only did you want be loved, as do we all, but you wanted to lavish love on your beloved. You wanted it with your whole being and you thought it had been denied you forever."

The way he said it embarrassed Kylar.

"Don't be embarrassed," the Wolf said. "What is more human than to love and be loved? Between loving and thinking that love was denied you, that tension amplified your power."

"That tension's with me still, isn't it?" Kylar asked. "For my love will always be dangerous to those I love."

"Clever, isn't it? Your power is tied to your capacity for love. The creator of the ka'kari gave you a gift and built into it the means to keep it forever powerful. No mean trick, that."

"A mean trick is exactly what it is," Kylar snarled. "What the hell am I supposed to do?"

"It's a problem," the Wolf said, shrugging.

But Kylar wasn't listening. He could feel the blood

draining out of his face. "Oh my God," he said. His heart was a thunder in his ears, a rock in his chest. He'd meant he was dangerous to those he loved because his enemies could always threaten them. That wasn't what the Wolf meant. He'd been telling Kylar for five minutes and Kylar hadn't understood. Breathless, Kylar asked, "You mean every time I've died someone I love has died for me?"

"Of course. That's the price of immortality."

Kylar's throat constricted. He was suffocating. "Who . . . ?"

"Serah Drake died when Roth killed you. Mags Drake died for Scarred Wrable's arrow on the trail. Ulana Drake died when the Godking killed you."

Kylar's knees buckled. He wanted to throw up. He wanted to faint. Anything, anything to not be. But the moment stretched on and in the midst of the gale, he found himself thinking, thank the God it wasn't Uly or Elene, and then he cursed himself for the thought. Who was he to weigh one life against another and be thankful that one should die, simply because he loved her less? He'd killed them. Count Drake had taken in a foul-mouthed, amoral guttershite and made him part of his family. And Kylar had murdered the Drakes through his carelessness, his arrogance. For every gift Count Drake had given Kylar, he'd repaid him with grief.

"And for my blasphemy? When I took money to be killed?"

"Jarl."

Kylar screamed. He tore his cloak. He pounded the ground with his fists, but there was no pain here, no body to mortify. The tears rolled down his cheeks and there was no comfort. "I didn't know. I didn't know. Oh, God."

The Wolf was astounded. "But of course you knew. Durzo left you a letter on his body. He explained everything. He told me he put it in his breast pocket."

"I couldn't read it! It was soaked with blood! I couldn't read a damned thing!" Then the last revelation hit him. "Who is it this time?" he asked, desperately. "Who dies for me this time?"

The Wolf was aghast. His lambent eyes and scarred face softened, and he looked fully human for the first time. "Kylar. I'm sorry. I thought you knew. I thought you knew all along."

"Please. I'll trade back! Let me trade back!"

"It doesn't work like that. There's nothing either of us can do. This time it's Elene."

58

Kylar woke on a cold stone slab in a cold room. He didn't open his eyes. If he could have willed himself never to wake again, he would have. He was still except for his breath and the currents of his life's blood rushing through his veins. As always when he came back from the dead, his body felt wonderful. Absolutely whole, powerful, bursting with energy. He'd stolen a life and it came to him abundantly. He was overfull, spilling life in every direction. His health was a mockery.

Tears welled in his eyes and spilled down his cheeks to his ears. No wonder the Wolf had thought him a monster. He'd thought Kylar was throwing away the lives of those he loved and who loved him.

He lay on his back, but it only got worse, so he opened his eyes. The air was stale, dank. The ceiling was ornate, cool white marble. He was in a crypt. Only feet away, on slabs like his, were a man's body and a woman's. The man was big, holding a big sword. The woman's throat had been cut, and from how she'd decomposed, Kylar guessed she'd been bled dry. The man had died around the same time, surely during the coup. They were Logan's parents. Around them, the walls were filled with row upon row of Gyre corpses, stretching back centuries. Logan had put Kylar in his own family's crypt.

Kylar stood, not even feeling stiffness from having slept on marble. He'd been dressed in a cloth-of-gold tunic and white breeches, and fine fawnskin shoes. It was, of course, pitch black in the crypt. There was no way of telling what time of day it was, and the mouth of the crypt was sealed with a massive rock cut into the shape of a wheel taller than a man. If Kylar remembered correctly, the crypt was located outside the city and sunk beneath the ground. If so, he had a good chance of getting out without anyone knowing. Regardless, he had to get out, so he grabbed the wheel and heaved with his Talent.

Slowly, the massive stone rolled a half turn and settled into another rest. Kylar went invisible and stepped outside.

It was night, but the harvest moon was bright and high overhead. In the narrow stairwell that led to the crypt stood a young girl, her eyes wide with fear. It was Blue, the little guttershite from Black Dragon guild.

Kylar stopped, still invisible, and rubbed his face. Blue didn't move. He could tell she wanted to run but refused to. Brave little shite. "Kylar?" she whispered.

What was he supposed to do? Kill her? Avoid her and let her blab stories about the crypt opening? It was unlikely, but someone might open the crypt to check it out. And what would they do when they saw Kylar was gone?

"Kylar, I know you're there. Take me with you."

Staying invisible, Kylar asked, "Have you ever killed anyone, Blue?"

She gasped and swallowed, looking for the source of the voice. "No," she whispered.

"Do you want to kill people?"

"I'd kill Dag Tarkus. He kicked Piggy in the stomach for stealing and the next day he died."

"What if I told you that to be my apprentice you'd have to kill a dozen kids like Piggy? What if I told you you had to kill your whole guild?"

Blue started crying.

"You just want out, don't you?"

She nodded her head.

"Then I need you to do two things, Blue. First, never—ever—speak about this. If you tell anyone, bad people will find out, and they'll kill lots of good people. You understand? You can't even tell your best friend."

Blue nodded. "I got no friends, not after Piggy died."

"Go to the corner of Verdun and Gar. I'll meet you in an hour."

"Promise?"

"I promise."

Blue left and Kylar closed the crypt. He found a safe house and loaded up everything he needed, including Retribution, which he had left before he killed the queen, knowing his weapons would be confiscated. He wrote a note to Rimbold Drake, first explaining about the laundress he'd maimed and asking Drake to pay restitution, and then explaining what the Wolf told Kylar he'd cost the Drakes. He grabbed several bags of gold and a few poisons and changes of clothing, took a cloak and pulled the hood over his face.

He found Blue sitting at the intersection. She scrambled to her feet.

"Inside that house lives a good man, Blue. He was poisoned and nearly died during the coup, and the Khalidorans killed his wife and two of his daughters. He's the best man I know, and I think he might need you as much as you need him. In my note, I've asked him to raise you. He'll give you the only chance you'll ever have to make something of yourself. But it won't be easy. If you go in this house, you stay until you walk out a lady. Is that what you want?"

"A lady?" Blue asked, her face lit with impossible yearning.

"Say it."

"I want to be somebody. I want to be a lady."

"I believe you." Kylar put his hand to a crack in the door, sent the ka'kari through, and opened the latch. He opened the door and they walked past the porter's hut to the front door. Kylar handed a bag full of gold crowns to Blue. It was so heavy she could barely hold it. Then he put the note in her hand and threw back his hood, so she would never doubt that it was him. "Blue, I'm trusting you. I see souls. I weigh them. From yours, I know you're worth it. Be good to Count Drake. I wasn't as good to him as he deserved."

With that, Kylar pounded on the door and went invisible. He waited until the bleary-eyed count opened the door. Rimbold Drake looked at Blue, confused. She was too terrified to speak. After a moment, he took the note from her hand. After he read it, he wept.

Kylar turned to go.

"You were better than you know," Drake said to the night. "I forgive you any wrong you think you have done me. You will always be welcome here, my son."

Kylar disappeared into the night. It was where he belonged.

59

*A*fter two days, they moved Solon to another room. It was still locked, the windows covered with bars, the cedar door banded with iron, but this room had a view of Whitecliff Castle's courtyard. The courtyard was decorated in a style fit for the wedding, greens the color of the vines and the seas, and the purples of wine and royalty dominating.

"I don't know who you are, Pretender," one of Solon's guards said. He was a paunchy man with heavy jowls and haphazardly polished armor. "But enjoy the wedding, because it's the last thing you'll ever see."

"Why's that?" Solon asked.

"Because the Mikaidon wanted his first order as emperor to be your death."

The other guard, a rail-thin man with a single eyebrow, looked nervous and guilty. "Shut it, Ori. Nysos' blood, it's gonna be a bad enough day as it is." To Solon, he said, "We'll make it quick, I promise." He exited, watching Solon for any sudden movement, and locked the door behind himself.

Solon was surprised to find a tub full of water and fresh clothes in the room. He scrubbed himself and donned the clean garments, thinking. Oshobi was already giving orders to Kaede's guards. That couldn't be good, but it didn't necessarily mean what Solon suspected. Solon had never learned how much power Kaede intended to share once she married. When she talked with him two days ago she hadn't seemed desperate enough to grant Oshobi total power.

It made him feel sick. For the last two days, he'd thought through every option he had, and he couldn't find anything that would assert his own rights without undermining Kaede's. He didn't know what any of the political undercurrents were, so anything he did could have the opposite of the intended effect. But the clean clothes laid out for him, clothing fit for a noble, if not quite royalty, told him that Kaede most likely hadn't intended him to die today. Was this his chance? Or was she punishing him by forcing him to watch a wedding that she saw as his fault?

Outside, the nobles were gathering in order of precedence, standing as Sethi always stood to witness a wedding. Soon, at least four hundred of them surrounded the platform where the Empress and Emperor-to-be would be wed. Solon could pick out many faces he recognized, and saw a frightening number of absences, too. Had his brother killed so many? How had Sijuron become such a monster without Solon knowing?

The ring of the singing swords announced the beginning of the ceremony. On the platform, the dancers faced each other. Each wore a mask, the man the suitor's mask, which today was deadly serious. A pubescent boy wore the woman's mask, today lovely but austere in keeping with the empress's dignity. Each held a specially shaped hollow sword that would sing in the dance, tones varied by the dancers' grip and where each struck the other. The swords were pitched at octaves, and the duel—symbolic of the couple's courtship—was always partly choreographed and partly extemporaneous. It was a perennial favorite, and skilled dancers were the most expensive part of a wedding. The dances, proclaimed sacred to Nysos, ranged from the erotic to the comedic. It was also usually the most anxiety-provoking time of a wedding for the couple. Dancers being the artists they were, there was no guaranteeing they wouldn't make the man or woman or both look like fools, and the sword dance was often the only thing remembered about the wedding.

The dancers bowed low, but kept their eyes up, as if suspicious of each other, and then they began. For a time as they danced, Solon forgot that he was in a prison. They gave the boy a quick hand for Kaede's quick tongue, and a wide range. A woman known as a scold might be given a single note for an entire dance, while an excitable man might be given only notes at the extremes of the singing sword. The man playing Oshobi was a huge presence, forceful and manly and, if slower, also stronger than Kaede. Whoever they were, these dancers were incorruptible, unafraid of even a man who would be emperor. In their dance, Solon read the courtship perfectly.

Oshobi had always pursued with a single-minded determination. Kaede weakened early, then rallied for years. Always, Oshobi pursued, and the dancer gave a lightly mocking tone to it that only a skilled eye would have seen. There was the suggestion that Oshobi wanted not Kaede, but that which was behind her—missing opportunities at the woman as he aimed at the throne.

Kaede slowly tired, but the dancers underplayed it, not suggesting that Oshobi beat her into submission, but simply allowing her to slow to his level and make him look more brilliant as he matched and overmatched her, cadences singing together until Oshobi took up Kaede's line. As the dance wound to a close, Kaede bowed to her knees and spread her arms to take the ceremonial touch over the heart. In apparent haste, the dancer playing Oshobi stepped forward too quickly and slipped, his sword tapped her throat for the barest instant before he righted himself and touched it to her heart.

It was so well done that even Solon believed for a moment that the dancer really had slipped. Everyone took it as that, or decided to take it as that: a slight error in an otherwise flawless performance. They cheered wildly and once the cheering stopped, the betrothed entered.

Solon's heart leapt to his throat as Kaede strode forward. She wore a purple samite cape with a long train, edged in lace. A crown of vines with ripe purple grapes was woven through her long black hair. It being her wedding, both of her breasts were bare, the nipples rouged, and beneath her navel her bare stomach was adorned with ancient fertility runes. A cloth-of-gold skirt hung low on her hips, trailing slightly behind her, her wine-stained bare feet barely winking out. Most women exposed more of their ankles, saying the juice of the grape is clothing enough for a wedding. Apparently Kaede really did believe that a queen was a queen first and a woman sometime later. But after a decade and a half in Midcyru, the modesty was lost on Solon. The sight of her here, like this,

filled him with every sort of longing. The skirt had neither
buttons nor clasps nor ties, nor underclothes beneath it. It
was finished the morning of the wedding with the woman
inside it. It was to be torn off by the groom in his passion.
Revelers outside the wedding chamber would call loudly
until the groom threw it out the window. In ancient times
and in some rural areas still, the skirt was always white,
and ripped open but not removed until the wedding was
consummated. Then the revelers would parade with the
"proof" of the woman's virginity, which as often as not
was sheep's blood. Most mothers provided their daughters with a vial of it, in case she had broken her hymen
licitly or illicitly. It was a tradition Solon was glad had
mostly disappeared, not only because he thought it was
gross, but also because he found it hard to imagine enjoying consummating his marriage with drunken screaming
assholes pounding on the walls.

In the courtyard, Oshobi Takeda walked forward.
Solon felt a stab of hatred. *He* should be walking forward now. *He* should be the one who tore Kaede's skirt
tonight. Oshobi Takeda came into the circle bare-chested
as well, runes of vigor and potency painted on the surface
of a stomach so muscular and devoid of fat that it wasn't
flat but ridged. He too wore vines through his hair and a
simple green cape, paired with cloth-of-gold trousers that
ended just below the knee.

Oshobi mounted the platform, barely looking at
Kaede. Solon thought he must be either blind or homosexual to disregard such beauty. He turned and addressed
the assembled nobles. "I came here today to marry our
empress. It was in my heart to unite this land as it hasn't
been united for more than a decade. I know all of us were

dismayed when we heard of Daune Wariyamo's infidelities, and though it strained my family's honor, I came here determined to wed."

From his position, Solon could see what the nobles below could not. At every exit, armored city guards had lined up, and with them in irregular ranks stood many of the royal guards. The strength was, so far, hidden, but they could move in on the assembled nobles in moments. What Solon couldn't see was how Kaede was taking this prologue to treason.

He didn't have to wait long.

Kaede strode up onto the platform directly to Oshobi and slapped his face. "If you speak treason, Oshobi Takeda, I will have your head," Kaede said in a clear, fearless voice.

An older noble Solon recognized as Nori Oshibatu, long a friend of the Wariyamos, shot a look at Oshobi and stepped forward. "My dear, Kaede, our beloved empress, you sound hysterical. This is not befitting. Please, he only speaks." Nori pulled Kaede back into the crowd, where several other family "friends" closed around her.

Oshobi smiled like the big cat he was. "I came here to serve Seth, but this very morning, I discovered something my honor could not countenance. Daune Wariyamo had on her person letters from the late emperor's brother Solon to Kaede. In these letters, he spoke of his trysts with her in the castle and of a secret marriage."

"You lie!" Kaede shrieked.

Solon's heart sank. The trysts in the castle had only been attempted trysts, culminating in the disaster of her mother coming in on them naked and beating Solon with a shoe. It would have been worth it if she'd come in ten minutes later or—well, he'd been a young man—maybe two minutes later. The marriage, of course, was a total fiction.

But Oshobi was quick. "I have the letters here!" he said, brandishing a sheaf. "And this woman was with Lady Wariyamo when she came upon you fornicating in the castle." A slave woman was thrust forward. "I do so swear," she said in a tiny voice.

"Louder," Oshobi demanded.

"I swear it's true!"

The nobles were in the predictable uproar, but Oshobi was wise enough that he didn't call his men forward. Kaede was screaming, but someone put a hand over her mouth, and numerous men were restraining her.

"So you see, even if we believe that Kaede wasn't incestuous in her sluttish trysts in our nation's very heart, we know that she married Sijuron Tofusin. A marriage null and void because she was already married—to the emperor's brother!"

Oshobi painted a sad look on his face. "I woke this morning, willing to dishonor my family because I wanted to do what was right for our country—"

Behind Solon, the door creaked open. He turned away from the courtyard to see his two guards enter. "All right," the paunchy one said, "we already let you see more of the show than we was supposed to. You can figure how it turns out from here. You ready?"

"Yes," Solon said. He drew in his Talent. "Which of you would like to die first?"

"Huh?" they asked in unison.

"Together then," he said, and stilled their hearts with his Talent.

The guards collapsed, one crumpling, the other falling full on his face. Solon took a sword and faced the barred window.

With a concussion that rocked the castle, Solon blew out the entire wall. Stones rained on the crowd fifty paces away. Everyone ducked and turned to see what had happened. *And Dorian always said I wasn't subtle.*

Solon jumped down lightly and strode toward the crowd. A guard stepped in his path, wide-eyed and gulping. Solon gestured as if shooing a fly and a wall of air flipped the guard aside.

"I am Solonariwan Tofusin, son of Emperor Cresus Tofusin, Light of the West, Protector of the Isles, and High Admiral of the Royal Fleets of Seth." It was a deliberately ambiguous construction, whether he was listing his father's titles, or claiming them for himself. "I have come home, and I call you a traitor and a liar, Oshibi. And even if your despicable lies were true, you have no claim to this throne while I live."

"We can remedy that," Oshobi snarled.

Solon advanced quickly onto the platform, not giving Oshobi time to think. "You would duel me?" Solon asked. He laughed scornfully. "A Tofusin does not dirty his hands with the blood of a dog."

Oshobi roared, drew his sword and hacked at Solon with all his considerable strength. Solon deflected it. His counterstroke cut halfway into Oshobi's neck. Oshobi's eyes went big, but he tried to complete one more slash while Solon's sword was stuck. A sliver of magic enervated Oshobi's fingers. The sword dropped.

"However," Solon said, "I'll make an exception for a Little Cat." He ripped the sword out of Oshobi's neck and blood sprayed over the platform as the big man dropped onto his face. Solon put his foot on the neck of his dying foe and pointed the sword at the nobles holding Kaede. "That's your empress," Solon said. "I'd advise you to take your hands off her."

60

After riding most of the night, Kylar camped a short distance off the road, merely unsaddling Tribe and throwing a blanket on the ground. A few hours later, Tribe's snort woke him. Kylar blinked and rolled to his feet.

"So you haven't forgotten everything I taught you," a brown-clad figure said, leading his horse to tie it next to Tribe.

"Master?" Kylar asked.

Dehvirahaman ko Bruhmaeziwakazari snorted. It was odd to hear the sound, so characteristically Durzo, coming out of the Ymmuri's mouth. He glanced at Retribution in Kylar's hand. "Good, I see you haven't managed to lose it again, yet. See that you don't, would you? You ready to ride?"

Kylar felt an odd excitement. He did feel ready to ride. The overflow of energy from his invocation of immortality hadn't worn off yet. "I'm not dreaming this, am I?" he asked.

Dehvi lifted an eyebrow. "There's one way to find out for sure," he said.

"What's that?"

"Go piss in the woods. If you feel wet and warm afterward, wake up."

Laughing, Kylar went and relieved himself. When he came back, Dehvi was seated cross-legged and had laid out a huge, albeit cold, breakfast.

Kylar tore into the food with gusto that surprised himself, though apparently not Dehvi. The scene still had an air of unreality, though, and Kylar kept glancing at him. Finally, the Ymmuri said, "If you're looking for Durzo's mannerisms, you're going to see fewer and fewer of them. I don't chew garlic anymore, for one. And I'm getting rid of the rest as fast as I can. A new face isn't much good if you still do everything else the same. I have done this a few times. So if you need me to prove who I am, let's get it over with."

"There is one thing Durzo told me that he never told anyone else. You've had all these names, and you always picked something with meaning: Ferric Fireheart, Gaelan Starfire, Hrothan Steelbender. Even the other wetboys had names that meant something: Hu Gibbet, Scarred Wrable. Why Durzo Blint? Is that another Old Jaeran pun?"

Dehvi laughed. "Trick question. I never told you why I chose it. But to answer, it was supposed to be Durzo Flint. I was drunk. Someone repeated it Blint, and I didn't care enough to correct them. Next?"

"Flint makes a lot more sense, you old bastard."

"Only by nature, not by birth. Anything else?"

Kylar got grim. "What does immortality cost?"

"Right to the gut, huh?" Durzo said. He cleared his throat and looked away. "Every new life costs the life of someone you love."

There it was, as simple as anything. If Durzo had told him that before the coup, everything would be different. Of course, Durzo had tried to tell him, in the letter.

"Is there any way to stop it?" Kylar asked.

"You mean stop your immortality or stop it from killing someone else?"

"Either. Both."

"The Wolf never told me the limits—maybe he didn't know himself. I avoided anything that would fully destroy my body like burning or being drawn and quartered."

"And Curoch?"

Durzo shot Kylar a sharp look. "A fatal blow from Curoch would blow apart the immortality magic. Jorsin feared the Devourer. He made sure there was at least one way to kill an immortal."

Kylar had a sudden feeling of dislocation. He was talking with someone who had known Jorsin Alkestes. Jorsin Alkestes! And Jorsin had feared the magic Kylar possessed. "What about stopping it from costing someone else's life?" Kylar asked.

Durzo sighed. "You think in seven centuries I didn't try? It's deep magic, kid. A life for a life. The Wolf can delay it, but not stop it, and it's not easy even for him."

Kylar cleared his throat. "What if, um, what if I were killed by Curoch during the time between me dying and the person who is going to die for me dying?"

The look on Durzo's face made it clear that Kylar's question was far too specific for him to dismiss as theoretical. "Boy, you have no idea what Curoch is like—"

"Yes I do, I threw it into Ezra's Wood."

"You what?!"

"I made a deal with the Wolf. I didn't get your note until afterward."

Durzo rubbed his temples. "And what did he give you in return for the most powerful artifact in the world?"

"He brought me back to life faster—and gave me my arm back, which I kind of cut off."

Durzo's flat stare was all too familiar, despite that it was coming through almond-shaped eyes. It suggested he was seeing previously undredged depths of stupidity. "And between assassinating a Godking and a Cenarian queen and rescuing a man from the Hole and making a king of him, when did you squeeze in the time to find and lose the world's most coveted magical sword?" Durzo asked.

"It only took me a week. Lantano Garuwashi had it. I dueled him for it."

"Is he as good as they say?"

"Better. And he's not even Talented."

"Then how'd you win?" Durzo asked.

"Hey!" Kylar protested.

"Kylar, I trained you. You're not the best. Someday, maybe. So either he's not as good as they say, or you got lucky, or you cheated."

"I got lucky," Kylar admitted. "Is it so bad though? I mean throwing Curoch in the Wood?"

"Do you know who the Wolf is?" Durzo asked.

"That was the next question."

"The better question is who the Wolf was. No one knows what he is now."

"I'll bite. Who was the Wolf?" Kylar asked.

"In Jorsin Alkestes' court, there was a mage with golden eyes. He was slightly less Talented than Jorsin himself in terms of raw power, but whereas Jorsin had to learn the arts of war and leadership and diplomacy in addition to magecraft, the golden-eyed mage had only magecraft to study, and he was the kind of genius of magic born once in a thousand years. He had few graces and fewer friends, but Jorsin meant the world to him. In the war, he lost everything: Jorsin, all his tomes of magic, his only other friend, Oren Razin, and his fiancée. He lost his sanity, too, and no one knows if he ever really regained it. He hid in a forest where he could work out his hatred. The forest, of course, took his name."

"Ezra's Wood," Kylar whispered. "The Wolf is Ezra?"

"Jorsin had a close friend who betrayed him, a man named Roygaris Ursuul."

"Oh God."

"During the war, Roygaris Made something—out of himself. We called it the Reaver. It was impervious to magic, faster than thought. It killed thousands of us." Durzo touched his cheek. "I was the first person to even wound it. My pockmarks are from where its blood sprayed me. Magic couldn't heal me. After the last battle, the Reaver was badly wounded. Instead of killing it, Ezra took it to the Wood. Fifty years later, there was a power struggle of some sort, and every living thing in that wood died—and dies to this day, whether animal, krul, mage, or the purest virgin. Armies from both north and south have perished there. Whatever it is, the Wolf has been collecting artifacts for seven centuries, and he gets the best of every deal."

Kylar felt suddenly cold. "What did you give him?"

"A couple of the ka'kari. He wants them all—and Curoch and Iures."

"Iures?"

"The companion to Curoch. The Sword of Power and the Staff of Law. Jorsin died the day Iures was finished, before he could use it. No one knows what happened to it."

"But what's the Wolf trying to accomplish?"

"I don't know. Kylar, we've held one ka'kari, and its power is awesome. Imagine what an archmagus could do with seven ka'kari *and* Curoch *and* Iures. Even if the Wolf is Ezra, would you trust a madman with that much power? Would you even trust yourself? What if the Wolf isn't Ezra, what if it's Roygaris?"

"So you've opposed him," Kylar said.

"After I gave him the brown ka'kari, I thought better of it. Since then, I've scattered ka'kari to the ends of the earth. This is no short-term ambition. It has taken the Wolf seven hundred years to get a few ka'kari and now Curoch, and perhaps Iures. He doesn't care if it takes another hundred years to get the rest. This is part of your burden. Make sure he doesn't get them all."

"But he might be on our side," Kylar said.

"You tell that to all the innocents he's murdered."

"What do I tell all the innocents you've murdered?"

Durzo blinked. He chewed on his lip. "The problem with the black ka'kari is that it doesn't work in a mirror. I could never see the state of my own soul, and you can't see yours either. But if you wish, bring it to your eyes now. Judge me."

Kylar didn't dare. Durzo had poisoned dozens during the coup alone. There were surely hundreds—thousands—more deaths on his soul. If Kylar saw profound guilt, he might not be able to stop himself from killing Durzo. Or at least trying. It wasn't a fight he wanted to win, and now that he knew the cost of losing, that was even worse. "What should I do about the Wolf?" Kylar asked.

"Nothing now. But if you hear that Mount Tenji isn't spitting fire for the first time in two centuries, or you hear that the Tlaxini Maelstrom has stilled, you need to move fast. Like I said, this is not a short-term threat."

"When does it end?"

Durzo snorted. His hand moved to his belt where he used to carry a small pouch of garlic cloves. He noticed and gritted his teeth. "It could be hundreds of years. It could be twenty. Giving him Curoch was a big mistake."

Thanks. "Can we win?"

"We? I'm mortal now, kid. At best I have thirty, forty years left? I'm not terribly interested in tangling with the Wolf. Can you win? It's possible. He can't live forever. His magic's only an imitation of ours. Yours."

"He made one black ka'kari, why not make another one for himself?" Kylar asked.

"Made it? No. Ezra found it. He studied it to make the others, but they were all inferior copies."

"It told me—"

"Let me guess, something about being crafted with 'limited intelligence'? The black ka'kari was ancient when I was born, Kylar. It told you that so it wouldn't scare the shit out of you. You're sharing your head with a being whose power dwarfs yours."

~I wouldn't say my power exactly dwarfs *yours.~*

"Give the fucker my regards," Durzo said.

~I loved you better than you loved yourself, Acaelus.~

"I have to say, though, if he tells you to move, do it," Durzo said.

Right. Thanks. The first time the ka'kari had spoken to Kylar, it told him to duck. He hadn't—and had taken an arrow through the chest moments later. "Wait," Kylar said. "You never answered my question about dying by Curoch before the ka'kari kills someone in my place."

"Don't," Durzo said. "It's not the ka'kari that kills anyone. It's us. You're twenty years old and you've died five, six times? That's not the ka'kari's fault."

"Fine, it's my fault. Curoch?"

Irritation passed over Durzo's face, but he let it go. "Dying by Curoch might leave the person you love alive. Equally possible is that it will kill *everyone* you love. It's a feral magic. Curoch means the Sunderer. It was not intended for gentle things. It's a bad gamble, kid."

Kylar exhaled heavily. "This is all kind of a lot to absorb at once."

"Then absorb while we ride. We're burning daylight."

They rode until dark, and ate together, speaking only of inconsequential things. Kylar told Durzo everything that had happened in his absence. Durzo laughed, sometimes in the wrong places, as if laughing at similarities to his own memories, but more frequently than Kylar remembered him ever laughing before.

Then Durzo began telling stories. Kylar was surprised to find him an excellent raconteur. "I was a bard one life," Durzo said. "I took it up to train my memory. I wasn't very good."

Some of the stories he told were familiar from bards' tales Kylar had heard, though the details were very different. He told of a young Alexan the Blessed caught with dysentery in the mountains during his first campaign taking off his plate cuisses and dropping his mail trousers to squat in the bushes and then getting ambushed. His descriptions of Alexan fighting with a sword in one hand and trying to hike up his armor with the other had Kylar howling. Then Alexan tumbled down the mountain and fell a hundred feet. They found him at the bottom without a scratch—or his trousers, which had caught in a tree ten feet from the bottom of the ravine, slowing his fall and saving his life. "The Tomii used *shitting* as an intensifier, like we might say someone was damn lucky, they said he was shitting lucky. That's why they called him Alexan the Shitting Lucky. Later some prude translated it Alexan the Blessed. He was a good kid." Durzo laughed. Then his smile faded. "Broke my heart to kill him. But he needed killing by the end."

Kylar looked at his master intently. He said, "You're different now."

Durzo said nothing for a long time. He was like a caterpillar half-metamorphosed. One minute he was the old, hard-as-nails Durzo. The next he was this laughing, reminiscing stranger.

"The Wolf has worked with me for almost seven hundred years. Ezra and Roygaris were the best Healers ever. Whichever the Wolf is, he's seen me die and come back dozens of times. He knows the magic and how exactly the ka'kari worked with my body. But he isn't a prophet. At least not a natural-born one, unlike Dorian. So even with all his magic, he can only get bits and pieces. When I died, I think he spent a long time trying to figure out if my being alive one more time would help him or hurt him. Then he decided to raise me."

Kylar wondered about that. The Wolf had said Durzo's resurrection was a mystery, a gift. Was he simply being modest, or did he really not know how Durzo had come back?

"Anyway, by the time the Wolf started working on me, my body had pretty much rotted away. So I feel like a new man." He grinned, then stirred their little fire, watching the sparks.

"So this life is different, isn't it?" Kylar asked.

"Sometimes to love is easy, but to accept love is hard. I used to always be the man who led the charge. The Devourer steals that. Tell me, what kind of man would put his eight-year-old daughter at the spear tip of a cavalry charge? A monster. But what kind of man would refuse to fight when his enemies threaten all he holds dear? That's why I trained relentlessly. That's why I became the perfect killer. Because every time I wasn't good enough, I murdered someone I loved. I thought I finally defeated love when the ka'kari abandoned me, but then there you were in the tower, standing athwart fate and crying, No! I realized three things as your crazy ass dove into the river. First, you . . . cared about me."

Kylar nodded silently. To hear Durzo say it without scoffing was alien, and the man seemed to marvel at it himself.

Durzo plowed ahead. "I knew your regard wasn't easily won, and I knew you'd seen darker sides of me than I'd let even most of my wives see." He chuckled. "You know, I can ignore it when Count Drake loves me. He's a saint. He cares about everybody. No offense, but you're no saint."

Kylar smiled.

Durzo studied the fire. "Second, I . . ." He cleared his throat. "I'd tried to root out feeling anything at all with drinking and whoring and killing and isolation, and I'd made myself into a monster, but I'd still failed. I still cared about you more than I cared about myself. That tells me something about myself." He grew quiet.

"And third?" Kylar prompted.

"Third, ah hell, I don't remember. Oh, wait. I spent years beating into your skull how hard and unfair life is. And I wasn't wrong. There's no guarantee that justice will win out or that a noble sacrifice will make any difference. But when it does, there's something that still swells my chest. There's magic in that. Deep magic. It tells me that's the way things are supposed to be. Why? How? Hell, I don't know. This spring I'll turn seven hundred, and I still don't have it figured out. Most poor bastards only get a few decades. Speaking of which . . ." Durzo cleared his throat. "I've got bad news."

"Speaking of which which?" Kylar asked, chest tightening.

"Life being unfair and all that."

"Oh, great. What is it?"

"Luc Graesin? Kid you died on the wheel to save?"

"It was more for Logan than for Luc, but what about him?"

"Hanged himself," Durzo said.

"What? Who killed him? Scarred Wrable?" Kylar could see Momma K deciding that even a remote threat to Logan would have to be eliminated.

"No, he really hanged himself."

"Are you joking? After what I did for him? That asshole!"

Durzo grabbed his blanket and lay down, resting his head on his saddle. "Letting someone die for you can be tough. If anyone should understand that, it's you."

61

. . . get up in three seconds, I'm gonna nail you with a biscuit." Kylar struggled to open his eyes, and the voice went on without even slowing. "One, two, three." Kylar's eyes shot open, and he snatched the hard biscuit out of the air with such force that it exploded into crumb shrapnel.

"Dammit," he said, combing biscuit pieces out of his hair. "What'd you do that for?"

Durzo was grinning from ear to ear. "Fun," he said.

Kylar scowled. There was something different about his master. His eyes seemed a little more round, his skin a little lighter, the shirt he was wearing tighter across the chest and shoulders. "What are you doing?" he asked.

"Eating breakfast," Durzo said, chomping into another biscuit.

"I mean your face!"

"What? Pimple?" Durzo asked, patting his forehead, the word coming out "pimpuh?" around the biscuit.

"Durzo! You went to bed Ymmuri, and you woke up halfbreed."

"Oh, that. What, you want to hear more? I talked last night more than I've talked in a hundred years." Kylar thought he might not be exaggerating. "You need to learn everything at once?"

"You're mortal now. And you're *old*. You could keel over at any moment."

"Hm, you have a point," Durzo said. "You saddle the horses, I'll talk."

Kylar rolled his eyes—and began tending to the horses.

"You've tried illusory masks. I've seen your whole little scary-black-mask thing that the Sa'kagé found so impressive."

"Thanks," Kylar griped. It had been impressive, dammit. "Wait, when did you see that?"

"In Caernarvon."

"You came to Caernarvon? When did you—"

"Too late to save Jarl, but early enough to save Elene. Now stop interrupting," Durzo said. "You might have noticed there are some drawbacks to making masks of real faces, especially with disguises of people of different height from yours. I made some good masks in my time, but it was horrible work, and if someone touched you or it even started raining, the illusion would break. Then one time I died. Got a leg hacked off and bled to death. When I came back, as always, my body was whole. Look at yourself—dead six times and not a scar. How can that be? How could I regrow an arm?"

"I thought you said it was a leg," Kylar said, throwing a saddle over Tribe's back. For once, the brute didn't try to bite him. "And what's that about Elene?"

"It was an arm. Just remembered. I'll tell you about

Elene later. What I figured out is that somehow our bodies know what shape we're supposed to be. I mean, when you cut any man's arm, arm skin grows back there, not a nose or another head. Why? Because the body knows what's supposed to be where. I figured that if that was the case, all I had to do to make a perfect disguise was change the instructions. Hah, if only it were that simple. I figured out a few things along the way. Like Ladeshians aren't just really tanned. And if you change your height dramatically, expect to be uncoordinated for a year. And don't mess with your eyesight. And don't change things about your body that you merely don't like. Pretty soon you'll be so damn beautiful people will stop on the streets to watch you—it makes for a lousy disguise. Anyway, it took me— I don't know—a hundred years? I have about twenty bodies I do now. That is, bodies I've spent enough time in that I know how they work, understand their stride, their movement, their quirks. Twenty is probably too many, but I got nervous once when I found two different paintings of me made two hundred years apart from different sides of Midcyru and obviously me in both of them. Some Alitaeran collector had the two hanging side-by-side in his study. I'd moved to Alitaera to start a new life and I was using that same damn body."

"Wait, you're telling me you could have chosen any face? And you chose the nasty ugly Durzo Blint face?"

"That's my real face," Durzo said, offended.

Blood rushed to Kylar's cheeks. "Oh, by the God, I'm so sorry. I mean, I'm sorry I said that, not that your face is . . ."

"Gotcha," Durzo said.

Kylar pursed his lips. "Bastard."

"Anyway, it takes time to make the transition, especially when you start, and doing it halfway can be rather horrifying. We're on the trail, so we may meet people. If the skin on the upper half of my body is blackest Ladeshian, but my legs are white, or if half my face is young and half old, folks don't take it too well. I can actually do it much faster now, but I figured I'd show you body magic that's merely intensely difficult before I show you the damnnear impossible stuff."

"Wait, does that mean you can make yourself look like anything? So you could be a girl?"

"I don't want to hear your twisted fantasies," Durzo said.

"Hey!"

"I've never been a girl or an animal. I have a small fear of getting stuck: once I made a disguise that I was a man without a trace of Talent. What was supposed to be a quick, one-month disguise while I infiltrated the Chantry instead took me a decade to undo and cost me my chance to recover the silver ka'kari," Durzo said. "Being stuck as a fat Modaini, bad. Being stuck as a woman, unthinkable."

"So why are you changing now? And what into?"

"I'll look like a fifty-year-old, rather affable Waeddryner count, who appears to have a small Talent that he's never tapped. Because the reason I'm leaving the woman I love behind and going with you to the Chantry—not my favorite place—is that I want to meet my daughter. In fact, I'd appreciate your help getting the disguise right. I'd like her to look at me and say, 'oh, I have his eyes.'"

But Kylar wasn't interested in that yet. He paused. "Master? What does it mean? The Wolf called me Nameless. If I learn to do what you do, I'll be faceless, too. If we can be anyone, who are we?"

Durzo smirked, and even in another face, that bemused smirk was Durzo Blint through and through. "The Wolf doesn't know what the hell he's talking about. I had a delusion once that every new life I started was new. Our gift doesn't give us so much freedom—or terror. What we are is Night Angels, of an order ancient when I joined it. What it means to be a Night Angel is a harder question. Why do we see the *coranti?*" At Kylar's questioning look, Durzo said, "The unclean. And seeing them isn't a compulsion, it's a sensitivity. There was a time when I could see a lie, but in the year before the black abandoned me, I could barely see a murderer. What does it mean? Why was I chosen?

"Jorsin sometimes had the gift of prophecy. He told me I needed to take the black. 'All history rests in your hands, my friend,' he told me. I believed him. I would have walked through a wall of flame for that man. But a hundred years later, all my friends were dead, the world descended into a dark age, and no one was even pursuing me. Maybe my grand place in history, my whole purpose, was to keep the ka'kari safe for seven hundred years until I could give it to you. You'll forgive me if that doesn't seem entirely satisfying. Imagine rallying an army: 'Come on, men! Let's get together and . . . wait!' But then again if reality is hard and flat and unjust, then it's better to adjust to what really *is* than to complain that it isn't what you wish. That was what made me lose faith in prophecies, in purpose, even in life, I guess. But having lost it, soon I doubted my lack of faith. There were niggling hints of meaning everywhere. At the end of the day, you choose what you believe and you live with the consequences."

"So that's it?"

"That's what?"

"'Choose what you believe and live with the consequences' is all you've learned after seven hundred years? We're fucking immortal, and that's all you're going to tell me of why?"

Faster than Kylar remembered his master could move, Durzo's hand lashed out. His backhand cracked across Kylar's cheek and jaw. It stunned Kylar. A backhand hurt the person who delivered it nearly as much as the person who received it, so the only reason Durzo would choose a backhand was for the contempt implicit in it.

They stood looking at each other, silent. Mixed with Durzo's frustration, Kylar could see regret, but Durzo didn't apologize. Apologizing was one skill Acaelus Thorne hadn't mastered in seven centuries.

"Kid, every place I've turned left, you've turned right, and now you want me to tell you your destiny? Would it mean anything to you if I told you?"

Kylar said, "It would tell me where to turn right."

Despite himself, Durzo grinned. But it wasn't enough to bridge the sudden gap. Kylar could see now that his rejection of the lessons Durzo had tried to pass on had cut Durzo deeply—even if Durzo now agreed some of those lessons had been wrong. At the same time, Durzo was saying the same thing that the Wolf had told Kylar long ago. Kylar had never accepted other people's answers: not Durzo's bitter practicality, not Momma K's cynicism, not Count Drake's piety, and not Elene's idealism. Durzo was right about choosing what you believe and living with the consequences.

"I just . . ." Kylar trailed off. "We're immortal. We're Night Angels. I don't know what it means. I don't know why we're this way, or what we're supposed to do with it. Sometimes I feel like a god, and other times I don't feel like I change anything. If I'm going to live forever, I want it to be *for* something. I mean, you can't tell me that your destiny has been to hold the ka'kari for seven hundred years until I came along. That's ridiculous. Terrible. It's not good enough. You're a great man, not a lockbox." Kylar scowled. Gods, he'd just given Durzo a backhanded compliment—exactly how Durzo gave compliments to him.

Durzo's little grin told him he'd noticed, but he could also tell that the compliment meant a lot to the man. In all the times Kylar had been irritated that his master never properly appreciated how well Kylar did, he'd never really thought that Durzo might want to be appreciated too. Kylar hadn't bothered to tell Durzo how excellent he thought he was; he figured it was obvious. Maybe that was another knife that cut both ways.

"Being a lockbox wasn't the destiny I chose," Durzo said. "Right or wrong—or right or left—I've chosen to seek the ka'kari, take them, and scatter them so those who would use them for evil can't. I don't know if that's what Jorsin foresaw, but it's what I've chosen. Has it been meaningful and satisfying? Sometimes. I've had some good lives and some that were just damn awful. Now that you bear the black, I can lay my burden and my destiny down. Now I get different choices. So I'll train you until spring and see my daughter as much as I can. Then there's a woman I have to ask to love a man who doesn't deserve it. Your choices? Well, that's your shit." He smirked, acknowledging he was being a bastard.

Kylar sighed. He loved Durzo, but the man sure was a pain in the ass.

62

"From an older brother, the compulsion weave is weak, Your Holiness," Hopper said. "It won't hold a determined aetheling for long."

"I know. I was the son who was able to break it when my father used it on me," Dorian said. He'd had another dream last night, and again couldn't remember it, but it had left him with a headache again. His Talent for prophecy was healing faster than he'd expected, but for the time being, it was useless to him. He couldn't remember his dreams, and the only thing that banished the pain was using the vir. It put him in a foul mood.

"I'm sorry, Your Holiness. I'd forgotten."

The plan had come together with frightening ease. Dorian was his father's son. He'd spent days thinking about what he might have missed, and had found no flaw. "The oath is a distraction. You tell them that their reward for swearing loyalty will be choosing a concubine to marry. That will sound like a very southron thing to do, very weak. It will give the aethelings hope. Hope—and lust—will keep them from organizing a defense. After each chooses, I want him led out by that concubine past his brothers, who will be waiting in line. The women should be dressed beautifully—and of course, they should know nothing except that they are to lead the aetheling to one of the empty upper apartments. Each aetheling should be very lightly guarded, but heavily watched. You understand? These are my brothers; they're not stupid. On the way, kill them. If you have a handful of soldiers and three or four Vürdmeisters you know we can trust, that should be enough to take care of all of them—at least with the compulsion spell in place. Their faces are not to be destroyed. I will require a precise accounting and viewing of the bodies. When you're done, isolate any of the Godking's seed who are too young to show whether they are wytchborn. Kill them. Induce abortions on the pregnant concubines. Letting any grow up to see who's wytchborn will give my enemies chances to smuggle them out."

"Very prudent, Your Holiness," Hopper said. His only expression was appreciation for a solid plan.

It was brutal, but it wasn't cruel. Dorian took no joy in this. He would strike once to the root, and rip out much of what made this kingdom a hell for its people. This way was kinder than waiting for dozens of aethelings to coerce hundreds of others into their plots. Dorian could wait, and have executions every month for years, and his people would live in terror as dark as his father had encouraged, or he could be as brutal as the north itself, and his people would live in peace, unafraid. It would be a clean slate, a new start. Dorian would be Wanhope not for his own despair, but because those who opposed him must despair.

"Yes," Dorian said. "Monstrous, but prudent."

Hopper didn't know how to respond. He bowed low. The Godking dismissed him.

It was a horror to be a god. On his wedding day, Godking Wanhope waded in blood. He'd known that his father had one hundred forty-six children, but seeing them dead and oozing and stinking, expressions frozen in death, bodies still warm, not all the blood congealed, was something else entirely. With vir, he blotted out his sense of smell as he examined the boys.

He'd run out of suitable concubines before he'd run out of aethelings to slaughter. That meant that some of the women—each of whom had witnessed the murder of an aetheling she had expected to be her new master—had to make two trips. Only those who'd been splattered with blood were excused. It had worked though, because the aethelings who'd come later were the youngest, and the least likely to pick up on a concubine's anxiety.

They'd got them all. Three of the older boys—three!— had broken the compulsion and fought, killing one Vürd-meister and two soldiers. In a perverse way, Dorian was proud of the boys.

Godking Wanhope took his time, steeled against the sight of dead children. Vipers, all of them. He was the fluke; he had always been the only one of his brothers with any moral sense. Vipers couldn't be tamed. He couldn't flinch now. He had to know if the job was done, or if he needed to be looking over his shoulder for the rest of his reign for a Vürdmeister who could hide his vir and betray the Godking himself—as he had in his own youth. He paid special attention to those whose faces had been damaged. But in each case, he could still smell the faint residue of his compulsion spell on their flesh, and he'd tied it in an unusual way so that he would recognize his own work. That was why he had to examine the bodies immediately.

If a Vürdmeister had betrayed him and hidden an aetheling, the traitor would have to find a boy of the correct age, kill him and destroy his face, change his clothing, examine the Godking's weave—and notice that it had been altered and how it had been altered—and lay it on the dead boy himself. It was all possible but barely, and by the time he was finished inspecting the boys, the Godking was sure it hadn't been done.

The next room was worse, though there was no blood in it except what came in on the Godking's white robes. Hopper had gathered all the wives and concubines. The fifteen women who had been pregnant were lined up against one wall. The Godking walked past them, touching swollen bellies and feeling no life within. Then he moved past the rest, feeling to see if any were pregnant.

He took his time. A weave to hide a pregnancy was easier magically than disguising the dead, but a bigger risk for a Vürdmeister. There was no guarantee that the hidden child would be wytchborn, much less suitable for an ambitious Vürdmeister to ride to the Khalidoran throne.

As he moved from woman to woman, he noticed something disquieting. There was no hatred in their eyes. He had made them help him murder one hundred forty-six children. He had killed their unborn, but few wept. More looked at him with adoration, worship. He had done something beyond their comprehension, and it had worked perfectly. In short, he had acted like the god they expected him to be—powerful, terrifying, inscrutable.

"This afternoon," he said, "each of you will have a choice. As you know, the tradition is for wives and concubines to join the late Godking on his pyre, except for those whom the new Godking wishes to save for himself. You have served me well. I would give all of you a place in my harem. Garoth's aethelings will join him in the fire. Let them serve him in the afterlife. But if it is your wish, I will not forbid you to join them."

Now, the women reacted as he would have expected. Some broke down and wept; others stood taller and prouder. Some were still uncomprehending. But in moments, all dropped prostrate, hands stretched out for his feet. *I am walking blasphemy.*

"Is there anything else?" he asked them.

One of the women, a curvaceous teen from the upper harem, raised two fingers.

"Yes, Olanna?"

She cleared her throat three times before she could speak. "Sia, Your Holiness. She wasn't counted among the pregnant girls. She got real sick and went to the meisters so she wouldn't lose her baby. She never came back."

Dorian's stomach twisted. It was like hearing his own death sentence, twenty years before the fact. He wondered if he'd dreamed of this and was only now remembering the dream, or if his dread was purely natural. He looked at Hopper, who'd paled. Hopper served the lower harem, so the detail had escaped him, but he still looked aghast to have missed it. Dorian gestured and the man shuffled out of the room as quickly as his stilted gait would allow. Wanhope would send men to hunt this woman and whatever Vürdmeister had taken her, but they wouldn't find her. Wanhope had forgotten the first rule of massacring innocents: one always gets away.

63

As Kylar and Durzo approached the Chantry, the Alabaster Seraph gleamed, presiding over a city freshly dusted with snow that made it match its mistress. The waters of Lake Vestacchi glowed light blue tinged with red in the early morning light.

They stabled their horses on the outskirts of town, and after speaking with an old woman who ran the tavern and seemed to recognize him, Durzo took a key from her. Eschewing the punts, Durzo led them across narrow, crowded sidewalks. Kylar gaped at the enormous Seraph and at the crisscrossing currents that made the city's streets, bumping into strangers. A few cursed him and shoved back, but stopped as soon as he leveled his cool blue eyes on them. Beneath his awe at the Seraph, though, was a growing dread. He could feel Vi. He adjusted his sword belt and blew out a breath uneasily. She was in there, up two or three stories. Her feelings were a mirror of his own.

Durzo took them into a small, dusty house with a thick door. Kylar noticed that his eyes and his master's checked all the same things: doors, narrow windows, rugs, plank flooring. Durzo was satisfied. He opened the bureau and lifted out the bottom drawer to reveal a false bottom. Kylar pooled the ka'kari in his hand. *I'm really going to miss your wit.*

~*If I wanted sarcasm . . .* ~ it began, but Kylar willed it to cover Retribution. ~*Wait!*~ He dropped the sword into the space beneath the bureau. Both Retribution and the ka'kari were magical. He couldn't bring either to the Chantry. They would stay here until Kylar left.

Durzo replaced the bottom drawer, locked it into place, and took a few minutes to place a trap on it. In the meantime, Kylar worked on his disguise as Durzo had taught him. After he'd finished with the trap, Durzo studied him. "Not too bad," he admitted.

Minutes later, their little punt had scarcely docked next to a fishing boat flying two black flags when a familiar face turned up.

"Sister?" Kylar asked.

"There's a king in Cenaria!" Sister Ariel said, making it an accusation.

"Is this a password?" Durzo asked.

"Glory to his name," Kylar said. "Can we get out of the boat?"

"In Torras Bend, I called you arrogant. You said we'd discuss your arrogance when there was a king in Cenaria," Sister Ariel said, unamused. "Was that your doing?"

"Me? Who am I to meddle with kings?" Kylar said, smirking a yes.

"What's your name, young man? I seem to have forgotten. And who's this?"

"Kyle Blackson. Nice to make your acquaintance

again, Sister Airy Belle, right?" She gave him a glare that could curdle milk. "This is Dannic Bilsin, Uly's dad."

"Seven hells," Sister Ariel said.

"Nice to meet you, too," Durzo said.

Kylar got out of the boat and Sister Ariel stepped close to him and sniffed. She stepped back, confusion rising sharply in her eyes. She looked around the docks to see how far away the other Sisters were. "What have you done to yourself?"

With Durzo's instruction, Kylar now appeared to be a man with a vast and untapped Talent. Otherwise, he smelled and looked like any man. As long as he didn't use the ka'kari or his Talent, his guise would remain in place.

"I'm here to see my wife," Kylar said.

"Vi's studying, but I can have her brought to you after lunch."

"I meant the wife I chose, not the one you did." Kylar smiled thinly. Sister Ariel's face drained:

"You have no idea what you're doing, do you?" she said.

"Maybe I'm not the only one."

"And you?" Sister Ariel asked Durzo. "Do you have demands that will cost lives, too?"

"I'm just here to see my daughter," Durzo said.

64

The funeral came before the wedding. Dorian didn't want the first thing he saw with his new bride to be insane women throwing themselves into a fire, shrieking as they burned to death. Nor did he want her to see the dozens of tiny bodies his men would throw on the fires first. He'd told Jenine that he'd purged the aethelings who'd been plotting against him, but he'd told her that he'd merely sent the younger ones away.

Well, hell counted as away, he supposed. Heaven certainly did.

Dorian, of course, had never seen the cremation of a Godking, but some of the older meisters had. There was a ritual to be observed, despite the fraud at the center of it: rarely had the body being cremated actually belonged to a Godking. But Garoth Ursuul's pyre wouldn't hold a substitute. Garoth had been a man deeply committed to evil, but he had been a great soul, too, a horror who could have been a wonder, and he was Dorian's father.

Only meisters were allowed to attend the divine funeral, but that restriction meant little, for nearly every ranking official in the Khalidoran government was a meister. Generals, bureaucrats, the masters of the treasury, and even the chiefs of the kitchens stood in attendance. Tax collectors and soldiers watched according to their rank. Dorian uttered the meaningless words of praise to Khali, and they uttered their meaningless refrains of devotion. The fires were started and Dorian could read the vir of every meister making a weave to block the acrid stench of human fat burning. When the fires roared hottest, Dorian had the harem brought before him and claimed almost all of them. There were raised eyebrows, but nothing more. A Godking was expected to be voracious. The eight wives and concubines who'd chosen death were brought forward, and that was regarded as a small, but adequate nod to tradition. The women had been provided with wine laced liberally with poppy, and six of them had indulged freely. Two were sober. All seemed content with their madness, not shrinking back even as the eunuchs lifted them to heave them into the fire.

The shrieking was awful, but mercifully brief. It was considered a greater sacrifice to Khali if their suffering were extended, but Dorian was already giving Khali more than her due. He should have forbidden the women to join Garoth. But if he had forced them to live and they truly had loved Garoth, such women might have become a poison.

Or they might have transferred their slavish devotion to me, the way a good dog finds a new master after its old master dies. Dorian watched their bodies sizzle, and pushed the thought away.

He nodded to the Vürdmeisters tending the fire and

the blaze leapt higher, consuming the flesh and even the bones to ash. In minutes, it was done.

Dorian lifted his hand to gesture that the wedding was to begin. It would be a simple affair, though lavish by Khalidoran standards. Godkings never wed. When commoners did, a man simply said, "I take this woman to wife." From the woman, only a lack of explicit protest was required. Dorian planned something grander for Jenine but not too foreign for his meisters to stomach. But with his hand still raised, he paused. The moment had taken the eerie lines of prophecy. Dorian felt a sick chill and readied the vir in case there was another assassination attempt. Hopper was whispering to a page, who strode respectfully to Dorian's side. Dorian was looking at his grand white robes, at the assembled faces. He'd seen this moment in a prophecy, why couldn't he remember?

He inclined his head to the page.

"Your Holiness, Hopper wishes you to be informed that a spy has returned from Cenaria. He reports that a man named Logan Gyre has been named king."

The world stopped. Jenine's husband was alive. Dorian felt as if he were outside his body, re-entering the madness he thought he'd left behind with his prophetic gift.

How dare you, God? What do you want from me? To tell her that he *lives? I've given my soul for this! For You. I am become a monster so I can redeem these people. Don't You care about me? Don't You care about this damned country?*

If You did, You would have saved these wretches Yourself. I did not seek these chains of office. I did not seek the Talent You gave me. I only asked for one thing: this woman. You made me with this yearning too deep for words, and You would have me sacrifice it at the moment the honey touches my lips?

I have not forgotten you. I know the plans I have for you.

Remembering me means nothing if You won't act for me. I have not betrayed You, You betray me. Non takuulam. I shall not serve. You and I are finished.

Godking Wanhope became aware of the stares of his meisters. He smiled and completed the gesture to Hopper. "Let our wedding commence," the god said.

65

A simple lunch was delivered to Durzo's room and Kylar and Durzo ate together in silence. "Guess you should head to your room, huh?" Durzo said. "They should be here any time." He cleared his throat, reaching for a garlic pouch he no longer carried.

"I'd give anything to see you meet your girl," Kylar said.

"I'd give anything to see you meet yours," Durzo said.

Kylar swallowed, realizing he was pacing.

"You can feel her?" Durzo asked.

"Three floors up, heading down. Almost as nervous as I am."

"I knew there was a reason I was never stupid enough to get ringed," Durzo said.

"Do you have any idea how Uly's going to react when she sees you?" Kylar asked.

Durzo shook his head.

"Then maybe you should shut your face."

"Ah, wook, wittle Kylie is all gwowed up. He mad at his massah."

In a flash, Kylar was on the verge of punching Durzo's face. Then he laughed. "Unbelievable, huh? Guess I'll go over to my room. Good luck."

Durzo patted his back as he walked out of the room. It was an oddly intimate gesture, but Kylar said nothing to draw Durzo's attention to it.

His room was even smaller than Durzo's, which barely had room for two chairs. Kylar's had only one chair and a bed. Kylar sat in the chair. Then he moved to sit on the bed. Then he stood so he could open the door before she even knocked. Then he changed his mind and sat again.

He cursed. She was just down the hall now, and she'd stopped—dropping Uly off at Durzo's room? Uly and Vi were together? Vi didn't seem to feel upset or guilty, which was weird, considering she'd kidnapped Uly, beaten her, and starved her only a few months ago. Then Vi was moving again, as tense as he was.

Kylar stood to open the door. There was a quick, firm rap, and then she opened the door, but Vi wasn't alone. Sister Ariel and another woman of a similar age but with long blonde hair stepped into the room, and Vi followed.

For the tiny room, it was too many people, even if three of them hadn't been magae. Kylar backed up to the wall.

"Kyle Blackson, this is Speaker Istariel Wyant. She's in charge here," Sister Ariel said.

"Nice to meet you," Kylar said. "Here the guest quarters or here here?"

"I'm the Speaker of the Chantry," Istariel said, annoyed.

"Then why aren't you the Chanter?" Kylar asked. What

was with him? That had Durzo written all over it, and Vi's eyes went wide.

Istariel's lips thinned. "We have problems, young man, they may even be bigger than your ego."

"Why are we meeting here rather than your office?" Kylar asked.

She blinked. "What was it you said, Ariel, reckless but not stupid? Kyle, the Chantry and all of the south is entering a perilous time. We need Vi's help if we are to survive."

"You do?" Vi asked.

"Silence, child," Sister Ariel said.

"All of this was supposed to happen much more slowly," Istariel told Vi. "We meant to give you some semblance of a normal tutelage, because the service we require of you entails serious risks for you and the Chantry. The bare fact is that you may be—"

Sister Ariel cleared her throat.

"You *are* the most Talented woman to come to the Chantry in a century, Vi. You were married before you arrived, so your marriage is not in violation of the Third Ali-taeran Accord. A woman's Talent isn't enough to guarantee her advancement, but a highly Talented woman is always conspicuous. Thus, you're highly visible, highly Talented, and married—to a man who's also highly Talented—and your marriage is not in breach of any treaty."

"Huh," Vi said. "What are the odds of that happening by chance?" She stared pointedly at Ariel, who had the decency to blush.

Istariel cleared her throat. "Yes, about that. Kyle, we never expected you to actually come here. In fact, Sister Ariel was adamant that you wouldn't."

"I wasn't aware how susceptible you would be to Vi's . . . charms," Ariel said blandly.

Kylar blushed. "That's not why I'm here."

"But here you are," Istariel said. "So you could destroy Vi—or at the very least destroy her usefulness to the Chantry."

"Which is why I get some truth. Right. Still doesn't answer why you have to sneak around to meet me," Kylar said.

Istariel's eyes flashed. "The Chantry has had a number of incidents involving Vy'sana wedding rings. A century ago, someone ringed a Speaker against her will."

"It's called ring rape," Ariel said.

Istariel turned a cold gaze on her sister. "Stop helping." She turned back to Kylar. "It was an attempt to subvert the entire Chantry in one stroke, and it came disastrously close to succeeding. That was only the most recent incident. There is enormous antipathy to forcible ringing."

"So if I tattle, Vi's finished. Why do you care?" Kylar asked.

"There's no reason for us to be enemies," Istariel said.

"I can think of one," he said, tugging his earring.

She averted her gaze. "Magae have been forbidden to marry magi for two hundred years, Kyle. The Alitaeran Emperor Dicola Raiis feared we had established a breeding program to make archmages so we could become the dominant force in world politics we once were. At the time, we were closely allied with the men's blue school, and the treaty required all the married magi to divorce. The men wanted to go to war, but the decision was the Speaker's, who was herself married to a Blue. She knew that they had no chance against the might of Alitaera, and she signed the accord. The split with the men was acrimonious. Relations have been strained since then. To protect ourselves, and perhaps for many other reasons including to stop the humiliating inspections of compliance, the Chantry has spread the prohibition of marriage to all men. Women who do marry are effectively finished. They are allowed no advancement within the Orders; they are sometimes denied further schooling, and they are often the objects of ridicule. Nonetheless, for their own reasons I suppose, many women choose this path."

"How many?" Kylar asked.

"Half."

"You lose half?"

"The only thing worse than losing them is getting them back the wrong way. There is a woman named Eris Buel who has become the de facto leader of a large number of these women. They want to come back. They want to reject the Alitaeran Accords—maybe all of them—and they want to establish a men's school here. At heart, though, they just want to be Sisters again. Our reports suggest that we may have more ex-magae here this spring than magae."

"How many are you talking?" Kylar asked.

"Eight to ten thousand. While we have that many active Sisters, ours are spread out throughout the world. If these Chattel—ummm, these married Sisters—arrive and demand to be readmitted and form their own order, we won't be able to deny them."

"What happens if they do form an order?" Kylar asked.

"Most likely? They immediately hold a vote of no confidence and oust me and put their leader in my place. At best, Eris Buel is angry, naive, and dangerous."

"You want Vi to kill her?"

"Light blind me, no!" Sister Istariel said. "We want Vi to replace her."

"What?!" Vi asked.

"You're more Talented than she is. You're prettier, and you're not as angry."

"Oh, you haven't seen Vi when she gets angry," Kylar said.

"Neither have you!" she snapped.

"The point is," Sister Ariel said, "Eris Buel doesn't lead the Chattel yet. These women come from all over Midcyru. Most of them don't know each other. They'll look for a leader once they're here. There's more. Istariel, tell them about the Khalidorans."

"Even though Khalidor doesn't occupy much of its eastern lands, they are still our neighbors," Istariel said. "After Garoth died, an unknown named Wanhope took the throne. We have reasons to doubt his rule will last. In the north, one of Garoth's other sons, Moburu, has joined up with the barbarians in the Freeze. They're rumored to have rediscovered how to raise armies of creatures that are less than human. Moburu is heading east either to fight or to join another group which we think has about fifty Vürd-meisters, led by a Lodricari named Neph Dada, at Black Barrow. The word is that he plans to raise a Titan."

"What's a Titan?"

"It's a myth. We hope. But as the mistress of a floating island, I can only think of one compelling reason a Khalidoran army would need a giant."

"You think they want to attack the Chantry?" Vi asked.

"I think they're fools," Istariel said. "But we only have a mercenary army of five hundred men and not a single battle maja. If the Khalidorans came through the pass with twenty thousand soldiers and a hundred Vürd-meisters, even without krul or a Titan, they could destroy us. Worse, the Lae'knaught plan to march north at the same time. While there's a small and tempting prospect that our two enemies would converge and destroy each other before our eyes, if either attacked us first, even if we won, we would be so weakened that the other would annihilate us."

"So you want to turn the ten thousand Chattel into an army so they can die saving women who reject them," Kylar said.

There was an icy silence.

"I'm responsible for the lives of the women in my care, and the caretaker of the legacy of a thousand years of learning and freedom," Istariel said. "So if it costs Vi's life and her honor and your life and your freedom and my life and my reputation and a war with Alitaera to save them, I will gladly pay that and more. Kyle, you can destroy my plans and your wife simply by telling the first maja you see that you were ringed forcibly. I can't stop you. But neither can I free you. In the centuries when these rings were Made, they were studied by magae greater than any now alive, and *they* found the bond unbreakable. You can ask anything for your silence, but you can't ask the impossible. So what's your price?"

"Tell me exactly what you're buying," Kylar said.

"In the coming weeks, I've arranged to have very ugly

and very public debate with some of my key councilors about the Chattel. Ariel will be one of those who splits with me. I'm going to take a strong stance that the Chantry will never allow the Chattel to rejoin. A few days later, some of the threats to our safety I've just told you about will be leaked. I will send to Alitaera asking for protection as per the Accords. My request will be impossibly large, so that even if Alitaera sends soldiers, the small number will be taken as an insult. Vi will begin training whoever wishes to join her and Sister Ariel in the arts of war. I will ban this training, but no action will be taken against those who 'defy' me. If Vi plays her part appropriately, she'll have a good chance to become the leader of these rebels. Come spring, Vi will negotiate with me on behalf of the Chattel. I will break down, the Chattel will be readmitted with certain conditions—mostly that they reside here for at least a year before they are given full voting privileges."

"Which," Ariel interjected, "will make sure that few of them actually do it. Most of these women have farms and shops and families to get back to."

"Yes, *thank you*, Ariel," Istariel said. "But those who truly wish to rejoin will be allowed to do so and still stay married. After we make it through the summer, we will renegotiate the Alitaeran Accords."

"What's to say you won't sacrifice Vi to the Alitaerans then?" Kylar said.

"Whatever goodwill she's built up with the Chattel will probably make her untouchable. If I betray her, it could be enough to make enough Chattel stick around to become full voting members and oust me. Regardless, the Alitaerans are next year's problem."

"So what's my part?" Kylar asked.

"You share a house with your wife. I don't care if you share a bed, but to all appearances, it must be a model marriage. You will spend enough social time together to maintain this fiction. Nothing elaborate, eat at an inn together once in a while, take walks, hold hands."

"Do you have any idea what it's like for me to be in the same room with her?" Kylar asked. "I'm in love with another woman, a woman I planned to marry. If I get aroused by a woman other than Vi, I nearly throw up. I can't control my dreams. I feel what she feels. I—"

"We can't fix it!" Istariel said. "Get rid of your old lover. Start sharing Vi's bed. After a while, you might even like each other."

"You cruel, cruel bitch," the thought was Kylar's, but it was Vi who spoke.

He was stunned, as were Ariel and Istariel.

"You want to pretend things are different, go ahead," Istariel said. "You ringed him. Are you going to make thousands die so you can feel properly guilty? Kyle, are you going to make thousands die so you can punish me or Sister Ariel? Is that going to make it better? Because you'll still be ringed next year, no matter what happens to the Chantry. Kyle, I'll give you whatever you want. Vi, you'll have more power and a better position than you could ever dream of. In time, you could become Speaker. It's your choice. You two figure it out and tell Sister Ariel. I can never be seen with you. Should we ever meet, I expect you to act as if you dislike me intensely. I suspect that won't be difficult."

She opened the door, glanced both ways, and left. Sister Ariel said, "Elene will come to your new house in a few hours. The story will be that she's your servant."

"I haven't said yes," Kylar said.

Sister Ariel looked at him gently for a long moment, then opened the door and went out.

"So what do we do?" Vi asked.

This close to her, Kylar was picking up flashes of images directly from her mind. There was Elene, throwing a knife aside. Kylar saw himself, flashing a grin, his handsomeness exaggerated. He saw himself reaching to touch her face gently. He saw himself holding her. He saw himself in the throne room, fierce and wild, slashing into Garoth Ursuul's head and saving Vi's life. He saw himself looking at her with horror as he discovered the earring. He saw himself above her, chest bare, muscles taut, his eyes locked on hers, pupils flaring. Then, again, horror and loathing.

Kylar looked at Vi, glad that she was wearing a shapeless sack of a white wool dress. But she was close enough that he could smell her. She wore no perfume. Perhaps her soap was lavender, but mostly, he smelled her, and she smelled incredible.

He saw Jarl go down in a sudden spray of blood and then he saw the shot from her perspective, her tears almost blinding her as she released the arrow. He felt her self-hatred, her guilt—and whether the compulsion had been magical or mundane, he forgave her.

It didn't need words. She felt it directly. Her eyes brimmed with tears.

Kylar cleared his throat, glanced at her breasts involuntarily, and blushed as she noticed. The image of holding her naked came back again, and he wasn't sure which of them it came from. "Holy shit," he said.

She glanced at the narrow pallet against the wall and

quickly away, but the image couldn't be hidden: Kylar on her, handsome, muscular, his touch setting her skin afire, her legs wrapping around his, pulling him to her, his weight anchoring her to something deep and real and better than she deserved. "Gods," Vi said, "this takes fore-play to a new level." He could feel the warmth rising in her body.

"No," he said. "I've betrayed Elene in every way but that. Please, we can't do that, not ever. All right?"

Her arousal was gone instantly, replaced with confusion and guilt. She stepped forward and reached out to him.

He recoiled. "I don't think we should even, you know, touch."

She averted her eyes, her feelings of rejection and unworthiness seeping through the air. He wanted to reassure her, but he didn't.

"Right," she said quietly.

66

*S*ister Ariel stared at Kylar in a way that made it obvious she was using her Talent, trying to figure him out again. "Elene will be here any minute. Is everything to your satisfaction?" she asked.

He met her gaze. He wished he had the ka'kari to bring to his eyes, but Durzo had told him that for his disguise as a highly Talented man who had only tapped his latent Talent a few times in his life to hold, he couldn't use either ka'kari or Talent at all. So Kylar had left the ka'kari covering Retribution in Durzo's safe house. Of course, he could reform the disguise afterward, but it was always a question of whether he wanted to spend eight hours fixing the disguise for a momentary use of the Talent.

Kylar was starting to appreciate why Durzo had taught him so many mundane skills that had seemed like they were obsolete after he'd learned to tap his Talent.

"It's fine," he said. The Chantry had given him an enormous sum of money to purchase this small manse on the shores of the lake. He and Vi were moving in today, and the house had room for Elene and Durzo as well, though Uly would continue to live in the Chantry. For the most part, Kylar wouldn't see Vi. She would rise early, go to the Chantry, and not return home until late. Later, when her "rebellion" began, she and the Sisters who accompanied her would train in the manse's large walled yard. The manse, of course, had been selected for exactly that purpose.

"When did you learn this disguise?" Ariel asked. "It's remarkable. I wouldn't have believed such a thing was possible."

"Maybe you were just mistaken before."

"Oh, I've made mistakes, *Kyle,* and you figure prominently in them, but I have a perfect memory." She cleared her throat. "I want to apologize. Your predicament is more my fault than anyone's. I didn't know exactly what I was imposing on you, but I did manipulate Vi into doing it."

"And would you do anything differently if you could do it again?" Kylar asked.

She paused. "No."

"Then it's not really an apology, is it?"

Sister Ariel turned and left, leaving Kylar rubbing his temples.

"Hi," a voice said from the doorway.

Kylar looked up and saw Elene. She was smiling shyly. A thrill ran through him. He was frozen, taking her in. First he was surprised again at her beauty, the fine balance of her features, the glow of her skin. Then his eyes were drawn to the uncertainty of her smile, the wide and fragile hope in her eyes, waiting to see how he would react to her. Even when she was scared, she lightened a room. A huge lump rose in his throat. Before he could think more, he crossed the room and pulled her into his arms.

She hugged him fiercely and didn't let go. He held her tight and all the world was well. He smelled her hair, her skin, and that forgotten scent was the scent of home.

He didn't know how long it lasted, but all too soon he came to himself.

Elene felt the change instantly. She pulled back and took his face in her hands. She stared him straight in the eye, and when he averted his gaze, she pulled him back. "Kylar, there's something you have to know," she said.

"Something *I* have to know?"

"Yes," she said. "I know about everything, and I love you." Her grip on his face relaxed, and she trailed her fingers down his cheeks. "I love you."

"Elene," Kylar said. He wondered what made her name sound different from all other names as it crossed his lips, "it's more than just Vi."

"Both things," Elene said.

Kylar stopped. "Both things" as in the both things he was thinking about, or was she forgiving him for something else he didn't even know he'd done? During their brief time as a happy family in Caernarvon, Kylar would have let it go, afraid of being hammered with something he hadn't seen coming. Now, he shook his head. "Honey, this is too important not to put into words."

Elene cocked her head fractionally, and he saw that she noticed the change in him, and respected him more for it. It was one of the things that made being with Elene so intense: she was so open, he knew immediately what she felt, and it was often overwhelming. "I know about the ringing. Vi and I have had a number of

long and uncomfortable talks. I know that you sold your
sword for those rings, and that one of them was supposed
to be for me. I know about Jarl." Tears came to her eyes
but she blinked them away. "I know that you've shared
some . . . intimate dreams with Vi because of the rings,
and I know about the Chantry's deal and why they want
you to act like Vi's husband. I don't like it, but it's the right
thing to do. Some things have happened that have changed
me, Kylar." She grimaced. "Kyle now, I guess, but let me
just call you Kylar for another hour. Is that all right?"

He nodded, that damn lump in his throat getting bigger. "I like it when you say my name."

She smiled and suddenly tears welled up in her
eyes. She fanned herself. "I told myself I wouldn't cry."

"You'll let yourself cry later?" he suggested.

She laughed suddenly, and it was better than music.
"How do you know me so well?" She took a deep breath.
"Kylar, in Caernarvon, I had some very firm ideas about
what sort of man you were supposed to be. There is something in you that is fierce and wild and strong, and it fascinated me and frightened me. And when I got frightened,
I tried to change you, and I didn't listen to you, and I
didn't respect you the way you deserved, and I didn't trust
you."

*You had this crazy notion that I was going to take you
to a far country and then leave you with nothing.*

"So I cloaked my fears in some really righteous-
sounding horseshit."

Kylar's eyebrows shot up. Elene, swearing?

She smirked, liking that she could shock him. But
then her expression grew serious. "All of our fights about
that stupid sword. . . . You couldn't sell Retribution be-

cause you are Retribution. That girl in Caernarvon, that shopkeeper's girl Capricia? You changed her life, and that was giving her what she deserved as much as it is when you kill bad men. The fact is, Kylar, I made my God look a lot like me instead of the other way around. I'm sorry. When I first found out that you'd sold that sword for me, I cried for myself, because I'd lost you. But later, I cried for you, because I'd told you that you weren't good enough for me.

"Kylar, what you do scares me. I can understand it in my head, but it's still hard to fit my heart around. It's, well, it's horrifying and terrifying for me."

"It's horrifying and terrifying for me, too."

She looked him in the eye still. "When I was escaping from the slavers, there was a Khalidoran who was going to kill a boy. I killed him. I killed the guilty so the innocent might live, and that's what you did with the queen, Kylar. I hope I never have to kill again, but I won't think that I'm better than you because you have to."

"What? Slavers? Wait, you got kidnapped?"

"There's a story more important than that, Kylar. When you died, I had a dream. A very short man appeared to me. He was handsome, with amazing white hair and yellow eyes and burn scars."

Kylar froze again. It could only be the Wolf.

"He told what immortality costs. Every time you die, someone you love dies in your place. He told me that this time it's me. He said that the most he could do was hold off my death until spring."

"I didn't know," Kylar whispered.

"Kylar, I think the hardest thing for me in Caernarvon was that I realized you were important and I wasn't. Now

instead of envying you or fighting against you, I'll fight
with you. All the good you do for a lifetime will be possible because of me. I guess this is a kind of heroism that
no one sees, but maybe that makes it better, not worse."

"I love you, Elene. I'm sorry I've been such a fool. I'm
sorry I left."

"Kylar, you love a girl with scars; I love a man with a
purpose. Love comes at a price, but you're worth it."

"How can you say that? I've killed you. I've stolen
your life." Kylar swallowed, but that damn lump wouldn't
go away.

"You can't steal what I freely give. I can live with eternity in mind because I know I'm going to be facing it
soon, and I'm not going to waste a second of what I have
left. Being here, with you, is exactly what I choose."

And then Kylar was crying. Out in the yard, he felt Vi
fumble a weave in shock, then go back to it, trying to distract herself, trying to give Kylar privacy. Elene hugged
him and in her arms he found such boundless warmth and
unqualified acceptance that his tears redoubled. All his
doubts and self-recriminations, his self-loathing and fear
washed away. And when his tears stopped flowing, she
cried. The tears were an ablution and, holding her, Kylar
felt clean for the first time in years.

When the tears had passed, they looked at each other,
tear-smudged face to tear-smudged face, and laughed and
held each other more. Then, slowly, they spun out their
stories. Elene told him of her trip to Cenaria and her capture by the slavers. Kylar told her of Aristarchos's attempt
at killing him, about Jarl's death, about fighting the Godking and being ringed, of his work to enthrone Logan,

and his death on the wheel, his discovery of the cost of immortality, and his reunion with Durzo.

Then she asked him about wet work, about his first kill, about his training, about the Talent and what he saw when he looked at people through the ka'kari. He told her the unvarnished truth, and she listened. She couldn't understand all of it, she said, but she listened without judgment, and she didn't draw back after hearing it.

As he spoke, Kylar slowly relaxed. He felt the tension of secrecy and guilt, the fear of discovery and condemnation—all the tension that he had carried for so much of his life that it was simply part and parcel of how he experienced life—begin to unwind. In Elene, he found rest. For the first time, peace.

He looked at her with new eyes, and her beauty was warm blankets on a cold winter morning. It was home after a long journey. It wasn't a beauty to covet, like Vi's; it was a beauty to share. If Vi's body was art shaped to stoke desire, Elene's whole being was shaped to share love. Elene had scars, her figure was attractive but not such as left men incapable of speech—and yet her beauty surpassed Vi's. The intuition that had kept Kylar from Vi even from the first time she'd tried to seduce him at the Drake estate suddenly crystallized: You don't share your life with a woman's body, you share your life with a woman.

"Marry me," Kylar said, surprising himself. Then, realizing that his mouth had only uttered what his whole heart longed for, he said, "Please, Elene, will you marry me?"

"Kylar . . ."

"I know it'll have to be secret, but it'll be real, and I want you."

"Kylar . . ."

"I know, this damn ring will probably keep us from making love, but we'll figure something out, and even if we don't, I love you. I want to be with you. I want to be with you more than I want sex. I know it'll be really hard, but I mean it. We can—"

"Kylar, shut up," Elene said. She smiled at the look on his face, smoothed her dress, and said, "I would be honored to be your wife."

For a moment, he couldn't believe it. Then, at her spreading smile and her delight in taking him off guard, light burst over a thousand hills. Somehow, she was in his arms, and they were holding each other and laughing and Elene was crying, and they were good tears, and then he kissed her and his whole body dissolved into that point where their lips met, and her lips were soft, full, warm, inviting, moist, responsive, eager. It was beautiful. It was amazing. It was the best feeling of his whole life, right until he threw up.

67

Their lovemaking was completely one-sided. Again. Jenine had been a virgin only a month ago, so Dorian told himself it was a lack of practice, that her awkwardness was an awkwardness of how. But Jenine was coordinated and Dorian was ravenous, so that justification was getting strained. She averted her gaze as he lay atop her, unable to match the intensity in his eyes. He buried his head in her hair, trying to ignore her body's lack of arousal. He finished alone.

He held her, inhaling the scent of her, trying not to feel lonely.

She never denied him, even when he came to her a second time in a day or a third, and that made it worse. She didn't pretend to climax, at least not yet. But even when she did climax, afterwards, the gap still wasn't bridged. In everything she didn't say, he saw a woman trying desperately to love him, and give love every chance to grow.

Even now as he held her, she held him. He'd tried everything short of vir to make her love him as he loved her. He had a kingdom to defend and administer, men to train, plots to unravel, reforms to institute, magic to practice, but every day, he carved out hours simply to spend with her, to talk with her, to listen, to dance, to recite poetry, to tend the garden together, to tell stories, to listen to bards, to laugh, and only to make love after all that. The hell of it was that it seemed to be working. Jenine seemed more comfortable with him, more delighted with his presence and humor, more in love—everywhere but in the bedchamber. Was that because she was sixteen and lovemaking was new, or was their love as much a lie as Logan's death? Or was everything fine except that it was poisoned in his own mind? What if she did love him, and he was simply going mad?

"What are you thinking about?" Jenine asked.

Dorian propped himself on his elbows and kissed her breast to give himself time to think. "How much I love you" would have been a partial truth. "How much I love you and you don't love me" would be too brutal. But love needed truth to grow. He rubbed his aching head. "I was thinking of how hard you're trying, and how much I appreciate it."

She burst into tears, and there was truth in how she clung to him.

Logan sat in his new throne. He had given the artisans three weeks to deliver it, and the men had barely met the deadline. He had wanted it simple, sturdy wood with no ornamentation, but Duchess Kirena had prevailed upon him that the Cenarian throne couldn't look like a dinner chair, so he had relented. This throne was sandalwood, almost glowing with a high polish, solid, elegantly shaped, and with a few fat rubies in each wing and in the front of the arms. By some magic, it was comfortable for Logan's enormous frame. He almost pitied the rulers who would succeed him. Sitting in Logan's throne, they would feel like dwarfs.

He lifted an eyebrow at Lantano Garuwashi, who knelt on a plain woven mat on the floor at Logan's right hand. It looked uncomfortable, but Garuwashi appeared at ease. He nodded and Logan gestured.

The Lae'knaught in Wirtu, their semi-permanent camp that was functionally their capital city, had sent a new emissary. The man had arrived on time, though not an hour early.

"Greetings, Your Majesty," the diplomat began. He went on for some time, listing Logan's titles and then his own, and then those of his master, Overlord Julus Rotans. Logan kept his face impassive. Going to Khalidor without the Lae'knaught would be suicide. By spring, Logan would have an army of fifteen thousand if he was lucky. Garuwashi's sa'ceurai added six thousand. Between them, they had less than a thousand horse. Cenaria's nobility were the only people in the realm who had the time and coin to become horsemen, and most of them hadn't bothered. Of those who had, many had been killed in futile resistance to Garoth Ursuul. Similarly, Lantano Garuwashi had attracted mostly peasants and hedge sa'ceurai and the masterless. His army was the best in Ceura, but not the richest by a long shot. Duchess Kirena's spies said the Khalidorans had at least twenty thousand soldiers and thousands of wytches.

Garuwashi's men were in charge of training all of

Logan's forces, and they would train them for at least three more months, four if the winter was hard, which was an eternity for a peasant army to train, but Logan didn't relish the idea of facing greater numbers and wytches on Khalidor's own land. However it worked, what they called the Armor of Unbelief did seem to make the Lae'knaught less susceptible to magic, and if they could neutralize the meisters, that would demoralize the normal Khalidoran soldiers, who were used to their wytches crushing the opposition before they even raised their swords. It came down to one brutal fact: if Logan wanted Jenine back, he needed the Lae'knaught.

" . . . after detailed discussion of your proposals," the diplomat said. "The High Command has come to a decision."

Logan stood abruptly. "Throw him out," he told his guards. They seized the diplomat by both arms instantly.

"You haven't even heard me out!" the man yelled as they dragged him backward, his feet barely touching the ground.

"Oh," Logan said, scratching his jaw as if that hadn't occurred to him. "Very well then, go ahead. But make it fast. You're boring me." The truth was, he knew their response as soon as the man said "proposals," plural.

"We agree with everything in the first and second articles, there are just a few minor details in the third that you may not be aware violate some very important Lae'knaught principles of honor. I'm sure quite unintentionally, you ask us to blaspheme against our most closely held beliefs."

"Oh," Logan said. "Let him go. I'm sorry, sir, I

didn't mean to offend. What articles in particular were troublesome?"

"As I said, uh, we agree that Khalidor is our mutual enemy and that the time to act is now. We agree that—"

Logan waved his hand petulantly. "You're boring me."

"We simply had some logistical problems with the distribution of our forces."

"Oh?" Logan said. He thought they'd have some problems with that. Lord General Agon had a low opinion of Lae'knaught loyalty, so he'd asked for a provision that specified that the Lae'knaught forces would be split and serve under Cenarian and Ceuran commanders. It was a trade-off militarily. The Cenarian commanders wouldn't use the lancers as efficiently as the Lae'knaught commanders could. The Cenarians simply hadn't commanded such forces before, so they didn't know their strengths and weaknesses. On the other hand, it would make treachery much harder to organize, especially with how active Duchess Kirena planned to keep her spies.

"If I may be blunt, Your Majesty, this idea of having lancers serve under your commanders is suicidal."

"Fair enough," Logan said.

The man was professional enough that he didn't show his surprise at Logan's sudden acquiescence. "There were also a few other small details, much less substantial, I assure you. But now that we're agreed in principle, I could meet with Your Majesty's officials to arrange—"

"Why would that be necessary?" Logan asked.

The diplomat paused awkwardly. "Uh, to work out the details of our alliance?" He asked, as if trying not to treat Logan like an idiot.

"Alliance?" Logan asked.

The diplomat opened his mouth, but no words came out.

"No, no, sir," Logan said. "This is no alliance. This is war. You rejected my terms. This summer, after Garuwashi's sa'ceurai are finished looting Wirtu and slaughtering all of your officers, I will propose the same terms again—with one small additional detail. Namely, the lancers will stay under Cenarian command permanently. And if you say no then, I will kill you all. Guards?"

The men grabbed the little diplomat again.

"Your Majesty, wait!"

Logan lifted a finger and the guards stopped. "The only words I need to hear from you are, 'Your Majesty, we accept your proposal.' If you have anything else to say, you can say it to Underlord Dynos Rotans, who accompanied you, oddly in servant's garb, though he outranks you and is known to have his brother's ear. Tell him he should have had the balls to come see me himself. It's an insult that he thought if things went really wrong, he could step in himself. I'm sick of Lae'knaught sycophants. Tell him he's forbidden to come to my court. I'll give you half an hour. Either come in that door with the words I told you, or find your horses." Logan nodded and the guards heaved the diplomat out the door.

When the doors closed, Garuwashi said, "You seemed to enjoy that."

"On the contrary, I'm within an inch of vomiting."

"Really? Because you just tried to provoke war over a senseless provision?"

"I knew this kid, small kid, nothing to look at. Someone picked on him once, and he flew at the guy like he'd lost his mind."

"Did the little kid win?"

"He got destroyed. But no one picked on that little kid again, because he approached every harassment as if his life depended on winning. There were no rules in a fight with him. He didn't care how badly he got hurt. He would win. I was always bigger and stronger than other kids, but I would fight fair and stop when someone conceded victory. I had to fight a lot more than he did."

"So you're basing your handling of the Lae'knaught on a metaphor from your childhood?" Garuwashi asked.

"Which is why I feel sick." But there was no way around it. Without the Lae'knaught, he couldn't get his wife back.

Lantano Garuwashi cleared his throat. "While we're on the subject of things that make us sick, I've had word that some members of the High Council are proposing that the Regent send an emissary to see if I am Ceura's lost king."

"You say that like it's a bad thing." Cenaria had enemies north, east, and inside, the last thing Logan needed was problems from the south.

"They will most likely send an army with the emissary." Garuwashi lowered his voice. "He will demand to see Ceur'caelestos."

"And?" Logan asked.

"Kylar didn't tell you?"

"Tell me what?"

"I am sorry you had to put such a man to death, Your Majesty. It is not many men who will guard another's honor when he owes him nothing." Garuwashi cleared his throat, and Logan could swear that the big redhead was flushed. "I, ahem, I no longer hold the Blade of Heaven. Kylar threw it into Ezra's Wood. A magus went into the

Wood after it and said he'd received a prophecy from the mad mage himself that told him how to make a second sword for me, but the mage has not returned."

"But you carry—"

"A scabbard with a hilt. If I have to show my sword, I'm dead. Should this become known, they won't even allow me to slay myself to expiate the dishonor."

And I'll lose the best part of my army.

"I see," Logan said. "We will do all we must to give your mage the time he needs. I'm sure he will return. No man swears idly to Lantano Garuwashi."

They sat in silence, each tense for his own reasons.

"How is your campaign against the Sa'kagé?" Garuwashi asked finally.

"Impossible to tell. Well, except that I'm still alive, as are all of my advisers. This war may actually help us. It gives us something to offer to men whose only trade has been violence. We call it an earned amnesty. A different number of years of service for different crimes. How we'll pay for a standing army for the next five years, I don't know, but these people have to do something, and I'd rather have them kill my enemies than my people."

"And you fill your military with the untrustworthy."

"Yes. But are not many of your own men the masterless? In Ceura, are not such said to have no honor? All I can do is give men who want to change the chance to try, and help them feed their families in the meantime. No one who was in the Sa'kagé will be allowed in the city guard, and taking bribes is a hanging offense for guards. We'll have a lot of problems, but for the moment, a lot of people hate Khalidor enough that they'll fight with me to defeat them before they start fighting against me again."

"You think you'll win," Garuwashi said.

"As long as Duchess Kirena and Count Drake stay alive, I'd rather be me than the Sa'kagé." Logan shrugged.

Garuwashi grunted, a sound that could have been assent or interest or neither, and they waited silently once more.

The massive doors of the throne room opened, and the diplomat came in. It had only been fifteen minutes. The man's eyes were filled with hatred. "Your Majesty," he said, biting off every word, "we accept your proposal."

68

$\mathcal{W}$ithin a month of their first secret meeting with Vi, the Chattel had dreamt up two dozen new spells. A gap-toothed farmwife with tobacco-stained teeth knew a spell that made food more filling. An Alitaeran widow had developed a weave to keep food fresh for months. Others added their knowledge and soon, they'd created biscuits half the size of a man's hand that would give him energy for the whole day, made him feel satisfied, and came in a dozen flavors. A village blacksmith's wife had crafted a spell that kept plows sharp, and it was easily applied to swords, but it had to be reapplied every day. Almost all the women had some experience as Healers, so they crafted bandages that stayed cleaner longer, packable spider webs to help blood clot instantly, potent salves for burns, poultices that could suck poison out of wounds. One could bond a simple repelling spell to fabric, making light tents or tunics stay dry even in a storm. A cowherd taught them a spell to firm treacherous, muddy roads. It would dissipate almost instantly, but if the magae spaced themselves along a column, an entire army could march safely through a bog.

Few of them could throw a fireball, but when a soft-spoken woman told Vi that she had crafted a spell-containing spell, they had something better. One woman would cast a spell-container, another would cast a simple fire spell, and a third would bind it to an arrow. The spell was smaller than a woman's fist, but the arrows wouldn't fly well until someone figured out how to smooth the spell over the entire length of the shaft. Then, the arrow flew true, struck the practice dummy's shield, and the spell-container burst, splashing fire over the shield and the dummy. The dummy was engulfed in fire in seconds. Magae around the yard stopped what they were doing and turned to watch.

Several of the herders knew spells that would temporarily sharpen sight, hearing, or smell. Working together, they made one spell that was more efficient than any of the three alone that would last the duration of a watch. It could be applied to sentries or scouts.

Then they took to reversing their spells. An enemy's food could be spoiled in a day. Making roads muddy was harder than making them dry, however, as a maja had to soften many layers of earth, rather than harden a few. Likewise, dulling the enemies' weapons during a battle was deemed impossible. Magically locating hundreds or thousands of moving swords and differentiating friends' from foes' was too difficult. They could make wounds fester and suppurate and attract flies, but most of the women were too sickened for such work. Those who had trained as Healers, who would have been best suited to it, said their vows precluded it.

The two fronts where they made no progress at all were the signal sticks and magically representing a battle. Garoth Ursuul had been able to see a battlefield and communicate instantly with his generals or men across his kingdom. In war, signal banners could be missed or captured or out of the line of sight. Trumpets' calls could be lost in the cacophony, and with either of those, the messages passed were both necessarily simple—withdraw, advance, come now—and public. Developing signal sticks would mean giving commanders the ability to hear scouts report from behind enemy lines, rather than hoping that they could cross back over and report hours or days later. It would mean ordering cavalry to reinforce a wavering line and having them move instantly, rather than minutes later. It would mean a general could split his armies and still coordinate their movements, or change their strategy as the situation changed, rather than being committed to meet on a specified day at a certain area and hope nothing kept the other half of your army from getting there.

The failure put Vi in an evil mood, which wasn't helped when Sister Ariel laughed at her. "Vi," she said, joining her on the field, "don't you see what you've accomplished?"

Vi grunted. "I've made war easier."

"Well, yes, you have, but you've done something more remarkable. Remarkable for any maja, but perhaps doubly so for you."

"What's that?" Vi asked, suspicious of any praise from Sister Ariel.

"You're teaching these women to wage war without trying to be men. The simple fact is, most women aren't really good at throwing fire or calling down lightning. If you'd insisted on these women becoming war magae as the Chantry thought of war magae, they'd have made little progress before spring. Instead, you've let them be who they are."

"It's common sense."

"By the Seraph's tits, Vi, a magus's fireball isn't any good if he can't cross a bog to get to the battle; his lightning bolt can't hurt anyone if he starves. We were right about you. It might be common sense, but the weaves you've encouraged these women to develop would never have been encouraged by anyone else. You want to know why? Because we all have blind spots, Vi, even you. The good thing is that yours are different from ours. Your commonsense answer violates one of our institutional creeds in place since the Third Alitaeran Accord, which is that the Sisterhood is complete. By abandoning certain areas of study, many would say you imply that men are better at those types of magic. That statement would be enough to paralyze most Sisters from doing the work you're doing. Even if they agreed it was true, they would spend a lot of energy trying to conceal the fact that they weren't studying fire and lightning and earthquakes."

"I'm not making any statements," Vi said. "I bet I can throw a better fireball than most magi, and I haven't even worked on it. I'm just trying to save our asses."

"Oh, just because a crisis threatens to wipe us out, you think we should stop infighting?"

Vi scrunched her eyebrows together. "Is that a real question?"

Sister Ariel laughed. "How are things, ahem, on the conjugal front?"

"What?" Right when Vi thought Sister Ariel was being

kind, the woman had to pull out her big words to make Vi feel stupid.

"How are things with your husband?" Sister Ariel asked, after making sure no one was close enough to overhear.

At even the mention of him, Vi felt Kylar, only fifty paces away, training in the basement of their manse with Durzo. He seemed happy despite his many bruises. Vi Healed them secretly from time to time when Kylar was asleep in the mornings.

The last month had been awkward, but not nearly as bad as Vi had feared. Vi had expected to feel malice leaking through the bond at all times, and if Kylar had hated her, there was no way she could be anything but miserable. Mostly, though, he didn't think about her. She was training and studying as many hours a day as her body could stand and so was he. When she got home, she went to bed immediately.

Meanwhile, Kylar and Elene had found a patr to marry them in secret. Durzo, Uly, Sister Ariel, and Vi were the only witnesses. Kylar had moved into Elene's room, though consummating their marriage was impossible, and any time cuddling even flirted with the erotic, Kylar began to get sick. Oddly, they still had that newlywed glow. Maybe it was all intensified because they knew Elene didn't have much time left, so they touched whenever they could—though carefully—and spent hours talking.

Vi knew Kylar felt the absence of sex acutely. Some nights she'd lie awake on the opposite side of the wall from where he lay awake, Elene snuggled into his chest. She could feel the ache of desire, but as soon as he entertained the desire, his thoughts veered to Vi and with an iron self-control, he stopped those thoughts and began admiring everything he loved about Elene. Sometimes, Vi knew, that iron self-control was rusted all the way through, but still he closed the door.

They'd met twice in their dreams.

"You don't hate me," Vi said in the first dream. She marveled at it.

"I hate the price we have to pay."

"Can you ever forgive me?" she asked.

"I'm trying. You did what had to be done. You're not a bad woman, Vi. I know that you've been giving me and Elene space and time, and I know it's hard for you, too. Thank you." He glanced down at her night dress; this one actually fit, and his gaze was admiring, but deliberately brief. "I just wish you weren't so damn beautiful. Good night."

The second dream had been harder. It had been one of those nights where Kylar lay on the opposite side of the wall so tormented he thought he would burst. In the dream, Kylar stood at the foot of Vi's bed, naked. His eyes were closed and Vi drank in the sight of him, his hard lean limbs, flat stomach etched with hard muscles. She was wearing one of Master Piccun's nightdresses, which she'd left behind in Cenaria. It was white silk and short with sheer panels, but more pretty than provocative: a make-love-to-me, not a fuck-me. It was one of the first things she'd ever bought from Master Piccun, and in four years she'd never worn it. Men made love to their wives or girlfriends. Vi got fucked. Her hair was unbound and combed out glossy.

Vi had a revelation at the very moment Kylar opened his eyes. Kylar had never seen this dress. This wasn't his dream. It was hers. She froze, feeling more exposed than she had when she'd stood naked in front of the Godking. Garoth Ursuul had judged her not knowing her. Kylar had far more power. He was here because she desired him. Vi had long been the object of desire, and she'd mocked men for it.

Now, the numbness that had sat between her legs since the first time one of her mother's lovers raped her was thawing. The ache there was so foreign that Vi hadn't been able to name it. For all the fucking she'd done, Vi had not once taken a man to bed for pleasure, much less love. The receding numbness, though, not only allowed her to feel desire for the first time, it also threatened her. Through the ice, Vi could see the outlines of a mystery: she could imagine bringing her desire—of which fucking was a part, but not the center—to Kylar and experiencing union, wholeness in a fragmented world. She'd made fucking a simple physical exertion, as monotonous but as necessary to her work as exercising. If she ever wanted to experience what was beneath the ice, she'd have to feel the pain and violation frozen inside it. If Kylar were to speak while they had sex, she'd remember all the bastards who couldn't shut up. If he were to remain silent, she'd remember the brutes who fucked silently. If Kylar were to twine his fingers through her hair, she'd remember all the assholes who pawed her hair like she was an animal. If Kylar ripped her clothes off in his passion, she would remember when Hu Gibbet did it and spat on her face. If Vi were ever to enjoy Kylar's desire and allow herself to reciprocate, she'd have to trust him with her brokenness, and she'd have to wade through all the hells her numbness had spared her.

She understood all of that in the very moment Kylar's opening eyes met hers. She tensed and immediately her hair was back up in its ponytail, tight enough to hurt. Two waves of feeling raced through Kylar, the second chasing the first, and even with her emotional stupidity or however Sister Ariel had said it, Vi could name his feelings through the very air. The first was desire, and though it was physical, it wasn't only physical. A month of cuddling the woman he loved had been a month of foreplay. But right after that, he withdrew.

"Vi," Kylar choked out. "I can't even be here." He ignored his own nudity, and her near-nudity, looking into her eyes and letting her read his.

Her rapists had shattered the bond between sex and intimacy, leaving her only with fucking. In ring raping Kylar, she'd left him with only intimacy. The difference was, the only person who could damage Kylar as she had been damaged long ago was Kylar himself. The integrity between what Kylar's body did and what his heart felt was still intact. He was sorely tempted, but so far unbroken. If he cheated on Elene, he would be a cheater in his own eyes—for the rest of a very long life.

He'd turned and walked out of her dream.

Vi cleared her throat and met Sister Ariel's gaze. "Things with Kylar are fine."

69

Dorian knew he was in trouble as soon as the dancing girl entered the throne room. He'd been meeting with the Graavar chieftain, a hulking highlander whose raven hair hung in great mats to his waist. The Graavar were a powerful highland tribe, and Grakaat Kruhn was highly regarded by all the tribes. He had come to test Dorian. It was a harmless bit of highlander play, mostly—the highlanders hadn't made a serious attempt at independence for more than a century—and Grakaat had found Dorian satisfactory in all ways. Until this.

"Your Holiness," Grakaat Kruhn said, his half-lidded eyes too self-satisfied by far, "I would like to present you with a gift to seal our treaty." He gestured and two girls came forward. The dancer was about sixteen, the other, who held a highland flute, was perhaps thirteen, and though they were both pretty, Dorian had no doubt they were the chieftain's daughters.

As the dancer began a sensuous *rondaa,* most of Dorian's guards and all of his courtiers averted their eyes.

The highland version of the dance was different from what Dorian had seen as a youth. The girl wore a wide garment with exaggerated wide shoulders from which were suspended strips of cloth. Around the hips, the cloth had bells sown in. As her sister played, each gyration of the dancer's hips made the bells tinkle and revealed glimpses of her nakedness beneath. As in the lowland dance, the girl appeared to float, chest and head immobile while her body tantalized, but the lowland dance was more focused on the stomach, which this girl had fully covered. Nonetheless, in moments Dorian was drawn in. The chieftain's daughter was talented.

The *rondaa* gave way to a *beraa,* and removed the last doubts from Dorian's mind about what that chieftain intended. The *beraa* was faster, more erotic. The girl clapped her hands in time over her head, exposing the sides of her breasts, her hips snapping side to side, but now also undulating front to back in a motion that would torment any man with a pulse.

Dorian was trapped. He wasn't sure if he was glad that Jenine was sequestered for her moon blood or if he wished she were here. Perhaps her presence would have changed things. Grakaat Kruhn wouldn't have his daughter dance a *beraa* for the Godking unless he planned to give her to him. A marriage to seal a treaty had far less weight in the north than it did in the southron realms, but the smile that had been on the chieftain's face told Dorian something else.

Dorian thought that taking many wives would have quelled the rumors he'd begun by entering the castle as a eunuch, but if anyone found out that he wasn't using his harem, the Halfman jokes would begin again. A highland

warrior like Grakaat Kruhn achieved his place through
the force of his *virtu,* which meant not only virtue, but
also strength and manliness. To the highlanders, the three
concepts were one. What manliness could a eunuch have?
How could a war chief submit to half a man?

Dorian made a small gesture and the throne room
cleared quietly of everyone except his guards and several
Vürdmeisters. Grakaat Kruhn looked disturbed, but his
daughter didn't miss a step, and Dorian kept his attention full on her, not giving the chieftain any clues. Inside, Dorian's stomach roiled. *God, give me strength for
what I'm about to do.* But he'd rejected the One God, and
the thought of what the God would think of this cooled
whatever arousal Dorian still had left. Would Jenine
understand?

Maybe. If she didn't have to see it.

Damn the highlander. Dorian's Hands had given him
news that Moburu was making a bid to take over the barbarian tribes of the Freeze. Moburu was calling himself
the prophesied High King, and the hell of it was that he
had been born on the right day—or missed it by three,
depending on which scholar's calendar you believed.
But even if Moburu died before spring and especially
if he didn't, Dorian needed this highlander to bring all
the other highlanders to him to face Neph Dada and his
Vürdmeisters.

If Dorian faltered now, the story would get out instantly: the new Godking was either impotent or a eunuch. A southron, then. No true Godking at all. Grakaat
Kruhn would have killed him with a teenage girl. *If I'm to
be Godking, I've got to rule like a Godking.*

The dancer finished with an exuberance and intensity

in her smoky eyes that surprised Dorian. Had she convinced herself to love him, a stranger? Or was there fear somewhere beneath, a terror she concealed, taking only its energy to fuel her dance?

Dorian wrapped his knuckles on his throne appreciatively, the Khalidoran equivalent of applause. He smiled and stood. "By Khali, Grakaat, they're amazing. They're stunning. Gorgeous. The younger one dances too?"

Grakaat looked confused. "I—yes, Your Holiness, but I meant—"

"I accept them. I've never had a more handsome gift. Child, what's your name?" he asked, turning to the flutist.

Her sudden fear confirmed what Dorian expected. Grakaat had intended to bait him with the dancer. The last thing he'd expected was that a eunuch would want both of his daughters. Between the young girl's fear and the older girl's incredulity, Dorian wanted to say, "I didn't want this. Your father used you as pawns against a god. A god can't let him win." But he said nothing.

"I'm Eesa," the girl said. She was barely flowered, pretty in an awkward girlish way. Dorian's stomach threatened to rebel. *Khali, give me strength.*

He remembered a spell to ease the girl's fright and accomplish his purposes. He'd used it often as a lecherous young man. "The Graavar seal marriage pacts publicly, don't they?" Dorian asked.

Fear shot through the chieftain's eyes and Dorian knew that the younger daughter was Grakaat's favorite. "It's a tradition we've not practiced in many—"

"A good tradition," Dorian said, "especially when

there are . . . *doubts* about the groom's *virtu.*" *Khali, give me strength.*

"I, I . . . Your Holiness." Grakaat was turning green. His men-at-arms averted their eyes.

Eesa still didn't know what they were talking about. Before she could figure it out, Dorian laid a tracery of vir on her. She visibly relaxed. Her pupils dilated, and she couldn't seem to look anywhere but Dorian's face. He continued the spell, delicately coaxing her body into deceiving her mind. Whatever he did to her now, she would enjoy. Later, if she were as horrified as she ought to be, they would tell her that he was a god, that there was no shaming in serving him however he desired, that she should feel honored to have attracted his attention.

"I don't know all the intricacies of your quaint barbarian customs, so a few pillows on the floor will have to do. That is, unless you object?" Dorian stood and shrugged out of his ermine over-robe. With the vir, he devoured the rest of his clothing with tongues of black flame. Naked, his flesh writhing with layer on layer of vir, thorns of it clawing out of his skin, a black crown of it springing through the skin of his head, Dorian glowered at the chieftain. The huge man trembled. He tried to turn his head, and found it locked in place. He tried to close his eyes, and found he couldn't blink.

The vir swept Dorian's courtiers' pillows into a pile three paces from Grakaat's feet.

Dorian let his glory fade and turned to the girl. He smiled at her. "Come, love." *Khali, give me strength,* Dorian prayed, and found he had it. God forgive him, his strength didn't flag for an instant.

Afterward, Dorian stood, his body gleaming with

sweat. Eesa lay panting, oblivious, obscene. For the first time, Graakat Kruhn was staring at Wanhope with the fear a Godking deserved. The Godking said, "I'll be expecting you come spring. If your warhost numbers seven thousand, I will put you over the Quarl, Churaq, Hraagl, and Iktana clans. On spring's first new moon, we march to Black Barrow. The girls stay with me."

70

$\mathcal{V}$i woke to Sister Ariel shaking her. The windows were still dark, and the only light in the room was from a single candle. Vi sat up and gazed blearily at the maja, who was red-eyed and wearing the same tent-like dress she'd worn the day before.

"What are you doing?" Vi asked.

"I found it. I can help you."

"Help me with what?" Vi asked.

"Get up, I'll tell you on the way."

Vi dressed and followed Sister Ariel. Sister Ariel said nothing until they were on one of the punts that would convey them to the Chantry. Even then, she spoke quietly, leery of how voices traveled over the water, even in the pre-dawn fog that wreathed the lake.

"Long ago, there was an Alitaeran emperor named Jorald Hurdazin. By all accounts, he was a skilled and wise leader. In his younger years, he solidified Alitaeran control from what is now Ymmur in the east to the west coast of Midcyru. What is now Waeddryn and Modai were his last conquests, and with his marriage to Layinisa Guralt, the Seeress of Gyle—essentially its princess—the lands that are now Ceura came under his control as well, and there he stopped, mostly because of her influence. He spent the next twenty years consolidating his empire and for the most part bringing justice and prosperity to the lands he had conquered. He was, however, magically poisoned by one of his many enemies. The poisoning was caught early, but the magi could only delay its effects. They treated him every day, but soon determined that Emperor Hurdazin would die within two years. Obviously, this was a closely held secret, and obviously, they called as many green magi and magae as they could. To make matters worse, there was no heir, and in agreeing to bring Gyle into the Empire, Gyle's king had insisted that Jorald and Layinisa be married with rings like yours. For a man of his power, finding such rings was no problem, and though their marriage was first political and magical, all the histories I've read agree that Jorald and Layinisa deeply loved each other. The green magi found nothing to heal Jorald, and they soon found that Layinisa was infertile. Women with great Talents sometimes injure themselves with their magic, and infertility is common in those who use too much magic, or too much too soon.

"The emperor put as many magi as he dared trust to work on both magical problems. He believed that Layinisa might hold his empire after his death, but if she were infertile, that would only delay the collapse, and he didn't want to be yet another emperor whose empire died with him. In the end, it was Layinisa herself who discovered a way around the rings' bond."

"She did?" Vi asked.

"Don't get excited. Now we're here, say nothing until we reach the library."

They walked silently through the dark halls of the Chantry. Vi wondered for a moment that the building was beginning to feel like home. The dim magical torches that illumined the walls and followed them seemed normal now, the austere marble arches comforting in their strength rather than menacing. In a few minutes, they were deep in the Chantry's storerooms, far below the waterline, a place Vi had never been allowed to go. It was neither dark nor dirty, but it did have an air of abandonment. Numbered oak boxes lined the room to the ceiling. The one small desk had an oak box already upon it.

Instead of opening the box, however, Sister Ariel closed it and put it back on a numbered shelf and grabbed a different box two rows down. Vi understood that she had left out the wrong box in case some spy checked what she was studying. At first Vi wondered why the boxes were oaken, but then she looked again and saw the spell sunk into the wood. Each oak box had one spell to strengthen the box and make it watertight, one to make it fire resistant, and one to suck air from the box as it closed to preserve whatever was kept inside.

"Magically reactive materials are kept in special rooms on the next floor; these archives are for mundane records only. Because of how they're preserved, they only have to be copied by industrious tyros such as yourself every few hundred years—if they're not frequently opened," Sister Ariel said. The box opened with a hiss, and she gently lifted out sheets of bound parchment that to Vi's eyes looked scarcely ten years old.

"At the time of Jorald and Layinisa's marriage, binding

rings had been forbidden for almost fifty years. They were still common among royal families, of course, who were rarely willing to surrender them. The rings continued to cause misery wherever they were used and all magi became more and more convinced that banning them had been one of the best decisions the Chantry and the brotherhoods had ever made. Every group eliminated knowledge of them and how to make them to the best of its ability. This did lead to bloodshed a number of times, especially among the Vy'sana, the Makers, who to this day are a small brotherhood. When Layinisa figured out how to circumvent the magic, there was a great debate among us. Some wanted to follow her research to find a way to fully break the bonding. The majority, however, feared that any dabbling in those arts again would lead to a full rediscovery of how to bond. The suffering of those few who were presently bonded was weighed against the possibility of vast suffering if bonding were rediscovered by the unscrupulous. I don't know if you've experimented with your bond, Vi, but it does have an element of compulsion. That's what made it break the Godking's compulsion on you. The order of the ringing makes the compulsion in your rings flow from you to Kylar."

"What?" Vi asked. "You mean . . ."

"I mean if you told Kylar to walk on his hands to Cenaria, you'd find his body somewhere in a mountain pass with stumps where his hands had been. It's a compulsion stronger by far than what the Godking used on you."

"But there's a way out?" Vi said, her throat tight.

"Not out, child. Because you're the mistress of the bond, however, you can do what Layinisa did."

"Which is?"

"She used the compulsion of the bond to force Jorald to divorce her and marry a princess. She was then able to suspend the bond to allow him to produce an heir."

"What happened?"

"He died but the empire lived, minus the country of Gyle, which was deeply insulted by Jorald divorcing their Seeress. Layinisa served Jorald's new wife and supported her regency for five years, until the new empress marched against Gyle, at which point Layinisa committed suicide. The enmity between Alitaera and Ceura didn't cool for centuries and would probably be raging right now if the countries still bordered each other. The point is, if you wish it, you can suspend the bond—partially. A maja named Jessa worked with Layinisa on the rings. Jessa was in the camp that wished to learn about breaking them, and when the Chantry forbade it, I suspected that she tried to defy them. Jessa was a Healer, but she was also interested in gardening, so I've been looking through her books. They're not terribly enlightening; others did far better, and she wasn't an important maja, so I think no one ever studied her books. If they did, they would have found what I have. She's hidden it in plain sight, and not well. She was no cryptographer. After I read the books, I began applying ciphers, then I worked on her marginalia. If you could read Old Ceuran you'd see how ridiculous this is—she'd capitalize a strange word in her margin notes and everything from that capital to the next capital was part of her secret message. If you look at all the marginalia from the last to the first, the message unfolds. I don't even understand everything Jessa wrote, but I think you will. Oh, one more thing: Vi, I haven't told Kylar or

Elene about this, and I won't. This is your burden. It is yours to decide if the price is worth it."

Twelve hours later, with dark circles under her eyes, Vi found a cheerful Elene making breakfast.

"What is it?" Elene asked. "Are you well?"

"I know it's a month late, but Elene . . ." A timid smile broke through Vi's fatigue. "I have a wedding present for you."

71

*T*hey were calling him Solon Stormrider. They said that his hair was growing in white because of the snow-laden seas through which his longboats had plunged. Or they said it had turned white after the winter sea had chewed on him and found him too tough and spat him back out. His boat had capsized once, and even his magic had barely saved him as he swam a mile through storm-whipped seas. Of course, his hair had been growing in white since he'd used Curoch—long before this mad winter—and he'd explained that to the soldiers and sailors who'd begun to follow him, but they preferred their own versions.

Now it was spring, and Solon was heading back to Queen Wariyamo, having destroyed her enemies. He had bowed before her after saving her life, and she had told him, fury edging her voice, that the price for her hand was cleansing the isles of the rebellion he had started by killing Oshobi Takeda. Kaede didn't like being weak, didn't like needing anyone, but her temper always cooled in time. At least, it used to.

Everyone had expected Solon to wait for spring and take an army to each of the Takeda isles. Instead, he'd begun at once, alone. In a canoe, he'd paddled the eighteen miles to Durai. There, he'd given the ultimatum he would give a dozen times through the winter. Surrender, swear fealty to the queen, and give me all your weapons, or I shall slay every man who fights and take those who surrender as slaves.

Gulon Takeda had laughed at him, and died, along with eighteen of his soldiers. Solon had returned with twenty-four awed soldiers in a longboat. He had delivered them to the new Mikaidon and slept in a dockside tavern, not seeking so much as a word with Kaede. By the time he'd woken and gone out to his canoe, a score of the craziest sailors he'd ever met and a captain with a vendetta against the Takedas volunteered to join him.

Soon, storms battered them every time they left port, and Solon's command of weather magic grew by necessity. But Sethi winter storms were tamed by no mage, and it was a fight every day. Several times, the Takedas who had faced them were so stunned that anyone should be able to make the crossing they had surrendered on the spot. And when Solon returned to Hokkai yet again, victorious yet again, he found the Takeda soldiers he'd conscripted were a fully trusted part of the Sethi army, oddly proud to have been defeated by the Stormrider.

Now it was done. The Takedas' home island, Horai, hadn't expected an army for at least another six weeks. The leaders were totally unprepared, and having almost three thousand men to Solon's four hundred did them no good. Before the Takeda army could be rallied, its commanders were dead, and Solon's magic-enhanced voice had offered generous terms to the living. The rebellion was crushed and nearly all the dead were Takedas.

With the first day of spring, the first day clear enough that the merchants would be on their boats preparing for the first spring runs, checking for damage, repairing sails and nets, shouting orders at men rusty from months spent ashore, Solon's little fleet sailed into Hokkai harbor.

They were greeted as heroes, and the crazy sailors who had joined Solon first were now soldiers in truth. Sailors dropped their gear to greet them, captains forgot their shouting, and the shorebound traders and vintners streamed through the streets to greet them. The flood carried them to the castle, and Solon's heart thudded with fear and expectation. *Kaede, please, my love, don't take my glory as an insult. Without you, it all means nothing.*

The crowd brought him to Whitecliff Castle, shining in the spring sun. Kaede stood on the dais where months before she had almost been deposed. She wore an ocean blue nagika and a platinum tiara with sapphires. She raised her hands and the men and women quieted. "How fare the isles, Stormrider?"

"The isles are at peace, Your Majesty."

The people cheered, but Kaede's face was still somber. She let the people cheer, then raised her hands once more. "They say you are a mage, Stormrider."

"I am," he said.

The crowd grew quieter, noting the queen's solemnity. That solemnity brought to not a few minds the questions people had asked when Solon had first been sent to school with the Midcyri magi: where would his loyalties lie?

"They say you are a god, Stormrider, to have defied the winter seas alone."

"Neither a god, nor alone, Your Majesty. A loyal son of Seth who tracked the seas with men and women fearless as tygres, fiercer than storms, and hungrier than the seas. Not even winter seas could stop such from serving you."

The crowd stirred with hope, and Solon's Stormriders swelled with pride that he should share the glory so liberally, but Kaede cut it off quickly. "They say you were our prince, Stormrider. They say I've stolen your throne."

Silence.

"A prince I was, of an ancient house that my elder brother debased and dishonored. He broke the holy covenant between king and country, and I stand a prince no more. Should you command, I will sail to the sunset or to death's rocky shores. I am but a man." He lowered his voice, but still it carried across the silent crowd. "A man who loves you, my queen."

She stood silent and the crowd held its breath, but Solon could see her eyes shining. "Then Solon Stormrider, Solon Tofusin, come forward and receive your rewards as a mage, and a loyal son of Seth, and a man."

He was in a haze as the crowd pulled him forward, laughing and cheering and shouting. Kaede first presented him with a pendant with a glowing ruby lit from within, burning with ancient magics. He'd never seen it before, never heard of such an artifact, but before he could consider it, she put a crown on his brow. It was his father's crown, a circlet of seven golden grape leaves mingled with seven golden waves. "A ruby fit for a mage, a crown fit for Seth's most loyal son, and—if you will have me—a proud and troublesome woman ill-fit for any man."

"Except one," Solon said, and he swept her into his arms and kissed her.

72

$\mathcal{V}$i didn't know how Elene had explained it to Kylar, though she had known when by Kylar's sudden burst of confusion and hope and longing through the bond. Tonight was the night. She'd gone over the magic a number of times with Sister Ariel. As Ariel had warned her, Vi wasn't severing the bond, only partially suspending it.

First, it was only suspended while Vi was actively using magic against it. If there was any good news, Vi thought, it was that Kylar was a virgin. That embarrassed him, but Vi thought it was extraordinary and kind of cute, which embarrassed him further. Now, though, she simply hoped it meant his lovemaking with Elene would be brief. Vi had told Elene—and Elene had decided not to tell Kylar—that the suspension of the bond worked only one way: Kylar wouldn't feel Vi, but Vi would still feel him.

Vi had her materials: an itchy wool robe that she hoped would distract her from whatever physical sensation bled through the bond, and a pitcher of wine for afterward to obliterate her thinking. Sister Ariel didn't exactly approve, but she didn't forbid it, either. Vi could only hope that Kylar was one of those men who promptly fell asleep after sex, because once she released the magic, he would feel her once more. If Kylar knew Vi was basically magically eavesdropping on his love-making, he would worry about it. Elene fully believed she would die by spring, and she deserved as much of Kylar's attention as she could get.

Kylar was coming up the steps. He and Elene had fin-ished a romantic dinner in the kitchen—of course they couldn't go out where people might see them—and Elene was leading him by the hand. Vi felt his anticipation and disbelief. He probed toward Vi, but she made herself a stone wall and began chanting.

According to Sister Ariel, the weaves themselves weren't that challenging; it was using them at the strength required for the time required that was difficult. Plus, Sister Ariel allowed, it was probably emotionally taxing. Ariel thought Vi could probably maintain them for twenty minutes.

Sister Ariel could probably withstand the emotional tax forever. The words Bitch Wytch made their way into Vi's chanting, but they didn't have the force they used to. After all, it was Sister Ariel who had done all the research to make this possible. Was that her way of saying sorry?

Layer upon layer of magic surrounded the bond, wreathing it like fog, and in moments Vi knew she was doing it right for two reasons. First, Kylar stopped, be-wildered, as he was leaning forward to kiss Elene as they sat on the edge of their bed. Second, Vi could tell that he stopped leaning forward as he sat on the edge of his bed.

Whatever Vi was doing to mute Kylar's side of the bond, it seemed to be amplifying her own.

Panic hit her, making it hard to breathe, but Kylar didn't feel it. She could tell he didn't feel her. He wondered at the absence and then joy spread through him like a fire. He pulled Elene into his arms and kissed her passionately.

It was hard to breathe. Vi could only choke out a series of curses to keep the magic going. She'd kissed men, of course, and had dozens more kiss her. She'd avoided it when she could, wishing she could be as numb there as below, but it was part of her work to kiss convincingly. Feeling Kylar kiss Elene was something different. It was fresh and innocent and full of rejoicing. Then it deepened, and Vi felt Kylar's surprise at the ferocity of Elene's passion. He fell—was pushed?—back onto the bed, and she settled on his hips. Then he was kissing her again, fumbling with the ties of her dress.

Vi cursed desperately, locking her eyes open, rubbing the wool across her forearm. It helped, a little, but Kylar's joy and free desire still lived in her head. Elene must have said something, because Kylar laughed. Vi could hear it through the wall, but as she felt it, she knew she'd never heard Kylar laugh like that. Maybe Kylar had never laughed like that in his whole life. It was playful and free and accepted and accepting, a joy wild and strong and content. This was the Kylar Elene had always seen, and with a pang, Vi knew Elene deserved him.

There was a tenderness so deep emanating through the bond that it ached, and Vi realized that of all things, Kylar was talking to Elene.

"Put him in a bed chamber with a naked woman and he

talks?" Vi said aloud, still working her Talent. "No wonder he's still a virgin." It was too bad the weaves weren't
harder, because she needed the distraction. Elene was
scared, Vi realized, and embarrassed because she knew
exactly what Vi was doing here in this room. Either way,
Kylar was soothing her, lying by her side, his left arm
under her head and his right arm embracing her, caressing
her while he spoke soft assurances and slowly awakened
her passion.

Vi had fucked so many times, with so many men, in so
many ways, she thought she knew pretty much everything
about sex. But Kylar and Elene, in their mutual ignorance,
were experiencing something she never had. Their lovemaking fit into a pattern bigger than itself. There was no
awkwardness even in their fumbling, because there was
no fear of judgment.

"Oh, fuck me, oh—" Vi's voice squeaked and she lost
the thought. Whatever Elene was doing, she was either
naturally gifted or Kylar was extremely sensitive. Either
way, the wave of pleasure through the bond was overwhelming. Vi's cheeks felt like they were on fire.

Then Vi felt Kylar's mischievous grin—dammit, it felt
exactly the same way it looked—and his own pleasure
faded into the pleasure of pleasuring.

"You bastard," Vi said. "I hate you. I hate you I hate
you I hate you." When Vi fucked, she put on a persona
like a mask, always. Kylar was making love as a whole
man. Every aspect of himself was present—and Vi knew
then that she loved him.

She'd been attracted to things about Kylar from the
first time she saw that damned mischievous grin in Count
Drake's house. She'd admired how he tried to leave the

way of shadows, how he treated Elene and Uly. She appreciated his excellence in fighting. She'd felt a twinge of infatuation long ago—but then, she'd once been infatuated with Jarl, who was homosexual. In the past month, she'd even come to accept that she desired Kylar. But all those things weren't love. Perhaps she never would have known what love was if she hadn't talked so much with Elene, and if she hadn't felt it daily in Kylar's feelings for Elene.

Something banged into the wall inches from Vi, and she gasped. Her eyes widened. The magic almost escaped her, and only her fear of what would happen if it did helped her regain control. She scrubbed the wool against her arm—fuck she hated wool! "Dead babies. Bearded women. Back hair so long you can braid it. Moon blood. The smell of the Warrens on a hot summer day. Unwashed whores. Vomit. Dead babies. Bearded women. Back hair so—oh shit!" Vi bit the wool and held onto the magic for dear life.

A few moments later, Vi could breathe again. She checked the magic as a deep sense of ease and restfulness and well-being and intimacy and peace with the entire world rolled over Kylar. The magic was still intact. Vi grabbed the pitcher of wine and drank from it directly. "It's a good thing you're a virgin, Kylar. Were a virgin. I don't think I could've handled that for much—"

Vi realized something at apparently the same time Elene did: Kylar was still aroused. He asked a question, and Elene's answer was unmistakably and passionately affirmative. Vi set the pitcher down with shaking hands. Pleasure arced through Kylar again.

Oh gods, it was going to be a long winter.

73

As winter slowly faded in Khaliras, Dorian arrayed his army on the plain north of the city to face the invaders from the Freeze. The ground was still covered in melting snow that their feet churned into freezing slush. Every breath steamed a protest against battle in such conditions.

The wild men who inhabited the Freeze always fought bravely, but their only tactic was to overwhelm a foe by throwing a larger army at it. Once engaged, they fought man to man, never as a unit. Since its founding, Khaliras had never been taken by the brutes, though a few times it had been a near thing. Garoth had always said that the wild men had proportionally more Talented men and women than any people in the world.

The armies faced each other as the sky turned from inky blue to ice blue with the rising sun. Godking Wanhope's lines were only three deep, arrayed over as much of the plain as twenty thousand men would stretch. The wild men's army dwarfed his, and stretched much further and more thickly. There was no way Wanhope could keep them from flanking his army. In the middle of the wild men's line there was one huge block that the men shunned. If Dorian's reports were correct, he faced twenty-eight thousand krul, and even more wild men.

Three-to-one odds. Dorian smiled, fearless. The current of prophecy was streaming past him, and he saw a thousand deaths. Ten thousand.

"Milord, are you feeling well?" Jenine asked. Dorian hadn't wanted her to have to see this, but he'd been counting on Jenine more and more, not only for her advice, either.

He blinked and focused on her. Her futures were splitting off so sharply that he could barely see her as she was now, pretty, lips pale from the cold, bundled in furs. Flickering in front of her was a woman hugely pregnant with twins, and a woman with a crushed skull, features unrecognizable under the gore. "No, not well at all," Dorian said. "But well enough that I won't let my men die."

From this distance, the grotesque features of the krul weren't visible, though their plainly naked gray flesh was. That nakedness gave Dorian hope. The krul were created with magic, but they were creatures of flesh. The cold would cripple and kill them eventually. It wasn't easy to force the krul to wear clothing, as it wasn't easy to rein them in from slaughter, but each could be done. That the wild men's shamans hadn't meant their control was tenuous.

Dorian gave an order, and the slaves lowered his palanquin to the ground. Godking Wanhope stepped out and advanced onto the plain alone. Palming an obsidian knife, he shrugged off the priceless ermine cloak and let it fall to the mud. It was a gesture that would have infuriated him had he seen his father do it. Now, he understood. To protect what he loved, he had to keep control. To keep control, Wanhope had to be a god. A god was above ordinary concerns like ruining a cloak that cost more than fifty slaves.

The currents of prophecy were rising at the pressure of seventy thousand futures that Wanhope held in his hands. On his choices, tens of thousands would live and die. He looked at the army opposing him and saw ten thousand ravens swirling over them, waiting to feed. He blinked, and the ravens were gone, then blinked again, and they were back. But they weren't ravens. Nor did they only swirl over the wild men.

Dorian turned, eyes wide. Wispy, dark figures swarmed over his entire army, clotted the air above his men, darting this way and that. Here six perched on a single man, their claws sunk deep into his flesh. There only a single dark figure spun around another warrior, stabbing in one place and then another, as if trying his defenses. But those were the exception. Almost every man in Dorian's army had at least one figure clinging to him. And there were ranks among them; some were far more terrible. Dorian looked at General Naga nearby. A trio of the monsters clung to the man, two perched on his shoulders, one licking ephemeral blood from the general's fingers.

This close, Dorian could see their features. One had a cancer that swelled one eye grotesquely. Open, suppurating ulcers dotted their golden-skinned faces, dribbling black blood onto robes so black with that blood that Dorian could barely tell that they had once been white. It was those shredded robes, dripping ephemeral blood that made them all look like ravens. The cancered one dipped his claws into General Naga's skull and drew them out again and licked its claws greedily. But they weren't claws, they were finger bones, denuded of their golden flesh. It turned its good eye to Dorian. "What is he looking at?" it asked.

The other cocked its head and it met Dorian's gaze. "Us," it hissed in wonder.

"Odniar, ruy'eo getnirfhign em. Dirlom?" Dorian heard the voice. It was Jenine, but he couldn't understand what she was saying. Why couldn't he understand her, but he could understand these things? What were they, anyway?

He looked back to the army across the plain. He saw the krul, but this time, he saw through their flesh. Each of them held one of these creatures. *My God, these are the Strangers.* Dorian saw them, and he understood. The Strangers carried hell with them wherever they went. They fed on human suffering not because it sustained them, but because it was a distraction from their own suffering; it was entertainment. Wearing flesh was no escape. Rather it was simply the best distraction of all, a chance to feel, if only for a time, to experience the pleasures of food and drink, if only in a muted way, and to kill. That was the pinnacle, to take away that which men had and which they had no more.

"Odniar!" the voice was in his ear. Dorian turned and for a moment, he could see with his natural vision once more. Every one of his men was staring at him, fearful. Then his vision bifurcated and he could see fear rise like a fragrance from his men—to the delight of the swirling Strangers. He felt the fingers on his shoulders, bony fingers, but before he could turn to face what he knew must cling even to him, he felt natural fingers grab his bicep and squeeze hard.

Jenine swam into his vision, which was natural once more, then it split. She was pregnant, right now, but not with twins. A Stranger spun in tight circles around her, but hadn't yet found a place to rest. It wanted—by the God, it wanted their baby!

Dorian cried out and saw a fresh wave of fear rise from his men. A mob of the Strangers, now aware of his awareness of them, had congregated around him. They were walling him in.

"ODNIAR! Rodnia! Adimmt! Dornia. Dorian!" Jenine was whispering fiercely in his ear, her body pressed against him, turning him away from his men. He blinked, and saw only ground, and soldiers, and krul, and his wife. She'd called him back from madness, maybe using the thing which best anchored him to reality: his own name.

"I'm back," he said. "I'm here. Thank you." He shook himself, willed himself not to see beyond the veil again. He looked over his shoulder, nodded to General Naga to let the frightened man see that Dorian was well, and then strode forward.

Beneath the cloak, Dorian—Wanhope—had decided to go bare-chested. A god felt not the cold. He strode forward, decisive to cover for his earlier hesitation, great knots of vir rising in his skin. He gestured and a young man was brought forward. Dammit, Wanhope hadn't wanted Jenine to see this. But it was too late, and there was no way she would go where she couldn't see him after he'd almost doomed them all by standing around looking lost.

The young man's name was Udrik Ursuul. All of the

aethelings in Khaliras had been killed, but seventeen who'd already left for their Harrowings still lived. Udrik had impregnated the wrong Modaini oligarch's daughter and had to flee, thus failing his uurdthan. He'd come home to beg mercy.

"Do you know, Udrik, if you raise thirteen legions of krul, you can command them yourself, but if you raise just one more, you have to master an arcanghul?"

"A what?" Udrik's brows were still heavily kohled, menacing despite his fright.

"It's a creature that these wild men didn't dare try to master," Wanhope said. "Tell me, brother, is it better for one man to die, or the whole people?"

Udrik's eyes widened, and then widened again as Wanhope cut his throat with the obsidian knife. He dropped to his knees, throat spurting, then tumbled awkwardly on his back. Dorian felt—or imagined—the jubilation of a thousand Strangers. He blinked. *Control, Dorian. Control it.* He didn't dare to watch what this next part looked like from that other reality.

Wanhope extended his arms and his wings toward the host before him. "*Arcanghulus!* Come! Be known to me!" The weaves spun out from him easily as if the vir itself was helping him, as if he'd done this a thousand times. Green lightning danced around him. A train of blue fire looped around him. Then the ground began to boil around Udrik's corpse. Clumps of dirt burst and stuck to the body. Flares danced over Udrik and the corpse's muscles tore, skin ripped.

The shamans saw their mistake. They hadn't dared raise an arcanghulus, and Dorian had. An aurochs-horn bugle called the wild men to charge. But only half did.

A bolt of lightning cracked the earth before Wanhope, blinding him, and thunder ripped over him and over both armies, dropping men to the ground on both sides.

When Wanhope's vision returned, the wild men's charge had faltered and broken. There was a man standing where Udrik had been and every eye was on him. He was easily seven feet tall, with hair of molten gold falling to the nape of his neck. Though his skin was the color of polished silver, it wasn't shiny or artificial. His eyes were an arresting emerald of a shade barely within human possibility. Perhaps one man in a million had such eyes. Perhaps mimicking Wanhope, he too was bare-chested, though his body was lean and angular. He was the most beautiful man Wanhope had ever seen.

The arcanghulus laughed, and even his laughter was beautiful. "We're Strangers, Godking, not monsters."

"What is your name?" Wanhope asked.

"I am Ba'elzebaen, the Lord of Serpents."

"Awfully cold in the Freeze for a snake."

"I'm not in the Freeze any more, am I?"

"I would have you serve me, Ba'elzebaen," Wanhope said. He desperately wanted to look at Ba'elzebaen as he was, but he didn't dare. If he lost himself to madness now, Ba'elzebaen might take Dorian's body instead of Udrik's.

The Stranger chuckled. "And I would have the sun and moon bow down to me."

"But one of these things will happen."

Ba'elzebaen laughed as if at a precocious child. "I am stronger than you."

"It is only the will and the call that matters. I have called you, and my will is implacable." The stunning green eyes locked onto his, and Dorian had only to think of how Jenine would be taken if he didn't compel this snake. He felt the arcanghulus's will rise against him, higher and higher. Ba'elzebaen was ever so much more than this body before Dorian. He was immortal, omnipotent, there was nothing Dorian could do to stop him. It was hopeless. He should bow and beg for mercy.

Dorian knew that this was the arcanghulus's attack, and he held onto what he knew. The arcanghulus would obey, would bow, would serve. *I am Godking. I am implacable. I will destroy those who challenge me. I will not serve. I am a god.*

Ba'elzebaen relaxed and the attacks stopped. "Very well, Godking, I will serve you."

"Where is my half-brother Moburu?"

"He attempted to take over the ten tribes. He failed. Only one tribe joined him, but he did take enough bones to raise a legion of krul. He's heading for Black Barrow." A legion was about two thousand krul. It wasn't good, but it was far better than facing Moburu at the head of this army. "But it isn't Moburu you have to worry about."

"Neph," Dorian said, his suspicions confirmed.

"Yes. Neph is the one who taught the wild men to raise krul. All this was nothing more than a diversion to keep any Ursuul away from Black Barrow."

"What's he trying?"

"To make himself Godking, whether by raising a Titan or by giving Khali flesh."

Surely Neph Dada didn't mean to raise Khali herself. It would be madness. If what Dorian had seen of the Strangers' nature was true, giving their leader flesh would be inviting the devastation of all Midcyru. The good news was that no one since Roygaris Ursuul had been powerful enough to raise Khali. A Titan, on the other hand, was far more probable, and plenty frightening enough. Where in the Strangers' hierarchy did a Titan fall? Two ranks above Ba'elzebaen? Three? By the God.

But all that was a conversation for another time. "To claim the wild men's krul, we must strike down the shaman who controls them, correct?" Wanhope asked. "Who is it?"

Ba'elzebaen pointed to a wild man covered completely in woad tattoos. The man had dozens of shields surrounding him, both his own, and other magi's, but as Ba'elzebaen gestured, the shields simply melted away. Wanhope threw a single green fiery missile at the man. The mage watched it contemptuously, secure in his shields—and it burned a hole in his chest. He died with a shocked look on his face.

Ba'elzebaen smiled and Dorian noticed something strange in how the skin crinkled at the corners of his eyes: the arcanghul's skin was made of thousands of tiny scales. "Master," Ba'elzebaen said, "what would you have the Fallen do?"

"Kill the wild men. No feeding until nightfall, and then load the bones onto the wagons. We may need them to make more krul at Black Barrow."

"As you desire." Ba'elzebaen bowed. By the time he straightened, panicked cries were already rising from the wild men's army as the krul in their own ranks turned on them.

74

"Spring is upon us," Elene said.

Vi joined her on the balcony, still sweating from her exertions with the hundreds of magae practicing in the yard below. Kylar was outside the city, training with his master again, and Elene had asked to meet. Vi tried to swallow away the lump in her throat as Elene turned and smiled at her.

"You've been avoiding me," Elene said.

Vi wanted to say that she'd been busy. She had. The Chattel were gathering; women were joining Vi's Shield Sisters every day; messages had to be passed secretly to the Speaker; and always tactics and magic had to be practiced. But all those weren't why she hadn't met with Elene. The past two months had seen them grow strangely closer, but the coming of spring was a naked sword.

"I need your advice, Vi. You know how Kylar's gift works, and you also know how his mind works. I'm afraid he'll try to do something stupid to save me, if . . ." She laid a hand on her stomach.

"If what?" Vi asked. Then it hit her. "Ah shit, you're pregnant!"

Elene blushed, and said quietly. "A Healer confirmed it for me this morning. I'm one month along. Haven't even had a touch of morning sickness. Lucky, I guess."

Lucky. That was one way to put it. If Kylar found out. . . . Actually, Vi had no idea what he'd do, but stupid heroism was likely. Unfortunately, she had no idea how stupid heroism would show itself.

"It complicates things," Elene said. Vi could see from her face that she didn't mean only for Kylar.

"I can make you tansy tea," Vi said.

Elene was incredulous. "If I wanted it to die, I'd wait a month! God, that's the most stupidly callous thing anyone's ever said to me."

Vi stood transfixed. *I'm stupid and callous. This is why you never let anyone in. If you do, they shit all over you.*

Elene closed her eyes and when she opened them, the anger was gone. "I'm sorry. I'm feeling really emotional and upset, but that doesn't make it right to take it out on you. You're not stupid. I'm sorry."

"But I am callous."

Elene paused. "You've been through hell, Vi. You are callous, but less and less every day, and I'm sorry I said that. Can you forgive me?"

The thing about Elene that made her a good friend and a pain in the ass was that she didn't lie, not even when apologizing. If she were less tender-hearted, the lack of guile would be infuriating. Hu Gibbet had "always told the truth" and used it to hammer everyone. Elene's gentleness made it hard to stay mad. "Yes," Vi said. "What do you need?"

Elene smiled slowly and it was like the sun breaking through dark clouds. When she smiled unself-consciously, she was beatific. It wasn't a courtesan's beauty—though the gods and Vi knew that Elene had spent a lot of time in the last two months exploring the courtesan's skills and pleasures—yet it was feminine and utterly alluring. When Elene felt joy, it was always joy shared. Her naïveté in expecting the best from others somehow drew out the best in them. "I'm glad you're my friend, Vi. I've been meaning to have this talk with you for a while."

She scowled, uncertain how to begin. Vi felt the lump rise again in her throat, but there was no leaving, no escape.

"I'm going to die," Elene said. "I'm scared, especially with this." She put her hand on her stomach protectively. "I've complained to the God a lot about it, to tell you the truth. I know you think I'm either totally holy or totally deluded, but I've asked God every way I know how to let me live without it disrupting His plan. I want to live, and I want Kylar to live, and I want our baby to live, and I want Kylar to do all the big things God created him to do."

"And what's your God say?" Vi asked. The way Elene related to her God wasn't at all how Vi had related to Nysos, but whether or not He was real, He was real in Elene's mind, and you don't mock the beliefs of someone so near death.

"He says He's with me."

"That's helpful," Vi said.

"Yes," Elene said, missing or deciding to miss the sarcasm. "Kylar thinks . . . Kylar fears that he's a man born to be forever alone. He thinks the last couple of months has been him cheating fate. He's not a man born to be alone, Vi, but some lies take a long time to heal. I don't have time. When I'm gone, I want you to take care of Kylar. In every way. He is the most precious thing in all this world to me, and I trust you with him. He'll need you. You'll know when he's ready, and when you are."

Vi had thought of it, of course. As she sat in her room with the newlyweds canoodling on the other side of a not-thick-enough wall, she'd thought of it a hundred times: this torture wouldn't last forever; Elene would die come spring. Worse, she'd thought that once Elene was dead, she might have Kylar herself.

"I've been selfish," Elene said, "I knew we only had a couple of months, so I've been selfish for myself and for Kylar. I know you've paid the price for that. I've seen your face some of the mornings after—" Elene cleared her throat, "after Kylar and I stayed up late. I know you love him, Vi, and I can't imagine how I would have felt if our places were reversed. If I were in your place, I'd look forward to . . . this ending. It's all right."

"It's not all right to wish your friend was dead," Vi said stiffly. Her eyes felt hot.

"For that and anything else you may have thought or done, I forgive you, Vi. Everything really is going to be all right. God has a purpose in this, even if we don't see it."

"You're leaving," Vi said.

"Yes."

"And you haven't told him."

"I've tried. Kylar's not ready to hear it. Vi, help him know that loving again is no betrayal. He's immortal, and living forever without love is hell."

"When are you leaving?" Vi asked.

"Now."

"Where?"

"King Gyre's marching into Khalidor in a few weeks. There are women in his army. I'll join them. At least that's my plan. God might have something different for me."

"Why join them?"

"To force Kylar to be there. He's sworn he wouldn't leave me again for Logan, but that's where he needs to be. If nothing else, I'll die fighting for something."

"You're not a warrior, Elene."

"No. But I am a fighter."

"Do you have any idea what Kylar will do when he finds out?" Vi said.

"I've left a letter for him on the table telling him that I'm staying at the Chantry overnight. I hope I lie better in writing than in person because I'll need the head start. But here's another letter that tells the truth." She paused. "Well, not the whole truth. I didn't tell him I'm pregnant. He's going to hurt enough. Please make sure he gets it." She handed the note to Vi.

"You're putting me in the middle of this?"

"He'd feel your complicity through your bond. You might want to stay at the Chantry for a couple days."

Elene hugged her. At first awkwardly and then fiercely, Vi hugged her back. Her eyes teared up faster than she could blink away, and through her bond, she felt Kylar's sudden alarm from a mile away. It wasn't in words, but she could feel his wonder: *are you* crying?! She sent a wave of reassurance to him, which left him even more befuddled.

"I don't want you to go," Vi said.

Elene pulled back and searched Vi's eyes. "You mean

that. I can tell. Even with how hard this has been, you mean it."

"I've never had a friend," Vi said. "I don't want to lose you."

"You're a better woman than you know, Vi. God bless you."

75

"The passes are clear," Durzo said. "The magae are going to march tomorrow."

Kylar had known there was something different in his master's attitude as they'd sparred today. They sat together on a table in the practice room of Durzo's house, each holding a towel and blotting the sweat from their faces. Durzo didn't make eye contact. "You're leaving," Kylar said.

"If you can believe it, Uly's kicking me out the door," Durzo said ruefully.

"I thought you were getting along great."

"She's worried about her mom. Says I should have gone to her first."

"I think Uly's smarter than both of us put together," Kylar said lightly, though his heart was lead. Durzo was leaving him again, and if for the first time Durzo was letting him know about it beforehand, it didn't make it much easier.

"Watch out for women smarter than you, kid. By which—"

"You mean all of them, I know." Kylar shared a grin with his master.

"Guess I need to give you your gear," Durzo said. "You going with the magae?"

"If I go, Elene will go, and she'll die. I'm steering clear of this fight."

Durzo examined his fingernails. "I told you that's not how it works. She can fall in a puddle and drown as easily as take a sword in the guts. Death won't be cheated, not in this."

Kylar took it like a shot in stomach. He said quietly, "I won't let her die. I won't let anyone take her away. Not Death, not the Wolf, not God himself."

"Kid, remember your first time in the Antechamber of the Mystery? Was there one door or two? It wasn't Death or the Wolf or the boogeyman that made you immortal. This was your own damn choice."

"I became immortal so I could save Elene, not so I could kill her."

"You want her to live forever? Go ahead. See if you can make another deal with the Wolf so someone else will die in her place. Maybe you can choose which one of the other people you care about dies. Won't that be fun? Maybe then you can get a ka'kari for Elene, so she won't age. But be glad that the other ka'karis' immortality isn't like our own. She won't age, but she can still be killed. And be glad for that too. Because when she becomes a monster, corrupted by the very gift you sold your soul to give her, you'll be the one who has to do something about it."

Durzo's anger was too focused, his description too detailed. "You did that?" Kylar asked.

His master didn't answer him, wouldn't even look at him. He opened the bureau, released the bottom drawer and pulled it out. He lifted Retribution, skinned black with the ka'kari, from the false bottom.

"I can't let Elene die for me," Kylar said.

"You haven't got any goddam choice. You've had a few months to get used to the idea. That's more than the Wolf ever gave me. Be grateful. Now take your shit and get out." Durzo tossed the big black sword to Kylar.

As soon as the ka'kari touched his skin, it began shrilling. ~Why didn't you listen! I tried to tell you! It's gone. Three months gone. Stolen!~

Dumbfounded, Kylar stared at the sword. Frustrated at his stupidity, the ka'kari sought to sink into his skin of his hand and he let it, forgetting that it would destroy his disguise. As the black metal rushed into him, it revealed a pitted, half-devoured sword blade. Retribution was gone, replaced with a counterfeit that Kylar hadn't noticed when they'd hidden the blade. It was impossible, but someone had stolen his sword before he hid it here, probably when he'd first been gawking like an idiot on the crowded sidewalks of Vestacchi.

Durzo was aghast. "Kid, you have no idea what that sword is. You have to get it back."

Then Kylar felt Vi through his bond. She'd been nervous since yesterday, and now he could feel her starting guiltily as she felt his emotions. Vi knew, and she was hiding in the Chantry, certain he wouldn't go there. For all his help, the Sisters had stabbed him in the back. They'd stolen Retribution.

"I know where it is," Kylar said.

The closer Kylar got to the Chantry, the more his anger grew. He became more and more certain from Vi's guilt that Elene was somehow involved too, and that lit a fire in him. He thought he could read her. Yesterday afternoon he'd gotten her note that said she had some things she needed to work on in the Chantry, and she still wasn't back. The timing seemed strange, but there was no doubting Vi's guilt as he came closer. Having the vastness of the Chantry against him blew his rage to a flame. They wanted him passive, tame, emasculated, obedient. He was sick and tired of it. Sick of being worked on by vast, remote powers he couldn't understand or counter. The Chantry was like fate, like the Wolf, like Death itself, working inexorably on the world, on Kylar, and turning a deaf ear to his pleas.

When he stepped out of the punt onto one of the Chantry's docks, two dozen pairs of eyes turned to him, scandalized. Some he recognized from Vi's training sessions; others were more hostile. A Sister was lecturing a class of teens on the workings of the punts. Others were doing maintenance magic on the little bay itself, reworking the rain shield overhead. He ignored them and strode toward the double doors that led inside.

A white robed woman stepped forward, "Sir, no men are allowed here."

He walked past her.

Before he could touch the double doors, magic bonds

latched onto him arm and leg. "Please, sir, we don't wish to harm you—"

Kylar shrugged the bonds off as easily as he might shoo a fly. He turned and looked at the faces of the two Sisters tasked with guarding the door. They were stunned. One of them was readying a lash of magic.

"Don't," Kylar said, staring her in the eye. As he held her gaze, something in his eyes turned her resolve to water. The weaves slipped away. He threw the doors open.

Vi was in a panic upstairs. *Good.*

Kylar walked straight down a long hall to a set of huge double doors three times a man's height. Doors along the length of the hall opened and Kylar heard cries of alarm. The smaller door inset in the double doors slammed shut by magic and a young maja yelped. The scraping of metal on wood told him that the double doors had been barred. Kylar didn't slow; he didn't turn to the right or to the left. He gathered power to his hands.

~I've seen stupider things, but it's been centuries.~

The voice was the buzzing of a gnat. There was something beautiful in this simplicity. Someone had stolen Kylar's birthright. He was getting it back. This door was in his way.

Kylar's open hands shot into the doors. They bowed and then crashed open. One half of the timber that had barred the door shot across the floor toward dozens of tables. Perhaps two hundred magae were seated in the great hall, enjoying lunch. The splintered timber skimmed down one aisle at great speed, shooting between a Sister's legs and finally crashing against the first step of a great curving staircase.

As Kylar stepped through in a shower of kindling, the

other great door sagged on its remaining hinge. Every eye turned to him.

Sisters began standing all around the room and shields blossomed everywhere, but the first woman on her feet was Sister Ariel. She moved faster than Kylar had ever seen her move, coming straight at him. "What do you think you're doing?" she shouted.

"Where's the Speaker? She's stolen from me," Kylar said.

"You will go no further!" Sister Ariel shouted. She was purple.

"Stop me," Kylar said. He could see that his smirk infuriated her.

Faster than he thought possible, she did. Giant chains of magic lashed his arms to his body, clamped his legs together. Magae around her openly gaped at her sheer power.

~*You deserved that. Take it, apologize, and come back later.*~

Kylar had had enough of taking it, apologizing, and coming back when it was convenient for someone else. He was sick of being trapped. He felt something mighty rising within him.

Fear flickered over Sister Ariel's face at whatever she saw. Kylar sucked in a great breath and flexed, tensing every muscle in his body, physical and magical. He felt suddenly gigantic, his body a tiny vessel for a giant soul. As he strained, a groan deeper than Kylar's voice came from his lips.

His chains shattered, blew apart with a magical concussion that swept through the room. The tables didn't move, the air didn't stir, but everything magical was flattened. Every nimbus in the room winked out. Only a few held for an instant before popping and blowing away.

A dozen of the standing magae simply folded and dropped to sit on their benches or the floor. No one else moved, not even Sister Ariel. "What are you?" she whispered. The question was mirrored in every eye.

"Out of my way," Kylar said. He strode forward. They got out of his way.

76

Istariel Wyant eyed the Alitaeran ambassador's untouched ootai. Marcus Guerin was bordering on fifty, bald with a fringe of blond hair, a small paunch, no bottom, and a restless intelligence in his blue eyes.

"There are some troubling rumors we've been hearing that I think we need to discuss," Ambassador Guerin said.

Istariel took the opportunity of taking a sip of ootai to cover her sudden rage. Someone had leaked this to the Alitaerans? If he'd learned about Vi's practices, that was one thing, but Istariel had only told three Sisters about her plan to withdraw from the Accords. If he knew about that, it was treason. She simply arched an eyebrow.

"What do you know about this 'High King'?" he asked.

Oh, those *rumors. Thank the Seraph.* "Little," she said. There was a twinkle in his eye that made her wonder if he had done that on purpose. Bastard. "What we've heard has only told us that you ought to know more than we do.

He's Alitaeran, or at least raised in your glorious country. His name is Moburu Ander, though he claims Ursuul blood. We know he's half Lodricari, he led a company of lancers, and he's found a position of some importance among the savages of the Freeze." She knew more, but there was no point telling Ambassador Guerin.

"He's the adopted son of Aurelius Ander, of a once-powerful family that has fallen far in the last two generations. Moburu was adopted at fifteen, before that, we can't find any record or recollection of him anywhere, so we give some credence to his claim of Ursuul patrimony."

"I doubt that an absence of records was enough to make you believe he's an Ursuul," Istariel said.

The ambassador stroked his moustache. "The captain is both intelligent and charismatic. Nothing was ever found to link him to the scandals and disappearances that seem to swirl in his wake. Last autumn, the king's sister bore a daughter, Yva Lucrece Corazhi. The child and her wet nurse disappeared. At the same time, Moburu led his company—all of them—to a place called Pavvil's Grove, where they fought beside the Khalidorans. There are wild tales surrounding that, but most of Moburu's company escaped and headed north."

"You believe he kidnapped the child?"

"What I believe has no relevance. Some very powerful people in Skon insist that he did not. They are having a harder time explaining why he has taken an entire company out of our country without leave, though some whisper it's a secret mission for the king. There are generals who don't wish to appear fools who have not discouraged such whispers. There are even those who claim that Moburu's company itself is trying to recover Yva Lucrece."

"It appears to me that this man must be declared a traitor," Istariel said. "Otherwise, if he joins Khalidor again, this time to attack us, Alitaera will be making war on the Chantry."

The slight wince that passed the ambassador's face told Istariel she had voiced an argument he had presented to his superiors himself. "Our response to Captain Ander will be determined soon, and I promise you will be among the first to know." Ambassador Guerin's face looked like he was chewing lemons. "Now speaking of sharing intelligence," he said, "you never did turn over that intelligence you told us about a few months ago," he said. "But let's return to that in a moment. First, we were hoping this house of learning might tell us some more about who this High King is supposed to be, and how one identifies him."

Ariel leaned back in her chair. "Meaning you won't move against Moburu until you know if he's the real thing."

"Meaning it is wise to know all one can about one's enemies—and friends."

Istariel took another slow sip of ootai, considering. "The High King is a legend mostly confined to the rural areas of Khalidor, Lodricar, Cenaria, and Ceura. His coming is not spoken of by any of the prophets recognized by the Chantry. We keep track of prophecies spoken by those who have the perishingly rare Talent of prophecy. We think of that one as simply a hope kept alive in Lodricar and Khalidor as a longed-for end to oppression. In Cenaria and Ceura, it's probably more a wish to be consequential, something Cenaria hasn't been for centuries."

"Your pardon, Speaker, but I'm not terribly interested

in why they believe as I am in *what* they believe. Does this have anything to do with the Ceuran Regency?"

"It could. The Battle of Mount Tenji was as crushing for the Ceurans as it was for Alitaera. King Usasi and his son and seven daughters were all killed; that was so devastating to the country that after that time Ceuran women were no longer taught the sword. The regency was established both because of the profound respect for tradition engrained in Ceuran culture, and the fact that the first Regent had no blood claim to the throne. The other contenders realized a regency meant that they themselves could hold power without needing a blood claim, if only they were powerful enough to take it. It suited everyone, and the myth of the coming High King gave them a hope of future glory. Our scholars' best guess is that there was a High King who ruled those lands for a single generation in the dark centuries that followed Jorsin Alkestes' fall."

"Wasn't Alkestes himself called the High King?"

"Rarely. In the early years of his reign, he ruled over seven kings and styled himself the High King. Three of the seven—Rygel the Blue, Einarus Silvereyes, and Itarra Lachess—rebelled. After that, Jorsin was Emperor Alkestes. We don't know if the latter High King claimed descent from Jorsin or not—almost all records of him were lost in the dark ages—but he only claimed the lands now encompassing Ceura, Cenaria, Khalidor, and Lodricar, not all of Jorsin's kingdoms."

The ambassador looked unimpressed. "So that's it? A long-dead legend?"

Istariel said, "Well, the magi give some credence to a prophet or two whom we don't recognize."

"And they know more?"

"They don't know more. They believe more."

"By the God's beard! I don't care what's true—I care what people believe! What are these prophecies?"

Istariel gave him a look that let him know he was treading on thin ice and didn't answer until he looked on the brink of apologizing. "They say he will be a dragon—the accepted interpretation is that he'll be Talented, though any conqueror brings fire. They say he will raise a standard of death—I hope that's clear enough, things aren't going to be all prancing ponies and cuddly kittens. Then the prophecies get strange. They say he'll bring peace— peace everlasting is a pretty normal staple of prophecies, right? Well, these prophecies say he'll bring peace for two years or eighteen. They say his coming will open the way for the return of Jorsin Alkestes, who will both be taken under his wing, and test the mettle or taste the metal—it's unclear which—of his sword."

"When was this prophecy given?" the ambassador asked.

"Five years ago. A magus named Dorian, who claimed to be a rogue Ursuul. Not exactly a reliable source."

"It sounds like a nightmare."

"Yes, and these things tend to spread with a religious fervor once they get started. Even if Moburu is the High King, I'd strongly advise King Alidosius to make sure he never sits in any throne—not unless you want to invite civil unrest or even civil war to Alitaera. Jorsin Alkestes still stirs all sorts of emotions. A High King would itself be bad enough, considering the sheer area such a man would rule, but in the Alkestian prophecies, he is a harbinger. Think what may happen in each of our lands if people really believe that the Lord of Hell is coming in bodily form, that creatures from their nightmares will walk again, that kingdoms are doomed to fall."

Ambassador Guerin looked moderately ill. "Yes, I'll convey all this to the king. Is that all?"

"No, I need to know if your lancers are on their way."

"You ask me this now, after you've only just given me the information which might make the king amenable to such a request?"

"I gave you the information when we got it. We need those soldiers now."

"I told you months ago that without access to whatever intelligence you had about an invasion we would be unable to grant your request. If you'll pardon an old military man speaking bluntly, we can't send five thousand lancers every time an old ally gets nervous. That's not what the Accords oblige."

An old military man? You haven't lifted a lance in thirty years. "The Accords oblige a robust defense of the Chantry, which seems even more pressing now that Moburu Ander's company—an Alitaeran company—fought for Khalidor at the Battle of Pavvil's Grove. We're facing two enemies here even without Moburu Ander's men, and each alone may be capable of annihilating us. The fact is, even the two thousand lancers you have across the border— yes, of course I know about them—probably won't be enough to defend us. The best I can expect is that they will hold our flank against the Lae'knaught while we go to Black Barrow."

"You're going to Black Barrow?" Marcus Guerin asked.

"The Khalidorans have learned to raise krul."

"Krul? A legend!" Marcus Guerin scoffed. "This is completely—"

"Have you been to Black Barrow, ambassador?"

His blue eyes looked troubled.

"Black Barrow is the only place where, once killed, the krul can't be Raised again. It's the only place we can fight them with any hope of winning."

"So you want us to help you invade your neighbor? That's an awfully bold interpretation of accords intended to curtail the Chantry's imperial ambitions."

Suddenly, from many stories below, the Speaker felt an unfamiliar magic. Though she'd only met a half dozen magi, and had never seen them use their Talents, she knew instantly that this was a magus—in her Chantry.

"Speaker, is something wrong?"

Istariel had only moments to decide how to react. Could she turn the presence of a hostile mage to her advantage? Would interrupting the meeting be to her advantage? Perhaps it could have been, if the Chantry's objective in this talk were anything positive. As it was, she wished only to back out of a centuries-old treaty without declaring war. "Yes, you slap us in the face with old, unfounded allegations, sir. We wish only to survive as a house of learning." A rush of magic much more familiar to her snapped in response to the intruder, whoever he was. Istariel was surprised at the force of it. It was a chaining magic, and the only maja she could imagine powerful enough to use it was Ariel, blessed oblivious Ariel. Or, perhaps, Vi.

"A house of learning?" the ambassador asked. "Does that include learning battle magic?"

So he knew. Dammit. "If our allies abandon us in the face of a massacre? Yes."

His lips thinned to a tiny line. "This is most precipitous."

Istariel opened her mouth to deliver a historical reminder when a magical concussion ripped through the Chantry. The constant buzz of magae's Talent ceased and, for the first time in centuries, perhaps the first time since it was built, the Chantry was utterly silent. The magic ripped through everything, though it destroyed nothing except whatever the Sisters were actively weaving. It had character, a distinct flavor: free and fierce, not hostile, but rather a strength unaware of itself. The impossible image that leapt to Istariel's mind was of a teenage archmage, and it shook her to her core. Ariel had tried to chain him, and he refused to be chained.

Magically, Istariel felt like a little girl trapped between screaming parents.

"Wh-what was that?" the ambassador asked.

By the Seraph, it was powerful enough even this unTalented toad could feel it.

"We hereby withdraw from the Accords, ambassador. If Alitaera wishes to expel the magae from its dominions, they will leave peacefully. I do request, however, that you give us six months to show our good faith. This is no declaration of war with you. Please let the emperor know that we fight only to live."

The ambassador sat silently. He sipped his ootai, which Istariel was certain was cold by now, but he didn't seem aware of it. "The king always thought you were one of the Chantry's more moderate voices, Istariel. Surely the discussion needn't end on this. You wouldn't throw away hundreds of years of cooperation and progress."

The archmage was climbing the Chantry, getting ever

closer. He'd used so much magic that he still burned with it. Istariel could almost see him through the floor. She didn't want to have this conversation now, but she couldn't exactly throw the ambassador out. "No," she said, "I don't wish to throw away anything, least of all our lives. Perhaps this fall I can come to Skon and meet with the emperor personally."

It wasn't some random archmage, Istariel realized. It was Vi's damned husband. What the hell was he doing? Was Vi attempting a coup? No, that made no sense, leading a coup with a man? Even Sisters with dual loyalties would automatically side against him. So it was something else entirely. That scared the hell out of her.

"Perhaps we could conclude this conversation later this afternoon," Istariel said.

"Your pardon, Speaker, but I can't imagine there's really anything more important than the dissolution or defense of an alliance three hundred years old. I must insist we finish."

Speaker Istariel sat back down at her desk and gathered her Talent to her, facing the door. He was almost here.

The door exploded inward, the hinges and latch ripping through the wood, the door slapping to the ground. A young man with his face set fiercely stepped in. Istariel unleashed a massive fist of air.

It turned aside in midair and smashed her collection of thousand-year-old Hyrillic vases. She lashed out again and punched a hole in the ceiling. Impervious, almost oblivious to her attempts to kill him, Kyle strode to her desk, put his hands on it, and leaned forward. She gathered her full strength; he blew in her face.

Her Talent scattered as if that puff had been a hurricane.

He said nothing. He looked into her eyes and deep within his eyes was something that made her want to gibber like a madwoman. It was like staring at the night sky after learning for the first time that the stars were not pinpricks in the raiment of heaven, but each its own sun, billions of leagues distant. To stare into this man's eyes was to realize how small one was.

Kyle sighed, not finding what he wanted.

The Alitaeran ambassador, either finding his courage, or seeing no magic springing from the young man, stood. "I dare say, you young lout, I'm not going to let you disrespect any woman while I stand by! Stand and deliver, sir!"

Istariel saw an alien magic stir deep in Kylar's eyes, then Kylar said, "We'll talk about respecting women when you stop fucking your wife's best friend."

The ambassador's hauteur shattered. Kyle turned on his heel and walked out.

Istariel and the ambassador said nothing for a full minute. She cleared her throat. "Perhaps," she said, "we can agree that nothing of this leaves the room."

He swallowed and nodded.

77

$\mathcal{V}$i was up here somewhere. Kylar's encounter with the Speaker had left him shaken. He'd been sure that she'd stolen Retribution. One look in her eyes told him otherwise. Now, what had looked like an unexpected move that would bring him to the center of the deceiver's web and deliver his sword back into his hand was looking like a colossal blunder. Nonetheless, Kylar bulled forward. He was committed now.

The floors this high in the Chantry weren't large. The Seraph's head held the Speaker's office, a waiting room, some storerooms, the stairs, and a classroom. In that classroom was Vi. Kylar opened the door to the last room before the classroom. He'd kicked down enough doors.

This room was at the Seraph's eyes. It was a broad, open room, but despite the light pouring in from the glass-clear eyes, it had a distinctly unused feeling, as if no one had set foot here in decades. In the center of the room stood a woman wreathed in light. Her arms were crossed over her chest, chin pointed at the floor, eyes closed. She wore a short gossamer robe that ended at her knees. Halfway down her shins, her skin changed from a shade too golden to be merely sun-kissed to the purest white alabaster. As Kylar stood, stunned by this unexpected beauty, he saw the alabaster recede to her ankles, to her toes.

The woman took a gentle first breath. Her chin lifted. She opened her eyes. The irises were pure platinum.

"You're the Seraph," Kylar said dumbly.

"Indeed, and you are a man and you have awakened me, but you are not the One."

"Uh, sorry?" Kylar said. The Seraph stared at him and as he met those platinum eyes, all he could see was magic, oceanic and mercifully at rest. "Are you going to do something bad to me now?"

The Seraph laughed. "Should I? You've frightened my little sisters badly." She glanced at the door. "Except for the one who holds your bond. I'll leave you to her tender mercies, Nameless."

"I like that dress better than the one your statue wears. You've got great legs."

Her eyes widened, but he saw that she wasn't displeased. "Me too," she said, "but when one is three hundred feet tall, it behooves one to err on the side of modesty."

"I can't believe I said that."

She arched an eyebrow at him.

"Um, Lady? Ma'am? Sorry, what should I call you?"

"Impertinence suits you better, Nameless. Ask your question."

"I lost a sword. I thought the Speaker stole it, but I

was wrong. Can you tell me if one of the other Sisters stole it?"

She tilted her head, weighing him. "You assume friendship quickly. I can't decide if that's a function of youth or naïveté or goodness or your singular powers. Not everyone can weigh a soul in a glance, Nameless."

"Sorry for the presumption, my Lady."

"Give me your sword hand."

He extended his hand and she studied the palm. He saw magic swirling over it. He said, "It's been three months since I—"

The magic died suddenly. The Seraph's eyes snapped up from his palm to his eyes, and in her platinum eyes, Kylar saw fear. "You fool," she whispered. "Do you have any idea what you've done?"

Between the intensity of her tone and her fear, Kylar felt a snake of terror twisting in his guts. What could make the Seraph afraid? "I lost my sword Retribution. It was my birthright—"

"Retribution? Was that Acaelus' attempt at a joke?"

Kylar said nothing. What had he revealed here? She'd told him he was naive to trust her. How much did she know now? "I don't know what you're talking about," he said woodenly. "It's a simple sword, inscribed with a word, either Justice or Mercy."

"And it depends on you to dispense whichever is deserved."

"Well, yeah."

"I don't suppose that reminds you of anything."

"Uh . . ."

"You see the state of souls. You mete out justice or

mercy, giving people what they deserve. What does that make you?"

Kylar remembered the Wolf's words, laughing at his name, telling him Kylar Stern was a title. "A judge," Kylar said quietly.

"And a judge decides the application of what?" the Seraph asked, equally quiet.

"The law?" *Together, Jorsin Alkestes and Ezra created two artifacts: Curoch, the sword of power, and Iures, the scepter of law.* "But it's supposed to be a . . ." his voice trailed off. He'd seen Curoch shift into any shape it needed to be. He'd seen Retribution raise the words Mercy or Justice in different languages. Why not hide Iures as a sword? Where better to hide Iures than with Durzo, whose ka'kari concealed him? What better place to keep the ka'kari of concealment than concealing one of the greatest artifacts in history? Kylar should have known Durzo wouldn't have retrieved Retribution simply to spare Kylar of the inconvenience of having his swords blunted. How many times had Durzo told him the blade was priceless?

"Do you know where it is?" Kylar asked.

Holding his hand, the Seraph closed her eyes and glowed golden. The light started in her forehead and expanded until it filled the room, then it whooshed. For an instant, Kylar swore the entire Seraph—the big one—was aglow. Then the woman opened her eyes.

"It is in Trayethell."

"Trayethell?" Kylar remembered the name dimly. Acaelus Thorne had been the Prince of Trayethell. "It's in Black Barrow."

The Seraph hadn't released his hand. "Nameless, the

Scepter . . . Iures gives a mage no additional power, but it gives a thousand times the control. A mage with Iures in hand could unravel anything given time."

So what was Neph doing? With Iures, he could take apart the shield around Ezra's Wood and take Curoch. What would he do once he had both? What would he not do? Even Jorsin Alkestes hadn't wielded both together.

There was no choice. Kylar was the judge. If Neph was invulnerable to magic, Kylar was the only one who could stop him. Kylar might be the only one who knew the full extent of the danger. He had to stop him. *God, how am I going to tell Elene?*

At the thought of Elene, Kylar felt Vi flinch through the bond. There was a deep guilt there, and fear.

Kylar turned from the Seraph, anger stirring once again. He opened the door to the classroom and strode in, slamming the door behind him. There were fifty senior students in the room, every one of them surrounded with a nimbus of magic. Vi stood in the center of them. She alone didn't hold her Talent. "What have you done?" Kylar demanded.

"She made me swear not to tell you," Vi said.

"What the fuck have you—"

"What have I done?" Vi shouted. "What have you done? Breaking in here and treating my Sisters like this? How dare you!" Kylar opened his mouth, but Vi cut him off. "No! Sit down and shut up!"

The words hit him like a whip through their earrings' bond. The compulsion made Kylar's mouth snap closed, and he sat instantly. There was no chair: he sat on the ground.

Vi was as stunned as he was. He tried to open his mouth,

but it wouldn't budge. He couldn't move. Vi had told him
that the rings broke her compulsion to Garoth because its
bond superseded Garoth's magic, but Kylar hadn't appreciated what that meant until now. The earrings' bond was
compulsive—one way. Vi could make him do anything
she wanted, and she had known all along, Kylar saw from
her expression. She simply hadn't invoked her power
before.

The Sisters stared round-eyed at Vi. A moment before,
they all had been terrified of this man who had violated
the Chantry and broken the chains their most powerful Sister had laid on him. In the next, Vi had defended
her Sisters, and he obeyed her command as if he had no
choice. Whatever other repercussions Kylar's foolishness
was going to have, he had certainly increased Vi's cachet
with her Sisters.

A riot of emotions flooded through the bond, but Vi
mastered herself quickly. "She went to join Logan's army,"
she said. "She was afraid you wouldn't fight otherwise."
Aware of the other women listening to her conversation
with her "husband," Vi said nothing more. She handed
him a note. "You can stand now, and speak."

Kylar stood and took the note, but he had no words.

The door on the far side of the classroom banged open,
and dozens of Sisters began pouring in, with Sister Ariel
at their head. Almost all of them, Kylar realized, were
magae who'd trained with Vi.

One of them threw something like a spear of coruscating red and silver light. It flew straight at Kylar's chest—
then dissolved in midair.

Around the room, Sisters began kneeling, mouths
dropping open once more. Kylar turned to see who had

saved him. The Seraph walked into the room, glowing gold. "I'm sorry if my friend frightened you," the Seraph said. "Forgive him. We needed to speak about a threat that faces us all. If he fails, all our fighting will be for naught." The awed Sisters parted. With one last glance at Vi, Kylar left.

78

I won't watch you kill yourself," Durzo said. For the last three days, Kylar and Durzo had been traveling west. Durzo was traveling to Cenaria, to see Momma K at last, so he'd joined Kylar. The pass had been muddy and snowy, so they were setting up camp only a few hours from Torras Bend and a few hundred paces from Ezra's Wood.

Kylar spread his heavy saddle blanket on a fallen log next to the fire and sat. "I don't plan to die," he said.

"Oh, so there is a plan? I thought you were making it up as you went. It's getting dark. Our little stalker will be along within the hour." They'd been followed, clumsily, since they left the Chantry. Today they'd ridden hard, trying to make it to Torras Bend, and their pursuer hadn't been able to keep up.

"I don't think Khali exists," Kylar said.

"I didn't realize you were in the habit of having religious epiphanies."

"I mean, it exists, but I don't think she's a goddess."

"Oh?" Durzo asked.

"She—it—is a repository of magic. The Wolf said magic is strongest when it's attached to emotions. Khali is filled by the Khalidorans' worship. As they hurt people for her, they chant a prayer. But it's not a prayer. It's a spell. It empties their glore vyrden into the repository. And it's from that repository that the meisters and Vürdmeisters and Godkings draw their power. Because the talents for drawing in magic from the world and using magic are different, that means they can often use far more magic than mages. It means they can use it at night. Don't you see? The entire nation chants this spell twice a day. The repository is the key to Khalidor's power."

"And this has something to do with why you're committing suicide?"

"Curoch is anathema to that power. I saw that when I killed a meister with it. Curoch makes the vir explode. It bursts it from within."

"A few months ago, you assassinated a man who called himself a god; now you're going after a goddess in truth. Unless you can figure out a way to kill continents, after this you're going to have to retire."

"You know it's not like that," Kylar said, flushing.

"So you're hoping to find Khali and put Curoch in her and what? Just see what happens?"

Kylar scowled. "You make it sound stupid."

"Hmm."

"It's a way to win, really win, once and for all. Come on, how many times have you fought Khalidorans?"

"More than I like to remember," Durzo admitted.

"Look, I lost Iures. That's a disaster. I know it. It's also a disaster you helped cause when you never told me what the damn thing was. With Iures in Neph's hands, we're going to have a hard time killing him."

"We?"

"But if we destroy the vir, Neph won't even be able to use Iures. If he survives the vir's destruction, even if he has Talent, it will take him a while to think to use it. He'll be vulnerable. Master, he's been spending the last three months figuring out how to break into Ezra's Wood and take Curoch for himself. If one man holds both Curoch and Iures . . ."

"It wouldn't be good."

"It would be a cataclysm!" Kylar said.

"You realize that if you put Curoch into the center of all the vir in the world, it might make a qualitative rather than a quantitative difference?"

"Huh?"

Durzo shot him an exasperated look. "Curoch blew the vir out of one wytch and nothing happened. If it blows up all the vir in the world, something might."

"If it blew up every wytch in the world, I wouldn't complain," Kylar said.

"And if it blows you up with them?"

"At that point, I won't be able to."

"It might not obliterate you. It might just kill you and invoke your immortality. You know what that costs now. Are you willing to risk a friend's life for this? Hell, it might be *my* life. I don't know if *I'm* willing for you to risk it."

"We were given this power for a reason, master. I don't want to lose anyone. I don't want to die, but if my death can change a nation, if I can save thousands, how could I not risk it?"

Durzo grinned ruefully. "You damn fool. You realize, even if all your assumptions are correct—even then, you still have to steal the world's most coveted sword from the world's safest place then be pursued by the ultimate hunter until you reach the heart of an enemy country in the middle of a war in which any side will happily kill you as a traitor, a spy, a wytch, or all three?"

"I thought you'd like it," Kylar said, eyes sparkling.

Durzo laughed. "The Wolf is gonna have puppies."

"Well, I'm hoping not to see him any time soon. But I figured if I could convince you, then there wouldn't be much he could do about it."

"Convince me of what?" Durzo asked.

"To help," Kylar said.

"Oh no," Durzo said. "Count me out."

"You can't!"

"I can. Kid, you took away my immortality. That gave me back my life. I—"

"You owe me!" Kylar said.

"Not like this, I don't. I have one life left. One. Because of you, I can do with it whatever I want. I can love."

And Kylar couldn't. "But we can change the world!"

"Kid, do you know how many times I've changed the world? The Tlaxini Maelstrom used to be a shipping lane. The Alitaeran Empire stretched from coast to coast. God-kings have threatened the southlands and nearly gained ka'kari half a dozen times. Ladesh used to—look. The fact is, I've done my piece. Adventures are for the young, and I'm young by no measure. There's a woman I love in Cenaria, and neither of us is getting younger. I need to go."

"I need you," Kylar said. "Alone, trying to steal the

world's most coveted sword from the world's safest place and being pursued by the perfect hunter into a war—"

"Yes, yes," Durzo said. "I've showed you most of my tricks—"

"Most of them?"

"—and you've developed a few of your own. You're not an apprentice anymore, Kylar—"

"Fine, but I'm hardly—"

"—you *are* a master. Your tutelage is finished."

"Don't cut me loose," Kylar said. His heart was in his throat.

"I'm cutting you free," Durzo said.

"But you're still better than me!"

"And I always will be," Durzo said. He grinned, and despite himself, Kylar couldn't help thinking that it was nice to see this once hard and bitter man smile. "In your memories. I'm smart enough to stop fighting you before you start winning. I reached the top of my game, and I had a good run. From here, I'll only get worse."

"But you still have so much to teach me."

"You think this isn't going to teach you something?"

"What if I fail?" It came out in a whisper.

"What if you do? It won't change how I feel about you."

"But I could doom the world! Don't you care?"

"If I spend my last hours in Gwin's arms, frankly, not much. Growing old with the woman I love would be my first choice, but dying reconciled with her isn't a bad second."

"So I'm alone."

"I told you that was the cost when you demanded to be my apprentice."

"I didn't know I was agreeing to eternity!"

"Cry me a river. You're pathetic. What's your plan for getting into the Wood?"

Stung, Kylar shrugged. "The ka'kari."

"The ka'kari." Durzo stated the question like Momma K would have. The old man really had spent too long with her.

"It absorbs magic, eludes magic, makes me invisible. I'll figure something out." Now he was sounding defensive.

"Whose Wood is this again?" Durzo asked. "Oh yeah, Ezra's. And who made the ka'kari? Oh, don't tell me. Ezra."

"Ezra didn't make the black."

"He understood it well enough to make six others. So tell me, fifty years after making six ka'kari he comes here—and at this point he and I aren't on such good terms—and he makes himself a fortress. You think it never occurred to him that I might try to come in?"

"Uh . . ."

"Kid, you can scare a few Sisters with raw power and bravado, but you're playing on a different plane here. If you live through Ezra's defenses—which by the way, you strengthened tenfold by throwing Curoch into the wood—you still have to get around a creature so powerful and so cunning that it may have killed Ezra himself, unless it is Ezra gone utterly mad. Either way, the Hunter isn't going to be impressed by raw magic. Your newfound confidence is inspiringly suicidal."

Kylar was silent. Then he said, "I won't be stopped."

"Shut up, she comes."

Kylar rolled the ka'kari into the center of the fire. The

flames collapsed into the ball, dying instantly, plunging the clearing into darkness. Kylar jumped left and Durzo rolled right even as purple magic blazed through the clearing in jagged hands. Kylar extended a hand and the ka'kari leapt into it, flooding him with the energy it had absorbed from the fire.

He leapt from tree to tree, sinking black claws into the sides of each, and saw a maja flailing about herself, suddenly blind. Fires flared around her. She flipped them back and forth wildly like great scythes in her fear. The magic slapped against the trees, singeing bark, sending up gouts of steam, but the recent rains and snows prevented any fires from bursting forth. Durzo, on the ground, was beneath the swipes, and Kylar was above them.

In moments, the maja had exhausted her Talent and with no sunlight and no fire to draw from, her magic guttered out.

In the sudden darkness, both men moved. Kylar was on her almost before she could scream. He flew straight over her head, grabbed fistfuls of cloak and robe as he passed, and used her body weight like a beam to flip himself over and stop, which transferred his momentum to her. She flew backward half a dozen paces and crashed into a tree trunk, the breath whooshing from her lungs. Kylar landed on one knee on the forest floor and stood, blue flame trickling over his features.

By the time she'd taken two breaths, something was rising from deep beneath her skin. It was vir, and it rose as rapidly as a shark striking from the deep, starting at her fingertips, over her hands, and wrists, disappearing in a wriggle that made her sleeves tremble, up to her neck like a black blush, and then—it stopped. Durzo stood behind the tree trunk, his arms wrapped around it, fingers poking into two points in the side of the maja's neck. She shrieked as the vir bulged against the blockage like a river at flood assailing a levee. Her cries crested and then fell as the vir receded, faded and sank beneath her skin once more.

Durzo stepped from behind the tree and grabbed her by the scruff on her neck. Holding her before him, he buried his fingers in those points on her neck again.

"A trick you didn't teach me?" Kylar asked.

"You expect me to teach you all I know in a couple months? The vir needs a physical expression. Block the physical expression and you block the magical. It's a weakness of the Ursuul family's hidden vir."

"She's an Ursuul?"

"What better use for Garoth's Talented daughters?" Durzo asked.

"I thought he had them killed."

"Garoth wasn't a man to throw away tools, no matter how blunt. What's your name, sweetie?"

She didn't answer, so Kylar did for her. "It's Eris Buel. You little bitch. We had our suspicions about you."

"Not enough to save your precious wife," she snapped. In her eyes rose such hatred that Kylar felt his gift unfolding, saw the murders littering Eris's path to power, but there was no dead Elene, nor Vi. He saw betrayals, broken vows, and, far down on the list, receiving Kylar's sword from a thief and then delivering the blade to Neph's spies.

All the darkness demanded an answer. "Justice has been denied you too long," Kylar said. His dagger punched through Eris's solar plexus, driving the breath from her lungs once more, and her guilty eyes flared wide, the light in them dimming.

A hand cracked hard against Kylar's cheek. Kylar staggered from the force of the blow. "Dammit, we need to question her, you fool!" Durzo shouted. Durzo grabbed Eris by her hair, holding her upright. "The ka'kari, Kylar, give me the ka'kari, quick!"

Kylar handed it to his master. The bastard had nearly torn off his jaw. Kylar put a hand to his face and took it off, sticky. Kylar looked at his fingers. It wasn't blood.

Durzo dropped Eris's body.

Kylar rubbed the golden liquid between his fingers. "Peri peri and xanthos?" Kylar asked. It was a contact poison, and though it would only leave him unconscious, the tincture still left permanent scarring. "On my face?"

"You deserve a permanent slap-print, but you heal too well."

"Why?" Kylar's legs were getting shaky.

"I needed this," Durzo said, lifting the ka'kari. "Sweet dreams."

Kylar crumpled to the ground and his lips smashed on a root. His mouth filled with blood. *The bastard could have at least caught me.*

79

Neph Dada strode through the dark streets of Trayethell. It was nearly noon, but he was inside the dome of Black Barrow, and the solid black rock dome above him cast the hidden city in perpetual darkness. He could only see his way by the bobbing yellow light hovering over his head and by the thousands of torches his Vürdmeisters had burning around the monolith at the covered city's heart.

Despite the darkness, Trayethell was an almost cheerful place. It had the air of a city whose inhabitants had stepped out and would be back momentarily. There was no dust, and the siege that had seen the city's death hadn't lasted long enough to destroy its beauty. Sections of the city were scorched and blackened or even leveled by magic, but many were pristine. Perhaps, though, the cheerfulness was all Neph's.

His fortunes had changed radically since winter began. He'd sent his thief to steal Kylar's sword, expecting to find that it was covered with the black ka'kari. As soon as he'd touched it with magic, he'd known it wasn't the ka'kari—it was something better. The sword was Iures, the Staff of Law. Like Curoch, Iures had been made by Ezra or perhaps by Ezra and Jorsin together. Unlike Curoch, Iures didn't amplify power, but it made vastly complicated weaves a hundred times easier to make—or unmake.

The cylindrical monolith was halfway up the hill to Trayethell Castle, extending up to the dome like a glass pillar. In the light of the torches, the monolith looked like a jar of churning smoke. The smoke betrayed only hints of the Titan imprisoned within. Here, a claw pressed against the glass, there, the side of a gigantic, disturbingly human-looking foot. It irritated Neph that he still felt a tremor at sight of the frozen monster. With Iures, he could destroy the monolith in an instant—after all, Ezra the Mad had used Iures to create the monolith, trapping the Titan until Jorsin Alkestes had killed it.

The glassy prison of frozen air was broken only by the Titan's death wound. Jorsin had unleashed a bar of fire from the top of Trayethell castle. It had burned through the prison and the Titan's chest in a perfect circle ten feet in diameter. The raw amount of magic necessary for such a thing made Neph hope Jorsin had been using Curoch.

Neph approached the monolith with small steps, coughing more from habit than necessity. Iures was doing wonders for Neph's health. The Vürdmeisters nearby made their obeisance and then returned to their work at his wave. Standing on scaffolding, they were lifting buckets of earth and packing it into the hole Jorsin had burned in the Titan. Soon, that earth would be made into flesh, and the Titan would rise. It would break open the great dome of Black Barrow, and then it would break any army that faced Neph.

Neph's tent was undisturbed. The fifty Soulsworn guards and his spells guaranteed that. Neph paused inside before entering Khali's room. Hiking up his robe, he touched his silver staff—the form he had chosen for Iures—and touched it to his ankle. It dissolved from his hand and wrapped smoothly around his ankle and calf. He willed it to be hidden, to remain inert even if touched with Khali's magic, to simply record all the magic that occurred around it. Khali didn't know about Iures, and Neph didn't intend for her to find out until it was too late. Iures changed everything.

Composing himself, Neph pulled back the flap. Tenser was sprawled on as fine a bed as they'd been able to make, his limbs loose, features slack, breath slow, eyes open but unfocused and rarely blinking. Neph pretended difficulty kneeling at Tenser's feet and extended the magic as Khali had taught him. "Holy One," he called. "I am here to serve."

Tenser's eyes closed then opened again, and She was present. Her presence filled the little tent like a sooty cloud, making it hard to breathe. "You have been neglecting your duties," Khali said. Her voice was Tenser's but the intonations were wrong, the accent unfamiliar. "This host has bedsores."

Neph's throat relaxed. "I will attend to it personally. Immediately. I've been about your business, collecting specimens for you." He cleared his throat but didn't cough. His coughing irritated Khali. "I was hoping we could talk about my reward."

Her laughter was amused, Neph thought. It was hard

to tell because though Khali controlled Tenser's voice and eyes, She didn't control his facial expressions. They remained blank, slack except when tongue and jaw worked to make words.

Khali wanted to be truly embodied, not the rude parody of it She had in Tenser. She needed three things: Ezra's weaves on Black Barrow to be broken, a willing host, and a spell that would require the blood of an Ursuul and the combined might of Neph's two hundred Vürdmeisters. Godkings in the past had delivered two of the three, but none could dismantle Ezra's work, because Ezra had used Iures to deny Khali embodiment. But Neph could undo Ezra's spells—because Iures remembered every weave it had ever helped make.

"I want two things," Neph said. "Godking Wanhope will arrive soon to kill me. I want to deny him the use of the vir. Second, I want to live another hundred years."

"Impossible," Khali said.

"Fifty then. Forty."

"Once embodied, I can give you a hundred years. But I can't deny Dorian the vir."

Neph's heart sank. *Dorian* was Godking Wanhope? Of all Garoth Ursuul's sons, the last one Neph wished to face was his old pupil. "I thought You controlled—"

"I do," Khali said, cutting him off. "The vir are magical parasites. Most of them were wiped out in antiquity, but Roygaris Ursuul captured several. What he liked about vir was that in the early part of an infestation, they broke open new channels in their host's Talent, adding to the host's power. Of course, they slowly devour their host's Talent itself, but Roygaris hoped to keep the vir in that first stage indefinitely. He failed, until I helped him. We slowed the progress of an infestation, but they can't be stopped. Try to use your Talent; you'll see it's a shadow of what it was when you were young. But I taught Roygaris something far more important. The vir is a like a grove of aspens. Each looks like a separate tree, but they're one organism. Control the right part, and you control the vir of everyone who's been infected with that strain. Your vir, Dorian's, Garoth's, every Khalidoran's—they are all one. Roygaris and I made a grand bargain: his blood line would control the vir, and I would control the reservoir of magic. The vow was made in a way that breaking it will destroy the vir and the reservoir."

Neph had expected Her to lie. He hadn't known the details, but just holding Iures had made much of Khali's magic plain to him. "If I can't stop him from taking the vir from me, Dorian will kill me," Neph said.

"When I am embodied, I shall protect you. Your service will not be forgotten. This I swear."

Neph wondered about that. Did Khali really need to be embodied to protect him from a mere man? Was she not a goddess? Or was it simply that she *wouldn't* protect him because if he wouldn't help her she had no reason to help him? He wondered what Khali would do to the world if she were embodied. Would she wreak havoc on everything, simply because she hated life as all the Strangers did? Or was her thirst for power more nuanced? Neph's interactions with her had been as infrequent as he could afford, but he hadn't sensed the same all-encompassing rage from her that he had seen in the other Strangers.

It was vital to judge correctly—Neph wanted to be Godking, but he wanted to rule over more than ashes and the dead. Still, he might not have much choice. If by not raising her, he would certainly die, but by raising her, all the world might die, he would risk the world.

"I am an old man," Neph said, defeated. "I have not the strength for this task."

Tenser Ursuul's arm flopped up as if lifted on strings, his hand limp. Neph touched the extended hand, and Khali's magic flowed into him, invigorating him, setting cool fire to his lungs. When it faded, he felt stronger than he had in years, and Iures had recorded every detail both of the Healing, and of how Khali herself drew from the reservoir of magic. It might be enough.

"Thank you, Holy One." Neph had only days to figure out the magic necessary, but with Iures in hand, he might depose more than Dorian.

"The latest ones approach," Khali said. "Bring them in."

Neph went outside and gestured to the Soulsworn. There were six young women chained together standing with them, and they all looked terrified. Khali's potential hosts were all peasant girls. Neph's men hadn't had much to choose from in this wilderness. Neph led them inside. They were surprised that the goddess was a drooling young man. Perhaps they'd expected claws and fangs. Neph studied the girls as they studied Khali. Four were either ugly or plain. Khali hated ugliness. Two were pretty, but Neph could See that one had been raped—against Neph's explicit orders. He would kill someone for that. Khali wanted any violation of Her host to come at Her own hands. The other girl was even prettier, with big brown eyes and radiant skin, but she was disfigured with scars.

"What's your name, child?" Khali asked the scarred one.

"Elene Cromwyll . . . uh, Mistress."

"Would you like to live forever, Elene?"

The girl's big eyes filled with such longing that even Neph couldn't help but pity her. "More than anything," Elene said.

80

Feir was standing at a table in Ezra's secret workroom under Black Barrow with a polishing cloth in his hand. He wasn't polishing the blade. He'd polished it a dozen times already, and it didn't need polishing in the first place.

"It's finished," he said aloud. "Except for one thing." Feir unveiled the sword. His fraud was nearly Ceur'caelestos' twin. He had held Ceur'caelestos, had marveled at it, had studied every whorl in the patterns of the mistarille. The heads of twin dragons were etched in either side of his blade, facing the tip, dragons of sun and moon, in accordance with Ceuran mythology. The blade had a single edge, curving slightly to give it more cutting surface. The thicker spine of the blade was to give it strength, the flexible iron core compensating for the sharp, hard fragility of the steel edge. This blade's form was pure show. It was mistarille, and it wouldn't break even if a man stood on the side of the blade and the wielder lifted it. Despite its incredible strength, Ceur'caelestos was lighter than it should have been. The mistarille, folded and refolded like steel, had the same steel patterns Ceur'caelestos' blade had borne. The difference between the original and Feir's fraud was that the original held the "fires of heaven." In response to danger or magic or its wielder's mood, the dragons could breathe what looked like fire out to the tip of the blade.

Feir knew the weaves to duplicate that, now. What he didn't have was a heartstone to hold the weaves. Certain stones resonated with different frequencies of magic. A ruby resonated with fire magics, specifically those having to do with red and orange light. If a stone was pure enough and exactly the right size, which varied by weave, a resonance could be built that sustained itself. This was nearly always imperfect, which was one reason magic imbued in items failed after a time. Feir needed as perfect a ruby as possible to be the dragon's heart.

"This part was supposed to be simple," Feir said. Even his own voice was depressing. "The prophecy was 'The greatest red gives dragon's heart and head.'" The greatest red had to be a big ruby, a heartstone, but placed at the dragon's head on the sword.

Feir had done a dozen impossible things over the course of the winter. With the barest of clues he'd been given in his time in Ezra's Wood, he'd come to Black Barrow and found the secret tunnel to this room. He'd found the magically hardened gold tools. He'd avoided the hundreds of Vürdmeisters who shared the shadowed city with him and found seven broken mistarille swords. He'd discovered Ezra's notes—a treasure any Maker would give his right arm to read. By all the gods, Feir had learned to reforge mistarille! He'd made the most beautiful fraud in history.

But he couldn't find a red rock.

"Could any other smith now living make this?" Antoninus Wervel asked, his voice low.

Feir shrugged. Antoninus waited. Feir gave in. "No."

Antoninus picked up the blade reverently, and in spite of himself, Feir was warmed. Antoninus wasn't a Maker himself, but he appreciated the mastery required for what Feir had done. He turned the blade over, examining it. "I thought you put your crossed war hammers on it."

In a moment of vanity—well, two hours of vanity—Feir had etched his smithmark near the hilt. As a boy, he'd loved the stories about Oren Razin, one of Jorsin's champions. Feir had been the only person he knew who could even think of wielding two war hammers as Oren had. Later, he'd mostly given it up. It was a lot easier to find someone to train you with swords. "It's not much of a forgery if you put your name on it. It's still there, but you have to know how to uncover it."

"You should be proud, Feir. You've made a thing of beauty."

"Without the dragon's heart, I've made nothing."

81

$\mathcal{W}$hat troubles you, my king? You've been fondling that rock for two days," Kaede said.

Solon pulled her into his lap and cupped her breast. "Only when you don't let me fondle better things."

"You beast!" she said, but she didn't pull away. "I'm serious."

The first days of their marriage had been bliss, except for the rock. Kaede's repentance at ordering him to subdue the Takedas by himself had led her to make all the wedding preparations. The very night Solon had arrived they had been married. Kaede refused to wait until later in the spring when the outlying nobles could attend. She said if they were offended, she would threaten to send her Stormrider to "visit" their isles.

But there were only so many hours a day that could be absorbed with lovemaking—though Solon and Kaede were doing their best—and that left Solon with time to consider the rock.

"I told you a little about my friend Dorian," Solon said. "And his prophecy over me."

"Something about killing your brother and a kingdom falling, right?"

Solon pulled back his white and black hair. "There's nothing quite as infuriating as having a man in a trance lay out your future in a sing-song: 'Storm-riving, storm-riding, by your word—or silence—a brother king lies dead. Two fears deriding, hope and death colliding, of the sword's man, regal third, true lies in your dragon's heart—or head. The north broken and remade on your single word.'"

Kaede looked puzzled. "Well, you got the storm-riding part."

"And before you ask, no, I didn't name myself that. I used to have no idea about the rest of it, except the brother king part. If I came home, I would have rallied the nobles to stop my brother Sijuron, thus my words would have left him dead. As it was, I served a man named Regnus Gyre, a man who would have been king and was like a brother to me. I didn't tell him I was a mage, and on learning it, he barred me from his company and was slain. The last part never made any sense to me, I only saw one king in the first part of the prophecy, my brother, so I thought Dorian was raving."

"But something has changed."

"This ruby, Kaede. I never heard of it. My father never spoke of it. Nothing is written about it in the royal records except to record its being in the treasury for at least two hundred years. It's listed as the dragon's heart. I think a third king, the regal third, the sword's man, depends on me bringing this ruby to him."

"What if you're the third king? What if you're the sword's man? You said it was a sword that turned your hair white. Perhaps a threat approaches here, and you need the ruby to withstand it. Solon, you can't leave. Not on some madman's word." Though she still sat in his lap, she was rigid, fear and anger rising in her.

Two fears deriding. The words were suddenly crystal. Damned prophecies could always be interpreted at least two ways, and usually both were correct.

"Kaede," Solon said, "there's a garrison called Screaming Winds that guards the pass between Cenaria and Khalidor. Dorian and I were there last fall. Dorian was unconscious most of the time, waking and scrawling fragments of prophecy and lapsing into trances again. One day he woke screaming. He demanded as much gold as I could get my hands on. I got it for him and we walked up into the hills to a stunted black oak. Dorian told me that Khali was coming and that she would tempt him. He said she would massacre everyone. He melted the gold and used it to cover his eyes and ears and made fetters for his arms and legs and asked me to drive stakes pinning him to the black oak. I wrapped him in blankets and left. The commander didn't believe my warnings. I wanted to leave, but I took too long, so I had the men bind me in ropes and I emptied my glore vyrden, but before the men could blindfold me or block my ears, She came."

"Khali?"

He stared into the distance. "I saw men throwing themselves off the wall. I saw a man tear his eyes out. And then, in a vision I thought was real, I saw you. I tried to go to you, but the ropes saved me. No one else survived. In fact, the Soulsworn came through and made sure everyone was dead. If a body hadn't fallen on me and covered me in blood while I was praying, they would have killed me too."

"So to what god should I offer sacrifices for saving your life?"

"None. It was a coincidence. A lazy soldier who didn't clean the blood from his sword in freezing weather and couldn't draw his sword."

"While you just so happened to be praying," she said. "That's quite some coincidence."

"Yes," Solon said, more roughly than he meant to. "That's what a coincidence *is.* Anyway, sorry, when I went to Dorian's black oak, he was gone. His tracks lead north, toward Khalidor, but I couldn't follow. I had to see you. Nothing else mattered. I signed on with a captain whose last run of the year was to Hokkai."

"So this is why you believe Dorian's prophecies," she said.

"This is the dragon's heart, Kaede. I'm the second king. A third king lives or dies by what I do with this."

"What are the two fears?" she asked quietly.

"My fear of Khali and my fear of speaking the truth. The latter was the fear that cost Regnus his life. I feel like I've been given a second chance, first to speak honestly with you, and second to face Khali again. 'Broken north, broken you, remade if you speak one word.' I've still got something broken inside, Kaede. I thought marrying you would fix it, and I can't tell you how happy I've been, and how much I want to stay here forever, but there's a part of me that still whispers 'coward.'"

"Coward? You're Solon Stormrider! You braved the

winter seas. You put down a rebellion single-handedly. You resisted a goddess. How are you a coward?"

"Dorian needed me when he went into Khalidor. He's probably dead because I didn't go. Regnus is dead because I wouldn't risk telling him who I was. If the prophecy is true, there's a word I have to speak, a life I can save, and I can be remade."

Kaede's eyes were troubled. "Will it be enough? Will there not be ever one more thing you need to do to prove that voice wrong? Will you chase valor until it kills you?"

He kissed her forehead. "I've already done the hardest part: I've told you the truth. I won't go unless you give me your blessing. My loyalty is all to you, Kaede."

Her eyes filled with a weight of grief. "My love, I won't give your death my blessing."

Solon held her gaze for a long time, then he tossed the Heart of the Dragon aside. "Then I stay," he said.

Kaede pivoted, sitting astride him. She put her hands on both sides of his face and looked deep into his eyes. "Please don't ask again. Please."

"I won't."

Her lovemaking was so fierce it left him breathless. She rode him to a silent climax, and even as her pupils flared and her breath caught and her fingers clawed into his shoulders, her eyes never left his. Then she clung to him, shaking, tears and sweat mingling on his chest, but she didn't say a word.

82

I don't know if I should have married you," Jenine said. "I think I made a mistake."

They were sitting together in the enormous Godking's carriage, slowly rumbling toward Black Barrow. Despite the dangers of bringing her to a battle, Dorian hadn't been able to leave her behind. Some plot might unfold in Khaliras that would take her from him. And if he had another episode, she was the only person he trusted to cover for him.

"But you love me," he said. "I know you do."

"I do," she admitted. "I respect you and I enjoy your company and I think you're brilliant and honorable. You're a great man. . . ."

"But?" he asked woodenly.

It came out in a rush. "But it's not like it was with Logan. I know it's not fair to compare you to a man who's dead—maybe I just remember all the good things about him now that he's gone, and I know—maybe it isn't fair to expect love to be the same every time. Maybe with Logan

I fell in love the way a girl falls in love and a woman's love grows slowly and protects itself. I don't know what it's supposed to be like, Dorian, but sometimes I feel so empty. Maybe I should have waited."

I'm a fraud. But what could he do? Tell her the truth? Send her back to Cenaria and her infatuation for some petty princeling she didn't even know? Together they were changing a kingdom, bringing light to a dark land. What could Logan give her compared to that? Why should Logan's love be more deserving than his?

Jenine's love was growing. Dorian knew it. It would grow more still when she realized she was pregnant with their child, he knew it. He'd seen that in his moments of madness on the battlefield, and hadn't trusted it or anything else he'd seen there, but in the days since then, he'd looked at her again, and he was sure it was true. Not twins, as he'd first foreseen, but a child, a son. Maybe the twins were to be their next children. He'd been waiting for the right time to tell her the news, but no time had seemed right.

He still spent as much of his days with her as he could. Their lovemaking was less frequent now that he was using his harem, but whatever jealousy she might feel seemed outweighed by the sudden reversal of the concubines' feeling toward her. Dorian had given her the credit for preserving their lives. That generosity cracked their envy and hatred. Instead of defeated rivals, Jenine suddenly had sisters, and her isolation melted with the spring snow.

This was real. It wasn't perfect, but it was the best they could do. This was what it was to be Godking. Besides, if he and Jenine simply ran away, one of the Vürdmeisters would rule with even more brutality than Dorian's father

had. Every relationship, every marriage, had its little lies.
He was king. A king made choices for other people based
on information they didn't have. That was the burden
of rule. Dorian had weighed Jenine's choices, and he'd
chosen.

"I'm sorry for laying this at your feet when you've got
so many other concerns, but I promised myself when we
married that I'd never lie to you, and silence was starting to feel like a lie. I'm sorry. I made my decision. I did
marry you. I do love you. I just—it's just hard to be an
adult all the time. You've trusted me to be your queen, and
I still keep acting like a little girl. I'm sorry for being such
a disappointment."

"A disappointment?" Dorian asked. "You've done better than I could have imagined. I didn't even begin acting
like an adult until I was much older than you are. I'm so
proud of you, Jenine. I love you more than anything. I
understand you're confused. This is a confusing place. I
understand you have doubts. We've been married for two
months, and you've realized that you're committed to
something for the rest of your life, and that's scary. Yes, it
hurts me a little, but our love is big enough to take a few
scratches. Thanks for telling me the truth. Come here."
They hugged, and he felt her unreserved relief. He wished
she would feel his hesitation, wished she would ask him
what was wrong. If she asked, he would tell her about
Logan. He would tell her everything.

After a few more seconds, she released him. He let
her go, and the moment passed. "I love you, Dorian," she
said, looking him in the eye and not seeing him.

"I love you too, Jenine." *I still don't call her Jeni. Why
is that?*

* * *

Kylar opened his eyes slowly. His mouth felt like it was stuffed full of cotton. His whole body was a chorus of complaints from sleeping propped against a tree. Working his jaw to clear the cotton feeling, he sat up. He touched his cheek where Durzo had smeared the poison. The new skin was tender, but there would be no scarring: Durzo was right. The bastard was always right.

It was dawn in the woods. Kylar was about to curse aloud when he became aware of a presence in the wood. He filled his lungs with a deep, slow breath, willing his senses to come alive. There were no animals in the forest this morning, but whether all the birds had migrated and the squirrels were hibernating or if the reason was more sinister, Kylar didn't know. He slowly flexed the muscles in his legs and back, judging whether they would cramp if he tried sudden movement. He scanned the forest, turning his head slowly. The sound of his fresh beard grinding against the collar of his tunic was the barest whisper. The length of his beard confirmed that he'd only been unconscious overnight.

There was nothing in the forest. No sounds out of place. He thought he could trust his body to respond. Wind sighed through the big oaks, the few remaining leaves whispering secrets against him. But something had woken him. Kylar was sure of it. Instinctively, he reached for the ka'kari to cloak himself in invisibility, but the ka'kari was gone. Kylar reached instead into his sleeves, loosening the daggers there. He scanned the trees.

A puff of air hit the top of his head.

Kylar threw himself to the side as he buried a knife in the tree above his head. He rolled once, threw himself to his feet and jumped backward a good ten paces, daggers in his hands.

Durzo laughed softly. "I always did like watching you jump." He was clinging like a spider to the tree Kylar had slept against.

"You bastard, where's the ka'kari? What have you done?"

Durzo kept laughing.

"Give me the ka'kari," Kylar said.

"All in good time."

"Wait, why am I asking? I can—" Kylar extended his hand to call the ka'kari to him.

"Don't!" Durzo barked.

Kylar stopped.

"The Hunter's nocturnal," Durzo said. "Its sense of smell is better than any tracking dog, its hearing is acute, and its vision rivals an eagle's, even when it's running full speed. If I timed things right, you'll have until dark before it starts hunting you."

"What—"

Releasing one hand from where it gripped the oak, Durzo unlimbered a black sword from his back. He tossed it to Kylar.

"Whatever you do, don't take the ka'kari off Curoch. Everything magical that goes into the Wood is marked. It's given a scent, so if it's taken out of the Wood, the Hunter can find it. The ka'kari can mask that scent, but I couldn't figure out how to erase it with the time I had. So the second you take the ka'kari off Curoch, the Hunter will come. I don't know exactly how fast the Hunter is, but if you really need to use Curoch, take the ka'kari off, use it, and then get the hell away from it. It might be minutes, it might be hours, but the Hunter will come. It will risk everything to get this sword."

Durzo had saved Kylar's life again. Kylar had known that his chances of making it into Ezra's Wood were dismal, and his odds of stealing Curoch and making it back out were even worse. Durzo had known it, too. In his typical way, Durzo wouldn't say anything to tell Kylar what he meant to him, but he'd do anything to show it.

"You old bastard," Kylar said, but his tone said, *thank you, master.*

"I can give you magic for the run. If you don't push too hard, you should get there in time and still have energy to fight. I'm going to Cenaria. This way, the Hunter has to follow us in opposite directions. It should be enough. Don't run flat out like you did when Sister Ariel gave you power, got it?"

"Got it," Kylar said. That was why Durzo was clinging to the tree. It made him harder to track. Plus, Kylar suspected the ground had all sorts of traps.

Durzo wasn't done. He spoke quietly. "Kylar, the fact Curoch was in the Wood tells me Neph's using Iures to break Jorsin's and Ezra's spells on Black Barrow. It makes Elene's talk of a Titan plausible. It also means that you're taking the thing he wants most straight to him. If he takes Curoch from you, he could break the world. I don't mean that metaphorically. For seven centuries I've done all I could to keep artifacts of such power out of the hands of men and women who will use them unscrupulously. If you fail, he'll undo everything I've spent seven centuries doing."

"You trust me this much?" Kylar asked.

Durzo grimaced. "Come here, you're wasting daylight."

Kylar stepped close.

"When Jorsin Alkestes commissioned me for this task, Kylar, he bound me with an oath he claimed was as old as the Night Angels themselves. If you so desire, here it is." Durzo's back straightened, his voice deepened, and Kylar knew Durzo was remembering his friend and king Jorsin Alkestes. "I am Sa'kagé, a lord of shadows. I claim the shadows that the Shadow may not. I am the strong arm of deliverance. I am Shadowstrider. I am the Scales of Justice. I am He-Who-Guards-Unseen. I am Shadowslayer. I am Nameless. The *coranti* shall not go unpunished. My way is hard, but I serve unbroken. In ignobility, nobility. In shame, honor. In darkness, light. I will do justice and love mercy. Until the king returns, I shall not lay my burden down."

"Who's the king?" Kylar asked.

"Vows are a bitch, huh?" Durzo grinned.

"This is what the Sa'kagé is supposed to be, isn't it?"

"The Sa'kagé's always been made of thugs and murderers, but there have been moments, like diamonds studding a pile of shit, when they've been crooks with a purpose."

"Thanks for the image."

"You gonna say the words?" Durzo asked.

"You'd make me commit to something I don't fully understand."

"Kid, we're always committing to things we don't fully understand."

"I thought you'd lost your faith in this and everything else," Kylar said.

"This isn't about my faith; it's about yours."

It was standard Durzo evasion. You don't ask someone you care about to swear their life to horseshit. Durzo was continuing the conversation they'd started months ago about Kylar's destiny. In choosing a life in the shadows, in choosing obscurity, Kylar would avoid one of the greatest temptations of the black ka'kari—the temptation to rule. Its power made him almost a god already, and the danger was always that he could become what he sought to destroy. Durzo hadn't even trusted himself with so much power. Did Kylar think he was that much better a man than his master?

A man serving the shadows also saw things that no king could see. A man serving in ignobility saw wrongs that were hidden from those in power. No one bothered to hide anything from Durzo Blint—except their fear of him.

The oath of a Night Angel wasn't enough to make a destiny, but it was a start. *What am I for?*

Whatever else he didn't know, Kylar knew he longed for justice. By serving in darkness with eyes that saw through the darkness, by being welcomed into the shadows, he could give justice to those who'd escaped justice. Those overlooked, too unimportant for mercy would find better than they'd hoped for. Those who should be stopped would be stopped. The faces of the Night Angels were already Kylar's faces. I will do justice and love mercy.

"I'll say it," Kylar said.

Durzo grimaced, but beckoned him closer and laid a hand on Kylar's forehead. Kylar recited the vow from memory—Durzo smirking at him, as if asking, how well did I teach you? But as Kylar finished, Durzo's hand grew strangely warm, his face somber. He said, *"Ch'torathi sigwye h'e banath so sikamon to vathari. Vennadosh chi tomethigara. Horgathal mu tolethara. Veni, soli, fali, deachi. Vol lessara dei."* Durzo withdrew his hand, his deep eyes limpid and, for perhaps the first time Kylar had ever seen, at peace.

"What was that?" Kylar asked. Whatever else the words had done, Kylar felt power suffusing him, more gently than when Sister Ariel had given him power, but also more solidly.

"That was my blessing." Durzo smirked, acknowledging he was a bastard for blessing Kylar in a language he didn't understand. With the way he'd trained Kylar's memory, he surely knew Kylar would remember the words until he was able to track down the outlandish language they'd been spoken in. But it wasn't in Durzo to just tell him. "Now get the hell out of here," Durzo said. "I've got trees to climb."

83

Logan and Lantano Garuwashi stood with their retainers on top of a still-pristine tower that guarded the mouth of the pass, surveying what would be the battlefield to the north. The great dome of Black Barrow and the dark stain of devastation around it were miles away on the opposite side of the Guvari River. Logan saw wonders to every side. Before Jorsin Alkestes had buried Trayethell beneath Black Barrow, it had been one of the great cities of the world in a world where wonders were common. To the east was Lake Ruel, which had been dammed in ages lost. The dam still stood, feeding the Guvari River not through the sluice gates on its front, which had been closed for centuries, but over the top of the dam itself. A series of locks, long since broken, had once made it possible for cargo ships to reach the city from the ocean. Half a dozen bridges or more had once spanned the river, but all had fallen except two, the wider Ox Bridge and Black Bridge near the dam.

The tower in which they stood guarded the entrance to

Ox Bridge. It commanded views of the pass behind them, the terraced slopes of Mount Terzhin to the southwest, and everything except whatever lurked on the far side of Black Barrow. Looking at the terraced hillside and the empty expanse at its base that they called the great market, Logan had a revelation. He'd always thought Black Barrow had enclosed the city of Trayethell. It hadn't. Jorsin had only enclosed the city's heart. Trayethell had spanned leagues. If what Logan was looking on was correct, the city had been bigger and more populous than any city now in the world.

"We'll have to move our men over Ox Bridge tonight," Garuwashi said. "It'll take maybe four hours for thirty thousand to cross. The camp followers will have to cross in the dark."

"Cross?" Logan said. "Do you see Wanhope's army? We have twenty-six thousand men, half of whom have never seen battle. Wanhope has twenty thousand, ten thousand more highlanders, and two thousand meisters— each of whom is worth a dozen men. You want us to fight with our backs against a river? No. We guard the bridges and put our men in the great market in case Wanhope tries to ford the river there. We'll see how well his men fight waist-deep in water. If necessary, we can retreat slowly into the passes."

"You're planning for defeat?" Lantano Garuwashi asked, incredulous. "This is lunacy. We cross the bridge, and we destroy it behind us. Desperate men fight best. If you leave them an out, they'll flee, especially your battle virgins. Give them no choice but to win or die, and they will fight almost like sa'ceurai."

"They outnumber us, and we have four magi. Four!"

"Numbers mean nothing. Each sa'ceurai is as a hundred men. We came here for victory." Behind them, several of Garuwashi's men voiced muffled agreement.

"I'll give you victory," Logan said.

"You'll *give* us nothing."

"That's not what I meant. Tonight under the cover of darkness, I'm sending ten thousand men west down the river. My Feyuri scouts say there's a crossing a few miles down. Ten miles downriver is Reigukhas. It's not a big city, but all Wanhope's supplies flow through there, and it's very defensible. We send our magi with my ten thousand, and they can take Reigukhas before dawn. If we can starve Wanhope's army, it will be his men who melt away in the night."

"They'll see our men heading west, unless you mean to march ten thousand without any light."

"The torches will only be visible for the first half a mile, then there's a forest between them and the Khalidorans. It'll look like men moving around among our campfires."

Garuwashi was quiet for a long time. Finally, he spat. "So be it, Cenarian. But I'm sending a thousand of my sa'ceurai with your men to take the city. None shall have glory greater than the sa'ceurai."

Thus it begins.

84

Dorian was meeting with his generals in the afternoon when he felt the first twinges of madness rising.

"Enough," he said, interrupting General Naga's report. "Here's what I want. Make sure our defensive positions are impregnable. I don't want them to even try us. Let them see our strength. In the meantime, I need better intelligence on Moburu's numbers. We know he has two thousand krul. How many men does he have? And where the hell is—" A vision flashed before Dorian's eyes of Khali herself, rising from the ground, perfect, whole, beautiful, embodied and smiling victoriously. The room had disappeared, and only she remained, potent, a black ocean of krul rising around her.

"And where the hell is Neph Dada?" he heard a voice say. Though he couldn't see the speaker, he knew it must be Jenine. "His Holiness demands you find out. He'll expect your report this evening. For now, begone."

Dorian blinked and the vision was gone. General Naga turned back as he reached the flap of the tent. He seemed reassured to find Dorian meeting his eye. "The queen speaks with my voice," Dorian said. "Is that a problem, general?"

"Of course not, Your Holiness. I will report when we get word." He bowed deeply, and left.

When the last of them was gone, Dorian let out a long breath. Jenine took his hand and he sat. "I need to use it," Dorian said.

"Every time you do, it's harder to stop," Jenine said.

She was right, but with so many armies in close proximity, Dorian needed to use his gift to make sure he didn't trigger a cataclysm. He'd done everything he knew to do militarily to discourage the Cenarians from attacking, but with Neph's men and Moburu's nearby, there were too many factors at play for him to not try to see the futures down the roads before him.

He'd studied his gift with a Healer's eyes, and he thought he understood why prophecy seemed easier to begin and harder to stop now. The vir had broken open new channels everywhere throughout his Talent, and it had penetrated his prophetic gift, too. All his magic, and now all his prophecies, passed through the tentacles of vir rather than their natural channels. Because the vir was thicker, everything passed more freely. It was quite possible that the vir, tainted itself, was tainting Dorian's gift with bizarre visions like those he'd had of the Strangers and his wife pregnant with twins, but there was no help for it now. He would stop using the vir and only use the Talent—after this.

"I love you," he said.

"I love you too," she answered. She had a quill and

parchment to write down anything he said, in case he couldn't remember it afterward.

Then he dove in. He tried to hold onto enough of himself to speak what he saw, but the current was too strong. He saw a Titan rise from Black Barrow, and then he pulled downstream fifteen years to Torras Bend. There was Feir, standing at a smithy, ordering his young apprentice to gather wood. Then Dorian was a hundred years downstream, in Trayethell, somehow magically rebuilt, celebrating something, a vast parade working through the street. Dorian fought it, tried to throw himself back to a time where his visions would help him. He found himself standing in the guts of Khaliras, deciding whether to take Jenine out through the sewage chutes or try to fight their way out, everything would turn from this one choice—no, that was the past, dammit.

"Rodnia? Nidora?" He heard the voice calling for him, but it was too distant, and he hadn't found anything yet. There was a whisper as it called again, and then it was lost.

Jenine drew the curtain that separated Dorian's throne, where he was quietly mumbling, from the rest of his tent. "Dorian!" she whispered one more time, but the king didn't stir. She shut the curtain and said, "Come in, General Naga." The man had been knocking for more than a minute.

"Your Highness," he said, coming in and looking conspicuously at the drawn curtain. "My apologies, but we've just had a report from a spy. His Holiness must hear it."

"His Holiness is not to be disturbed right now."

"I'm afraid this requires immediate action."

Jenine lifted her brows as if the general were perilously close to being rude. "Then deliver your report."

General Naga hesitated, open-mouthed, as he struggled with the idea of reporting to a woman, much less a woman young enough to be his daughter, then wisely closed his mouth. When he opened it again, it was to say, "Your Highness, our spy reports that the Cenarians and Ceurans are planning to attack our supply lines at the city of Reigukhas. They plan to have ten thousand men sneak away tonight under cover of darkness. The Cenarian king said—"

"The Cenarian king?" Jenine interrupted.

For an instant, General Naga seemed stricken. "Sorry, I meant, the *Ceuran* king said that we would think any torches we saw tonight were merely men moving between their campfires. In truth, such movement would only be visible to us for a short section. The Cenarian queen—your pardons, Highness, I obviously am having a slight problem adjusting to so many queens—the Cenarian queen concurred." He swallowed nervously.

"Do you trust this spy?" Jenine asked. She didn't know whether she more wanted Dorian to wake up instantly and make the decision for her, or if she feared that he might wake up with a scream as he had the last few times.

"Absolutely, Your Highness."

"If we wait until we see the movement of torches tonight, will our men be able to get to Reigukhas in time to defend it?" Jenine asked.

"It will be a near thing."

"Then send fifteen thousand men now. If we don't see the torches moving tonight, we can send riders to get them to turn back."

"Fifteen thousand? From a defensive position, five should be more than adequate to defend Reigukhas, and would still preserve our superiority of numbers here."

He was probably right, and Jenine would have conceded to his experience if this had been a war, but it wasn't a war. Those were her people on the other side, too. Fifteen thousand men would be such an overwhelming defensive force that the Cenarians would call off an attack on the town as hopeless. Jenine was saving lives on both sides, and tomorrow, they'd be able to send emissaries to the Cenarians before blood was spilled. "Fifteen thousand, general. That is, unless you're still having a problem adjusting to this queen."

General Naga barely hesitated before he bobbed his head and withdrew. For an odd moment, Jenine thought he looked relieved.

As night fell, Logan and Garuwashi met once more at the top of the tower, this time alone, though each had bodyguards stationed out of earshot on the stairs. They watched the line of sa'ceurai, every one bearing a torch, heading down river. Then the kings turned, scanning the thousands of campfires dotting the plain around Black Barrow. The Khalidoran army and the highlanders stayed outside the circle around Black Barrow that was carpeted with those oddly non-decomposing bodies. They called it the Dead Demesne.

"Do you think it worked?" Logan asked.

"Wanhope's a wytch, not a warrior," Garuwashi said. "I think he'll believe everything his spy told him we said earlier."

In truth, Logan had sent ten thousand men west, but only until they were blocked from the Khalidorans' sight by the forest. Then the men were told to extinguish their torches and make their way back to camp. Logan was sure no small amount of grumbling was going on right now: the men had no idea why they'd been sent marching in circles, and he couldn't tell them in case more spies lurked in their ranks. Meanwhile, Garuwashi's thousand were continuing west. They would ford the river and come back on the opposite side as stealthily as possible. Dressed in muddied garb, they would crawl through the Dead Demesne. When the sun rose, they would lie in the shadows and huddle next to the corpses as if dead themselves. They would circle the long way around Black Barrow. Garuwashi figured it would take them two nights to get into place, but then, either on his signal or when they saw the opportunity, the men would don their armor, rise from among the dead, and attack the command tents. If Momma K's spies were right, Jenine was there. If not, they still might kill some of Wanhope's generals or even the Godking himself.

It was likely a suicide mission, but there had been no lack of volunteers. But the only Cenarians going were a hundred of Agon's Dogs, former sneak thieves and burglars and his wytch hunters with their Ymmuri bows.

Of course, as Agon and Garuwashi kept telling Logan, timing was everything. Those thousand men were among the armies' best. If Wanhope did split his forces and tomorrow went as planned, Logan and Garuwashi might be close to victory. Those extra thousand veterans could turn a Khalidoran retreat into a rout.

"The Feyuri scouts say that the Ceuran force following

us is led by the Regent himself," Garuwashi said quietly. "I will be obliged to kill myself when he discovers I have no sword. My men will be invited to join me in suicide or return to Ceura immediately."

"How far back is he?" Logan asked, his throat constricting. Now he understood why Garuwashi had been so adamant that the thousand who snuck through the Dead Demesne be sa'ceurai. It was a service to Logan. Separated from command, they wouldn't know that their leader had been disgraced, so they would keep fighting.

"They will arrive tomorrow night."

"We can stop them in the passes," Logan said. "There are narrow—"

"He has twenty thousand sa'ceurai. My men would wonder why we were fighting the Regent, who only wants to see the Blade of Heaven. Even without him, they will expect me to lead them into battle. This is my last night."

They turned as a man cleared his throat at the stairs. The man was nearly as big as Logan, not quite as tall, but wide as an ox. He carried some flab, but it was only a thin layer over rock hard muscle. "Maybe not, my lord," Feir said, dipping his head. "I don't suppose either of you has a big ruby?"

They looked at each other, and Logan saw a thin, desperate hope in Lantano Garuwashi's eyes. He knew then that this man would kill himself in a heartbeat if he needed to, but there was nothing in Lantano Garuwashi that desired death.

"No?" Feir asked. "Damn. Well, I hope we can find someone who's good with illusions." The big man stepped forward and unwrapped a bundle to produce a sword. "My lord, I present you with Ceur'caelestos."

85

$\mathcal{V}$i and three hundred of the fittest war magae made it through the eastern fork of the pass an hour before dawn. Sadly, fittest wasn't the same as most Talented. The journey had taken longer than anyone had expected. Ushering eight thousand women—most of them middle-aged and every single one more than willing to share her opinion—through the mountains had been a nightmare. Most of the rest would arrive sometime during the day, but a sizable number wouldn't arrive until the next day, or the day after that. Even with bodies that appeared decades younger than their years, eighty- and ninety-year-olds were simply not going to hurry. Vi thought that if she never saw another woman in her life, she'd count herself lucky.

After some bickering with sentries that had ended when Vi lifted both men off the ground with her Talent and shook them, Vi was brought directly to King Gyre. He was among his men, reassuring them with his presence, and as Vi approached, he was cinching the leathers of a young horseman's pauldrons. Vi cleared her throat and Logan turned.

Vi had heard of Logan Gyre, of course, but seeing him was altogether different. He was perhaps the tallest man she'd ever seen, and perfectly proportioned. In his white enameled plate armor, gilded with a gyrfalcon with wing-tips breaking a circle, he was the perfect picture of an energetic young king at war. He was muscular, his carriage erect, and though he walked with the knowledge that eyes were on him, he didn't seem to revel in it. There was also something odd about his right forearm. It seemed brighter than the other, somehow. "My lady," he said, nodding. "Is there something I can do for you?"

She stopped staring. "I'm Vi Sovari of the Chantry. I bring three hundred magae, and seven thousand more by tomorrow. We have come to help you."

"Thank you, I dare say we will have need of healers, but so many . . ."

"Your Majesty, we're war magae."

"War magae." The king's eyes widened.

"We have withdrawn from the Accords, that we may help you."

He scrubbed a hand through his blond hair. "This changes things. . . . They may have two thousand meisters, two hundred Vürdmeisters among them. We have ten magi. How can you help me?"

"Two thousand?" Vi despaired. "If they bring two thousand meisters against us before the rest of my Sisters arrive, we'll be worm food in an hour."

"I may have drawn off half of them. How long could you and your three hundred hold out against a thousand?"

"We might make it, and some of the Sisters should arrive during the day. My war magae are mostly good at defensive magic, Your Majesty."

"Good, then I want half of you to hold Black Bridge and the dam. Spread the others out through the lines." A messenger trotted up and Logan held up a finger, forestalling the man. "Oh, and thank you, Sister. Your aid is desperately needed and greatly appreciated. I hope to speak more with you this evening."

"You're welcome, and . . . Your Majesty, I know you were a friend of Kylar's. He'll be here."

Logan got a strange look on his face. "Yes," he said, "I'm sure he shall."

Vi was stationed with a hundred and fifty of her Sisters at Black Bridge, almost in the shadow of the great dam, when she realized what that look meant. Logan thought Vi meant Kylar would be here in spirit. Logan still thought Kylar was dead. *Stupid, Vi, stupid.*

Logan and Garuwashi were astride their mounts in the Great Market as the first rays of dawn revealed the Godking's armies arrayed across from their own. "They fell for it," he said. "They must have sent fifteen thousand men to Reigukhas. Last night, they had six thousand more men than we did. Now they have ten thousand less."

Lantano Garuwashi grinned. "Only two things can undo us now."

"Magic?"

"And young men so drunk on glory they forget their discipline," Garuwashi said.

"So when do we attack?" Logan asked.

"Right now."

* * *

It was still dark in the royal tent. Dorian ran a hand over Jenine's bare shoulder, down her back, and over her hip. Her beauty made him ache. He shouldn't have brought her here. It was too dangerous in too many ways. She wasn't asleep, but she feigned it for him. She knew how he enjoyed her. He inhaled the scent of her hair once more and sat up. He began dressing.

"That army is Cenarian," Jenine said in the darkness. "Those are my people."

"Yes," Dorian said.

"How do I find myself in my enemy's camp, my lord?"

"Have you ever wondered what would happen if someone threw a war and nobody came?"

"What do you mean?"

"I have no intention of killing any Cenarians," Dorian said, "though I understand why they won't believe that. We're here only to destroy Neph and Moburu. At dawn our emissaries will let the Cenarians know that we will not attack, but I don't think we have to worry about them. They've already taken a defensive position, as have we. They'll stay until they see us withdraw, and then they'll go home."

Jenine stood, and Dorian couldn't help but glory in her beauty. The familiar panic-edged desire swept over him. He wanted to grab her and make love frantically, right now, as if he might never have a chance to again. But it was almost dawn, there were things he needed to do.

"My people are aggrieved at your father's predations, and that savage Lantano Garuwashi is with them. They say he bathes in blood. What will we do if they attack?

I will be our emissary," Jenine said. "They will believe me."

"No!" Dorian said.

"Why not?"

"It's dangerous."

"They will not attack a woman approaching under flag of parley. Besides, better a hazard to me than to forty thousand lives."

"It's not that," Dorian said, thinking furiously. "Your presence might precipitate war, my love. What will Terah Graesin do—even under a flag of parley, if she sees you alive? Your life would be the death of all her power. People will do horrible things to keep what they love, Jenine." The fact was, if he sent Jenine to Logan, the threat of Cenarian attack would end in one second—and so would his marriage.

Unless . . . what if Jenine chose him? She'd barely known Logan. What Dorian had built with her was . . . *real? It's built on a lie. Oh, Solon, what would you say if you could see me now?*

"You're right, my lord husband. I just wish there were something I could do."

Dorian kissed her. "Don't worry. It's going to be fine." He stepped through the tent flap and saw a young man sweating, obviously bearing a message for him, and obviously too afraid to wake a Godking. "What is it?" Wanhope demanded.

"Your Holiness. The warchief wishes me to tell you that the attack on Reigukhas was a ruse. Our spies were wrong. The Cenarians outnumber us by more than ten thousand now, and . . . Your Holiness, they're attacking."

86

*F*ighting in these damn robes was going to be a chore, but Vi was glad she hadn't worn her scandalous wetboy grays. Well, she'd worn them, but under the robes. Going into battle without her grays would be like going into battle with her hair unbound.

A blond man wider than he was tall brought his horse into the line next to her. A mage, she could tell. "Feir Cousat," he said. "You Vi?"

She nodded. They were positioned ten ranks back, behind pikemen and shield bearers who were guarding the bridge in front of the dam. From their elevated position, they could see the whole valley.

A flag went up among Garuwashi's men down in the market. The third time it waved, the Ceurans began marching toward the river. Lantano Garuwashi himself rode beside the front lines, and when he drew his sword, it glowed in the low light. A cheer went up.

Vi squinted at the sword. There was something wrong with it.

"What's wrong?" Feir asked.

"The glow . . . did you make that?"

"What?! You can see that from here?"

"It just looks like you. Like your work, I mean. I don't know."

The highlanders who made up the center of the Khalidoran line were slow to react. They did nothing until half of Garuwashi's five thousand had made the opposite bank. "What are they doing?" Feir asked. "The Khalidorans didn't shoot any arrows." Then the highlanders began trotting forward.

Garuwashi's flag dropped when the highlanders were thirty paces away and a shrill keening shriek sounded from every Ceuran throat. Shrieking, they charged. To a man, the sa'ceurai ran with their long swords trailing behind them, the other hand extended forward. Charge was too inelegant a term.

Then the lines crashed together. The average highlander was taller and thicker than the average sa'ceurai, but as the clash of arms and rattle of armor resounded to where Vi watched, it was highlanders who fell ten to one. The sa'ceurai whipped their swords under and up, or over and down, or feinted and threw their shoulders into the highlanders instead.

"Best solo fighters in the world," Feir said. "There are twice as many highlanders out there—and look."

Within minutes, the rest of the sa'ceurai had made the crossing. As Feir had said, both sides fought man-to-man, breaking into a thousand duels, though neither side was above hamstringing an enemy whose back was turned. Despite the bulkiness that made the sa'ceurai's lacquer armor look heavy, the men danced.

Lantano Garuwashi presided over it all, dealing death every time highlanders pushed through the lines to get to him, but mostly watching. The air around him winked and sparkled, and Vi figured those were arrows or magic the Khalidorans where shooting at him. A terrified-looking magus sat on a horse directly behind Garuwashi, making constant gestures as he protected the war leader.

Vi saw the effect of the meisters before she could see the meisters themselves. The sa'ceurai lines seemed to ripple back as if all of them had been struck at once. Then she saw green fireballs arcing over the highlanders to splatter among the sa'ceurai, the flame turning blue where it hit flesh and sizzling, black smoke rising from a hundred bodies on fire.

In that instant, the sa'ceurai advance faltered. Lantano Garuwashi waved his hand forward frantically, and his standard bearer was waving a flag furiously, but his men sank back. A dozen green fireballs splattered against Garuwashi's shields and they nearly collapsed. He sawed his horse's head back toward the river and joined his men's retreat, waving his hands and cursing them all the way.

A cry went up from the highlanders and they surged forward. They'd routed the Ceurans.

But from the rear, where the Khalidorans couldn't see, it looked all wrong. While those in the front made big, panicky gestures, none threw down their weapons as they fled. The sa'ceurai closest to the river sheathed their blades and calmly carried the wounded between them in twos. Lantano Garuwashi's frenzied waving, the whipping flag—it hadn't been the same flag he'd used for the advance, had it?—it was all a setup.

"Palies comin'!" someone shouted.

Across the bridge in front of Vi, hundreds of Khalidoran soldiers were running to their places. Their archers loosed a flight of arrows. Feir threw his hands up and a shimmering transparent blue sheet of magic unrolled above the Cenarians, covering those at the foot of the bridge. The first arrows hit the shield and, to Vi's surprise, didn't burst into flame. Rather, they hit the shield like it was a pincushion, poked through it, and robbed of all speed, simply dropped the last five feet onto the Cenarians.

"Archers, shoot from outside the umbrella!" Feir shouted, but not before several of them had loosed shots into it. The outgoing arrows stabbed through the umbrella, flew half a dozen feet, then came to rest back on top of the umbrella again, lacking even the energy to make it back to the ground.

"Meisters!" someone screamed.

Before Vi found the dark figure across the bridge, something blasted her from her saddle. She met the rocky ground with far less speed than she had any right to expect.

"Make that 'vürdmeisters,'" Feir said, helping her up. "The bastards."

"You saved me," Vi said, noticing the unfamiliar shield around her as she stood.

"You owe me. Now do something. I'm tapped out."

A dozen green fireballs of various sizes arced across the bridge. Vi fumbled for her Talent, but her ears were still ringing. She was too slow.

Nonetheless, every one of the Khalidorans' falling fireballs was lifted like an arrow catching a sudden updraft, then curved in the air and smashed back into the Khalidoran lines. A woman whooped, and Vi recognized Sister

Rhoga's voice. Vi's battle magae had practiced that weave for four days straight, but seeing it actually work took Vi's breath away.

Vi couldn't find her horse, though she had no idea how it could have gone anywhere through the massed ranks of pikemen, archers, and shield bearers who were holding the foot of Black Bridge. She pushed her way to the front.

The men maintaining the shield wall at the front line looked at her. Their shields were studded with dozens of arrows each. The Khalidoran archers had figured out that if they shot at a low enough trajectory, they could find targets here. "How much cover you want, Sister?" a skinny officer at least twenty years her senior asked. The first row of soldiers were on one knee, their shields covering them completely; the second row held their shields at an angle and a third held theirs overhead despite the umbrella. They were packed as tightly as possible.

"You, rest," Vi told a man in the second row. She pushed her way into place and poked her head through the shields.

She found the Vürdmeister by the swirling black vir-shield spinning in front of him. A moment later, half a dozen darts of mage fire plunged into his shield, magic breaking and spitting and sizzling in chunks on the bridge at his feet, but the Vürdmeister barely seemed to notice. He was looking down the river toward the ford at the Great Market.

The Khalidoran highlanders had pursued the sa'ceurai across the river, and thousands had now gained the Cenarian side. Vi's heart jumped into her throat.

A blue flare streaked into the sky over the Great Market. To Vi's right, a magus struggled out onto the narrow stone walkway that ran across the face of the dam. Because the waters poured over the top of the dam rather than through its centuries-closed sluices, the magus made his way through a deluge as water poured from fifty feet overhead. He held the handrail and climbed forward, hand over hand, struggling to keep his feet anchored to the stone. At the center of the walkway were two enormous pulleys, the chains wrapped around them still pristine. The chains themselves disappeared into the face of the dam where they would open the sluice gates. The magus threw thick blue ropes of magic at each of the pulleys, straining.

He had barely started when half a dozen Vürdmeisters who'd been hiding in the Khalidoran ranks burst forward. Fire, hammers of air, gales, and missiles engulfed the lone magus from every direction. The magus's shields held until a gleaming white homunculus winged its way to him. The magus screamed as the air ripped open and a pit wyrm struck.

The wyrm's jaws crunched through shield and man and one of the huge pulleys, then it pulled back into whatever hell it had come from and disappeared.

A moment later, half a dozen green fire missiles ripped into the other pulley, cracking it and snapping the chains.

Only as they destroyed the second pulley did Vi realize that she'd just seen Garuwashi's trap defanged. Garuwashi had feigned the rout to draw the Khalidorans into the river where he meant to drown them. But the Khalidorans had known. Why else would they have concealed the presence of six Vürdmeisters? Now Garuwashi had just had his trap turned back on himself.

"Feir!" Vi shouted. She turned and was surprised to see he was right behind her, the dread in his eyes telling her he understood. "Can you protect me?"

His eyes flicked to the Vürdmeisters, who to Vi's eyes looked all the same. "Three seconds, two thirds, and a sixth shu'ra. Shit. Maybe?"

One of the younger Vürdmeisters laughed, turning his head over his shoulder to say something. Vi lashed out, grabbed the hem of his robe, and yanked. If Vi had thought about it, she wouldn't have tried. She couldn't reach that far. She never had.

The man was halfway down the gorge before he screamed.

Feir's eyes were huge. "Nice grab."

"This is the stupidest thing I've ever done," Vi said. With her Talent, she pushed men aside right and left. The dam's walkway was a good thirty feet out and twenty down. She ripped off her robes.

"Distract them. Now!" she shouted.

The battle magae complied, flinging dozens of fireballs.

Vi ran through the space she'd cleared, a few quick steps taking her to a full sprint. She leapt into the void, barely remembering to shield herself. The jump was perfect. She landed with both feet on the middle of the walkway, splashing water every direction, then her momentum carried her into the wall of the dam. Her shield helped, it was still a twenty-foot fall. Vi crunched into the wall and then rebounded. She clawed blindly and felt stone under her fingertips for a brief instant, then she was flying into space.

Stupid, Vi, stupid.

She imagined she could hear Nysos laughing. She hadn't thought of the god of potent liquids in months, and here she was, killed by water.

She tensed for impact, but it never came. Vi opened her eyes and couldn't see anything through the torrent. Then she was clear of it. She saw a thick rope of Talent knotted around her and extending all the way back to Sister Ariel, who was grimacing with the effort. In another moment, Vi was next to one of the chains. She grabbed it and Sister Ariel released her.

Vi was instantly swept off her feet and spun by the force of the water, but with effort she regained her feet. Above her she saw the Vürdmeisters—there were only three now—throwing fiery death toward her, but nothing came even close. On the Cenarian shore two hundred women glowed like torches with Talent: her Sisters. They were protecting her, and nothing could stop them. Vi's heart swelled to bursting. These women would die for her. For the first time in her life, she belonged.

She was crying and laughing even as she found the other chain. She stood with one chain in each hand, each link as long as her forearm. She heaved, but without the pulleys it was just too heavy.

She moved back a step, out of the dam's shadow into the sun. It wasn't quite noon. She felt sunlight drenching her skin and she opened herself to it, opened herself until it burned, until it filled every pore with heat.

Then she heaved again. At first, nothing moved, and then she felt as if deep within the dam mechanisms were threatening to give way, protesting deep in their iron throats, and finally . . . turning. Her Talent extended beyond her arms, gripping the chains like half a dozen hands, grabbing, pulling, and grabbing again. Hissing filled her ears, and she opened her eyes. Something was glowing, blindingly bright. It was her. She was luminous. Vi glowed like the Seraph herself. Steam rose in great hissing billows where the water washed over her limbs.

The sluice gates cracked open, three on the left and three on the right. Vi pulled, feeling her strength waning. She had to finish. She pulled one more time and felt the gates lock open. The water pouring over the top of the dam onto her slowed, stopped. She could see again.

The six open gates below her jetted water into the valley with incredible force. The water blasted into the thousands of highlanders crossing into the Great Market. Men clambered for higher ground, stampeding toward shore, crushing their fellows underfoot.

Only Garuwashi's men were unfazed by the flood. Whether or not they had seen how near their trap had come to collapsing, the sa'ceurai were ready for it to work. Through all the high ground surrounding the Great Market, they closed ranks and shut down choke points expertly. Then they surged back, pushing Khalidorans to a watery death. In places, men clawed their way over the sa'ceurai's shields, but they were quickly cut down.

Vi became aware that everyone on the bridge was staring at her. They were all shouting, cheering. She was still holding the chains. They were suddenly unbearably heavy. She dropped them and staggered. Hands grabbed her, steadied her. A dozen Sisters had ventured out onto the slick walkway to come to her.

Sisters. My sisters. Vi started crying, and no one looked at her like she was stupid.

87

Lantano Garuwashi was the first to understand the implications of what occurred at the dam. The trap he and Agon and Logan had worked up had always assumed that they would be able to close the sluice gates after they opened them. With the destruction of the pulleys, it was a miracle they'd been opened in the first place. After flooding out the highlanders, he and Logan had planned to throw everything at the shaken Khalidoran army. Caught between the Ceurans and the Cenarians and the cursed ground of the Dead Demesne, the Khalidoran army would have broken in minutes. Instead, the allies' armies could only advance across the narrow bridges.

Garuwashi ordered the crossing and ordered magae to protect the bridges. If he'd been the Khalidorans, that's what he would try to destroy.

He was right. The counterattack was almost solely magical. Hundreds of meisters had hit each of the bridges, but then, suddenly, they'd been called off. The magae told him they could see a magical conflagration on the far side of Black Barrow itself, Khalidorans fighting barbarians, but they couldn't tell him anything else. Had he been able to ford the river, he could have taken advantage of the Godking's splitting his army. But that was water literally under the bridge. He established beachheads and put engineers to work widening the bridges by whatever means they could, but the situation looked grim.

As soon as the Khalidorans saw that his men were establishing fortifications and not attacking, they withdrew to high points hundreds of paces away and began working on their own.

In the early afternoon, Garuwashi found King Gyre in their command tent, which had been moved to the foot of Oxbridge.

"Today was a great victory," Logan said. "They lost more than nine thousand highlanders. I lost ninety men holding the market. How many sa'ceurai?"

"One hundred fifteen in baiting the trap. Eight in springing it."

"Two hundred men, to kill nine thousand," Logan said. He didn't elaborate. It was a victory, but it was a victory that was a prelude to defeat.

"Tomorrow their fifteen thousand come back from Reigukhas, and you lose my sa'ceurai," Garuwashi said.

"How long until the Regent arrives?" Logan asked.

"An hour. His messengers have asked that he see me immediately." It wasn't right. After such a great victory, he should be looking on the morrow with relish. Instead, this night he would kill himself. Many of his sa'ceurai would join him. The twenty thousand sa'ceurai who accompanied the Regent would simply turn and go home.

"Can't you just use the illusion you used today?" Logan asked.

Garuwashi sighed. "Feir said there's something about the magic of the blade that interferes with illusions. The glow looked good from ten or twenty paces while the sword was cutting back and forth, but from up close? It wouldn't withstand a child's scrutiny."

"Your Majesties, if I may?" Feir asked. Garuwashi hadn't seen him arrive, despite his huge bulk. It was a measure of how exhausted he was. Logan gestured Feir to continue. "I made that sword. If we can find a ruby to hold the spells, I dare say I'm the only person in the world who could tell the difference between the new Ceur'caelestos and the real thing. We don't even need a special ruby. It just needs to be big. King Gyre, I'm sure your treasury has something that will work. It seems ridiculous that we'd give up this close."

"It's not giving up," Garuwashi snapped. "It's having our fraud discovered."

"What if they didn't discover it?" Feir asked.

"The Regents have been waiting centuries for this," Logan said. "I'm sure they have some kind of test to determine if the blade is real."

"So what if they do?" Feir asked. "The Regent's not Talented and you have magae at your disposal. With a little preparation, we can—"

"Get out," Garuwashi breathed. "I listened to you once and dishonored myself. No more. You know nothing of sa'ceurai. Begone, snake."

Feir's face drained of color. He stood slowly. Garuwashi turned his back to him. He almost hoped Feir would strike him down. Let Garuwashi die betrayed. Then any

flaw found with the sword would be assumed to be the
work of the betrayer. Something would be left of Garuwashi's name.

"If you would save this army and all these thousands
of souls, the magae and I will be near," Feir said quietly.
"If you would save only your precious honor, you can go
to hell."

When Garuwashi turned, the big man was gone. King
Gyre looked at him silently.

"What is a king without honor?" Garuwashi asked.
"These men mean everything to me. They have followed
me from villages and cities to foreign lands. Where I have
gone, they have gone. When I have told a hundred to take
a hill, knowing it would cost ninety their lives, they have
obeyed. They are lions. If they are to die, they should die
in battle, not dishonored by their lord. Tomorrow, you
will face twenty thousand Khalidorans and two thousand
meisters, who barely fought today. Without the sa'ceurai,
your men will be shaken."

"Seeing six thousand men and their unbeatable general
kill themselves may do that," Logan said dryly. "As will
looking at the backs of twenty thousand sa'ceurai who
could have been allies."

"You are a king. What would you do?" Garuwashi
asked.

"You ask me that when I have such an interest in your
answer?"

"I saw you put your closest friend to death for honor."

Logan looked at his hands. He said nothing for a long
time. "The night before Kylar went to the wheel, I sent a
man to break him out of my own gaol. Kylar refused to
leave because it would hurt my reign. He believed in me

that much. To be king means to accept that others will pay the price of your failures—and even your successes. Part of me died on that wheel. Whatever you decide, doen-Lantano, it has been an honor to fight beside you."

"King Gyre, if I choose expiation, will you be my second?"

Logan Gyre bowed low, his face rigid. "Doen-Lantano, I would be honored."

88

He'd been mad. Feir had followed the instructions of an insane archmagus who was seven centuries dead. Feir had made a sword that even he didn't fully understand. He had bent even Lantano Garuwashi to his will. He had believed, and now fraud would build on fraud unless Lantano Garuwashi chose to end it all.

Having sworn himself to the warleader, Feir would be expected to suicide along with Garuwashi, but he wouldn't. He knew that. Of course, the warleader might slay him. But Feir didn't think he'd allow that, either. So he would cheat again, and defend himself with magic. Every sa'ceurai in Midcyru would despise him. Perhaps one would hunt him down. That was Feir's future. Either that, or serving forever as Lantano Garuwashi's illusionist-in-chief, threading pretend flames onto his beautiful sword for the rest of his life.

That deception would destroy Lantano Garuwashi. If he ruled, he would rule badly, knowing himself to be dishonored. Garuwashi was not so young that honor was the only important thing in his life, but he was sa'ceurai to the roots of his soul. The best thing for Garuwashi would be to bury a blade in his own guts.

The sun sat low in the sky as Feir ducked to step into the council tent. Inside the tent sat King Gyre, Lord General Agon Brant, a wan Vi Sovari, and an older maja Feir didn't recognize. Feir took an empty seat. King Gyre sat with folded hands to Feir's right. His face was emotionless, but that in itself told Feir that the king was worried. As Feir pulled his chair in, something about Logan's right arm drew his attention. There was some magic there, woven small and tight into Logan's vambrace or his arm.

Logan noticed his attention and folded his hands in his lap, under the table. Feir dismissed it and continued looking around the table. Vi Sovari had covered herself with a modest maja's dress, but at the wrists and neck her gray-black skin-tight wetboy's garb was still visible. She had dark circles under her eyes and her skin was pale from her magical exertions at the dam. She was four places down the table, almost at the end of Feir's magical vision, but he could see she hadn't overextended her Talent. After Solon had used Curoch, he'd looked broken. His hair had grown in white, and he'd only escaped permanent injuries because Dorian was such a gifted Healer. With her escapades at the dam, Vi hadn't hurt herself at all. She'd come near the limit of her gifts, but hadn't exceeded it. Feir suspected that with a good night's sleep, she'd be ready to do as much tomorrow. She was easily the most powerful mage here. She might even equal Solon. And, sitting up straight now at a word from the old maja at her right hand, Vi felt huge. As a man's muscles looked most impressive after hard labor, so now did Vi's Talent feel enormous. It made Feir feel small, and he didn't like it.

The tent flap opened suddenly, and every eye turned to it, but the man who stepped in wasn't Lantano Garuwashi. It was a dark-haired, dark-eyed Alitaeran with a waxed mustache and an eagle sigil on his cloak pin. A Marcus then, from one of Alitaera's most important families, and certainly the leader of the two thousand Alitaeran lancers who'd arrived with the last of the magae this afternoon.

"I didn't realize this council had anything to do with the Alitaeran military," Lord General Agon Brant said. Clearly there was some bad blood there.

"This council decides if we've got an extra twenty thousand sa'ceurai or if we lose the six thousand we've got. I'd say that makes it a council of war. I'm Tiberius Antonius Marcus, Praetor, Fourth Army, Second Maniple. We're to defend the Chantry. Sisters, Your Majesty." He nodded to them.

"An honor, Praetor, please join us," Logan said.

Before the man sat, the flap opened again and Lantano Garuwashi strode in. He rested his hand over the pommel of his sword and walked to his seat and sat before acknowledging anyone.

"Well, everyone's here now except the Ceuran Regent himself, and of course, the dear Lae'knaught Overlord, who I suppose will walk in half an hour late and ask that we repeat everything," Lord General Brant said.

"I suppose he will," Logan said. "Since I told him this council wouldn't meet for another half an hour."

There were some snickers, but Feir breathed easier. A Lae'knaught overlord would likely have all sorts of magic-dampening paraphernalia that would spoil a perfectly good illusion.

What little chatter had been going around the room soon died as the sound of thousands of marching feet approached the tent. All twenty thousand sa'ceurai were coming.

This could get ugly.

The tent flap opened and a teenage boy and a middle-aged man with a fringe of auburn hair around an oiled pate stepped in. The middle-aged man had four locks of hair bound to his, all of them Ceuran, all of them old. He stood aside to make way for the boy, who couldn't have been more than fifteen. The boy had fiery orange hair, cropped close to his skull, and a single, very long lock bound into his hair. He wore ornately embroidered blue silk robes and a ruby-encrusted sword.

Feir had the insane thought of breaking off the biggest ruby and using it for his fraud.

"Sisters, Lords, Praetor, Your Majesty," the middle-aged Ceuran said, "may I introduce Sa'sa'ceurai Hideo Mitsurugi, sixth Regent Hideo, Lord of Mount Tenji, Protector of the Holy Honor, Keeper of the High Seat, Lord General of the Held Armies of Ceura."

People around the table greeted the boy. Logan stood and clasped his forearm. The boy was a little overwhelmed, but even as he followed protocol to the best of his ability, he could barely take his eyes off Lantano Garuwashi. He must be the boy's hero, Feir thought. Of course, Lantano Garuwashi was probably every young sa'ceurai's hero.

Garuwashi eyed the middle-aged man more than the boy. Was he the real power? The boy a figurehead? As the boy and his minister got closer and took their seats, Feir's heart dropped. The middle-aged man was a court mage of some kind, his Talent formidable. Garuwashi caught Feir's eye and shook his head slightly. It was the signal to abandon the fraud.

It was over. Only death would follow.

Hideo Mitsurugi cleared his throat. "I guess, uh, we might as well do what we're here for, shall we?" His eyes flicked upward as he tried to remember his lines. "It has been brought to our attention that claims have been brought forward by you or by your followers, doen-Lantano Garuwashi. We understand you have claimed to wield the Blade of Heaven, Ceur'caelestos."

"I have made such claims, doen-Hideo," Garuwashi said. There was something almost cheerful in Garuwashi's face. He'd been doing something wrong that he hadn't liked, and now it was finished.

"By ancient law and prophecy, the holder of Ceur'caelestos is to be Ceura's king, a man to usher in the return of the High King, whose reign will announce the birth of the Champion of the Light." Mitsurugi paused. He'd lost his place. A panicked look came into his blue eyes.

The middle-aged mage whispered a prompt in the boy's ear. It seemed to embarrass Hideo almost to tears. "Do you claim the High Seat of Ceura, Lantano Garuwashi?"

"I do."

What was he doing? Feir shot a look over at Garuwashi's sword. The dragon of the pommel grinned emptily like a boy who'd lost both front teeth.

"Hold on," Lord General Agon said. "It was my understanding that Ceura's Regent is doen-Hideo Watanabe.

How do we even know that—pardon me—this boy has the authority to test Lantano Garuwashi?"

"You dare!" the middle-aged sa'ceurai said, putting a hand to his sword.

"Yes, I dare," Agon said. "And if you draw that sword, I'll dare feed it to you."

"Ha. You're an old cripple."

"Which will make your death all the more embarrassing," Agon said.

"Stop!" Mitsurugi said. "Hideo Watanabe is my father." He looked down. "Was. He gathered this army. But before he marched, I learned that he didn't intend to test you, doen-Lantano. He intended to kill you—whether or not you held the real Ceur'caelestos. I confronted him for dishonoring the regency." Tears came to Mitsurugi's eyes. "We dueled, and I slew him."

Feir couldn't believe it. The boy killed his father for the *idea* of Lantano Garuwashi.

"I am Regent now, and by my father's blood that stains my hands, I have the right to test the man who would be our king," Hideo Mitsurugi said. "Please, doen-Lantano, show us Ceur'caelestos."

There was the sound of something tearing and everyone stopped and looked to the back of the tent, where a knife was cutting a vertical slash all the way to the ground. Instantly, every maja and magus embraced their Talent and a dozen hands went to the hilts of swords. An assassin would have a hard time with this crowd.

A hand poked in and waved. "Pardon me," a man's deep voice said outside the tent. "If I step inside, am I going to be skewered?" Not waiting for an answer, he stepped inside.

He had pure white hair with black tips, deeply tanned olive skin, and a muscular bare chest beneath a rich cloak. He wore loose white pants and a thick gold crown sat snug against his brow.

"Solon?" Feir asked, astonished.

Solon smiled. "Only to you, my dear friend. As for the rest of you, pardon my unconventional entrance, but you have twenty thousand surly sa'ceurai blocking the front of the tent. I am Solonariwan Tofusin, King of Seth. I would say emperor, but as of ten years ago we have no more colonies, so 'Emperor' is a tad pretentious. Your Majesty, King Gyre, I bring a thousand men to your efforts. I did also bring five ships, but someone flooded the river this morning and now I have only two and I'm lucky not to have lost any men. Sisters, should we emerge from this conflict alive, I will be asking the Chantry for reimbursement. Feir, it seems you travel in exalted company these days. Ah, this must be Sister Ariel Wyant, a legend in your own time, and Vi Sovari, both buxom and brilliant—I've heard so much about you."

"Eat shit," Vi said.

Gasps arose around the table, and Sister Ariel put her hands on her temples.

"Apparently all I've heard is true," Solon said.

He wasn't acting like himself. Solon never prattled, but now he was speaking so quickly that even if anyone had known what to say they couldn't have fit a word in.

"I have to tell you, on my way here, I saw a very dour Lae'knaught gentlemen speaking some rather choice words at being denied entry by the selfsame sa'ceurai who barred yours truly from said engagement. But here I stand, at considerable cost to my kingdom, and most especially my marriage—it took me weeks of moping about Whitecliff to secure my wife's permission to come. Oh, you married men can pretend to be the masters of your castles and keeps and so forth, but the mistress of the bedchamber is the mistress of the master, eh? Regardless, here I stand, and I must say, the crowning jewel of my visit is this: Lantano Garuwashi, it is a great honor to meet you." Solon strode over to the sa'ceurai and extended his hand.

"I don't clasp hands with fish," Lantano Garuwashi said.

Hideo Mitsurugi snorted, but no one else said a word.

Suddenly, Solon's rushed and—to Feir's eyes—panicky demeanor shifted. Solon had tripped over his tongue to get to Lantano Garuwashi, but now that he had the man's attention, he was utterly patient. "It seems to me," Solon said, "that a man born to an iron blade should not scorn the friendship of kings."

Dead silence settled on the room. No one spoke like that to Lantano Garuwashi.

Solon continued, "You have no peer when it comes to the spilling of blood, Lantano Garuwashi. If you died today, your only legacy would be blood. Wouldn't you rather your legacy was that of a man who spilled blood to quench the fires of war? Can butcher's hands become carpenter's hands? As a brother king, I ask you once more, and once only, will you take the hand of friendship?" Solon stood with hand extended.

It was an odd thing to ask a doomed man. Feir expected Garuwashi to spit in Solon's face. But Garuwashi stood. "Let there be peace between us," he said, and took Solon's hand.

Standing right next to them, his own bulk blocking most of the table from seeing what transpired, Feir saw sudden confusion in Lantano Garuwashi's eyes. He withdrew his hand from Solon's clasp with one finger still pressed against his palm, concealing something. Then he rested that hand on Ceur'caelestos's pommel. With a tiny sound, something clicked home, and Feir understood. Gods! "The greatest red gives dragon's heart and head." Feir had thought it meant the greatest red ruby, and it did, but it also meant the greatest red mage: Solon.

Garuwashi whipped the sword out of its scabbard and slammed it on the table.

A perfect ruby redder than ruby-red burned in the pommel, and it swam with deep magic, though Feir hadn't imbued it with any weaves. The mistarille blade had patterns like a folded steel blade, but its patterns glittered like diamonds, sparkling and then transparent, letting a man see all the way through the blade into the heart of its magic. As they watched, every diamond-like ripple faded to a purer translucence like a slow shockwave as the twin dragons breathed fire. The fire blossomed in a thick bar from hilt all the way to the point of the sword. The heat of it warmed Feir's face.

Feir had created something beyond himself. He was a great smith, but he wasn't this good. Awed, Feir turned to Solon. The new King Tofusin grinned at him.

"Call me fraud or call me king," Lantano Garuwashi said, and if there was a trembling of wonder in his voice, no one noticed it through their own.

Hideo Mitsurugi's jaw was slack. "Lantano Garuwashi, I declare you—"

"My lord!" the court mage interrupted.

Mitsurugi acquiesced. "My ancestors have looked forward to this day for centuries. We've wanted it and feared it. Perhaps the regents most of all. Frauds have been attempted, so the Regent's sword carries a test. I beg your pardon, doen-Lantano, but it is my duty." He drew his ruby-encrusted blade and gave the pommel a sharp twist. It clicked and he pulled half of the hilt off. Inside was a thin scroll woven with preservation magics. Mitsurugi read it, his lips moving as he puzzled out the old language.

"Lantano Garuwashi, banish the fires from the blade."

Garuwashi took the blade and the fires died. How did he know how to do that?

"I need a candle," Mitsurugi said, and someone slid one down the table to him. He picked it up and brought it toward the blade.

Terror seized Feir's breath. Mitsurugi brought the candle to the very spot Feir had hidden his vanity, his own smithmark. The crossed war hammers practically leapt out of the metal.

Mitsurugi sighed.

Feir's heart stopped.

Mitsurugi said, "Down to Oren Razin's crossed war hammers, it's real. This blade is Ceur'caelestos. Lantano Garuwashi, you are the lost King of Ceura. The sa'ceurai stand at your word."

Real. Not a forgery. The very things that made it different from Curoch were what convinced the Regent that Feir's blade was real. Feir's limbs felt weak. He had a single moment to think, *how embarrassing, I can't possibly pass—*

Then he passed out.

89

After Feir collapsed—and what was that about? Ariel wondered—the odious Overlord of the Lae'knaught, Julus Rotans, finally won his way through the waiting sa'ceurai and made it into the tent. Hideo Mitsurugi wanted to go immediately and announce that Ceura had found its king, but Logan had asked him to wait. Ariel still didn't know why.

Julus Rotans was in his late forties, his figure still trim and military and his features pure Alitaeran. He wore a white tabard emblazoned with a sun and a white cloak with twelve gold chevrons. Sister Ariel couldn't make out any other details: the man emanated such a deep aura of ill health she almost gagged. He didn't remove his gauntlets as he sat, and mercifully there were no open sores on his face, but Julus Rotans was a leper. Worse, his strain of leprosy was the simplest kind to Heal. Even Sister Ariel could do it—but it would take magic.

"So, everyone's here already," Julus Rotans said. "I see. No need to include the Lae'knaught in the planning, huh? Just throw us at the thickest part of the enemy, and whether we live or die, you win."

Logan Gyre didn't look perturbed. "Overlord, I have wronged you," he said. "Your representatives told me it was unfair and unwise—actually, I think the word was 'stupid'—for me to assume direct control over your men. Forgive me. I was worried they would betray me. That was unworthy of me, and it was indeed stupid."

The overlord's eyes narrowed, wary. Everyone else watched carefully.

"Today, due to the terrain, your men didn't fight, but tomorrow, we will rely on you. Your losses may be significant. You have our only heavy cavalry, and you will indeed hold the center. There have been . . . ugly rumors that your men wish to withdraw and let 'all these wytches' kill each other." Logan sighed. "I know you feel compelled to be here, Overlord Rotans, so I wish to drop the compulsion now. And I do so hereby: Overlord, I freely grant you the fifteen-year lease to the Cenarian lands for your use. I hereby release you from fielding an army and putting them at my service."

"What?" the overlord asked. He wasn't the only one incredulous at the table. Without the Lae'knaught's five thousand, the armies would be seriously weakened.

Logan held up one finger, and the overlord sat up, sure this was the teeth of the trap. "I only ask that if you wish to withdraw from this fight, that you declare your intentions immediately so that we may know how much of an army we will have."

Overlord Rotans licked his lips. "That's all?" It was too fair a request for him to protest. Logan didn't want the Lae'knaught fielding the army and then melting away at the first Khalidoran charge. He still looked puzzled, so he hadn't seen the teeth of Logan's offer yet, and the damn fool was about to speak. He was going to accept the offer if Ariel didn't do something.

"I'm only a woman," Sister Ariel said, "but it seems to me that such cowardice will make recruitment a challenge in a few countries. Let's see. Cenaria, of course, will feel betrayed. Ceura too. Oh, and I doubt the praetor would be impressed, so definitely Alitaera—that's a tough one to lose. Waeddryn and Modai may still send recruits; pity they're so small."

"And their people so historically reluctant to die for the light of reason," Praetor Marcus said with some satisfaction.

"And this is such a bad time to have trouble with recruitment," Sister Ariel said.

"Why's that?" Marcus asked, playing along.

"Some superstition in Ezra's Wood recently slew five thousand Lae'knaught."

Marcus whistled. "That's some superstition."

"You're vile, all of you. You're the friends of darkness," Overlord Rotans said.

"There's the crux," King Solonariwan Tofusin said. "You see, friends, the Lae'knaught have no country; they have only ideas. If they abandon us, they can survive the allegations of betrayal and cowardice; what will cut them is *hypocrisy*. They can betray us, what they can't betray is their principles. Today we faced perhaps a hundred meisters, but this Godking Wanhope brought two thousand. Where were the rest?"

"Do you actually know the answer to that question?" Lantano Garuwashi asked.

"We passed a town called Reigukhas on our way up the river," Solon said. "It was dead. From the magic still in the air, hundreds—perhaps thousands—of meisters worked for at least twelve hours raising krul. Those krul then devoured the city's inhabitants. Tomorrow we will face actual, real creatures of darkness, Overlord. I'd estimate their numbers to be in excess of twenty thousand."

"Shit, there goes our twenty thousand sa'ceurai advantage," Vi said.

"One sa'ceurai is not offset by one krul," Hideo Mitsurugi said, offended.

"Do you even know what a krul is?" Vi asked.

"The point is," Sister Ariel broke in, "when they have a chance to fight the spawn of darkness, the world will see that the Lae'knaught are hypocrites who prefer to turn tail."

Julus Rotans was actually shaking with rage. "Go to hell, wytch. Go to hell, all of you. Tomorrow you will see how the Laetunariverissiknaught fight. We will take the center of any charge. I will lead it myself."

"A generous offer. We accept," Logan Gyre said immediately, "with the caveat that I ask that you not lead any charge yourself. I'm afraid, Overlord Rotans, that there are simply too many who would wish to see you fall in this battle."

The obvious target of the comment was the magae, but Sister Ariel saw that what Logan feared was the Lae'knaught's own men, who were doubtless chafing at having to fight beside wytches. If Julus Rotans fell, the Lae'knaught would retreat. In offering an honorable exit from rash words—or had the Overlord actually hoped to die and thereby allow his men to retreat and the Cenarians and everyone else to be betrayed and slaughtered?—Logan Gyre not only kept the Overlord alive and his army at Logan's disposal, he also might have gained some goodwill from the man, who if nothing else had shown that he was willing to talk. Sometimes the devil you knew was better than the one you didn't.

Sister Ariel looked at Logan Gyre with newfound respect. In this meeting of kings and magi, praetors and overlords, he had taken command without the least effort. He must have had some intelligence of a Lae'knaught betrayal or he wouldn't have brought the matter up. Now he had effectively defanged the threat, and managed to look magnanimous doing it.

"Now, before we discuss specifics of our disposition on the battlefield, does anyone else have anything to add? Sister Viridiana?" Logan asked. He looked at Vi, who looked like she'd been on the verge of offering something for a while.

Vi bit her lip. "There was an explosion of magic earlier this afternoon on the other side of Black Barrow. Our source said there was a fight between the Godking's meisters and a bunch following one of his rivals, a man named Moburu Ursuul."

"May the God see fit to send that traitor's soul to hell on the edge of my sword," the praetor whispered.

"Moburu is claiming to be some prophesied High King," Vi said. "Apparently, he seems to fulfill the conditions. I didn't think anything of it until the Regent said that making Lantano a king would clear the way for a High King."

Sister Ariel wondered if her own face was as pale as everyone else's around the table. She probably knew more about the High King than any of them, but it had never occurred to her that it might be a Khalidoran who fulfilled the prophecy.

"You said Moburu fought the Godking. Who won?" Logan asked.

"Moburu was driven to Black Barrow."

"In our prophecies," Lantano Garuwashi said, standing, "When Ceura has a king once more, that king will fight beside the High King. I will never fight beside this Moburu. This I swear on my soul." He put his hand on Ceur'caelestos and it flared to life in answer. Then he sheathed the blade and sat.

"That's good enough for me," Praetor Marcus said. "In Alitaera the prophecies of a High King speak of days of turmoil and woe, so I don't envy you the troubles the next decades may visit on you. But I think that's one problem we may safely dismiss for now."

"Sister Viridiana, you said you had two things?" Logan asked.

Vi glanced at Sister Ariel, "I'm not actually a full Sister yet. Anyway, I'm sorry to bring a personal matter before this council, but does anyone know where Elene Cromwyll is?"

No one showed any sign of recognition. "The name sounds familiar," King Gyre said. "Who is she?"

"She's Kylar's wife," Vi said. "And he's going to come for her."

Logan's face lost all color. Everyone else looked curious but unknowing, except for Solon and Feir, who both looked afraid. Afraid of Kylar? Regardless, they knew him. Sister Ariel's fear was for Vi. The damn fool girl had casually spilled a truth that could spell her own destruction. "Oh, by the way, I'm not married to Kylar." If Logan had proved how excellent he was at this kind of council, Vi had shown herself to stand at the antipodes.

"You're right, that's more of a personal matter. I'll speak with you about that later," Logan said. He thought Vi was crazy. Thank the gods. "Are there any other questions?"

"I have some," Praetor Marcus said. "What if Black Barrow isn't meant to keep things out? What if it's meant to keep something in? What if Moburu wasn't driven there? What if he went to get something?"

"Oh, gods," someone said.

90

The armies formed up while it was still dark. Stomach knotted with tension, Logan tended to his horse, checking the straps a third time. The allied armies were stretched left and right, extending further and deeper than anything he'd ever seen. The Lae'knaught's five thousand would lead the charge. Behind them, twenty thousand Cenarian infantry would take the center, flanked by twenty thousand sa'ceurai. Lantano Garuwashi's original five thousand sa'ceurai would secure the forest to the west to make sure the Khalidorans didn't have any nasty surprises hiding there, and if possible sweep from the forest into the Godking's camp. A thousand of Vi's Shield Sisters would hold the dam and the bridges from magical attacks. The other seven thousand had spread out among the armies according to a logic they didn't deign to share with Logan. The two thousand Alitaeran light cavalry and one thousand Sethi light infantry would be their reserves.

Much would depend on the first Lae'knaught charge. With twenty thousand krul added to their ranks, the

Khalidorans would have forty-five thousand to stand against the allies' fifty-three thousand—or sixty thousand if one counted the Shield Sisters. The Khalidorans would have their backs to the Dead Demesne. If the first Lae'knaught charge could shatter them against it, the army could be halved and separated from command.

Of course, no one really knew how krul fought. The magi had offered centuries-old accounts of brutes with great strength, poor eyesight, and an inability to feel pain. That last was the most worrying. "What kind of a monster can't feel pain?" Garuwashi asked. Overlord Rotans jerked in his chair. "They'll die like anything else," he said, angry at the curious glances.

Odd man, never took off his heavy gauntlets in six hours of deliberations. And through it all, Solon had offered excellent suggestions that reminded Logan of how much time Solon had spent on tactics with Regnus Gyre. Solon, Logan's tutor, was now a king. It was all Logan could do to keep from demanding an explanation from the man right in front of everyone.

"Your Majesty," his guard Aurella said, "do you remember last month, when you went down to the Hole again?"

Logan made it a habit to go every month. He was sorry to inflict it on his bodyguards, but he hadn't stopped. Logan looked at Aurella, sitting ahorse, holding her sword like she knew what to do with it now. She was one of the few women of the Order of the Garter who'd chosen to join Logan's bodyguard rather than go back to their lives after Pavvil's Grove. Logan hadn't been surprised when Garuwashi had singled her out as a natural talent with the sword. Not as strong as a man, he'd said pointedly, but damn good for a woman. Aurella had wisely chosen not to take offense. Logan said, "You asked me what kind of idiot I was to keep going down to that hell, when it gives me nightmares every time." She had, of course, been more diplomatic.

"You told me it was to prove nightmares had no power over you," Aurella said.

"You're making me nervous."

"I think you should mount, sire."

Logan mounted. The gloom of night was lifting by slow degrees, revealing nothing more than the deeper blackness of the Dead Demesne advancing toward them. It took Logan far too long to understand what he was seeing. It was krul, bodies dark gray or mottled black or even white, loping forward in a massive wave. There had to be eighty thousand krul alone. The Khalidoran army was at least a hundred thousand strong, and every one of them stood between Logan and his wife. His right arm tingled as rage washed over him.

"Vi," Logan barked. "Give me light!"

"Look away!" the maja shouted. The order was an exercise in futility. The Sisters had given Vi a new dress, deeming both the scandalous wetboy grays and the plain robes of an Adept ill suited to the woman they were now calling Battle Mistress. The new dress was red, with skirts divided for riding. Logan suspected it might be woven entirely of magic. It shimmered despite the low light, and—as Vi's figure did in any garb—it demanded attention. "Luxe exeat!" she yelled.

Logan barely looked away in time, and despite his closed eyes, the light was blinding. There was a rush and when he looked, a white fireball was arcing out over the plain, then it froze in midair. Moments later, a dozen more followed from points all along the line, illuminating the charging krul, who'd already closed half the distance.

"Signal ready!"

Another maja in Vi's cadre gestured and a magical version of the signal flag flew into the air over Logan's head, glowing and big enough for the entire army to see.

The rattling of armor and stirrups, low curses and prayers, the creaking of leather, the popping of knuckles, and the synchronized clash of the Lae'knaught lances on shields yielded to the sudden ululations of the sa'ceurai battle chant.

"Advance!"

The magical signal winked out and was replaced with a waving red banner. The sa'ceurai ululations pitched higher, and the army rumbled forward.

91

Kylar came through the pass as the armies on the plains below sprinted the last paces toward each other. He was too far away to hear the crash, but he could see the shock of it passing through the ranks. He continued running, not slowing as he passed the camp followers who had gathered to watch the battle, many of them carrying all their possessions in case the battle turned out badly.

He lost sight of the battle as he sprinted down the valley. Those few armed men he encountered he passed before they could raise a challenge, until he got to Black Bridge. There, half a dozen men with pikes and short swords at their belts turned from the battle to watch his approach.

"Hold!" a young man shouted.

As Kylar stopped in front of them, a crack like thunder shook the earth. Kylar was the only one who kept his feet. He turned his eyes to Black Barrow. The slight rises and dips of the plain between him and the great dome were covered with warriors, both human and krul, but the battle slowed as those not in the front line looked to the great shining black sphere. Another thunder crack shook the plain, and this time, jagged cracks raced from the highest point of the dome down its sides. Men cursed in fear and wonder.

The third crack shattered the dome from inside. Huge chunks of black rock three feet thick exploded into the air and rained onto the Dead Demesne and the battlefield, crushing krul and men alike. Most of the dome still stood, quivering, edges sharp around the hole in its crown.

More sharp blows followed and the rest of the dome fell in, raising a huge cloud of black dust like a stain of night across the morning. Something huge moved inside it.

"What is that?" the young man guarding the bridge asked.

Kylar was already running.

Most of the fighting men had noticed nothing. The grim business of war took all their attention. The allies' armies were doing extremely well if what Kylar had seen of their relative numbers was accurate. He saw one of Agon's archers fit an odd arrow to his Ymmuri bow and shoot. Two hundred paces away, one of the Khalidoran signal flags went up in flames. It was obviously on purpose, because only one or two Khalidoran signal flags remained on the entire plain. Kylar wondered briefly whose good idea that had been.

Curoch was still strapped to his back and the black ka'kari concealed it. Kylar drew neither as he closed with the rear of the Cenarian line. His battle senses seemed to explode, obliterating conscious thought, blotting out everything but the sharp outlines of the figures in his path. This group was spearmen, packed tightly and surging forward. There would be no slipping through these men. They pushed against the backs of the men in front of them with oblong shields, holding their elbows up so their spears wouldn't become entangled in the press.

Kylar leapt lightly and pushed off one man's shoulder, twisted, pushed off another's spear hand, then planted both feet on the shoulders of a man in the second row and jumped as hard as he could. He was over the Cenarians so fast he didn't even hear their cries of surprise.

His leap took him over the first six lines of krul. Kylar read the bodies of those among which he would land. Five black creatures and one a diseased flaky white that seemed their leader. Two saw him. Kylar tucked his knees to his chest, flipped, then threw his feet forward at the last second. His feet connected with a big black krul over its eyes. Its head snapped back and its neck cracked. Kylar rolled to his feet.

He'd never seen krul before. They were shaped like men with grotesquely bulging muscles, their eyes small and piggish, brows prominent, shoulders heavy, necks almost nonexistent, but beyond that, each was different, as if they were the products of many different hands. The one closest to Kylar's left was covered with fur, two others were hairless. The one directly in front of him had a nose smashed upward into a snout. It also had thin curling horns. Three had an extra knuckle's worth of finger on their hands, sharpened into claws. Their skin or fur was the black of a bloated corpse, and they smelled of rot. None wore armor or clothes except the white one, and few had weapons other than their claws or horns. The white was taller than the others, more than six feet, and recovered first, swinging a huge dull blade at Kylar.

Kylar dodged it and crushed the white's throat with a kick. Kylar darted behind another, grabbed its horns, and broke its neck before he realized that perhaps a dozen black krul weren't moving at all; they simply stared at their dying white leader. It was hissing, trying to breathe. Unnerved by their sudden listlessness, Kylar paused for a moment—a pause that in a normal battle could have been lethal. He pulled a tanto from his belt and jammed it into the white krul's heart. Krul apparently kept their hearts where men did, because it died as he withdrew the blade.

What little light had been in the piggish eyes around him guttered out. The ten krul looked lost. For three impossible seconds, they didn't move. Kylar could sense them searching for something. Then, as if each had been yanked on a leash toward a new master, the krul bolted in ten different directions.

A jolt of fear more intense than any he'd ever felt lashed through Kylar's bond with Vi. She was two hundred paces to his left.

Kylar ran through the Dead Demesne, over corpses that looked oddly fresh but didn't stink. He was behind the main line of krul, but there were still hundreds that saw him. His Talent filled him like a fire. He was a blur.

As always, he could feel Vi more intensely the closer he got. She was in the middle of a thick knot of fighting. The sheer volume of magic was astounding. Magae flanked Vi and they faced a dozen Vürdmeisters with vir clawing through every inch of exposed skin. On a white charger in white enameled armor, Logan and a score of his bodyguards faced dozens of monsters. A great sword-

tooth cat leapt for the king. Logan slashed his sword into
the top of its head. Its claws scored his horse's armor as
it fell dead.

A wash of fire spurted from a Vürdmeister toward
the king and lapped against a shimmering shield one of
the magae had put around him. A squat red krul, a head
shorter than most of its kin but three times as wide, with
skin that looked like it was entirely made of bone, grabbed
a horse's leg. The horse whinnied as its leg cracked. It
fell, spilling one of Logan's bodyguards to the ground. He
jumped up and slashed at the creature, but his thin blade
rang off its skin. He stabbed it; his blade bowed but then
pierced the creature's skin. It ignored it and grabbed his
arm, then his face. Gnasher grabbed the man's other arm
and tried to pull him up onto his horse. His scream was
muffled against the krul's palm until it crushed helmet
and head together. Gnasher kept pulling, not understanding the guard was already dead.

Greenish krul with splayed legs like frogs leapt at
Logan, trying to knock him from his saddle. Vi blasted
them aside with Talent and bodyguards opened their
throats.

As Logan's knot of warriors ground slowly toward
the Dead Demesne, a Vürdmeister beyond the fighting
chanted calmly. Kylar saw the sword-tooth cat's split head
mend, and moments later it stood. Everywhere, the scene
was repeated. The Vürdmeisters were instantly replacing
the most powerful krul they lost.

Kylar unlimbered Curoch and decapitated that Vürdmeister, and then another before it could raise the red-
skinned ogre, and cut a third in half. Through the press of
bodies, he saw Vi. A krul claw slapped into her arm, but

bounced off as her blood-red dress hardened like armor. She sliced off the krul's arm and met Kylar's eyes. She pointed behind him.

It was the Titan, looming huge. It had cracked open Black Barrow and now it was coming to war. The sheer size of it was hard to believe. It was shaped almost like a man, its skin a coolly luminous blue under scale armor, its hair gold and short and spiky like an unruly boy's, its eyes black with silver vertical irises like a cat's, its muscles smooth and beautiful. But if it was a god from the front, it was a demon from behind. Huge spikes extended from its spine, reptilian wings draped from its shoulders, and a rat-like hairy tail dragged behind it. It wielded a spiked pole as a cudgel.

"Kylar!" Vi shouted. "Kill it!"

He could feel her intimately enough to know she hadn't meant to invoke the bond, but she'd done it anyway. Like he'd been lashed with a cat o'nine tails, his attention focused instantly, irrevocably on the Titan. He had no choice.

92

Kaldrosa Wyn was lying in the shadow of a huge krul corpse. This one was shaped like a bear with scabby pale skin devoid of fur. She was near the crest of a hill in the Dead Demesne, north of Black Barrow—or north of where Black Barrow had been. The dome had come down minutes earlier, scaring the hell out of her. From her position, she could see several hundred of the other soldiers. Most of them were sa'ceurai, the rest were Agon's Dogs. She'd come because her husband Tomman had, and if he was going to take a mission this dangerous, she was going with him.

A low whistle trilled in the distance, and seconds later, was repeated by someone closer. It was time. Kaldrosa pulled the muddy bag at her feet up and opened it. She dressed slowly, carefully, trying to work blood into her stiff arms and legs. They'd been crawling and lying in muck for two days, and it was a wonder she could move at all. They'd blackened their armor and weapons so they wouldn't reflect sunlight, but she was still as quiet as possible. They didn't want to spoil their gambit this close to its fruition.

The Ymmuri bows were the biggest problem. To string them, the Ymmuri warmed them by a fire for at least half an hour. That wasn't an option. Someone had foreseen it, though, and the archers gathered around an odd, kohled Modaini magus named Antoninus Wervel.

Otaru Tomaki, one of Lantano Garuwashi's advisers, was in command. Kaldrosa didn't know what he'd seen to make him decide they should attack now—or if he had seen anything. Tightening the last stubborn leather strap between Tomman's shoulder blades with numb fingers, she poked her head over the bear, not shrinking from its touch. Her horror at the monsters had peaked the first night. She might have gone mad if Tomman hadn't lain next to her, his fingers interlaced with hers. Now, the monsters were just meat, and oddly unstinking meat at that.

The Khalidoran command tents seemed almost abandoned. There were a score of rich pavilions in a rough circle, but only a half dozen guards patrolled the area, and they focused on a pavilion beside the largest one. Four female meisters stood around it. That confirmed it for Kaldrosa. It was the concubines' pavilion.

The Dead Demesne ended a hundred paces from the pavilions. Tomman and the other archers were creeping as close as they could. She knew Tomman could make the shot from two hundred paces, but they didn't want to take chances; everything depended on being quick and lethal.

Turning to sit against the bear, she stretched her arms and rolled her head. South of her hill, the black dust from the dome was settling in the city that had been hidden beneath Black Barrow. In the center was an expansive white castle. The city itself was at the highest point of the plain, so Kaldrosa could see nothing of the battle beyond it. She pulled on her helmet and turned in time to see every guard and meister in sight tumble to the ground with arrows stuck in them.

There was another whistle and a thousand men jumped to their feet and ran toward the pavilions. The sa'ceurai usually shouted war cries, but now they were silent. A few stumbled and fell with muscles cramping from their nights of exposure, but most reached the pavilions in seconds.

Otaru Tomaki held up a hand with four fingers extended, gave a tempo, and cut. A hundred sa'ceurai ringed the pavilion that had been guarded while the others fanned out. On the count Tomaki had given, they cut through the walls of the pavilion on four sides simultaneously and stormed in.

By the time Kaldrosa arrived, maybe five seconds later, the six eunuchs inside the tent were dead, and the lone woman was ringed by wary sa'ceurai. The woman was dark-haired, of a slender build, maybe sixteen. She was dressed richly and held a sword, waving it wildly. "Get away! Stay back!" she shouted.

It struck Kaldrosa that a hundred sa'ceurai were probably not the kind of rescuers a Cenarian princess would expect. "Your Highness," Kaldrosa said, "be calm. We're here to save you. We've come from your husband."

"My husband? What madness is this? Stay back!"

"You're Jenine Gyre, aren't you?" Kaldrosa asked. The girl fit the description, but she'd never seen her.

"Time!" Otaru Tomaki said. "We've got to go!"

"Jenine *Gyre?*" the girl laughed, twisting the name. "That's been one of my names."

"King Logan sent us. He's missed you terribly, Your Highness. You're the reason we're here," Kaldrosa said.

"Logan? Logan's dead." Their puzzled looks must have convinced her it was no trap. She went white. "Logan's alive? 'The Cenarian king.' Oh gods." The sword tumbled from her fingers. She passed out.

Otaru Tomaki caught her before she hit the floor. He hoisted her over a shoulder. "Good work, easier this way."

"I've never seen someone actually swoon," Antoninus Wervel said. The kohl connecting his eyebrows had smudged and run from his days in the Dead Demesne, making him look more freakish than menacing. "Very well, are we ready?"

"Thirty seconds," Tomaki barked.

The sa'ceurai, who'd held perfect order to that moment, bolted, looting every pavilion they could in a frenzy. Kaldrosa counted, and every last warrior was back by twenty-eight. At thirty, Antoninus Wervel extended his hands to the sky and a blue flame whooshed out, turning green at its apex.

Then they waited. A tense minute later, an answering green flare arced into the sky from the opposite side of Black Barrow.

"We go east, through the Dead Demesne," Tomaki said. "Go!"

93

In the tumult of clashing arms, grunts, curses, clashing sword on sword or sword on shield, the thump of cudgels hitting flesh, the muted crack of breaking limbs or shattering skulls, the whistle of air escaping from a throat instead of a mouth, the familiar stench of blood and bile and death-loosened bowels and the sweat of exertion and the sweat of fear, Kylar was suddenly serene. He kicked low into a white krul's shin, snapping it. He slid past the falling beast, lunged to slide Curoch into another krul's throat, reversed his grip on the sword, and stabbed it through the white krul's skull before it hit the earth.

Its death and the sudden slackness in the krul nearest him gave Kylar a moment to look at the Titan. It had reached the thick of the fight, a hundred paces away. It swept its spiked club in a savage swathe. Krul and men alike were lofted into the air, pierced by spikes longer than swords and then flung free on its next slash.

Kylar plunged back into the maelstrom like a diver into a cool lake on a blistering day. Vi's command to kill gave the world a beautiful focus. There was no fear about protecting others less capable. No worry about advancing at a slow enough rate that the rest of a line of plodding sword-swingers could keep pace. No thought of concealing how good he was. Not even the muted horror of killing men. A dark facsimile of a Harani bull reared up before Kylar, lashing stump-like feet, slashing mighty tusks. Kylar dodged backward, hesitated until it was about to land on all fours, then dove beneath it. Curoch passed through the bull's abdomen like a comb passing through a princess's hair on the hundredth stroke. It was beautiful. The creature trumpeted in pain and its bowels squirted onto the ground. Kylar was already killing something else.

He'd acquired a stabbing spear somewhere, and now he spun into another knot of krul. None had time to swing weapon or claw at him. The spear spun and Curoch darted like a hummingbird, and eight beasts died. He wasn't fighting, or killing, or butchering. It was a dance. He didn't decapitate a krul unless he needed to change the direction of its falling body; it was faster to clip a single artery. Faster to cut a hamstring. Faster to cut across a face to take both eyes. He stopped killing the black krul half the time, focusing on the white, the bears, the aurochs, and the Harani bulls—anything that was in his path to the Titan.

He blinded a Harani bull in one eye, made it spin, slashing at him with its tusks, then speared its other eye. Blinded and mad with rage, it charged, plowing through line upon line of krul, trampling and killing. Kylar found himself laughing.

When the Titan was less than thirty paces away, for the first time, Kylar had a cut parried. This krul was different from any he'd yet seen. Where most krul seemed to be crafted on the idea that stronger-is-better, bigger-is-best, this creature was man-shaped and as lean as Kylar. Instead of skin, it had a blood-red chitin exoskeleton. Its face was a featureless chitin oval. It held two swords of the same material and stood in a perfect ready stance. It countered Three Daisies with Garon's Stand. Kiriae's Crouch with Boulders Falling. But when it tried to stop the Knot Loosed with Sydie's Wrath, Curoch punched through its chitinous chest. Kylar decapitated it to be sure and saw that the exoskeletoned red warriors were the only krul around the Titan. As the Titan swung its club, they easily rolled out of the path of every swipe. There were thirteen thirteens of them, swarming like fire ants.

Between the fire ants and the Titan, the Cenarian center was close to collapsing. The Lae'knaught, the Cenarians, the Ceuran reserves, and the Alitaeran reserves had all come here, but the center could not hold. The Titan was as tall as seven or eight men, and neither stupid nor slow. Where the cavalry bunched, it killed half a dozen horses and men in a single swipe. Where they spread out, the fire ants darted into the gaps and killed men at every turn.

The Titan lifted a foot to stomp on a horseman charging him, and the ants scattered. Kylar leapt through the gap. The Titan's foot came down, crushing man and horse to jelly and shaking the ground. Kylar jumped and grabbed its calf. The Titan wore scale armor made of scales so big that Kylar didn't dare imagine what they had come from, but the straps holding the armor together were thick leather and enormous hemp ropes. With Curoch sheathed, Kylar clambered up to the Titan's belt.

The Titan noticed him and spun so fast Kylar's feet

lost their grip and swung out horizontal. Kylar saw chitin warriors crushed by the unexpected move. The Titan swatted at him and Kylar was batted into the folds of its furled wings.

Cocooned in soft, stinking leather, Kylar slipped toward the ground. He grabbed a wing bone as thick around as his thigh. He climbed as quickly as he could and Curoch came to hand as the Titan noticed that he was still hanging on. Kylar slashed once, twice, three times, and the soft, hand-thick membrane parted. He slapped Curoch onto his back and slipped through the hole as the Titan unfurled its enormous wings with a snap. Caught halfway through the wing, Kylar was almost knocked unconscious by the whiplash. The Titan furled its wings to try to shake him loose again and Kylar pushed through and jumped.

He caught himself on one of the huge spines protruding from the Titan's back. The Titan spun again, but didn't see him, and then was distracted by some attack Kylar couldn't see. Kylar's feet found purchase on a lower spine, and timing the movements of the Titan's body, Kylar clambered from spine to spine.

There was nowhere to brace himself for a blow to cut into the Titan's spine, so Kylar kept climbing until he reached the broad gorget that protected the Titan's neck. A fringe of metallic hair protruded over it, and Kylar grabbed a handful, bracing himself to ram Curoch into the back of the Titan's head.

Magic arced through the metallic hairs and blasted him off his feet. Kylar spun, hanging on by one hand.

He lost his grip and caught the gorget itself, his hand between the metal and the Titan's skin. Kylar swung around and hacked blindly into the Titan's neck. Magic burst from the Titan in a shockwave. The world went black and Kylar felt himself spinning into space. There was nothing to grab, no possible way to stop his fall—and from this height, falling would surely be lethal. It was like a dream: the rush of air, the sick emptiness in his stomach, the twist as he braced for the inevitable impact—but he didn't wake up. He crushed something, and heard as much as felt his bones snapping. His collarbone, right arm, every rib on the right side and his pelvis crunched and crackled.

When he blinked his eyes clear, he was flat on his back, a fire ant crushed beneath him. Kylar tried to move, but there was no way. Pain arced through him, so intense that black spots swam in front of his eyes. If he tried again, he'd black out. He was dead. Just like that, Kylar's battle was finished.

The Titan had staggered back several huge steps. Its neck was fountaining blood from the right side. Kylar had caught its carotid artery. It screamed. Then it caught sight of Kylar. If Kylar could read emotion in those silver and black cat's eyes, he would have thought he read satisfaction. The Titan stepped forward. It was dying, and it knew it, and it was going to fall on top of Kylar to crush him.

Kylar extended one finger to the Titan and lay back and looked at the sky. A speck floated in front of his eyes and he blinked, but it didn't go away. In the sky, diving from mountainous heights was a bird of prey, diving at great speed. Even in a dive, it was clear it must have had a thirty foot wingspan, and it was diving straight at Kylar.

Great, crushed by a Titan or by some huge bird. Beautiful.

There was no question of moving. So many bones were broken that breathing was excruciating. Kylar looked back at the Titan. The blood-fountain from its neck still gushed. It was rocking forward, its perfect white teeth bared at Kylar.

The bird snapped its wings open at the last second and swooped into the Titan's face with bone-shattering force. The Titan's head whipped back with a crack and it dropped like a stone—backward, onto the lines of krul.

Kylar lay back. He'd hoped to do more. He might have even been tempted to think his destiny would have been to do more, but he knew better. Anyway, at least he'd killed the Titan. That was surely worth something.

There was a ululating cry from the Ceuran lines, and the allies surged forward. Kylar saw men and horses leaping over him.

He'd barely closed his eyes when he felt magic sliding into him. With a sure and brutal hand, his bones were wrenched into place and reconstructed in rapid order. When the magic receded, Kylar lurched over and threw up. He hadn't even known he could be Healed so quickly. Who else would have tried?

"One of these times, you're really going to have to save my life. This is really getting old. By the way, I thought I told you to hold onto this."

Kylar gaped up at Durzo. His master was extending Curoch to him. Durzo was wearing a huge pack on his back that extended several feet above his shoulders—except it wasn't a pack. "Oh, hell no," Kylar said. "You cannot fly. Tell me you can't fly."

Durzo shrugged. "Hollow bones, changes to the heart and eyes if you want to see while you dive, careful reapportionment of body mass—it's a real bitch. Helps if you study dragons."

"Dragons? No, don't tell me." Kylar stood, shaky from the vast amount of magic that had coursed through him. "I didn't think I could heal that fast—" he cut off as Durzo's wings melted into his back and his form subtly changed proportions. Durzo had taught him that shifting his features, even the relatively minor shifts from one human face to another, took eight to twelve hours. Now his master had lost thirty-foot wings in a matter of seconds. "Unbelievable," Kylar said.

"It's too hard for you," Durzo said, a note of apology sneaking into his voice.

"Do you know where Elene is?" Kylar demanded.

"Not for sure, but I know where the party is." Durzo looked like he was about to say more, but he stopped. His face drained of humor.

A moment later, Kylar caught what dismayed his master. By degrees, the ground beneath them seemed to sigh. The stench of the newly dead was magnified tenfold. Jorsin's spell locking the ground had been broken. The Dead Demesne shook off its chains and breathed.

94

Godking Wanhope saw the Cenarian flare arc high over his command tents and his heart stopped.

Jenine. They were taking Jenine.

He stood on the last flight of steps before a great dome of the ancient castle. It was the tallest building he'd ever seen, with towering arches and flying buttresses that scraped the very heavens. Inside, he could feel Khali—and Neph Dada. Dorian was surrounded by a dozen highlanders and two hundred Vürdmeisters: more than enough. The real battle would be between himself and Neph, his old tutor. Neph, who was making his play at usurpation. Neph, who had raised a Titan and the red *buulgari*—the fire ants, the bugs—which had been imprisoned near the Titan.

Nor was Neph Dada the only one making a play. Wanhope's brother Moburu had spent almost all his strength in cutting through Wanhope's forces yesterday to get to Black Barrow. Now he was emerging from one of the tunnels under the city. He had a ferali.

From the stairs, the Godking had a vantage of everything north and east of the castle. To the north, he could see the small Cenarian force cutting through the Dead Demesne to the east, where they would meet Logan Gyre's troops, led by the king himself. Moburu's force looked to be only a few hundred, and it would meet Logan's troops before the Cenarians who'd taken Jenine got there. Without the ferali, the Cenarians would obliterate Moburu's force. With it—well, it depended on how good Logan's magae were.

All in all, the resulting clash should give him plenty of time to go inside, take Khali and cut off Neph from the vir. Without vir, Neph and Moburu would be helpless, and the entire army of krul would finally be united. Wanhope had made mistakes, but the day was far from lost. He was turning to go inside when he saw Moburu's men turn and head for the Cenarians holding Jenine.

His heart pounded. He'd seen this scene as his gift came back. Moburu's ferali would demolish the kidnappers, and he would seize Jenine. Wanhope saw the picture vividly. Moburu held Jenine, his eyes wild, a spell wrapped around her head that would crush it like a melon if he released it.

It was too late for Jenine. Wanhope could see her head popping, brains squirting out of the narrow holes in the spell. He blinked. Even if he saved her, his marriage was finished. The Cenarians had taken her. She must know now that Logan was alive. If he rescued her within sight of Logan, would she thank him for it? Inside, at least, was power. With Khali, Wanhope had magic, wealth, every pleasure of the flesh, comfort. There was the study of things lost, of magics no one could teach but a goddess. There was everything but friendship, companionship, love—but what were those things if he was going to go mad and couldn't enjoy them anyway? This was his birthright, and people had been trying to take his birthright for as long as he'd lived. He'd given everything to be here. What would happen to his harem if he left? He'd given those girls a decent life, a better life than they could have imagined. He couldn't live without the vir. He'd quit it once, and quitting had nearly killed him. He couldn't do it again. Jenine was dead to him anyway. Besides, he wanted to crush Neph, to teach him finally who was the master and who the student, to avenge all the cruelties Neph had inflicted on him growing up.

Wanhope turned to go inside.

"Dorian?" a man shouted from halfway down the hill. "Dorian?!" In the cobblestone street, a hundred paces away, Solon emerged around a corner, riding a chestnut destrier. He gestured with one hand to what must have been soldiers in the street behind him, telling them to stop. "Dorian! My God, Dorian, it's good to see you! I thought you were dead!"

Godking Wanhope was wearing his white robes and heavy gold chains of office. The vir were darkening his skin, and Solon pretended not to see any of it.

Solon rode toward him, not touching his Talent, not holding any weapon, not making any move that might seem threatening, as if he were approaching a wild animal. "It is you. *Dorian.*"

He said the word like it had power, like he was calling a dead man back to life. And it was life. Even with all the luxury and the fulfillment of every whim, Dorian had lived these last months hunted. There had been no rest, only stupor. There had never been communion, not even with Jenine.

The two hundred Vürdmeisters were getting nervous at Solon's approach. They could smell the potency of his Talent, and even to Wanhope's nostrils it reeked. He hated it. It smelled of light, scouring, revealing, shaming light. But the Vürdmeisters wouldn't attack Solon, not without the Godking's word. Solon ignored them. The man always did have brass balls. "Dorian," he said. "*Dorian.*"

Dorian had spoken a prophecy over Solon once. Ten, twelve years ago? It ended: "Broken north, broken you, remade if you speak one word." The cheeky bastard was asserting that the word was "Dorian"? He was turning Dorian's own prophecy back on himself? Solon had a little grin twisting his lips in the way Dorian knew so well. A laugh burst out of Wanhope and then was strangled in a sob. It sounded insane to his own ears.

He looked down the hill. Moburu had closed with the Cenarians holding Jenine, and the ferali was plowing through them in a cloud of black dust, tearing them apart, sticking their bodies to its flesh—growing.

Inside, Neph was working to give Khali flesh. The goddess would enslave all Midcyru, maybe all the world. Enslave and destroy. Without a body, she had turned Khalidor into a cauldron of filth, a culture of fear and hatred. What could she do with a body? The best thing Dorian could do was stop him. Godking Wanhope could stop Neph. He knew Neph. He knew how Neph would fight. The girl was a tangent, a distraction in the big picture. Dorian was too important, his skills too valuable to go after a girl when the real battle—the battle that would determine the fate of nations, perhaps of all Midcyru—was only paces away.

Dorian would go inside as Godking Wanhope one last time. He would take the vir one last time, and destroy all Neph had wrought. He would destroy Khali's works—and he would die. His fighting would be done at last. Unable to live well, he would at least die well.

Besides, Jenine was dead to him.

"Dorian," Solon said. "Dorian, come back."

Jenine was dead to Godking Wanhope, she was dead even to Dorian—but she wasn't dead. This delusion was the same temptation that had snared him a hundred times: allow this present evil for some grand, future good. To change an entire nation, to undo the evil his father had wrought, he had taken a harem, raised krul, slaughtered children, raped girls, and started a war. In fact, he'd accomplished most of the things for which he hated his father, and in far less time. The truth was, Dorian had always been more interested in being known as good than in simply being good. And he was about to do it again. No wonder he'd been so willing to throw away his prophetic gift at Screaming Winds: he'd seen then what he was going to become.

"Go inside, kill the usurper," Godking Wanhope ordered his Vürdmeisters. "I'll follow momentarily." They went inside instantly. They might even obey. It didn't matter. He couldn't keep them here. They might try to stop him. "You too," he told his bodyguards, and they, too, obeyed instantly.

With his stomach revolting at even touching his Talent, weak and frail as it was, Dorian readied the weaves, not giving himself time to think. He knew these weaves; he'd used them once as a young man. It was probably too little, too late. There was no way he could pay for what he'd done. He should just smash Neph and die.

No, that was the same old voice he'd obeyed too many times. Every time he decided to think about the temptation, he fell into the temptation. Now was the time to act. To simply do good, whether or not anyone ever knew, whether or not it was enough.

With a deep breath and as much Talent as he could hold, he ripped the vir out of himself. Parts of his Talent ripped away with it, as he cut deep, deep. It ripped so many parts open that he knew he would never again control when his prophetic gift came or went. The madness he had feared and fought for so long would come, and it would stay, forever.

Finally, sickened, Dorian threw off the gold chains and the white cloak of his office. "Solon. Friend," he said, heaving a deep breath, "ride with me. Quickly. The madness comes."

95

Logan had no idea how the battle was going. Shortly after the signal had gone up that Jenine had been recovered and he'd committed himself to meeting those soldiers on the east side of the hill below the castle, flares had gone up behind them, calling for all of the reinforcements. But for the moment, none of it mattered.

At the base of the hill beneath the huge castle, the expedition Logan had sent to recover Jenine was caught in a battle with a few hundred Khalidorans. The ground here was covered with the black dust that was all that remained of Black Barrow. It had settled quickly, but as the forces fought and as Logan's men rode forward, they kicked it up once more, obscuring the battle.

With six inches of dust on the ground, Logan didn't dare a full charge. If that black snow concealed pitfalls, horses would fall. The riders behind, blinded by thick black dust, would ride right over their companions.

Logan and his foremost riders were within thirty paces when he saw something looming through the black dust. It was vaguely bear-shaped, but men were stuck to its skin, screaming. "Break! Break!" Logan shouted. "Ferali!"

He veered left. A crowd of Khalidorans appeared out of the dust before him, all pressing to get away from the ferali. The Khalidorans were panicked, totally unprepared for the sudden appearance of cavalry, and Logan's line plowed through them. His destrier trampled half a dozen before the press of bodies became so thick it stopped them.

A vast arm, its skin writhing with gaping little mouths, passed over Logan's head, brushing his helmet with a scraping sound as little teeth tried to chew through metal. Logan couldn't see the rest of the creature except as a shadow against the lesser blackness of the dust.

He lurched as a horse collided into the back of his destrier. It jarred him forward and the men before him slowly yielded, either crushed, or faces laid open from his destrier's teeth.

A crackling ball of mage fire whizzed through the air and exploded against the ferali's hide, doing nothing. The magae didn't know what they were facing.

More screams rose as the force of Logan's charge pushed his men directly into the ferali. Logan found horses wedged to either side of him. Gnasher on one side, Vi on the other, her red dress glowing from within as she hurled a flurry of fist-sized fire balls, some into the Khalidorans packed before them, and some at the ferali. "It's not doing anything!" she shouted.

The ferali suddenly disappeared, hunkering down into the earth.

"Ah, shit," Logan said. He'd seen this before. The ferali wasn't leaving or hiding, it was rearranging itself to use all its new meat. The press of the lines pushed men toward it.

The ferali exploded upward, and men and horses were flung into the air in every direction. They fell and crushed their fellows.

"Spread out! Spread!" Logan shouted. Vi threw up a flare, but Logan bet no more than a hundred men saw it.

Suddenly, he saw magic rippling through the air over his head, diffuse as a cloud.

With a sound like a slamming door, the magic plunged to the ground. Within a square a hundred paces on each side, the black dust dropped to the earth and was held there. The air was clear.

Logan looked up the hill and saw the source of the magic: Solon Tofusin, the man he'd thought he'd known for a decade. He stood with a dark-haired man on a promontory. The other mage was crackling with light, weaving a dozen strands of magic. Logan barely registered their presence before looking back to the battle.

He saw that they were caught in what had been an estate's garden. There were walls on two sides, and it was toward those walls that Logan had been trying to retreat. The ferali sat in the middle. It had foregone legs to simply squat with half a dozen arms, plucking men and horses from the ground indiscriminately, and if the clear air helped Logan and his forces, it helped the ferali too.

"Second, Third, Fourth battalions, circle behind!" Logan shouted. Vi threw up the signal, but getting an army to change direction wasn't a quick process. The Fourth Battalion might arrive in time to stop the Khalidoran force from retreating, but nothing could save the thousand men trapped with Logan in this garden.

Vi began attacking the ferali again, but now she was throwing a stream of balls of light toward the ferali's eyes. She wasn't trying to hurt it now, merely blind it, distract it, slow its killing. In moments, a dozen other magae followed her lead and dazzling streams of light flowed toward the great armed blob in the garden's center.

For moments it was paralyzed, then it picked up a horse from the Khalidoran side of the garden, where it could still see. It hurled the horse toward one of the magae, crushing her and half a dozen others. It extended an arm, and dozens of swords and spears bubbled to the surface and floated into its hand. It hurled all of them at the next maja.

Logan craned his neck to see how much the press had eased. Not enough.

"Jenine!" someone yelled. It was the man on the promontory with Solon, and it was a cry of utter despair. His arms were spread out, each hand swimming with intricate weaves—Logan wondered for a brief moment how he saw them; he'd never been able to see magic weaves before—then the man brought his hands together, squeezing the weaves into one ball. Magic leapt from his hands like an arrow and hit the ferali, and unbelievably, stuck. Magic never stuck to ferali.

The ferali was lifting another horse from the Khalidoran side of the circle. There was a woman in the saddle, clambering back, trying to throw herself off the back of the horse, but the ferali's hand was clamped over her dress. It was Jenine. Logan's heart jumped into his throat, but there was nothing he could do.

The man on the promontory screamed, and the magic in his hands went taut, like a rope tied to the ferali. Shrieking, he yanked.

The horse dropped from the ferali's hand and Logan lost sight of his wife. The ferali's gray skin was shimmering. In a wave of black smoke, the skin evaporated. With a hiss of escaping gases, the ferali slumped, died, and burst apart, the maze of magic that held it together clipped like a Fordaean knot.

Logan's heels were into his destrier before the ferali's last arm hit the earth. He rode over mounds of stinking entrails and crashed into the first Khalidorans he saw between him and where Jenine had fallen. Logan caught a glimpse of the Fourth Battalion coming into place and sealing the northern exit from the garden.

A Ladeshian and two dozen men had dismounted and climbed onto a raised stone balcony. The mansion the balcony had been attached to was a ruin, but the balcony itself was pristine, commanding views of the whole garden. The Ladeshian raised his arms and threw fire into the sky. It faded slowly until it burned around him, forming the outline of a dragon.

"Behold!" Moburu shouted. "The High King is come! King Gyre, come make your obeisance!"

Moburu had no more than thirty men left, all of them stuck on the balcony with him. Logan ran up the steps. When he reached the top, he saw Jenine. Her rich velvet clothing was torn and dirty, smeared with black dust like soot, but she appeared uninjured. Her arms were bound to her sides and a spell sat around her neck and head, with vicious teeth dimpling her skin. The jaws were held open only by a thin weave Moburu held. If Moburu were killed,

the jaws would snap shut and crush her skull. Logan
didn't question how he knew it, but he did.

Seeing Jenine, Logan's heart surged with a mix of feelings too powerful for words. To see her alive after giving
up hope took his breath away. No one would take Jenine
away from him again. No one would hurt her. Logan held
up his hand, forestalling those following him from attacking Moburu.

Moburu was raving, "It is written:

> "'He passeth through Hell and waters below and rises,
>   marked with death,
> "'Marked with the moon dragon's gaze,
> "'In the shadow of the death of the barrow of man's
>   last hope he rises
> "'And fire attends his birth.'

"I tell you," Moburu shouted, "this prophecy is fulfilled this day in your sight. I, Moburu Ursuul, son of the
north, rightful Godking, rise this day to take my throne.
Pretender, I challenge you. Your crown against mine," he
lowered his voice, "and her life."

"Done," Logan said instantly. "Hand over the death
spell to one of your wytches."

"What?" Vi asked. "Your Majesty, we have him! He's
got nowhere to go!"

"No interference!" Moburu said.

"Done!" Logan shouted.

"And done!" Moburu turned and handed over the
weave to a Vürdmeister at his left.

Logan tore off his helmet and pulled the crown from it.

He tossed it to the same man. "Jenine," he said, meeting her wide eyes, "I love you. I won't let them have you."

The battle had ended. There were no Khalidorans left to kill here.

"I was born on the day foretold, twenty and two years ago. I bear the signs," Moburu shouted, his eyes shining. He raised his right arm, and displayed a glittering green tattoo reminiscent of a dragon. "Be prepared to greet your High King!"

"This is madness, Logan," Vi said. "The man's a Vürdmeister! You can't face him!"

Logan's eyes finally left Jenine. "Nice tattoo," he told Moburu. He drew his sword.

Logan's right arm felt burning heat. Logan looked down. The incandescent green pattern etched into his arm had melted through the chain mail of his sleeve. It burned as bright as the moon dragon's eyes. Logan caught one glimpse of fear in Moburu's face before Moburu's skin was overwhelmed with black knots of vir.

Moburu threw out a hand and a gout of magic leapt for Logan. Something burst from Logan's arm to meet it. All Logan saw was rushing scales and the burning green of the moon dragon's eyes, as if the entire creature had taken up residence in his arm and was now springing free, full-sized. Its mouth snapped shut on Moburu. Then it disappeared.

Moburu stood immobile. At first, Logan thought the moon dragon had been illusory or his imagination. It appeared to have done nothing at all to his opponent. Then, every tracery of vir within Moburu's skin shattered.

With a dragon's strength, Logan swung his sword down on the pretender. It caught Moburu at the crown of his head and sheared through him. Before the halves of Moburu's body hit the ground, Vi was on top of the Vürdmeister holding the death spell on Jenine.

He and every other Khalidoran and Lodricari and wild man on the balcony raised their hands slowly. The death spell dissolved. The Khalidorans dropped to their knees and looked at Logan with something in their eyes uncomfortably close to worship.

"Battle Mistress!" a voice called out in the sudden silence. It was the odd mage who'd killed the ferali. His eyes were unfocused. He smelled strange to Logan's sensitive nose. He laughed suddenly, then stopped and said somberly, "Battle Mistress, you're needed in the Hall of Winds! Come, quickly, or Midcyru is dead!" He turned to Logan. "High King, summon every man you'd have live to see the night!"

Jenine was staring at the madman with horror.

"Who is this man?" Logan demanded. *High King?*

The mage had made it onto the balcony. He held a thick gold chain in his hands, but abruptly seemed lost.

"Dorian," Jenine said. "Gods, what have you done?"

"Dead to me. Not dead but dead to me," Dorian mumbled.

"He's a prophet," Solon said, following in Dorian's wake. "What he speaks is true. There's no time, Your Majesty. We must go!"

Jenine was crying. Logan pulled her into his arms, not knowing exactly what her tears were for.

The ground trembled and sound rolled over the whole land, like the earth itself was sighing.

Solon swore a string of curses. "Neph's done it. Damn him. He's broken Jorsin's spell." Solon was staring at the black dust that covered everything within miles. It suddenly congealed, forming a thin sludge everywhere.

Logan turned to the Sethi king. "You're sure of this man? You'd bet sixty thousand souls on his word?"

"That and more," Solon said.

Dorian wept. Solon took the great gold chain from his hands and draped it over Logan's shoulders.

Logan turned to Vi. "Send up flares. All our armies to the castle, immediately. And then get yourself there. Fast."

96

Kylar and Durzo approached the Hall of Winds together, unlimbering their swords as one. Both men were liberally spattered with blood. They paused outside a rosewood side door. "You ready?" Kylar asked.

"I hate this part," Durzo said.

"Relax, I killed four Vürdmeisters once, didn't I?" Kylar asked, grinning evilly.

"There are two hundred Vürdmeisters in there."

"There is that," Kylar admitted.

"All right, we do the highlanders guarding the door in no more than five seconds. Then you draw the Vürdmeisters' attention, and I go for Neph Dada," Durzo said. He shrugged. "It might work."

"Not likely." Kylar patted Durzo's back.

Muted light flared to the tip of Curoch. Kylar threw open the door and Durzo dashed inside.

The four highlanders guarding the side door had their backs to them. In less than two seconds, all four were

dying. Only after killing his two did Durzo allow himself
to take in what everyone else was staring at.

The Hall of Winds was a vast circle topped by a high
dome without any interior supports. The entire panorama
of the ceiling and the walls themselves was imbued with
magic. Looking east, it was as if the walls weren't there:
he could see Logan's men battling a ferali. The presen-
tation of what was happening outside continued as he
looked south, but ended abruptly at a crack that had sliv-
ered down from the top of the dome. From south to west,
the scene portrayed was of sunrise over the bustling city
this once had been. It was a summer day; ships crowded
the river. The terraced hills were a tapestry of gardens,
bearing a thousand different kinds of flowers, and the city
was vast beyond comprehension. Beyond the next crack
was the night sky, half a moon shining brightly enough to
cast shadows. Beyond that one was a narrow panel of a
thunderstorm, with lightning flashing and rain falling in
torrents. Other panels were dark, the magic gone, leaving
plain stone.

But none of these wonders were what held the highlanders' and Vürdmeisters' attention.

In the middle of the domed room, the Vürdmeisters
stood in concentric circles around Neph Dada, who held
a thick scepter. At his feet, clutching a wrinkled leather
fetish, was a slobbering Tenser Ursuul. Every one of the
Vürdmeisters held the vir, and every one of them was
linked to Neph Dada, who stood at the center of a vast
web of magic. Thick bands of every color disappeared
into the floor and the earth itself, and he was manipulating
the weight of two hundred Vürdmeisters' vir, expanding
that web. Iures was shifting in his hands, morphing faster

than the eye could follow, twisting the web, expanding parts of it, pulling parts together.

Neither swordsman hesitated. Kylar dashed along the outside of the circle, his sword at neck level like a kid running a stick along a slat fence, except this stick cut throats, leaving twenty men dead. Then, even as the first yells went up, he leapt ten feet in the air and light exploded from him.

Durzo ran straight for Neph Dada, up one of the aisles, passing between dozens of chanting Vürdmeisters. He was within five paces of the wytch when Neph raised a hand. Durzo stopped instantly. He couldn't even bounce backward. Magic wrapped him every way.

Neph extended his hand again and air gelled in a wall, cutting off Kylar and another score of Vürdmeisters from the rest of the hall. Kylar plowed into them, and they—their vir still connected to Neph—could do nothing. In seconds, they were all dead. Neph reached with magic to grab Kylar, but the wetboy moved too fast. After a few seconds, Neph gave up. He threw up three more walls to make a wide cage, and then ignored him.

Returning his attention to Iures in his left hand, Neph began chanting once more. Iures morphed again into Retribution. Neph wrapped liver-spotted fingers through Tenser's hair and cut his throat open. Blood spilled all over the leather fetish Tenser held, hissing and spitting as if it were white hot. Tenser pitched over, dying as the magic released.

There was a second sigh through the land.

"It is finished," Neph Dada declared. "All Jorsin's works are broken. Khali comes." He released the vir back to the two hundred Vürdmeisters in the room. He slipped into a coughing fit, and when it stopped, he turned to Durzo. With a gesture, the bonds holding Durzo fell away. "You must be Durzo Blint. Or should I say Prince Acaelus Thorne? Oh, surprised? The Society of the Second Dawn has let its standards for membership slip, I'm afraid. I know all about you, Durzo Blint—even that you gave up the black ka'kari. Poor choice."

"Seemed good at the time," Durzo said, never shifting from his ready stance. "We gonna do this or not?"

"No," Neph said. He turned to Kylar and gave a little mocking bow. "Well met, Kylar Stern, Godslayer, ka'karifer. You're not using the black ka'kari. Why?"

"Lost it in a card game," Kylar said.

"Not a very good liar, are you? When a ka'kari is surrendered willingly, it must serve its new master. They can be broken, but it takes time. I'm an old man. I'd like to bond the black as soon as possible, but I can take it from your corpse if need be. If you don't give it to me, I'll kill your master. If the Society's right, this time he won't come back."

Kylar's face twisted. "My master understands about necessary sacrifices."

Neph turned to Durzo. "There you have it," he said. A sliver of magic jutted out of Durzo's chest. Neph had stabbed him from behind. The magic faded and Durzo stood, weaving.

"Dishonorable," Durzo said. His legs folded.

"What's honor? A ninety-year-old man fighting you with a sword?"

But Durzo made no reply. He was already dead. Kylar made a wordless sound of protest, staring at the corpse with disbelief. It was like seeing the sun set at noon. He'd known that Durzo would die someday, but not now, not so easily. Not without a fight.

Neph turned back to Kylar. "One more chance. Give me the black ka'kari. That's all I want. I'll leave you to Khali. You may even escape."

Kylar drew himself to his full height, and rolled his shoulders, loosening his muscles for action. "That sounds like a great deal, but there's three problems," Kylar said. He smiled. "First, I'm not Kylar." He laughed, and his face morphed into one leaner, pock-marked, with a wispy blond beard. He was Durzo Blint. "Second, that corpse isn't Durzo."

"What?"

"Third," he continued, "if someone would move his ass. . . ." He cleared his throat.

Neph turned belatedly. In a smooth motion, the corpse stood—and was Kylar. Shields flew up around the Vürdmeister.

Skin sheathed in black metal, face covered by the mask of Judgment, Curoch sliding out of his fists as white-hot claws, Kylar punched. The Vürdmeister's shields popped like soap bubbles. Claws of Curoch crossed on either side of the Vürdmeister's spine, eight bloody points poking out of his back. "Third, I'm not dead," Kylar said, lifting Neph off the ground. "And this is Curoch."

"Shit, that's four things, isn't it?" Durzo said.

Neph Dada screamed. He threw his arms out spastically. The vir leapt to the surface of every inch of his skin. Neph shrieked and shrieked as white light blasted through every vein of vir. Kylar roared and ripped the claws in opposite directions, shearing the Vürdmeister in half.

The walls surrounding Durzo evaporated into nothing

and there was silence in the Hall of Winds. Kylar sheathed
Curoch on his back and gingerly picked up Iures. He
tossed it to Durzo. "You could have given me a few
more seconds," Kylar said. "You just taught me rapid
healing ten minutes ago. What if I hadn't got it right on
the first try?"

Durzo grinned. Bastard.

An earthquake rocked the ground.

Kylar looked at the dome, hundreds of feet overhead,
swaying out of time with the ground. At Kylar's feet, he
saw the focus through which Neph had been pulling all
the power he'd worked on with Iures. It was a leather bundle, ancient, cracked, and yellowing, with gems sewn to it
and a horrid, desiccated, hairless, boneless skull grinning
formlessly from the front. It could only be one thing. This
horror was Khali.

He hefted Curoch and jammed its point through the
fetish.

A dozen Vürdmeisters cried out, but nothing happened.
There was a hiss of escaping air, and the section of the
floor beneath the fetish and Curoch sank.

Kylar stepped back and the floor opened like a coffin
lid. There was a woman inside. Her hair was long and
blonde, carefully arrayed in small braids and curls. Her
long-lashed eyes were closed, her cheeks flushed, full lips
pink, skin flawless alabaster. For some reason, to Kylar's
eyes, the girl was a collection of details that refused to
coalesce into a woman: a familiar dimple here, the sweep
of her neck. Her dress was white silk, slim cut to her figure, backless, more daring or more scandalous than anything Elene would have worn. Elene. Kylar staggered
back. "Elene!"

Her lips curved into a smile. She drew a breath. Lovely brown eyes opened. Kylar's knees went weak. She reached out a regal hand, and when he took it, she rose almost magically to her feet. Every move spoke perfect grace.

"You—you don't have any scars," Kylar said.

"I can't stand ugliness. I want to be beautiful for you," Elene said, and she smiled, and every part of her was beauty. "Kylar," she said gently, "I need Curoch."

He looked into her smiling face and was lost. Through the ka'kari, Elene looked like an archmage. Magic swirled thickly around her. Elene wasn't Talented, but this *was* Elene.

His heart froze.

Distantly, he heard the main doors of the hall bang open. His knees hit the floor.

"Kylar! No!" Vi shouted. Numbly, Kylar watched the doors open wide. Following Vi was Logan, one arm glowing green; Solon, Logan's old adviser, wearing a crown; the mountainous Feir Cousat; four magae, all greatly Talented; Dorian the prophet; Lord General Agon Brant; and Captain Kaldrosa Wyn with fifty of Agon's Dogs.

The scent of Elene filled Kylar's nostrils as she stepped close. What had she done?

His eyes snapped open as Elene snatched Curoch from his limp fingers. The look in Elene's eyes was foreign. She looked intoxicated as she gazed at the blade. She laughed and twirled.

"Trace, that's enough," Durzo said suddenly.

She stopped abruptly and stared at Durzo, disbelieving. "Acaelus? No, it can't be."

"Hand it over, Trace. And the white ka'kari, too. Release that girl's body."

Elene's eyes narrowed. "It is you."

"What happened to you, Trace? You were one of the Champions. Jorsin trusted you. We all did. What have you become?" Durzo asked.

"I am Khali." At the word, the Vürdmeisters dropped to their faces. She laughed again. "Look at my pets, so humble, and every one of them scheming even now." She looked around the Hall of Winds. She gestured with Curoch, and every crack in the dome was sealed, the scene unified: a spring day, mountains purple in the distance, flowers everywhere. "Do you remember this, Acaelus? We were supposed to be married here." Her white dress shifted like liquid metal, shimmering into a high-necked full green gown with thousands of crystals sewn into it.

"You were beautiful."

"I was a hag!" she shot back. "Bad teeth, bad skin, crooked back. Then Ezra gave me the white ka'kari. I heard you quarreling with him. You betrayed me first, Acaelus. You left me here in my wedding gown, shamed me in front of everyone. I waited hours. I was finally beautiful, and all you were was jealous."

Durzo's face was gray, and bits and pieces that Kylar had heard over the years fell into place. To save the black ka'kari and keep its incredible power secret, Jorsin had given it to "The Betrayer" Acaelus. Acaelus hadn't even been able to tell his fiancée that he had it, and knowing that he would soon have to act the betrayer, Acaelus had fled rather than marry. All without a word of explanation. Kylar remembered Durzo snarling at him when he was a child: "I will not allow you to ruin yourself *over a girl*." Momma K had said women had always been Durzo's downfall. The Wolf had said Durzo had once done something worse than take money for a death. Kylar had guessed it was suicide, but it was worse than that. Knowing the price of immortality was that someone he loved died in his place, Durzo had killed himself, hoping to kill Trace.

But Trace, an archmage in her own right and the smartest of the Champions, had figured out a way around the black ka'kari's death sentence. *~Acaelus and I always knew there was something strange about that death. We knew she fought the magic for months, but then her body died. We tried never to think of her again.~*

"Jealous?" Durzo said. "I had the black ka'kari, the most powerful of them all. Ezra and I quarreled because he gave you a ka'kari that confirmed a lie you believed. You weren't ugly then, Trace; you're ugly now. Look what you've done. For seven centuries the north has labored under your darkness. This is what Trace Arvagulania turned her mind to? This is what you created? Why?"

~For immortality,~ the ka'kari breathed to Kylar. Kylar could tell it was understanding for the first time. *~The white ka'kari can create a glamour so powerful it can be used for compulsion. She tried to turn her ka'kari into a dark imitation of me, using it to compel worship, and then trying to steal life from her "willing" worshipers. But it didn't work because the soul of my magic is love—and love cannot be compelled. Trace has been disembodied until she could find someone who loves in a way that is totally foreign to what she has become. Someone willing— without compulsion—to let Trace have her body.~*

Now she'd found that person at long last: Elene.

"Why? I do it because I wish it. I am Khali. I am goddess. Someone has to pay the price for immortality. Tell me, Acaelus, who's paid for yours?"

Durzo paled. "Too many people. Come, Trace. Our time is done."

"My time has just begun." Curoch became a slender staff in her hand, and she raised it. A black cloud exploded in every direction, then disappeared. The walls of the Hall of Winds became clear as glass, showing the dark battlefield to every side. "Do you remember when Jorsin faced the grand armies of the Fallen?" Khali asked. "He could have stopped them, if he'd listened to me. He didn't have to fight them. He could have controlled them. He was a greater mage than Roygaris. These armies could have been Jorsin's, he could have simply taken them from Roygaris. We could have won."

As she spoke, it slowly became clear that the sudden darkness on the battlefield was moving, standing up. The black blanket was countless thousands of krul corpses rising from seven centuries of death, standing, healing, and moving into ranks. Earlier in the day, even with a hundred and fifty thousand men and krul fighting, all the armies together had occupied only a wedge of the plain south of the Hall of Winds. At Khali's gesture with Curoch, krul rose in a writhing black ocean north, south, east, and west as far as the eye could see. Kylar saw the Titan he'd killed get back to its feet. Dozens more like it stood around the battlefield. Beasts that dwarfed even Harani bulls rose. Birds great and small rose in clouds. Fire ants by the thousands. Flying beasts. Beautiful, fanged children. Brute wolves. Great cats. Horses with bone-scythes extending from each shoulder. Ferali by the hundreds. Kylar's mind couldn't take it all in. Jorsin had faced *this?*

The allied armies had reached the Hall, and now they turned outward, back to back, guarding the hilltop in a circle dwarfed by the numbers of krul they were about to face.

"I can banish them," Khali said. "All of them. But I need Iures to banish the Strangers. What do you say, Acaelus? Will you watch everyone you love die a second time?"

"You'll not have Iures from my hand," Durzo said.

"So be it," Khali said. "Kylar, kill him. Kill all of them." Her words washed over him with the whipcrack of authority. He recognized it as a compulsion spell even as he rose to obey. The spell was the full-grown older sister to the spell Garoth had laid on Vi, akin to the glamour Vi had used on him the first time they'd met, when she'd tried to kill him. But where that glamour had been anchored only by Vi's attractiveness, this compulsion hit every note from lust to awe at standing in front of another immortal, a goddess. It pulled on his adoration for Elene, his loyalty and trust for her as his wife. She was princess, goddess, immortal, lover, companion, wife—and all those bonds were amplified a hundredfold through Curoch. There was no question of disobedience.

Kylar stood. The black ka'kari formed twin swords in his hands. It was trying to speak to him, tell him how to combat the magic she was bombarding him with. But to use the ka'kari, he had to want to use it, and the compulsion stole his very willpower. He looked into Elene's big eyes and nothing mattered but pleasing her. Even as his heart despaired and he wanted nothing more than to throw himself on his own swords, he wanted to please her more.

"Kylar! Stop! I command you!" Vi shouted, advancing alone from among the magae. The command flashed like lightning through Kylar's compulsive wedding earring to the core of his being. It felt like he'd been falling from a great height only to have a rope tied around his wrists suddenly stop his fall. Kylar gasped with pain—and stopped.

Khali paused, surprised. She looked at Vi. "Dear girl," she said, "don't you know what happens when a woman contends with a goddess?" She turned to Kylar and put a hand on her stomach. "My love, you wouldn't betray the mother of your child, would you?"

He couldn't breathe. Elene's stomach was indeed slightly swollen. His child. The sudden delight on Khali's face told him it was true. Elene was pregnant. She'd known. She hadn't told him. The new claim to his loyalty added another layer to the power of the compulsion spell.

"Darling, kill them. Starting with that slut," Khali said. The command snapped tight like a rope around his ankles. He felt himself being torn between compulsions like a man on the rack.

One of the mages chose that moment to loose a fireball. It fizzled before it went an arm's length. Khali made a little snatching motion and Kylar saw every glore vyrden in the room emptied in an instant. The magi were left gasping.

"Kylar, help me," Vi cried. She fell to her knees, concentrating on him, sending strength to him. She reached for the nearest elements of their bond: His guilt at what he'd put her through, how he owed her better, and his desire for her.

Khali matched those and overmatched them. Khali tugged on what he owed Elene, on his desire for her, on the moments they'd shared making love. The compulsion spell worked by magnifying whatever hold a person had, whether authority, or love, or lust, or obedience. Fueled with the might of Curoch, it almost obliterated Kylar's mind.

Kylar raised his swords and started walking toward Vi. He could feel Khali's triumph, her pleasure at her mastery of him.

Vi's eyes held his as he walked closer. She reached up and pulled out the band that held her braid. Her hair spilled down like a copper waterfall. For the first time in her life, Vi made no attempt to protect herself, no attempt to cover this one thing that she had kept private as she had lost all else.

She spread her open hands and dropped the threads of lust and guilt in their bond. Kylar saw her then as he'd never seen her before. He saw the nights of agony with which she had paid for his nights of pleasure with Elene. He saw how gladly she'd done that for him, and at what cost. Vi loved him. Vi loved him fiercely. Kylar missed a step as she clung to that single cord—love—with all her might.

She looked up at him as he drew the twin swords back. "Kylar," she said quietly, at complete peace, "I trust you." Then, impossibly, she released the bond. Every claim she had to him, she dropped. She let him owe her nothing— not friendship, not honor, not dignity, not friendship, not her life—nothing at all.

With no claim to magnify, their wedding earrings failed.

It shook him like a bell had been rung from his ear through his whole body. It shook him from his suddenly freed wrists down to his bound ankles—and there, Khali had no answer to this kind of love. She knew only taking. It was like two people had been playing tug-of-war and one released the rope. All the magic held in tension by the wedding ring rushed outward—toward Khali. Kylar felt the huge wave of power passing through him as the vast pressures of the bond released into her, their force doubled and redoubled by her own pull on them.

There was a giant crack that rattled Kylar's teeth. Something tinged on the marble floor. It was Kylar's earring. The earrings were broken. The bond was broken. The compulsion had vanished. Kylar couldn't feel Vi—or Khali. He was free of both of them.

Ten paces away, Khali was rocking on her heels, stunned.

"I'm so sorry, Kylar," Khali said, but the tone was Elene's.

Kylar was at her side in an instant. "Elene?"

She pushed Curoch into his hands. "Quickly, quickly. I can't stop her. She's recovering."

"What are you talking about?" Kylar asked. "Honey?"

Tears were rolling down Elene's face. "Wasn't Vi magnificent? I'm so proud of her. I knew she could do it. You take care of her, all right?"

"I'm not letting you go."

Her eyes filled with sudden pain and her jaw tightened as a convulsion passed through her. "You know how I used to think I'd never be important like you are? I found it, Kylar. I found something I can do that no one else can. The God told me. Khali could only possess someone who let her, but she didn't know I can hold her in. You can kill her once and for all. You can kill the vir."

"But I can't kill them without killing you," he said.

She took his hand and smiled gently, acknowledging it. She was more beautiful than anything he'd ever imagined.

"No!" he shouted.

The ground shook. Kylar looked through the clear walls and saw one of the Titans pick up an entire building and hurl it at the allies. It crushed hundreds. There was no time. He looked back to Elene just as another spasm passed through her frame.

"But . . . Curoch," he said. "It can kill me. If it does, the spell that makes people die for me will be broken. I can still save you."

Kylar heard Durzo curse behind him, but he ignored him.

"Kylar," Elene said, "when Roth Ursuul killed you, that first time before we knew you were immortal, I prayed that I could trade my life to save yours. I thought the God said yes. I was so sure of it that I dragged you out of that castle. Later, I told myself that it was just a coincidence, but God *did* say yes. Yes in his time, not mine. My death then would have accomplished nothing. Now I can do something no one else can. Please, Kylar, don't be too proud to accept my sacrifice."

He clutched her hand convulsively. He was crying. He couldn't stop. "You're pregnant."

Tears coursed down her cheeks. "Kylar . . . there are so many people we love here. I'd give our son for them. Won't you?"

"No! No."

Elene held his face in her hands and kissed him gently. "I love you. I'm not afraid. Quickly now."

The ground shook again, and outside, choruses of

magic rose into the sky. Whatever krul had been raised, some of the newer ones had Talent. But inside, no one moved, they all knew that their fates and the fates off all Midcyru's nations were balanced on Curoch's edge.

Kylar pulled Elene into his arms and hugged her fiercely. Sobs burst from him. He drew back Curoch, and slid it into her side. She gasped, squeezing him.

As Curoch pierced Khali, light exploded, engulfing him in fire. It was clean and hot and purifying. Kylar thought he might be dead. He hoped he was.

97

$\mathcal{A}$ voice in the darkness: "I thought it was finished. He killed Khali. Why are they still coming?"

"She lied," another voice said, Dorian's voice. "She wasn't the queen of the Strangers, only an ally. Our work isn't done yet. Not by half. We need Curoch."

Kylar opened his eyes as someone touched him. Sister Ariel stood over him, and he was curled on the floor with Elene. "We need the sword, child." Her voice was gentle, but firm. "Now. Khali's dead, Kylar, but Elene's not, not yet, but her wound can't be Healed. Nothing can mend what Curoch cuts," Sister Ariel said. "We need you. Both of you. Or we'll never stop the krul."

Curoch was buried almost to the hilt in Elene's side. Her eyelids fluttered briefly but didn't stay open. "I can't," Kylar said.

Sister Ariel put a thick hand on the hilt and drew it out swiftly. Elene grunted weakly and a wash of blood poured from her ribs.

"Open the doors!" Dorian shouted. "Both sides!"

"Do it!" Logan shouted. "Do everything he says."

The two hundred Vürdmeisters lay in concentric rings, all dead, all bleached white. The vir itself was dead.

But the krul hadn't been affected. They still surrounded the Hall of Winds in a vast, churning black ocean. And even now, some of the most frightful of them were winning their way to the front of their lines. Shoulder to shoulder, Ceurans and Lae'knaught and Cenarians and Sethi and Khalidoran soldiers fought the horde. Kylar had somehow thought that killing Khali would mean a total victory, but the krul on every side—tens of thousands, hundreds of thousands, millions of them—told another story. The army of men in the center was like a lonely rock in the face of the incoming tide.

God, there was no way they could stand up to so many.

Someone squeezed Kylar's shoulder. It was Logan. His cheeks glistened with tears of mingled joy and sorrow. "Kylar, brother, come. We have a chair for her." Logan squeezed his shoulder again, and that touch was worth a thousand words.

The earth shook again, but Kylar didn't turn from Elene, who was breathing lightly now. The flow of blood had slowed. The open doors had magnified the cacophony of the battle. Kylar barely heard it. He allowed himself to be prodded into place in a tight circle between the open doors. Sister Ariel laid Curoch unsheathed across a dozen palms.

Pushed by Durzo, Kylar put his hand on the blade. Durzo took Kylar's other hand in both of his. It was an uncharacteristically tender gesture, and Durzo held it until Kylar looked up at him. As ever, Durzo didn't have words, but there was a respect in his eyes, and shared heartache, and pride. It was the look of a father whose son has done something great, and that look from Durzo, told Kylar he was an orphan no more. Then, with Kylar's hand still in his, Durzo cupped his hand, a request in his eyes.

Kylar understood, and let the ka'kari flow out into his hand, and gave it to Durzo. Durzo nodded and released his hand. Then Vi put her hand next to his on Curoch, just touching him. Conscious once more, Elene put hers on the other side of Kylar's. Several powerful magi of both genders knelt, each reverently resting two fingers on the blade. Solon and Sister Ariel did the same. Durzo had Retribution—Iures—in hand. It was black-bladed but its grip was uncovered, and Durzo spoke quietly to Dorian as he handed the prophet the Staff of Law.

As he touched Curoch, Kylar became aware of everyone else touching the blade. They sounded like an orchestra warming up, each on his own instrument and pitch. Then, beneath them, Curoch began humming. As Dorian laid his right hand on the blade, his left still holding Iures, a gust of wind blew through the Hall.

Solon found his pitch first, a bass as deep as his speaking voice, wide and strong, oceanic. Sister Ariel matched him, a powerful mezzo, broad but sharper. Then the magi joined in a chorus of baritones and basses, pure and simple and masculine, laying the foundation. The magae settled over them, fine and feminine, adding depth and complexity. Vi joined, her Talent like a high note with a rapid vibrato, higher than any of the others could possibly go. Then a startling new voice joined, richer than any of the others, layered in mystery, a baritone with such depth and range it dwarfed all the others put together.

Kylar's eyes shot open, and he and everyone else stared at Durzo, who had laid a single insolent finger precisely on Curoch's point.

Then Kylar felt his place. He sang a tenor, soaring over the other men, interweaving with Vi. He himself was startled at the power of his voice and noticed that all eyes had turned to him, as awed as they had been when Durzo joined. Fierce pride filled Durzo's eyes.

Through the euphony, Kylar noticed something else, suffusing the whole. It was hope. And that voice, if voice it could be called, was all Elene. Her hope—even as she was dying—drew forth hope from each of them. And with that revelation, Kylar saw that Curoch wasn't a simple tool of magic. It wasn't an amplifier of Talent. Curoch amplified the whole man.

Elene's beacon of hope, Durzo's titanic determination, Dorian's penitence and astounding focus, Ariel's intelligence, Logan's courage, Vi's longing for a new beginning, Kylar's love of justice, the bonds of brotherhood and sisterhood, sacrifice, hatred of evil, feelings martial and impulses nurturing. Through it all, the glue that made the magic was love, and love sounded each instrument from its top to its bottom notes—and each man and each woman performed beautifully, heroically, some capable of only a few notes, some with huge range but little depth, and some of them true masters, but each giving all.

The Hall of Winds itself reacted to the perfection of magic building inside its walls. Tapestries of colored light danced through the walls, magic made visible even to the non-Talented, and wove together as the magic wove together. Radiance bathed them, and the magic growing inside was echoed to the world. The warriors outside, battling incredible odds, felt a sudden assurance, as if they were children fighting a bully and the bully had just caught sight of their father coming.

As the music climbed, directed by Dorian, Kylar could see the score laid out before them. His vision widened and he saw not just his own part—climbing, climbing— another voice was needed. One beyond any of the people in the Hall. Their Talents built to a crescendo, and every one blazed like the sun. There was so much magic in Kylar's blood and in the air it was almost intolerable. He was standing in a furnace. Everything Kylar had was sinking into Curoch, and still the magic Dorian was attempting demanded more.

A distant whistling sounded, high over the roar of battle.

Kylar's eyes flicked open. He looked at Dorian.

The mage shifted his grip on Curoch, leaving the hilt free, shifting their holds so that the hilt pointed toward heaven.

The man was more audacious than Kylar could believe. Even with all these mages working together, they didn't have the power needed to end this. So Dorian had set a trap to join their will to the one beast that had the power to impose that will on the world. Kylar was aghast. He couldn't even understand everything Dorian was trying to do. Dorian grinned at him, and Kylar wasn't sure if what he saw in the man's eyes was sane or mad. Through the southern door, Kylar could see all the way to the pass to Torras Bend, and as he watched, a streak of fire appeared.

It crossed the river, not bothering with a bridge, and plunged through the lines of krul without slowing. It moved too fast to see. Kylar could only judge its progress by the cloud of dust and smoke and blood that trailed it; the shockwave rippling through bodies crashing back to the earth long after it was gone. In seconds, it had gone from the distant pass to the old line where Black Barrow had stood. Kylar realized why Dorian had opened the doors: if he hadn't, the damn thing would have blasted right through the walls.

The whistling and the magic crescendoed as one. Through Curoch, for a split second, Kylar felt the Hunter as it seized the offered hilt of Jorsin Alkestes' mighty blade to snatch it away from them. And Kylar knew him.

A crack of thunder leveled everyone in the room. Magic obliterated everything.

98

*W*hen Kylar became aware, he was standing on the roof of the Hall of Winds. The Wolf stood next to him, and the world had the indistinct sheen Kylar had come to associate with the Antechamber of the Mystery. "So I'm dead," he said. He had no passion left in him.

"No," the Wolf said. "I can come into your dreams, it just takes a lot of magic. I have some to spare now."

"You're Ezra."

He inclined his head.

"Then what's the Hunter? I felt you in it."

"It's my hubris."

Kylar glanced at him. This was not an explanation.

"I tried to undermine the Dark Lord's own work by twisting the twisted back on the twister."

"The Dark Lord? You mean that metaphorically, right?" Kylar asked.

He chuckled. "You are still Kylar, aren't you? But not to worry, the Hands of Hell are still bound for another fifteen or twenty years. Until then, the Hunter and I will battle for control every day. I can only be here while it sleeps."

"What?"

"Do you see this, Kylar?" The Wolf—it was still hard to think of him as Ezra—gestured to the city. Kylar gave it a cursory glance.

"This is how it was when you lived here?" It was beautiful, but Kylar didn't care.

"This is real. This is what you and your friends have done."

Kylar looked with new eyes, stunned. The city was completely restored, and it was a marvel. The streets were straight, perfectly paved. The houses were immaculate, from the largest manse to the tightly packed row houses in the artisans' quarter. Fountains pumped sparkling clean water in squares throughout the city. Hanging gardens flowed over white marble walls. The dome of the Hall of Winds was covered with beaten gold. Nearby, the castle shone white and red. The fields below the city were carpeted with the green shoots of growing crops. The docks on the lake and the locks on the river were restored. The dam was closed and the water level rising. Every sign of war and death was gone.

"The krul's very bodies were turned into vegetation," Ezra said. "It's a better trick than anything Jorsin or I ever managed."

Flowers were budding everywhere, at every corner, bordering every field, rows of beautiful red flowers bursting from bulbs. Kylar had never seen their like, or known any flower to bloom so early in spring.

"How did Elene trap Khali?" Kylar asked. "I'm certain that she isn't Talented." Kylar paused. "Wasn't, I guess."

"There's more to magic than the Talent, Kylar. You've seen that yourself. When have you been most powerful? When you've acted in harmony with the deepest parts of your own spirit. Elene trapped Khali through love. It was a love that said *I love you too much to let you do more evil—not for the sake of your victims only, but for your own sake.* If it had been a rejection, Khali could have escaped and become disembodied once more. It was only Elene's love that made your justice possible. If I hadn't seen it, I wouldn't have thought such a thing could be done. Obviously, Khali didn't either."

Kylar had felt rejected when Elene had left him without telling him where she was going or that she was pregnant. This cast her in a different light. It hadn't been a rejection. She had simply seen that he wasn't mature enough or selfless enough to let her do what she needed to do. Elene had taken Khali not out of a rejection of Kylar, but out of a profound acceptance for who he was not only as a man, but as the Night Angel. Her only purpose in trapping Khali was so that Kylar could kill her. Elene had believed Kylar would do the right thing in the end so much that she had bet her very soul on it. For if he'd faltered, unable to give Elene up, Khali would have taken her over completely.

"What happens now?" Kylar asked, tears coursing down his cheeks.

"Your friend Logan will be crowned High King of Ceura, Cenaria, Khalidor, and Lodricar. He'll establish his capital here and rename it Elenea—not for you, but because he is a man who believes in honoring sacrifice. Within a few years, it will be one of the great cities of the world again. I suspect he will reign well." Ezra shook his head. "Feir Cousat will go to Torras Bend and set up a forge and start a family as he's always wanted. He'll take care of Dorian.

"Dorian was the architect of all this magic, but he's now completely mad. I don't know if it was the vir infecting his prophetic talent, or him ripping the vir completely out of himself, or the death of the vir that caused the madness. I don't suppose it much matters. But that he rooted out his own vir did save him. Indeed, he is probably the only Vürdmeister in Midcyru who didn't die along with the vir. Godking Wanhope will be declared dead. Durzo will be reunited with Gwinvere Kirena, who will eventually rule Cenaria, and rule more capably than any king or queen has ruled there for four centuries. Vi will return to the Chantry to finish her schooling. There will be calls to make her Speaker, which will scare the hell out of the current Speaker, Istariel Wyant. Vi will decline, but not before using her influence to make the Speaker swear that no Sister pursue you. To a surprising extent, they will actually obey."

"And what happens to me?" Kylar asked.

"You will be welcomed wherever you go in this guise. Sooner or later, the world will have need of you again. You are not a man to fade into oblivion, Kylar Stern. Secrecy, perhaps, intentional obscurity certainly, but never oblivion." He cocked his head to the side in his wolfish way. "I have a question."

"Yes?"

"You were four days away from the Wood when you unveiled Curoch. You knew that it would draw the Hunter?"

"Yes."

"How did you know that the Hunter would make it here in time to make a difference in the battle? Indeed, as it happened, *all* the difference. Without it, you didn't have nearly the power those spells required."

Kylar remembered removing the black ka'kari from Curoch before going to face Neph Dada. It had barely been a conscious act. He'd known that the Hunter hated krul and that it would be drawn to reclaim its stolen sword. Maybe he'd thought it would come earlier and kill a lot of krul. But more than a plan, it had simply been something that felt right. It felt like he was moving in consonance with the universe, with his own deepest character. If the Wolf was right, that was its own kind of magic. "I didn't know," Kylar admitted. "I believed."

The Wolf got pensive. "In this world of shadows, you believe? Despite all you've seen?"

Kylar took a breath, looking over the city in all its splendor and remembering what it had looked like not so long ago. "We live on a great battlefield, and you and I fight behind enemy lines," he said. "Like it or not, my lupine friend, you are one of the lights that helps me believe."

Ezra hmmed. "I will consider what you've said. The creature stirs. The day's battle begins."

"May the light shine on you, my friend," Kylar said.

"That's twice you've called me friend." Ezra seemed to taste the word as if it were a flavor long lost. Then he smiled, accepting it. "Thank you."

Ezra turned away, then hesitated. He turned back. "There is . . . one other thing. The red flowers? They're a modified tulip not native to Midcyru. They're known as the Heralds of Spring. They're the first flowers to bloom every year. They're a symbol of hope. I studied the magic, and . . . Elene made them, Kylar, all of them. She made them for you," Ezra's voice cracked. "I couldn't save her. I owed you that much, but I couldn't save her." Ezra pursed his lips, and his jaw clenched as he crushed his own emotions. He touched Kylar's shoulder. "I must go. May I not see you in the Antechamber of the Mystery for many, many years."

Tears flowed down Kylar's face. There were tens of thousands of red tulips. Every intersection, every field, every house was adorned with them. They were Elene's sign to him of her presence, her joy, her acceptance, her love. Only Elene would put such beauty in the middle of his pain. How was he ever going to live without her?

99

Logan dispatched perhaps the fortieth messenger of the day. Not being Talented seemed to have saved him from the brunt of the cost the magi who'd used Curoch had borne. Half of them were still unconscious, including Kylar. Vi had a white streak in her fiery red hair now, and Dorian's hair was gone utterly white like Solon's, though Solon retained his sanity, while Dorian had completely lost his. It was, perhaps, the better part of why Logan had spared the man. Dorian had turned at the end, and he'd certainly saved Logan's life and the lives of everyone else—but they wouldn't have been in jeopardy if Dorian hadn't stolen Logan's wife in the first place. Or not in jeopardy today, at any rate.

Scrubbing his hands through his hair, Logan almost knocked his new crown off. A soldier had found it waiting in the castle and had presented it to Logan, who'd lost his Cenarian crown in the fighting. They'd wanted to start the coronation celebrations to crown him High King immediately, but Logan insisted on taking care of his men first,

and with Lantano Garuwashi and Hideo Mitsurugi reporting to him, as well as one of the magi telling him about
the conditions of Khalidor's human soldiers, the number
of men Logan regarded as his own had exploded. Mercifully, he also had the services of eight thousand Sisters,
most of whom had some ability with Healing. With more
than one in ten of his people a Healer, far fewer died than
would have otherwise. And Curoch's magic had left them
in a paradise where they'd expected a wasteland.

Still, he'd had more than enough work to keep him
busy until long after dark. Part of him was glad for it. It
was one thing to raise an army to rescue your stolen bride;
it was quite another to figure out how to repair a marriage
when your wife had thought you dead, had remarried, and
had been sharing another man's rule and his bed.

Logan rubbed his temples again and set the crown
down on a desk. He looked around the room and realized he had no idea where he was. He'd left an immense
throne room and walked at random. Kaldrosa Wyn and
Gnasher and several other bodyguards had followed him,
but they'd said nothing as they took up their positions outside the door. He guessed they knew he needed nothing so
much as a quiet place. He sat.

There was a gentle knock and the door opened. It was
Jenine. She looked small, fragile. Her face was gray.
"Your Majesty," she said formally. "I'm pregnant."

"I know," Logan said flatly. "Solon told me you bear
Dorian's child."

"I've just met with a Healer. It's twins. Boys." Her
voice was wooden.

It was a disaster. Sons. Nor would they be simple bastards who could be put aside: they were the offspring of

a Godking and a Cenarian queen, with ample claim to the High King's throne on the basis of their blood alone. Their very existence would be destabilizing. If Logan had sons of his own, it would only be inviting civil war.

"I found a Healer who said . . . she said this early it would be safe to abort them." Jenine's eyes were dead.

"That isn't what you want," Logan said.

"There's more you have to know, Your Majesty," Jenine said. "I—I loved Dorian. Not the way I loved you, but even as I watched him descend into the madness and evil, I cared for him. You can scrub his sons from my body, but I will not come clean so easily. I'm sorry. You waited for me, and I didn't wait for you. If you wish to put me aside, Your Majesty, I will make no trouble for you. And if you wish me to purge my womb, I will. My duty to my lord husband and my country is greater than my own—"

"I've always wanted to be a dad," Logan said.

"What?"

"Can you love me, Jeni?"

She blinked up at him. "I love you so much it hurts."

Logan took her right hand in his left. "You are my wife, my lady, my queen." He put his right hand on her stomach. "Let these boys be my sons."

She jumped into his arms and squeezed him so hard he coughed. Then they laughed together and cried together and sat talking together for hours until Logan asked a question and Jeni didn't answer. She was staring at his lips.

"What?" he asked. He brushed his lips, but there was nothing on them.

Then her mouth was on his and there was roaring in his ears and the room faded and her softness and warmth was better than anything Logan had ever imagined. Somehow she was on his lap straddling him and her hands were on his back, in his hair, on his face, always pulling him closer, and he was pulling her in to him, crushing her against him, begging, demanding to be closer than clothes would allow.

When he surfaced from that kiss, her eyes were warm, dark pools of desire, reflecting only him. Somehow her hair had become disheveled, but it had never been more perfect. He'd surfaced for a reason, but he had to kiss the curve of her neck, so he did—and then her throaty murmur demanded more kisses and he gave them gladly. Following the curving of her neck to his lips, her back arched and her hand was behind his head, pulling him down toward her breasts.

Damn, the girl knows what she wants. Guess Dorian taught her a thing or three. What if Logan the Virgin doesn't measure up?

It was like catching a lake of cold water on his lap. He must have tensed because she pulled back.

She looked in his eyes. She knew.

Now I've spoiled everything. It wasn't just one moment he had destroyed; he could have just destroyed the easy, unfettered spirit of her sensuality. Every time they made love she would have to be conscious of Logan thinking, "Did she learn this from Dorian? Was Dorian better?"

"I'm sorry," she said. She swallowed, and he could see her wilting inside.

He breathed. "I forgive you." She moved to get off his lap, but he caught her and held her against him. It wasn't an emotion, it was a decision. He forgave her, even of the things that weren't her fault. This was too precious to let the past destroy it.

"Jeni," he said as he had said the night of their wedding. "Jeni, will you kiss me?"

She smiled and laughed and almost cried—and kissed him, still laughing. She pulled away and beat her fists on his chest.

"What?" Logan asked, alarmed.

"You can't do this to me. I can't feel all this at once!"

He grinned, and felt that he was himself once again. The idealistic, noble Logan and the wry, carefree Logan and the fierce, primal Logan were being reunited, reintroduced to each other—and Logan would need all of them to be the man and husband and king that he wanted to be. "Then just feel this," he said.

He kissed her again softly, slowly drawing her in, and in the pleasant blur of minutes that followed, they rebuilt their passion.

The thoughts came again like buzzing flies, but Logan ignored them. *No, you won't have this. This is precious. This is ours.*

As their kisses became more heated, those thoughts—and all thoughts—dimmed into the background and disappeared altogether beneath the scents of lavender and faint sweat and her breath, and the feel of her weight on his lap and her hands on his body and her skin beneath his lips and—finally!—his hands won through all the layers of skirts and he felt slim, stockinged calves and his fingers traced that silk up to silkier skin. Jeni moved her hips against him.

Logan jumped to his feet and set Jenine on hers. Eyes

wide, he cleared his throat, "The royal apartments can't be far," he said. "If you can wait five minutes—"

Jenine grabbed him. They didn't wait.

When Kylar opened his eyes, he was lying in a soft bed. High overhead, the ceiling was covered with an elaborate mosaic of a warrior hanging onto a Titan's neck, a huge black sword drawn back in his hand for a killing blow. It was Kylar, but the mosaic was centuries old. Kylar turned.

At first, he didn't recognize Vi. For the first time he'd ever seen, she wore her luxurious, wavy red hair unbound. A single streak of it was stark white. She was seated beside his bed, holding his hand, her green eyes closed in sleep. There were red tulips on the bedside table.

Epilogue

Elene's funeral was simple and small, despite being held in the Hall of Winds. The high king and queen joined Vi and Kylar and Durzo and Sister Ariel. Dorian sat cross-legged on the ground near the back, oblivious. Thankfully, he was silent. Feir stood near him, mostly watching Dorian to make sure he didn't do anything offensive. Amazingly, Elene's old patr from Cenaria had accompanied Logan's army to help with the wounded, and he preached with a simple eloquence that bespoke his long friendship with her. The walls and dome of the Hall of Winds showed the beautiful spring day outside, ripe and bright with promise.

Vi caught herself glancing at Kylar again and again. After being bonded to him, it was strange to have to read his emotions from his face. He wept freely, and there was something clean and healing in those tears. The patr finished the final prayer, and one by one, they made their way to the open coffin.

Kylar and Vi went last. Elene was absolutely stunning.

Sister Ariel and Vi had made her gown. It was white silk, like the one she'd died in, but in line with Elene's modesty and taste. Her face was radiant. Unscarred, it was the face God had intended for Elene, but without her gentleness to animate it, it looked too austere. Here was the face of a queen, but Elene's beauty had always been warm and comforting, never intimidating. As Vi tried to sketch in the details that this husk couldn't capture, the vastness of the loss overwhelmed her. She had to brace herself against the coffin.

Finally, Vi drew a little weave Sister Ariel had taught her around the splay of red tulips Elene held against her chest. It would preserve the flowers for all time. Then Vi touched her friend's cold cheek and kissed her forehead. As she touched Elene's body while still holding her Talent, Vi was struck by something.

Elene wasn't pregnant. Vi straightened, her tears forgotten. Had Elene simply been mistaken? Elene had never been pregnant before, so she wouldn't know exactly how it felt. Vi joined the departing line of mourners. Her eyes fell on the High Queen, pregnant with twins, and then on Dorian, sitting by the door. The mad mage grinned at her, and that grin reminded Vi that Dorian the Mad had held both of the world's most powerful magical artifacts at the same time. Dorian had been responsible for guiding the magic that had wiped out all the krul and restored this entire city. Dorian had been magically linked to all of them. Dorian had been the most Talented Healer in living memory.

Vi's mouth dropped open. Then the insanity of voicing her wild suspicions made it snap shut. What was she going to do? Challenge a madman, tell a king his wife was carrying two different men's sons, and throw an insane hope at Kylar as if it would make up for Elene's death?

No, she would say nothing, not until she knew, maybe not for a long time. But if Elene and Kylar's child somehow lived, Vi swore—swore!—that no one would hurt him.

As the ceremony ended, Vi looked surreptitiously at Kylar. He stood tall. Even as tears coursed down his face, he seemed unburdened, more at ease, more confident, more . . . himself, than Vi had ever seen. She came and stood beside him as the mourners walked into the glorious spring sunshine to look out over their clean white city. Ten thousand red tulips were a reminder of the blood that had purchased it. Kylar took Vi's hand and squeezed.

extras

orbit

meet the author

BRENT WEEKS was born and raised in Montana. After getting his paper keys from Hillsdale College, Brent had brief stints walking the earth like Caine from *Kung Fu*, tending bar, and corrupting the youth. (Not at the same time.) He started writing on bar napkins, then on lesson plans, then full time. Eventually, someone paid him for it. Brent lives in Oregon with his wife, Kristi. He doesn't own cats or wear a ponytail. Find out more about the author at www.brentweeks.com.

introducing

If you enjoyed BEYOND THE SHADOWS,
look out for

ORCS

by Stan Nicholls

Stryke couldn't see the ground for corpses.

He was deafened by screams and clashing steel. Despite the cold, sweat stung his eyes. His muscles burned and his body ached. Blood, mud and splashed brains flecked his jerkin. And now two more of the loathsome, soft pink creatures were moving in on him with murder in their eyes.

He savoured the joy.

His footing unsure, he stumbled and almost fell, pure instinct bringing up his sword to meet the first swinging blade. The impact jarred but checked the blow. He nimbly retreated a pace, dropped into a half crouch and lunged forward again, below his opponent's guard. The sword rammed into the enemy's stomach. Stryke quickly raked it upward, deep and hard, until it struck a rib, tumbling guts. The creature went down, a stupefied expression on its face.

There was no time to relish the kill. The second attacker was on him, clutching a two-handed broadsword, its glinting tip just beyond the limit of Stryke's reach. Mindful of its fellow's fate, this one was more cautious. Stryke went on the offensive, engaging his assailant's blade with a rain of aggressive swipes. They parried and thrusted, moving in a slow, cumbersome dance, their boots seeking purchase on bodies of friend and foe alike.

Stryke's weapon was better suited to fencing. The size and weight of the creature's broadsword made it awkward to use in close combat. Designed for hacking, it needed to be swung in a wider arc. After several passes the creature strained with effort, huffing clouds of icy breath. Stryke kept harrying from a distance, awaiting his chance.

In desperation, the creature lurched toward him, its sword slashing at his face. It missed, but came close enough for him to feel the displaced air. Momentum carried the stroke on, lifting the creature's arms high and leaving its chest unprotected. Stryke's blade found its heart, triggering a scarlet eruption. The creature spiralled into the trampling mêlée.

Glancing down the hill, Stryke could make out the Wolverines, embroiled in the greater battle on the plain below.

He returned to the slaughter.

Coilla looked up and saw Stryke on the hill above, not far from the walls of the settlement, savagely laying into a group of defenders.

She cursed his damned impatience.

But for the moment their leader would have to look after himself. The warband had some serious resistance to overcome before they could get to him.

Here in the boiling cauldron of the main battlefield, bloody conflict stretched out on every side. A crushing mob of fighting troops and shying mounts churned to pulp what had been fields of crops just hours before. The cacophonous, roaring din was endless, the tart aroma of death soured the back of her throat.

A thirty-strong flying wedge bristling with steel, the Wolverines kept in tight formation, powering through the struggling mass like some giant multi-stinged insect. Near the wedge's spearhead, Coilla helped clear their path, lashing out with her sword at enemy flesh obstructing the way.

Too fast to properly digest, a succession of hellish tableaux vivants flashed past her. A defender with a hatchet buried in its shoulder; one of her own side, gore-encrusted hands covering his eyes; another silently shrieking, a red stump in lieu of an arm; one of theirs staring down at a hole the size of a fist in its chest; a headless body, gushing crimson as it staggered. A face cut to ribbons by the slashing of her blade.

An infinity later the Wolverines arrived at the foot of the hill and began to climb as they fought.

A brief hiatus in the butchery allowed Stryke to check again the progress of his band. They were cleaving through knots of defenders about halfway up the hill.

He turned back and surveyed the massive wooden-walled stronghold topping the rise. There was a way to go before they reached its gates, and several score more of the enemy to overcome. But it seemed to Stryke that their ranks were thinning.

Filling his lungs with frigid air, he felt again the intensity of life that came when death was this close.

Coilla arrived, panting, the rest of the troop close behind.

"Took your time," he commented drily. "Thought I'd have to storm the place alone."

She jabbed a thumb at the milling chaos below. "Weren't keen on letting us through."

They exchanged smiles that were almost crazed.

Bloodlust's on her too, he thought. *Good.*

Alfray, custodian of the Wolverines' banner, joined them and drove the flag's spar into the semi-frozen earth. The warband's two dozen common soldiers formed a defensive ring around the officers. Noticing one of the grunts had taken a pernicious-looking head wound, Alfray pulled a field dressing from his hip bag and went to staunch the blood.

Sergeants Haskeer and Jup pushed through the troopers. As usual, the former was sullen, the latter unreadable.

"Enjoy your stroll?" Stryke jibed, his tone sarcastic.

Jup ignored it. "What now, Captain?" he asked gruffly.

"What *think* you, shortarse? A break to pick flowers?" He glared at his diminutive joint second-in-command. "We get up there and do our job."

"How?"

Coilla was staring at the leaden sky, a hand cupped over her eyes.

"Frontal assault," Stryke replied. "You have a better plan?" It was a challenge.

"No. But it's open ground, uphill. We'll have casualties."

"Don't we always?" He spat copiously, narrowly missing his sergeant's feet. "But if it makes you feel better we'll ask our strategist. Coilla, what's your opinion?"

"Hmmm?" Her attention remained fixed on the heavy clouds.

"*Wake up,* Corporal! I said—"

"See that?" She pointed skyward.

A black dot was descending through the gloom. No details were obvious from this distance, but they all guessed what it was.

"Could be useful," Stryke said.

Coilla was doubtful. "Maybe. You know how wilful they can be. Best to take cover."

"Where?" Haskeer wanted to know, scanning the naked terrain.

The dot grew in size.

"It's moving faster than a cinder from Hades," Jup observed.

"And diving too tight," added Haskeer.

By this time the bulky body and massive serrated wings were clearly visible. There was no doubt now. Huge and ungainly, the beast swooped over the battle still raging on the plain. Combatants froze and stared upwards. Some scattered from its shadow. It carried on heedless in an ever-sharper descent, aimed squarely at the rise where Stryke's Wolverines were gathered.

He squinted at it. "Can anybody make out the handler?"

They shook their heads.

The living projectile came at them unerringly. Its vast,

slavering jaws gaped, revealing rows of yellow teeth the size of war helms. Slitty green eyes flashed. A rider sat stiffly on its back, tiny compared to his charge.

Stryke estimated it to be no more than three flaps of its powerful wings away.

"Too low," Coilla whispered.

Haskeer bellowed, *"Kiss the ground!"*

The warband flattened.

Rolling on to his back, Stryke had a fleeting view of grey leathery skin and enormous clawed feet passing overhead. He almost believed he could stretch and touch the thing.

Then the dragon belched a mighty gout of dazzling orange flame.

For a fraction of a second Stryke was blinded by the intensity of light. Blinking through the haze, he expected to see the dragon smash into the ground. Instead he caught sight of it soaring aloft at what seemed an impossibly acute angle.

Further up the hillside, the scene was transformed. The defenders and some attackers, ignited by the blazing suspiration, had been turned into shrieking fireballs or were already dead in smouldering heaps. Here and there, the earth itself burned and bubbled.

A smell of roasting flesh filled the air. It made the juices in Stryke's mouth flow.

"Somebody should remind the dragonmasters whose side they're on," Haskeer grumbled.

"But this one eased our burden." Stryke nodded at the gates. They were well alight. Scrambling to his feet, he yelled, *"To me!"*

The Wolverines sent up a booming war cry and thundered after him. They met little resistance, easily cutting down the few enemy still left standing.

When Stryke reached the smoking gates he found them damaged enough to offer no real obstacle, and one was hanging crookedly, fit to fall.

Nearby, a pole held a charred sign bearing the crudely painted word *Homefield*.

Haskeer ran to Stryke's side. He noticed the sign and swiped contemptuously at it with his sword, severing it from the upright. It fell and broke in two.

"Even our language has been colonised," he growled.

Jup, Coilla and the remainder of the band caught up with them. Stryke and several troopers booted the weakened gate, downing it.

They poured through the opening and found themselves in a spacious compound. To their right, a corral held livestock. On the left stood a row of mature fruit trees. Ahead and set well back was a sizeable wooden farmhouse.

Lined up in front of it were at least twice as many defenders as Wolverines.

The warband charged and set about the creatures. In the intense hand-to-hand combat that followed, the Wolverines' discipline proved superior. With nowhere to run, the enemy was fuelled by desperation and they fought savagely, but in moments their numbers were drastically depleted. Wolverine casualties were much lighter, a handful sustaining minor wounds. Not enough to slow their advance or impede the zeal with which they plundered their foes' milky flesh.

At length, the few remaining defenders were driven back to bunch in front of the entrance. Stryke led the onslaught against them, shoulder to shoulder with Coilla, Haskeer and Jup.

Yanking his blade free of the final protector's innards, Stryke spun and gazed around the compound. He saw what he needed at the corral's fence. "Haskeer! Get one of those beams for a ram!"

The sergeant hurried away, barking orders. Seven or eight troopers peeled off to run after him, tugging hatchets from their belts.

Stryke beckoned a footsoldier. The private took two steps and collapsed, a slender shaft projecting from his throat.

"Archers!" Jup yelled, waving his blade at the building's upper storey.

The band dispersed as a hail of arrows peppered them from an open window above. One Wolverine went down, felled by a shot to the head. Another was hit in the shoulder and pulled to cover by his comrades.

Coilla and Stryke, nearest the house, ran forward to take shelter under the building's overhang, pressing themselves to the wall on either side of the door.

"How many bowmen have *we?*" she asked.

"We just lost one, so three."

He looked across the farmyard. Haskeer's crew seemed to be taking the brunt of the archers' fire. As arrows whistled around them, troopers gamely hacked at the uprights supporting one of the livestock pen's immense timbers.

Jup and most of the others sprawled on the ground nearby. Braving the volleys, Corporal Alfray knelt as he improvised a binding for the trooper's pierced shoulder. Stryke was about to call over when he saw the three archers were stringing their short bows.

Lying full-length was a less than ideal firing position. They had to turn the bows sideways and aim upwards while lifting their chests. Yet they quickly began unleashing shafts in a steady stream.

From their uncertain sanctuary Stryke and Coilla were powerless to do anything except watch as arrows winged up to the floor above and others came down in exchange. After a minute or two a ragged cheer broke out from the warband, obviously in response to a hit. But the two-way flow of bolts continued, confirming that at least one more archer was in the building.

"Why not tip the shafts with fire?" Coilla suggested.

"Don't want the place to burn till we get what we're after."

A weighty crash came from the corral. Haskeer's unit had freed the beam. Troopers set to lifting it, still wary of enemy fire, though it was now less frequent.

Another triumphant roar from the pinned-down grunts was followed by a commotion upstairs. An archer fell, smacking to the ground in front of Stryke and Coilla. The arrow jutting from its chest was snapped in half by the impact.

At the livestock pen, Jup was on his feet, signalling that the upper storey was clear.

Haskeer's crew ran over with the beam, muscles taut and faces strained with the effort of shifting its mass. All hands to the improvised ram, the warband began pounding the reinforced door, splintering shards of wood. After a dozen blows it gave with a loud report and exploded inwards.

A trio of defenders were waiting for them. One leapt forward, killing the lead rammer with a single stroke.

Stryke felled the creature, clambered over the discarded timber and laid into the next. A brief, frenzied trading of blows pitched it lifeless to the floor. But the distraction left Stryke open to the third defender. It closed in, its blade pulling up and back, ready to deliver a decapitating swipe.

A throwing knife thudded hard into its chest. It gave a throaty rasp, dropped the sword and fell headlong.

Stryke's grunt was all Coilla could expect in the way of thanks.

She retrieved the knife from her victim and drew another to fill her empty hand, preferring a blade in both fists when close-quarter fighting seemed likely. The Wolverines flowed into the house behind her.

Before them was an open central staircase.

"Haskeer! Take half the company and clear this floor," Stryke ordered. "The rest with me!"

Haskeer's troopers spread right and left. Stryke led his party up the stairs.

They were near the top when a pair of creatures appeared. Stryke and the band cut them to pieces in combined fury. Coilla got to the upper level first and ran into another defender. It opened her arm with a saw-toothed blade. Hardly slowing, she dashed the weapon from its hand and sliced its chest. Howling, it blundered through the rail and plunged to oblivion.

Stryke glanced at Coilla's streaming wound. She made no complaint, so he turned his attention to this floor's layout. They were on a long landing with a number of doors. Most were open, revealing apparently empty rooms. He sent troopers to search them. They soon reappeared, shaking their heads.

At the furthest end of the landing was the only closed door. They approached stealthily and positioned themselves outside.

Sounds of combat from the ground floor were already dying down. Shortly, the only noise was the distant, muffled hubbub of the battle on the plain, and the stifled panting of the Wolverines catching their breath as they clustered on the landing.

Stryke glanced from Coilla to Jup, then nodded for the three burliest footsoldiers to act. They shouldered the door once, twice and again. It sprang open and they threw themselves in, weapons raised, Stryke and the other officers close behind.

A creature hefting a double-headed axe confronted them. It went down under manifold blows before doing any harm.

The room was large. At its far end stood two more figures, shielding something. One was of the defending creatures' race. The other was of Jup's kind, his short, squat build further emphasised by his companion's lanky stature.

He came forward, armed with sword and dagger. The Wolverines moved to engage him.

"No!" Jup yelled. *"Mine!"*

Stryke understood. "Leave them!" he barked.

His troopers lowered their weapons.

The stocky adversaries squared up. For the span of half a dozen heartbeats they stood silently, regarding each other with expressions of vehement loathing.

Then the air rang to the peal of their colliding blades.

Jup set to with a will, batting aside every stroke his opponent delivered, avoiding both weapons with a fluidity born of long experience. In seconds the dagger was sent flying and embedded itself in a floor plank. Soon after, the sword was dashed away.

The Wolverine sergeant finished his opponent with a thrust to the lungs. His foe sank to his knees, toppled forward, twitched convulsively and died.

No longer spellbound by the fight, the last defender brought up its sword and readied itself for a final stand. As it did so, they saw it had been shielding a female of its race. Crouching, strands of mousy hair plastered to its forehead, the female cradled one of their young. The infant, its plump flesh a dawn-tinted colour, was little more than a hatchling.

A shaft jutted from the female's upper chest. Arrows and a longbow were scattered on the floor. She had been one of the defending archers.

Stryke waved a hand at the Wolverines, motioning them to stay, and walked the length of the room. He saw nothing to fear and didn't hurry. Skirting the spreading pool of blood seeping from Jup's dead opponent, he reached the last defender and locked eyes with it.

For a moment it looked as though the creature might speak.

Instead it suddenly lunged, flailing its sword like a mad thing, and with as little accuracy.

Untroubled, Stryke deflected the blade and finished the matter by slashing the creature's throat, near severing its head.

The blood-soaked female let out a high-pitched wail, part squeak, part keening moan. Stryke had heard something like it once or twice before. He stared at her and saw a trace of defiance in her eyes. But hatred, fear and agony were strongest in her features. All the colour had drained from her face and her breath was laboured. She hugged the young one close in a last feeble attempt to protect it. Then the life force seeped away. She slowly pitched to one side and sprawled lifeless across the floor. The hatchling spilled from her arms and began to bleat.

Having no further interest in the matter, Stryke stepped over the corpse.

He was facing a Uni altar. In common with others he'd seen it was quite plain: a high table covered by a white cloth, gold-embroidered at the edges, with a lead candleholder at each end. Standing in the centre and to the rear was a piece of ironwork he knew to be the symbol of their cult. It consisted of two rods of black metal mounted on a base, fused together at an angle to form a simple X.

But it was the object at the front of the table that interested him. A cylinder, perhaps as long as his forearm and the size of his fist in circumference, it was coppercoloured and inscribed with fading runic symbols. One end had a lid, neatly sealed with red wax.

Coilla and Jup came to him. She was dabbing at the wound on her arm with a handful of wadding. Jup wiped red stains from his blade with a soiled rag. They stared at the cylinder.

Coilla said, "Is that it, Stryke?"

"Yes. It fits her description."

"Hardly looks worth the cost of so many lives," Jup remarked.

Stryke reached for the cylinder and examined it briefly before slipping it into his belt. "I'm just a humble captain. Naturally our mistress didn't explain the details to one so lowly." His tone was cynical.

Coilla frowned. "I don't understand why that last creature should throw its life away protecting a female and her offspring."

"What sense is there in anything humans do?" Stryke replied. "They lack the balanced approach we orcs enjoy."

The cries of the baby rose to a more incessant pitch.

Stryke turned to look at it. His green, viperish tongue flicked over mottled lips. "Are the rest of you as hungry as I am?" he wondered.

His jest broke the tension. They laughed.

"It'd be exactly what they'd expect of us," Coilla said, reaching down and hoisting the infant by the scruff of its neck. Holding it aloft in one hand, level with her face, she stared at its streaming blue eyes and dimpled, plump cheeks. "My gods, but these things are *ugly*."

"You can say that again," Stryke agreed.